Positively Indecent!

Positively Indecent!

The Story of Dr. Lana Jean Masters

Jack Bentley

Writers Club Press
San Jose New York Lincoln Shanghai

Positively Indecent!
The Story of Dr. Lana Jean Masters

Writers Club Press
an imprint of iUniverse, Inc.

For information address:
iUniverse, Inc.
5220 S. 16th St., Suite 200
Lincoln, NE 68512
www.iuniverse.com

Any resemblance to actual people and events is purely coincidental. This is a work of fiction.
Original Cover Art from an oil painting by Hyacinthe Kuller Baron

ISBN: 0-595-22028-2

Printed in the United States of America

I dedicate this novel to world peace.

Jack Bentley

Acknowledgements

For their valued assistance I should like to thank my lovely wife Jean for her patience, quite incredible actually, and my great kids Michael, Marlee and Allyson for their understanding.

My very close friends Hyacinthe and Ed Baron for their encouragement, guidance, editing and sound advice.

Contents

Acknowledgements vii

From the Author xix

Foreword xxi

Preface xxiii

Introduction xxvii

Precursory 3

Dr. Lana Masters And Her Guest, Father Donnely 6

Russell strikes it rich with Lana.

Kupangg 18

Lana's Chambre De Execution 35

Warning-Unusual Sex

Lana's Remarkable Childhood 41

Sir Galahad And Big Buster; The Ranch Hands 49

Lana's Heroism At Age Nine 56

Lana's Net Worth At Age Fifteen...Lana's Nightmare 64

Warning! One Beastly Sentence.

Resentments By Others Of The Young Lana 71

Lana's Registration In Nyu At Thirteen 73

The paparazzi.

Lana's First Date, Franklin Foster 80

Franklin's Summer Vacation With Lana 88

At her Father's Ranch.

The Rustlers 93

Virginity...Lana At Age Fifteen 100

Lana's Mother's Abhorrence 101

Virginity Lost...Lana At Age Fifteen 104

Athens Greece: Lana And Franklin 109

The Singles Bar: Los Angeles 115

Lana Lectures 90,00 People In Baton Rouge. 118

Clark St. James at home in L.A. watches on TV.

Metaphysical Mention Of The Twelve Cosmic Controllers 121

The St. Jame's Family. Historic, 1907 123

Santa Monica High School, 1907 130

Phillip Foster and Silken Hendrick's tryst

Maria St. James, Phillip Foster And Mousey: 1908 141

Maria, Bat Masterson And Harley Earp 148

Maria, Phillip, Mousey 161

Warning...Vicious rape scene.!

The Rats, May 1997 181

Warning! Graphic mutilation!

The Female Rat's Escape: Dreadfully Inelegant 184

Istanbul, Turkey, May 5, 1997 186

Lana must have a guardian angel...the bruising battle

The Origin Of The Universe…Eve One 197

Warning! Extreme bestiality.

The Controllers Decried 207

Intelligence…Deletrious Acts 223

Dr. Samuell Marshall: The World's Foremost Scientist 232

Lana's Would Be Assasin 235

The Controllers revenge: Itanya Koslosky

Lana's Frustration 258

Lana Lectures On Money And Finances 267

More Money And Finances 271

H&B Financial And Poors, Inc. 272

Vito Apostli and Washington Jefferson's murder

George Washington To Bill Clinton…U.S. Debt 274

Holly Hoxdale, stunning hooker

Atrocities 284

Lana And Clark St. James 287

Dr. James Bell-Irving And Eve Three: Cosmic Love 293

Mesozoic Era And Upper Paleolithic Period 301

Istanbul, Lana And Stone King, The Big U.S. Network 308

Lana And Dr. James Bell Irving 319

Lana And Stone King Interview Continued 324

Lana's Sister Margaret's Plea 338

Margaret Masters And Christeen Barlow's Love Affair 342
Margaret And Christeen 380
Lana Meets With Margaret And Christeen 386
Ten Years Ago 395
The Ivy Leaguers 396
H&B Financial And Poors 414
Trent Logan, The Equalizer And Billy Wheaton 417
Christeen's Answer 423
To Lana's Seductive Question
The Ivy Leaguers Contract Father Donnely 431
To assasinate Lenny (the pimp) Chimos
Father Donnely Doesn't Miss 444
Lana's Twenty-Third Birthday 459
Lana's Twenty-Third Birthday Party 460
Franklin Foster et al.
The Twenty-Third Birthday Rape 465
Warning! Orgies. Repulsed, Lana becomes a Manhattan Bag Lady.
Lana's Questions 473
Lana's Transition Into Polly The Bag Lady 474
Polly's First Sortie Onto Manhattan's Streets 477
Mcmaster College Of Arts And Sciences 485
Polly's Flight To Los Angels, First Class, Shocking! 489

Polly Visits Santa Monica High 493

And St. James, Rogers, Struthers and Co. C.P.A.'s

Lana Visits The Morning Telegraph, Manhattan 504

Lana Meets With Trent Logan 507

Trent Logan Evens The Score 510

Polly's Entourage 511

Polly meets Clark St. James

H&B's Manhattan Office 515

Polly Disrobes 520

And discloses her secret to Clark

Three Years Later Polly Disrobes To Wall Street Yuppies 523

Polly discloses her secret. Hold on to your hats!

Lana's Rape By Father Donnely And The Ivy Leaguers 534

Instanbul 541

Clark's Journey 554

Clark's Journey 561

Clark's Journey 570

Warning…one loathsome scene

Clark Incorporates H&B Financial And Poors 574

Clark's Skid Row Committees For H&B 578

H&B's First Shareholders Meeting 592

3000 skid row derelicts attend

Polly's Financial Expertise 608

Istanbul, Lana Discusses Religion 611

Istanbul, Lana On Celibacy 617

God's Banker, Catholics and Muslims, grand theft.

Istanbul, Lana Discusses Politics 630

Istanbul, Lana Summarizes Her Five Days Of Lectures 639

Father Donnely's Demise 651

Warning! Abject horror.

Author's Secret 659

Postscript 661

About the Author 667

The Female of The Species

Rudyard Kipling

When the Himalayan peasant
meets the he-bear in his pride
he shouts to scare the monster
who will often turn aside.
When Nag the basking cobra hears
the careless foot of man,
he will sometimes wriggle sideways
And avoid it if he can.

When the early Jesuit fathers
preached to Hurons and Choctaws,
they prayed to be delivered
from the vengeance of the squaws.
Twas the women, not the warriors,
turned those stark enthusiasts pale.
For the female of the species
is more deadly than the male.

Man's timid heart is bursting
with the things he must not say.
For the woman that God gave him
isn't his to give away.
But when hunter meets with husband,
each confirms the other's tale…
The female of the species
Is more deadly than the male.

Man, a bear in most relations…
warm and savage otherwise…
Man propounds negotiations
Man accepts the compromise.
Very rarely will he squarely
push the logic of a fact
To its ultimate conclusion
in an unmitigated act.

Fear, or foolishness, impels him,
ere he lay the wicked low,
to concede some form of trial
even to his fiercest foe.
Mirth obscene diverts his anger-
Doubt and Pity oft perplex
Him in dealing with an issue-
To the scandal of the sex.

But the Woman that God gave him,
every fiber of her frame,
proves her launched for one sole issue,
armed and engineered for the same.
And to serve that single issue,
lest the generations fail,
the Female of the species
Must be deadlier than the male.

She who faces Death by torture
for each life beneath her breast
may not deal in Doubt or Pity
must not swerve for fact or jest.

These be purely male diversions-
not in these her honour dwells.
She the Other Law we live by,
is that Law and nothing else.

She can bring no more to living
than the powers that make her great.
As the Mother of the infant
and the Mistress of the Mate.
And when Babe and Man are lacking
and she strode unclaimed to claim
her right as femme (and baron)
her equipment is the same.

She is wedded to conviction-
in default of grosser ties:
Her contentions are her children,
Heaven help him who denies!
He will meet no suave discussion,
but the instant, white-hot, wild,
Wakened Female of the species
warring as for the spouse and child.

Unprovoked and awful charges-
even so the she-bear fights.
Speech that drips, corrodes, and poisons-
even so the cobra bites.
Scientific vivisection
of one nerve till it is raw
and the victim writhes in anguish-
like the Jesuit with the squaw!

So it comes that Man, the coward,
when he gathers to confer
with his fellow braves in council
dare not leave a place for her
where, at war with Life and Conscience,
He uplifts his erring hands
to some God of Abstract Justice-
which no Woman understands.

And Man knows it! Know, moreover,
That the Woman that God gave him
Must command but may not govern-
Shall enthall but not enslave him.
And She knows, because She warns him,
and Her instincts never fail,
that the Female of Her Species
Is more deadly than the Male.

From the Author

Dr. Lana Jean Masters is a genius! A stunning, enticing, brutal and POSITIVELY INDECENT 29-year-old.
A ravishing goddess who stirs the hearts of men…and women. Lana is the very fulfillment of men's dreams; and yet manifests men's worst fears.
A scintillating woman, her breathtaking beauty, statuesque body and acerbic tongue makes Lana a role model for all women struggling against injustice and terrorism.
POSITIVELY INDECENT! is full of suspense, mystery, unforgettable characters, unmitigated sex, metaphysical intrigue …and unsavory truths.

* * *

The handsome, enormously wealthy Californian ***Clark St. James*** is so aghast at the inequities of the world he gives up his life of opulence to become a denizen of Manhattan streets. His trek as a vagrant from Los Angeles, California to New York City is terrifying, humorous and somewhat libidinous.

Lana posing as a bag lady for six years has heard of Clark's ingenuity. They meet and together form ***H&B Financial and Poors.*** The company, whose goal is to reward indigents, becomes highly successful and wildly profitable.

Not until Lana discloses her secret disguise as a bag lady to Clark do they share an out of this world love affair. Together they wend their way through the dark sides of sin and violence in the squalor of the back streets of Manhattan.

Lana spends a remarkable week lecturing in Istanbul, Turkey. Readers are introduced to **The Universe's 12 CONTROLLERS.**

She also encounters many of the world's leading emissaries, an egomaniacal man of the cloth (who Lana ravages…hang on to your hats for this ride) two voluptuous lesbians (one being Lana's sister and they will blow your mind) two devilish Ivy Leaguers, and ***Stone King*** (Lana's interviewer) and ***Trent Logan*** (Lana's equalizer) and a bevy of prostitutes and a garish bunch of low-lifers.

Here is the setting for POSITIVELY INDECENT!

Lana has her abhorrent guest in a most indelicate situation in her father's barn. She is about to…

Well the Preface gives you a hint of things to come.

A nightmarish storm howls outside, yet the tormented skies make no impact of the psyche of 'cool' Lana.

It is hot inside the barn. Lana dangles her long shapely legs from a stack of baled hay, strips to her panty and bra, and looks down at her guest, whom she has shackled to the floor…

Okay readers…you have the scene.

Enjoy!
Jack Bentley

* * *

Foreword

Readers, here's the setting for **POSITIVELY INDECENT.**

Dr. Lana Jean Masters has her abhorrent guest in a most indelicate situation. She is about to…well the story's preface will give you a hint of things to come, so let's just wait and see.

* * *

They are ensconced in a barn on the prairies. It is nighttime, yes, and the prairies are being battered by a fierce storm. Lightning is so close it sizzles before exploding in ear-splitting thunder. Hail flattens grain crops and gardens, dents tops and sides of cars and pockmarks buildings. The howling winds of the nightmarish storms blow down granaries and silos and remove some housetops in the cute little city of Swift Current.

But these tormented skies make no impact on the psyche of the cool Lana Masters. She sits unruffled on double stacks of hay bales in her father's barn. Her long curvy legs hang nonchalantly down the sides. (Yes, the bale she sits on has a blanket.)

In spite of the rampaging storm it is hot inside the barn. Our provocative heroine removes all her clothing, except for her panty and bra. Lana looks down on her guest whom she has shackled to the floor of the barn.

* * *

Okay! You've got the scene, so as Michael Buffer would say, "*Let's get ready to rumble!*"

Preface

POSITIVELY INDECENT! Enters into many facets of life. Its contents include fact, fiction, intrigue, suspense, sex, humor, cruelty, horror, malfeasance as well as the panning of economics, politics and religion. Often its narration is reprehensible, unrelenting and defiant. I have taken the liberty to head those chapters whose words and actions may be too much for some readers. But make no mistake about my novel's heroine Dr. Lana Jean Masters, she can be gentle, loving, caring, yet, when called upon to do so she can be as fierce as a grizzly.

Throughout the novel Lana leaves you gasping, she shocks you, and she assaults your imagination, tantalizes your sex drive and toys impishly with the inner sanctums of your mind. Lana will numb the very marrow of your bones as she takes you step-by-step throught the chilling execution of her one time heinous lover. Lana's executioners are three rats. Rats caged on her lover's lower gut! Rats whose escape route is so singular, so ghastly, and so gross!

Lana Masters is a charming, crafty twenty-nine-year-old. She has an intelligent quotient of 205. Her intellect, stunning beauty and delectable body have endowed her with all the necessary attributes and skills to take her into a most ebullient and fascinating many-sided life.

From a child of six to womanhood, Lana triumphs in so many different and defiant ways that those ways make her eminently unique when compared to others. Over the years she reached dizzying heights of success in education, teaching, lecturing, monetary and self-fulfilling riches, provocative controversies, human dignity, exigent propitiousness, love, adventuresome sex, yet, by her own decision she entered into the squalid depths of depravity. For six hellish years she took on the roll of a Manhattan Bag Lady.

Lana is the daughter of Carl and Beatrice Masters who farm and ranch thousands of acres of land in Southwest Saskatchewan. The Masters are wealthy. They raised five children, two girls and three boys. Lana Masters, born on October 29th 1967 is the youngest of the children. Her stunning sister Margaret is gay.

Lana's exploits will engross you.

Thirty-one-year-old Clark Rodney St. James is a big, quiet, unassuming, handsome Californian. In 1991 he comes to terms with himself after a year of "gut" wrenching decisions. He enters into an unforgettable life of poverty after leaving his highly remunerative profession and his huge fortune. His family, friends and associates in Beverly Hills are stunned, broken-hearted and at a loss trying to understand what caused him to leave so suddenly, and they are baffled as to his whereabouts.

Clark becomes a Manhattan skid row dweller. His bizarre journey from Los Angeles to New York City as a penniless tramp abounds in filth, defilement, rough and tumble fights, horrifying sights and sex filled interludes. His meeting with Lana the Bag Lady is inevitable.

For three years, Lana keeps her secret as a withered crone from Clark. Finally when she removes her swaddling clothes to reveal her true being to Clark in her luxury condo in the St. Pierre opposite Central Park, Clark is traumatized.

There Lana stood, a statuesque nude.

Subsequently, their involvement is filled with intellectual sparring, adoring love, exciting sex, enterprise, entrepreneurial wizardry, thrilling adventures, debased gutter living and philanthropic munificence.

*　　　　*　　　　*

P.S. I almost forgot to tell you Lana's unique way of measuring time. It is almost childlike. This storybook beauty relates time to "grandfathers". By figuring the average life expectancy of a grandfather to be sixty-years-of-age over the past 2000 years, the Civil War of the 1860's in the U.S.A. was, as Lana reckons, less than three grandfathers ago. Slavery was rife in America just three grandfathers ago. The dark ages were a scant eighteen grandfathers ago. The sacrifice of Our Lord Jesus by some thugs was a mere thirty-five grandfathers ago. Lana quite liked this method of measuring time. She found it most revealing. It brought her closer to the rationalization of time. Heck, flying machines were invented just two grandfathers ago, that is just a moment ago in the scheme of universal things.

Introduction

May 18, 1997

Dr. Lana Jean Masters was deep in thought as she sat in the den of her luxurious mid-Manhatan condo. She was analyzing herself as she had done once before in her life, when she was just twelve-years-old. Now Lana's 30th birthday was only five months away. Seventeen years between serious bouts of self-analysis. She knew her fame placed her in a special global category of her own. She was looked up to by many millions of people as a model of integrity, kindness and forgiveness. She was the very quintessence of *summum bonum.* Both men and women admired her. They made concerted efforts to emulate her. In her scant twenty-nine years of life Lana Jean Masters had evoked and instilled thoughts of decency in many of the world's masses.

Now here she was sitting cat-like in a comfortable oversized lounge chair contemplating her second murder of the second "someone" she loathed. "A colossal enigma," Lana Masters reasoned. Her superior mentality, her respect for human lives and her inalterable mindset for justice caused her to have a frustrating exchange of thoughts on the matter of her having the right to impose the death sentence on the gentleman who in five days would become her guest.

Arguably, she thought, she was the only jury capable of finding the fellow guilty on all counts of his violations against her. Yes, she would find him guilty as charged and her recommendation to herself as the judicial head of her personal court would be the death penalty. Yet she pondered over the question of her right to take someone else's life without due deliberation being given by a jury of his peers. How would they view the verdict and the sentence? Probably they would give the culprit a scant five-year jail term with time off for good behavior for his crimes against her. Now as for his crimes against others, that was quite another matter. No doubt a jury of his peers would find him guilty on all these coutns. His uncaring executions of Vito Apostli and Washington Jefferson; his classic disposal of that pompous pimp Lenny Chimos; his murder of the two Ivy Leaguers by suffocation; the carnage and murders he was responsible for in the pitiful Asian monarchy which was left in chaos after his well-executed sabotage. Without question these acts would call for the death sentence (a penalty in law Lana loathed) in many States in America. "Yeah, so I don't like death row 'lover boy', but you lousy bastard I'm in charge here, I make the rules, so fuck you and death row, it's '*Good Night Irene*'."

* * *

May 9, 1997

Dr. Lana Jean Masters departed New York City on Air Canada flight 739 at 10:20 a.m. May 19 and arrived Regina Saskatchewan at 3:20 p.m. central standard time. Awaiting her at Regina's airport was one of her father's ranch hands. John "Cowboy" Ellis, who was not only a capable ranch hand but, as well, an excellent pilot of smaller aircraft. The twin engine Cessna Cowboy Ellis flew belonged to Lana Jean's father. It was just one of her father's multi-million-dollar holdings. Lana had made this trip many times in the past: From New York's J.F.K. airport to Saskatchewan's capital city Regina. Her final destination point was almost always her hometown, her place of birth, Swift Current, Saskatchewan. She had made it a point to visit her parents, both of whom were native Swift Currentonians, at least twice yearly. Her visits were always fun visits. She loved and adored her mom and dad. She loved and adored her brothers who were all married, who lived in Swift Current, and who were all working shareholders in her dad's massive land holdings. Lana loved her brothers' wives and their kids. She adored her gorgeous sister Margaret, a medical doctor and a smoldering but rather shy lesbian.

* * *

Lana loved getting busy on the farm, once she got there, everything from helping her mom in the kitchen to driving tractors, combines and heavy-duty trucks. What a life! But what a contrariety! What a contrast from Lana, the world's most intelligent and beautiful woman, a five-foot-eleven-inch statuesque Goddess to Lana a tomboy in overalls and cowboy boots with a straw of hay held between her incredible lips.

While Lana deemed herself to be a small-town prairie girl, she was in fact the world's heavyweight in raw and learned clinical intellect, sophistication and benevolence. No one in the world of science, health, cosmology, business acumen and perspicuous rational could stand up to this female Titan. She did, after all, have an intelligence quotient in excess of 205.

But here she was from time to time, a grubby farm girl, dust covered or muddied, grease on her face and clothing, helping the farm and ranch hands with chores ranging from baling hay to seeding crops to helping pregnant cows give birth to cute little calves. Thence, following a shower, tidied up, clad in short shorts and a halter-top, no make-up and barefooted, she would emerge as a startling, radiant masterpiece.

However, the trip she was now taking was not for jocularity. This trip was being made for a single purpose…to destroy another human dispassionately. Although Lana Jean Masters was tender, kind and humane, her brain had complete control over her ego and emotions. Lana's brain had concluded her soon-to-be arriving guest must be put to death by way of an unrelenting, iniquitous, disquieting torture. "Damn my brain," Lana thought, "Damn my pragmatism."

The execution chamber for her one-time lover was to be a huge barn on one of Lana's father's farms; a farm just eight miles north of the delightful little prairie city of Swift Current. She had made certain her father's farm would be uninhabited from May 21 to May 26th. These six days would give her ample time for the preparation of the deed, the deed itself, and for the disposal of all incriminating evidence.

THE STORY OF DR. LANA JEAN MASTERS

CHAPTER 1

PRECURSORY

May 5, 1997

Dr. Lana Jean Masters knew from early childhood that she had been given life for a very special reason. While she went through her daily routines in much the same way as others, her ego told her her soul overlapped into the cosmos itself. She knew she was a genius, an incomparable beauty and someone who could agitate, excite and captivate others. She knew she was different from all other humans, not as an alien, not as a spirit, not as a divinity, not an imaginary external perception, no, none of these, no hallucinations, no ethereal dreams, no illusions of grandeur, simply a matter of fact.

At birth she had been blessed with an indefatigable inner spirit replete in macrocosmic awareness. While Lana Jean knew of her resplendency and probity since childhood, she was unaware until two weeks ago from whom she had inherited her celestial bliss. Now she knew. **It was the 12 Controllers of the universe. But what did they expect of her?**

Lana knew she would be giving her life to the betterment of people. This feeling was elementary, but what about the other feeling? While it never cluttered her brain to the extent of diminishing its brilliance it did nevertheless frustrate and frighten her. When would she know the special reason for her birth and the ultimate expectations of her?

Now, as she stood at the podium in the huge convention hall in Istanbul, she knew whom her masters were. Quite innocuously they had come to see her in her condo in Manhattan on April 20 just passed.

They had made themselves known to her as the **Controllers of the cosmos** and they made it clear their leader **Eve One** was, without question, ***Primus Inter Pares.*** They made no specific demands of Lana, nor did they outline any expectations they had of her during their visit. They were friendly, chatty yet discriminating and judgmental. In a most matter of fact way, they told Lana she had been selected as their "choice" among the earth's 6 billion people. Choice for what? Lana wondered. They gave her no indication or sign of what she was being chosen for. But just before leaving they did give her a frightful warning of just how close humans were from being extinguished by them. 'And holy shit, what a warning,' the unabashed cussing Lana thought, 'shape up you 6 billion numb-nuts out there or you're history.'

* * *

Dr. Masters knew these Controllers were aware of her thinking at all times, yet this did not frighten her. She knew, at least for now, the Controllers would not interfere or dally with her thought processes. She was at liberty to think and do as she wished. Too, Lana now was aware of the fact it was the Controllers who held the secret of her inner being and it was they who would choose the time for her secret to be revealed. As well, Lana knew when the enactment of her secret inner being was to come about it would be trying, enriching, but most terrifying. In any event, Lana Jean Masters was certain it was her responsibility to inform the world's populace of the genesis of the Controllers and the reasons for their foreboding warning.

In addition she was to lecture the world's citizenry on economics, religion, and politics and to weave these topics into their rightful place in the ethics of human rights and equity both in spirituality and in materiality.

And what better forum than the upcoming meeting to be held in Istanbul, Turkey? Lana was to be the sole speaker. It would be ideal.

Over 2,000 well-known dignitaries were to attend the meetings while Television, radio and various other media were to take her messages to over one-half of the world's people.

* * *

Lana was right. Istanbul was the perfect forum for her. It was ideal. It was fun, exciting, magnetic, electrifying. And bizarre, hell, the word bizarre was too ordinary a word to use considering some of the non-conforming exotic, ecstatic even frightful absurdities that occurred during Lana's five-day stint in Istanbul.

Enveloped in a charismatic aura, Lana smiled as she began her address to the 2100 attendees who were gathered in Istanbul's magnificent convention center.

CHAPTER 2

DR. LANA MASTERS AND HER GUEST, FATHER DONNELY

Russell strikes it rich with Lana.

Lana looked across the table at her guest. 'Damn, you are so alluring,' she thought.

'But you are such a loathsome bastard. And your naiveté surprises me. You still think I love you and you still think we are going to frolic in the hay. But handsome, in a matter of hours instead of making love to you I will be preparing you for your execution. What a waste though, 'cause you are dreamy.'

It was eight P.M. May 23, 1997.

* * *

"So Father, it was you who screwed up Kupangg's political way out of it's mess wasn't it?" Dr. Lana Masters asked with a feigned smile.

"That's correct."

"You are a monster, a cute one, but nonetheless a monster."

"If you say so Lana, as long as I'm cute."

'Yeah, and you're a sanctimonious prick too,' Lana thought. 'A slick intellectual. A cross between Jack the Ripper and Hannibal Lector. No matter how hard I try to convince myself that you deserve to live, I can't make it. You've got to die.'

The Priest looked smug as he smiled at her.

'Yeah baby, in a couple of hours you shan't be so smug, you'll be nothing but a delectable tidbit for my genus rattus norvegicus threesome.' Lana thought.

They were dining at O'Tool's Restaurant on Swift Current's north hill. Lana's guest had ordered a bottle of Chateau Clinet Pomerol. When it was brought to their table he checked the wine bottle's cork, lifted it to his nose, sniffed it, placed the cork on the table and nodded. He swirled the sample the waiter had poured into his high-stemmed glass. He closed his eyes as he inhaled its bouquet. He raised the glass to his lips, sipped judgmentally and said, "Excellent."

They supped on sesame-topped perch. Perch caught that day in the cool waters of Duncairn Dam. They had Buffalo wings for starters followed by a spinach salad touched lightly with an exquisite house dressing.

"Mighty fine vittles they serve in this here one-horse town," Lana's guest said, mimicking John Wayne.

"Yes Father," Lana replied.

Lana kept the hatred out of her eyes for the present. Yet even her powerful ego was stretched to the limit. She wanted to get to this bloody monster's quietus now. But first things first. Hear him out. Be patient.

"How did you know it was me Lana?"

"It was easy. After I read the details of the killings I knew it was you. I know your style. It's my bet of the seven assassinations you fired only five of the shots. My intellect tells me you had the other tyrants murder themselves…after you set them up."

"Right as usual. And pray tell what is my style Dr. Masters?"

"A neat bullet hole in the center of the forehead…then brains exploding out the back of the skull leaving just a face."

"Right again."

For a moment they supped in silence.

While he appeared cool, Lana's guest's mind was racing. No longer did he want to act the smart-ass. He wanted her. He wanted to hold her in his arms. He wanted her love. He wanted to tell her that his love for her was forever, that he couldn't live without her. He wanted them to be husband and wife. He wanted children with her. He hoped all of this would be possible. No more of his treachery, he would promise her that. Perhaps in the next few days he could win back her love and trust. He must do everything in his power to prove his worthiness to her.

"Lana, I love you," he blurted out. He hesitated as he looked pleadingly into her eyes. "Please, answer me my darling, do you love me?"

"What a question. Why do you think I brought you here? Didn't I express myself rather clearly a few days ago after you and your Ivy Leaguers raped me?"

Her guest looked ashamed.

"Cheer up Father, in an hour or so you'll be bound up in ecstatic rapture on my Dad's farm. You'll see." She winked as she told him to be patient. In the distance Lana saw flashes of lightning. "Common' baby, tell me about your priesthood and your heroics in Kupangg."

Still looking shamed Lana's guest took her hand in his and began his strange story.

* * *

"My priesthood, yes, well it was an amusing start. I had never given religion much thought during my life. One day a few years ago I was thumbing through the New York Times' real estate section when I spotted two interesting Manhattan properties listed for sale. A small Catholic Church situated on a 10,000 square foot site and adjacent to it a 7200 square foot lot housing a thirty-year-old bungalow. I made an offer on the two properties and my offer was accepted. So 'voila' I became an owner of a church. Cute hey?

"You know I've loved you from the first time I saw you Lana. It's been a damnable nightmare to say the least. I've tried everything short of suicide to forget you. I thought if I 'took on' some religion I might luck out; hence my ownership of the church. Hallelujah, I had chortled, God will replace that voluptuary in my mind. Shit, this reasoning was about as effective as a fart trying to requite a hurricane."

"Splendid analogy, lover boy."

"In any event doll, after I moved into my new house I began to think about the parish and its parishioners. Would the parishioners want to continue to use the church facilities, you know, for bingo, weddings, funerals, meetings, Christmas parties and the like? And would they want me, a fucking farce, to be their priest? I put a notice on the front door of the church asking parishioners and the public to attend a meeting to discuss these matters, not including though Lana, the fucking farce bit. The little church was swamped with people. They were delighted. They ensconced me as Father Donnely. I found that to be quite delightful.

"I had a blast playing the church game Lana, and I did find my ego to be somewhat free of you, but not free enough dammit.

"Then along came Lenny 'The Pimp' Chimos, a dreadful excuse for a human. He was a parishioner before I bought the property, a good strong Catholic lad, and he was one of the people who attended my meeting. The parishioners who knew Lenny thought highly of him. They didn't know he was a pimp. They thought he was a successful businessman, generous to a fault as witnessed by his substantial donations to the church. In time I got to know him. He was most generous to me sweetheart. Every Saturday Lenny would bring me one of his most sought after tidbits. All of these tidbits were gorgeous young girls. My latest one is known as Twinky. Thoughtful of him wouldn't you agree Lana? But even these tidbits could not expunge my thoughts of you. Incidentally babe, I shot good old Lenny right between the eyes one fine evening.

"No comment Lana?

"No, no comment."

Dr. Masters was enraged at the thought of his imbibing in youngsters. Even her great mind could not jail her feelings about this lump of humanity. How she wanted to throttle him now, on the spot. 'Be patient,' she said to herself, 'it won't be long until I have him wishing he was dead, a couple of hours at the most. The rats are waiting and they are hungry.' Lana had seen to it the 12 year-old 'Twinky' now was being properly cared for.

"Ok my sweet, would you like to hear about my heroism in Kupangg?

"Yes Father Donnely, I would."

* * *

"The CIA was impressed with my work as a government agent. In particular the closeness with which I held the federal government's classified information and my ability to deliver 'the goods' no matter how unsavory the chore. The Kupangg assignment was designated red because of its life-threatening risks and its secretive intent. The CIA offered me the job. I accepted. Frankly Lana I wanted to be killed on the assignment. I wanted my death to do two things. One, end my misery about you and two, die a hero hoping my 'emblematic' death would cause you to grieve. Even though the CIA considered the assignment to be suicidal and my chances of survival to be worse than one in a thousand I found the assignment to be rather mundane. Shit baby, I outwitted both sides in the Kupangg struggle. Debauched bastards the ruling class, good dudes and dudesses leading the proletariat. How'm'so'ever, fucked up me saw to it that both the good guys and the bad guys were slaughtered.

"The deal I was to peddle was in exchange for money, goods and technical expertise from the USA the totalitarian Screw leading Kupangg would agree to a democratic election within one year, release all political prisoners and begin a reformation in human rights. Our Feds agreed if all went as planned the Screw would get the credit for the 'do-gooding'. However, if I failed in my mission and been killed, the whole world was to know of the treachery of good old Screw and his henchmen and their lives would be up for grabs. In this latter event you would have heard of my heroism and hopefully your psyche would have been shattered.

"That's kinda' sick."

"Yes I guess so Lana. Do you want to hear more?"

"Yes."

"Ok, well, the instructions given me by the CIA pooh-bahs were clear on all matters but one. The unclear one had to do with the secret disposal of a man and wife, the good dude and dudess. This was a part of the deal insisted on by the Screw. Reluctantly the CIA agreed. But it was made clear to me if I was caught in the act of killing the couple the CIA would refute any connection with the assassination and with me. I would be made the scapegoat. Quiet and discreet were the operative words pertaining to the eradication of the couple. And, my precious beauty, another covenant given by the CIA to the Screw was he and his henchmen would be able to keep, without the threat of garnishee, all of their personal wealth. I will touch on this fun stuff later.

"My buddies in the CIA knew my proclivities. They knew I would have no remorse in disposing of those salt-of-the-earth people. The CIA was right; I didn't give one big black rat's ass about the two goody goodies. My thoughts were about you Lana, your guilt and remorse if I was killed."

"Why didn't you feign their deaths, hide them, kill the Screw and his henchmen then set the couple up as de facto leaders of the country until democratic elections were held. This would have made me proud of you. Dammit man what's wrong with pride?"

"I don't want your pride Lana, I want you."

"Carry on."

Thunder rumbled in the distance. Heavy raindrops began to fall.

"Carry on? Is that all you have to say. No sympathetic words like I'm so sorry about your dreadful assignment or 'poor baby' or any fucking thing, just 'carry on'?"

"Ok, poor baby. Is that better?" Lana said smiling, "but you have made me so curious about your escapades in Asia. Please, be a good boy and carry on."

* * *

'Well I'll be darned,' Lana said to herself as she glanced over Father Donnely's shoulder. A young man in work clothes along with three other men had just entered O'Tools restaurant. They began to chat with the pretty hostess. The hostess was shaking her head. It was obvious that, at the moment, nothing was available in the restaurant or bar for the men. It was obvious too the pretty lady knew the men. They were all smiling as she entered their names in the reservations register. Lana overheard the young man say 'forty minutes is perfect.' The men turned and left the restaurant.

The young man's name was Russell Chandler. It was two years ago when Lana and he met for the first and only time. And what a meeting it was. Lana had taken a few days away from her self-imposed role as a bag lady in New York City's Manhattan to visit her mother and father in Swift Current.

It was early September, the weather had been perfect. Lana had taken her father's Land Rover to drive to scenic city of Saskatoon for the weekend. Saskatoon, where Lana had begun her university studies when she was 11 years old. She loved traipsing around her home province of Saskatchewan. On this particular trip Lana had stopped a few miles out of Saskatoon at a Best Western. It was only 2 in the afternoon. After checking into the motel she had put on her bathing suit gone to the pool nestled down on a deck chair and began reading New York's latest best seller, **THE OCEAN TURNED MILKY.**

The sun's rays were warm and the breeze from the west seemed to whisper it's way through the leaves of the alders. Lana was alone. Kind'a nice. At around three thirty she strolled over to the pool's side sat on the steps and put her feet in the water. My, even the water was delightful. She heard the gate to the pool open. She turned and looked to see who was coming. It was a young man about her age. Farmerish looking, lean, pale skinned except for his tanned face, neck, arms, and legs. He was an obvious wearer of sleeveless shirts, shorts, and boots. A typical prairie farm boy. He looked a little like Brad Pitt, the actor. Bigger, not as handsome as Mr. Pitt, but with those same sensational lips. He made Lana feel a twinge of sensual excitement. 'Perhaps he will be my prey this evening,' she thought.

The young man was making his way toward a lounge chair. Then he spun. Spun hell, he vortexed. He had spotted Lana. His brain unhinged, his stomach flipped, he gaped, his eyes bugged out, he stumbled over a deck chair then flubbed around about as gracefully as a pregnant giraffe pirouetting to the music of Swan Lake.

"Good afternoon," Lana said smiling.

"Hi," Russell responded showing a lot of teeth.

"A lovely day."

"Yes I believe so, I think so, they are breathtaking." His eyes were locked on Lana's breasts. She must be from another planet, she has to be an 'it' not a 'she,' she's so breathtaking. Those eyes, my God, and her hair, her face, her lips and her mouth.

Lana stood.

Russell straightened up. He tried to look cool, but instead he was shell-shocked. 'She's so tall, and her body, it's, it's positively indecent, and that bathing suit, Jeeze, it's so tiny.' His mouth was dry. 'What if 'it', I mean 'she' talks to me, I won't have a voice. I'll mumble. I'll mumble like a rube.'

"Am I bothering you sir?"

"No, no, heck no."

"I'm so sorry. You're shy, I can tell."

"I am shy. And in front of you I am in full regression. I'm, I'm shit faced scared.

"Don't be frightened. Come, sit with me on the pool steps." Lana said.

Russell, with a whole lot of trepidation, came to the steps and stopped.

"Truly, are you afraid of me?"

"Yes."

"Why?"

"Look at you. You are overwhelming. I'm a prairie clod. You're a feast."

"Common, sit. I don't bite."

Russell sat. He felt his thigh touch hers. Ooooohhh Sweet Jesus. The feeling sent wild, tingling, erotic, gooey sensations through his whole body. Like a numbskull, he tried to cover his deranged dink, (which was at full mast and throbbing shamelessly inside his bathing suit) with his hands…what a hope.

"My name is Lana."

"I'm Russell I think."

"Hi Russell."

"Hi Lana."

Lana from time to time tantalized men on purpose. It was a fault she recognized about herself. But her teasing was not for the purpose of being vindictive or mean it was done because she had fun doing it. And Lana never left her victim unsatisfied. She was most gracious about her game playing. Russell just happened to be in the right place at the right time. Yeah, he was next. He won't know what hit him. But be assured, the good lad will live happily ever after.

"Do you live around here Russell?"

"Yes, I think so."

"You think so?"

"Aw heck, I…

Just as he was about to explain himself Lana expropriated his entire psyche…she slid the tip of her pink tongue over her full sensuous lips.

'Ah damn, that does it," he mumbled.

"Pardon." Lana said. *Lana knew his feelings. This move had left many men, women and even massive audiences in a state of impious passion. Lana knew that along with her genius, she was the world's leading beauty. Whenever she made an enticing move of any kind she overwhelmed her beholders. She was after all 5' 11" of seductive femininity.*

"Please excuse my mumbling Miss Lana, you see you still frighten me. Anyway, I live in Kyle, Saskatchewan."

"Cool Russell, I was born in Swift Current. Practically neighbors aren't we. And what is your profession sir?"

"I work for the government. I am an agricultural engineer, U of S. graduate."

"How nice."

"And you Lana."

"Presently I am unemployed."

Russell sat stoically. He looked rather pathetic as he peeked at her from time to time.

Lana decided to shake him up a bit. She took his hand and pulled him into the water. They swam for a few minutes. At the three-foot level of the pool Lana stood. Her tawny mane flowed over her shoulders down her back to the tops of her buttocks. Her magnificent breasts rose and fell with each breath. Her tiny bikini did its best to cover her secret parts. Her face, which seldom had need of make-up, glowed. She beckoned Russell to come to her. When he came she had him stand toe to toe with her.

"We are about the same height aren't we Russell?"

"Yes we are." *Russell was beginning to feel more at ease with this Goddess until she spoiled it all by touching his lips with hers. He felt giddy. He wasn't sure if his legs were going to hold him. 'Damn me, damn me all to hell, I've got the Madonna here with me and I'm about to faint. What kind of a dork am I?'*

"Do I trouble you Russell?"

"Yes."

"Do you want me to leave?"

"No."

"Are you sure?"

"Yes."

"Look me in the eyes Russell." Lana knew her eyes were verboten to the uninitiated. They could send messages faster than any man made medium. They could express any emotion Lana was wont to express. They teemed with power and smoldered with sex.

Russell looked. He smiled. Her eyes expunged his faint-heartedness.

"Now, do you feel more like yourself?"

"Yes, I do Lana."

"Good." *Lana leaned toward him. She kissed the corners of his mouth, ran her fingers over his shoulders, up and down his arms then onto his chest. She parted her lips as she kissed his firm nipples. She lifted his arms and slid her tongue lightly under them. These moves demolished the poor beleaguered Russell.*

Russell knew he was on the front line of an impending love battle with the esoteric Love Goddess, Lana. "This is going to be one frenzied joy filled war," *he reckoned as he fell victim to her first onslaught.*

She took both of his hands and slipped them under her thong-like bottoms. She guided them onto each of her buttocks. She pulled herself tight up against his body. She worked her tongue into Russell's mouth as she kissed him. She reached under the back of his trunks and placed her hands on each of his buttocks. She pulled him to her. She felt his hardness. He was moaning.

Lana herself began to feel pleasure in her antics. She glanced around the pool. She satisfied herself that no one could see their upcoming sexual encounter. She was certain that Russell had not finished in his bathing trunks. She went down on her knees, took Russell's penis in her wet mouth then moved her mouth up and down his shaft as she sucked. Russell groaned. He filled his hands with Lana's hair, gritted his teeth, lifted his head skyward, and in exquisite ecstasy, and desiring nothing more in his young life than this precious moment he finished.

Lana rose and came face to face with him. He didn't look like the man who had come to the poolside an hour or so ago. He looked spent. But he looked golden. His gratification reached beyond cosmic splendor.

Gently Lana bunched her hands in his hair and pulled him down to her love nest. Sort'a quid pro quo you might say. Without ever having done this before Russell became exhilarated as he used his tongue to massage Lana's vagina. Lana moaned, called out, murmured, "Yes oh yes, don't ever stop, yes, this is heaven, yes, oh what are you doing now? Please Russell further that way, yes you are wonderful."

Russell's first encounter with cunnilingus was a gold medal performance. Lana's sensational orgasm was proof. In one short lesson Russell became a pro. Their love battle in the pool ended in a breathtaking stalemate.

Their night together at the Best Western was lively, cheerful, erotic and adventurous. Their acrobatics brought a new meaning to sex.

Lana remembered slipping away before Russell awoke.

When Russell arose several hours later, he found her note. It said, "You are adorable Russell." She had signed it Lana. Russell's life subsequent to his affair with Lana was lived on a higher, happier plane. He knew the woman whom had he had made love to was **the** *Dr. Lana Jean Masters. 'Why say anything,' he thought, 'heck, even with her note no one would believe me anyway.'*

* * *

"Are you with me Lana? You seem miles away. Is something bothering you, or are you just getting bored with me and Kupangg?" Father Donnely asked.

"No, no Father." Lana said with a devilish grin. "I thought I saw someone I recognized leave the restaurant a moment ago. Someone with whom I had a rather odd experience a year or two ago. Nothing of any consequence my dear man, please carry on with Kupangg"

CHAPTER 3
KUPANGG

"Ok Lana. To begin I was to meet in secret with Kupangg's dictator, QuaTang and his two associates, brothers actually, Lin and Loc Ng. I was flown into Kupangg under obscure wraps, James Bond like. I felt embarrassed, like a kid playing guns. Hell, I could have gone as motherfuckinggoose for all anyone cared. I even had a mysterious contact who was disguised as a hooker meet me at the airport. Believe it or not she had long blond hair. Quite a spectacular mix with her tawny skin and sexy Asian eyes. She was some broad. Nice name too, Jayleen. Anyway, it was like spy meets spy…dumb.

"I walked straight to her, no folderol, no spy meets spy crap. I did, however, like a good little boy, introduce myself to her as Stefan Boyce, my CIA given name. After I picked up my luggage she whisked me off to a waiting cab and away we went. We stopped at a luxury hotel in the affluent part of Keelung, Kupangg's capital city. "The city was made up of two parts, a tiny affluent one and the other one huge hellhole. The hellhole would make perfect grist for your so called humane drivel mill Lana, you pinky you."

"Careful lover boy."

"Sorry Your Highness."

"Carry on."

"The affluent part was isolated from the shack town by a "Y" in the Kwang River which flows through the city. The rich part was nestled in the crotch of the "Y" and tall hedges of oleander surrounded the top of the "Y." This kept the grand elite segregated from the scruff. Quite proper wouldn't you say darlin'? In any event when Jayleen and I arrived at the hotel I registered, and guess what?"

"Jayleen escorted you to your room."

"Right."

"Then?"

"It wasn't just a room with a bath, it was a beautiful suite. Two bedrooms, two baths, a john for guests, a living room, den and sauna, a wet bar, hell, even chocolates, cookies and other goodies. A fridge, coffee maker, microwave, and, best of all, yummy, delicious, Jayleen. Seeing she was a mere woman she occupied the smaller bedroom. This exotic chink needed no luggage because her walk-in closet was full of her clothing, shoes, et al, and her boudoir's dresser held all her scanties. Am I making you jealous Lana?"

"Not yet handsome."

"You piss me off Lana."

"I hope so Father."

"Anyway, other than the greetings we proffered one another when we first met, not another word was spoken between us until we were in our suite. I showered, put on a T-shirt, shorts, then repaired to the living room. Jayleen was snuggled up in a corner of a huge sofa clad in a silk, mini type kimono. She looked at me in a most analytical way as if to determine whether I was capable of doing what was expected of me on this mission. I didn't know from shit what her role was. I soon found out."

* * *

Ominously lightning flashed in the west.

Dessert along with small decanters of port and sherry were brought to their table.

"O'Tools is quite the place Lana. Is it new?"

"It's two years old. It has the reputation of being the finest place to dine throughout southwestern Saskatchewan.

"I'm sure it does. Should I carry on?"

"Please do."

"Jayleen began to impress me as someone in the know. She spoke in a soft Asian accent. 'Stefan,' she said, 'it is time for me to bring you up to date on certain matters of state. Please listen carefully. My government has been wavering between agreeing to change into a democracy with all the human rights attached thereto, or else becoming an even more militaristic dictatorship. Our leader is a strong, demanding, autocrat. He believes the masses are primitive creatures who have been put on earth to serve their masters. In fact Stefan, if it was my country's leaders choice he would line up all the dissidents among our country's peasants and blow them away. He would dismiss any thoughts about Kupangg becoming a democracy. He feels the masses are too stupid, lazy, uncouth, too everything to be burdened with governing. All these plebes know is food, shelter and having babies. Animals essentially. They are dullards who pay homage and taxes to their masters and who pay their last pennies to their church. They need to be led because they are incapable of leading. We, I mean our leader; can govern these primitives efficiently and effectively while their church can teach them to be meek and beholding. Good deal for the elite wouldn't you say Stefan?"

'Yes, quite, Jayleen.'

"However Stefan, our country's ruler has opted for a democratic nation. One of your ex-presidents is a very persuasive gentleman. He outlined the cons of remaining a totalitarian state. In particular he warned that inevitably, a bloody revolution would occur led by the masses against our governing body. Very much like Vietnam. The result would be communism. Then wholesale executions of our nobility would take place along with the dispossession of their wealth by the filthy reds.

"As to the idealistic couple, your former president was adamant about their safety. No harm was to come to them. Our esteemed leader agreed, but he had no intention of keeping such a promise. He and your CIA had other plans. This, of course, is where you come in. You have been commissioned by the CIA to execute the two would be revolutionaries in obfuscation just as Oswald was in the case of J.F.Kennedy. Our master will see to it that you will be rewarded if you are successful.

"Now hear this Stefan and hear this well. You must make certain the killings look as if they were done by a person or persons unknown to our ruler. Publicly our ruler will show great sorrow over their deaths. He will announce world wide that 'our great nation's' constabulary will hunt down the murderer or murderers relentlessly. He will offer a handsome reward for the capture of the killer or killers, dead or alive. So, as they say in America Stefan, be cool."

"Jayleen provided me with everything there was to know about the two assassinees. Pictures of them, their ages, height, weight, their friends, their habits, employment, address, where they shopped for their measly goods—everything.

"And Lana, do you know what my thoughts were pertaining to this job being asked of me? 'Piss on the bunch of them,' I thought, 'why not shoot them all, the ruler, his henchmen and the two 'pinkies.' Wouldn't that be something? Why traipse around like a god dam idiot spy? Why all the cloak and dagger stuff. Fool everybody. Sumbitch huh? So I worked out a nasty scheme of my own, one I effected and executed brilliantly.

"Jayleen was one smart broad. Before she got the ball rolling on her government's and the CIA's plot, she balled me. She indulged me. Best damn sex next to you. I knew she was using sex as a doggie treat. Perform for your master, roll over, sit, and shake a paw and all that shit and you get your doggie treats. Here Fido all the tits and ass you want as long as you 'be' a good puppy.

"Jayleen beckoned me to join her on the sofa. She was some stacked for a god dam chink, beautiful ass, tits out to here and a delicious mouth. And guess what Lana, that Bentley guy who wrote 'The Ocean Turned Milky' was right, Chinese girls' peepees do go up and down not sideways like some people think."

"No shit Father."

"No shit."

"Anyway Jayleen teased me for a good hour. She had me pulsating. We made love 'til I was rendered erectless.

"Isn't that a shame? Rendered erectless."

"Yeah, and the next day my work began."

* * *

"Jayleen and I were taken by limo to the big man's grand palace. Jayleen went through all the security stations as if she owned the place. I was surprised at the ease with which we swept through all the barricades leading to the dictator's pad. Yes my dear, an 86,000 square feet pad of decadent luxury Lana. A doorman ushered us into the palace. The dude bowed to Jayleen and in perfect English said her father was expecting us. Her father, holy sheeeit, this beautiful tart is the great one's daughter. Cock a snook I said to myself. Wadda ya know, just a few hours ago I banged his kid every way known to man.

"Now are you getting a wee bit jealous sweet one?"

"Never mind, just carry on lover boy."

"I shall. Jayleen escorted me to a very large study. A study filled with goodies. Huge leather bound chairs and sofas, two desks, lap tops, other computers, TV screens, a sound system, old masters paintings, everything Lana. I sat next to Jayleen on one of the grand sofas. No sooner had we sat than a maid, quite an exquisite maid I might add, brought us tea. Jayleen and I chatted as we sipped our tea until a short, handsome, husky, black-haired gentleman entered the room. Jayleen stood as this distinguished looking man strolled over to her, kissed her cheek, gave her a hug, backed away from her as he held her hands and beamed at the sight of her. Smiling at one another they spoke in their native tongue. Jayleen kissed her father's cheek then turned to me and beckoned me to come join them. When I reached their side Jayleen introduced me to her father. I must say Lana; it was exciting meeting this man whom I had read so much about.

"He was polite, genteel, well spoken, with, of all things, a Bostonian accent. He appeared to me to be quite shy. It seemed odd that a man with a masters degree in engineering, a doctorate in political science, the dictator of several million people and a billionaire many times over would be shy. As I found out later, he was about as shy as ants at a picnic. His accent, well he lived in Boston for 10 years as he attended school there. He moved back to Kupangg after he received his degrees from MIT. In any event, his accent was quite charming.

'I am delighted to meet you Stefan. I have heard a great deal about your exploits. You are an accomplished person sir, and I admire you for that.'

"For several minutes we talked about everything but the topic of murder. Family, kids, weather, sporting events, the good old religious right and his adoration for this group. I was in no hurry, hell, I could tolerate this luxury as long as they wanted to heap it on me.

"In due course Quan Tang summoned two of his cohorts to join us, the brothers Ng, Lin Kong and Loc Pen. They were short dudes, but they looked fit. They spoke flawless English. They did not appear to be suck-ups, obsequious obviously, but not suck-ups. They knew who was boss, no doubt about that, but they gave a clear impression of being independent thinkers, yet devoted to their master, Quan Tang.

"Now the Big Man brought about the topic of his country's politics. First he made it clear he was the State's fuehrer. He alone made the final decisions pertaining to State matters. He alone knew what was best for the unwashed and he alone knew how to rule and govern the affairs of his State. He was pissed off with the US, Canada, et al for their democratic pettiness. How dare they insult his ego and intelligence?

And how dare they carry on with their heartless sanctions. His country's coffers were running low. And that meddling past president of the USA, what right has he got to proffer his warnings about internal strife and civil war by 'my' loyal subjects.

"In truth Lana, the only reason why the lousy bastard bowed to our past president's warning's was his fright of losing his personal wealth. Good old Quan Tang, money was his main object. With the covenant given him by us good guys about the preservation of his wealth turned him from his nationalistic stance to just another greedy s.o.b.

"By damn Lana, he carried on with his rantings for a couple of hours. Finally he said to me 'Stefan believe me, after I give up my rule in favor of democracy, my countrymen will wallow in their own stinking ineptitude. They will drown in their own cesspool of ignominy and thousands will die in countless revolutions. Don't you know this Stefan? My country's people go back over 2000 years all under my kind of rule. My people know nothing but totalitarianism. But Stefan, in spite of all that I have said I have acceded to your country's wishes, Kupangg will become a democracy. Now sir, it is your move. You must assassinate those two unspeakable revolutionaries, Soo Ling and her husband Yen Poon Ling.'

"After berating Ling and Ling for several minutes he gave me some documents which he needed verified and signed by me attesting to their accuracy. These documents disclosed the cash assets owned by 'his greatness' along with Jayleen's and Lin and Loc Ng. Our governments, who had covenanted the preservation of these peoples' wealth following Quan Tang's abdication, wanted independent proof of ownership. Christ Lana, Tang's net worth was a whopping $38 billion US of which $5 billion was held in cash in various Swiss banks. Jayleen had ½ billion in US dollars in Swiss banks; Lin Ng had 1.2 billion and Loc 1 billion. Tang informed me that I would be leaving the next day for Zurich, Switzerland where I was to verify the ownership of these monies. Yes babe, I was flown by Tang's jet the very next morning.

"While we were discussing my assignments I had the opportunity of seeing Quan Tang's iron rule in action. A ruckus had broken out on Keelung's main drag, Ming Alley. Some peasants had tried to abscond with some discarded food from a dump truck. They had broken one of the truck's windows during the melee. The truck driver called the police on his cell. When the police arrived they contacted their chief who in turn contacted Tang. Within minutes the scrambling ceased. 22 riddled bodies lay strewn on the street. The police hung the bodies upside down from poles lining Ming Alley. They looked like slaughtered pigs in an abattoir. Shit Lana, some of the bodies were not dead. They fuckin' howled, screamed, wailed, kicked, bucked and convulsed as they bounced around on the meat hooks hooked through their feet. Quan smiled as he said 'See Stefan how I handle such disobedience.'

"Following this episode Jayleen escorted me to a smaller room. She wasted no time with me, Lana. She slipped out of her clothes disrobed me, led me to a chaise lounge, pushed me down on it, then snuggled in beside me. Huh I thought, fornication time. Rather an odd activity after such weighty business we had just concluded. Oh well, what the hell, who am I to question Kupangg's culture. No such luck. Jayleen reached down to the floor, picked up some papers, nipped my neck then touched her lips to signal sssshhhh. Now she began to read the details regarding the Ling couple whom I was to blow away. I must say we did indulge ourselves after she clued me in.

*   *   *

I arrived in Zurich the next evening. I had not gone 20 steps into the terminal before being met by 2 well-dressed men, Max Werner and Frederich Sholtz. They were good. They handled my luggage pickup and my security clearances. They escorted me to a waiting limousine whose chauffeur drove us to the Hotel St. Moritz. They gave me all the information about the banks I would be attending, the names of the banks' chairpersons and all that jazz. They told me the limo and its drivers were at my disposal 24 hours a day, and that they themselves would be available to me at any time. But Lana Jean, they were unaware of the fact that I would not need their help. I had the whole shitereee planned out as a solo act.

"My scheme was simple, no spy hijinks, just good old common sense. I concluded the audit on Tang's bank holdings and found them to be in order, yeah, $5 billion principal in US funds plus a coupla 100 thousand bucks interest. Tang probably forgot about the 200 grand. Following my audits I returned to the bank, which held the preponderance of Tang's funds. Again I met with the bank's Chairman who also held the title of C.E.O. Nice guy, family man, wife and six kids. It was a pity I had to stiff him."

"So it was you who went on the murder binge in Zurich back then? You are a monster aren't you Father?" Lana said.

"Yeah, 'twas me." Lana's guest said with a smile. "In those days and up to two or three days ago I was a monster. Now I am a real sweetheart.

"Should I go on Lana?"

"Yes, please do."

"Before I left Kupangg for Switzerland I had the good sense to have Jayleen get me some of her father's letterheads. I had become an expert in forging names. You would have been proud of my expertise therein. I used the good old onionskin paper and needlepoint punch caper in crafting these plagiarisms. I'm sure you know from whence I speak?"

"Yes, Father, I know."

"When I met with the banker the second time I had this cleverly drafted forged letter with me. I had sealed it with Quan Tang's wax. I presented it to him. He swiveled his chair around so his back was to me, opened the letter and after a few moments muttered 'my, my.' He turned his chair back around looked at me and said 'my good man, if you would be kind enough to wait in my outer office I shall dictate a response to Mr. Tang and forthwith give you a sealed envelope containing my reply.'

"In just 15 minutes I had the reply to my forgery in a closed envelope under the bank's official seal.

"Now Lana an odd thing occurred while I was still in Kupangg. I was left alone for a few moments in Tang's office. Lying beside a shredder was a balled up piece of paper, which, I suspect, missed being shredded. Curious old me picked the wad up, opened it and tilt, the words were in Kupangg's language. I stuck the thing in my pocked and never gave it another thought until I was relaxing in my room in the St. Moritz. For some unknown reason I got the paper out of my jacket pocket and deciphered it via my translation book. I laughed to beat hell. I knew Tang and his henchmen were going to wax me when I completed my assignments, and here the order was in writing proving me right. It read,'To L. and L., have Stefan killed immediately after his work is completed. Quan T.'

"Nice guy hey Lana?"

"Yes lover boy, about your caliber."

"You don't mean that do you sweetie."

"Like fuck I don't. Get on with your story Father."

"It's not a story Lana, it's fact."

"C'mon get on with it."

"Ok, when I got back to the hotel from my meeting with the banker, I was able to open the banker's letter to Tang, read its message and, of course, close it as if it had never been disturbed. The response was what I wanted. It read: 'Thank you your highness. Our bank will be pleased to deposit the funds of Lin Kong Ng and Loc Pen Ng into your account when such funds are transferred over to our bank etc., etc. I confirm the amounts to be $I.2 billion I.0 billion US and US respectively etc., etc.

"What thinkest thou my dearest one, are you with me?"

"Of course I'm with you. Now with a forged letter to Lin and Loc's bankers you had Lin and Loc's monies transferred to Quan Tang's account. I see the picture. You're cute Father."

* * *

Lana could hear rain falling on the skylight above them. She noticed too that the wind had picked up and that lightning flashes in the west had become more numerous. 'Damn,' she thought, 'sure as hell I'll get caught in the middle of this storm just as I'm about to take lover boy to his final destination. Ain't that just loquacious ferret farts.'

"As you can guess Lana, I wanted to cover any fuck-ups pertaining to my actions with the rascals I was dealing with. To be certain of this my agenda was filled with the word 'kill.'

Yeah, smoke the turkeys. First one on the agenda was Tang's banker. I hit this dude while he was enjoying his lunch at an outdoor café. Got him right in the middle of his forehead, yeah, a clean, bloodless hole. Face ok, but the back of his skull became a part of the wall behind his chair. Remarkable, my silencer had worked its wonders. The only sound audible was the hubbub of the crowd. I waited around for a few minutes. He just sat there dead 'r'n a doornail, upright, eyes wide open, no blinking, his face getting whiter and whiter. I strolled back to my hotel, which was only two blocks away. I dropped off my briefcase, sponged, and then walked back to the scene of the crime. The good old stiff still sat there but his body was slanted slightly to the right. A pretty young waitress seated me next to two ladies who were talking French. They nodded as I sat. I used a sexy French accent to order tea. My back was to the banker. Both ladies hiked up their skirts as they talked. Nice gams too. Suddenly there was a loud terrifying scream. I twisted about in my chair shock written all over my face as the scream continued. The two ladies looked in the direction of the screamer. Soon the whole cafeteria was in an uproar. The banker had slumped forward. His face filled his salad bowl while the rest of his head was dripping off the wall.

"Like a good person, I along with others, rushed over to the screamer. When I saw the mess the banker had made, I feigned nausea and returned to my seat. The police came. I was free to go following a few questions. I left for Kupangg the next day.

"I was met by Jayleen at her father's private landing strip. On the way back to the palace she asked me if I was the one who slew her father's Swiss banker. What? I said, acting dumbstruck, your father's Swiss banker. He was alive and well when I left Zurich. What the hell are you talking about? Jesus I was cool Lana. Jayleen believed me. She showed me her country's only newspaper, Quan Tang's of course. The paper told of the banker's murder as reported by Reuters. No arrests as yet, but plenty of suspects. Yeah, in a pig's eye. I showed shock and sorrow at the news of his death. I told Jayleen I found him to be a good sort, and a most obliging servant of the bank. "I'm so very sorry," I said to her.

"Jayleen instructed her driver to take us to our hotel. Her driver was a smart looking, 30ish, raven-haired Chinese beauty. She parked the limo in front of the hotel's entrance, let herself out, came around to our doors, opened them for us, bowed as we exited, then for Chris sake escorted us into the elevator. She stayed at our side until we were safely in our room. Imagine Lana, a 5' zip, 100 lb. slender little Oriental body guarding me.

"Groovy lover boy."

"It was 5:30 when we arrived at our suite. Jayleen joined me in the shower. We played with one another, soaped one another and dried one another. We lounged in the buff as we sipped some excellent wine unknown to me. We ordered a light dinner from room service. We went to bed just after nine. I lay on my side exhausted. Jayleen snuggled up in front of me. My rod layeth twixt her curvy buttocks. We slept until 8 the next morning. Then we banged each other. Once again we showered. I felt goooood, in fact I felt so good I made our breakfast. The fridge was full of goodies and the bowl on the dinette table was loaded with fruit. The omelet I made was so tasty we both had seconds. And surprise of all surprises, Jayleen had Starbucks coffee for us; yes Starbucks, the nectar of the Gods.

"Jayleen and I discussed the two revolutionaries I was to kill. She made it clear to me once again that her father and the Ng brothers could not be associated nor appear to be associated with the couple's death. I must be most circumspect in my disposition of the duo. I assured her I would."

* * *

"I had no intention of sitting by a window on the second floor of some crappy old building with a high-powered rifle in my hands waiting for the exact moment to shoot the couple as they soap-boxed from the steps of a beaten-up, run-down, old post office building. I wanted to be close enough to my quarry to see the neat round holes my bullets would leave in their foreheads. No picture show shit. Just put on some seedy old duds, go unshaven a coupla' days, wear a floppy wide-brim hat, messy hair, walk up to the post office steps and bang, shoot the two fuckers. But see Lana, I needed a little diversion, not only for the fun of it, but to get the crowds' attention away from the couple. It was so simple baby, I felt a little guilty in hamstringing the pathetic proletarian dweebs.

"I bought a few packages of small firecrackers, and strung them together. I put an extra length of fuse into the first package so the little cuties would not start to pop off 'til I was near the intended victims. I stuck the little mothers on a window ledge across the street from the post office, and then waited for the crowd to thicken and the duo to be well into their orations. Then I lit the fuse. All hell broke loose as the firecrackers exploded. The crowd was sure Quan Tang's Gestapo was on the scene. I tucked my hands into the floppy gunnysack jacket I held over my arm got hold of the butts of my pistols and let fly. The Ling commies hit the ground just like everyone else did Lana, 'cept'n they each had a neat hole in their foreheads, and, essentially, lacked a full cranium. Oh I forgot to tell you sweet stuff, I had stuck a dozen blockbuster 'crackers' among the little ones, you know, for special effects.

"Many of the deadbeats cowered, some screamed, some shit themselves and some ran like scared rabbits. I was one of the rabbits. I hightailed it outta there waving my arms and hollerin' my head off. I was back in my hotel room in 30 minutes with blood all over my face.

I had done the job to perfection but I had screwed up removing my old rags. I shot myself as I disrobed the rags for Chris sake. Not a serious wound, just a grazing along my left temple. But damn if it didn't make me fall face first on the ground. Not only did I feel foolish Lana, but it hurt. Lucky for me no one saw my swan dive. By the time I got to the hotel I had the bleeding under control but I looked terrible. I went directly to the hotel's doctor's office. He took me to a hospital, shaved my head, stitched me up and bandaged my wound. He made me spend the night in the hospital. I phoned Jayleen. She came immediately. At first she cried when she saw me then laughed when I told her my sad story. You see Lana, she thought I had been wounded in action. When she finished poking fun at me she climbed into bed with me and stayed the night.

* * *

"Two days later I was back in Quan Tang's drawing room along with Quan, Lin, Loc and Jayleen. Tea was served. Some idle chatter took place including Whitewater, Jessica Flowers, some Jones broad and a White House intern. I kinda' missed the name of the intern. 'Goodness,' Quan said, 'I have 17 beautiful maidens as my playthings at all times. I see nothing wrong with your Chief Executive having some toys. My countrymen admire me for my masculinity.

"Finally I handed Messrs. Tang, Ng and Ng the sealed envelopes I had carried back from Zurich. You would have been proud of me Lana, I was so cool, but doll, I couldn't wait for the inevitable eruption. I was like a kid inside...wheeeee...anti anti eye over...anti anti eye over...pig'sfuckingtail. 'Hurry dudes read the shit' I said to myself, 'lets get it on.' 5 then 10 minutes went by without a sound. All three read and re-read the shit several times. Lin and Loc's faces went from pink to red to crimson. They were seething. They began to speak then shriek at their 'grand master' in Chinese. Good old Tang looked terrified. Lin and Loc now knew of the expropriation of their funds by Tang. Whoooeee! Tang cowered. No question he was trying to tell his hench men there must be some mistake. He appeared to be begging. I'm positive Tang was blaming me for the mistakes because he kept pointing his finger at me. He walked over to them and attempted to hug them to show his sincerity. They just pushed him away. Tang made a sudden move for the door. Loc tackled him. Damn fine tackle too Lana. Lin ran to a panel of switches and immobilized them all by a pull of a master control.

" 'You lying dog son of a mongrel,' Loc roared in English. He pulled a revolver from his belt and shot Tang 3 times in the gut. Jayleen screamed. Tang didn't fall. Panic-stricken, bewildered and frightened he looked down at his bleeding gut. Like a helpless child he tried to stop the blood flow with his hands. Then he looked up at me, pointed in my direction and shrieked 'he's the one you should be shooting, not me. The wretched cur of a Yankee must have done this when he was in Zurich, shoot him.' He took his bloodied hands away from his wounded gut and let out a chilling cry. He wept as he began to sway back and forth like a drunk. He reached for his desk for support. He looked down at his blood soaked shirt and jacket in disbelief. 'How could you not trust me?' he said as he looked up. 'I am your beloved benefactor. For the love of God shoot the slimy Yankee, not me,' he wailed.

'You lie you filthy pig,' Lin shouted. 'Your whole life has been one big lie. Yet we did trust you you son of a whore. 28 years serving you and this is our reward.' Blood began to trickle from Tang's mouth. Loc fired another shot hitting the 'little dictator' in the heart. Jayleen screamed again as she pulled a pistol from her purse. Her father sprawled onto his desk sending papers and desk paraphernalia flying. Before Jayleen could shoot either of the brothers guess what Lana? I got 'em both with my big 45. Poor Jayleen, she threw herself on her father's corpse as I did my clean up. I strolled over to Loc's body, slipped on a glove, retrieved Loc's revolver with my gloved hand just as the sobbing Jayleen looked up at me. 'No, Stefan don't, please, I love you,' were the last words ever spoken by Jayleen. She fell on her dead father after I put a bullet through her glistening forehead."

"My hero," Lana said sarcastically. "You shot Jayleen. What the hell for? I'm sure she did love you, and…

"Fuck her Lana, I love only you."

"Finish your story Father."

At that moment the lights in the restaurant dimmed as a monstrous crackle sounded as a lightning flash exploded.

"Holy shit Lana, that was one close mother."

"Go on Father, I'm here so don't be frightened."

"Me frightened, don't be silly sweetie cake. Anyway, there's not much more to tell. I shot Loc and Lin only after I was satisfied that Quan Tang was dead. You see I wanted the world to know that I tried to kill the Ngs before they stiffed the 'big man.' But, dash it all big world out there, I was too late. And, of course, the neat correspondence pieces I delivered the three men from Zurich spoke for themselves. As for poor Jayleen, hell, the police would find it was Loc's gun that killed her and they would presume she was whacked because she threatened Loc and Lin with her piece. So my whole plan worked as I had intended. If I got killed along the way I didn't care. If I pulled the stunt off I would have the satisfaction of knowing I fucked up a whole nation's political position. Yeah, from a hard line fascist dictatorship to ruddy bedlam. And you know as well as I do Lana, the place is still up for grabs. Every religious faction is battling for control. Maybe when a new regime is established in Kupangg the CIA will hire me for another kick at the cat. Who knows?

CHAPTER 4

LANA'S CHAMBRE DE EXECUTION

WARNING—UNUSUAL SEX

The storm was centered above the city now. The mix of wind, hail and thunder was deafening. Lightning was so close it sizzled before it exploded into ear splitting thunder. Lana sat unperturbed. Some diners were terrified. Even Father Donnely appeared to be jumpy. He wanted to get to Lana's father's farm before the city of Swift Current was blown off the map. He rose, excused himself and made his way to the men's washroom. This gave Lana time to slip a knockout drop in her guest's after dinner drink. The drug would keep 'lover boy' out for about two hours, just time enough for her to complete her plans. After her guest returned to their table and finished his drink they decided to leave for the farm. By the time they ran to her car they were soaked. After getting settled in their seats, seat belts done up Lana's guest's head fell to one side. He was 'out.'

Lana cursed the storm because she knew it could cause her to take more time than she had bargained for to drive to the farm. Why hadn't she just stayed in Manhattan and forgotten this shit? No, she had vowed the deed she was about to perform must be completed as she had planned. She turned right onto number-four highway north from Central Avenue and began the eight-mile trip to the farm.

They arrived at the farm in about 20 minutes, ten minutes longer than usual. She drove to the barn's main entrance pushed the automatic door opener and drove into one of the huge barn's parking stalls. She wrestled her guest's body out of the car, and then dragged him over to the spot she intended to use as her killing field. Lana had made certain her father's farm other than herself and her guest would be vacant for seven days. This would give her ample time to carry out her plans.

While Lana busied herself with the task of securing her guest to the barn floor she thought about Uncle Fred. It was seventeen years ago in this very barn she had done away with the rotten old bastard. Even though she was just 12 years old at the time, she had planned his demise well. It was during the re-roofing stage of this grand old barn back in 1979 when Lana had put her plan into action. She had seen to it that the stanchion Uncle Fred was going to use for support broke when he leaned on it. Indeed, good old Uncle Fred leaned. This caused him to fall 30' onto two upright pitchforks held in clamps that jutted out 2' from the south wall of the barn. Uncle Fred had made a dreadful mess. He had screamed blood-curdling screams as he writhed on those abominable forks. He died before the ambulance arrived. How she despised her Uncle Fred. She remembered his dreadful forays into pedophilia, and the sickening sexual advances he made towards her from the time she was little. 'Cummon,' she said to herself, 'forget Uncle Fred, get on with your current project. Lover boy here will be awake in less than an hour.'

First she placed a blanket on the spot where her guest was to be reposited. She did after all want him to be comfortable. She removed his clothing, laid him on his back, spread-eagled his nude body, strapped down his midsection, secured his arms to the metal cleats on the cement floor at 45 degree angles from his shoulders above his head, fastened his legs to metal cleats about 30 inches apart at his feet and then secured on his lower torso the dreadful surprise she had in store for him.

Now she inserted a CD into the barn's sound system, turned it on and listened to the lyrics she intended to play during her guest's last few hours on earth. Perry Como's beautiful ballad, "*Alone from night to night you'll find me, to weak to break the chains that bind me, I need no shackles to remind me, I'm just a prisoner of love....*"

Next she fitted with foolproof care the major portion of a large sturdy birdcage over her guest's genitalia, one that reached down past his anus and stretched back to just below his ribs. She attached it so it could not be dislodged regardless of her guest's struggles. She had chosen this birdcage because its construction was such that the prisoners Lana had just put inside it could not escape through its bars. Lana then moved her guest's body in a position so his anus and genitalia were over one of the barn's sewer holes.

The day before all these shenanigans began, Lana, using every muscle in her body and with great caution, installed a large mirror on the rafters above where her guest was to lie. This she had done to be certain her guest would have the best seat in the 'barn' to contemplate his performance as the lead actor in Lana's play. As well Lana had seen to it that ample lighting was available day and night not just for her, the audience, but for him the star performer of his upcoming quietus.

To the right of her guest were several stacks of baled hay, the top of which was perfect for viewing the play. Lana clamored up the side of the bales then at the top she unfolded a blanket and proceeded to make herself a comfortable nest in the hay. Being a hot muggy evening Lana stripped down to her bra and panty. There she sat, knees apart, the soles of her feet together, elbows on her knees and her chin cupped in her hands. She waited for her guest to waken.

Lana's guest was in some respects her professional counterpart. Her feelings toward him over the years ranged from unbounding love to despicable hate. In the beginning their love was soft, gentle, fun and adventurous, as well it was fulfilling. Fulfilling to the extent that Lana felt certain it was impossible for life to get any better. She was wrong. During their nine years of friendship, love and devotion he transformed from a warm caring man into a ruthless, sadistic sex-starved monster. He was hell on earth.

*   *   *

Lana relaxed as she listened to Perry Como's soft baritone voice. She knew that over the next few days she would get little or no sleep. After a few minutes she looked down at lover boy and saw through his bleary eyes he was looking up at her. He smiled, winked and mumbled, "what the hell happened to me baby? The last thing I remember is running to your car through that fucking storm?"

Father Donnely, the improbable farce, yawned, stretched, and tried to pull himself up. He began to put some real effort into rising after his first efforts failed. He yanked his arms, struggled to draw his legs up, tried to arch his back and when he convinced himself he was tied up tight he winked once again at Lana and with a wry smile said, "Okay doll what's this all about? Sex. I'm nude right Lana? And why the shackles?"

"Cause Romeo I want to watch your reactions through what I think will be the most memorable sexual experience you have ever had. Yeah and while you are shackled, you know, shackled vis-à-vis some of our past tidings, pari passu and all that rot.

Her guest was silent for a brief period of time while he squirmed and wiggled in an attempt to free himself.

*I need no shackles to remind me I'm just a prisoner of love...*filtered through the solitude of the barn.

"Hey Sweet stuff, some furry things are moving around down there," he said as he lifted his head and looked toward his groin. "Yaaah, they seem to be nipping at my dick...man...it feels good. Are they rabbits? Cool...nice touch Lana." He fantasized as only he could fantasize. He wanted to maximize his pleasure. He wanted this feeling to go on and on. This was a first; soft harmless bunny rabbits toying with his thing.

Wow. He revolved his hips, closed his eyes, bit his lower lip and moaned "so furry Lana, so tickly…so squirmy…so ecstatic." He wanted to hold back ejaculation as long as possible. 'Lana was right,' he thought, 'this could be a most memorable sexual experience, it could be the greatest. Hare hijinks, what next? "Hear that Lana, hare hijinks, get it, hare spelled h-a-r-e." Lana smiled. He glanced up at her magnificent face and saw her slide her pink tongue over her moist, full, lips, and then he saw her pull her bra down so that her incomparable breasts were bared. "Shit Lana, what are you doing to me?" he asked grinning. "Son of a bitch, look out world, here I come, whoooeee." He could hold back no longer. Like a small Vesuvius his penis erupted. Father Donnely groaned with pleasure. He was breathless. His body relaxed. He was spent. "Night, night Lana. See you later. Don't forget to unchain me. Love you." The wanton killer fell into a deep sleep.

Dr. Masters had evoked a most frightful plan for the execution of her guest. The prisoners in the sturdy cage were not rabbits; they were in fact three starved rats, an adult male, a juvenile male and an adult female. Their escape route was singular. The only exit for the hungry rats was through Father Donnely's soft gut.

Lana busied herself adjusting her nest in the hay. She squirmed, pushed the baled hay hither and thither, wiggled, patted down her soft comfy blanket, laid on her tummy put her elbows down and put her chin in her cupped hands. Dr. Masters then began to think back on her life. What a life it had been in her scant 29 years. She remembered most everything about herself from the time she was just two years old. Her mom, dad, sister, brothers, her chickens, her fun on the farm-ranch, her friends, teachers, her holidays, her dad's hired hands, the cattle, horses, the farm machinery…and her stallion Sir Galahad and her dad's behemoth bull, Big Buster. She thought back on her academic achievements, her worldwide lectures (in particular in Istanbul) her six-year stint as a Manhattan bag lady and her incredible association with the Universes' 12 Controllers.

And her awful Uncle Fred!

Lana's thoughts were in the deep recesses of her brain. Her mind was weaving itself through her past. She was drowsy, yet her thoughts were as clear as an unblemished television picture.

Her guest whom had had that vigorous ejaculation just moments ago, together with his long journey from New York City that day and, of course, the little 'shot' Lana had slipped in his glass of port at dinner left him exhausted.

He slept as if he was comatose.

The hungry rats began to feed.

CHAPTER 5

LANA'S REMARKABLE CHILDHOOD

Lana Masters had told Uncle Fred to leave her alone. He just leered at her as he walked out of the barn. Without her family's knowledge she hated him. Lana was just six years old, yet she knew he was a bloody pervert. Lana had read about pedophiles, sex, masturbating, gays, and all these strange things before she was five-years-old. Masters and Johnson's; *All You Ever Wanted To Know About Sex*—she had read them all. "Damn Uncle Fred and his sticky out pecker behind his overalls anyway. The next time he rubs it against me I'll whack it one. I should tell mom and dad about the horny old fool (Uncle Fred was 36). "But dammit all, I like to work things out on my own." And she did. Lana had seen and felt Uncle Fred's thing eleven times since he started these latest escapades three months ago. Before that he had patted her cute little behind just like her mom and dad did, you know, like any living, devoted family member. "The bastard," she thought, "patting my behind like mom and dad was just an excuse to touch me, the old fart," she thought, "he'll be sorry, I'll git him, yes Uncle Fred, keep this shit up and I'll have your balls."

Lana Jean Masters was born in the Swift Current Union Hospital, in the charming little city of Swift Current, Saskatchewan. The date was October 29th, 1967. She was a good size baby at birth weighing eight-pounds, five-ounces. She differed from other babies following her delivery. Instead of looking like Edward G. Robinson as most wrinkled squalling little primates do, Lana Jean, within 24 hours of her life, looked adorable. The birth of this child was the beginning of a life that would prove to be unequaled. She was to excel in everything she did.

Her parents, physician, church minister and her parents' friends recognized that little Lana Jean was unlike all other children they knew or had read about. She walked at nine months, spoke her first words at five months and she could carry on a reasonable conversation by the time she was one. She could read the local newspaper, books, periodicals and the bible by twenty-four months. She could read and understand mathematics, certain sciences, chemistry and physics by the time she was four, and at that age she could read music and play the piano. On top of all this, she was a frisky, healthy, tawny-haired, beautiful child.

She loved the farm. She tussled with her older sister Margaret and her older brothers Raymond, Steven and Carl Jr. She had swings and teeter-totters to play on. Old, inert, well kept machinery to pretend all kinds of things on. She had sheds and huge barns to play in. She cared for a few chickens and a cocky old rooster her parents had bought her. She had her own little vegetable garden to tend. Every winter three farm hands, and three rough and tumble cowboys employed by her father would build and flood a skating rink for the kids and adults to play on. She had her own pretty bedroom that was furnished in soft pinks, yet with plenty of farm reminders. Pictures of prairie sunsets, swaying wheat fields, a cowgirl on a huge, shiny black rearing stallion. She had her own television set, a radio and a "record player." Best of all, Lana Jean had her very own tawny-haired stallion, a huge regal looking stallion. Lana Jean had named him Sir Galahad.

When she was just six-years-old, her Dad had taken the family to a state fair in Great Falls, Montana. The reason for the trip was business. Carl Masters and his foreman, Hank Drennan, had heard that some 'mighty fine' Hereford bulls were 'going for' a mere $70,000. Carl thought it would be fun for his children and a good learning experience for them, too, to see a cattle auction in session and the things to look for in a prize breeding bull. Carl drove his Lincoln accompanied by his wife, Raymond, Steven and Margaret while Hank took Carl Jr. and Lana Jean in the Land Rover.

The kids had a ball. They rode every ride on the fair's midway. They tasted every tidbit sold by the food hawkers. The fair's "smell" was captivating…hamburgers and onions, hot dogs, hot tamales, sauerkraut, buttered corn; and the cotton candy, wowee, just everything. The sideshows, to Lana Jean the sideshows were fun but 'phony.' This child's mind was so sapient, so erudite, so sagacious that she could describe in detail animals that had been extinct for millions of years, yet whose pictures or write-ups she had never been privy to. Take for instance the mighty saber tooth tiger and its saber-shaped upper canines. Or any of the flying reptiles known as pterosaurs, including the frightening pterodactyl. Lana Jean, without ever having seen a duplicate of them before was able not only to describe these extinct species in detail, but she was able to relate the time period in which they lived. Scary. This child was far more than just a genius, she was an intellectual phenomenon. Yes, the sideshows to her were just places to pay to get in, but fun.

It was time for the children to attend the auction with their father and Hank. My, what a show. The animals were groomed like high fashion models. A magnificent one-year-old Hereford calf in due course was shown. His pedigree line was perfect…a perfect young bull. His legal name was Sir Percival Smyth-Evans, his moniker was Buster. Carl Masters paid $76,000 for this future revenue producer. Carl just kept bidding for the young bull until he owned him. His investment paid off. Buster's hourly fees made doctors and lawyers' fees look like tooth fairy droppings. The kids jumped for joy knowing this bovine beauty was to become part of their dad's herd.

While this auction was taking place, Lana Jean had spied another beautiful animal, a tawny golden haired gelding colt. It was tethered to a rig not unlike the hitching posts seen in western movies. Neat, Lana

Jean thought. The colt held his head high. His body glistened, his muscles rippled. His tail and mane were long and flowing. He would rear up on his powerful hind legs; toss his majestic head and neigh. "He is going to grow into one huge fatha," Lana Jean mused.

Lana Jean had to do some high power convincing to get her dad and mom to buy the gelding for her. No wrangling, just be straightforward. Get Mom and Dad together and tell them she needed this foal. Assure them she and her brothers and sister would care for him. They would feed him, brush him down, clean his stall, train him (Hank and she could break him in for riding), exercise him…do everything for him.

After Carl Masters and Hank had cleared up all the paper work needed to consummate the purchase of 'Buster' Lana Jean was able to get her father and mother, brothers and sister together. Without ceremony she led them to the gelding. "Mom and Dad," she said, "I want him!" She pointed to the young stud. "Whatever his cost, I give you my covenant that I shall repay you that cost, plus interest thereon at 100 basis points above the Royal Bank of Canada's prime rate, by the time I am seven."

"Lana Jean," her father replied, "we don't need another stud on our spread."

"I know that father. I want him for my own enjoyment, not for studding."

"Lana dear, you are too young to manage a growing young stallion."

"I beg to differ with you father. I would have him 'eating out of my hands' within one week."

"Lana Jean," Lana's mother broke in "his asking price is $60,000. He's not a racer, nor a good range horse for round-ups like a quarter horse is. He's a lot of money for just a fun horse. My goodness child, we have plenty of horses and you know you can have your pick of any one of them."

"Mom and Dad, I want that horse. I will pay for him just as I said, by the time I am seven." Lana Jean's deep blue eyes were not in a pleading mode. No, they were flashing power, albeit loving power.

"Lana don't talk foolish about raising $60,000 in the next year and a half. All of us know you are an extraordinary child, but my darling girl, $60,000," her father replied.

"Mom and Dad, look at this." Lana Jean fetched a bank passbook from her small purse, opened it and showed them the latest figures in her book, dated just the day before. The book showed a balance of $312,000.

"Great Scott," Carl Masters bellowed, "Who at the bank made that up for you child, its either a play thing the bank does for you, or a terrible bank error, which is it?"

"Neither Dad, I earned every cent of it myself. Mr. Evers, our bank manager, made me a good trade-off. He and his staff gave me their word they would say nothing about my account to anyone provided I waived all interest that otherwise would be earned on it. I was the one who demanded both conditions. You see, Mom and Dad, if the account earned any interest, such interest would be added to your annual income, thus you and Dad would be subject to paying the income tax thereon. I wasn't going to see that happen. I was four-and-one-half years old when first I met with Mr. Evers. I had foreseen that some great action was going to take place on three different penny-mining stocks in Northern British Columbia and in the Northwest Territories. Two of the stocks were at five cents and one was at eight cents. I had purchased 80,000 shares in total at an average cost of six-and-one-quarter pennies, and within five months I had sold all the shares at a net price of $5.06 gaining therefore some $400,000. Of late I've been trading in grain futures, $80,000 worth to be exact, and by gosh, Mom and Dad, I could sell my position now for over $120,000. So I can buy that beautiful foal with my own money if you don't want to buy him for me."

"Lana Jean," her father said in astonishment, "where did you get the four or five thousand dollars to buy the penny stock in the first place? Don't tell me Mr. Ever's bank loaned you the money?"

"No Daddy, I had sold lots of eggs from the time I was three. I saved some of my allowance, I gathered pop and beer bottles and cans and sold them, and I won $800 in a poker game in Grant's Pool Hall. That's how I raised the money."

"In a poker game?" Carl and Beatrice Masters screamed, "Poker?"

"Only once, Mom and Dad."

"When you want money you come to me Lana," Carl exploded. "You hear me child? "Poker, God Almighty."

"I will Daddy, I will."

"Grant's Pool Hall. I'll see that old reprobate Silas Grant and I'll, I'll…"

"No Daddy. He's a good egg customer. Besides I talked him into letting me in his pool hall because I told him I was looking for someone. I knew guys played poker in a smoky corner of the pool hall. I rushed over to the poker table while the pool players patted my head and kidded me as I went by them. When I got to the table I asked the guys to deal me in. They were flabbergasted. The poor rubes said, "Beat it kid," and I responded, "fuck you, you bunch of penis breaths," and I plunked down six twenties on the table.

Lana Jean's mom and dad, Raymond, Steven, Margaret and Carl, Jr. all gasped in unison when they heard five-year-old Lana use the word 'fuck' and 'penis.'

"Lana Jean Masters, where did you learn to say that horrid word? Shame, shame on you. We know you swear, but never, never did we suspect that you would use that vile word."

"Penis you mean, Mom?" Lana Jean said laughing.

"That's quite enough young lady."

"Sorry Mom. What about the horse?"

"Never mind about the horse, what about the poker in that awful pool hall and your terrible language?"

"Well, as to the terrible language, I'll always cuss. As to the poker, I won $800 bucks in just three hands before Mr. Grant realized I had been in his snooker parlor too long. When he found me playing poker with Dale, Dennis, Ken, and three other men I didn't know, he paled, then lifted me in his arms and carried me to the street. That's all that happened Mom and Dad."

"I cannot believe our child, Beatrice."

"Nor can I, Carl. What in heaven's name are we going to do?"

"Mom and Daddy I love you both so very much. I love you more than anything. You are my world. I am ashamed of myself for saying that word in front of you and for playing poker. Please don't hate me." With that, little Lana Jean rushed to her parents' sides and hugged their legs. She sobbed.

"How can anyone ever get cross at such a captivating little girl?" Carl moaned. "What are we going to do with you, Lana dear, my oh my, what?"

"Mommy and Daddy, I know I am different from other kids. I know I could start university any time now and get straight A's. I know too, I shock you in many ways with my intellect and the adult things I do. I am sorry for these unusual traits I have but you must realize I was born this way. On occasion, like the silly three hands of poker I played, I get an overwhelming urge to do something adult, and I do it. The poker was so easy for me to play and win at. My opponents were like babes in arms. I could play 100 games against them and win them all. Stare and scare, bluff and....whatever. Please accept me as I am. You both know in a very few years I will be studying at some university. I am frightened at the thought of being away from you, but I know my leaving you by the time I'm 11 or 12 is a *fait accompli*. I want now to have my life packed with being a kid. What to do with me Dad and Mom? Just love me, always. I promise my love for you will be unending. I will always try to do things you will be proud of, and, I'll try my best not to swear in front of you. Oh! How I love all of you and how I love our home. Mom and Dad you are what makes our home, home."

Carl lifted Lana Jean up in his arms. She buried her little head in his shoulders. Beatrice joined in. Soon the whole family had their arms around each other. Carl, Beatrice, Margaret, Carl Jr. and Lana Jean were all snuffling.

The statuesque gelding was purchased by the Masters' that very day.

CHAPTER 6

SIR GALAHAD AND BIG BUSTER; THE RANCH HANDS

Lana Jean was captivated with Sir Galahad, as was Sir Galahad captivated with Lana Jean. After he was 'broken-in' Lana Jean rode him everywhere. Sir Galahad didn't disappoint the Masters' family or the farm and ranch hands. He grew to be an immense size. For a stud, he was surprisingly gentle. He was cared for by Lana Jean and her sister and brothers, just as Lana had promised. Kids from all around Swift Current came to see the beautiful steed and some were even brave enough to ride him. But through all of the attention given to him by everyone, the big stallion's allegiance and devotion was to Lana Jean.

*　　　*　　　*

The Hereford bull calf Carl Masters had bought at Great Falls seemed never to stop growing. At age four he was like a snorting freight train. A one-ton horny, cantankerous, money producing fucking machine. Every cattle owner in Northern Montana and Southern Saskatchewan wanted Sir Percival to sire their cows. The big bovine, known country wide as *Big Buster,* came through. His owners would permit him only three $1,000 bangs daily, grossing therefore $3,000 each day. Much to Big Buster's chagrin, he was allowed to work just five days each week for only 90 days each year. "I'll have to start a labor union with other bulls from around here and see if we can't get longer hours of work. Shit I could work seven days a week, 365 days a year at this job," Big Buster lamented. The Masters' were delighted with Big Buster's labor and revenue production. For those 90 days a year, Big Buster's gross prostitution revenue was a whopping $270,000. The big bovine's worth at that rate of annual gross was bordering on $400,000.

Lana Jean loved Buster but she obeyed her father's orders not to pet him unless he was in his pen. She wanted so much to prove her father was wrong. She was sure she could win over Big Buster's nastiness and make him her friend. But, she respected her dad's wishes; she petted him only through the steel bars of his pen.

* * *

School to Lana Jean was perfunctory. Dutifully she attended play school and kindergarten. She mastered these two weighty academics in about two seconds. As a matter of fact she was, at age four, the equivalent of a senior high school student. But Lana Jean was a thoughtful, caring child. She had no desire to denigrate in any way her little friends because of her superior talents, nor for that matter, her teachers. She had fun doing all the little games presented at play school…finger painting, Lego building, stories read by the teachers, learning to count, skipping rope, sleep and rest time.

Carl and Beatrice had a dreadful time trying to decide what they should do with their wonder child. On advice from the Dean of Psychology at the University of Saskatchewan they had Lana Jean attend grade one. The dean had reasoned that the little girl must experience growing up along with her same-age friends in order for her to be exposed to 'normalcy.' Whilst the Dean's reasoning was sound, Lana Jean's psyche was such that it timed her degree of maturity in all aspects (other than her immeasurable brainpower) to perfection. The child was as much at home playing hide-and-go-seek with her little friends as she was with mastering calculus or computer technology. The Dean had met with many of his colleagues to discuss Lana Jean's quintessence. Together they formulated an educational plan for this pretty young prodigy. The several Deans had charted out a variety of subjects for Lana Jean to study as she attended grade one, subjects ranging from mathematics, physics, chemistry and astronomy to economics, history, and the arts. Lana Jean 'had a ball' attending grade one with her friends and digging into the texts pertaining to the courses of studies put together by the Deans and sending off her weekly assignments, together with her own postulations, to the University of Saskatchewan. A veritable 'ball,' she mused. The results of her grade one fun and her university courses were quite extraordinary. Straight A+'s for her university work and one 'F' for 'behavior' in her grade one report card. 'F' for her use of bad language. The teacher warned her over and over that the word 'motherfucker' was not acceptable, nor were the words 'shit' and 'cocksucker.' Lana Jean listened to her teacher and her school's principal each time they lectured her about her vile language, but 'what the fuck,' she would say to herself, 'who gives a shit,' and the lectures would dissolve in the depths of her great mind. Lana Jean's parents were at a loss of what to do about Lana Jean's foul language, as were the teachers at Begg School. Together they tried. Together they lost. The University of Saskatchewan Deans had no answer. Laughing the University of Saskatchewan professors wondered about giving Lana Jean Masters her Doctorate Degree in Profanity. And how did little Lana Jean become so proficient at swearing?

At first, it was 'kinda' cute to hear this beautiful, angelic child use some off-color words before she reached her first birthday. "Thit Mommy, where did those bright thstars cum frum? And the big friggin moon?" or "Hi Mithhus Gween, howths your athhole of a husband?" Dear me, Beatrice would wonder, where does this child of mine pick up these words?

But as she grew, Lana Jean's vocabulary blossomed including her use of the 'vernacular.'

Often when hiding in her father's huge barn, she would overhear the farm and ranch-hands talk. Their glossary defied the language of the genteel, especially in the evenings when their day's work was done and they sat around in the barn having a beer or two and telling jokes. Often too, little Lana Jean's sides would be bursting from wanting to laugh, but she would 'hang in there' soundless. She recalled a few jokes told one night by the 'hands.'

"One guy," a hand named George related, "was constipated so bad he went to see his doctor. The doctor gave the guy enough suppositories for a week and told the guy to come see him in a week. The guy came back to see the doctor one week later and when the doctor asked if he had a bowel movement the guy said, no, he hadn't. So old sawbones prescribed another week of suppositories. No luck! After a coupla' more weeks of the same thing, old sawbones asked the guy, Well?

"Shit, doc, no luck, for all the good them suppositories done me, I might as well of shoved them up my ass."

All the hands guffawed. Little Lana Jean caught on…she knew from whence a suppository goeth…she smothered her laugh.

"Hey Ray old chap, you got any good 'uns?" She remembered Bobby Riley asking. "You Britishers wouldn't say shit if ya' had a mouth full of it. Ray didja' hear 'bout the Polack in a barn standin' in a fresh cow-pie…you know Ray old chap…fresh cow shit? The Polack looks down at his feet and yells, My God, I'm melting."

Ray whacked Bobby on the head. "You want to hear a joke you degenerate cowpoke?"

"Yes sir I do," Bobby retorted.

"It's a golf story," Ray said huffed. "But mine is not crude nor offensive. You see a British Lord gasping for air, holding his throat rushed up to the bartender at the golf clubhouse and gurgled, 'double scotch barkeep…quick.' The barkeep had the double scotch ready in a trice. The chap gulped it down and ordered another…swoosh it was gone…and yet another. Now the chap could breath. 'Pheeeuu,' he said to the barkeep, that was a close call.

'What in heaven's name happened your lordship?' the barkeep asked. Well, my good man, my wife and I were playing the ninth hole; you know chappie, the fairway that runs alongside the fenced field with all the smelly cattle? "Yes of course your grace, I know the one." Well dash it all if my wife didn't hit a rather good ball straightaway into that nasty field."

"I'm sorry your greatness."

"Tut, tut, lad, I'm not finished."

"Please go on Sir."

"I joined my beloved in the field, ripping my plus fours on the dashed barbed wire fence while getting in. Another double scotch good lad please."

"Get on with it," George said in frustration.

"Be patient my good fellow."

"Hurry up Limey," Pistol Pete yelled.

"Yes, well as I said, the golfing chap joined his wife in the field and began to look for her ball. It was, after all, a brand new Titleist. You couldn't just walk away from a ball worth 15 bob now, could you gentlemen?"

"Yore a pain in the ass Ray," Tim Thompson said.

"Well chaps as it turned out, the snooty golfer, whilst looking everywhere for his wife's ball, glanced up and saw a cow flicking flies away from her bottom with its tail and woe-betide if our good man didn't see a ball lodged in the middle of the female bovines vulva."

"Her what?" George asked.

"Her vulva you ninny," Ray elucidated.

"What the hell's a vulva…a car?"

"No, dummy, it's a cunt," Pistol Pete answered.

"Jesus Ray, why didn't you say so?"

"Oh, you hopeless Canucks."

"In any event, the lordly golfer walked over to the cow, lifted its tail up, and said to his wife in a voice so loud that many other golfers could hear him, 'Lovey, does this look like yours?' he asked. And dash it all, with that the poor golfer's wife rushed over to his lordship and struck him across his throat with her putter. Now, my good men that's why…"

"We get it Ray, we get it."

Lana Jean doubled over to hold back her laugh.

Everyone but George laughed. George was still back at the vulva.

"C'mon, Georgie boy, at least smile," Pete said.

"Does what look like yours?" asked George.

"Aw forgit it pardner," said cowboy Ellis.

"No, I want to know why yer all laffin?"

"The inference is, dear friend, does this look like your, your pussy," Ray cajoled.

Everyone waited a few moments to let Ray's explanation sink in. It worked, first a smile crossed George's face, then a toothy grin (you could see the gears working in George's brain), then a belly laugh. "Lovey, does this look like yours?" he wailed. "Har, Har, I get it now, does this look like your thing…the cow's that is…mighty good joke Ray…har, har. Got any more like 'at Limey?"

"Listen did you hear something?" Pistol Pete whispered.

"Shore did," George replied. "Shh."

Another rustle was heard near the hay bales. George put a finger to his lips and began to move toward the bales.

A louder noise erupted from behind the bales as Lana Jean's foot got caught up in some twine. "Damn," she said under her breath. The next thing she knew she was in George's massive arms.

"What are you doing here, Lana Jean?" he asked shocked.

"Listening to all the funny jokes George."

"Shame, shame, you shouldn't be here listening to us growed-ups, child." All the men gathered around Lana Jean and George.

"Little girl, yore ma and pa are going to be mighty mad at all of us if' they hear about this," Cowboy Ellis admonished.

"No they're not, Cowboy, 'cause I'm not going to say anything to them. I love all of you too much."

"We love you too baby girl, but yore far too young to hear adults tell jokes."

"Cowboy, I thought the jokes were great."

"But we use lotsa' cuss words Lana Jean. Words you shouldn't hear."

"I know, but I don't care. Hey, fellas I've got one that will tick you off reeeal goood. Wanna hear it?"

The cowhands looked at each other and nodded a reluctant O.K.

" Pistol Pete," Lana Jean said, "why do men have a hole at the end of their peepees, you know their peckers?"

Red-faced Pete replied "I do not know and I could not even guess."

"So they can get air to their brains silly."

For a moment the gang sat motionless and quiet, then a twitter was heard from Cowboy Ellis, then Ray chuckled, George said hah, Pete laughed, Ray roared, the gang broke up and in a trice all hell broke loose as the barn filled with booming guffaws.

Teary eyed from laughter Pete looked up at Lana Jean and said,

"Now child, it's nearly eight o'clock so's you better be gitten' home. Scoot now."

"Night-night, guys."

"Night-night, Lana Jean."

"Damn it all guys, that little one should not hear the kind of jokes we tole' tonight. I'll bounce it off Hank tomorrow and see if he feels we should tell Carl," cowboy Ellis said.

"Naw, forgit it Cowboy, all's okay. We just have to be more careful in the future." Pete said.

"Yeah, and what about her joke?" George said in a flustered manner.

CHAPTER 7

LANA'S HEROISM AT AGE NINE

Lana's guest was rousing. He mumbled and coughed a bit. His eyes squinted open. He attempted to turn over but found he was unable to do so. He heard Perry Como's voice singing…*to weak to break the chains that bind me….*

Now he remembered…Lana…restaurant…thunder storm…groggy sleep…shackled…a few words with Lana…furry crotch tickles…humungus hard on…bang!…a huge 'come'…another sleep.

He looked up and there he was, reflected back by way of a huge mirror above him. He glanced to his right and there she was, Lana the world's ultimate brain, the most caring and heedful person about all of Mother Nature's life and surroundings. The champion of rights for everyone, the kind, beautiful Lana, sitting unperturbed in her bra and panties just above him on some bales of hay, smiling down at him. "What's with the mirror gorgeous?" her guest questioned.

Lana didn't respond.

It was 12:45 a.m., May 24th when Lana's guest had awakened. He yawned. His eyes were bleary. He was still exhausted from his travels, the mighty 'come' and the shot Lana had administered him earlier. The poor man had left J.F.K. airport at 6:30 in the morning on May 22nd, arrived at O'Hare in Chicago at 8:00 a.m., met with a diplomatic corps from South Korea and the I.M.F. for three hours. Departed O'Hare at 12:37 p.m. for Winnipeg, Manitoba. Laid over in Winnipeg for 30 minutes. Departed Winnipeg for Regina, Saskatchewan at 2:30 p.m. arrived in Regina 3:00 p.m. Central Standard time. Walked to parking space 21-G in the airport's public parking, picked up Lana's father's Lincoln and drove to Swift Current arriving at Lana's parents house at 5:45 p.m. Lana was alone in the house. Her parents were visiting friends in Vancouver. And her guest, on arrival at Lana's door, ordered sex.

Lana laughed. She feigned joy on seeing him. They embraced, he kissed and he fondled her. Fondled, Lana thought, just like dear old departed Uncle Fred had done to her so often. Christ, how she hated her fucking guest. She poured him a drink. They chatted. Her guest grabbed Lana from behind as she was pouring him another drink. His hands went under her snug mini skirt as he grabbed at her crotch. Abruptly Lana turned forcing him to let go of her. She reached up to his lips with her finger, whispering, "Wait darling until we go to the farm. I promise you nights you will never forget when we get there!"

"Jesus Lana, you are sheer heaven. I can't wait."

"Yes, yes my sweet. But now we must be away to O'Toole's Restaurant on North Hill. I reserved a special table there for us at seven. Following dinner we shall retreat to the farm, okay Father?"

"Oh yeah, baby. To the farm."

Lover Boy would have followed her anywhere.

Ominous lightning flashed in the west.

* * *

Once again her guest felt those squirming furry bodies down on his lower abdomen. Only now the nippings were beginning to be more painful than sensual. Not only were those razor-like little teeth biting his proud manhood, but also they were biting his hips, scrotum and anus.

Somewhat frightened, he looked up into the mirror. Then squinted his eyes to be sure they were focused. He was aghast when he thought he saw a cage on his lower abdomen and, by damnation, holding three rats, deleterious rats with long ugly rope like tails. No cute furry bunnies as he had thought, instead scrawny sick looking rats.

"Jesus Christ, Lana," he yelled, "You've got a bunch of rats caged on me."

"That's right handsome," she replied smiling.

"Well get them off me…now!"

"Simmer down, baby, don't make me angry."

"What are you trying to do to me, Lana, is this shit intended to punish me for some of my past?"

A moment of silence except for…*too weak to break the chains that bind me…*

"Lana darlin, you know how much I love you. I always have, even after our break-up. Life is empty without you. I admit I was a scoundrel, and that I, God forgive me, abused you. And I feel so much remorse for having forced you to perform some despicable acts of sex for me. But Lana, you are the very essence of sex. No man can hold back his feelings when it comes to you. You know full well you attract the whole gamut of sexual adventures, both good and bad, from all men who meet you and that includes me."

Another moment of silence.

"And Lana, I admit I borrowed that million bucks from you and you know I have every intention of paying it back to you, with interest."

"Hell Father, I deemed the million to be a gift the moment I gave it to you and as for the rest of your short sermon, bullshit," Lana retorted.

"Please Lana, I beg of you, let those damn rats out, you know how much I hate rats, they carry disease, mercy baby, rats can be omnivorous, in fact they are chewing on me right now."

Lana had made certain her hideous rodents were hungry before she put them in the cage. She was satisfied they were doing their job. Lana in addition to her first priority, that is her guest's demise, wanted to observe and study the rats' reaction to the predicament they were in. A rather interesting study to be sure. Will the rats try for a quick escape, or will they enjoy feasting on their host before absconding to freedom. Perry Como's music continued...*I'm just a prisoner of love...*

Lover boy moaned, his eyelids flickered, slowly they closed. Once again he slept. He snored. It looked as if he was going to be out of it for sometime.

Half awake and half-asleep herself, Lana continued her reminiscing. The reminiscing was important to her. Important because she had no idea where she would be a week from now, only the 12 Controllers of the universe knew the answer to that confounding riddle. She had her execution plan of Father Donnely well mapped out, including her escape from justice. His body nor any telltale clues will be left for policing, simply he will disappear from the face of the earth. The last trace of him will be at Chicago's O'Hare. His travel documents will end there. From Chicago to Swift Current, at Lana's request, all his passenger information was in the name of Orest V. Semchuk of Simmie, Saskatchewan. Orest V. Semchuk's name had been used as a ruse. She had told her guest her fiancé would get word of it if her guest used his real name, and Lana said her fiancé was a fearsome jealous fellow. In addition she told lover-boy if he wanted to carry on an affair with her after she was married, her future husband better not know lover-boy's real name or whereabouts. Orest V. Semchuk was the answer. Orest V. was just a six-month-old baby flying home from Chicago on the very flight lover-boy was on. A week earlier, little Orest had stuffed an oversized bead up his nose, such bead ending close to his eye and brain. The little fellow was rushed off to Chicago to a specialist who had the expertise to remove the bead without harm to the child. That's one good thing about the two Swift Current newspapers, Lana thought; they devote a lot of space to stories like Orest's. Yeah, right from the time of Orest's misadventure, to the precise time he was to return home. And, by damn, I get these two newspapers mailed to me in Manhattan and *voila*, I now had my solution for the dissolution of lover-boy. But, Lana opined, like Murphy's law, anything that can go wrong will go wrong, so where will I be one week from now?

* * *

Lana's thoughts returned to her childhood. Thoughts about her schooling in the public school system, grades 1 to 12, which she waltzed through, in five years. She remembered the exciting challenges of numerous subjects provided her by various universities throughout North America and the United Kingdom.

She captured every award for excellence in education from the time she began her formal education in grade one until her latest graduation from the school of medicine at UCLA. Whilst she was envious of her everyday school chums and their well-plotted out lives, she did mix well with them. She was aware of her superiority over her fellow students and even her teachers, her parents and most of her university professors. She knew, in due course, her intellect could lead her to a life of loneliness. 'So Lana Jean, have friends, cherish them, play with them, socialize with them, go camping with them, cry with them. Make them an integral part of your life. Never act dominant over them.' But, dash it all, she was always the top athlete in school, the best pianist, the best painter, the best orator, the best dancer, and, as an aside, the best rifle and pistol shooter anywhere. Always she was the tallest of her girlfriends. Her astonishing beauty was incomparable. Her hair, her face, her torso, her legs, her personality, her enchanting charisma, her modesty and her power-laden personality placed her in a domain all her own. She found it a bit of a challenge for her not to get a wee bit vain.

Her physical endowments at age 15 were a startling 36, 23, 36, her height was five feet, ten-and-a-half inches, and she weighed 127 pounds. Right from childhood Lana remembered herself as being a stunning, radiant beauty. My, how she used to wish she could have been just *your average pretty girl*." Now almost 30 years of age she is the most beautiful girl in the world. Her vital statistics are an awe-inspiring 38, 24, 38". She stands 5', 11" and her weight a delectable 130 pounds.

Damn I've had some dramatic ups and downs in my friggin life, Lana thought as she shifted herself to a more comfortable position on the bales of hay.

She knew her years at home had some crazy and unusual happenings that were not the norm. 'Fuck me, no,' she said with a wry smile on her face. Like the time when ten-year-old, Jerry Thomas fell through the ice on Lake Pelletier, wild. Hundreds of kids and adults were skating or playing hockey, racing or just ice fishing. Jerry-Boy, as he was known, was speed-skating only about 100 feet from shore when he plunged through a large rectangular piece of ice that was barley frozen over. Some careless person had cut out several large pieces of the stuff and had neglected to put the usual red warning flags up surrounding the spot. As the surprised and frightened Jerry splashed into the opening, he flailed his arms then he let out one hell of a 'whoop.' Many saw the incident happen and screamed for help. The people closest to Jerry hesitated to rush to the spot in case the ice was thin all around where Jerry had fallen in.

His head disappeared in the frigid water, then reappeared as he tried to reach for solid ice. Not succeeding in his attempts to hold on to the slippery top of the thick ice he slithered back into the 6x10 foot death trap crying and sputtering. His chances of survival in the cold, uncaring waters were slim if someone didn't get to him fast. The water was 15 feet deep at that spot. In a trice he could get lodged under the ice. Many skaters rushed back to their cars and trucks in search of ropes that could be used as lifelines to be thrown out to the helpless child.

Lana Jean saw the whole frightening affair. Yet she maintained her composure as she rushed the quarter mile between Jerry Boy and herself. She put her skates into high gear. As she was rushing to the site she removed her long scarf, her jacket she just gotten for Christmas and her sweat-pants. My God, she was nimble. She didn't seem to lose a stride as she undressed. 'Dammit,' she thought, 'if Jerry goes under the ice I'm going to have a bitch of a job trying to save him.' Lana Jean was just nine years old. There was no doubt in her mind she would save her friend; it was just the degree of difficulty in doing so. 'Jerry, show-up please,' she pleaded under her breath as she tied her scarf, jacket and sweat-pants together. "Out of my way everybody," she yelled as she neared the hole. "Thomas and Justin come behind me," she screamed. The two skinny ten-year-olds gawked but obeyed her. Lana Jean took a flying leap at full-tilt about 20 feet from the hole, and slid to the edge of the hole on her stomach. The two skin and bones came behind her…scared shitless. "Hurry up you two," she yelled, "take hold of this shit I've tied together, and don't let go, hear? The ice is safe where you are. Don't let go you shitheads 'cause I'm going in after Jerry." In she went. People could see the water splashing from Lana Jean's frantic kicks, then nothing. God they're both gone many thought. A good minute passed before two heads appeared. "Now dig your skates in and pull like hell," Lana Jean blubbered at Thomas and Justin as she and Jerry broke the water. "Pull." Thomas and Justin pulled with all their might. They were doing it. The two boys saw that they were succeeding. "Pull hard you motherfuckers," Lana Jean screamed. Soon Jerry and Lana Jean's stomachs were on solid ice. "Good goin' fellas, keep pullin," Lana Jean sputtered. Then their whole beings were out of the water as Thomas and Justin gave a final Herculean tug. "Awesome, guys," Lana Jean called out to the two skinny ones, "you are the greatest."

But the rescue was not over. "Now take off your parkas and put them down on the ice," Lana Jean ordered. The boys were grateful for getting their buddy out of the water, but they looked frightened, even horrified, as they took in the awful ghost-like pallor of Jerry. "Let go of the fucking clothes of mine and get your parkas on the ice now," Lana screamed. "Now!" The boys, shivering not from the cold but because of their trepidation, still stood stone-like. "Now, assholes," Lana barked. This time they moved their butts. Off came their parkas. Lana Jean rolled Jerry onto the boys' jackets and began her resuscitation of Jerry. Grown-ups began to inch their way towards Lana, Jerry, Thomas and Justin. Lana Jean paid them no heed. She just kept on with her mouth-to-mouth and her pumping until water spilled out of Jerry Boy's lungs onto the jackets and his breathing kicked-in.

When she was satisfied Jerry was okay she screamed at the crowd, "Get Jerry to the rink house and warm him up. Move!" Some adults rushed to her side, picked Jerry up and carried him to the warmth of the rink house. God how I shivered from the cold that day I was wet, exhausted, freezing. Herman Weibe was the man who picked me up and carried me to the rink house. I shivered for days after that ordeal, but otherwise I was fine and so was Jerry. Christ, you would have thought I had saved the world rather than Jerry Boy from the plaudits I received. Mom, dad, my sister and brothers thought I was a bona-fide heroine. Shit, I never did tell anyone about the struggle I had with Jerry Boy under the water, it was damn near a catastrophe. But we survived. Even the Saskatoon Star Phoenix, the Regina Leader Post and, of all things, the New York Times, told the story of my 'heroism.' My favorite coverage in any of the newspapers, however, was the Moose Jaw Tribune's "BOPPER LANDS WHOPPER. Frigid water's *death grip* gives up to cussing nine-year-old wonder girl." Asked about her intemperate language, words that would make a grizzled mariner blush, the youngster replied, "My forceful language makes people jump."

"It does?" the Tribune's reporters asked.

"You're f—king right it does," she replied.

CHAPTER 8

LANA'S NET WORTH AT AGE FIFTEEN...LANA'S NIGHTMARE

Warning! One Beastly Sentence.

Her guest groaned and snored as the rats filled their guts on his lower body.

*　　　*　　　*

Lana continued to think back on her life. How by age fifteen her net worth exceeded 29 million dollars. Over a period of 9 years she had accumulated capital gains of $29 million. These gains came about from trades of $6 million on United Kingdom gilts; $5 million on Canadian and U.S. bond trades; $6 million dollars on insurance, mining and brokerage stock trades; $3 million on grain futures; $2 million dollars on gold and $7 million dollars on real estate deals. She recalled how she kept her assets in a liquid form following the economic 'bust-up' in1981 until the mid-eighties, at which time she began to dabble in certain markets once again. She remembered keeping the preponderance of her 29 million-dollar fortune in long-term government bonds she had purchased at substantial discounts in the years 1979, 1980 and 1981. These bonds, 22 million dollars worth, were returning an average yield of 15 percent on her investment. The average cost of her bond portfolio was only $67 for every $100 bond she owned. Her annual interest income on these bonds amounted to a whopping $2.2 million. Her income taxes amounted to $1.1 million leaving her $1.1 million to play with. Most of the $1.1 million she had to play with went right back into liquid and other investments. By 1990 her net worth had grown by $22.0 million to $51.0 million. Her latest computation showed her net worth to be $282.0 million.

'Yeah,' Lana reflected, 'my early life was unusual compared to the norm. How many kids by the age of fifteen had earned on their own, before tax, a gross of over $50.0 million bucks. Yeah, and what becomes of my ass if I don't cover my tracks with the demise of Lover-Boy here and when the Controllers begin to run my life. Son-of-a-bitch! Why did he go off the rails about me? Christ, I am game for damn near any kind of sex, but the sick shit he was pedaling for me to do was too much. Suck-off a German Shepherd dog while he videotaped it. And that was one of the more innocent sex acts he made me do.

"Suffer you bastard you. I've got all the tapes," Lana said. "The way you had me coerced into doing these despicable things. You rotten S.O.B. Using my sister Margaret and her lover Christen as hostage. And your stinking buddies, ugh! You were a good man. Christ—like what changed you? Damn it all, the courts can't deal with your kind. Only I can. The million bucks…stuff it," she murmured.

Her guest paid no heed to Lana. He just snored.

Lana noted trickles of blood coming from his sides. The rats squeaked, their noses twitched.

"Suffer you bastard, suffer."

Lana wept. She couldn't get her mind off Clark now. "What will become of him if I get caught and put to death, or if the Controllers remove me from planet earth. Oh Clark, how I love you, your strength, your qualities, your humanitarianism. Your wonderful brain-child H&B Financial and Poors, your positive actions, your intelligence and your boyishness, why couldn't I have just settled down with you somewhere in *small town* USA and raised a family? Why?" she said, tears streaming down her face.

Lana dozed for a few minutes but her mind still swirled around her past life as she dreamed. She saw herself in jeans, wide western belt, western denim shirt, cute little cowboy boots, six years old, six guns blazing shooting the necks off pop bottles from 30 feet away. Her mentor, Hank Drennon, had taught Lana Jean everything from A to Z regarding guns. Safety and respect he hammered into her receptive brain. "Guns," Hank insisted, "are not for killing or maiming of any living thing, man or beast. Guns," Hank emphasized, "should be used only as an instrument for sports. Target shooting, trap shooting, speed of the draw and most of all guns which can use only dum-dum bullets. Not for murder, not for hunting, not for wars, terrorism, only for sport." Lana Jean knew this to be true, but hearing it from Hank, her mom and dad, Pistol Pete and the other ranch hands comforted her to know that some grown-ups felt as she did. She wanted guns to be outlawed worldwide. No Heston and Selleck rubbish. Can anyone imagine Jesus condoning firearms.

Lana Jean and Hank put on shows showing their prowess at gun handling, shooting, quick draws, rifle action, shot gun pumping at several rodeos held in Saskatchewan and Alberta (Swift Current Frontier Days and the Calgary Stampede being the biggest) as well as some Texas, New Mexico and Arizona rodeos.

Pistol Pete, the rugged, handsome, always the showman did the introduction of little Lana Jean and Hank. Following the acquisition of her huge beautiful stallion Sir Galahad, riding him (as saucy as an imp) Lana Jean would make her entrance to the show in a charismatic display of horsemanship. As he strutted into the rodeo arena the giant horse would rear-up on his hind legs march forward, front feet flailing, huge head tucked into his chest, his magnificent neck arched, his elegant mane flowing and his tawny tail sweeping the ground. Atop Sir Galahad in her western saddle the very cocky little Lana Jean standing in her stirrups, reins tied to the saddle horn, her six-guns firing off loud flaming caps, would heehaw as she rode the huge beast into the arena. Adorned in a cowboy shirt, a red handkerchief around her neck, chaparejos with colorful frills, cowboy boots and her tawny hair flying akimbo, Lana Jean would put on a show-stopper every time she performed.

Hank Drennan was no slouch. He made the old TV show star of The Rifleman look indolent. Hank could do wonders with his rifle. Not just shoot with dead accuracy, but with class he would flip his gun around himself every which way topping Buffalo Bill's best. After each show Lana Jean and Hank would get a standing ovation. Every penny they earned at these events would go to an impoverished country. That was so much fun, Lana's brain would recall.

Sir Galahad's death, his horrid death. He was the bravest most faithful friend Lana Jean could ever imagine…and Sir Galahad's executioner. Glory be. Suddenly Lana jumped, startled as Uncle Fred slapped her across her face. Lana fought to awaken. She clawed at the straw, tried to scream, tried to stand. She knew she was in that terrifying half-awake, half-asleep state. No matter how she tried she remained in this semi-conscious coma fighting off Uncle Fred, fighting off this dreaded comatose feeling. Uncle Fred, naked, his disgusting cock flip flopping as he tried to maneuver it between her legs. "Wake-up Lana," her mouth would want to say to her, "wake-up". Lana could not shake the ominous stupor. Uncle Fred descended on her, his drooling mouth searching for hers, phallus thrusting back and forth between her legs. "Get off me you bloody animal," Lana tried to shout. But only jumbled sounds came from her throat. Uncle Fred grinned an ugly grin at her. Jagged holes where his eyes should have been leaked blood and yellowish pus on Lana's face. He winked at her—his torn eyelid devoid of lashes. "Lana Jean, see what you've done to me, you wicked child?" Look at my crotch if you dare to. Look, it's ugly. Look child, it's bleeding on your sweet thighs. Look Lana Jean, look. And my eyes Lana Jean, see the pitchfork prongs sticking right through my eyes? You little devil you." He giggled imbecile-like. "That was very clever of you cutting part way through the 2x6 I needed to lay across between those flat-head joists on the barn's rooftop. Yes child, clever. And only a brain of your caliber could place those pitchforks in such a position as to impale me so exacting. Ooh, you are something, Lana Jean, but now it's my turn. You're going to get what I've been wanting to give you ever since you learned to walk."

Lana fought her wire-bound brain. "Why can't I waken myself?" She tried to shout. But no sound left her throat. She recognized the stupor she was in, she had experienced it a few times before but never so foreboding as this. She remembered one time a few years ago when she was in one of these horrid spells, she had jerked, shook and flung her body every which way to break the spell and it worked. She tried it now. But Uncle Fred had her pinned down. This time it didn't work. Blood from his eyeless face was now streaming down onto Lana's face and seeping into her mouth. Uncle Fred had now succeeded in getting his penis through her volvo, good old George and his Volvo. Vulva, George baby, not volvo. How can my brain think of George's Volvo when dear old Uncle Fred is trying to stuff me with his torn up prick?

Uncle Fred had no breath. He didn't need to breathe. He was dead. Lana Jean had seen to it that he was dead. Uncle Fred stunk. God how he stunk! His vile penetration of her was foul, incarnate, diabolical. How do I kill this freak again? He was so monstrous. No breath, Jesus Christ, no breath yet the heathen monster can copulate. "God, how I've always hated you, Uncle Fred."

"I know that child," the distorted warp spake. "If you had just played with my thing over the years, if you had just let me fuck you up your cute little ass. If you had just let me take pictures of you in the nude, if you'd…

"Shut-up, you bloody monster."

"Yes, my sweet, like you left me alone. I wanted you, you little bitch. How I wanted you when you were growing up. Then you killed me.

Accidental death, my Death Certificate read. Accidental death, bullshit! Christ, how I wanted to tell the police. I hung around in the air like a handful of fog. I was dead. I could not get through to the police…they couldn't hear nor see me…I couldn't make them understand that you were my killer. God damn you, Lana Jean. Now I've got you and I intend to keep you. I am going to have you forever." He put his slimy wet mouth on Lana's. Lana gave a great heave.

She wakened. Uncle Fred was gone. She wiped her mouth then spit, she looked down at her legs. No slobber, no blood, nothing but sweat. Lana was covered in perspiration. She rubbed her face, again no blood. Thank the Lord I am awake, she glanced down at her rat-infested guest. He was still there, mouth agape, breathing stertorously. "Yes I'm awake, pheeuuu, what a relief, damn Uncle Fred, he seemed so real…those horrid semi-comatose mind grabbers…pheeuuu." She wiped her brow. Her brow felt sticky. She looked down at her lap then howled. Lying there across her lap was a blood stained pitchfork holding two pus-running eyes. Shit. She reached for it, her hand shaking. "No, Lord no," she sobbed as she saw the back of her hand she had just wiped her brow with was covered in blood. "Eve One, please, I need you," she begged. Lana knew Eve One would not come to her. Get a hold of yourself, woman, Lana thought. This can't be happening. Use your brains. Figure this out. She stood up letting the pitchfork fall from her lap. It bounced off the hay bales and fell towards the barn floor. It bounced on the barn floor then settled itself. Lana peered down at it. The pitchfork was clean. Clean as a whistle, no blood, no eyes. Lana checked the back of her hand again. Damn it, it was still bloody. Again she put her fingers on her forehead. There was a sharp pain. She could feel quite a long cut on her forehead. How did she cut herself? The mysteries confounded her, a bloody pitchfork and a cut forehead. So Lana did some detecting. She looked at the hay bales to her right, then kneeled down feathering the hay delicately as she scanned it, then she began to move to her right in a semi-circular way. Touching and scanning. "Aha," she said, "gotcha." Just to the right of where her head was while she was under that horrible half-awake, half-asleep brain grabber was a piece of wire that was an inch long sticking straight up from the bale binding. A small piece of her forehead skin was attached to the wire, and blood. "Whadda ya know, it was you, that was the culprit, not Uncle Fred. As to the pitchfork, I guess when I was twisting and turning and grasping for anything to get a hold of while under that fuckin' spell. I grabbed a pitchfork which is kept on top of the bales for easy access to the ranch hands, and quite by accident it ended up on my lap. As to Uncle Fred's eyes and blood being on the pitchfork tines, who gives a shit? They're not there now."

Lana's guest slept through the din caused by Uncle Fred's mad appearance. He must be tired, Lana thought. The noise! The rats! I hope he's not dead yet. Lana, don't be stupid you can hear him breathing. He's not dead. The rotter has to live long enough for the rats to escape, eh!

"Eh. I wonder what Canadian introduced that retard euphemism eh? I know David Letterman finds it to be quality English, both he and Paul, eh David? And Big Dave, ain't we Canucks an exciting bunch. Ain't we daring, dashing and full of fun, eh? If you want to be blown away by ebullition Dave, come visit Piapot, Saskatchewan some time. Ya', Piapot Saskatchewan, its about midway between Swift Current, Saskatchewan and Medicine Hat, Alberta. Or maybe Dave, you'd rather visit Uren, Saskatchewan. Uren's just a little Southwest of Moose Jaw, Saskatchewan. Uren, is a breath of fresh air, Big Dave. Or maybe Biggar, Saskatchewan 'what says,' New York is big but this is Biggar. Go ahead, Dave ask Paul. No shit!

CHAPTER 9

RESENTMENTS BY OTHERS OF THE YOUNG LANA

Lana dozed again, but her mind kept busy. Her schooling, what a snap everything was. No real challenges in any grade, class, subject, study, and research…none. Her leaving home at 12; just a few months after the unfortunate demise of good old Uncle Fred; attending two semesters at the University of Saskatchewan, Saskatoon. Straight A+s in arts, commerce, pharmacy and the sciences in eight months; too easy! Eight long months! Eight months away from home. She cried every night until after Christmas. She cried even though her mom and dad flew to Saskatoon almost every weekend in their Cessna to be with her. A few times Hank Drennan and his crew piled into the Land Rover and drove to Saskatoon to visit her and take her to the movies.

By 13 Lana was more than gorgeous. She stood an awesome five-foot-seven, slim and graceful, classic, flowing, polished. She turned every head on campus. The fact is, she turned every head everywhere. Lana Masters knew her beauty was breathtaking. She knew, too, that she was flowering. Her periods had started back in July and she was beginning to grow some cute fur around her pee-pee and under her arms. Her breasts were expanding. Her hips were widening and her rump was rounding. She was Miss Universe without ever having to be contested.

Not only was the child a genius she also excelled in athletics, drama and music. Many of the other coeds on campus, who saw her in classes, labs, theater and the like, were jealous of her. Some downright hated her. "How dare this 13-year-old invade *our* campus. Looking as she does and showing off her tits and ass. We are not angry with her because all the hunks on campus want her. No, we are not the jealous types. It's her…her…how should we put it? Her overtones, her lack of modesty, her exhibitionism, and her foreboding damnable sexy eyes. She makes them up to be smoldering. The way she rolls her ass. Disgusting. Sure she is smarter than any of us, she is after all a genius. We give her that. And she is better than anyone in sports, music and drama. But her shameless swearing. How revolting is that? She's nothing but a shameless guttersnipe."

At first Lana Jean, other than her effusive swearing, did everything she could to disguise her beauty. She did what she could to be plain. She didn't want to antagonize anyone. But her trying to look plain was like trying to make the Taj Mahal look like a shack. Lana Jean, if she wished, could cover her beauty by hiding herself behind facial covers and huge ankle-length dresses. However, in due course she said to herself, "Fuck it, this fucking campus will have to take me as I am." And that it did. Soon Lana was the campus ruler. She just turned her charisma up several notches and there she was in complete control of her fellow students. While most of the females remained jealous of her, they found they were unable to dislike her. Lana befriended everyone. She was kind, thoughtful, an excellent listener, and charming. She was the antithesis of conceit or egoism. She allowed the student body to fall under her congeniality. She was the University's sweetheart. With the campus' male population things were different. Even though the males knew she was just 13 years old, it didn't stop them from wanting her.

CHAPTER 10

LANA'S REGISTRATION IN NYU AT THIRTEEN

The paparazzi.

Without any hesitation, the young genius would help anyone from any of the university's colleges with their studies. She had an amazing ability to help others learn. Her fellow students on receiving Lana Jean's words of wisdom felt as if she had entered their minds and deposited her intellect therein.

Lana Jean returned to Swift Current at the end of May 1981. She remained there until August 30th, 1981, at which time her parents, sister and brothers flew with her to New York City. Lana was no longer called Lana Jean, after all she was going to be 14 in October, so now she deemed herself to be a young woman, and she was after all now five-feet-nine-and-one-half-inches tall. She was no longer a baby girl, but when it came time for the goodbyes with her family she felt like an infant. She was crushed with sorrow knowing that in a few short days she would be parted from her family, her friends, the U of S. campus, her dad's big beautiful spread, her wonderful sod busters and Big Buster.

Lana was to register as a very special student in two NYU schools, Science and Business Administration. Diverse schools indeed, but it was what Lana wanted. Her goals for her formal education seemed to most of her advisors to be incongruous, not necessarily conflicting but somewhat mismatched. Her mind set could not be altered by anyone.

She was going to have her doctorate degrees in science, medicine, psychiatry, law, business administration and economics and have certification as a Certified Public Accountant in the United States and a Chartered Accountant in Canada, despite anyone's objections. She was determined to have these degrees tucked under her belt by the time she turned 27…13 years from now. Shit, she could master these degrees in half the time if she didn't have to waste her time on interning and apprenticeships. However Lana was realistic when it came to the subject of one putting time in on the job, vis-a-vis interning and apprenticing for medicine, law and accounting. This she knew was necessary for the proletariat who sought the highest of education. But damn she thought, for me, a total waste of time. Apprenticeships cost me four good years of my life, but what the hell, that's the name of the game.

* * *

It was nearly 3:00 a.m. May 24th, 1997. Lana's guest slept on in spite of the rats disgusting derangement of his lower torso. Now her guest's anus was being chewed on by the juvenile rat. This made her guest squirm, but for some unknown reason did not waken him.

Lana could not sleep even if she had wanted too. She had vowed to herself that she would be attentive to her guest right from the time she had secured him to the barn floor until his soul departed his body.

* * *

She remembered landing at La Guardia Airport at 2:00 p.m. August 30th, 1981, and the maze of media awaiting her arrival. This was a shock to the Masters family save for Lana. Carl and Beatrice knew their daughter was rather famous in Canada as well as Montana and North Dakota in the U.S. but heavens, in New York City? Lana's exploits as a youngster had been reported on by many in the media in both North America and Europe. Hence, she was seen as an intellectual behemoth, an incomparable beauty and a child of immense heart. However, these facts were not known to Carl and Beatrice. But Lana knew, Lana knew everything. The moment the family deplaned on the tarmac at La Guardia they were swamped by the media. Carl, Beatrice and the three boys were culled out of the little family like heifers from a herd.

Margaret was left with Lana, because Margaret, too, was beautiful, and the more glamour captured on TV and the newsprint the more sales for the mighty media industry moguls. The media types were awe-struck with Lana. They couldn't believe she was real. The girl made the word beautiful insignificant. This girl is incomparable, they thought. "Statuesque, shit," she has to be a mythological nymph.

"Lana, how old are ya really?"

"You're a dream boat."

"Is that your sister?"

"Are you real Lana?"

"You have no make-up on and you still outdo any other girl in the world."

"Are you going to model while going to NYU?

"Is it true that you are a multi-millionaire?"

"Yeah and by your own devices?"

"Are you really as smart as you're written up to be?"

"How long will it take you to graduate from NYU?"

"Are you really a farm girl from that funny named Province, County, State or whatever in Canada?"

"Is it true you cuss like a trooper?"

"How big are your tits Lana?"

And on and on the questions came. Flash bulbs never stopped. TV cameras zoomed in on her from her feet thence up her legs, to her mini skirt where they hesitated, to her flat tummy, zoomed to within inches of her incredible breasts, then settled in on her face.

Margaret was embarrassed. She squirmed, blushed and her face turned wine-colored. The TV boys loved this. They captured all of

Margaret's moves on camera. She oozed glamour, her boobs bobbled, her lush-lips quivered, the suggestive tip of her tongue would emerge to moisten her lips, she turned around to talk to her brothers, begging them to rescue her and Lana. The boys only laughed at their sister. TV cameramen caught her as she turned then focused in on her adorable butt. Frightened (she was now five-eleven-and-one-half) Margaret broke through the frenzied paparazzi like a *Packer fullback* unheeding of who she slammed into. She went right to the outstretched arms of her father.

Lana stood among the reporters, posed for pictures, answered most questions thrown at her. Yes, she will do some modeling, but far more important she said she intended to tutor, lecture and teach kids and adults from the slums, ghettos and those from any other area of Greater New York which have been treated unfairly by the general politic.

"Are you going to pose for Playboy Lana…in the buff?"

"Maybe."

"What about Sports Illustrated?"

"Maybe."

"And Lana, are you still a virgin? If so, I can sacrifice some of my time to correct this unfortunate aberration," one smartass offered.

"That's quite enough ladies and gentlemen," her father ordered. "You can ask her questions about her intelligence and other similar topics, but cut out the rest of the garbage or I'll whale the tar out of the whole darn bunch of you."

"Is zat so?" one pushy bastard threatened Carl. Like taking candy from a baby, Carl took the camera away from the pushy one, handed it to his big son Raymond and, with ease, he lifted *is zat so* up in his arms. "Here, take the camera Ray and do some panning," Carl said. Ray obliged.

Iz zat so hollered blue murder. "I'll sue you, you hay-seed farmer."

"Why?" Carl asked.

"Because you've stolen my camera and you've hurt me."

"Hand him back his camera Raymond."

"And let me down you A-hole, now."

"Okay lad!" and Carl let go.

Is zat so landed on his butt screaming his head off and threatening Carl with all manner of misfortunes. The rest of the media types encouraged their sue-screeching brother.

Lana stepped in, laughing. "You paparazzi are a bunch of insipid weak-kneed snot-noses. You don't give a damn about the abuse you heap on your subjects, but let one of your subjects so much as touch a hair on your pathetic little bodies you yell blue-murder. Then every one of your compatriots far and wide holler blue-murder along with you condemning the interference of free speech, and freedom of the press by your itty-bitty body toucher. You haven't the guts to stand up to your subjects like men. No, like curs you hide behind the legendary shield provided you by the millions of people who have died fighting for free speech…free speech without defilement, slander and smear tactics. Your pathetic attestations and dialectics are not about free speech, they're about pedaling your shit to the highest bidder or to your money grubbing editors.

"In any event, you media men and women can say write or picture me anyway you wish. You can ask any questions you want, regardless of its *reduction ad absurdum* its unrelated critique or insensitiveness. If you wish to be boorish about me fine.

"But for Christ's sake get some individualistic backbone. Don't be gutless wonders. Believe me, the world's populace sees you as a pack of trashy cowards. Any other questions?"

"Yeah bitch, are you a good fuck?"

"I don't know? I haven't tried it yet. Ask me again in a few years."

So much for Lana and her family's introduction to the media.

*   *   *

New York gave off its famous aura of excitement to the Masters. It welcomed Lana with open arms. Before meeting with the Chancellor and the head Dean of the New York University, the Masters' rented a condominium unit in a high rise self-owned apartment near Central Park for the month of September. The suite was situated in such a spot in the building that the southeast view gave the Masters' an opportunity of seeing much of mid-Manhattan's skyline. They were within walking distance to Central Park, its zoo, the Plaza Hotel, Bergdorf Goodman, Schwartz' toy emporium, the Waldorf-Astoria, Bloomingdales department store, the Museum of Modern Art, Carnegie Hall, even Rockerfeller Center. My, Lana remembered, what a thrill it was to see all of New York's world reknowned sights and to see, feel and enjoy its culture. What a lucky girl I am, she thought.

After getting settled down into their temporary quarters, Carl and Beatrice along with Margaret took Lana to NYU's Chancellor's office. There they met with the Chancellor, the University's bursar, the Head Dean of the University, the Deans of the Schools of Science and Business Administration and with the University's chief security officer. The bursar of the university opened Lana Jean Masters' file and briefed the attendees on Lana's educational qualifications, her studies and graduations to date, her mind-boggling grades, her maturity and her intelligence quotient. Each of the attendees other than Carl, Beatrice, Margaret and Lana had duplicate copies of Lana's file and had, on numerous occasions, studied the material therein. The files included Lana's life, other than her scholastic background, in all other matters. NYU had corresponded with all of the educational facilities Lana had attended from grade one to the present time for information not only on Lana's scholastic abilities but as to her personal life as well. The reports on the youngster's activities and lifestyle were as astonishing as her intelligence. NYU had called for and received remarkable reports from Lana's physicians as to her physical well being. The child's health was perfect.

NYU knew it had quite a serious, if not a profound responsibility in meeting this young woman's expectations, and of equal seriousness was NYU's responsibility for the guidance and care for this child's welfare. Teaching Lana, after all, is academic re a person of her talents. But students who would trail Lana's intelligence and who may be offended by Lana's mental superiority could cause Lana Masters to try to suppress her brain power in order to be like the others. What a terrible thought! But, while Lana's psyche was complex her brain was in complete charge of its workings, allowing, therefore, Lana to dominate any eventuality that faced her. No, Lana Masters would not try to suppress her brain power. She, Lana Masters, was always in controi of all her faculties.

Lana, after experiencing her two semesters at the U. of S. was comfortable with persons of any age, mental prowess or sophistication. As well, Lana could direct people of all ages to come around to her way of thinking if she desired. Her compelling, even overriding influence over other people's minds was astonishing even at the age of 13. Lana knew this fact. Without interfering with her brain's celerity and its deep-seeded intellect, she could place it on any level needed in order to meet any circumstance.

CHAPTER 11

LANA'S FIRST DATE, FRANKLIN FOSTER

Lana's three years at NYU were exciting and rewarding. She obtained her Masters of Science and her Masters of Business Administration degrees in just two years. She stayed at NYU an extra year and gobbled up a degree in Education. She cruised through the required lessons for her CPA designation in the USA and her C.A. designation in Canada. As was the case at the University of Saskatchewan, Lana captivated the hearts of the students and faculty heads at NYU. Academically she outshone every student of the various schools she attended. She was supreme in debating, she stole the show as the most popular person in her schools and she was the star in athletics, music and drama. She experienced her first date just before her 14th birthday and she lost her virginity at 15 years of age.

Lana lived in the university's dormitories for the full time she was attending NYU. All the while her fortune was mounting by way of compounding interest on her bonds, and the profitable way she dodged in and out of various securities. Then in 1983 just before her 16th birthday, Lana bought a 4,500 square foot condominium on the 29th floor of the St. Pierre on Fifth Avenue facing Central Park. Cost, $3,200,000.00. Lana visited her condo weekends. Here she relaxed reading novels, newspapers and letters from home. While her investments in equities seemed to her broker to be spontaneously chosen, they were in fact well thought out. Lana's brain had the capacity to remember the intricacies of most of the blue chip, growth and glamour stocks. She knew the various companies' management capabilities, their union contracts, their product acceptance by the public, their merchandising techniques, their financial position and earnings capabilities, their cash flow, their debt to equity ratios, price earnings, dividend records, trading volumes and on and on. But, most of all Lana had intuition, intuition that dovetailed absolute knowledge with specious reasoning or perhaps absolute awareness with idealistic intellect. Who knows? Lana made whatever it was work. It was in her condo where most of her investment decisions were made.

Lana's parents visited her often and, of course, had the condo as if it were their own. Often the whole family came to visit, and from time to time Margaret came alone. What a blast Margaret and Lana had shopping.

* * *

Lana met 18-year-old Franklin Foster in a Science Lab class. The class was split up in pairs. Every young male tried to pair-up with the about to be 14 year-old 'to die for' Lana Masters. Even the girls tried to be with Lana 'cause they knew she knew everything' and grades could only flourish if some of Lana's intelligence 'rubbed-off' on them.

Franklin Foster was the lucky one. Franklin was the person all the girls would choose. He was *the* hunk. Yeah, a six-foot-one, 185-pound sophomore. *The* number one quarterback for NYU's football squad. Smart, handsome, polite and charming. What a delicious screw he would make, the girls thought. Even Lana was delighted with the choice. Poor Franklin fumbled and bumbled his way through the first few classes because of his nearness to Lana. "Christ," he told his friends,"how can a guy concentrate on Lab class info when you're standing next to 'Princess' Lana. Sheeit, we touch, look through the microscope together, my thigh often rubs up against her ass. I shake, get a hard-on. Is it worth it?"

"I'll trade ya anytime Franky, anytime," Jeremy Todd piped in.

"Like hell you will Jeremy, I'll tough it out. I'm a big boy."

"Are the front of your boxer shorts starched in come?"

"All the time."

"Poor bastard," Lucky Ainsworth said laughing. "I get a bone-on every time I see her. Just think of a ring of her lipstick around your old pecker."

"Yeah," they all moaned.

"How old is she Franky Boy?"

"She just turned 14 or is just going to be 14…sumpin' like that."

"Fourteen, probably she's still a virgin."

"No doubt she is."

"Why'n'cha' ask her for a date Franky?" Jeremy asked.

"I'm gonna, as soon as I get enough nerve to ask her. I just hope I don't catch hell for wanting to date a kid."

"Some kid, Franky. Five-ten, five-eleven or so and with a body to die for. I wouldn't care if she was only ten. I'd go for it."

"Bullshit man, I like kids and I would punch-out any bastard that hurt one."

"Soorrry man, I was only kidding."

Finally, Franklin Foster made a decision to approach Lana for a date. He would ask her during or right after the next Lab class. "Yeah, tomorrow morning," Franklin averred. The poor dude tossed and turned in bed all night wondering, have I got the guts to ask her or haven't I? He was excited, scared and anticipatory all at the same time. When he saw her chatting with some other girls just outside the Lab the next morning, he began to get chills. She was too much. His nerves faltered.

Lana was dressed in jeans, huggy-huggy jeans. Her top was a western soft denim shirt open at the front down to just above her cleavage. She had the bottom of her shirt tied around her waist leaving a couple of inches of skin showing. She wore classy cowboy boots over the bottom of her jeans. Her tawny hair tumbled down her cheeks, flowed over both sides of her shoulders down past the skin that her tied shirt had allowed to be seen. She wore no make-up. Her jewelry consisted of a plain ring on the third finger of her right hand, a plain wristwatch with an artificial leather strap, and medium sized gold colored earrings that were visible only when Lana's hair permitted them to be seen. Simple enough clothing! Quite ordinary one might think. But on Lana, 'wow' too, too much. She looked edible.

Franklin was stunned. "Do I dare ask her for a date? A movie perhaps, or a Broadway musical? Or a nice dinner in one of those neat bistros facing Central Park, then a pleasant walk around the Plaza and the Plaza's coterie. Possibly a goodnight kiss. Do I dare ask her? Damn me. No damn you Lana Masters, why do you have to be so confounding luscious?"

The girls turned and began to make their way into the Lab. Lana spied the baleful-looking Franky Boy. She stopped, then marched toward him smiling. When she reached him she took his hand in hers, looked into his eyes and said, "Hi handsome what's the trouble? You look like you've lost your best friend. You look so sad." Lana touched her lips on his. "Don't be sad. Tell me what's troubling you, maybe I can help." Franklin near passed out when he felt Lana's lips touch his. His voice box went spastic….

"It's you Lana," he squeaked.

"Me?"

"Yes you," his voice still sounding silly.

"Why me?"

"Because you are so you, so inviting, so attractive. You should be against the law. I can't stop dreaming about you. My life was so organized, so simple before you came along. Now look at me. I'm a blithering idiot. My brain has quit working all because of you."

"I'm sorry Franklin. Do you want to trade partners with someone else in the Lab for me? I'll…"

"No, God no. Don't even think that way. It would kill me if you weren't my partner."

"Okay, then what?"

"I want to date you," he blubbered. "Yeah, I want to date you."

With that, he took Lana in his arms and kissed her. Lana waited until Franklin was through kissing her then said,

"Why didn't you say so, silly?"

"What, you're not going to slap me?"

"Why should I?" You haven't hurt me."

"You mean you would go out with me on dates?"

"Of course I would. At least at times suitable to me."

"Lana, you're not shitting me?"

"No, I'm not shitting you."

"Okay, I'll tell you what, I'll go get an all day sucker for you and we'll head for a motel right now," he said panting.

"Don't be smart, big guy," Lana said, warning her suitor. "I know I'm only going on 14, but my parents warned me about bad guys like you who offer little girls like me candies if I get in their cars, so you can't fool me Franklin Foster."

"Okay Lana, *touche*." He laughed.

They became very close. Often they went out to a movie or a play on Friday nights, had Sunday afternoons together and an occasional hour or two during the week. Lana tutored Franklin when he became mired down in this or that subject. Franklin, like professors, lecturers and other students were dumbfounded by Lana's intelligence.

Lana, Franklin, and their friends enjoyed being together. They would go on picnics together in Central Park when not studying. They played touch football, frisbee throwing, badminton, tennis, all sorts of activities to get their bodies alive and vibrant after sitting all day in classes or studying. In winter they would ice-skate, ride sleds and toboggans, hike, anything that would lighten the load of their studies. For Lana, it was fun having such nice friends. To her, though, she needed no recreation to ease her study load because she had no need to study. Anything Lana read would store itself in the microchip section of her brain. She sopped-up all information as a blotter and retained the information like the universe retains the stars.

One day during Christmas holiday, a gang of them decided to go for a swim in a pool situated in NYU's student building. The pool was huge. Olympic-size for swimming and deep enough at one end for springboard and tower diving. Several other students were at the pool that day. All hell broke loose when Lana stepped onto the pool deck. She wore a black bikini. The bra was scanty as was the thong type bottom. Lana's skin gleamed. Her perfect figure was overwhelming. It wasn't fair for her to be among mere mortals.

Lana's compelling physical attraction was so strong that the male swimmers were like iron filings around a magnet. They flocked to her. Most were gentlemen. Most tried to be nonchalant even indifferent as they sidled up to her. But others were simply rude. One student in particular was brazen with Lana. He came up next to her saying "What gash you are baby. We must jolly-well fuck." He reached out and went for her breasts. Lana smiled as she drove her right knee into his crotch. The guy yelped as he flopped to his knees holding his pecker and testicles. The guy's girlfriend heard his cry of pain, and unable to see Lana, broke through the circle of males calling, "Brad, are you hurt?" At first she thought her boyfriend had tripped or slipped on the pool deck injuring himself. Then she saw him on his knees gasping for air and holding his privates…on his knees facing a ravishing beauty…a beauty with a smile on her face.

"What happened?" Brad's girlfriend shouted.

Lana explained what happened.

"Well look at your skimpy bathing suit and all, no wonder he joked at you."

At that very moment Brad let go of his genitalia reached up to Lana's lower suit, grabbed it in both hands and pulled it down to her knees, leaving her front and back exposed. The male students went wild.

Rather unladylike, Lana hit the kneeling Brad with "one hellova punch" flush on his chin sending him sprawling on his side.

Brad's girlfriend screamed as she lunged at Lana. Lana stepped aside, caught the girl's back with her right hand and propelled her into the pool. Lana then eyed the circle of gawkers just as Franklin burst in on the scene.

"What the hell's going on Lana?" Looking at her half nude body and seeing Brad lying on his side in front of her, hand on his chin, holding his nuts with the other and a half-crazed broad sputtering explicit expletives at Lana as she fumbled her way out of the pool.

"What the hell's going on?" Franklin repeated.

Smiling, Lana pulled up her suit covering once again her sought after parts.

"Spoil sport," some guy yelled. "Let her strip numbnuts."

"Shut the fuck-up," Franklin hollered. He made some menacing moves toward a couple of students who just wouldn't give up. Recognizing Franklin as the star quarterback of NYU, a footballer, the two backed off.

Lana told Franklin to calm down. She explained the whole episode to him and to their friends, who had just now gathered around her.

"Shit," Jeremy said, "I missed all the fun. Lana, maybe you'd be a good girl and replay the scene where your panties were down. I'd, you know, like to see the..."

"Jeremy dear," Jeremy's girlfriend said, "hush now, or I'll break your face."

"Oui mademoiselle, pardon e' moi, or whatever. But dear, I have asked Lana to do this only for scientific reasons, you know, to find out the extent of the growth of her pubic hair at her tender age of 14. Oh yes, and to see if that buffoon lying there holding his doohickey hurt our charming Lana. Lana please pull down your…"

Swack! Jermey's girlfriend Lorriane let him have it. All of Lana's and Franklin's friends laughed. This wasn't the first time Jeremy had been belted by Lorriane.

"Wow that stung sweetie-pie."

"I hope so."

"Lana, c'mon, lets see your pee-pee and bummy," Jeremy begged once again, ducking just as Lorriane swatted at him.

"Okay," Lana commanded, "everyone but Jeremy and Franklin, and you too Brad baby, turn your backs to me and close your eyes."

They did.

"Now Jeremy and Franky come close to me."

They did.

Lana removed her entire bikini. Slowly she turned around for them. Then she faced them, eyes veiled and translucent.

"My God," both men moaned.

She called Franklin to her. She pressed herself against him, her firm breasts fused against his tight clear skin, his nipples just inches above hers. She took his hands and placed one on each of her bare buttocks. Then smiling, she moved away from him as he gasped. She handed him her bikini and asked him to put it back on her body. He did.

"Okay eva'body the show she is over. You can turn around now and open your eyes."

After an hour of swimming and having fun at the pool, the gang departed and retreated to one of the university's cafeterias.

Franklin Foster would never forget that sultry moment with Lana. Jeremy was in a daze for days afterward.

CHAPTER 12

FRANKLIN'S SUMMER VACATION WITH LANA

At her Father's Ranch.

Franklin and Lana became head over heels in love with one another. In three short years Lana had accomplished her goals in NYU. She had completed her studies on May 3rd, 1982. She was now 15 years old, soon to be 16.

During her years at NYU she and Franklin were inseparable when time permitted. Lana's effective tutoring of Franklin brought him from a C+, B—student to a straight A student. He earned his athletic and academic scholarships with hard work imposed on him by Lana. Franklin's bias changed from a life of wanting to a professional athlete to wanting to be a "somebody" in diplomatic circles. His goal now was to obtain a Doctorate Degree in Political Science and Economics.

* * *

During the summer breaks between semesters Lana would go back to her 'cute little city, Swift Current.' While she spent a fair amount of time in, as the locals called it, 'Speedy Creek' the preponderance of her time was spent on the ranch-farm helping the same old hands, Hank, George, Pete, Cowboy Ellis, Ray, Bobby and Tim. She couldn't get enough of her dad's spread. The chickens now were now gone, but in their place were over 1,000 turkeys…1,000 gobblers kept in a half section of land over a mile from the farmhouse. The pens and feed and equipment for those birds were all state-of-the-art. Three young high school students looked after the turkeys on weekends under George's watchful eyes. The entire net proceeds from the 'turkey' department went to the Federal Government of Canada for the purpose of employment.

Lana spent hours with Big Buster. The huge bull snorted hatred at everyone who came near him, save for Lana. She brushed him, sprayed him with insect repellent, fed him vitamins, snoozed beside him when he chewed his cud, made him run to exercise him, sang to him, even tickled his nose with foxtails. No one could believe their eyes when they saw her fussing over this behemoth, a behemoth which could destroy her in seconds. Lana's explanation to those who asked her how she could keep 'this killing machine' from harming her, she said simply, "I love and trust him, and he loves and trusts me." But for heavens sake, don't try to emulate me with Big Buster, no, my goodness no, keep yourself a safe distance from my pet.

In the spring of 1982 Lana had asked her dad and mother if Franklin could come and work on the ranch-farm from the end of June through Labor Day. Her parents, who had met Franklin the year before, thought the idea was a splendid one.

"Yes dear, by all means. It should be fun to see a big city boy on our 'little old' spread," Carl said. "He can live in the farmhouse with the other hands. It will be a delight to see Franklin in with the tough cowhands and plow-jockeys." Lana and her dad laughed.

Bernice didn't, she said, "It's cruel to leave a city boy with our men. They'll play all kinds of tricks on him. And what about your brothers, they'll have poor Franklin not knowing whether he's coming or going. Franklin is such a nice boy. If your brothers or your dad's men overdo it, I shall have him come and stay at our house here in Swift Current and have him work with me in my garden."

That broke Carl and Lana up. They laughed until tears came into their eyes. "Work alongside me in my garden," they mimicked then roared again.

"Mom, Franklin is over 200 pounds now, he's a quarterback on a squad of 250 to 300 pound footballers. He's tough."

"He's still a boy, and besides footballers can't wrangle cattle or wrestle 800 pound steers."

* * *

Franklin had never enjoyed a summer break as much as he did this one. The summer was hot and dry. Franklin relished every chore he did, with the exception of hosing down and cleaning out the barn. He helped repair machinery. He learned to drive tractors and combines. On his own Franklin 'summer fallowed' two sections of land. He learned to ride horseback and often he would accompany Pete, Cowboy Ellis and Tim herding the cattle. By the end of the day he would be exhausted but gratified.

The meals made for the hands were delicious, hearty and nourishing. Franklin never ate so well. Lucy, the cook, looked after the men as if they were her own kids. Before bedtime every night she had fresh fruit, sandwiches and tea, coffee or milk set out for them on the kitchen table. Farm and ranch work was not a nine-to-fiver as Franky Boy found out. Daily work could stretch out to 20 hours on some occasions, and could be as short as six hours on others. But it seemed to be the norm that chores ran twelve hours each day.

Franklin became tough, rugged and mature. His muscles were stretched, pulled and tested for strength many times during each day. He gained 15 pounds over the two months and, by damn, if his body hadn't reached six-feet-two-inches. He was a smooth, rippling muscled, non-fat 220-pound stud. 'Bring on those mean sons-a-bitches linebackers. I'll show them some fuckin' steer wrestling. They'll think twice about trying to tear my head off. I'll kick the shit out of them. Ha!' He worked in Izod shorts, no shirt, heavy woolen socks and cowboy boots. His body was a glistening bronze masterpiece. Every time he had to go to town in the open little go-anywhere Jeep, girls would drool for a piece of his body. He would wave at them smiling his million-dollar smile.

Lana worked on the ranch-farm as well. She never shirked tough chores. She ran the hay-baler as good as any man. She always worked the round-ups. She tended newborn calves, assisted the veterinarian with vaccinations of the cattle, or with the sick or injured stock. While tears came to her eyes when she thought back on her big stallion Sir Galahad, she had replaced her memory of him to some extent with a beautiful deep brown six-year-old mare she named Tess. The mare was excellent for moving cattle from one grazing ground to another. Just a touch of her neck by the reins was all that was necessary for Lana to do to direct Tess. Lana would not have been surprised if her pretty little mare could herd the cattle on her own.

Lana's mother was right. Lana's brothers and the hands had a ball getting to Franklin. They teased him every chance they had and the tricks they played on him were non-stop. But at no time were the "guys" mean. The tricks and teasing were all done in good fun and if the guys went a little overboard, both Hank and Big George would intercede. Franklin accepted all the jokes played on him in good spirits. He knew when he left New York that he would be the typical 'city slicker' to the westerners, and the brunt of the westerners jokes. In fact Lana's brothers and the hands liked this city dude one hell of a lot. The guys found Franklin unafraid to tackle any chore they gave him to do. Franklin got Carl Sr., Lana, her brothers and the hands good one afternoon.

Everyone was in the barn having some homemade lemonade. Pistol Pete began jabbing Franklin with a few barbs about how all tough cowpokes could only make the grade if they were able to milk a cow just as the cow was getting set to be humped by a bull—and would Franky Boy like to try it? Franky Boy feigned astonishment and fear.

Lana had told him the story about her mom saying that if her sons and the hands teased him too much that, "I shall have Franklin come to my house in Swift Current and have him work with me in the garden." Then to Pete, "just as I understand you did a few years back Pete when it got too hot in the kitchen for you…hey boys?" Everybody guffawed at Pete.

"No shit, Pete, you did that?" Tim shouted. Pete laughed too. Up he got, grabbed an empty gunnysack, ran over to Franklin, pulled the gunny—sack over Franky Boy's head and shoulders and wrestled him to the ground.

"Yippy-i-o-k-yea" the guys all shouted.

CHAPTER 13

THE RUSTLERS

The Masters', in addition to the 12,000 acres of land they owned eight miles south of Swift Current, had a huge 30,000-acre ranch in the Cypress Hills in Southwest Saskatchewan, some 100-plus miles west of Swift Current. The ranch was the grazing ground for a basic herd of 100,000 Hereford cattle. The range was picturesque with its wide expanse of green grasslands leading up to a forest of lodge pole pine. The scenic wonder known as the Cypress Hills came about by an oversight of Mother Nature some 10,000 years ago when she was busy with the last ice age. She had erred as the huge ice floes she had concocted began to move out of the area as she directed. The poor Dear hadn't consulted enough with her computer, drafting boards and measurements in the beginning. The result was the ice age dashed well missed the 30-mile wide and a couple of hundred miles long beauty stretch, now known as the Cypress Hills. On either side of the majestic hills are the prairies, the bald somewhat boring prairies. Then right in their midst is this island, an island with forests of lodge pole pines, luscious green grass, exquisite fauna not found anywhere in the world except in the Cypress Hills, fauna that existed prior to Mother Nature's ice-age gig. Deer, elk and antelope abound. Beaver and muskrats busy themselves in the cool streams. Streams full of brown trout. Bobcat's and lynx' shrieks fill the night air. The hills roll with showy punctillousness. Some of the hills are without pines. Pine-less peaks known as Eagle Butte and Bald Butte. Exciting and adventurous riding trails weave their way throughout the hills. There are several small lakes and one large lake in the park. The large lake, known as Cypress Lake is surrounded by pretty cabins, cabins tucked away in the pine forest so that they are scarcely noticeable to those walking, cycling or driving around the lake on a narrow paved road. The lake teems with sporty good-sized rainbow trout. A new lodge snuggles itself deep in the pine forest. The lodge in no way disturbs the uniqueness of the surroundings.

* * *

One of the cabin owners on the lake are Carl and Bernice Masters. Every summer, when their children were growing up, much of Bernice's time was spent at the cabin with her brood.

During the summer months the cattle are attended to by three old cowboys and a host of young high-schoolers who live in a cow-town known as Maple Creek, a town just a few miles from the Masters' spread and 80 miles west of Swift Current.

During the winter months, wranglers Cowboy Ellis, Pistol Pete and Tim Thompson are transferred from the Swift Current spread to a cozy house on Maple Creek's main street, a house owned by the Masters. The cowhands have a F.W.D. Jeep and snowmobiles to get around on the huge acreage during the winter months. The work is downright brutal. Cold, mean, treacherous, blizzards sweep across the plains and the hills from the northeast. Wind-chill factors reach 60 degrees below zero on the Fahrenheit scale. The cattle must be fed. Haystacks that become hidden in deep snow must be cleared so the cattle can feed. Sick cattle must be attended to and brought to the large shelters built for this purpose. Cattle rustlers must be thwarted. Rustlers are cute. They drive high-powered snowmobiles into the herds scattering them. They then herd stragglers to hidden cattle trucks that whisk them away to whom knows where. Cowboy Ellis came across three mobile rustlers moving 50 or so head belonging to the Masters' herd during a vicious storm one

Sunday morning in January 1981. He called Pete and Tim on his walkie-talkie for help.

Pete and Tim were working separate areas of the huge spread but they received Cowboy Ellis' S.O.S. Pete called the R.C.M.P detachment in Maple Creek and gave the mountie on office duty the message. The mountie called his fellow officers informing them of the cattle rustling taking place on the south slope of Bald Butte. Three officers each took a snowmobile from their storage shed and each floored their machines. They carried carried high-powered rifles and 22-gauge shotguns on their vehicles.

Cowboy Ellis came at the three rustlers from the lee side of the storm so that the roar of his mobile would not be heard by the thieves and so they would not spot him until the last minute. Cowboy Ellis' goggles kept getting covered by the driving snow. He would lose sight of them. "Damn it, wouldn'tcha know it," the cowboy said as he saw several heifers stranded up to their bellies in snowdrifts. Cowboy now was in a dilemma. Save the eight or ten yearlings or continue after the rustlers. Shit. The cowboy opted for the rustlers. He called Pete and Tim about the stranded heifers and gave them the approximate location of the 'burgers.'

Around noon the cowboy spotted the three rustlers at the bottom of a small ravine, their mobiles side by side and the cattle hugged together in a tight circle. The cowboy knew this would be the designated pick-up spot for cattle trucks. "Nice thinking you bastards," Cowboy Ellis mumbled to himself. The roadway for the get-away trucks came to within a few hundred yards of the cattle, and the roadway was always clear from snow, so long as a northeast blizzard was blowing and this was one hellova Nor-Easterly. The cowboy grimaced. "What'll I do?" The tough cowpoke thought to himself as he laughed, "I'll jest do what ma ole pal Evel Knieval would do, I'll come off that there lil ole ledge yonder and land this mother on all three of their dune buggies." Shifting his machine to its fastest torque, turning right to get on the hill above the ledge, Cowboy Ellis, hit the top of the hill, pushed his iron horse to its top speed, barreled down the slope hitting the ledge at about 60 M.P.H. He howled like a madman, arms flapping, as he and his mobile flew through the air.

"What the fuck?" yelled one of the rustlers looking up. "Jump fer chrissake." The three jumped just a part of a second before Cowboy Ellis and his machine landed smush on their three mobiles. Dumbfounded the rustlers scrambled away from the big bust-up. The cowboy bounced crazily in his seat-belted seat hooting and hollering his bloody brains out, as his machine crashed on the dune buggies. Cowboy swore his machine farted on impact. He grabbed for his Howitzer, a big menacing shotgun, and fired the loud shoulder-kicking monster over his head. Hearing the shot the three rustlers flopped down in the snow covering their heads. Cowboy Ellis despite being knocked silly by his Knieval stunt, clamored down from the steaming mess of twisted mobiles and landed on one knee. Pain shot through his whole body, and almost falling, he slammed the butts of his shotgun and 30-ought-three into the snow using them as canes to hold him up.

One of the rustlers, wondering what in hell came out of the sky busting up the mobiles and the crazy hooting alien that accompanied the U.F.O. shooting off his alien gun, peered back at the mess. He saw a cowboy alien leaning on a shotgun and a rifle. The cowboy saw the peeker. 'Ha,' Cowboy Ellis said to himself as he raised his shoulder kickin' loud mouthed Howitzer up and blasted a shot just over the rustler's head. The rustler dove into the snow and wet his pants.

Cowboy Ellis yelled at the three rustlers, "Stay put or you'll be a feelin' hot buckshot drivin' up your bony keesters." They stayed put. The cowboy grabbed a lariat from one of the defunct mobiles and holding his two guns under one arm and the lariat in the other, he waddled over to rustler number one. Kneeling down in agony and dropping his guns down behind him the cowboy in about three seconds had rustler number one hogtied. Like a calf-roping contest, he smiled grimacing, head aching, for sure a busted rib or two, Cowboy Ellis crawled to the next dude. In about three seconds rustler number two was hogtied. The cowboy looked up just in time to see rustler number three standing over him, driving an eight-inch bone-handled blade at him. The cowboy knew he couldn't get out of the way in time to miss the knife. God how it stung when it plunged into his shoulder!

But Cowboy Ellis knew no fear. He remembered the awful whippings he got from his pa over nothing while just a kid. They hurt awful bad. They were torture. His back, buttocks, thighs and arms would be covered with bruises and cuts. John Clement Ellis, the cowboy would whimper as he got beaten but he was never fearful of his religious bible thumpin' miserable pa. No, the cowboy's hatred of his father was so ingrained in his mind it smothered any fear that might have been lurking in the cowboy's subconscious. When he was just 16-years old the cowboy beat the crap out of his old man just before his old man was about to lay 'God's' leather on him once again. That same day the cowboy left home for good. He had heard tell that his old man was still preachin' the gospel at open air Sunday gatherins' in the summer and at the big old church just outside Assiniboia, Saskatchewan in winter. "Yeah brethren, good old Rev. Cyrus P. Ellis, some folks says. I say fuck the good old Rev. Cyrus P. Ellis."

The cowboy pushed himself backward with his aching legs. He tried to grab his guns as he slid through the snow. He got to them just as rustler number three was on top of him. The cowboy knew that with his wracked up body, which was now playing host to a big knife sticking out of his shoulder, he would not be the odds on favorite to win this fight. But who gives a dang about odds. Cowboy Ellis, like a Man Mountain Dean his psyche hitting mach two, heaved the rustler into the air a couple degrees west over his shoulders onto a barren embankment. A loud snap followed by a piercing scream punctured the air. Surprised, the cowboy twisted his ravaged body to see why the rustler was screaming so loud. "Well, ain't that a bearcat now, you mafa weasel?" the cowboy twanged as the rustler howled in agony. "So ya got yer ass caught in a coyote trap." Just as sure as night follows day, the rustler's lower left leg was snagged within the steel jaws of a leg hold trap. An illegal leg hold trap set there by old Walter Demchuck to catch a coyote that old Walter had been after for months.

The cowboy stood, weaving a bit, listening to the rustler holler and cuss, then looking at the bone handle sticking out of his shoulder. "Hell who gives a shit." He had captured all three of the rustlers. He started to hip-hop around like a drunken sailor. He pow-wowed from one side of the tiny coulee to the other as the 50 or so heifers eyed him stupidly, mooed suspiciously, while the leg trapped rustler howled like a beaten cur. All the while the two hog-tied dudes rolled around in the snow trying to free themselves from their tethers. The four pitiful flattened mobiles sat motionless but farted on occasion from gas leaks. That's how it looked when Pete and the Mounties arrived (Tim had stopped to free the ten yearlings). "What in Christ's name?" Constable Kent Oliver said to Constables Irwin, Clemson and Pistol Pete, as they looked down at the impiety below them. The blizzard had abated to a stiff breeze. The drifting snow had eased. The sun shone. The heifers bellowed at the cowboy. The cowboy leaped and pow-wowed around like a madman. The trapped rustler hollered to be freed. The two holy rollers rolled in the snow and the smashed tangle of mobiles sputtered and farted as they rested.

When the cowboy woke up in the hospital he wondered where all the snow and shit had gone to. He looked at his shoulder. "Huh," bandages, no knife. He went to sit up. Pain shot through his whole body. He laid back. He saw a pretty face. He pawed at it. Pretty face took his hand and said in a cheerful voice, "Hi Mr. Hero, so you decided to wake up. What a good boy you are, and after all you've been through, you look so cute."

"I did, I am and I'm what?"

"You're a cute, tough guy, hero."

"I am?"

"Yes, you are."

"And you're a nurse?"

"Yes, I am. I'm Janey Walker."

"Dang, you're a purdy one aren't you?"

"If you say so cowboy."

"I says so. I guess I'm in the hospital eh?"

"Yes you are."

Cowboy Ellis fretted after NurseWalker left him. He wondered if Mr. Masters and Hank would be angry with him. Now he remembered. He had smashed up a $20,000 rig trying to emulate Evel Knieval in a high-flying stunt. A $20,000 rig owned by Mr. Masters and under Hank's care. "Dang it, it was only a few years ago that I took Big Buster to the wrong quarter and almost had little Lana killed. Shit, they'll kill me."

The cowboy was wrong. Carl Masters, Hank...everyone...considered the cowboy to be a hero. His actions had brought about the round up and arrest of the most notorious band of rustlers west of the Pecos and north of the Mexican border. His actions had saved the Masters' ranch over $35,000 for the heifers and the yearlings, and the good big old mobile was insured. Carl Masters sent all the hands for a four-day, full-paid weekend to Las Vegas along with a thousand U.S. bucks each for spending. Yah, good ole Cowboy Ellis, the hands thought.

CHAPTER 14

VIRGINITY...LANA AT AGE FIFTEEN

The summer of 1982 saw the gorgeous Lana become a woman. A woman attuned in providing immense pleasures to others. Pleasures she too relished as she gave and received fulfillment. She saw her intellectual achievements strung-out behind her. Achievements she had accomplished from the time she was a baby. 'Now,' she reasoned, 'I have several bachelor degrees, master degrees and some doctorates, whilst yet a 'teener' so why am I not doing my articles in sensuality? I realize I won't be 16 until October,' she observed, 'but to date I have worked without boy girl physical intimacies, sure I have masturbated, and I have even felt some exciting impulses when Franklin has touched my yolvo...' she smiled thinking of George, '...and my breasts. But now, at my mental age of 40-plus amongst my peers and my physical age of 15, I want to experience complete sex with a man. And Franklin baby, without your knowing it, in three days you are going to be the terminator of my maidenhead at which time I will complete my entrance into womanhood. I am looking forward to the experience, it should be fun.'

CHAPTER 15

LANA'S MOTHER'S ABHORRENCE

"Lana, it is so difficult for me to give you orders or directions. You know that child. You are a mental giant…a most sensitive caring young lady. Your father and I love you beyond words. Your brothers and sister, well what can I say, they adore you.

Everyone who knows you loves you. And your physical appearance, well again what can I say? But my dear Lana, for you to expect me to approve of your next conquest, or as you termed it, 'an erotic sensual experiment with Franklin in the pristine environs of the Cypress Hills,' well my dear young lady, I do not approve. Regardless of your mental superiority, you are still a child, my child, do you understand that Lana? I will always feel it is my God-given right as your parent to refuse to let you do certain things. And this, Lana, is one thing I will quash. You have been menstruating only for the past two or three years. You are not one of those children in certain parts of this world who are expected to produce young the moment they can do so, nor are you a floozy. Good gracious Lana, you are making me angry."

"Mom," Lana sighed.

"Now don't Mom me."

Lana smiled at her mother and went to her and hugged her.

"Lana don't try to appease me. You cannot have intercourse outside of marriage."

"Mom."

"Lana, don't Mom me I said."

"Okay, Bernice." Lana laughed.

"I shall call your father if you don't stop patronizing me."

"Mommy my darling."

"And don't Mommy my darling me."

"Please listen to me for a moment Mom" Lana said kissing her mother's cheek. "I am so different from the norm, you know that. Fifteen and 16-year-olds are babes in the woods. Twenty-year-olds I can tolerate, but, by and large they are just big kids. Thirty and 40-year-olds…" Lana flip flopped her hand to designate neutrality. "So, the sweetest of all mothers everywhere, I doubt I will ever marry. I would never make a good wife, and, it is doubtful I will ever have children, except perhaps for experimental purposes. Who in their right mind would want me as a long-term hold? Once the sexy part of a marriage ebbed with me no man would find me a ball of fun. No, they would find me a walking encyclopedia. Heck no Mom, an ordinary everyday working man would shun me, a political would run from me, a religious would want to burn me at the stake and a professional would tire of me because I won't smoke pot, get drugged up or get drunk. Sex, sweetheart, is simply a physical phenomenon. Men, whilst many force themselves to be monogamous, most are polygamists. They want pussy."

"Lana Jean. Don't be crude."

"I'm not crude Mom. Men want pussy. And you know darn well mother that a lot, a heck of a lot of women want a wide variety of sexual partners, too. But that's not what we're now discussing. We are discussing my intended rape of poor little old Franklin."

"Lana Jean," Bernice scolded, covering her ears.

Lana kept on.

"Mom, no matter what you say, and with my absolute respect for you, my love and devotion to you, I am going on with this experience. I deem the experience to be no more than a physical activity. A pleasant physical activity I should hope for both Franklin and me, but nonetheless a physical activity. Much like breathing in the aroma of a beautiful rose and the pleasure the aromatic sweetness gives to one's sense of smell. Or Mom, the titillation given one's taste buds by the feasting on delectable fruits. Kissing is an acceptable activity to most societies as is nose rubbing in others and these activities tend to heighten the senses of eroticism. The playing with one another's pee pees, breasties, bummies and toes or whatever simply is a physical stimulation of another sense of a person's being. So Mom, I intend to take Franklin to the Cypress Hills. We will do a little hiking, fishing, swimming and riding. Then at the base of either Eagle Butte or Bald Butte, Franklin and I will pitch a tent for a three night stay, roll out our sleeping bags and after we get settled I shall invite Franklin into my lair at bedtime. I shall indulge myself.

"Lana Jean, I forbid you. Do you understand me? I forbid you to...to...even consider such a thing. I will talk to Franklin and tell him of your plan to seduce him. You are just 15 child, 15. I was 22 when your father took me."

"Mom, please do not say a word of this to Franklin. If you do, and even if Franklin does promise you he will not go to bed with me, I shall select one of the handsome boys from Swift Current to..."

"Lana, stop it, this instant!"

"No, Mom, I won't. I intend to have sex by Friday."

"Oh my dear child, what am I going to do with you? You are so strong, so very strong. I know I can't stop you. But Lana darling, I can impress on your mind my absolute abhorrence of your scheme."

"Common" Mother, not abhorrence for goodness sakes?"

"Yes child abhorrence. I will not speak to Franklin, no, but I shall tell your father."

"That's fair Mom."

They hugged one another as Bernice wept.

CHAPTER 16

VIRGINITY LOST...LANA AT AGE FIFTEEN

They pitched their tent mid-morning on Friday, July 17th, at the base of Eagle Butte just under some graceful rustling birch trees. The weather was ideal and it was to stay that way for the next two weeks. Mid-day temperatures were to be in the high 80's while the early morning hours were to be a refreshing, dewy 55 degrees.

They had two spirited well-groomed quarter horses for their transportation. Two quarter horses owned by Carl Masters.

After pitching their tent they hiked for miles around Eagle Butte. In time they came to a gravel road just a few hundred yards from a pretty cabin owned by the Bookers. They began to walk north on the gravel road. They came to a small lake, surrounded by tall grass and reeds that abounded in both beaver and muskrat. They watched in excitement as one big male beaver sounded loud, sharp, splashes with his broad tail on the water announcing the presence of nosy two-legged animals who don't grow fur. He was a beaut! Franklin was astounded when he saw Lana stroll out through the grasses and reeds into the shallows of the lake and in a gentle yet compelling voice call the beaver to her side. He came to her. She petted him, talked to him and even rubbed his cute little under tummy until he turned over on his back wanting her to rub his tummy with more vigor. After two or three minutes of vigorous patting, Lana touched the beavers nose with her fingers and said good-bye. The beaver understood. He righted himself, gave the water a mighty spanking with his tail then swam to the center of the lake looking back occasionally at the nice two-legged non-furry creature who had just made his day.

They walked another 15 minutes until they reached the Government's Public Park area. They stopped for some lemonade, sat and looked onto the sparkling Cypress Lake from their lodge pole pine bench. They held hands and stole an occasional kiss. Lana wore her sexy blue-jeans shorts. Shorts that just covered her secrets, and a white singlet that accentuated her 37-inch bust. Her long silken legs were tanned a deep glistening brown. She wore hiking boots and woolen gray socks. Her hair tumbled down her back to the top of her rump and fell declivitously over her shoulders and her breasts. Her face was without make-up. Tanned. A face so beautiful it was without equal. Her mouth and lips were moist, wet, inviting. Not a soul within eyesight of her could take their eyes off of her. She was breathtaking.

Poor Franklin knew that wherever Lana was, she would captivate everyone by her beauty. 'What chance have I got to keep her? It pisses me off. There will always be someone who will take her away from someone else. Damn you Lana,' he thought, 'damn fucking you.'

At that moment Lana was thinking of her upcoming seduction in the soft comfy sleeping bag in just a few hours, a sleeping bag which can be zipped open. Open so that both she and Franklin can watch what each one does to the other. This'll be fun. My first experience with a penis. A cock! She leaned over and pecked Franklin's cheek with her lips.

"Why are you looking so grumpy Franklin?"

"Never mind."

"Tell me, please?"

"It's you Lana. Just like always, I feel lousy when I know you will tire of me soon and fall for someone else."

"You don't know that Franklin."

"Look Lana, or Dr. Masters, you know full well I am just an intermediary. You may not know this now but, shit Lana, it won't take long for you to find out."

Lana knew what Franklin was saying was true. As she had told her mother, she doubted that she would ever marry, but she didn't know at age 15 if she would ever be able to have a lasting meaningful relationship with anyone.

"Forget it handsome, for the nonce I am smitten by you."

Franklin didn't reply. He just sat watching the lake, the swimmers and the boaters…without motors…fishing for that elusive big one.

"C'mon Franky baby, its nearly four o'clock. By the time we get back to our tent it will be close to six and I'm getting hungry for the filet mignon we're going to barbecue."

She took his hand, kissed his lips and said "my big quarterback, tonight, under the silvery moon, we're going to have one hellova football game. No holds barred, everything from blind siding to quarterback sneaks, from opening holes to roughing the passer, to fourth and inches, to loss on downs. From non-sportsmanlike conduct, to goosing the tailback. From passes completed to piling on, from converts to missing the uprights. You know baby, the whole nine yards.

That night before undressing, Franklin's mouth actually watered. They had eaten, gone for a walk holding each other around the waist and talked about everything but love making. Franklin had not stopped drooling from the time Lana had said, "the whole nine yards." God he was horny. On their walk he could hardly refrain from raping her. Back at the tent Lana told him to watch her. First she removed her hiking boots and socks then stretched her long tanned legs out as she sat in the folding lounge chair. She parted them—just enough to show her silken inner thighs. She stood, removed her singlet and jeans shorts. There she was all five-feet-ten inches of her guarded by only the briefest of undies and bra.

"Now," she said, "it's your turn."

Franklin was down to his boxer shorts in a flash. They kissed. They fooled around like kids as they wrestled in and out of their sleeping bags. They tumbled and rolled, they growled like a tiger and tigress, nipping and biting. Abruptly Lana stopped the action. She had seen many men's organs on cadavers in anatomy classes. She'd seen her dad's a couple of times when she peeked. She'd seen her brothers' things when they showed off, and she'd seen all the ranch-farm hands by peeking, Pistol Pete had the biggest, the rest were all about the same size. After peeking Lana Jean would cover her mouth and snuffle and giggle. That asshole Uncle Fred had had his hard reddish brown dick near her face many times. It was huge and loathsome. Now she had Franklin's. Franklin's was nice. His had a foreskin. Franklin was wild.

"What the hell ya 'doin' Lana?" He said.

"I'm checking out your throbbing wet-headed penis baby boy and the rolling movement of your testicles. I've read about their vigorous activities when under siege." With that she fondled his penis and testies and told him to cough. He coughed. "Your private parts are very healthy sir—that'll be one hundred bucks for the examination."

"Fuck you Dr. Masters."

"I'd hoped you'd say that sir."

With that she mouthed his wet-headed cock.

"Oh God," he moaned. He panted. He almost blasted. They tussled. Ready now for her maidenhood to be made extinct, she rolled away from Franklin onto the lush grass just outside the tent. Franklin followed. She beckoned him to lie atop her. He did. She lubricated her vulva with her spittle then directed his penis inside her. Lana grimaced. She held him from going further inside her by grasping his erection. "Please go slow babe, it hurts me."

Franklin's near delirious mind said, 'I want to hurt you, I want you to scream bloody murder. You are so fucking clean and tender. I want to dirty you up and ravish you.' He tried to drive his penis further inside her.

"Please Franklin, go easy"

Again, Franklin thrust hard using the force of his powerful hips.

Lana yelped as another two inches of Franklin's penis found its way into her vagina. The hymen now was close at hand. "God it hurts Franklin, please. I thought you would care about me and go slow." The hand she had around his phallus was now so lubricated that it did little to stop Franklin's powerful drives. Lana screamed when her maidenhead's membrane was ripped by Franklin's penis. He quickened his humping. His foreskin was rolled back. His bald penis head was so inimitably sensitive without the interruption of his foreskin that the feeling it generated was electrifying. He humped like a wild man until his cock felt that ultimate inexplicable feeling, ejaculation. He put the palms of his hands on either side of Lana's head onto the grass covered ground and lifted his upper torso from her perspiration covered breasts and shoulders. This allowed him to force his hips to drive his penis even further into her womb. He gasped as his sperm kept coming and coming inside Lana. After several seconds of ejaculation, Franklin's body went limp. He lowered his body onto hers. Perspiration rolled off his face onto Lana's.

Lana was crying. She hadn't felt any pleasurable sensation, only pain. Lana knew the first time would be painful. She hoped the next ones over the next few hours would be gratifying. Lana knew intercourse would be painful from time to time in the future, but, damn it all, she hoped most often it would be a delectable experience.

CHAPTER 17

ATHENS GREECE: LANA AND FRANKLIN

It was now 5:00 a.m., May 24th, 1997. Lana's guest had made boorish nightmarish screams all through the night, God-awful screams. It was annoying. Lana was getting sick and tired of his damn sleeping. She wanted him awake. **Awake so he could feel the ripping and the tearing the rats were inflicting on his lily-white skin.**

* * *

Lana's mind never impinged on itself while viewing her guest's revolting appearance. She watched those persistent flies hovering over his mouth, torso and anus. Again she let her mind wander back over her life.

* * *

For the next five years Lana attended many universities worldwide, both in the absorption of upper level knowledge and in the dissemination of her own postulations. She was a teacher in the most basic of dialectics. She could teach a class of kindergarten children with the same degree of ease, dispatch, skill and clarity as she could a class burdened with intellectual genii.

From time-to-time Lana would meet up with Franklin at designated locals. Franklin, by the age of 23 had obtained his Masters Degree in Political Science. Because of the excellent marks he received during his university years, his athletic accomplishments and his charming demeanor, he had no trouble in procuring a rather responsible position with the Diplomatic Corps under the jurisdiction of the Secretary of State. One of his first appointments was to attend meetings in Athens and Trieste along with senior personnel of the Corps and some private business heads. Essentially Franklin was being taken along on the trip for the purpose of gaining experience in diplomacy. The group was to be ten days in Athens and eight days in Trieste. Franklin was an astute, mindful trainee. He listened attentively to all that was said. He ingrained in his mind what he deemed to be the highlights of discussions that took place between the old pros. He listened to their polite voices, he watched their oft' phony gestures, their exquisite conduct and their tactful pussy footing. He found it most interesting when the attendees dove into subjects such as trade balances, interest rates, inflation, government deficits, trade barriers, free trade, immigration policies, labor sensitivities, unemployment figures, foreign cash holdings and the like.

Franklin, other than taking the occasional Saturday night and Sunday off worked 18-hour-days. He would attend mandatory cocktail parties but would remain at them only as long as necessary. Then he would be off to his hotel room to write-up in detail the notes he had made during the day. Franklin was careful when he entered into discussions with the old pros. Before doing so, he would think out the merits of his contributions. Were his contributions going to be substantial thus beneficial to the subjects at hand, or was it that he was trying to make an impression by talking intellectual flabbergast to the old pros. Thus Franklin, by eliminating sheer bullshit, often added to many assemblages' discussions and conclusions. The old pros agreed this young man, Franklin L. Foster, had the makings of either a political bigwig or a diplomat of the highest order. A fine young man indeed!

* * *

Lana met Franklin in Athens on Franklin's free Saturday night. Franklin had arranged for a suite in the Hyatt Athenea. The hotel was within walking distance of the ancient citadel wonder, the Acropolis. Lana flew in from New York City where she had just concluded a day's lecture to the supranational peace-seeking organization…the United Nations…on global human rights, basic human dignities, laws, and elimination of poverty. Lana just 18, verbally spanked every last member of the UN for their abysmal lethargy toward these subjects.

"Human rights," she hammered, "and financial equity are considered by too many to be solely the domain of and at the behest of big brother governing bodies, dictators, divine rulers, religious hierarchies, paternal heads, and condescending dictatorial con artists. These few mighty moguls love, adore, worship and kill for power and wealth. This lethargy must end now and be replaced by positive action. Everyone on this globe is entitled to, and has the sovereign right to be free to live well, to enjoy human dignity and all the positive concepts pertaining to human rights. No one in the United Nations Assembly or anyone else should have the audacity, the recklessness, the presumptuous damnable nerve to think they are supreme, thus have unfettered rights over others." Lana as well, gave the Assembly a stern lecture on fair and just laws and the required adherence thereto by the populace.

Lana and Franklin found one another in a cute little coffee shop in the hotel. This they had planned. Franklin was seated at a tiny table for two at a window. Lana spied him as soon as she entered the little bistro. She called his name. Franklin leapt up, knocking his chair over as he rushed to her. They embraced. They kissed. They stood back and admired one another. They laughed for joy. Once again, they embraced. Tears flowed. "I love you," was murmured, intermingled with, "I have missed you so."

Finally, other patrons of the cute little coffee shop began to applaud the two romanticists. No one's eyes left Lana. Franklin was not oblivious of the stares directed at Lana. He hated this. But he was so overjoyed at seeing Lana he was able to put this emotion aside. "God she is lovely," he thought. At last they sat at their tiny table. They held each other's hands. Their eyes were locked on each other. Finally, in unison they said, "How have you been?" They laughed. "You look so good," again, in unison. Again, they laughed. "Great minds think alike." They ordered a fine Greek coffee and the tasty Greek yummy baklava. They reminisced, they laughed, they cried.

Every eye in the cafe was fixed on Lana. Lana was used to this adoration. But Franklin swore he would never be able to take the staring. Damn the damn people. Isn't one look enough, must they ogle her incessantly?

They left the little coffee shop, took the elevator to the ninth floor and stopped at suite number 729. Franklin took out the plastic key, inserted it in the lock then opened the door. He bowed, swept his right hand forward like a gentleman and ushered his beautiful mistress into the room. Lana entered ladylike. The suite was charming. Lana, not an effusive ooer and aawer over niceties, did in this instance ooo and aaw over the niceties that made this unit so charming. The suite was exquisite. Models of various famous Greek philosophers, and paintings of exciting Greek Mythology were placed tastefully throughout the rooms. A plentiful library of books covered one wall in a comfortable den. The suite's bedroom was consummate. Lana and Franklin were delighted.

That night they made love seven times. Gentle and loving to begin. Franklin caressed and kissed Lana's body everywhere. He was so thoughtful of Lana's feelings even when they became somewhat acrobatic in their embraces. As the night wore on Lana detected an ever so slight change in Franklin's demeanor. He seemed to get a little rougher on each occasion he was romantic with her. The last climatic rapture that night was more than just adventurous, it was alarming. Franklin seemed bent on hurting her. She knew she would have some bruises on her inner thighs and on her posterior. Even on her flat belly. Finally Lana asked Franklin why he insisted on hurting her, why he was so gentle on his first few explorations of her body then almost abusive as they got into some serious love-making.

Franklin's stock answer was, "I just can't help it. You excite me so. I love you and hate you because of your singularity among humans. I get totally pissed off the way everyone, even women and kids for chrissake, seduce you in their minds. I get infuriated and dreadfully jealous of you Lana. When I hear you squawk and yelp when I'm sexing you I feel I have some control over you. That's important to me. Otherwise I don't feel like a man when I'm with you, because shit Lana, you're always in control. Don't you think I deserve some measure of control over you? And, what if we married, in no time I would mean diddly-squat to you. I know I would lose you married or otherwise. No one will ever be able to control you. What more can I say?"

"Hmm," Lana responded, "so you like to hear me squawk and yelp and you want to control me?"

"No not really. Yeah maybe squawk and yelp. That's kinda fun. Fact is Lana, your yelp is sexy. Makes me hoorneey. As to control, I do not have a natural inclination to control people, just you. You because, I know it's impossible to do so. I'm sure you of all people understand what I am saying. Dammit Lana, anyone who dominates you doesn't do so for long. You gain control over them by sheer ascendancy. So, by and large, to me it's a huge challenge for me to have even the remotest control over you. Even if it's just for a few moments babe, and even if its only when we make love. Yeah Lana, I love it when I'm in control."

"So it's a game you play is it Franky Boy?"

"I guess so."

That ended the conversation. They slept until 10:00 a.m. the next morning. Lana arose and as she stood nude, Franklin reached out from the bed and took her by her perfect buttocks. He pulled her to the bed, eased her legs apart then with his tongue and his lips tenderly he administered her with cunnilingus. Lana moaned. She finished in a torrent of delight. Lana offered him reciprocity. Quid pro quo.

"No," Franklin said. "I want this to be very special for you. I want it to be lasting in your memory forever. I love you Lana and I always will."

Lana thanked him and kissed him.

They enjoyed the remainder of the day sightseeing the splendors of the magnificent city.

They would not meet again for three years.

CHAPTER 18

THE SINGLES BAR: LOS ANGELES

Franklin rise through the ranks of the State Department was swift. While many politicals disagreed with his wholesome outlook for the poor they recognized his winning personality and skills. Franklin often led the way in peaceful negotiations between warring and near warring nations. His skillful ways in diplomacy had changed several countries from the stock phase, *Yankees Go Home* to *Welcome Yanks.* Soon, some diplomats thought, Franklin will understand the truth in what one good old GOP President said, "You can't make the poor richer by making the rich poorer." They were right. Franklin did change as his career flourished, particularly when he was 'loaned out' to the War Department, the F.B.I. or the C.I.A.

*   *   *

Lana Masters continued with her education in the United Kingdom at Cambridge University. There she both lectured and took classes. Her travels were extensive between university years. Russia, France, Germany, China, Malaysia, Australia, New Zealand, Chile, Argentina, Brazil, Columbia, Peru, Nicaragua, Kenya, Zaire, the USA and Canada. Her travels were three-dimensional experiments to her, fun, education and teaching. She conquered all three.

She was now 23-years old. Her net worth was something in excess of 51-million dollars. Her annual net income from all sources was over 6-million dollars. But Lana was lonely. It was her fault. She could make friends with anyone and she knew that. As a matter of fact everyone who met Lana even on the briefest of occasions wished they could befriend her. Her magnetic pull was enormous. Yet Lana kept most people at bay. She wanted no part of emotional tie-ups. She wanted complete freedom. When she wanted a companion she could have one at a moments notice. If she bar-hopped she bar-hopped alone. When she did bar-hop it wasn't for the purpose of a pick-up. It was done just to be among people who were not stuffy intellectuals. She would even sip some fine white wine as she observed members of the opposite sex consume time on mating. Men, chests swelling, macho machinations, looking cool, and big (like fucking peacocks fanning their tails), shirts open and trousers bulging. Yeah he-men pretending they don't give a damn about the winsome highly made-up T and A women, who, on their part, tended to ignore the line up of studs. Everyone's cool, everyone's aloof, everyone's horny. After a few drinks the cool guys and gals begin the sniffing out process. Soon the cool aloofness begins to disappear. The boys and girls start to get at it. First they join tables. Yeah. Then the females put on their coy, covetous, come hither look while the poor dumb egotistical males begin their tiresome bragging. Soon they are buying each other drinks. Finally they have come to their senses, no more wasting of precious time cat and mousing. Yeah, they get at it.

They begin to dance as if all of a sudden they became mentally and physically unhinged. They fling their poor bodies around like wild cannibals. Like cannibals going ballistic while boiling a missionary in a huge iron pot. They wiggle, leap, roll their arms, kick their legs, shake their shoulders, rock their asses, flip flop their breasts, make complete asses out of themselves while standing a couple of feet apart from one another vibrating their brains out. "Yeah," Lana mused as she watched, cool. Soon a slow piece of rock is played. The beat calls for the sweaty, heaving chests to come together. The girls slide their arms over their partners' shoulders and push their breasts against the boys' chests. They push their rounded thighs between the boys' legs. The hard-ons are in ecstasy. The boys get firm grips on each cheek of the girls' cheeky asses. The boys are in heaven, the girls are wondering if or how or whether they can say no.

Lana takes it all in as she chats to the bartenders. During her bar-hopping Lana is propositioned by most males, and often by females. The men, even if drunk, never become abusive when she refuses their naughty propositions. Lana knows why she can refute a casual suitor. It's her compelling eyes, and her powerful charisma. She knows these two attributes overpower men. However one night in a star-studded club in Los Angeles Lana came close to a disaster. A medium-sized young man, cool, handsome, dripping in riches came on her real hard. He was not taking "no" for an answer. First he offered her $10,000 for a weekend in Malibu. Lana decided she would taunt the guy for awhile.

"Ten grand, Malibu, don't waste my time little boy blue." Lana turned back to the bartender. The next thing she knew she lay sprawled on the floor, thanks to a couple of tough looking Afro-Americans. No one interfered on her behalf. Lana glared at the two blacks then stood. "Fuck-off you black bastards." She continued to glare at them with eyes that tore into their very marrow. They made no move toward her or away from her.

"Haul her out to my car, damn you Carl and Cleaver," the rich guy ordered. Lana stared at the Afros. They stood still. "Sorry Jay, she's too nice a lady. We're sorry Ma'am," said the man named Carl.

"Thank you Carl."

Jay slapped Lana with his open palm. Lana didn't so much as wince. He slapped her again. Lana glared at Jay. The "fucker" was so doped up on some kind of shit her glaring eyes made no impact on him. She had to try another tack. She kneed him.

Lana turned to the bartender and the patrons around her, and with her voice full of scorn said, "Thank you for your heroic intervention you bunch of lilly fucking pads. Good-night Carl, Cleavor, and Jay." She gave them all a rude finger as she made her way to the club's exit.

Jay's last name unbeknownst to Lana was Foster.

CHAPTER 19

LANA LECTURES 90,00 PEOPLE IN BATON ROUGE.

Clark St. James at home in L.A. watches on TV.

It was now 5:50 a.m., May 24th, 1997. Her guest continued to sleep. Lana began to think he was in a coma and may be comatose and die that way. She scrambled down from her nest, went to him and checked his vital signs. Heartbeat was good. Pressure 140 over 90. No respiratory congestion, bleeding, but not profusely. Trauma…must be high. Give him two more hours. If he doesn't waken by then, jar him awake. "Damn you, why don't you make me feel at least some remorse for you? I can't be thinking straight to be doing this. Just because you got the best of me a few times shouldn't entitle me to do this to you."

Lana, now sleepy, worn out, hungry yet nauseous, wormed her way back to the top of the bales. She could see through the skylights in the barn roof that the sun was toiling its way up past the horizon. She lay on her stomach, elbows dug in, chin in her hands and watched her guest and the rope-tailed, now pot-bellied rats as they snuffed, squeaked and rummaged around on her guest's lower belly looking for an escape route.

* * *

November 2nd, 1990, the applause was deafening. The huge crowd of 90,000 people chanted, sang and roared, "Dr. Lana, Dr. Lana, you are the one." Placards, signs, everything imaginable including "Dr. Lana, our Joan of Arc."

Lana had just finished speaking to this big gathering in a huge amphitheater a few miles outside Baton Rouge Louisiana. Lana had held nothing back. She patronized no one. No one, rich or poor, skin color, ethnic background, religious or non-religious, political conviction, Asian, European, Jew, Arab, Yankee, Canuck, Aristocrat or Scum. She faulted all of them for their combined cohesiveness in their struggle to keep over one-half of the world's population in poverty.

"Why…" she asked, "…why do the inane poor combine with the rich in their efforts to maintain inequities in the sharing of wealth? The poor have been doing this for centuries. The rich don't even have to coalesce to get the poor to suck along. Dumb. 'Blessed are the meek for they shall inherit the earth.' You better get at it you meek bunch of S.O.B's, before the rich despoil the whole fucking planet."

She lambasted the rich for their incessant greed, the poor for lacking the guts to unite for a better share of the globe's pie and their intolerable laziness, colored people for their constant bellyaching, the religious for their pussyfooting weak-kneed chameleonism and the non-religious for being non-entities. She hammered politicals for their lack of leadership, their lack of honesty, integrity and business acumen, and those politicals who look more to their re-election than to overcoming the plights of their constituents.

Dr. Lana Masters took everyone to task. But, she was fair. She congratulated and gave full credit to those people she deemed deserving. She was a compelling orator. She knew she would have a diverse audience. An audience made up of males and females, old and young and of various ethnic backgrounds. She knew as well she could, if she chose to do so, entice a riot whilst espousing her views. She avoided such nonsense by bringing her entire audience to her side at the outset of her address much like Mark Antony did when he addressed his audience regarding Julius Caesar's murder by Brutus. 'Friends, Romans, Countrymen, lend me your ears,' etc.

Lana Masters concluded her punishing oration on four notes. Four priorities she insisted the globe's populace must follow in order to put a stop to the ominous tumor which has been creeping insidiously through the guts of society for the past 40,000 years. First the family. Its coherence, love, care and devotion always must be the populaces' most important single consideration. Second, the care and flourishment of the globe's environment. Third, the care and respect of one's own country and its citizenry and all other countries of the world and their citizenries. Fourth, the fulfillment of sensible productivity of private and public businesses, the erasure of scurrilous business practices and the adherence to the economic practice of the laws of demand and supply.

At the conclusion of her address Lana did not need a bodyguard or security as she made her way into her crowd of "worshippers." Everyone there was her bodyguard. No one in the huge crowd would dare harm her. Lana was free to roam among her attendees without fear. She loved her fellow citizens as they loved her. She chatted,joked,answered questions, all the while showing her sincerity through her awe-inspiring eyes. She stayed among them for two hours before she was whisked off in her little Ford Escort. The media had had a heyday with her. She was open to all the marauding media's guys' and gals' inquires, even answering and laughing off some of their offensive sexist questions.

* * *

Sipping a glass of *Fonseca* vintage *Porto* and watching the six o'clock national news, Clark St. James was taken by this eye-popping intellectual. He had seen her before on TV and had seen her picture and read a number of articles about her in newspapers, *Forbes, Fortune Magazine, Time, Newsweek, The Rolling Stones, People* and even in some of the gossip rags.

'She is one fine crusader,' Clark thought. 'It would be great to meet her someday.'

CHAPTER 20

METAPHYSICAL MENTION OF THE TWELVE COSMIC CONTROLLERS

Lana lectured at educational institutions, acted as guest speaker at different conventions, spoke at various functions and orated at massive gatherings on topics ranging from the practice of good citizenship to the intimacies of the ever burgeoning cosmos.

Her unusual frankness, her doctrines and unswerving mind-set were unequivocally accepted by many, but were provoking, invidious and exasperating to a good many others. Lana's continued foray into the morass of world population seemed to set the stages of near dementia for many family-loving couples. How dare this young upstart suggest population control? Lana didn't waver. She had professed from the time she was 13 years old that a well managed world could support adequarely only eight billion people. "Our global garden could not feed 'properly' populations in excess of eight billion," she had said. "At the world's present rate of people growth, by the year 2027, the eight billion number will be reached. And based on past and current inequities, proportionately the numbers making up the poor will grow much faster than will all other classes of people. There could be as many as five billion hungry, homeless, destitute people by the year 2027.

On one occasion when Dr. Masters at age 16 was traumatizing her audience pertaining to the treacherous global increase in people her voice blurted out the words, "The 12 cosmic Controllers have so informed me of this outlandish overpopulation tragedy."

Lana had no idea where these words came from. When questioned about the words she had used and who the 12 Controllers were she, for the first time in her life, had no answer.

This troubled Lana. "Twelve cosmic Controllers"? Lana searched her great mind for an answer but to no avail.

CHAPTER 21

THE ST. JAME'S FAMILY. HISTORIC, 1907

Clark St. James, for seven years, was a partner in his father's firm, "St. James, Rogers, Struthers and company CPA'S." The firm, is a large statewide California partnership, with offices in Redding, San Francisco, Sacramento, Monterey, San Luis Obispo, Santa Barbara, Los Angeles, Anaheim, Rancho Mirage and San Diego. It was started by Clark's great grandfather in 1909 as a single proprietorship. In 1997 the number of partners totaled 352. The company, for its fiscal year ended October 31st, 1996, grossed in excess of $600 hundred million. Christian Farley St. James, Clark's father, the senior partner of the firm is its managing director.

Clark received his designation as a Certified Public Accountant when he was 22 years old. Because he was such a positive contributor to the firm at age 23 he was made a partner. He had found learning to be a bit wearisome because it came so easy to him. He was always the top student throughout his public school years. He was number one in his University years at Berkeley, wherein he received his Master's Degree in Business Administration, and was number one throughout his student apprenticeship years in obtaining his degree as a Certified Public Accountant.

While quiet and unassuming (cool, as his peers thought of him), Clark possesses not only a brilliant mind but he exudes a special warmth to all those he meets. He is charming, dignified, has a magnetic personality, and by the by is ruggedly handsome. He has a deep moral feeling of right and wrong. His conscience tells him he should be expending his considerable energies on behalf of the poor not on the rich.

He has struggled with his conscience about these persuasive and persistent feelings since he was a child of six or seven. When traveling with his father through the hellish slums of Los Angeles, destitute desert towns and many a ghetto, Clark wondered why more efforts were not made to help those poor souls who needed help rather than the mighty efforts put forth in making the rich richer. A real conundrum for a child!

Now as an adult, Clark understood why grown-ups when given the opportunity (through initiative, hard work, brains, personality, nervous breakdowns and mademoiselle luck) put their "best foot forward." It's because they worship money. The poor are not a source of funds, why chase them? Go with gusto after those who can afford to spend. Think of every circuitous route that will lead to that pot of gold at the end of the rainbow. Money equates not only to purchasing power but also to power-power, social prestige and class status.

As far as Clark was concerned the distribution of wealth between the grand super-rich, and the most wretched, stinking, unemployed human was abysmal. He felt the Lord Jesus Christ himself would find this bold discrepancy to be other than inconsequential. 'Jesus,' Clark thought, 'will be watching this pathetic charade and may well reverse the roles on the next few steps leading to Utopia. Every Christmas we see old Scrooge getting his whatfors.'

Clark like his great-grandfather, his grandfather and his father, believed in the democratic way of life, in a laissez-faire economy, hard work and positive productivity. He believed also in fairness. But does fairness necessarily mean compuction for the low end of humanity? Often he questioned himself about his pity for the poor. Are the downtrodden just a way of Life? Regardless of political reform, will the poor always exist? Is it God's wishes that their must always be a an abundance of low life? Thus is it an exercise in futility for anyone to try to raise the standards of livings of these poor plebs?

To search for an answer to these confounding questions, Clark St. James soon would make a gut-wrenching decision. He would disappear into the world of the poor. He would tell a select few of his intent to give up the "good life" and he would receive therefrom each one's covenant to keep his intent their secret.

* * *

Clark's great-grandfather, Simon Christian St. James began his accounting and audit firm in the city of Los Angeles in 1909. At that time it was a sole proprietorship called simply "St. James, Certified Public Accountant." Simon St.James, had completed his apprenticeship in 1907, the year he married Maria Nancy Sanchez. Maria and Simon were childhood sweethearts and a handsome couple they were. She was beautiful, waist long dark glossy hair which surrounded her angelic face, mystic dark smoldering eyes under endless eyelashes, full lips, tilted nose, and an athletically cared for curvaceous body. Simon was just a big raw-boned, good-looking guy. They were a couple whose marriage was, without doubt, made in heaven. They worked infinite hours together (Maria as a secretary, treasurer, bookkeeper and confidant) not only to ameliorate the exemplary services they provided their clientele, but to enhance their business in accordance with their entrepreneurial goals. They were successful.

Maria and Simon had three children who, on their own volition, joined their father's practice after having received their Certified Public Accountancy designation elsewhere. As fate would have it the girls wed Certified Public Accountants whose last names were Rogers and Struthers. By the year 1935 "St. James, Certified Public Accountant" had a practice comprised of some 60 C.P.A.'s of which 35 were full-fledged partners. Offices by 1935 had opened in several communities throughout California. Maria and Simon concluded that it was now time for a name change. It was clear that their two girls, Maria born in 1909, and Nancy born in 1913 and their son Rodney born in 1912 (who, incidentally, married a nurse) together with their sons-in-law Harold Rogers and James Struthers were established inalterability in the firm. Hence, in 1935, a formal partnership agreement was entered into and it was agreed to by all parties that the firm name be changed to "St. James, Rogers, Struthers and Company, C.P.A.'s.

As a result of the years of careful and thoughtful management given by Maria and Simon St. James to the affairs of their beloved accounting practice, the practice flourished in both economic good times and economic bad times. The proprietorships cash resources built up over the years were plentiful, its accounts receivable were always current, and its accounts payable were never overdue. In addition they maintained a large reserve balance in the proprietorship's capital account. The drawings the St. James' took from their practice while a proprietorship seldom exceeded 70 percent of its net cash earnings. It was these well-crafted policies that Maria and Simon passed on to their children.

* * *

The First World War began a scant five years after the St. James' had become operative as an accounting firm. Both Maria and Simon were unsure of the history that led up to the assassination of Archduke Francis Ferdinand of Austria-Hungary on June 28th, 1914, but like most people, they believed his assassination caused the outbreak of World War I.

They knew Archduke Ferdinand was assassinated by a Serb nationalist in the city of Sarajevo. Sarajevo in 1914 was the capital of the Austro-Hungarian province of Bosnia. Austria-Hungary in 1908 by annexation took over Bosnia and Hercegovina. At the same time a Pan-

Serbian movement in Serbia had as one of its objectives the annexation of the southern part of Bosnia. However Serbia needed the back-up of Russia to fulfill this objective, but the Russians simply said *nyet*. Thus the Serbs and the Austro-Hungarians were at violent odds with one another. Then when Gavrilo Princip, the Serb nationalist, assassinated Archduke Ferdinand on June 28, 1914, Austria declared war against Serbia.

The St. James' being staunch supporters of democratic principles believed the Triple Entente to be the savior of democratically run countries. The Triple Entente, which was made up of Great Britain, France and Russia, was designed in the late 19th and early 20th centuries to counterbalance the military coalition of Germany, Austria-Hungary and Italy known as the Triple Alliance. Clearly, the need for the Triple Entente became obvious. On August 1st, 1914, Germany declared war on France and on August 4th, 1914, Great Britain declared war on Germany. On May 23rd, 1915, Italy broke away from the Triple Alliance, and declared war against Austria-Hungary, Japan declared war on Germany on August 23rd, 1914, and on April 6th, 1917, the United States of America declared war on Germany.

From the beginning of the war, Simon, then 31-years of age, had an impassioned desire to wage his own war against Germany. He tried to enlist in the armed services of Great Britain so that he could become active as a fighting man against the ambitious *Huns*. His age was against him and he was turned down. When the United States entered the war in 1917, Simon tried to enlist in the U.S. Navy, but again his age was against him and once again he was turned down.

Simon was devastated because he was unable to become an active participant in the war, doing what he considered to be the most obsequious role he could play in order to help save the world from tyranny. He then did what he thought would be second best to "soldiering," to wit early in 1915, jointly he and Maria sent $25,000 to the British government as a punctilious contribution to Britain's war effort. They repeated this gesture by way of a $30,000 contribution in 1917 to their own country when it declared war against Germany. Whilst the funds he and Maria had sent to the governments of Britain and the United States mollified Simon's anguish to some extent he still felt he had not done his share in the defeat of the Alliance. As a result, it took some years to reconcile his thoughts that the $55,000 contributed by his tiny C.P.A. practice was, under the circumstances, the very best he could have done in assisting in the overall war effort. During the years of self-recrimination, Simon strove even harder to build his practice. He wanted to be able, through his selfless energy and endless hours of work, to provide employment for as many men and women as possible who had fought for democracy and freedom.

* * *

Maria and Simon had agreed that any investment they made would be made only after unanimity was reached between the two of them as to the propriety of the investment. These investments included their own personal dwelling, other real estate holdings, high-grade debt instruments, blue chip equities, as well as a few investments which could be deemed to be more speculative in nature. The St. James' were thoughtful investors. They kept themselves current and knowledgeable regarding the stock market. They would spend an hour or more most evenings, perusing newspaper reports on the market and on business affairs, pouring over subscriptions they received from various stock brokers and economists and any other relevant periodicals that would be helpful to them. From their personal experience and their perspicacious studies they knew that from time to time the stock market would be due for a significant 'correction'…'a big sell-off"…'a bargain sale.' Because of their cash and other liquid holdings, they were always in a financial position to take advantage and buy when these sell-offs occurred.

In the judgment of Simon and Maria, real estate (properties) provided a better hedge against inflation than corporate equities. They recognized, too, that real estate was "wont" to be quite illiquid.

However land values, they pondered, would become more and more in demand as California grew as a destination point. Many people, they thought, from outside the United States as well as influxes of thousands of other Americans would migrate to the attractive sun-drenched state.

As a result of their care, study, timing and jolly well good luck, by 1935, in spite of the stock market crash of 1929, and the worldwide recession of the 30's, their portfolio of stocks had a market value in excess of $3 million. Their bond portfolio's value was some $2 million, and their real estate holdings had a market value of $600,000. Maria and Simon's net worth which included their home, automobiles and other household items totaled $6 million.

The overall average annual return on all their investments in 1935 was two-and-one-third percent. This provided an investment income of $129,000 for the year. Maria and Simon's share of the profits of their partnership for 1935 was $68,000. They had come a long way since 1909. In 1909 their total liabilities exceeded their total assets by $500 and their annual income amounted to a scant $1,300.

Maria and Simon were grand people. The people of the community idolized them. The St. James' were recognized as community leaders, leaders because of their devoted efforts to community affairs. They held no biases, they had no racial, religious or other ugly tendencies. Everyone who came in contact with them considered them to be a remarkable couple. They were loved, cherished, respected and admired by their friends, associates and clients. Maria and Simon had a flawless life together with but one exception. The exception being a man by the name of Phillip Rupert Foster.

CHAPTER 22

SANTA MONICA HIGH SCHOOL, 1907

Phillip Foster and Silken Hendrick's tryst

Santa Monica High was a grand, eloquent, co-educational school, pupiled by children from well-to-do families. The school boasted of an above average 'faculty' of 'Schoolmasters,' an intricate schedule of classes, a well-balanced curriculum, superb drama classes, dancing classes, debating classes and an enviable physical education department.

Each of the school's educators were chosen not only for their eminent qualifications, but for their ability to pervade the school with an air and a chemistry of charismatic inspiration. This air, or chemistry had to be able to complement the canonization of the school itself which was designed and built with the magic of affluence and genteelism in mind.

Phillip Rupert Foster was the Head Master of the Physical Education Department. Phillip, born in 1884, boasted of Masters Degrees in both Physical Education and Mathematics from the University of California, Los Angeles. He was a handsome sort standing just over six feet tail with reddish blond hair and weighing 210 muscular, well-proportioned pounds. His smile was infectious, his personality absorbing and his attitude friendly but with a slight touch of aloofness. He was adored by his pupils and was a favorite among his peers. Phillip was married to Elizabeth Ashley, a beautiful debutante who made her debut into society in 1905 at the age of 19. Phillip and Elizabeth had two wonderful boys, Charles Jr. and Lawrence.

Phillip took pride in himself because of the masterful performances and the record-breaking accomplishments achieved by his students over the years. Each of his teaching assistants so admired Phillip's instructing skills and his ability to teach so (and always with the students respect, hero-worship and obedience) that they were disposed to clone his every move in their assiduous drive to meet his standards.

Save one unknown standard, one that was hidden from the world around him, one that was calamitous. Phillip had a grave weakness when it came to sex and alluring females. He was a womanizer. Not only did Phillip fantasize about "Glamour Girls" as he secretly thought of them, but indeed, he had his share of direct encounters with the ladies, including an arduous, steamy affair with one of the school's coeds. However, always, he considered Maria St. James to be the most fascinating, appealing woman he had ever seen. He damn well wanted her.

Phillip had first met the St. James' at a Church Social. The social was held in the school's auditorium, and its purpose was to help raise funds for the church's purchase of a new organ. It gathered in over 600 enthusiastic members of the local congregation. Everyone had fun. The evening 'take' from the social was $3,259.39, well over everyone's guess. And to make the evening even more fun, the person who guessed the closest to the evening's 'take' won $25 as a prize. Maria was the closest, and of all people, Phillip, the evening's master of ceremonies, was obliged to make the presentation to Maria. It was the first time Phillip had come face to face with Maria. He had seen her at a distance from time to time around the neighborhood and often at church but never close-up like this. He had fantasized about her daily. Within his own psyche, as he made the presentation to Maria, he was drinking in her Mexican sensuousness, her hair, her eyes, her mouth. God how he longed for this miraculous woman. Maria, on her part, presented the

$25 right back to Phillip, such moneys, she hoped would be used to purchase much needed Sunday school supplies.

Attending the church social was a debilitated rather ugly little scruff named, Carl Mousey, known to everyone as 'Mousey.' Without exception, everyone at the social was delighted to see him there. He had $3.65 to spend that evening. Quite properly he left $55 at home (hidden so that even Pinkerton's men couldn't have found them, which was his entire life's savings). Mousey had turned 23 years of age the day before the social. However he had forgotten to tell anyone about his birthday and for the life of him he couldn't remember why he hadn't at least told Maria and Simon. Before joining in on the social's fun and games he wended his little body through the crowd, through to the Church's Minister, Reverend James Colfield. In secret Mousey handed Reverend Colfield the $3.65 as his contribution towards the purchase of the new organ. A lump came in Reverend Colfield's throat. He knew Mousey had no possessions, he knew Mousey could not seek employment because of his handicaps and he knew Mousey would not, no sir, not by a long shot, accept charity. The Reverend knew that when feeling well, Mousey would sweep sidewalks in front of the storekeepers' shops in the neighborhood. He would take out their garbage, he would water their potted plants, he would do anything within his capabilities for his neighborhood friends and, as he referred to them, his business associates. It wasn't until he finished these chores for his "associates" would he accept their stipends.

Mousey knew he would not be able to fathom out the games of chance being played at the social and certainly his pride would not allow him to be embarrassed for being so dumb. This was why he had made his contribution directly to Reverend Colfield. Just one week later Mr. Carl T. Mousey's name appeared on the Church's bulletin board, as one of the many people who donated cash towards the purchase of the new organ.

After being thanked by Reverend Colfield, Mousey made his way to the bingo section of the church social. He ducked under one of the tables, walked up to the students of Santa Monica High who were running the bingo game, made himself available to the 'Teeners' who, with shouts of glee on seeing him, put him to work distributing bingo cards. This was living, Mousey thought—what fun to be among friends.

At the close of the night's festivities Mousey, escorted by many of his teenage friends, made his way home. His home was a small two-room abode of some 210 square feet located behind the storage room of Maria and Simons C.P.A. offices. The abode consisted of a small bedroom, which held Mousey's cot, a tiny chest of drawers, a night table, a small rocking chair, and was lighted by a 60-watt bulb hanging from the ceiling. The other room, a tiny kitchen, had a small table with two matching old chairs Mousey had found at the garbage dump. He had cleaned, sanded and painted them, and now they looked just like new. There was a small cupboard to hold his few dishes and cutlery as well as a tiny sink that had two taps, one for cold water and one for warm water. On top of the cupboard Mousey had a hot plate he had found at the garbage dump as well. He had cleaned and repaired it and had it working like a 'charm.' His 'refrigerator' was an oval good-sized old turkey-cooking pan.

As part of Mousey's bargaining processes he consummated what he thought to be a wonderful deal with Mr. Hymie Lipschit,(who always attended church socials, and, who donated $20 toward the purchase of the organ that very night), who ran the finest deli in Los Angeles. As for his part of the deal, (for the chores Mousey did for Mr. Lipschit), Mr. Lipschit daily gave Mousey all the unusable ice left over in his deli. Mr. Lipschit insisted that nightly Mousey take home some 'leftovers' from the deli, which Mr. Lipschit said would go bad if Mousey didn't take them, which of course was not true. It seemed so peculiar to Mousey that the amount of the each night's leftovers always made up one fine evening's meal. For years now Mousey was quite adrift in trying to 'figure out' why each night something different in the deli could go bad. One night chicken, another night thick tasty soup, another night turkey, another night kosher meatballs etc., etc., etc. Poor Mr. Lipschit, Mousey thought, it's too bad he Mousey could not find a way to help this fine man stop the food from going bad. Oh well, he conceptualized, every day I am well, I will clean the sidewalk in front of Mr. Lipschit's deli with the utmost of care. This should provide some relief for him. He is such a kind man. Now Mousey could put the ice from the deli into the turkey pan and keep his milk and food quite fresh "thank you." And thanks to his friend and associate Hymie Lipschit.

* * *

Phillip Rupert Foster became sex crazed every time he laid eyes on 'that' classic coed, Silken Hendricks. He knew the distorted weakness he had for lovely ladies. Most often he was able to corral his sensual desires. He loved his wife just as he did his two boys. He savored his family's togetherness. His wife and he enjoyed their brisk walks together, their gardening, sharing house routines, their music, their exciting sex, their social life, and above all the rearing of their children.

Elizabeth was so very proud of her husband's abilities. She knew Phillip was the favorite of the school's headmaster, of his peers and of the student body.

Without question the school was elitist and snobbish. Most of the students' parents were wealthy professionals, doctors, lawyers, certified public accountants, engineers, architects and the like. Even wealthy business tycoons, hearing of the schools *chef d' oeuvre* began to take their children out of private schools and, by simple bribery, enroll them in Santa Monica High.

The school facilities for its various departments, classes, offices, cafeterias, were pretentious, grand and glorious, pompous and even ostentatious. Yes and even its johns were fucking outlandish. What the school board couldn't fund for budgeting purposes the wealthy parents could. Each department was not only equipped with every modern convenience of the day but headed by the very best dons, educators and instructors.

Miss Gina Sovanti, was deemed to be the pre-eminent dancing instructor in California. Originally from Genoa, Italy where she was a child protégé in the art of dancing, she was secreted away from Italy to New York City with her parents who feared the barbaric threats of the Triple Alliance. Miss Gina continued her studies and her dancing in New York where she became quite a Prima Donna. But at the age of 30 she left the hubbub of the big city to become the head of the dancing department at Santa Monica High. She was now in her third year at the school and she loved every moment she was there. Gina considered Silken Hendricks to be the very best dancing student she had ever taught. Gina did her utmost to convince Silken to make dancing her career. She was certain that if Silken did continue with her dancing she would become a world famed Prima Donna by the time she was 20 years old.

Silken, a very bright young lady, cherished her dancing, but her mind was made up as to her future. She was going to study medicine and become a doctor just like her father. She adored her dad and admired the unselfish work he performed in helping the sick. Throughout high school Silken excelled in most subjects but her specialties were mathematics, and the sciences. She was a graceful athlete. While she loved tennis, swimming, basketball, track and field, she had her heart set on learning golf of all things. She knew Mr. Foster (yummy Mr. Foster as far as the coeds were concerned) was reputed to be an outstanding golfer, and she knew by the sly glances he made her way during basketball practices that he would be a willing instructor. How exciting, she thought, to be in the rough with Mr. Foster.

Phillip Foster was a hardworking man. He was one of nine children all of whom were born and raised in San Francisco. His father, Steven, a fisherman, was a big muscular friendly soul, who delighted in playing all kinds of sports with his five girls and four boys. His mother too joined in the fun when she wasn't baking, sewing, making meals and washing clothes ad infinitum. The family was a close one. They laughed together, cried together, prayed together and despaired together when one day their beloved father failed to return home to them from one ill-fated fishing trip. Steven and his three-man crew on his 50-foot commercial fishing boat were never found. Steven's wife Teresa, in spite of her terrible loss, carried on with the raising of her children and proud she was of the fact that all nine of them became university graduates. At the time of Teresa's death in 1905 all of her children were married except Phillip. How happy she would have been had Phillip too been married like his brothers and sisters. Oh well, she had thought, Phillip was bright, well schooled, handsome and so popular with the ladies that she knew he would marry soon enough.

Phillip had not only loved his father but also admired the way he kept his physical well-being. Like Steven, Phillip drank very little and then only on special occasions and he would never dream of smoking a cigarette. Phillip kept his mind stimulated by voracious reading, his body well muscled by strenuous exercising and his hornies well oiled by fantasizing about that voluptuary Maria St. James.

Following his graduation (with his Masters Degrees in Physical Education and Mathematics) Phillip applied for the headmaster's position of the Physical Education Department of Santa Monica High. He was selected for the position from among some 80 applicants. He began his first year in August 1906. He was delighted with his department. He found everything therein to his liking. In addition he enjoyed his partisanship with his fellow teachers, his respect for the student body, and he was in awe of the school itself.

Phillip had first noticed Silken Hendricks in an intimate way at a girl's basketball practice that was being held in the school's auditorium. Miss Gloria Stevens, one of Phillip's departmental teachers, was the coach of the girls' team. She had asked Phillip if he would be available to attend the practice that day and make whatever recommendations he judged would be helpful in improving the team's lot. Even though Miss Steven's teams had won all the major women's basketball tournaments against every high school in Southern California over the past five years, many of her players had now graduated from Santa Monica High leaving her now with a large group of neophytes.

Phillip was impressed with Miss Stevens' fledgling group of girls. They were tall, graceful, quick passers, fair shooters, and defensively quite skilled. He was pleased to advise Miss Stevens about his opinion as to the quality of her players and, as Phillip recounted to her, it looked like she had another strong contender for more championships.

One of Miss Stevens' top players, Silken Hendricks, would graduate in June of 1908, and therefore would remain on the team from the start of the basketball season in October of 1907 through to the season's finale in April 1908. Silken was well versed in the game. Silken's heart jumped the day she spotted Mr. Foster sitting on tier one at ground floor level in the center of the auditorium.

Silken knew her luscious body commandeered men's disgusting catcalls and lecherous looks, even though her body was always properly covered from her shoulders to her ankles. Mayhap, Silken knew all too well her ample breasts and her curvy hips stood out in any outfit because of the tight bodices she wore and, too, wasn't she flattered by the attention her anatomy garnered.

Now here was Phillip Foster, a man she would enjoy showing herself to even under the guise of a basketball practice. Didn't all girl basketball players rotate their derrieres during the play of the game and didn't they bend down from the hips from time to time exposing perhaps a part of their bosom. Well Phillip Foster, old man, "I am going to give you a bird's eye view of these girl things as best I can so that you are made aware of the fact that I am after your...mmm...," she said to herself.

And she did.

Phillip, somewhat remorseful, was sexually stimulated by this vixen's basketball antics.

Shit. Now Silken was making her way towards him. "Hello," she said, "My name is Silken Hendricks."

"Hello Silken," he replied. "I know who you are. I have followed the progress you have made through Santa Monica High and I must say your progress is most enviable, and tonight I watched your moves on the floor and I was—well—impressed. You are a picture of grace and agility," he said. Damn, he thought, imagine her moves in bed.

"Mr. Foster, I want to ask a great favor of you but I am hesitant to do so because I…I feel embarrassed…."

"Please Silken, do ask me, I will be straightforward with you, I promise."

She blurted out, "Will you teach me to play golf. I so want to learn the game.

Phillip smiled and said. "Of course I will, why would you be embarrassed asking me that?"

"Because I thought you would consider me a nuisance," she replied.

"Silken, please don't feel that way. I am going out to the golf course tomorrow to practice some of my shots and I would be delighted if you joined me. I will be there at around four o'clock."

"Oh, thank you so much Mr. Foster. I will be there at four with a new set of clubs my daddy gave me for Christmas." She brushed his cheek with her moist full lips, and was gone.

Phillip was at the golf course at four o'clock and standing by the club house in a knee-length skirt, knee-high socks and a full blouse with sleeves down to her wrists was Silken Hendricks. As she rushed over to meet him she tripped over an errant water hose and fell into his arms.

"Hello Mr. Foster," she said, "I just knew I would do something foolish and embarrass myself. I'm so sorry."

"It's all right Miss Hendricks," Phillip replied. "There will be times you will be in my arms as I teach you the proper strokes for the different golf irons and woods."

Oh, I do hope so, she said under her breath.

They looked into each other's eyes, unaware they were still in an embrace. She felt herself getting damp between her legs. God, he is so handsome, so muscular, so 'yummy', she thought. She could swear she felt his wonderful, whatever, hardness, against her lower "tummy". He was so tall.

They parted, each one blushing. They both knew what glory was in store for them. Phillip forgot his practice shots. By the fifth hole they were out of sight of all other golfers.

Phillip teed up her ball, took her driving club, as she called it, out of her bag, had her stand ready to address the ball. He came up behind her, put the club in her hands wrapped his arms around her, pressed his body close to hers, and told her to wiggle her hips in preparation for shifting her weight as she needed to do when ready to hit the ball. Then everything collapsed. Silken wiggled all right, she wiggled without a thought about hitting a golf ball. The horny little neophyte wiggled so hard she could feel Phillip's swollen cock (through his knickers) placed between her gorgeous (skirt and panty-covered) buttocks.

Dropping her driving club she turned around to face him took his hand and led him into the lush forest which surrounded the fifth fairway. Now, the lovemaking would begin but what position, or more to the point how would they seduce one another. Would Silken, as she professed, want to remain a virgin. Phillip stroked her body, ran the tips of his fingers up and down her arms, breasts and shoulders. He played with her hair, touched her lips with the tip of his tongue, whispered in her ear, licked under her arms, toyed with her vagina, mouthed her breasts, talked softly of erotic lovemaking, put his tongue in her mouth as she had climax after climax. He did not enter her with his penis but he did enter the delectable, secret entrances to her body with his tongue and fingers. He kissed her everywhere imaginable. She cried, sobbed and moaned with pleasure, she even kissed the end of his cock, then took it in her mouth. Together they finished. Together they rested in each other's arms.

In a few minutes they were getting prepared for round "two". Phillip knew he must suggest to Silken that she remain a virgin. He told her when she got married her fiance¢ would expect her to have been virtuous and thus, a virgin. He went on to explain that if he, Phillip, entered her the "fashionable way" he would surely end her virginity thereby causing her untold distress in the future.

Silken smiled a devilish smile and startled Phillip by saying, "You, Mr. Foster, are my future." With that, more frenzied lovemaking took place, Silken was not disappointed. She left for home by 7 o'clock, exhausted and deliriously happy.

Phillip went home limp, frightened and ashamed.

They carried on their blistering romance until Silken graduated. Then the romance stopped. They parted as friends but no longer lovers. On August 10, 1908 Silken departed to New York City for entrance into the School of Medicine at NYU.

CHAPTER 23

MARIA ST. JAMES, PHILLIP FOSTER AND MOUSEY: 1908

Phillip Foster's desire for Maria St. James was frantic. His direct encounters with other women occurred only (with the odd exception while attending teachers' conventions outside the greater Los Angeles area) prior to his marriage to Elizabeth Cuthbertson. With these few exceptions when away from home and, of course, only with those adventurous lady teachers who consented to his amorous advances Phillip stayed chaste. His sizzling episodes with Silken Hendricks were not considered to be unfaithful acts of fornication by him. He reasoned that he did not provoke any exigency that would cause her to lose her virginity. "Not good old Phil," he thought to himself, "I was just performing my extra curricular duties as a conscientious teacher tutoring Silken, to the best of my abilities, in the art of striking a golf ball and in the upgrading of her sexual qualifications."

After Silken's departure to New York, for several weeks Phillip remained faithful to his beautiful 'debutante' wife Elizabeth except, that is, for his numerous forays into fantasyland with Mrs. Maria St. James.

"But, damn it all, it's no fault of mine that, that voluptuary Maria, whom I feel was designed for the sole purpose of being the recipient of men's phalluses, seems always to be in my vision, which utterly and inalterably demolishes my sexual well being. I must put a stop to this before I become mad with desire for her. I know she works alone on Saturdays. Surely I can pop in on her and one way or another put a stop to this incessant craving I have for her. Tomorrow's Saturday, so Miss Mexican Beauty I will be at your office around two in the afternoon. I will unlock your office doors with my trusty 'all purpose key' and desensitize this whole misunderstanding betwixt you and me. Yes, Maria my dear, and excuse my French but, we'll fucking well have it 'out' by mid-afternoon Saturday October 26th, 1914, as I say one way or another."

* * *

Maria Nancy Sanchez was born into a very poor Mexican family in Tijuana, Mexico on July 4, 1886. She was one of eight children. Her memories of her childhood in some instances were clear while in others they were clouded. By the time she was ten, her brothers and sisters had all either left home or died. Maria's mother was of Indian descent whilst her father was a Mestizo. Maria dearly loved and admired her mother, but deplored her father for his drunkenness, his abusiveness, his frequent attempts at beating her mother and her brothers and sisters. She remembered with horror the fearful beatings her runt of a brother Jose' received from her father. Punishments that resulted in the loss of all Jose's fingertips, a disfigured spine, multiple obscene scars, loss of both earlobes, improperly healed broken bones and above all the discontinuance of the development of his brain which resulted from numerous concussions inflicted on him by his contemptible father.

Jose' in 1894, at age nine, escaped with his life from his father when his mother was able to smuggle him through the United States border and into the arms of waiting Mexican outlaws. These Mexican outlaws knew the plight of thousands of Mexican children who had suffered similar abuses as Jose'. Mexicans who swore on an oath to the Great Benito Juarez that they, the rough and tumble outlaws, would free these children from their subjugation and hope the youngsters would find a new safer life in America.

The outlaws were outraged when they saw the pathetic ruined little boy known only as Jose'. They cursed as they wrapped the wretched little Mexican lad in a warm blanket and began their secretive journey through the wilderness toward Jose's final destination in the City of Angels. Several days later the bandits left a crying Jose' at a small general store located in San Clemente, California.

The storekeeper, Abraham Wilson, knew what the bundle contained. He picked Jose' up, turned down the store's lanterns, locked up, and made off to the San Clemente Hotel, there to inform Mr. and Mrs. Alphonse T. Mousey that their parcel had arrived from Tijuana. He left Jose' with his new guardians, the Mousey's, and with twenty crisp ten dollar bills (minted in the U.S.A.) tucked away in his trousers pocket he proceeded back to the store to do more of the business he was wont to do. Two hundred good old somolies, green-backs, Yankee bucks. "Good day to you Mrs. Albright, I'm just about to open the store again, you see I had an errand to do, please excuse my delay and do come right in," he chortled in his joy.

Mr. and Mrs. Mousey, quite aside from the law, had proper papers drafted showing them as having full guardianship rights over young Carl T. Mousey. The whole of the plot to bring Jose' to the Mousey's was organized by Jose's mother, his aunt and the Mousey's. The plan's conditions were quite straightforward. Jose's name would be changed to Carl Timothy Mousey. He would do most of the chores required by the Mousey's, household, garden etc. He would chop wood for kindling and larger pieces for the kitchen stove. He would pile the chopped wood on the lee side of a shed. He would carry coal from the coal bin in scuttles to the furnace, fireplaces and kitchen stove. He would get up at five in the morning to start the fires. He would paint the inside and outside of the Mousey's house and shed when needed. He would carry groceries from the store that Mrs. Mousey had bought, and in reality be a nine-year-old slave to his "guardians". In return Jose' would be fed three times each day, and would receive two hours of tutoring each day by Mrs. Mousey. The Mousey's would clothe him and, he would have the right to sleep on his own straw-filled mattress in the very shed that the wood was piled up against. He would however have no days off unless of course he was ill. Jose's mother and aunt would never have agreed to these terms had they known how the Mousey's would violate the agreement by making tiny Jose' their personal slave.

Jose' escaped this entrapment six years later. Neighbors were happy to hear that young "Mousey" had run away. They knew the suffering he had gone through all those years he lived with the dreadful Mousey's. While many of the people in the community had reported to the authorities the abuses young Carl Mousey received at the hands of the Alphonses nothing was ever done to alleviate Carl's plight.

Jose' despised both Mr. and Mrs. Mousey since he met them that fateful day six years ago and he knew they despised him for what he was, a gnome-like sickly "wet back" who could work only 12 to 15 hours a day. They disliked him, too, for his refusal to attend either high mass or low mass in their elegant, richly appointed Roman Catholic Church.

Somehow Jose' (as he referred to himself) and his dull mind could not reconcile the differences between the enormous riches of the catholic church, its palatial palaces called churches, the finery of its bishops, its demand for tithes from the poor and his pathetic state of well being. Had he not heard somewhere that a man called Jesus proclaimed, 'Blessed are the meek for they shall inherit the earth,' and 'lay not up for yourselves treasures upon earth, where moth and rust doth corrupt, and where thieves break through and steal.' And he thought, too, he had heard that this same man had said, 'Blessed are the merciful: for they shall obtain mercy.' Ho! Ho! Well just maybe he, Jose', needed only to bide his time and await his inheritance to come to fruition because wasn't he just a "meek wet back?" It was clear to him that he would never be able to lay up treasures upon himself which will rust or get stolen, so no worry there. As for mercy for himself and all others (in particular his courageous, loving mother, and his wonderful younger sister Maria) who suffer unjustly, won't this good man come and show mercy for all us low life people?

One evening Jose packed up his few miserable belongings, left the shed, and without a word to anyone disappeared into the labyrinth of the unknown. Without being conscious of the subliminal state of his mind he was propelled by some unknown force to search for and find his beloved sister Maria Nancy Sanchez.

* * *

Mousey survived the ongoing years using all sorts of tactics to keep body and soul together. Only once did he succumb to stealing. He became so famished and weak on one occasion he took three oranges off a tree whilst trudging north to Santa Barbara. He had to lean over a fence in order to fetch the fruit and, by heavens, right next to a sign that read, (but undecipheral to him) TRESPASSERS WILL BE PROSECUTED. Mousey bowed his head and prayed to his mother for her forgiveness for this theft and to this wondrous man called Jesus.

In late June of 1903 Jose' saw and recognized his beloved sister Maria. His heart pounded, "Merciful God", he sighed, "She is still an angel." Tears flooded his eyes. How he wanted to run to her, to hug and kiss her, to kneel at her feet. She meant so much to him. She had protected him years ago from those who taunted him and from ruffians who wanted to hurt him. She nursed him after his father beat him. She was kind and thoughtful of everyone. Surely Maria must be a child of God.

She was seated with many young men and women her age, all of whom were dressed in long black gowns. The women wore attractive white caps while the men wore black. Maria rose from her chair when called upon by an older gentleman who was standing at a dais. With her eyes sparkling she ascended a set of stairs leading to a platform, a platform where several elderly ladies and gentlemen were seated and wearing clothes similar to the young people. The gentleman at the dais handed Maria a rolled up scroll of paper, then hung a gold medal around her neck, and with a broad smile on his face shook her hand as she curtsied.

Unbeknownst to Jose', the man at the dais was the headmaster of Santa Monica High. He was distributing diplomas to those students who had graduated from their senior matriculation year, Grade XII, and gold medals to those youngsters who excelled in their schoolwork throughout the year.

Mousey had been criss crossing Los Angeles for the past several days. His childish mind reasoned that his sister, now 17 years old, could have made her way from Tijuana to Los Angeles without too much ado because he knew how she could charm people. He knew people trusted her, and he knew people could not help but like her. He felt confident she would persist in obtaining a formal education, and at the expense of all other eventualities. Jose' was certain the ceremonies taking place before his own eyes must be associated with education.

He attended many of these strange events for a week now, and his psyche had told him if he persisted in pursuing this line of searching indeed he would succeed in locating his sister.

From the day he found her Jose' promised himself he would refer to himself only as Carl T. Mousey, Mousey for short, in order to keep secret that he, this rag-tag misfit was not in any way related to the sister he was so proud of. No longer was he Jose' Sanchez. He wanted Maria to have a clean slate, a slate never to be tarnished by his piteous intrusion. This promise was followed by an even stronger covenant. A covenant that would see him place himself as near as possible to his sister for the remainder of his life in order for him to act as her perpetual guardian angel.

Jose knew that even if he kept the name Carl T. Mousey and even if his slavemaster Alphonse Mousey found him, that Alphonse would stay quiet about his purchase of Jose' Sanchez and would not pursue his rightful guardianship of his peon, Carl T. Mousey. This Jose' was certain of, because Alphonse by now would have a new slave boy and likely of greater stature than Mousey.

* * *

Saturday afternoon, October 26th, 1914, Phillip was in the process of sneaking into the offices of St. James, Certified Public Accountant. Now he was kneeling down in front of Maria's office door peering in on her while she was leaning over a credenza behind her desk with her back to him. He drooled as he saw her dress fall delectably between her buttocks. Phillip was quite safe from her detecting him at her door because only the upper half of the office door was glass, and he was crouched down in such a way it would be difficult for Maria to spot him. He checked again the contents of the bag he had brought with him. A switchblade knife, a bottle of chloroform, a clean rag, a good-sized artificially made penis, several feet of sturdy rope, a leather strap from his school, and handcuffs. "By Jesus, Lady, are we going to have fun," he thought.

Phillip began to open her office door with his passkey. He was ready for the inevitable confrontation. His intent to escape any foolish accusations of rape by Maria was to claim that she, Maria, had begged Phillip to come to her office while she was alone so she could seduce him because of the mad, inflamed passion she had for him. The only thing he had to concern himself with was his bag of goodies. Shit, surely he could hide them after he and Maria finished their sexual acrobatics. Too, he was prepared to testify in any court of law that Maria St. James threatened suicide if he, Philip, did not (much to his revulsion and disgust of course) make degrading love to her. In fact it was his intent to report the afternoon lovemaking right after he had "finished" with Maria to Dr. Wilfred Schnider and to the local Sheriff Sean O'Flarity. With pity in his voice he would inform them of Maria's derangement, and her gross unladylike demands of him for depraved sex. "Poor soul," Phillip would say to them, "poor dear soul, so outwardly strong and yet so inwardly weak. I beg of you gentlemen, be merciful with her and please be understanding, she is, after all, not well."

CHAPTER 24

MARIA, BAT MASTERSON AND HARLEY EARP

Maria stayed close to her mother. She was a street-wise and a well educated 13 year old. She was fluent in Spanish and English. Maria was devastated when her mother passed away suddenly in the spring of 1899. She cried for days. How could she live without her mother? Why couldn't she, Maria, go on the journey to heaven with her mother. She suffered wave after wave of lonely despair and emptiness, she prayed, sobbed, tried to expunge her desperate feelings by burying her head in her pillow. Nothing worked. She swore vengeance on those horrid unearthy beings who took her mother from her. She would never get over her mother's death, she thought. Her father drank himself into oblivion at his wife's funeral and remained that way every day including the day Maria decided to take hold of herself, pack up her few belongings and leave her home of 13 years. She had but 100 pesos to her name. Perhaps these pesos equaled five dollars in American money, she didn't know.

Maria was so proud of her mother for the way her mother could handle her father during his fits of rage and his drunken tirades. While her mother was much smaller than her father yet in all of their married years her wretched father would find himself dumped on his ample Mexican ass by his wife if he tried to abuse her or the children while either drunk or sober. These occasions, whilst dreadful for the children's psyche, nevertheless were excellent remedies for curing their concerns about their personal comfort and safety. It was only when the children were home alone that their father could whip them. Because Jose' was the runt of the litter he was beaten far more often than his sibling brothers and sisters.

Maria, even at the tender are of 13, could take care of herself. Now on leaving her home and without saying a word to her father, she knew she had to prove to herself that she could survive in this lonesome, uncaring world. She knew she was capable of enduring hardships of all sorts, hunger, beatings, street filth, drunken sex crazed men. Hadn't she experienced all of these things in her past. She knew she was made of good stuff, good hardy stuff from the Indian genes passed on to her by her mother (much too, like her hero, the great Mexican Indian leader, Benito Pablo Juarez, a man who was famous for his integrity and his unswerving loyalty to democracy). She knew, too, that she possessed ample quantities of cunning and wiles which she could count on when necessary as she made her way along the circuitous, bumpy road ahead of her. Her destination was the city of angels, Los Angeles, California.

She wanted to get to a school in Los Angeles she had heard about called Santa Monica High. She was determined to be at Santa Monica High for enrollment by mid-August 1899 for the eighth grade, a scant three months from now. She had brought along all of her report cards from the school she attended in Tijuana, a school named after Maximilian the Archduke of Austria's wife, Carlotta. Ugh, Maria thought, that dreadful Maximilian was given the crown of the Mexican Empire in 1864 by, of all people, Napoleon III of France. "In any event," she mused, "my report cards show me to be excellent in all the subjects I have taken. This should hold me in good stead."

Maria had only a few troubles making her way to Los Angeles. The border crossing was easy. She told the Gringo customs official she was on her way to Los Angeles (walking of course) to enroll in a school called Santa Monica High. The Gringo smiled at her and sent her on her way. Cute kid he thought.

She walked north on graveled roads, hiding from time to time when she heard the thunder of horses' hooves and the laughter of men. Her first frightening encounter occurred when she stopped at a strange town called National City. There she had gone to a noisy hotel to find a place to sleep. She went to the clerk who was on duty to find the cost of a room for the night. She was exhausted from her long walk from Tijuana and being used to sleeping in a "so-called bed" she wanted a bed for the night. The night clerk, with a nasty grin on his face said, "For you, you pretty little Latino, no charge, no charge if yo're willin to share a bed with one of those fine young gringo's standin' over thar." He pointed at five half-drunk young men.

"No," she replied angered, "I want a bed of my own, I am so weary, please sir, I have ten pesos I can give you for one night's lodging."

"D'ya hear that boys?" the desk clerk hollered. "This little Mexican beauty, she won't sleep with any of you upstandin' cowpokes, even if I let her off with no charge. Shit boys, wadd'a ya say? Wad about you Luke, yo're good lookin, would you like ta stuff your fuck stick up her furry little cunt?"

"Ya, I shore wood Andy," Luke replied. With that Luke, whiskey bottle in hand, six-gun clinging to his leg, clomped his way over to Maria, grabbed her around her waist picked her up and was about to "cart" her off to a room, when whoa, Luke screamed in pain. He let Maria drop, he doubled over and spewed vomit across a poker table splattering the tables' six players, their drinks, their cards and their chips.

Old Andy farted, belched and farted again. He spotted a long thick needle like thing sticking out from the back of Luke's balls. "Jesus Christ," Andy yelled.

Now a blazing eyed Maria pulled a pistol and a baby rattler out of her travelling bag. Next she extracted a small box from her bag which she warned contained enough of a new secret 'atomic' powder inside it to blow the hotel and its occupants to Kingdom Come if she chose to unleash it. She turned to the desk clerk, "Now, please sir, let me pay you ten pesos for a private sleeping room for me and me only. I suggest that you and those hombres over there stay away from my room or I promise you, your hotel will disappear from the face of this earth." She held the little box just under Andy's nose.

Andy remained motionless. He looked down his nose at the box. "Yes, senorita, please be my guest. I promise you will have a good peaceful night's sleep."

"Thank you," Maria replied. "Here are your ten pesos."

She walked over to Luke, had him lie face down on the floor, then showing great expertise pulled an 18-inch knitting needle out of his testicles. He yelped. She rolled him over onto his back, pulled down his pants and his bloomers, took a bottle from her pocket along with a cloth, poured a few drops of liquid from the bottle onto the cloth then swabbed Luke's wound. A chorus of cheers and laughter erupted from all the other gringo's as one by one they congratulated her for her spunkiness.

Then, a huge gringo spoke up and said, "If any man, any man Jack goes near your room tonight, senorita, I will hawg tie him and brand his behind sos he won't fergit. Yes'm that's my promise to you."

"Good night little lady," the tough hombres said laughing.

"Good night gentlemen," she responded.

Maria slept well that night.

The next morning following her toilet and her five-peso breakfast, Maria stepped out of the hotel ready to proceed to "Santa Monica High." She was astounded to see the large hombre who had made that promise to her last evening, standing at the hotel's hitching post looking toward her with eyes that said, *come to me child, I wish to speak with you.* Maria walked over to him and thanked him for his courageous assurance of the night before.

"T'warnt nuthin' chile, I have a daughter of my own living somwhars hyar in Cal-ee-for-ney, 'bout yer age I reckin, and God strike dead any man jack who touches her. You look like yore travlin' north to go somwars. Ain't I right?"

"Yes" Maria replied, "I'm on my way to Los Angeles to start my eighth grade in a school called Santa Monica High."

"Are you goin' by coach, or how?" the big man asked.

"How sir…well I'll tell you," and pointing down to her feet, laughing she said, "by those."

"Little girl, I don't like that, I fear for yor' safety, sum'un'll hurt you. No, I wont let you go by yerself. Either I take you thar or I take you to the local sheriff, for yor' own good mind, and let him decide. You don't hafta be scairt of me senorita. I'd pretect you from everone, 'cluding me, 'n that's the actual truth so hep me God. When yor' sleepin' I'll be close by alookin' after you an daytime you can ride b'hind me on my good ole pony Cochise, so's yor' safe then too. I swear no'un'll hurt you when I'm about and anytime you don't wannabe be with me a'carin' for you I'll make certain yor' on a coach to go to yor' school. What say you to what I'm sayin' chile?" he questioned.

"I don't know you sir, so I don't know if you would just carry me off somewhere and kill me even with all your promises. I don't even know your name," Maria responded. "How do I know I can trust you? I'm sorry for saying such a thing but what else can I say." Tears trickled down her cheeks. "I have no one left in my family to look after me since my mother died," she sobbed. "My father's a drunk and, and I have no idea where my brothers and sisters are, or even if they're alive. I'm so alone sir, and I don't know who to trust…I'm sorry."

"Please, please don't cry…."

"My name is Maria Nancy Sanchez sir."

"All right Maria Nancy, please hush up yor' crying little one." (Maria Nancy was tall for her age standing five feet two inches, but beside the gringo's six-feet-five-inch frame she did feel like a "little one.") He came nearer to her and patted her head saying, "My name is Harley Earp, neffu of the lawman Wyatt Earp, have you ever heard of him Senorita? He is very famous in these hyar parts, spech'lly Air-eee-zooni-a.

"Yes, I've heard of him.

"Come along then Maria Nancy, w'er going to see the Sheriff." He took her dainty hand in his large callused "paw" and marched her off to the local Sheriff's office.

Sheriff Bat Masterson was seated in a hard-back chair with his feet up on a rather ancient but tidy desk. He had his nose stuck in a month old copy of The Morning Telegraph, the New York City's number one daily newspaper. He was oblivious to the sudden appearance of Maria and Harley Earp.

"Good morning William Barclay Masterson," Harley shouted.

Bat was up in a second, dropping his newspaper and going for his gun, "Jesus Christ Harley, you scared the shit out of me."

"Har de har," Harley laughed.

"Lucky I didn't blow your brains out, asshole." Bat replied.

"Sorry Bat," Harley said slapping his thighs and guffawing even louder. "You and your newspaper. Someday you'll be in New York writing a column in the Telegraph, I swear. Anyway Bat, I'm sorry if I startled you."

"It's okay Harley, but dam it next time go easy. By the by, who's the cute little girl?" Bat asked.

"Excuse me sirs," Maria interrupted, eye's ablaze, "how dare you swear like that in front of me Sheriff Masterson and you, Mr. Harley Earp, what's happened to your funny 'yorns' and 't'warnts' and 'reckin's' and all those other crazy words. Were you just fooling me cause your all grown up?"

Both men looked with askance at this haughty, bossy little Mexican firebrand who stood facing them with her tiny bunched up fists planted on her hips waiting for their answers.

The two men looked at one another, grinned, then laughed. Harley picked Maria up in his arms, hugged her, kissed the top of her head and like a caring father carried her over to Mr. Bat Masterson. First, to introduce him, and second to receive his apology, and third to seat her by Sheriff Masterson so he, Harley Earp, could explain his sudden grammatical departure from good old cowpoke jargon.

Harley told Maria his job as a "sort of policeman" necessitated he pretend to be someone other than who he really was when he was out and about catching a bad person who had broken the law. So he said that on occasion he must talk like he did last night and this morning when among strangers who talk funny, lest they become suspicious of him and won't talk about certain secrets they know and he needs to know. Otherwise he said he talks just as Sheriff Masterson does.

Maria now understood, and a little teary she put her arms out to hug both Messrs. Earp and Masterson. They both seemed so nice and caring quite the contrary to their loud manliness. They liked this spunky kid.

Harley took time to tell Maria, too, that last night when Luke was going toward her that he, Harley, would have taken Luke by the seat of his trousers and thrown him out of the hotel before Luke went too far. Harley grinned as he told Bat about Maria's episode last night at the hotel. The fear of the Lord she had put into everyone there with her pistol, her sidewinder and the confounding box containing a secret death dealing explosive that she had warned everyone about.

"What is in that box Maria?" both men asked simultaneously and with a good degree of apprehension.

Now it was Maria's time to smile and play possum. "Tee Hee," she giggled.

"Come child, this is no laughing matter. As Sheriff of this county you must tell me what is in that box. If you have something that will endanger lives I must confiscate it," he said rubbing his chin, "you know, take it away from you. Now stop giggling."

"No," Maria teased, taking the box from her traveling bag. "I know what confiscate means Sheriff." she said.

"Maria, do as Sheriff Masterson asks, please?" whispered Harley as he backed away from Maria and eyeing the box with uncertainty.

"No Harley," she said walking toward her big, brave hero, who was now moving backward with his arms outstretched as if to protect himself from this unknown weapon.

"Gentlemen if you two big men let me lock you in one of those cells I promise I will tell you what's in the box. I cross my heart and hope to die I will let no harm come to either of you…ever," she chided, crossing her arms across her chest.

Bat and Harley glanced at one another wondering what sort of mischief this little Mexican child was up to. As much as their hearts were taken with her, they didn't know her. Was she going to blow up the jailhouse with them in it? "Christ," Bat murmured to Harley. "Can you see the headlines in the newspapers, BAT MASTERSON ANR HARLEY EARP KILLED BY KILLED BY A 13 YEAR OLD MEXICAN GIRL. Our reputation would be ruined. Son of a bitch."

"I heard that Sheriff, yoouuurr naughty. But I promise you I won't hurt you. Now get in that cell 'afore I gits angry," she threatened, waving the box at the two men and backing them into the cell. Clang, the door shut on them. "That's good boys," she said patronizing them as she tittered once again.

"Now, my brave conquistadors, I'll show you all my toys. First, my Spanish pistol is real but, alas, I have no bullets for it. Second, my baby sidewinder is not a live rattler, it's just a short piece of rope covered in a baby rattler's skin. And third, this box, this devilish box, is filled with a frightening substance." In a quick thrust she poked the box through the bars of the cell causing the two men to leap backwards. Maria laughed, her childish eyes sparkled. She was enchanted with her cunning victory over two of the most feared lawmen in the west.

With great care she removed the top of the box then put it aside. Maria placed the tips of her fingers of her right hand into the box, moved them around in the box's secret holdings, removed her fingers, and with a happy, childlike gleam in her eyes patted her cheeks with the baby powder that made up the contents of the box. Yes, ordinary, everyday baby powder used the world over. Grinning, Maria asked Bat and Harley to inspect the box's powdery contents.

A mite frightened they came to the bars of the cell and peered into the box, then into Maria's face. They put their noses down to the box and sniffed at the powder and detected a light, pleasant perfume like odor.

"Please Maria, what is that stuff?" Harley asked.

"It's…it's…well…promise first you wont get mad?

They nodded. It's just baby powder Mr. Harley Earp sir and Sheriff Masterson, that my mother always bought for me at the general store and always made me use."

"Baby powder," Bat yelled "baby powder, for shit sake, you mean to say you bamboozled Harley and me, and others last night with nothing but baby powder? If I was your father you would get spanked so hard…."

"No, Bat," Harley broke in. "No, our little bambino is one smart kid. She seems to have learned how to take care of herself. And she knows how to frighten people without the use of weapons that kill. But damn it Bat, she can't go on like this, fooling people who may want to harm her. Think on it Bat, someone down the line may not be fooled by her bravado and then what?"

"Yea, I know what you're saying Harley," Bat responded. "Kid, you let us out of this cell NOW, and I mean it."

"Yes Sheriff," and with that Maria set the two humbled men free. Oops Maria thought, will I get a spanking, will they lick me like my father used to do? Was I wrong to frighten them? Soon she was answered. The men came out of the cell smiling. Together the three of them hugged and laughed.

"Now mischievous one, we have to make some plans for you, and get you to Santa Monica High, come hell or high water. So be a good girl and sit you down over there on that bench, take Bat's newspaper and read it from front to back." Harley ordered.

"Yes sir, I will."

Harley and Bat put their heads together and within the hour had come to a solution satisfactory to both of them.

"Come here now Maria," Bat called. "Harley and I have decided to take you to Los Angeles ourselves. We think we can have you there in eight days."

"But you are such busy men," Maria responded.

"Listen, no argument kid, we are taking you there," Bat insisted.

"I hear you sir and I would be so happy if you took me there but I don't want to be a burden on you. I want to be able to support myself." Again tears came to her eyes. "You and Harley, you are so kind and thoughtful. But, if you please, will you let me try to earn my own way. I sing kinda nice. Maybe you would let me sing songs at the hotel tonight and just perhaps someone there might have a guitar I can borrow. Often back home in Tijuana I would play and sing on a street corner with a sombrero in front of me. People would drop pesos in it and that would give me some money to take home to my mother. At the hotel tonight I could put one of your stetsons, I think you call them, in front of me and see if any gringos would drop some American money in it. If they did, then I would have some money to give to you. Pulleese," she begged.

"Sounds like fun to me Bat. What do you say?"

"It's fine by me Harley," Bat replied.

"Okay, that's settled. Now lets get down to the business of getting you to Los Angeles and, in particular, your enrollment in Santa Monica High. Harley and I feel that our personal attendance at the school and our brand of persuasiveness with the school's top-level authorities will ensure your enrollment. That's one thing. Now Maria, can you ride a horse?"

"Yes, I'm a good rider."

"Good, our plan is to buy you a horse today so the three of us can ride together to Los Angeles. That means Harley and I will be with you from now until you are settled in Los Angeles and enrolled in the school. I know a very nice elderly couple who live in Los Angeles whom I'm certain will be happy to have you live with them. You could help with their housekeeping and gardening chores and in return probably they will care for you rent free. In any event, I will discuss these things with them. Their names are Honus and Kathleen St. James. Now, two things more, the horse we will buy you will be a gift from us to you, and I'm sure you will be able to stable it and feed it in the barn the St. James' have on their property for seven or eight dollars a month. I will pay the St. James' $168 to cover the cost for your horse's upkeep for 24 months."

Maria couldn't believe her ears. Why are these two gringo's doing this for me, a grubby little Mexican kid?

Before she could interrupt Bat went on to say, "I am playing a little poker tonight at the hotel and I expect to win enough to cover the cost of caring for your horse at the St. James' and to buy you some clothes for school."

As if miracles were happening around her Maria put her hands over her face and peeked through her fingers, first at Bat then at Harley in disbelief.

"But…" she started.

"No buts," Bat refuted. "And, if it makes you feel any better I need to be in the Los Angeles vicinity within a few days anyway, and now is as good a time to go as any so don't feel any untoward Maria. I have a Deputy Sheriff whom I will leave in charge of the county while I'm away and today I will deputize two men from town whom I trust and who will be proud to serve their community."

"Maria," Harley spoke up "you will have Bat and me to look after you for at least a month until, as Bat just said, we are satisfied that you are settled in and ready for your studies."

'Son of a bitch,' Harley said to himself, 'how can one Mexican kid wrap two supposed tough guys around her little finger so easily?'

Again Maria cried. She was not accustomed to being treated so father-like. Bat and Harley took her outstretched hands in theirs and waited for her tears to stop.

That afternoon Harley bought a graceful 3 year old little filly named Princess and delivered it over to Maria at the Sheriff's office. Maria, between oooooohs and awwwwes hugged and nuzzled her new horse and vowed *this horse* would be the best cared for horse in the whole world.

That night Maria Nancy Sanchez had the hotel's lobby, its outside steps and its staircase, jammed with people. They applauded and cheered after every song she sang. She sang contemporary ones with an angelic voice, Mexican songs with zeal, and cowboy songs with a twang. The people loved her music, her Mexican liveliness and her special charm. Harley's hat at ten o'clock was filled with coins and bills. When counted in her hotel room, just before bedtime, the cash taken in totaled $39.50. Maria and Harley were overwhelmed. Harley took the room next to Maria's and he was asleep before eleven.

Bat swaggered back to his office some $392 "ahead" and by one-thirty he, too, was asleep in his bed.

It took 16 days and 15 nights for them to reach Los Angeles.

It was a playful trip for all of them. A little fishing now and then, hide and seek twix two burley men and a Mexican kid, laughter and tears from reminiscing, seeing pumas, coatis, marmots, countless birds, snakes, deer and even a grouchy old bear, picnicking, berry picking and so many fun things Maria had never before experienced.

And every evening, on their travels to Los Angeles, Maria would sing and entertain townsfolk. Harley's hat filled up every night and by the time they reached Los Angeles Maria had gathered in over $500.

Maria looked downcast when Bat and Harley refused to share her $500. "After all," she said, "it's your money, not mine. You have cared for me, bought me a horse, bought all of our food and all the feed for the horse, and you say you are going to pay the St. James' $168 to feed and stall Princess, and buy me new school clothes and, and…"

"Hush," Bat admonished, "not another word, I mean it, not another word."

"But?"

"No more," Bat cautioned.

"Oh, I do love you both," Maria cried, and with that hugged them with all her might.

CHAPTER 25

MARIA, PHILLIP, MOUSEY

Warning…Vicious rape scene.!

Maria was introduced to Honus and Kathleen St. James on August 1, 1899. At the outset the St. James' were taken with Maria. There was no need for William Masterson to brag about her and to assure Honus and Kathleen about how tidy, polite and caring she was, because they, the St. James', saw her as a most welcome addition to their home.

Maria on the other hand wanted to spend the rest of her life with Sheriff Bat and Harley Earp. No need to go to school if she could be with them. They were the greatest. But she knew starting today she would be living with the St. James', and soon she would be starting school, and soon, too soon, they would be leaving. She daresn't think about it, about them being gone, about not being with them, seeing them, she felt ill and dejected and even hateful with the whole world because she could have only one month of her life with them. She promised herself she would beg them to stay in the Los Angeles area so she could see them as often as she wished, yes, she would make them promise.

Maria was escorted by Mrs. St. James to Maria's bedroom on the second floor of this mansion (as Maria thought of it) and, my, oh my, what a beautiful room. It was furnished with a huge four-poster bed covered by a thick inviting comforter adorned in gay colorful flowers. It had elegant light-colored furniture which included a chest of drawers, vanity and stool, full length stand-up mirror on French designed feet, a large study desk with a sturdy chair, a night table, a wash stand holding a cream-colored basin and ewer, and a comfy chaise lounge. The high-polished hardwood floor had beautiful scatter rugs hither and thither throughout the room, one on the left side of the bed, one at the foot of the bed, a large one in the center of the room, and a small one under the study desk. A good-sized clothes closet was situated behind a door just to the right of the four-poster bed. This, thought Maria, is a bedroom for a princess not for a poor little Mexican girl.

After being shown the whole magnificent house, Mrs. St. James and Maria joined the men who were seated in the home's ample sitting room enjoying coffee and Danish all sorts.

"Well darling girl," Bat asked, "what do you think of your new home?"

"Wonderful," she said, eyes still popping from the grandeur of it all. "It's unimaginably unimaginable, and Mr. and Mrs. St. James are so nice."

"Good, Maria," Bat acknowledged, "Harley and I are staying here the night at Honus' and Kathleen's kind invitation and I understand, too, Kathleen has instructed her kitchen staff to prepare supper for all of us. "Thank you Kathleen," Bat nodded. "And Maria, tomorrow morning at nine o'clock you, Harley and I will leave here to go to Santa Monica High School. There we will meet with the school's Headmaster, Dr. Bartholomew Westwiggins at ten o'clock sharp. So attire yourself on the morrow in the dress and shoes we bought at Merryweather's today."

The next day, August 2, 1899, William Barclay Masterson and Harley Jonathan Earp succeeded, through implicit *force majeure,* in having Maria Nancy Sanchez enrolled (as the first Mexican student) in the formidable Santa Monica High School. Bat and Harley suggested to Dr. Westwiggins in a most persuasive way that the schools trustees, the headmaster, the school's department heads, teachers and staff treat Maria just as they would their other students.

"Because, let us assure you Mr. Westwiggins, we will be' in touch with Miss Sanchez frequently and, in fact, we will from time to time, make surprise visits to the school to ensure Maria's fair and just treatment."

They all shook hands when the meeting adjourned.

Maria cried every night and in secret several times each day, miserable with the thought of her two idols leaving her. How will it be possible to live without them? Who will take her hiking in the wilds to see all the pretty birds and the exciting animals? Who will play fun games with her? Who will take her to places where she can sing and entertain people? Who can she love as she loves them and who will love her as they love her?

"Please stay and live in Los Angeles," she begged of them.

"Son of a bitch," Harley and Bat thought, "how did we ever get tied up with this little sidewinder? Christ, we've got our work to do, what is it about her that captivates us so?"

"Maria, we can't stay here in Los Angeles," Harley replied. "Bat is meeting with the sheriff in the county of Pasadena today and I have to go back to National City to round up some cattle rustlers. We will be leaving tomorrow morning and, of course, we will come to say our good-byes to you before we leave."

"I won't let you go," Maria retorted, stamping her feet.

"Maria," Harley continued, "we promise we will write to you at least once a month and we promise to visit you at least twice a year. Remember Maria, Bat and I damn it, we love you just as if you were our own daughter."

The next morning Bat and Harley arrived at the St. James', saddlebags full and ready to go. Both were feeling dreadful. They felt they were being traitors to Maria.

They dismounted.

The front door of the St. James' house opened. Maria emerged. She was wearing a colorful Mexican dress and shirt. Her sombrero's tie string was around her neck allowing the sombrero to hang haughtily behind her head. She had brushed her magnificent black hair straight, letting part of it cascade over the front of her shoulders down to her waist, while the rest of her hair was done in such a way that it tumbled down her back to reach the top of her buttocks.

Maria had put rouge on her cheeks and a touch of lip-gloss on her lips. She wanted to impress Bat and Harley that she was not a child, that indeed she was a mature young lady who could ride with them on equal terms. Quintessentially, between the three of them, *quid pro quo*.

Bat and Harley saw through Maria's guise. Damn it, she just won't give up.

Honus and Kathleen St. James appeared at the doorway and came no further. Bat and Harley walked up to Maria and each took one of her hands in theirs. Tears streamed down Maria's cheeks, her cute little nose ran. She squeezed their hands; she looked into their eyes, they pleaded. One by one they knelt down beside her to hug and to kiss her, to encourage her to excel in her studies and to tell her how each of them loved her. No, they couldn't take her with them into their rough and tumble world. They said they were going to miss her just as she will miss them. But they must show their deep caring for her by having her go to her new school to complete her education and for her to meet many youngsters her own age, to have a normal life.

"Good bye, little sweetheart," Harley said, tears now welling down his cheeks. 'God almighty what's become of me? a blubbering sissy,' he said to himself.

"Yes, good bye, little sweetheart," Bat said, brushing his tear-filled eyes with the back of his hand. "I love you my darling girl. We both love you." They turned and walked to their horses.

Maria screamed, "You can't leave me, please, I'll die—don't leave me, don't, don't." She ran to them…she grasped their hands…she sobbed uncontrollably, "I'll die, I'll die without you. I don't want to live unless I'm with you."

"Please Maria, go back to the house. That's where you belong. Go now, go," Harley pleaded, crying aloud now.

"No," Maria screamed once more. She fell to both knees, bowed head in her hands, whimpering, crying, terrified that she would never see them again.

Both men stood transfixed, lost.

Maria stood up, her angelic face red, pinched up, wet with tears. She looked at them and moaned, "How can you leave me? You both know you will never see me again…you will forget me…in a few days I will mean nothing to you," she sobbed.

They moved to her.

"We will never forget you Maria. We love you. We will do as Harley said, as God is our witness, we will write to you at least once a month, and visit you at least twice a year. And you can come visit us when school is out on vacation. You are part of us now Maria, remember that." The men kissed and hugged her, turned to their horses, mounted them and rode off. Each man turned to look back.

Maria was on her knees waving, her little face scrunched, crying.

Honus and Kathleen came to her lifted her to her feet and escorted her into the house.

* * *

Maria first met Simon St. James in mid-August 1899 at Simon's grandparents' (Honus and Kathleen St. James) home. Simon was 16-years-old, and in grade 10. He was a brilliant student at the ostentatious Santa Monica High. Straightaway he was awe-struck by Maria. Maria too was awe-struck by Simon, even though her idols remained Bat and Harley. They became school sweethearts. And woe-betide any young man who made even the most perfunctory advance toward Maria. Big Simon would straighten out that chaps' feelings "post haste".

By Christmas that year Maria was the most popular student in the entire school. It wasn't because of Bat and Harley's "persuasion" that her popularity became so dominant. No, it was Maria's charm, her angelic beauty and her remarkable brain. Maria's spellbinding charisma was such that no one, male, female, adult or child could dislike her. She was an enchantress.

Simon and Maria wed in 1907.

* * *

Mousey stayed near Maria from the time he first saw her in June of 1903. His dull mind over the years was able to maintain the 2 covenants he imposed on himself back in 1903, one, no family relation to Maria and two, act as her guardian angel.

However, Mousey was able to acquaint himself with both Maria and Simon by attending church, community picnics and the like. Mousey knew that Simon St. James was articling under Thomas Sontag, C.P.A. in order to obtain his degree as a Certified Public Accountant.

Mousey knew Simon would start up his own practice soon after receiving his C.P.A. designation. One day at a community picnic Mousey overheard Simon and Maria discuss this matter as they sat on a bench while he, Mousey, was lying, and pretending to be asleep, on a blanket right next to the bench.

Mousey heard them discuss where their future office was to be located. This was a real boon to him. He checked out the office building. Much to his delight he saw jutting out of the back of the building a small "lean-to" like structure that (by peering through a window) had two small rooms. "My! Oh my! God intends me to live here," Mousey thought. "Thank you God."

Soon Maria and Simon moved into their new office and, to their delight, they had Mousey housed in the two-room "lean-to." Just like everyone else who knew Mousey they too thought a great deal of him and, like everyone else, had no idea where Mousey lived and slept. Now everyone would know his "whereabouts."

It made Maria and Simon happy to see Mousey assured of proper living accommodations and they were overwhelmed when Mousey insisted he pay them one dollar each week as rent.

Without his knowledge Maria banked each dollar she received from him into an account in his name.

* * *

Phillip entered Maria's office quietly. He stood for a few seconds marveling at Maria's beauty. Slowly Maria turned from her credenza to her desk mulling over some papers. On hearing a rustle she glanced up and saw a wild-eyed Phillip staring at her with the front of his trousers being pushed out by his hard penis.

Phillip had lost all his composure. Lust had taken over his sanity. All the sexual fantasies he had choreographed for Maria and he to perform since the first day he had seen her was now crammed in his brain, ready to explode.

Maria spoke first after taking in Phillip's frightening appearance. She knew he was not drunk. The nice things she had heard about him as a school departmental head, she had always considered Mr. Foster a gentleman, certainly not a drinker. 'Now, for heaven's sake, how could Phillip change so to become this ghastly intruder,' she wondered.

"Good day Mr. Foster," Maria said. "I should like to inform you that our office is closed for business now, and I do apologize if I left the office doors unlocked. If you will excuse me Mr. Foster, I must clear my desk because Sheriff O'Flarity will be here in the next few minutes to discuss with me a picnic we are arranging." Maria still knew how to use her wiles. She had no meeting scheduled with the sheriff, but with Mr. Foster's fearsome countenance, his shameless ogling and his jutting trousers she knew she must do something to dissuade him from his obvious evil intentions. By using an upcoming fictional meeting with the sheriff may make Mr. Foster leave lest the sheriff enter to find Mr. Foster here in Maria's office.

"No Maria, or should I say Mrs. St. James, you did not leave the office doors unlocked, I unlocked them. As to Sheriff O'Flarity you are not telling me the truth. I know he will be meeting with Dr. Schneider, at least until six o'clock this evening on an accident-related matter. The sheriff volunteered this information to me when I told him I would like to see him at his office at 5:30 this afternoon. SO DON'T LIE TO ME YOU MEXICAN HARLOT," Phillip screamed. He rushed for her. Maria tried to dodge him. Phillip had taken Maria by surprise at the outset. She had no time to consider an adequate defense against his barbarianism.

Phillip caught her. Spittle drooled down his chin. His muscular arms pinned hers. He tried to catch her mouth with his. With Herculean strength he ripped open the front of Maria's dress and slip, pulled off her brassiere, letting her plentiful breasts be at full mast displaying themselves unwittingly.

With that Phillip, his fly buttons already undone, flipped out his angry red penis and rubbed it against Maria's bare stomach. Maria did not panic. She was frightened and horrified but she did not panic. Phillip slapped her hard across her cheek and blood oozed from the corner of her mouth. This pleased him. He'd show this married cunt a thing or two.

*　　　*　　　*

Mousey stirred. It was Saturday afternoon. On most Saturday afternoons he rested on his bed until 4:30 at which time he rose to start his chores for his "associates" along the street. But did he not hear someone scream? Did he not hear a noise coming from one of the St. James' offices?

His slow-witted mind searched back to earlier in the day, Maria was in her office alone, he remembered seeing her. He was her guardian angel therefore, he must go check on her at once.

* * *

Maria tugged one arm free and with all her might she hit Phillip on the side of his face with her closed fist. Phillip bellowed with anger, she bloody well hurt him. Yeah! All the better he thought, now I don't care how I screw her and how I make her suffer. He lifted her up, pulled off her bloomers, ripped them to shreds, then jammed his face into her crotch biting down hard on her smooth gleaming inner thighs. She bled. Maria held back a shriek of pain. Phillip was becoming distraught by Maria's silence.

He held her long glistening hair in one hand and drove the fist of his other hand onto Maria's jaw. Maria moaned and fell semi-conscious to the floor. Good, Charles thought. He reached for his bag and retrieved his switchblade knife, his school's leather strap and the artificial penis. Maria stirred.

Mousey peeked through the window of Maria's office door, the same door Phillip was behind a few minutes earlier. Mousey wasn't sure but he "thought" he was horrified. No he wasn't quite sure. His dull mind had difficulty contemplating the scene before him. Were Phillip and Maria just playing and having fun? He watched as Phillip took the switch blade knife and made a thin cut just over Maria's navel. Blood oozed from the wound. Maria was conscious now. Phillip licked up the blood like a vampire. He rolled Maria on her side. Laughing like a lunatic he thrust the well-lubricated artificial penis into Maria's anus then, with the switchblade knife at Maria's throat, he rolled her on her back and with cold fury he sank "His Royal Highness Phillip the First" into her vagina. He pumped furiously while smashing the school's leather strap across Maria's hips and legs. No longer could Maria hold back her pain. She screamed for help.

In a panic Mousey tried to open Maria's office door. Phillip had locked it. He now understood Maria's terrible plight. Yelling at the top of his voice Mousey stepped back several paces from the door and without thought for his own well being, super charged with adrenaline, he ran, and like a rocket he hurtled himself through the glass on the upper half of the door. Shreds of the glass tore at his clothes, cut his bare arms, his face, his neck, his hands and his body. Blood streamed from his wounds. He howled like the devil gone mad. When he reached the floor, legs driving, he flung himself onto Phillip's back and like a constricting snake he wrapped his puny blood covered arms around Phillip's neck and his misshapen legs around Phillip's midsection. Dog-like he sunk his teeth into Phillip's right cheek. Blood flowed as part of Phillip's cheek came off into Mousey's mouth.

Phillip roared in rage and pain. He leapt off Maria's shuddering body, he shook himself like a wet dog dislodging water from his soaked fur in an attempt to rid his back of this satanic gnome. The goddamned 'thing' stuck like a fucking cowboy riding an enraged stallion. "You little piece of shit," Phillip bellowed. "I'll get you, you ugly little bastard." With that Phillip charged straight ahead then in mid-air spun himself halfway around smashing Mousey against a wall. Mousey's warped back was shattered by Phillip's 210 pound, battering ram body. Mousey squeaked, squealed and gasped trying to suck some precious air into his flattened lungs. Mousey hung on.

Maria screamed at Phillip calling him a devil, a pig, a bully, an evil demon. "Leave Carl alone you monster, you hellish snake you sc..."

Mousey interrupted Maria by screaming, "SISTER, MY BELOVED SISTER MARIA...RUN...GET OUT OF HERE...RUN PLEASE. I"M YOUR BROTHER JOSE...I WILL GLADLY DIE FOR YOU...GO..."

Maria gasped, "Jose?"

Phillip, catching Maria's stunned surprise, rushed at her while his rider screeched at Maria to run. Phillip's violent kick caught Maria's left cheek, she collapsed, the artificial penis fell to the floor, Maria was knocked unconscious. Phillip reached backward in an attempt to grab his nemesis and fling him to the floor.

Mousey was too quick, with another splurge of adrenaline and amid all the confusion Mousey had gotten hold of a letter opener which was lying on Maria's desk. With ghastly intent he plunged the letter opener into Phillip's left eye. Phillip's frightful scream was bloodcurdling. Much to Mousey's surprise, Phillip grasped the letter opener and pulled it from his eye. This left a gaping hole where the eye should have been, a hole that drooled an ugly pus-like substance. A frantic, bloodied Phillip reached behind himself and drove the letter opener into Mousey's leg and body over and over again. Mousey fell to the floor, eyes aflame with hatred and fury as he looked up into Phillip's remaining right eye. Mousey watched the savage brute sink slowly to the floor onto both knees. Phillip lifted his hands to cover the opening that was once his left eye. Blood and pus trickled through his fingers.

Maria's office door flew open, Sheriff O'Flarity, Dr. Schnider and Hymie Lipschit barged in. "My God," each man whispered. "My Good God."

Maria, Phillip and Mousey were a frightful sight. Maria's office was in a shambles. Dr. Schnider rushed to Maria's side. He was horrified. As he was taking her pulse, she stirred, moaned, opened her eyes, and expecting another punch or kick, pushed herself away from the good doctor and called out "Jose, Jose."

Dr. Schnider said "Maria Dear, it's me Dr. Schnider, you're all right now, you're safe, the sheriff and Mr. Lipschit are here with me."

"Oh, Doctor, is Jose all right?"

"I don't know a Jose, child."

"Jose, my brother…Mousey."

"Your brother, Mousey…your brother?" the doctor questioned, astounded.

"Yes." Maria pulled herself into a sitting position. Then with superhuman effort she was able to stand. She teetered and groped as the doctor held her. She searched the room for Jose. Was she hallucinating or did she actually hear Mousey call her sister? She saw him bunched up on the floor. He was looking toward her smiling. Maria went to his side hugged him and held him and whispered in Spanish, "Are you truly my brother from Tijuana, my brother Jose?"

"Yes my darling sister, I am truly your brother Jose from Tijuana, son of Conchita Consquela, our wonderful mother, and Benito our dreadful father."

Maria fell to the floor and wrapped her arms around Jose's pathetic body.

They both wept. "Why, oh why, Jose didn't you tell me you were my brother years ago, why? We could have been so close. Jose, why?"

"Because Maria, it's because I love you so much."

"Jose, that doesn't make sense…if you love…"

Jose broke in and hushed Maria by placing a stub-like finger over her lips, "Maria, you are such a lady. Your husband is such a gentleman. You have three wonderful children. You are the most respected and loved couple in all of Los Angeles. You are rich, you are giving, you are…"Jose moaned.

"Dr. Schnider" Maria screamed.

"No, no my angel," Jose whispered, "let me finish."

Dr. Schnider knelt down beside Maria and Jose.

"Shhh," Jose beckoned at the good doctor and speaking again in Spanish said,"Sister dear, you are a princess, an intelligent princess. I looked for you when I broke away from my masters, who you do not know and by diablo, I hope you never know. Something inside me at that time directed me to look for you, for which I will be forever grateful, and Maria, I found you, I found you, oh…my baby sister I found you."

They wrapped their arms around one another and wept. Dr. Schnider could not look at them. He turned away and wept. Jose moaned again, squeezing his eyes shut in pain. The doctor recognized the moan to be a physical distress signal, he reached for Jose, but once again Jose displayed the 'shh' sign.

"Maria, I am nothing but a wasted piece of humanity. Even though we are sister and brother, I am not as you are, stately, aristocratic, so grand and dignified, yet so human. Somewhere in the past there must have been nobility in our family, an Aztec prince perhaps. And you my wonderful sister, you must be the recipient of this nobility. Feeling as I do about you, I could not have had your name blemished by my relationship to you and have you brought down to my wretched level. No Maria I could never have done that. Countless numbers of time I wanted to hug you and kiss you, and tell you how much I loved you. But I fought off those feelings, because your position in life was of greater importance to me than my selfish thoughts. Sister Maria I am so glad we can hold one another now. I know my life is to end soon, and being with you makes my whole life worthwhile. Shhh, please Maria. When you and Simon let me live in your offices, I became the happiest person in the world Maria, because I knew I would be able to see you daily. I knew too I was to be your guardian angel. Maria, even though we have just had this terrible happening with Phillip, I have to say to you that now being together as sister and brother, the man known as Jesus of Nazareth has fulfilled his promise to me, that the meek shall inherit the earth. Because Maria, I think of you truly as the soul of the earth, and now my life is complete…we are together."

"Jose, no, you shouldn't have thought that way about me, I am your sister, your sister, only that, your sister, you are precious to me, why Jose, oh my God why?" Maria sobbed.

Jose's head fell to one side, he coughed, blood trickled from his mouth. Fumbling, Jose took the doctor's hand and directed it under his left arm a few inches above his lower ribs.

The doctor winced when he felt the jagged end of a huge splinter of glass at the spot where Jose's hand had directed his. Gently he parted Maria and Jose and lay Jose on the office floor. He lifted Jose's left arm and saw the ugly protrusion of the glass splinter. He observed the frothy blood oozing its way out from around the wound. He knew that Jose's left lung had been punctured. He saw, too, all the vicious punctures that Phillip had inflicted on Jose with Maria's letter opener. "God, how does he still live?" Dr. Schnider thought.

Maria moaned on seeing the dreadful injuries Jose had sustained in his protection of her. She put her head down beside her brother; she knew he was near death; she sobbed as she prayed in her mother tongue."Phillip, you are cause of all this, you depraved monster, you, you God be damned monster!" She struggled to her feet, saw Phillip's switchblade knife on her desk. She grabbed at it screaming, knife glistening in her upraised hand she rushed toward the inert Phillip. Kill blazed in her tear-filled eyes. Just as she was about to drive the blade into Phillip's chest, her arm was caught by a powerful hand. She looked around, eyes still ablaze. She looked like a mad woman. Kill was her intent.

Destroy that inhuman monster was all she could think of. But here now was her husband. Where did he come from? With a shriek she cried, "Simon my darling, you're here, thank God, you're here." She held onto the knife as she wrapped herself around Simon.

Simon was devastated by what he saw. His precious wife, half naked, her breasts exposed, bloody from Jose's wounds, her hips and legs a scarlet red from Phillip's beatings with the school strap, brandishing a knife above her head, Dr. Schnider on his knees beside a bloodied wounded Mousey. An eye-less Phillip crud falling from one socket, his trousers around his ankles, his bloomers down, his penis and testicles exposed. Sheriff O'Flarity looming over Phillip and Mr. Lipschit standing with his hands at his cheeks crying.

"What in God's name has happened?" Simon gasped.

Maria outraged and frantic told him the whole gruesome story, as she held Jose and Simon's hands in hers. Simon cursed the day Phillip was born.

Jose, knowing it was time for him to die, again in Spanish blessed Maria. He reiterated his love for her and told her how happy he was to be near her for the past 11 years. He smiled and said to her that in a few moments he would be joining their mother in heaven. "We will all meet in heaven when God calls us. Goodbye Maria, my darling sister, goodbye Simon, Dr. Schnider, Sheriff O'Flarity and Mr. Lipschit. I love all of you."

Jose died.

Maria could not be comforted. Jose's surprise admittance to her, his sudden death, the horrid molestation and abuse handed her by a respected teacher from the renowned Santa Monica High. Simon held her close to him as she sobbed.

Sheriff O'Flarity called the doctor over to examine Phillip. The sheriff was unable to detect a pulse on Phillip's wrist. The doctor sat beside the fallen rapist, and after several tests found that when Phillip was stabbed in the eye by Mousey the letter opener penetrated deep into Phillip's brain. Phillip was, in fact, dead. The sheriff and the doctor saw to it that Jose's and Phillip's bodies were taken to the morgue.

* * *

The newspaper and wireless were given an account of that hellish day, Saturday, October 26th, 1914, but with many variations to the actual events. The press release stated Phillip Foster for reasons unknown to Dr. Hendricks had become maniacal and had broken into Simon St. James, Certified Public Accountants' offices with theft in mind. The release said he was so demented that that like a brute he attacked Mrs. Maria St. James for not giving him money and coupon bonds. The article told about Jose, known in the community as Mousey, giving up his life to save his sister and how he, Jose, slew the frenzied Mr. Foster. The story made no mention of rape in order to save the reputation of Phillip Foster's wife and children and to keep the much-loved Maria's name away from any untoward publicity. The story was successful.

Phillip's wife Elizabeth and her children Charles Jr. and Lawrence moved back home to live with her parents James and Joan Cuthbertson in Santa Barbara. Charles Jr. was an exemplary student throughout his public school years right through to his graduation in 1935 from the University of California, Los Angeles, gaining therefrom a doctorate degree in political science. Charles Jr.'s grandson Franklin graduated with his doctorate degree in political science in the spring of 1987 from New York University in the City of New York.

* * *

Hymie Lipschit became a hero to the city of Los Angeles as a result of his part on that fateful October day. That day while out of his deli for a brief stroll, he thought he heard screams coming from Simon and Maria's offices. He wasted no time in making a decision about what to do. He chose to err on the side of caution. At first he tried to get into the offices in order to assess the situation. Dammit, how do you break into locked offices, he thought, burglars know how but, dammit, I have never been a burglar. Dammit, Dammit, Dammit. Frantically he looked up and down the streets to see if anyone was about. He saw a gentleman who frequented his deli coming toward him. Hymie, almost in hysterics, called out to the gentleman to rush to the sheriffs office "now" and have the sheriff come "this instant, to Simon's and Maria's office, there's trouble...go." The gentleman went. Unbeknownst to Hymie, Dr. Schnider at the time was with the sheriff.

Approximately 15 minutes later Sheriff O'Flarity and Dr. Schnider arrived at Simon's and Maria's offices and found that Hymie Lipschit had just broken through the offices front double doors and was about to enter Maria's private office. Hymie looked abashed, but damn well determined to get to Maria's rescue. Hymie at this point looked so "pumped up" that he could have whipped the old "Boston Strong Boy" himself, John L. Sullivan, even in John L's prime. Hymie was not at all interested in the accolades he received from his friends and the press, but he received them with dignity and in the spirit in which they were given. Mr. Lipschit wished only that he could have been there minutes earlier so that he could have done all in his power to prevent the horrendous carnage. "To have helped in saving the life of Maria, the city's angel, was reward enough," he said.

* * *

For several weeks after the horror show of October 26th, Maria was miserable, upset and confused. She was devastated about Jose's death. He remained in her thoughts until the day she died. Over and over again she searched her mind for reasons for Phillip's unreasonable sexual attack against her. Her troubled life as a child and from having witnessed drunken men's sexual abuses against women and children in the back alleys of Tijuana was one thing, but, to try to equate these drunken reprobates' actions to Phillip's actions was quite another. After all Phillip was an upstanding member of the community. To her knowledge he was not a drunk, nor did he roam the alleys of Los Angeles. He had a beautiful wife and a family. He was noted as a renowned teacher. 'My God, why did he assail and batter me? Why did he refer to me as a Mexican harlot and why did he scream 'you teased me long enough Mrs. Maria St. James?' I have never paid any particular attention to that man. I have seen him only a few times in the past and most often Simon and I were together. Our acknowledgment of him was always a simple, 'a good day to you sir.' Maria was anything but stupid. She knew she was beautiful and had an envious figure, but, she adjudged, 'Simon has, is, and always will be the only man I will love. Good gracious, I would never dream of teasing another man.'

Simon was the essence of manhood following the despicable day of October 26th, 1914. He comforted Maria. He swore vengeance on any person who dared threaten her in any manner. He assured her of his undying love for her, his pride in her, and that she Maria, was his life. "Maria my darling, you and I are one person. Phillip has, by his warped brain and his cruel actions crystallized our oneness even firmer if that is possible. Maria, I love you, cherish you, and I am, and always will be devoted to you."

Bat Masterson, who had moved to New York City in 1902, and who now, as Harley Earp had predicted way back in 1899, was a sportswriter for New York's daily Morning Telegraph. Bat had heard through news sources coming across his desk about the mayhem that occurred in Los Angeles on October 26th, involving his beloved Maria St. James. Straightaway Bat contacted Harley Earp in Phoenix and arranged with Harley a date they would meet in Los Angeles to see their beloved Maria. Bat and Harley met at the railroad station in Los Angeles on November 29th, 1914. From there they went directly to Maria's and Simon's home for their surprise visit.

Maria all but swooned on seeing Bat and Harley. She could not believe her eyes. She could not speak. She cried, just as she had done years ago when Bat and Harley had left her on the steps of Honus' and Kathleen St. James' home. Tears streamed down her cheeks, and her cute little nose ran, she hugged them, she smothered their faces with kisses. Her tear-filled eyes and her crinched up pretty face told Bat and Harley their coming to her was necessary.

Both big tough hombres cried without shame. This here Maria was still the most precious person in their lives. How in the world did this girl captivate them so? The three of them stayed clutched to one another for many minutes. Not so much as one word was spoken. No words at this time were necessary. Bat and Harley's love for Maria, and Maria's reciprocal love for Bat and Harley was so deep, so heartfelt that this love transcended all else. No words were necessary.

Simon watched the entire proceedings twix't Maria, Bat and Harley with a huge lump in his throat and with his own cheeks covered in tears. By damn he thought, these two men are something else.

"How do Simon?" Harley eventually interceded.

"How do my friend Harley," Simon responded.

Bat, now putting on a show that he was no blubberer said, "Okay, you two uncouth Westerners, what's this 'how do stuff?' You are now in the presence of a man with *savoir-faire*, a genteel gentleman from the great city of New York who speaks in only the grandest of his majesty King George V's English, to wit, Good Day Master Simon St. James, not 'how do Simon.' What say you my dear Maria St. James to my greetings to your husband compared to 'ole tree trunk' Harley Earps boorish words?"

"My response to you is that I love all of you. I am blessed by having the three greatest men in the world as mine, therefore Sheriff Masterson I love each of your greetings to my darling husband." With that she had her massive husband Simon join in on the hugs.

During their stay with Maria and Simon, Maria introduced them to Sheriff O'Flarity, Dr.Schnider and Mr.Lipschit, as well as many other friends and acquaintances. People could not believe they were meeting the great William Barclay (Bat) Masterson, and Wyatt Earp's nephew, Harley Earp. The Los Angeles Times newspaper also informed its readers that Messrs Masterson and Earp were in the city visiting the St. James'. The newspaper repeated its October 27th, 1914, story of the brutal attack against Maria St. James by the maniac Phillip Foster. Masterson and Earp, being very close friends, came to bring their sympathy and comfort to the St. James', and to remind the public that if anyone so much as ogles Maria wrong, they would answer directly to Messrs Masterson and Earp.

After Bat and Harley satisfied themselves Maria was well and her mind was quite settled, they agreed it was now time for them to leave her and get back to their own affairs. They knew the scene that would occur when they announced to Maria that they must go…a tumultuous fuss at the very least, shameless tears, begging them to move to Los Angeles. They were not wrong. Maria, without humility, cried just as she did 15 years ago.

Simon came to the rescue by picking up his weeping wife and carrying her into their home comforting her by assuring her she would see her guardians many more times. Simon's assurances to Maria were well founded. Bat and Harley visited Maria and Simon often. On one special occasion Maria, Simon and Harley together traveled to the awesome metropolis of New York City to visit Bat. What a time they all had. Bat, on Maria, Simon and Harley's departure put on a show, tongue in cheek, mimicking Maria when he and Harley left her. While they all laughed and joked at Bat's performance, Maria sobbed on leaving them.

William Barclay Masterson passed away in 1921. Harley Jonathon Earp passed away in 1925.

CHAPTER 26

THE RATS, MAY 1997

Warning! Graphic mutilation!

May 24th, 1997, 8:00 a.m. Lana's guest stirs. He awakens in a stupor.

During the night the rats acted as if they were under the influence of a drug. But no, Lana knew their quick body and beady-eye movements were attributable to the abundance of food and drink available to them (human flesh and blood) and their frustration of being caged.

As well, from time to time, short rather meaningless squabbles occurred between the rats over certain parts of Lana's guest's body that each rat wanted as his or her own to dine on. But, by and large, the rodents appeared to be quite respectful of one another and not as pushy or grabby as many humans.

At the start of the play the rats were somewhat skittish when Lana's guest howled with pain as they went about demolishing his lower body. But as the nighttime passed, they became used to these frequent noisy interruptions. In addition they appeared to enjoy the soothing sound of Perry Como's voice, particularly when they took time to snooze after gorging themselves on their host's succulent meat.

The mess being made on Lana's guest's lower belly now was becoming ugly and revolting. The head of his penis had been eaten away almost in its entirety. Left only was the tube on its underside, you know, the tube that carries away unwanted urine and that spurts out semen on copulation. What remained of his shaft was disgusting. Small irregular gobs of skin dangled hideously from it where the rats had gnawed and feasted "au naturel" while blood fell in small droplets from these gobs into his pubic hair.

Suddenly urine squirted out of her guest's mutilated pecker and rained on the three rats. Her guest screamed. Like a dying fish on the bottom of a boat, his body flip-flopped every which way, mind you, under the confining constraints of his shackles. The pain, Lana thought, must be like urinating through a urethra plagued with gonorrhea.

Again and again Lana's guest begged her to release him. He pleaded for mercy. He apologized over and over for his past indiscretions against her. "For God's sake, Lana, you are known as the kindest, most thoughtful person imaginable anywhere. Why are you being so iniquitous, depraved, so horrible now? And that dreadful mirror above me, you have put it there so I can see what is being done to me just as you do, right. How can you have me tortured so cruelly…and…and…just sit there as if I was some…some…whatever the fucking hell? Merciful Jesus, Lana! And please turn off that fucking music!"

A gut-wrenching scream convulsed his body. The big adult male rat was ripping out Lana's guest's left testicle from its sac. Blood spurted everywhere. The two other rats opened their mouths and slurped up the delicious nectar. Satisfied with his drink of blood, the young male now darted to the other testicle. His whiskers disappeared into Lana's guests other sac. Not having mature teeth like the adult rat he had to rip and tear at the testie like a snarling dog shaking a rag doll. The young rat, out of frustration and for leverage, jammed his hind feet into Lana's guest's anus, placed his forepaws against each cheek of "lover boys" buttocks sunk his teeth into the base of "lover boy's" ball then ferociously shook his head until the ripe testie came loose. "Lover boy" screeched. Blood splattered everywhere. The young rat dined on the succulent meat.

"Lana," Father Donnely sobbed, "please let me go. It hurts so. I am terrified. I will do anything for you if you free me. You don't know the hellish pain I'm in and how frightened I am. Lana, my love, are you going to let me die like this?" he moaned. He began to sob. "Jesus Christ, Lana, now I feel one of the rats tearing at my intestines." Her guest's mind whirled as he thought of his final hours on earth. Always, he had wanted to die peacefully and with dignity as an elderly gentleman absolved of all of his past indiscretions. Not dying by being eaten alive by three belly-bloated, fucking rats.

"Lana," he begged, "water. I need water."

"Your wish is my command, lover boy."

As she let herself drop to the barn's floor from the hay bales, she noticed something slithering toward her guest's body. "How sweet," she murmured, "two uninvited snakes to join in the play." She noted that one of the snakes proceeded to her guest's unclad anus. Its forked tongue picked off flies that buzzed around it. Then, cobra-like, the slinky snake, with lightning speed, drove its head through Lana's guest's anus right into his tattered rectum.

Lana's guest shrieked.

CHAPTER 27

THE FEMALE RAT'S ESCAPE: DREADFULLY INELEGANT

Soon, Lana returned with a glass full of cold water. She lifted her guest's head and placed the glass to his lips. He drank until the glass was emptied. As Lana's guest was drinking his water, the female rat, wanting her freedom from the cage was searching for 'an escape route.' She nuzzled every part of her host's body within the cage before deciding where to "dig." She proved to be very perceptive. She chose to make her escape through a hole that appeared to be already started, Lana's guest's navel. She sank her sharp teeth into his skin tearing it open. Then she began to rip away at his intestines disgorging mouthfuls of colon, feces and blood as she went. In due course her head disappeared inside her host's lower abdomen, then after several minutes and more disgorging, her whole body was inside his. At this point just her ugly rope like tail had not disappeared. At first it flopped aimlessly on Lana's guest's torso, then inch by inch, it began its entry into his body as if it was being sucked in by some bloodthirsty leach.

Father Donnely, looking into the Lana's diabolically placed mirror, watched in horror as the female rat burrowed its way into his gut, then disappeared therein. Inside him, Lord God, a live rat was inside his body, inside him, a part of him. The priest vomited and shat all at the same time.

The next thing he saw was the twitching nose of the female rat appear out of his lower back just above his pelvic bone. Again he threw up.

Then, like the birth of any baby mammal, the head poked out of the rat made "womb." Seconds later, its bloodstained feces covered body made its appearance on the barn's floor and finally its six-inch-long tail slithered out of Lana's guest's body completing therefore it's hideous "birth." On reaching its freedom, the rat shook off it's "placenta" covered body, ran to the center of the barn, squatted, licked away some blood and feces, squeaked, turned, and looked back at the overstuffed male rats. They appeared stupid and unimaginative to her.

No hole was left as Lana's guest's body had repositioned itself as if nothing was wrong. But his bowels, where the female rat had entered him, were now mangled and torn. Feces and yellowish crud oozed out of these ruined intestines making a mess of the rest of his innards.

The sight of the female rat's escape through her guest's body traumatized Lana. Even her great mind could not dismiss the scene it had just witnessed. She, like her guest entered into a semi-conscious stupor. Her mind whirled. Finally it settled. She peered over at the female rat who seemed to be content to just sit and squeak out messages to her slow witted cohorts.

Lana's great mind took hold of her psyche. She instructed her thoughts to go back to May 5, 1997, Istanbul, Turkey.

CHAPTER 28

ISTANBUL, TURKEY, May 5, 1997

Lana must have a guardian angel...the bruising battle

With equanimity, Dr. Lana Masters stood at the podium as the 2,100 mix of politicians, scientists, economists, religious leaders, and business and labor heads from around the world waited to hear, digest and critique her address. They had heard of her remarkable intellect, the methods she professed she would use in planting the seeds of harmony, humanitarianism and common sense in the entire globe's populace. The soluble answers she claimed to have within her vast repertoire of knowledge and the solutions of everything from worldwide 'holocausts' to lesser problems of inter-country spats. Hence the attendees except, of course, for the preponderance of the politicians and religious leaders, were prepared to hear, without predisposition, Dr. Lana Master's upcoming dissertation.

The Convention Hall being used was palatial. It could seat 2,100 people. The air-conditioning, lighting and sound systems were flawless. The attentiveness of the center's staff was precise and polite. Its location in the city was a delight. Parking, both valet and public were ample. The parking lot was not an eyesore. A variety of palm trees surrounded it, while the lot itself was splashed with a multitude of beautiful flowers, ferns and shrubs. Yes, the City of Istanbul was an excellent choice for this high profile gathering.

The planning and preparation took one year subsequent to the selection of the country, city and site in which the event was to take place. The competition among the numerous countries vying for this prodigious happening was intense. The "world-wide" media coverage, following the announcement by the United Nations of the happening, was "front page." Hawks considered her words and writings to be socialistic drivel while Doves considered her words to be seraphic.

"Is this Masters woman a communist?"

"Is this Masters woman a nut?"

"Is this Masters woman just an unparalleled beauty who earned her reputation by being unparalleled between the sheets?"

"Did the Masters woman get to her elite position by being a slick compelling orator?"

"Is this Masters woman an atheist, or just someone who claims to know the origin of the universe through a word or a thought not yet discovered nor defined in any global language?"

"Is this Masters woman a person who is blessed with a brain capable of being a productive genius but whose brain is 'garbled' leaving her a misguided misfit?"

"Isn't her kindliness among all the earth's populace just wishful Utopian thinking?"

"How dare this Dr. Masters attack today's religion?"

"Dr. Masters, you are rife for a religious terrorist's bullet."

"Dr. Masters how dare you attack big business?"

"Dr. Masters how can you be so naive as to think global problems…people…territorial disputes…religion…human respect and dignity…politics…economics…the wealthy and the poor, etc., etc., etc.…can be overcome through simplistic solutions? Good God, Dr. Masters get real."

All during the complex task of selecting a country and city to host the five-day assemblage Dr. Masters insisted she be informed of any unscrupulous behavior, trickery, gerrymandering, manipulation, or the like among the nations seeking the convention. The council in charge of the entire organization of the event assured Dr. Masters she would be so informed. No such improprieties surfaced, at least, not overtly. The council was recognized around the world as being one that was representative of all nations regardless of their political predominance. The council members were selected by the membership of the United Nations.

The convention was scheduled for five days, Monday May 5th through Friday, May 9th, 1997. The Agenda was uncomplicated, a call for the meeting to come to order, an introduction of the Council and of the Chairperson, Dr. Phillip Carruthers by Dr. Fergus MacTavish, Ph.D. in Science, of Edinborough Scotland, followed by five-days of lectures by Dr. Lana Masters.

Dr. Masters' introduction by Dr. Philip Carruthers of Canada, even with brevity, took a full hour to cover her educational background and her worldwide accomplishments.

Dr. Lana Masters (Ph.D.sc., CPA, C.A., LLB, M.D., M.B.A.) was ready. She needed no notes or files. She stood at the podium without pen, pencil, paper, voice recorder, computer or any of the 1990's intracellular marvels. Her great brain sufficed.

The huge press gallery was one floor above the attendees, but located (in a circular fashion) so that the media personnel could see most all of 2,100 people seated, and with a clear view of the head table and podium. TV cameras were placed throughout the huge center.

Security was not a concern to Lana Masters for herself. She felt impregnable. She did however insist security be intense so as to provide, to the greatest extent possible, the safety of the residents of Istanbul and for the safety of the attendees at this event.

Lana Masters had reason to feel impregnable. She felt certain the Universe's 12 Contollers were her special guardian angles. In addition, this mighty titan was sure her incredible ego would shield her from the most terrifying of incidents.

Hadn't she diffused the terror of Uncle Fred's sexual advances when she was just 12-years old and without recourse? Hadn't she shot out six knees of those three trusted insiders who were attempting to rob H&B Financial and Poors Inc.'s nightly deposit (a wealthy company in which she was an officer) being picked up by Loomis. Hadn't she disappeared into the evening like a mysterious phantom while those three bastards rolled in agony holding their shattered knees? Not one soul out of the hundreds of people who witnessed the whole daring, gory scene had seen Dr. Masters fire those six telling shots. She knew the three men she took out. They were elected members of H&B's 12 member board of directors. At the last moment she and Clark St. James became aware of their plot. These three turncoats were trying to make the heist look like the work of ordinary, everyday thieves in order to divert attention from themselves, so, as brains and bullets would have it, in the end the three "would be" bandits became the set-up-ees rather than the set-up-ers. Lana had chuckled as she disappeared into the thick Manhattan crowd.

Yes, and what about her most life threatening episode? The horrid scare she had on her parents' farm. Her miraculous escape from the big, 2,000 pound Hereford bull when she was just eight years old.

Yes, Big Buster the bull purchased in Great Falls, Montana, by Carl Masters a few years back. This big bovine earned his way on the Masters' huge spread by his valuable fees; fees for the impregnating of high-priced Hereford cows. It was the time of year when the cows were in heat when little Lana Jean's awful experience took place. Big Buster was not scheduled for his regular duty that day, the same day little Lana Jean Masters became within an inch of being "snuffed out." Big Buster was never known as Ferdinand the Bull, the bull with the delicate ego, hell no, no delicate ego for Big Buster. Ever since puberty he had earned the reputation of being one mean Fatha. Other than when eating, chewing his cud, sleeping or fornicating he kept his temper in high gear. His wide rock solid 20-inch brow was capped by two upright thick frightful horns. His balls hung between his massive hind legs like two large grapefruits inside a gray dufflebag. His cloved hooves were big, splayed and sharp. He used his hooves for pawing the ground while snorting unabridged hate through his huge nostrils. His eyes were sinful, foreboding. During his four years following puberty, this huge bovine had rammed through fences thereby freeing himself to roam side roads and even some main highways terrifying drivers as he plunged headlong toward their vehicles. He had gored three farm hands. Each one had been rescued and survived. Subsequently all three entered new fields of endeavor. He had smashed corrals, damaged tractors, combines and other farm machinery. He had even barged through the big metal barn door on one occasion ripping the door off its upper track and its bolted down bottom and dented it, as if it was made of paper mache. Everyone was scared shitless of Big Buster. But the big S.O.B. was worth $400,000. "Waddaya going ta do?" Big Buster was worked up this day because of his lack of a good fuck.

Showing his provocation for this unforgivable oversight he pawed, snorted and bellowed like the raging bull he was. Cowboy Ellis had herded Big Buster to the wrong quarter section of the farm that day, the very quarter section and the very day little Lana Jean Masters had decided to ride her huge stallion Sir Galahad.

It was a beautiful day. Indigenous meadowlarks' singular, glorious sounds filled the air with their delightful songs. A gentle west wind blew causing the fresh new leaves of the young birch trees (that stretched several hundred yards along the trailway that Lana Jean Masters and Sir Galahad were moving) to touch one another in a delectable, sensual unending symphonic rustle. Throaty frogs made their presence known in the pretty creek that flowed alongside the trailway. "What a 'neat' day for a ride," she mused "on my magnificent Sir Galahad, the biggest, strongest, bravest stallion in the whole wide world. I love you Sir Galahad," she murmured as she patted his well-muscled glistening neck.

Once past the tree-lined trailway, Lana Jean touched Sir Galahad's flank with her riding crop and whispered in his ear "faster big guy." Sir Galahad picked up his pace and moved into a smooth gallop. Lana Jean's body fit just right in her western saddle. In order for her to reach her stallion's ears she had to take her feet out of the saddle's stirrups, pull her legs up, place her knees on the upper part of the saddle, take hold of the saddle horn in both hands, and lean as far forward as possible. Once there she could murmur instructions into the ear of her massive steed. Lana Jean was certain this marvelous beast understood her and ergo, like an "Equine Gentleman" accepted her directions. Too, she felt certain that at any cost, he would be her protector.

* * *

Big Buster gave up his bellowing. His angry mind was convinced no female body of his ilk was going to be available for his hot pecker this day. "Shit! I may as well settle myself down, relax, and just chew my cud. But, by God, don't anyone or anything dare get in my way while I await my next bang with Ms. Clarable Cow." He farted.

His eyelids began to droop over those abominable eyes. His tail flicked at those oppressive fucking flies. He slept.

* * *

The farmhouse was about two miles away from Lana Jean and Sir Galahad as Sir Galahad galloped toward the steep prairie rise where Buster was reposing. It was now 3:30 p.m. Lana Jean had promised her mother she would be back by five o'clock to do her homework. She saw the ominous black thunderclouds gathering in the southwest. She estimated the storm would reach the farm about an hour and a half from now. She decided to have Sir Galahad race up to the top of the rise, go down the other side, then ride back to the farm in plenty of time to beat the storm. There she could rub down Sir Galahad, and see to it he was fed, watered and in his stall before the storm hit. Lana Jean loved these spring thunderstorms, they excited her, but she knew these very storms with their blazing lightning and fearful thunder made all the farm animals (other than Big Buster) skittish. At that moment Sir Galahad stumbled. Lana Jean screamed as she flew over Sir Galahad's head. Big Buster awoke with a bellow.

*   *   *

It was 4:00 p.m. when Cowboy Ellis noticed the black menacing clouds advance over the once peaceful horizon. Something since morning had been bothering him. 'Damn it, why can't I settle down,' he thought.

Once again he reviewed his days work. 'My first chore was to ride out to the south west quarter of section 102 where Big Buster was grazing and move the hulking, scary, fucking behemoth to the south east quarter. Shit! That's it, I moved old Buster to the north east quarter by mistake. Dammit all anyway,' Cowboy Ellis admonished himself. 'I'd better tell Hank before he finds out or I'll be in the deep stuff.' As he tugged at his Stetson, his face paled. 'Jesus H.Christ, I think I overheard little Lana Jean say earlier this afternoon she was going for a ride on Sir Galahad out to the northeast quarter and wouldn't be back until five. Dammit, Big Buster won't take kindly to her visit. Shit, shit, Big Buster didn't get his daily porkin' today either. He'll be snortin' horny and mad. I hope Hank's at home.' Cowboy Ellis ran off toward Hank's cottage.

*   *   *

Big Buster pawed his way to the top of the rise. He saw the huge stallion testing his left fore leg which moments ago had met up with a large prairie dog hole. He knew that stallion. He had seen him daily for as long as he could remember. "How I'd like to massacre that big mother fucker," Buster thought. Too, he saw a pathetic little human body sprawled out in front of the stallion. Within seconds the little body began to squirm and groan. Buster lowered his head, snorted, and charged straight at the small bundle called Lana Jean.

*　　　*　　　*

"Hank," cowboy Ellis yelled as he banged open the foreman's cottage door, "Hurry, please hurry, I think little Lana's in danger."

*　　　*　　　*

Buster scooped Lana up between his horns and tossed her in the air like a rag doll. She flew several feet but landed on some prairie brush that softened her fall. She was conscious now. She saw her dad's bull charge Sir Galahad. "No," she screamed. Big Buster was just three or four yards away from Sir Galahad. Sir Galahad turned, reared up on his hind legs, neighed a ferocious scream, and began to flail his front legs in the direction of the big Hereford's head. As Buster reached the stallion, the stallion's hooves, which were covered in steel horseshoes, struck the bull's skull. The hooves sheared off Buster's left ear and sliced open a gaping 12-inch gash down the right side of his massive head. Blood spurted everywhere. Big Buster reeled for a moment or two but was oblivious of any pain. He had no intention of altering or slowing his charge. He smashed into Sir Galahad's slick gut and twisting and turning his head he drove his horns through the stallions skin, but the horns did not penetrate far enough into the big steed's innards to prove fatal.

Blood gushed out of the two horn-made holes in Galahad's gut and mixed with the blood spurting from Big Buster's head wounds. Big Buster attempted to gore out the stallion's huge balls but Galahad moved to his left leaving the bull's horns slashing at air. Now Galahad had his hindquarters at right angles to the bull's plentiful body. The beautiful stallion unleashed his muscular hind legs in a tremendous kick, catching Big Buster flush in the ribs. Buster grunted in pain as Galahad's hind hooves smashed into his side, cracking some of his ribs like kindling. The force of those jackhammer hooves broke Buster's tough hide, which caused more blood to flow. Buster fell winded. Galahad now screaming with fury reared up again and once more drove his front hooves into Buster's face. Buster's left eye exploded leaving a blood filled hole where the eye should have been. Buster was 'non-plussed' with his performance. Now he was hurt. He ached. He was dazed. His eyesight from his remaining eye was blurred. Blood gushed from the terrible wounds inflicted on him by Sir Galahad, but the big bovine was determined not to lose this battle. He saw the stallion glaring at him with blood streaming down the inside of his rippling muscular legs. Lana watched frightened but fascinated. A loud crack of thunder punctured the still forebodiong air. Big Buster struggled to his feet. He bunched his hind legs, tightened all his powerful muscles, lowered his disfigured head, bawled a frightful scream and with the force of a Sherman tank charged straight at his much taller adversary. This time when the stallion rose on his hind legs to pummel the bull's head with his flailing hooves, he was just a part of a second too slow. His flailing hooves struck each side of the bull's back instead of its head. This did nothing except to slice up more of Buster's hide, no crippling damage, just more blood. Sir Galahad was caught by this bloody freight train. The one-ton bull with its horns planted in Sir Galahad's midsection lifted the 1,500 pound stallion (now whinnying an ungodly sound) into the air then brought him down with bone-crunching force onto the hard prairie ground. Sir Galahad snorted, grunted and gasped for air as his lungs constricted from the force of the impact. Now he felt his insides being torn apart by the grinding motion of Big Buster's horns. He screamed as his body convulsed. Big Buster drove his head into Galahad's midsection until his brow touched Galahad's hide. Buster then threw his head back, pushed his horns upward, ripping

Galahad's midsection wide open allowing Galahad's viscera to spill out. Yellowish bile together with blood gushed from the dreadful wounds. Guts poured down the magnificent horse's side. Lana vomited.

Lightning flashed above them followed by despicable booming thunder. Rain spewed. Lightning dazzled the sky again lighting the surroundings which displayed a huge raging bull standing stiff legged on a prairie rise. Galahad was making one last painful effort to rise. He failed. Buster, with blood and snot drooling from his flared nostrils, had lowered his head ready to begin to gore other parts of the stallion's body. Lana, still retching, saw a large rock, a good eight-inches in diameter, not two feet from her right hand. She slithered through her vomit over to it and grasped it in her small hands. She picked it up and rushed at Big Buster. She reached him just as the blood-covered bovine was about to deliver the *coup de grace* to Sir Galahad. She smashed the rock hard against the bull's grapefruit like balls. Buster bellowed, crossed his hind legs, then squatted. Still bellowing and in a frightful rage he looked up at the demonic sky which was now assaulting the earth with ear-shattering thunder, unmeasurable volts of death dealing electricity and slashing hail.

# # #

Carl Masters, Hank and Cowboy Ellis had sped out to the rise situated in the farm's north east quarter in the Masters' powerful Land Rover hoping that's where they would find Lana Jean and Sir Galahad.

"Jesus, good Lord Jesus" Carl Masters howled when he saw his little girl and the bloody carnage surrounding her as another bolt of lightning discharged lighting up the grotesque picture on the prairie rise. Hank was just raising his high-powered rifle to shoot Big Buster, when Lana stepped in front of her recent nemesis. "No Hank," she screeched. "No, please, no, I think my stallion is dead," she cried. "No more deaths please…it's pointless…Sir Galahad proved to me to be a hero beyond description today. He could have left me. He could have run away and left me alone with Big Buster. But no, he stayed and fought for me. Daddy, Hank and Cowboy Ellis, I have just witnessed a combat between two gallant warriers that never will be equaled. Buster and Galahad were fearsome. As monstrous as it may seem to each of you, I wish I had the whole exciting match on tape. My good God, I am sure no such battle as this one has ever been witnessed before by a human. It was a combat of terrifying beauty. Yes…and Big Buster could have killed me at any time he chose. But for some reason he chose not to."

Thunder crackled in the distance.

Sir Galahad was dead. Later that night, the farm's veterinarian injected the wounded bull with a powerful tranquilizer. Buster's ear was found and stitched back in its rightful place. His eye socket was treated and stitched closed. His sliced up sides and face required some 500 stitches. The damnable beast, within a few days, was back on track prostituting his high-priced sperm for one thousand bucks a "lay." Big Buster lived to be the ripe old age of 27. His servicing fees continued on until he was 22. He remained a cussed beast for the rest of his days. Yet Lana and he bonded. Their friendship started the day Sir Galahad died. Lana spent endless hours with the big bovine. She was heartbroken the day he died. Often Lana sobbed when she thought of her two magnificent beasts.

"The Controllers and my robust ego must be watching over me," she concluded.

CHAPTER 29

THE ORIGIN OF THE UNIVERSE...EVE ONE

Warning! Extreme bestiality.

"Good morning. My warmest greetings to each of you here in this grand theater, and to each of you who may be watching or listening to me over the various media. I must say, your patience and understanding will be tested over the next few days."

She turned to Dr. Carruthers and thanked him for his thoughtful introduction. The microphone, TV cameras and Internet were now hers. A splendid means of mass communicating with the estimated two billion people expected to be listening to her "week-long" lecture.

Quiet muffled choruses of laughter along with a gentle smattering of applause met the sophisticated Dr. Masters with her joking emulation of Michael Buffer's "Ladies and Gentlemen, Llllllllllllet's get ready to rumble." She guessed it would take some magic to warm up this crowd. Lana Masters knew, however, if she turned her charisma up a few notches it wouldn't take her long to have most everyone in the convention hall 'eating out of her hand.'

She was dressed in a cool powder-blue suit, whose jacket and skirt hugged her miraculous form. The suit was tailored exquisitely. Without intent it showed clearly Dr. Lana Masters was the most gorgeous, curvaceous woman in the world. The skirt was very mini. The jacket's lapels were long and narrow and met at a single powder-blue cloth button just in from the mid-part of her well rounded hips. She wore a cool, soft white cotton crewneck sweater under her jacket. Her jewelry consisted of simple pearl earrings and an emerald green brooch in the shape of the world, which was pinned to her suit's left lapel. Her tanned legs were bare. Her shoes were Ponti originals, semi high-heeled and finished in a soft almost cloth-like material. They too were powder blue. Some of her sensational full, long tawny blond hair flowed over the front of her right shoulder, the remainder cascaded down her lovely back. Dr. Masters knew she had an immense problem on her hands. She knew she had to take both men's and women's minds off her tantalizing beauty if she wanted to get their attention to her forthcoming words. Her confidence did not waver in the slightest. In order to shake the audience out of its stupefaction over the sight of her, she knew just what to say. She woke them from their lustful dreams following her "Lllllllllllets get ready to rumble," with words never heard before from a public speaker who was about to address such a genteel audience. In a loud clear level voice she trumpeted, "Hear me, my fucking brethren and my fucking sistren."

Shocked, the attendees sat up, they gasped at this verbal assault.

"A cloud of lust appears to have engulfed your minds this pleasant morning. I can see it in your 4,200 eyes. Is it my appearance that has each of your egos entrapped in your sense of sight? Are your expectations of a night in bed with me is irrefutable? Please, put your lust back a couple of notches. Let's check out my socialistic drivel, my naiveté, my utopianism, my religious bombardments, my daring attacks on big business, big government, big unions, my humanist wishes, my solutions to worldwide problems, femininity, ad infinitum. Now my friends thank you for attending this symposium. Whilst I recognize a symposium is limited to the discussion of a single subject, my selection of the word is quite proper. You see friends, every topic I will be discussing for the next three days will relate inexorably to one issue and one issue only, the inherent dignity due every human being living now and in the future on our globe.

"Ladies and gentlemen I know of your individual powers, prowess, grittiness, intelligence and unending endurance. Dr. Phil Carruthers, my gracious mentor from the rodeo capital of the world, Calgary, which is located in the pristine province of Alberta, which in turn is located in my stunning homeland...Canada...has told me so on many occasions. He likened your interminable tenacity and strengths to last year's winner of the prodigious Calgary Stampede award, 1996's All Around Cowboy, and ladies and gentlemen, that cowboy was 67 years old at the time." A few titters were heard among Lana's audience. "The 67 year old was being interviewed by Calgary's number one sportscaster, Ben Dover. Ben marveled at great length about the elder cowboy's physical prowess. After several minutes of the sportscasters words of praise, the somewhat bored cowboy drawled, "If ya' think I'm so great, you should meet my pa...he's 89 years old and still plays corner linebacker for the Dallas Cowboys."

"You must be joking," Ben responded in awe.

"Nope, it's true," the 67 year old countered.

"Great Heavens," Ben gasped, "what an extraordinary family. Here you are, an amazing physical specimen at 67, the Calgary Stampede's All Around Cowboy, and your father...my God...89 years old and still a professional football player. Sir, with respect I must meet your father and interview him."

"Sorry son, you cain't. Pa's not home. He's in High River stadin' up for my granpa. My grandpa's 114 years old and he's gettin' married agin.""

"Well now this is, uhh, how can I put it?" Ben Dover choked, eyes bulging. "Hail Mary, Holy Moses and may the saints preserve us. As I said a moment ago, here you are an amazing 67 year old physical specimen, your father's an 89 year old footballer, and now your grandfather, your family's mighty sire is 114 years old and wants to get married.

"No son," the cowboy grunted, "ya got that all wrong, grandpa don't want to get married, he has to!"

The laughter was sparse.

Dr. Masters understood. This was after all, the nineties.

She peered out at her huge audience in a most captivating way. **"Genesis,"** she said. She took her microphone in her hand and moved out from behind the lectern. "With utmost respect to past and present day scientists, astrologists, archaeologists, to anyone who has sought the elusive answer to the tantalizing question, where and how did it all begin? That is, the universe, galaxies, the stars, planets, suns, moons, asteroids, nebula, supreme beings?

Bell, Uranus, Newton, Laplace, Kant, Hubble, all the great scientists of the world to date have theorized, hypothesized, and struggled to answer this confounding question. All have come up empty. God suffices as answers for a huge proportion of the world's population to this humbling question. The bible exhorts in a mere two pages the creation of the universe and earth. In Genesis 2, the Bible states '*and the earth was without form and void.*' There's no question about that statement. In fact the Bible is quite convincing through to Genesis 31. However the Bible, like every other text, fails to answer the gnawing question...**who created the creator?**

The scientific community seems to hypothesize the universe was a dense something or other that began to expand (the big bang) some six billion years ago and evolved into its present structure. Perhaps it did, but what pray tell, created this something or other?"

Lana studied the congregation. Then smiling she said "I know the answer my friends. I shall take but one day to explain and answer the question in its entirety." She took a few steps away from the podium, then, rather dramatically. said, **"nothing."** Then she repeated the word, **"nothing."**

"There was no universe before the beginning. There were no gases, no space, no air, no time, no energy and no gravitational pull. There were no galaxies, stars, planets, suns, moons, asteroids, nebula, supreme beings. Some of her attendees squirmed when Lana concluded, "nothing, sweet fuck all."

"Before the beginning it wasn't truly a void, it was nothing. How many years, or how long was there nothing? Because there was nothing, there were no years, no months, weeks, days, hours, minutes or seconds, there was no length of time before the beginning because, ladies and gentlemen, there was no such thing as time."

Lana Masters grasped the microphone, moved out from behind the lectern, stopped mid-stage, legs spread slightly apart, and in a Churchillian voice paraphrased Dr. Martin Luther Kings famous words, *'I've had a dream.'* "Yes ladies and gentlemen I too thought I had had a dream." A pause ensued. "Without derogating in any way from Dr. King's dream, I must say my dream was not a dream at all. IT was in fact a reality. It was a message brought to me by **12 beings.** ***Beings not of this world, but of the universe. 12 Controllers who not only manage the Universe but who are the Universe.***"

A giant screen had been installed behind the podium at the behest of Dr. Phillip Carruthers. Dr. Carruthers wanted every attendee to be able to see "up close" Lana Masters as she spoke. He wanted the 2,100 "attendees" to see her eyes, her expressions, her every movement all of which were so important to note in conjunction with her words. Dr. Carruthers knew that Dr. Masters' sincerity would never be in question if audiences could look into her eyes as she addressed them. The giant screen made this possible.

"These beings explained to me how the universe began," Dr. Masters said. "I was busy in my study the day I was visited by them. It was Sunday, April 20th just past. They made no jarring, thunderous appearance when they came and they were not frightening. They introduced themselves as ***Eves One, Two, Three, Four, Five, Six and***

Adams One, Two, Three, Four, Five, Six. They came to the front door of my home like any other guests might, rang the doorbell, and when I opened the door there they were six women and six men dressed in casual attire. I must say at the outset I had the feeling they were not of this world. Not aliens, but beings of some other status, even though they looked like any young woman or man from the neighborhood.

I invited them in. Why did I ask them in? They could be trouble yet I was not one bit concerned about my safety with them. They entered, made themselves 'at home' and began exchanging pleasantries with me. They asked how I was. I thought in my heart they knew how I was and every other thing about me yet I answered, 'well, thank you.' After more small talk, I asked if I could get them a drink. They said that would be nice and, as one, they requested a glass of the *King of Beers, Budweiser*, of all things ('hoh khay' I said to myself disbelieving what I had just heard). I obliged. (Jesus Christ, I thought to myself these are not beings of another status they are just some scam artists on the prowl for more suckers.)"

"No," Eve One said, "we are not 'just some scam artists on the prowl for more suckers. No Dr. Masters, we are the Universe. We know your every thought Dr.Masters. ('Shit,' I complained secretly). "Shit," Eve One said. ('Blank your mind,' I said) "Blank your mind," Eve One mimicked with a smile.

"Lana," Eve One continued, "We are here to visit on you **the origin of the Universe,** the basic secrets of the Universe, and our position pertaining to our tiny planet earth. As well we want you to understand the one hundred and twenty three billion trillions of formations which earthlings refer to as galaxies, planets, stars, asteroids, suns, moons, dust and gaseous formations are **an assemblage of cells which in total are us, the 12 Controllers.** These cells make us the Universe just as surely as your cells make you a living person. You see Lana, beyond the Universe there is nothing and as we visit the information on you, we will explain the danger of nothing as it pertains to the Universe. You will find that the complexities of the Universe from its beginning are not as complex as you earthlings think. In fact the complexities of the Universe are no more complex than the birth and the growth of the computer age which you are now experiencing here on our earth.

However, the confoundedness of the human race during its evolvement is shameful. We shall come to that shameful subject in due course Dr. Masters. For the nonce it suffices for us to say we shall not interfere in our earthling's evolvement, even though we decry the dreadful inequities humans have imposed on other humans from their beginnings. I must say Dr. Masters, on thousands of occasions we have discussed the possibility of exterminating all the earth's humans because of their depravities and displace them with some other life form, much in the same manner as we did with the reptiles some seventy million years ago.

However, Doctor, whilst we say we will not interfere with our earth's peoples evolvement for the nonce, we give no covenant thereto. In the event humans fall a mere three-quarters of one percent more into the inhumane abyss they have sunk into at this moment in time, starting from this day forward, Sunday, April 20th, 1997, by your calendar, we will displace all humans with some other life form. Please keep this in mind. We have no intention of warning our world's population when the three-quarter percent is exceeded. Quite simply, we will rid our globe of people without any fanfare. You, Lana Masters, can inform the peoples of our message to you in any fashion you like, but be assured, you, Lana Masters, will receive little help from us."

"Eves and Adams," I said somewhat angry, "how in God's name do I know you are who you say you are? You could be 12 human cranks from anywhere. Doom agents. Just a bunch of fanatic assholes! Militants! Whatever?"

"No, Doctor, we are none of those. Come with us for a moment."

Suddenly I was facing my beloved deceased great grandmother.

"Believe child," my great grandmother said.

The next moment I was back in my living room with the 12 'whoevers.'

"So you mesmerized me for a moment. Hypnotic nonsense," I said.

"No, my dear, we refrain from doing magic of any kind," Eve one stated, "and I must say, Lana Masters, it is not necessary for us to prove our authenticity to you or to anyone else on Earth for that matter."

"But, Lana Masters, as we now toy with your psyche and karma, please observe."

Dr. Lana Masters closed her slightly parted legs. She moved back to the lectern, re-set the hand microphone back in its place and gasped. 'What in God's name is happening to me? As I sit here in my living room in my Manhattan condo staring at 12 whoevers April 20th, 1997, coincidentally, I find myself on May 5th, 1997 behind a lectern in the beautiful convention center in Istanbul, Turkey. How can this be? How can I be in two places at once, and on two different dates?'

Suddenly the audience burst into a resounding applause and stood cheering and hooting like 2,100 frenzied rock fans at a beer guzzling, pot smoking rock concert. "More Lana, more yes baby, more," they hollered, "sock it to us—whooo eeee. Keep on coming, Lana. Rock us and roll us."

Dr. Masters wondered at the burst of applause, the rude cheers, and the standing ovation being given her by the 2,100 attendees. What had she done to this point to deserve her audience's boisterous reception? She was unaware of the sight on the huge screen behind her. She turned, "Oh my good God," she screamed.

Drs. Mactavish, Carruthers and the council members seated at the head table all gasped, hyperventilated, and with their hands raised to cover their mouths, their eyes riveted on the big screen, prayed that all the lights in the center would extinguish themselves.

"Can you see this damnation of a scene, Lana Masters?" Eve One bellowed in a voice that sounded hollow as if in an echo chamber miles away, yet ominously close.

"Yes, yes," Lana Masters shouted pitifully. "Please, oh please get rid of that…that…"

"Listen to your appreciative audience, Lana. Everyone loves every degrading moment of this sight. Why?" Eve One questioned.

"I don't know why," Lana cried. "Please, I beg of you, stop this deviltry."

"Are you enjoying any erotic feelings from this experience, Lana?" Eve One questioned.

"Yes, oh yes, oh dear God I am," Lana responded gasping.

The 2,100 crazed invitees clamored for more, screaming, "Sock it to her Fido! Whoooeee, fuck, screw, blow, Lana and a 21-skidoo too," they shrieked.

The big slobbering Great Dane pumped his huge red prick between Lana's buttocks like a piston. Lana held two upright bars in each hand, her stomach lying flat on a velvet covered table, her back to the Great Dane, legs spread revolving her hips in perfect unison with the Great Dane's thrusts. She was moaning and sobbing all at the same time. The big dog had its front paws fixed on the table and his hind feet placed against a settee. He was positioned in such a way that he could ravish Lana Masters without restriction. Lana was sucking, the dog was howling. In front of Lana was a nude, handsome devilish-looking man who had his swollen cock in Lana's mouth. The man had his head tilted back groaning ecstatically as Lana mouthed his manhood. All three were ready to come in an avalanche of delight when…suddenly it all ended.

Lana was back at home with the 12 'beings.' She was panting, perspiring. Her panties were soaked. She looked abysmal. She cried as she looked at the 12 unknowns.

"Dr. Masters," Adam one spoke, "I think we have demonstrated in a most disgusting yet quite significant way our authenticity to you. We have the power to do anything we wish to do. In front of your very eyes we could remove our sun and our moon, your sun and moon in your glossary, in a twinkling of an eye. The episode we have just put you through is trifling, it's infinite, it is not worthy of debate, it is the smallest in the scheme of cosmic things but, to you and your audience it was beastly, bestiality, gross, horrid. To us it was a despicable example of what humans refer to as 'kinky' and unacceptable sex. We will touch on this later.

"Now, my dear we wish to visit on you the origin of the Universe, but before settling in on this subject, we want to assure you the scene just passed will be remembered by you alone. Please, Lana, take some time to freshen up.

CHAPTER 30

THE CONTROLLERS DECRIED

When Lana returned from a thorough scrubbing, Adam One began his dissertation.

"To start you off on the right foot Dr. Masters you should be aware of the fact that at the moment, in your earth's time dimensions, you are experiencing a closed time frame causing April 20th, 1997 and May 5th, 1997 to be one and the same day. While you are listening to our discourse to you on April 20th, you are at the same time preparing mental notes of this discourse on the morning of May 5th so that you can relate the Universe's beginning to your audience as told to you by us. Now, at this very moment, you are continuing your lecture to your 2,100 attendees as if no interruption occurred. Please note, unseen by your audience, we will be in your presence until we advise you otherwise."

*   *   *

"Yes," Dr. Masters said, "these 12 beings, whom henceforth I shall refer to as Controllers, explained to me how the Universe began and how it evolved to its present state. They told me, without equivocation, they have absolute control of the Universe. They told me they continue to expand its size. And they told me they are able to change with precision, at any time, the structure of any or all solar systems in the Universe including the placement or replacement of the most minute nebulae and any molecular entities therein.

"And, ladies and gentlemen, these Controllers do exist, believe me. They are not incorporeal. They are real. Do not slight them. They control the Universe's destiny in every respect. They can produce more extraterrestrial bodies, granite, gaseous, molecular, whatever at their whim. In a trice they can destroy any universal object if inclined to do so. As I stated earlier, the Controllers refer to themselves as Eves One, Two, Three, Four, Five, Six and Adams One, Two, Three, Four, Five and Six. They are cheerful entities who emphasize happiness and love, however, be clear on the fact they can be brutal and dispassionate. If after minutes, hours, months, years or centuries of misbehavior by any universal organism these Controllers can dispatch with such an organism by replacing it in its entirety, destroying it outright, or simply leaving it defunct."

At this juncture some attendees shouted disparaging remarks at Dr. Masters. Lana waited until the hubbub stopped. Thunder rumbled outside the convention center, yet no clouds occupied the skies. Some invitees got the jitters knowing the skies were clear, yet they heard thunder. Lana stood unperturbed. "As I stated earlier," Dr. Masters continued, "we humans must not fall three quarters of one percent below our present level of human behaviors lest we, the world's populous, is made extinct by the Controllers."

More disparaging remarks.

More intense thunder is heard from the blue, unblemished skies.

"Remember, my distinguished audience, we haven't the slightest idea of what position we hold on the Controllers' chart marking our present behavior. Did it take only a short while for we humans to fall 99-1/4 percent from perfect behaviors (our beginnings) to our present troubled worldwide state? Are our beginnings as intellectual beings deemed by the Controllers to be a scant 40,000 years ago? Think ladies and gentlemen, that is only 800 grandfathers ago, just a blink of an eye in the Universal scheme of things. If we humans have fallen 99-1/4% from 40,000 years ago to now, on a predetermined (Controller behavior) scale then we have been most irresponsible for some 39,700 years. Aren't we an enviable group? And friends, assuming a continuing rate of behavioral decline in the future computed at the same rate experienced as it may have been in the past then, by jove, we will be extinct in a mere 300 years from now. Only some six future grandfathers."

"Blasphemous, you cursing witch," some religious attendees shouted.

"Shame, shame," others taunted.

Lightning hit the building with a dreadful bolt of death-dealing electricity. Ear splitting thunder crackled all at the same time. Every light in the building was 'knocked out.' But for some eerie, inexplicable reason the screen behind Lana stood out untouched by the hellish bolt. It remained lit and focused without blight on Lana's unchanged countenance. People screamed. Many were ready to flee from this frightful show from the heavens.

But now the large screen showed Lana Masters raising her arms denoting that as long as she was present in the convention center everyone was safe.

"Please take you seats friends, the electrical show is over." With that the frightened attendees sat. Lana's soothing voice assured them of their safety. At that moment all the lights in the amphitheater came on.

Some, however, continued their harassment. "Set-up" they shouted, "set-up for God's sake. We have been royally set-up by this scheming woman, this pinko, this despiser of good old capitalism, this whole damn show was orchestrated by this Masters woman and her hired sound effects men. She's a flaming fraud. How can there be lightning with no clouds? How can all the lights go out except for the screen light from a non-existent bolt of lightning? Come on everyone, let's get real, let's vacate these premises, let us leave Lana Masters alone with her non-existent beings. She's a "well trained" fraud and manipu…"

The building shook as Lana Masters begged the upstarts to 'cool down.' "Please, I have no idea what the Controllers may be planning now. Please, just hear me out."

"Fraud," they continued to shout.

The building shuddered as lightning filled the building's interior and thunder howled in agony. Then silence, an eerie silence. The attendees sat as if frozen wondering what was to come of all this. A loud rasping, grating noise was heard above them. With trepidation the crowd looked up. The Convention Center's roof was grinding its way open, even though the roof was not a retractable one. Now the bright daytime sky was in plain sight, with a gray full moon hanging in the center. The full moon when darkness abounds, allows the countryside to become festooned with werewolves. Some attendees gasped when they thought they saw the moon shudder. Now blood, shit, puke and guts gurgled down the convention center's aisles while disgusting phlegm, mixed with squirming maggots hung from the noses and mouths of the dissenters.

Christ, the moon did shudder. It settled back for a moment. Then it began to whirl in an oblong uncontrolled manner. It seemed to enlarge itself. No, it wasn't enlarging itself, it was fucking well hurtling itself toward earth. Jesus Christ, it was. It was headed for earth. It became bigger and bigger. It began to block out the sunlight. Observatory personnel around the world at first were curious but now they cowered in fear. The air mass in front of the moon was pushed toward earth at a terrifying speed. Oceans blew apart as if they were puddles. Mountains flew into space as if they were pebbles. But the convention center stood erect. The moon continued its reckless propulsion as it drove itself toward its inevitable collision with the earth. People fainted, farted, puked, prayed, shat themselves. Lovers geared down. Blowjobees lost their dicks to clamped teeth. 6 billion people scurried every which way looking for refuge. Golfers hesitated before putting. The Vatican tried to abscond with its treasures. Bill Gates said 'shit.' The Donald said 'ah fuck.' Monica said no not yet I haven't flavored the cigar. Traders on Wall Street thought someone had pulled down the blinds and turned up the heat, after all the markets were booming, no need to look out the windows.

It hit.

With the exception of the people in Istanbul's convention center, the lovers, blowjobbers, golfers, Vatican, traders, Gates, The Donald, Monica together with 6 billion people in unison "hit" the dust on their bellies. Everyone covered their ears, clamped their eyes shut, prayed to any old God and waited for the end. They waited and waited. Shit, the waiting took an eternity. Things seemed calm. People stirred. They looked up. They let go of their ears and by damn if at that precise moment a tiny "pop" was heard around the world. Adam 6 had passed wind. The moon was back up in the sky where it belonged. The aisles cleared. The building resumed its original structure, clean, palatial and comfortable. The dissenters once again became listeners. They noted a rather foul taste in their mouths.

"Hurrmph! It must be the Turkish coffee," they presumed.

* * *

The foregoing trauma was forgotten by everyone with the exception of Dr. Masters. She continued her lecture as if nothing had happened.

"Within the hour I will cover people's actions considered to be unconscionable by the 12 Controllers. These actions, if continued by the world's citizenry, will contribute to the dreaded three-quarter percent total befalling us. But be comforted ladies and gentlemen because if peoples' future actions are considered to be humanistic by the Controllers this will cause the Controllers to reduce that 99-1/4 percent level, thereby lengthening the human race's occupation of this planet.

"It is well to remember the 'Mesozoic Era' in the life of Planet Earth. A period of some 155 million years, give or take a year or two, known by our scientists as the 'Age of Reptiles.' Dinosaurs, as we believe, flourished during those 155 million years and were the dominant form of animal life on our planet.

"Now here we humans are, existing in a so-called intelligent manner for some 40,000 to 50,000 years yet we may be ready for extinction in another 300 years if we carry on in so many of our perverse ways.

"If obliteration is in store for us 300 years from now, good old 'Dinny' will have outlasted us by about 154,960,000 years," Lana said smiling.

Dr. Masters turned to Dr. Carruthers. Dr. Carruthers announced that the meeting's agenda called for a 15-minute 'coffee break.' The time was now 10:30 a.m., Monday, May 5th, 1997.

* * *

Lana returned to the Lectern. She was 'worn' by the morning's foreboding exhibitions. She knew she alone had any recollections of them. She reached back into her ample reservoir of strength.

"Ladies and gentlemen the Controllers have informed me of the 'beginning.' I now bring you this information. Before the beginning, as I said earlier, there was nothing. Exactly 51 billion, 963 million, 507,000, 323 years, 9 months and 12 days at zero hours the Universe began. It began as a sub-microscopic movement of nothing. Nothing, as we know, means non-existent. How then could there be a movement in something that is non-existent? None of our current mathematical formulae abides by this.

"Given that worldwide vocabularies are prohibitively restrictive in instances of great depth, I will use the most simplistic terms to explain this phenomena.

"It happened thusly. ***Nothing moved.*** Nothing moved can be looked at as a double entendre, a dichotomy…a division into two…thus 'nothing moved' can mean no movement, or it can mean movement vis-à-vis it moved, nothing itself moved, it took action, nothing moved and rubbed against itself. **Taken in the last instance and going back 51 billion plus years, nothing moved sub-microscopically and caused, by**

minute friction, a sub-microscopic bubble. This finite stripling," Dr. Masters said, "was the beginning of the universe."

"Yes friends, this tiny bubble was the beginning. "Not six days per the bible, not sperm and ovum, and not a massive explosion known as the 'big bang' six billion years ago," she said. "This bubble was the birth of life, it was the birth of the Universe. As a result of that infinitesimal friction there came about within the sub-microscopic newly born bubble, space, energy and time, albeit, the minutest space imaginable to allow for energy and time to exist. Like all newborns, energy within the bubble was boundless. To begin, like any infant, matters within the interior of the bubble squirmed and kicked and floundered without reason thereby, enlarging themselves within the domain of nothing. You see my friends, the ceaseless energetic bumping against the unwitting, lethargic encirclement of nothing allowed the bubble to grow unheeded."

Dr. Masters scanned the audience. She waited for calls of disagreement from the scientific communities' representatives. None were forthcoming. "Damn," she thought, "have the Controllers taken over the senses of her attendees?"

"No," spake Eve One in Lana's ear, "we have not taken over the senses of your attendees."

"Oh shit," Lana said under her breath.

"Oh shit," Eve Three laughed. "Go on, my dear, your audience awaits you. Remember we are at your side."

Lana continued, "It will be an exciting challenge for scientists worldwide to isolate nothing and discover how it moved those 51 billion years ago. In my view this discovery by our scientists will be made within a year from now. Compared to past scientific achievements, this challenge will be child's play."

She took a sip of water. She awaited her next thought. "The Controllers informed me that the bubble grew rapidly in relation to size, but slow in relation to solar management. During its embryonic stage, which lasted for some 3,000 years, the bubble, which will be referred to as the Universe henceforth, grew to the size of Earth's moon. By the end of the bubble's first year of existence several billion molecules were formed as a result of the static caused by the relentless energy bombarding every 'which way' in the bubble's confines. The groups of atoms, protons and neutrons, making up the molecules whirled about like kids in a play yard battering the walls of nothing, thereby ever increasing the universe's size. Good fucking stuff eh gang?

"Careful," Eve One warned, "you swear too much, Lana. We don't care one whit about what humans call swearing, but in spite of the '*non-sequitur*,' paradoxical pretense of the bulk of the human species who claim to be righteous, yet think and do foul things, become virtuous and shocked only when the word fuck is spoken."

"Adam Six," Lana questioned, "do you think morally I am corrupt?"

"No, Lana, all 12 of us chose you as our favorite among the five billion, nine hundred and seventy-six thousand, two hundred and twelve people who were alive April 20th, 1997. However we do despise the cruelties you visited upon your Uncle Fred, your upcoming rat infestation of your guest, your shooting out the knees of H & B's directors and your rather foul tongue. You will hear later on in this assembly as you speak to invitees our judgments of morals because you, Lana, will be reciting our judgments to the assembly as to what constitutes, shall we say, good and bad."

"Thank you Adam Six," Lana said.

Lana looked straight into the eyes of her audience. "With respect, ladies and gentlemen, do forgive me for my outbursts of profanity. As I'm sure you know, my 'cussing' is known as my Achilles heel." Many in the audience "twinged."

"To try to detail every stage of the growth of this bubble and the evolutionary changes therein over the last 51 billion years would take an enormous length of time. But I must tell you I have the knowledge, I know the history, I am acquainted with the most subordinate intimacy from the beginnings of the Universe to date. I have been so informed of these facts by the Universe's Twelve Controllers. As well, these Controllers have informed me that the task of learning the detail of the Universe's beginnings to modern times will be left in the hands of our scientific community. The Controllers 'hope' humans will have the good sense to reverse the trend toward obliteration and make progress in 'clawing back' the 99-1/4% morass we have plunged ourselves into in order to give scientists time to complete their study. Let it be made clear, the Controllers congratulate scientists for their in-depth foresight and their remarkable achievements to date."

Lana turned to Dr. Carruthers.

Dr. Carruthers called for a break in the meeting. It was twelve o'clock noon. News people rushed to communicate with editors. Television anchors spoke their pieces to the masses. Interviews abounded. The Hubbub was deafening. Who was this magnetic beauty, a goddess? Damn, this bubble theory makes sense. Three hundred years…? doesn't sound unrealistic. Was Stephen King writing her speeches? Blasphemy! Good old-fashioned bullshit! The meeting reconvened. It was 1:15.

* * *

"Now, ladies and gentlemen, I will outline the advent of the Twelve Controllers. I must inform you while the words I speak come from my mouth, their meanings are not conceived by me. No, ladies and gentlemen, my voice mechanism is simply a conduit being used by Eve One to bring you the information pertaining to their advent. Please be assured friends, in a twinkling of an eye the Controllers could convince the masses of their authenticity. Do not dismiss this fact out of hand. It could be tragic if you do so…" At that moment, Eve One spoke using Lana voice.

"We the Controllers can in an instant make known to every living cell in our Universe our Existence, Domination and Control. But this is not our intention, nor our policy. Our ongoing policy has been to create matters within our Universe and with a 'jump start' given by us, watch each creation grow and develop on its own without our interference. If, during the course of any developing physical matter, we see the development going astray, we may straighten it out, dispense with it in its entirety or leave the cell devoid of living things. We have other alternatives too numerous to mention here. Now Lana, you have our permission to carry on with your deliberations about our genesis and our presesnt day status. Just one codicil though my sweet one, we can depart your presence at any time and leave you on your own, so Lana, be discerning.

Lana continued. "I repeat, Ladies and Gentlemen, the words I speak to you are those of Eye One. She has permitted me to carry on. Now, as I was saying..."

"Excuse me Dr. Masters," Dr. Carruthers interjected, "what you are saying as regards these so-called Controllers seems to us at this head table, and, I am certain too, your esteemed audience, to be rather preposterous. Why on earth would these dominant Gods and Goddesses of yours use you, a mere earthling, to bring this far-fetched, super-powered information to us in such a circuitous fashion? Why don't they speak to us directly? Why don't they show themselves to us in whatever 'fashion' they choose and prove their authenticity themselves? Why all the secrecy? Good gracious Dr. Masters, you have spent this morning and part of this afternoon bringing us this 'tale' of 12 Universal Controllers without one shred of evidence. You say to us, 'in a twinkling of an eye these Controllers could convince the masses of their authenticity,' you say they are almighty powerful...that they have ultimate control of the Universe...and on and on and on."

"One moment Dr. Carruthers," Lana Masters interrupted. "Considering the God Christians have worshipped for so many years, has appeared only once in our Biblical times and that was in the form of a burning bush to an aging Moses. What proof do you have of his existence?"

"Well, Dr. Masters, he did give us his son Jesus," Dr. Carruthers replied, "An ultimate act of supreme sacrifice."

"I am not attempting an exegesis of the scriptures, Dr. Carruthers. I am not promoting agnosticism. I am relating to the world the facts pertaining to the beginnings of time, space and energy, not some mumbo-jumbo bullshit emanating from graspers."

"Dr. Masters, as much as I admire, love and respect you, I find your cursing to be disrespectful, crude, boorish and…"

"Yes," Eve One whispered in Dr. Carruthers ear. "Give Lana a good tongue lashing for her swearing, but, Dr. Carruthers, believe her every word, she tells the truth. It is me Eve One whispering in your ear."

Dr. Carruthers all but swooned.

"Yes my gentle man, it is me, Eve One. Please note at this moment you are in the main boardroom of this assembly hall with Dr. Masters and my 11 associates. Now Dr. Carruthers, I should like you to meet Eves Two to Six and Adams One to Six and me, Eve One."

Dr. Carruthers paled. He shivered. Gad. Suddenly he was back at the head table in the assembly hall sitting in his position as chairperson, ready to continue to debate the issue of the Twelve Controllers with Lana Masters. Dr. Carruthers found his thinking to be clear, why? His mind told him he just may have met Lana's 12 Controllers, so how is it possible his thinking be clear? Gad, if it is true what a…a happening…gad, no word in any language would be able to express his wonderment, his emotional exaltation and his jubilation…Great Jehovah. "Dr. Masters, Lana, my dear, please," he gasped then hesitated. His mind was still fixed on his immaculate perception of these 12 Goddesses and Gods. Dear me was I "hornswoggled" by this clever Dr. Lana Masters?

"No," Eve One murmured in Dr. Carruthers ear. "You were not hornswoggled by the clever Dr. Lana Masters." The good doctor flinched. Can Eve One read my thoughts, he wondered. "Yes Dr. Carruthers, I can read your thoughts as can the other Eves and Adams.

We can read the minds and we can influence, if we wish, every living thing on our planet Earth."

"Dear me, I must be dreaming. This can't be happening to me. The presence of these so-called Controllers must be an illusion."

"You are not dreaming, Dr. Carruthers, it is happening to you. We 12 are not, as you think, illusionary. We are the Universe. Please take my hand." Dr. Carruthers obliged. "You and I are now on the speeding nucleus of ice and gas known to earthlings as the Hale Bopp Comet."

"Please Eve One, I am terrified. I see the comet's tail behind us streaming out forever. God forgive me for my transgressions," Dr. Carruthers prayed. "Why am I having this…this exciting…this euphoric cataclysm. I must be delusional. But I see the tiny Earth below me. It seems so real."

"It is real Dr. Carruthers, you are traveling with me and the comet. And, Dr. Carruthers, I do know the transgressions you are praying to God to forgive you for. Be assured, you are considered by us as a fine member of the human community. Your transgressions are minimal, you have no need to pray."

Dr. Carruthers once again was seated in his chair at the head table in Istanbul's convention hall. "Dr. Masters, I am sorry I interrupted you during your discourse, please continue." Dr. Carruthers otherwise was speechless. Now he began to feel Lana's words may be factual. His mind still was clear. 'My goodness gracious' he thought 'it appears to me I am to be privy to the solution of the most perplexing, inexplicable mystery ever known to mankind. *In media's res.* Inexplicable does not in any way describe the mystery, but what word does?'

"No word in any language is comprehensive enough to describe the mystery," Eve one stated in Dr. Carruther's ear.

The doctor all but jumped. 'Holy Mother Mary,' he thought.

"Holy Mother Mary," Eve One mimicked.

The good doctor smiled. “Please Dr. Masters, continue with your extravagant explanation of the advent of the Twelve Controllers. I feel your discourse pertaining to the Controllers to be most imaginative…”

“Have care Dr. Carruthers, we are not imaginary, we are real. We are the Universe,” warned Adam Three. “Do not annoy us lest we create a cataclysmic event of sufficient proportions to expunge the people of this human ant pile of ours you call earth.”

“Please Adam Three, let’s not bully these earthlings,” Eve one stated. “We must give them some time to recognize our warnings through Dr. Masters.”

“*Touche*,” Adam Three said smiling.

“No, not imaginative, Dr. Masters. I meant to say instead, probably. In any event, I shall not be so impolite as to interrupt you again. Please carry on,” Dr. Carruthers said, his voice quavering. He felt perspiration under his collar, sweat dripping down his back, while beads of moisture stood out on his forehead. ‘Adam Three has frightened me. No more dreadful blunders by me,’ he thought.

“Good thinking, Dr. Carruthers,” Adam Three warned.

“Thank you Dr. Carruthers,” Dr. Masters acknowledged. She continued, “The advent of the Twelve Controllers occurred almost simultaneously. The first organized formation of certain elements was created out of the energetic inner chaos of the undisciplined Universe. Gaseous elements, which we refer to as oxygen and hydrogen, evolved through years of interstitial action then, finally, by natural selection closed the interstice between the two of them to become water. Frictional lightning became a constant occurrence as ever increasing cold unstable masses of oxygen and hydrogen battered into warm masses of oxygen and hydrogen causing raging rain storms. Air itself, as you know, is a fusion of oxygen and nitrogen, together with small amounts of argon, carbon dioxide, water vapor and dust. Nitrogen, the greatest contributor to any atmosphere, was born like oxygen and hydrogen from the frantic bombardment by electromagnetic waves and the blistering movement of molecules. Friction itself increased in intensity as it fed on its own energetic impulses.

"All the while, ladies and gentlemen, a most delicate impasse was developing as the Universe grew. You see the scorching heat resulting from the repetitious friction threatened to burn out the new Universe thus returning it, sans a few dead ashes, to the state of nothing. However energy consisting of heat and electricity from the rambunctious friction as well as light, sound and chemicals combined to do its work…work as defined by our physicists…and finally, after three millennia overwhelmed the frictional heat allowing the newly created Universe to live. To you folks who are not acquainted with work as defined by scientists, simply put, energy is the capacity of matter or radiation to do work and work it did. Energy along with cloudbursts of rain snuffed out the danger of the Universe's fiery extinction.

"A positive balance of power favoring the dynamics of energy, that is matter, over the destructive hellish characteristics of overwhelming heat came about as chaos within the large bubble began to ebb as a result of several managing forces."

* * *

"Dr. Carruthers, with respect I do feel it is time for a short break before I explain to my audience the advent of our Twelve Controllers."

"Thank you Dr. Masters. Friends, coffee is being served as it was this morning. Please be back in your seats in 30 minutes. Thank you."

Only a handful of people left for coffee. The rest remained seated and were offered fruit juices in Kolinski glass tumblers by the convention hall's polite attendants. During the break very few words were spoken by any of the 2,100 attendees. They appeared to be awaiting Dr. Master's oration pertaining to the "advent of several managing forces."

Dr. Masters returned to her lectern in 30 minutes as did her audience. Dr. Carruthers called the meeting to order then asked the stunning Lana to continue her expose.

"Ladies," she said, "are not those Kolinski tumblers awesome?"

"Yes, yes," was their enthusiastic response.

"Can we keep them Lana?" they chorused.

"Of course, please do, but none for the men," Lana said smiling and exuding deviltry.

"That's fair ladies…isn't it? You get the tumblers without having to tumble in bed for them."

The crowd split into happy yells of "Yea," by the women and "Boos," by the men.

But some *Neanderthals* in the audience shouted, "Real men don't give a hoot about your femmy tumblers," then laughed with hardy guffaws.

Lana waited until the fun noise subsided, then she said,"Say ladies, don't those *Neanderthals* remind you of that conceited Yankee mosquito?"

"What conceited Yankee mosquito is that Lana?" came their loud and cheerful response.

"You know," Lana gushed, "that Yankee mosquito who was floating on his back down the Hudson River with a glorious hard on yelling 'hey men, open the draw bridge, I'm coming through.'"

The ladies gave Lana a standing ovation. The men snickered.

Lana waited until the convention hall's noises subsided.

Then she moved from behind her lectern. Her eyes were piercing, overpowering and magnetic. She stood silent. A few moments passed before she spoke.

"The advent of the several managing forces was not spiritual, not driven by Gods, not holy, not divine, nor inspired by sacred or religious dogma. No my learned friends, none of the aforementioned had anything to do with the advent of the Universe or the advent of its beings and management. Instead, a collection of matter during the Universe's erratic beginnings occurred as living molecules began to mass together kinetically forming three states of matter, gases, liquids and solids. These matters, which all took up space, were without intelligence. They spun undisciplined in the cosmos. However the gas, liquid and solid matters in the early stages of the Universe's growth became dominant because of the their physical power called *energy*. Matter, you see, which has weight and mass, is endowed with unequaled inertia, elasticity and impenetrability. Science today seems satisfied matter cannot be created or destroyed. Please note, my dear colleagues, a change in form of any of the three states of matter to another is physical only and does not alter the molecules making up the changed matter. I bring these latter facts to you because each of the Twelve Controllers of the Universe is a combination of every gas, both liquid and solid, contained in the cosmos. Perforce they are the Universe. And," Dr. Masters emphasized, "they can change into any form of matter they wish. Through their powers, they control every portion, however minute, of the Universe. As agreed, they can never be destroyed or recreated. Thus, as matter, they are infinite."

CHAPTER 31

INTELLIGENCE…DELETRIOUS ACTS

Dr. Masters returned to her lectern, "Yes, ladies and gentlemen the **Twelve Controllers are infinite, they are the Universe.** They have dominion over space, time, energy, matter and life. But, how, my dear colleagues, did these Controllers evolve into intelligent entities?" Dr. Masters questioned. "Their physical formation from gases, liquids and solids is not too perplexing to understand," she said. A bit of a hubbub arose from Lana's audience pertaining to this latter statement. Yet it subsided without any direct confrontation. "But the injection or the genesis of intelligence into Eves One, Two, Three, Four, Five and Six and Adams One, Two, Three, Four, Five and Six, that's quite another 'matter'. Intelligence is the ability of an organism to utilize understanding obtained from past experiences in order to meet the challenges of similar and future happenings. Intelligence, too, is the ability to collect information, utilize it and retain it. It is the capacity of matter to learn to think and to understand. Now," Lana said, "first let us look at a cell. Each cell, as you know, consists of cytoplasm and a nucleus enclosed in a membrane. Cytoplasm is the protoplasmic content of a cell apart from the nucleus. Protoplasm is the material comprising the living part of a cell, consisting of a nucleus embedded in membrane…enclosed cytoplasm. Protoplasm is the fundamental material of which all living things are composed. Protoplasm consists primarily of water, protein, fatty substances, carbohydrates, inorganic salts as well as carbon, oxygen, hydrogen and nitrogen. Sulfur, phosphorus, potassium, iron and magnesium, too, are present. Protoplasm is living material, it exhibits the properties associated with what we humans call life, thus it has the capacity to respond to environmental influences and has the ability to perform physiological functions."

Lana, unbeknownst to her 2,100 attendees, was perspiring. She wanted to remove her suit jacket in order to cool down her body. 'Dammit' she thought, 'men can take off their suit jackets under similar circumstances, roll up their shirt sleeves, loosen their ties, and no one complains or whistles at such action. If I take off my jacket my tits will be so fucking noticeable under my cotton crew-neck that my audiences attention to my words will vanish in favor of my 'bloody' bosom.'

Adam Six interrupted her thoughts, entered her mind and joshed her by saying, "Loosen up my beautiful...ahem...Goddess. Don't be so serious. Take off your suit jacket. Be proud, yes, make your breasts swell with pride. Strut in front of your audience showing them your glorious beauty...then...when you feel the time is most propitious...hit them with a bang re: Eve One's origin. Okay? Now child, off with your jacket."

Lana obeyed.

Like a graceful tigress she left her lectern. She smiled in a seductive manner at her attendees, ran the moist tip of her tongue over her full delicious lips as she slinked out of her suit jacket. Oozing sex Lana turned and strolled over to the head table, revolved her beautiful full rounded hips making certain that all eyes were on her tight powder-blue mini skirt which outlined her wondrous derriere. Winking she handed her jacket to Dr. Carruthers.

After thanking Dr. Carruthers, Lana turned again facing her audience. She walked back to the lectern, hips swaying, chin held high, tawny hair flowing, and her tits held at full mast. She stood an impressive six-feet-one-inch in her semi high-heels. Four thousand two hundred mesmerized eyes were fixed on her. Without question Lana was the most beautiful human structure ever conceived.

"Please excuse me for this delay," she murmured, "when I become involved in such a profound subject as the Universe, my body heats up. Men, ladies and gentlemen, when they perspire during their lectures, can shed jackets, loosen ties, roll up sleeves without condemnation but when we women remove our suit jackets because of our body heat we are accused of contriving a sexual move," Lana said smiling. "Of course, nothing could be further from the truth," she teased. A few people in the audience whistled. Without question, Lana's moves evoked sexual thoughts among most of her male attendees as well as a rather wide smattering of her female attendees.

"On April 20th, the Twelve Controllers explained to me in simplistic terms the advent of Eve One as an intelligent, distinguishable, all powerful entity and the subsequent heralding of the 11 other Controllers."

"Was Eve One created by accident as a consequence of the turmoil within the young Universe or was her advent a predetermined strategy of certain gamete sexual cells? In whichever event, I should like to inform you a single fertilized living cell evolved out of the turmoil. The cell, by its very nature, multiplied into an embryonic mass early in the history of the Universe. The living cell was conceived by the fusion of nuclear materials contained in two sexual reproductive cells called gametes.

"This single fertilized cell, called a zygote, then underwent a series of cell multiplication's and divisions...morphogenesis...and in due course created an ovum atmospheric coordinating center, such center being capable of intellectual activity. This, my learned friends, was the birth of Eve One," Dr. Lana Masters proclaimed. The Eleven other Controllers believe Eve One masterminded her own birth.

Eve One became supreme!" Dr. Lana Masters stated. The lights in the convention room dimmed. The attendees squirmed wondering what next? An eerie silence followed. A bright aura enveloped Lana. Lana was dumbfounded. She glanced over at Dr. Carruthers. Dr. Carruthers' eyes met hers. He looked confused.

* * *

At that precise moment a serial killer in Detroit, Michigan, about to add another person to his grisly list of those he had slaughtered became drenched in benevolence. With tears of remorse he released his would be victim.

The board of directors of a huge conglomerate prostituting its main product, nicotine, changed a resolution it was about to pass. The resolution was changed from, 'promoting vigorously the sale of its tobacco products to the teen market in Western Industrialized Nations, and in South East Asia', to 'management is instructed to donate one billion dollars to cancer research worldwide.'

A rabid dog in Kiev, Ukraine, about to sink its diseased fangs into a child's face, suddenly was cured and instead began to wag its tail and lick the child's face with its untarnished tongue.

A vicious lightning-packed tornado about to touch down in Montgomery, Alabama, surprised thousands of frightened residents when the twister and hail-laden clouds suddenly vanished, leaving a scene of beauty and serenity as the evening sun displayed a miraculous setting.

A bruised and bloodied eight-year-old boy living in a catholic orphanage in Italy about to be raped by a "so-called gentle but husky priest" leveled the big priest with a vicious punch (from out of nowhere) to the priest's sacrilegious jaw.

Mahatma Gandhi appeared to all of India for ten minutes, one minute for each letter in Gandhi's coined word Satyagraha (truth and firmness).

Adam One entered Lana's mind and informed her that her explanation of Eve One's birth was correct. Then, in a matter of fact tone, he told her of a few interferences the Controllers were now invoking in their world, the serial killer, the cigarette conglomerate, the rabid dog, the tornado, the eight-year-old boy and Mohandas Karamchand Gandhi.

In a trice the lights in the convention room brightened. The eerie silence was replaced by the rustling of the 2,100 invitees' movements. The aura enveloping Lana disappeared. Dr. Carruthers apologized to the audience for the brief electrical problem. He nodded toward Lana for her to carry on.

"My friends," Lana said, "with respect, I beg of you to watch channel three tonight at eleven o'clock. If you are intending to be at our social gathering in the main ballroom here at the center this evening, our hosts have assured me we will have the use of their huge TV screens. At that time you will see six rather startling events in various parts of the world which have taken place just moments ago. I will recount them for you now in detail." Lana described each event.

*   *   *

"The birth of Eve One occurred 3,010 years after the advent of the Universe. The Universe had grown to about the size of planet Earth's moon, some 2,160 miles in diameter. The disorder taking place within the confines of this massive moon-sized balloon would, in due course, cause it to destroy itself leaving only particles of dust scattered about in the space-less nothing.

"When the zygote became a reality 3,001 years after the Universe was born, it multiplied with precipitance and within nine years its capacity as an atmospheric coordinating center with intelligence was a fait accompli.

Hence, the advent of Eve One.

"Intelligence. Yes, how did this puzzler come about? All of you through your formal schooling or, perhaps *idee recue,* will be well aware of the make up of the brain; gray and white matters, the thalamus, mid-brain, pons and medulla, the cerebellum, cerebrum and so on which conjoin to induce intelligence. Clearly, without their coordinating center...the brain…humans would be nothing but forest vegetation. Humans, as we know them, would not exist without this coordinating center."

"You mean politicians, Dr. Lana?" one voice offered. Laughter from various parts of the audience ensued.

"No comment," Dr. Lana Masters said smiling.

"The ability to think is the key. How does a cell or a combination of cells provide the answer to this devilish conundrum? Well, as Eve One explained to me, an interstice between cells has not been identified at this time in our history thus not named as yet by our earth's scientists. This space is filled with CIESP's…Microbes as I will call them so earthlings may understand…which the Controllers call Cerebralionicenzymaticsensorprect A.K.A. C.I.E.S.P.'s. These minuscule life forms have tiny fiber-like antennas covered with innumerable ultra-vision seeing cells and sensitive hearing cells all of which permeate the Universe. These cells are in constant contact with all matter throughout the Cosmos. They relay their findings to a porous filtering mass of large molecules which with instant speed, separate the billions of visual and audio messages it has received into specific categories within the coordinating center. C.I.E.S.P's of various forms gather information on a continuous basis through their structures on all other activities taking place in the cosmos. The Trailing C.I.E.S.P's for instance have anchor neutrons that are attached to the control center. The trailing C.I.E.S.P.'s are made up of trillions of C.I.E.S.P.'s fanning out over the entire Universe. They send their messages to the porous filtering mass for categorizing all activities, big or small, from the coordinating center itself to the most remote areas of the Universe.

"Eve One found she was able to decipher and understand the information contained in the categorized material. She arranged and rearranged this information many, many times until it made sense to her. Her categorization of all materials became a depository of facts. Hence a centralization of facts occurred for the first time in the history of the Universe, and for the first time in the history of the Universe these facts were laid out by the first living entity in such a way as to be useful. Eve One used a thought process. She, ladies and gentlemen, initiated thinking and intelligence."

Because Eves Two to Six and Adams One to Six are a part of Eve One they enjoy the use of the same coordinating center as Eve One, and, they have the same abilities as she to think and to be intelligent.

"Please note, my friends, we earthlings have inherited Eve One's ability to think and to reason. She gave earthlings a *jump start* at the beginning of the *Upper Paleolithic Period*, some 40,000 years ago. It is interesting to note that several million years after the Earth was created certain other animals were given brains with limited intelligence. None, as yet, have evolved with the intelligence of we humans.

"Following her ability to reason Eve One realized she must eliminate the Universe's inner chaotic turbulence and in so doing create a system of uniformity and harmony in order to prevent its own destruction. Eve One found this to be a prohibitive task. She found when she arrested the turbulence in one section of the Universe that, that very section would resume its turbulent action when she left it to arrest another section. Yes, friends much like the human body's defense mechanisms against rampaging germs or viruses.

"She needed to re-think her whole hypothesis pertaining to the harmony, order and uniformity of the Universe. Should she freeze time on the spot, then release each individual piece of matter into a time slot deemed by her to be proper, until all matters were released back into the atmosphere to become active again, but active solely under her control? Or, should she begin the process of vast multiplication of her own atmospheric cells so she would pervade the entire Universe and by so doing become the Universe itself including therefore all matters living therein. Eve One thought of many other permutations that she might follow in addition to 'holding time still' or 'further multiplications of herself'"

Lana continued. "Eve One's decision was made after just two hours of deliberation. She concluded she would divide herself into 11 more parts, five of which would be female and six to be male. She reasoned that 12 coordinating centers, rather than one, would have a greater mental and physical capacity to bring about her plans for the Universe.

"Please be clear on this fact, my dear colleagues, Eve One was a collection of countless trillions of cells. Yet only one percent of the cells were basic structural units such as plants and animals. However these basic structural cells in Eve One's make up are infinite, they never die. They are Eve One's brainchild. They are the nucleus of Eve One's unequivocal, unequaled brain…her intellect…her mental power…her utter dominance as the single universal intelligence. Eve One, in a matter of minutes, dissected these structural cells then, on defining their make-up, altered them biologically and in so doing made them supreme both physically and mentally, as a part of her.

"The remaining cells, oxygen, nitrogen and all other gases, solids, liquids, energy, time, ad infinitum were the constituents which made up the other 99% of Eve One's being i.e., ladies and gentlemen, the whole of the Universe. She realized at her birth as an atmospheric center, **that only she had intelligence.** All other masses around her were mindless. Yet her intellectual prowess gave her dominion over the other 99% of her being. Eve One's decision to make herself into 12 parts was so damned incisive. It relieved the burden (not recognized enough in today's world) of attention span.

"It is interesting to note science is satisfied that each individual cell in plants and animals lives its own life as an independent entity, and, I might add, rather selfishly. Yet these selfish little devils allow themselves to live in harmony alongside other cells. Hence, it makes it possible for a plant or an animal as a whole (with kadrillions of cells) to carry on with its life's activities. This my friends is not dissimilar to Eve One's make up.

"However, the fundamental difference between plant and animal cells on planet Earth compared to Eve One's cells is physical. Plants and animals die as their cells become seriously diseased, or are destroyed by accidents, wars, or the like. They cannot replace worn out cells in perpetuity. Thus they age and die.

"Eve One within seconds of her birth knew this fact.

"She decided all of her cells would have endless lives simply by keeping her cells clear of all misadventures. After all, this would be a simplistic solution for her, because she had supremacy over all matter.

* * *

"Eve One, as I stated earlier, divided herself into 11 more coordinating centers, which she referred to as Control Centers. Thus, she and each of her 11 progenies would be referred to as Controllers. However, Eve One would be and forever remain *Primus Inter Pares.*

"Her division into 11 more Controllers was engineered through a process known to science as mitosis and fertilization. The remainder of her being, that is all other constituents in the Universe, would be shared equally among all 12 Controllers, but divided territorially for the purpose of effective cosmogonic management.

CHAPTER 32

DR. SAMUELL MARSHALL: THE WORLD'S FOREMOST SCIENTIST

A scant week ago Clark Rodney St. James (known as Barney or "Pots" to some of his new friends) reported an after-tax profit of 73 million dollars to New York City's skid row shareholders' company called **"H&B Financial and Poors Inc."**

* * *

Clark met Lana after she descended the meeting hall's stage. "She is so enchanting," Clark thought. He took her hand in his hoping to take her away from crowds that were now muscling their way towards her, "Dr. Lana," many shouted, "over here." Lana smiled and winked at Clark. She turned to the gathering, smiled engagingly and waved to them.

In moments she was surrounded but her attendees were thoughtful enough not to shove and jostle her. Yet Clark was concerned about her safety. Elitists, he knew, were not above murder, especially those who were inexorably opposed to Lana's views.

In moments, security guards were at her side. Lana welcomed them but begged them not to disperse the impassioned attendees. She smiled and chatted with the people and tried to answer the myriad of questions being thrown at her. Some in the group hurled insulting remarks her way. The religious right damned her for her sacrilegious postulations. "God will punish you by leaving you in eternal hell," they vowed.

However most attendees were gracious, patient, and proud to be near this remarkable woman. It seemed everyone wanted to touch her to see if she was real. Lana was patient and understanding with all those who surrounded her. She knew she had overwhelmed them during the day. She knew, too, many of her observations were most controversial.

Out of the crowd emerged an elderly, very distinguished-looking gentleman, a gentleman who Dr. Lana Masters recognized but whom she had never met. He came to her without fuss. "Good evening my dear Dr. Masters." he said. "My name is Samuel Marshall."

"Oh my," Lana gasped, "at last I have met you Dr. Marshall. I am so overwhelmed. Please excuse my gushing over you Doctor. I have admired and hero-worshipped you since I was a child of five.

"Dr. Masters, you flatter me, and I must say such flattery is inspirational for an old goat like me." Dr. Marshall responded.

Lana Masters reached out, took his hands, kissed his cheek, and embraced him.

"My, my, you are a charming girl."

"Forgive me for being so bold," Lana said.

"Tut, tut, my child, you are forgiven," the good doctor chuckled. "Now, Dr. Masters, I know you are a brilliant person and you have various doctorates in the sciences and in other worthy degrees, but you failed to convince me with your hypothesis on the Universe's beginnings and on the Universe's Twelve Controllers." Samuel Marshall stated.

"With the utmost respect, Dr. Marshall, the two subjects are not based on assumptions, they are fact," Lana responded smiling.

"But, your scientific factum was terse, not detailed, perhaps even paralipsis in what you say."

Lana replied, "As to scientific factum and paralipsis it's true only to some extent, Dr. Marshall. You see Eve One wants it this way. She wishes to see if her Earth's scientific community will have the ability to prove the reality of the Universe's birth and the advent of Eve One and her offsprings some day. I daresay I extolled these facts during my address on more than one occasion, Dr. Marshall. Please believe me Eve One wants it left this way."

"Thank you dear Lana." With that Dr. Marshall smiled, took Lana's hand and kissed it. "I look forward to your address this evening." Bowing he turned to leave Lana.

At that moment Eve One entered Dr. Marshall's mind and said, "she speaks the truth my good man." Dumbfounded, Dr. Marshall made his way out of the assembly hall.

Clark, along with the security guards, escorted Lana to the ladies powder room. Thence to Lana's table in the dining room, where she would dine with Dr. Carruthers and others from the council.

However, as she was moving through the dining area, she saw Dr. Marshall beckoning her to come to him. Lana obliged. When she arrived at Dr. Marshall's table she noted he looked pale and apprehensive. He stood and whispered in her ear, "Did you delude me, my dear, when I was about to leave you a few minutes ago and whisper these words to me 'she speaks the truth my good man?"

"No Doctor," Lana answered. "I would never delude you."

"Then, by the Holy Grail, who did?"

In a booming voice, audible only to Doctors Marshall and Masters, Eve One thundered, "It was me Dr. Marshall, Eve One, and I command you to believe. Lana Masters speaks the truth." Then in a gentle soothing voice Eve One said, "Please be seated now Dr. Marshall, I have just lowered your blood pressure. I want you to enjoy your meal."

Dr. Marshall sat. He looked up at Lana. She winked. Dr. Marshall knew, he smiled. Color returned to his face.

Dr. Carruthers called the meeting to order at eight p.m. Not one attendee was missing.

CHAPTER 33

LANA'S WOULD BE ASSASIN

The Controllers revenge: Itanya Koslosky

Lana took her place at the lectern. She looked stunning. She had taken a few moments during the recess to change her clothing. She stood tall in a breathtaking dark-green evening gown. Again her jewelry was simple, a pearl necklace and pearl earrings. Many of the attendees gasped on seeing her.

"Good evening friends. Was that not a most sumptuous meal…mmm? And our gracious hosts, my, all of Turkey can be proud." The attendees applauded.

"Ladies and gentlemen, I should like now to bring you the Twelve Controllers' precept of good and bad. All 12 have agreed if the world's entire populous abides by the good and shuns the bad the Controllers will reflect the improvement by bringing about a reduction in the 99-1/4 percent benchmark hovering over the extinction of mankind. We have touched on this before.

"First, friends, the management of our planet Earth has been abysmal over the years. Industrialized nation's had their beginnings in the Industrial Revolution, from 1760 through the 1800's. Entrepreneurs had little or no concern about using child labor. They inflicted dreadful abuse, killer punishment, horrific working conditions, scant pay for the children as well as a complete lack of health care and education for them. The industrialists had no feeling of remorse over using child labor…their motives were profit driven. Profits, profits, profits…not children's welfare. And they had little or no interest in keeping cleansed the air we breathe, the waters we need, nor the rape of our lands, forests, seas, et al.

"After hundreds of years of despoiling our garden-like planet, a few people began to have serious concerns about such carelessness. Many species of animals and fish had become extinct at the monstrous hands of people. Many species existence is threatened by cavalier attitudes even today.

Our planets' heroes have in many ways stalled this despoiling through their activities as environmentalists.

The resurrection of the good earth can become a reality if nations act responsibly as one in the sound management of our globe's resources. It is imperative that all peoples of our planet share in these resources so everyone can enjoy a bountiful standard of living. Let us be clear on one thing, people are the real assets of our world. All capital assets and natural resources are inert until put into motion by people.

For the past 40,000 years we have divided up the world and its riches without interference by the Controllers. And what a jolly fuck up we've made of it. Think on it. Between the rich and the poor, the strong and the weak, racism, religion and its hypocrisy, brutality, guns and other weapons of destruction, air space, ground space, sea space, grab, grab, grab. As the beggar weeps for alms his hands stay empty and as Microsoft's shares bounce up a buck or so sweet William Gates' net worth increases by $1 billion. Now Mr. Gates' shares could plummet by 50 bucks too, you say, leaving therefore his net worth at a paltry $40 billion. Yes $40 billion…double the net worth of the Bank of America. Shit. In any event the world and all its inhabitants, plant and animal, is an experiment started by the Controllers some 5 billion years ago. The Controllers will decide when the experiment has been completed. The 99-1/4 percent has only to do with the activities of people in the scheme of things, thus is only one part of the whole experiment.

"As you know, the division of lands has come about through skullduggery, discoveries, wars, barter, monetary exchanges, legal claims, squatter rights, mortgage foreclosures, seizure, usurpation, which has resulted in rivers of blood being spilled over the centuries.

"Miseries, indignities and injustices have abounded. Laws for goodness sake have had to be enacted to keep people from cheating, lying, killing...every manner of deception and savagery...against others. Is this not incredible? Laws to keep us from one another's throats. Hard to believe is it not? We cannot live in harmony can we? We must behave like beasts. I guess by our present standards, the world would by one big bore if we couldn't have evil and suffering. The media would be starved, politicals as we know them would not exist, the religious would become true ambassadors of good will, surely you know what I mean.

"We have religious groups, kings, queens, princes, dictatorships, wealthy individuals and corporate entities who own massive tracts of land, while others do not own one square inch of the earth's surface. This inequity is seen as grossly unfair by the Controllers, and is one of the main factors that has pushed human extinction to the 99-1/4 percent level.

"I presume my remarks here and remarks I have made elsewhere have much to do with my being branded a communist and an enemy of big business and capitalism. Well, ladies and gentlemen, I should like to inform you by my wits and daring I was a multimillionaire by the time I was nine years old. I expound on my financial adventures as a child in a book that I am currently writing.

"I am not a fucking communist.

"I believe in fair competition and in a *laissez-faire* economy. But does my belief in pure competition foreclose my right to stand up for equity. I believe no person in this world should live in poverty and be in need. Every person is entitled to a decent share of the world's output of goods and services.

"In any event, I favor fair and just rewards for people's ingenuity, hard work and entrepreneurial guts. The Controllers have told me there should be spirited competition among people in all walks of life and at most ages. Fair competition keeps people on their toes, keeps them plucky, healthy, happy, and feeling productive—on top of the world—looking forward to the next challenge.

"But the enormity of unfair, heavy handed, money backed, government backed, religious backed, manipulative gerrymandering non laissez-faire economies, results in painful, adverse, horrid inequities. Daily, billions of people puke their empty guts out yet are starving.

"Homeless, starving wretches living in degrading poverty (living among lice, rats and all manner of filth from non-existent sewage disposals, in hapless countries ruled by wealthy ruthless dictators, cruel monarchs, religious bigots et al, and in large cities throughout the world) make up the preponderance of people on our planet. Just over one-third of the world's people enjoy the world's bounties while the rest either grovel in misery or live a hand-to-mouth existence.

"Of the 99-1/4 percent precipitous chasm we are now hanging over, 90% is attributable to this one malignant scourge, man's inhumanity to man.

"Take some time my distinguished colleagues to visit the slums of the world. Then watch some of the television reruns of The Rich and the Famous."

* * *

A shot rang out.

Lana stood her ground.

Those at the head table ducked.

The attendees screamed and slid under their seats.

Lana continued, "Then you will see the unjust differences. All of you understand what I am saying and you know what I say is true."

Another shot rang out, the bullet zinged past Lana's ear taking with it one of her pearl earrings.

"Whoever the fucking gunman is out there take your slimy weapon and shove it," Lana shouted.

Suddenly the gunman was on the stage not 20 feet from Lana. He wasn't a crazed wild-eyed sort at all. He looked normal in his priesthood attire. The next moment his mini 303 rifle was flying through the air. His knees buckled as three shots erupted from Lana's tiny Beretta.

The priest groaned in agony as he pitched forward on his face, screaming, "The good lord will punish you, you godless slut of a whore. You and your sacrilegious fantasies about Twelve Godless Controllers, you wicked profane blasphemous witch. How dare you preach such impieties, such buffoonery? How dare you lie in the face of God? You know the poor and the wretched are God's children and it is their lot to suffer unto him. You know full well the rich and powerful are God's children as well, and they love God, and they bear gifts to him in the form of money so magnificent altars can be erected in his name. God thanks them for these generous bestowings and he rewards them with riches just as he did for Abraham '*neither shall thy name any more be called Abram but thy name shall be Abraham; for a father of many nations have I made thee. And I will make thee exceedingly fruitful, and I will make nations of thee, and kings shall come out of thee.*' Don't you see this you sinful voluptuary…you harlot…you Jezebel?"

Lana rushed to his side and held his head in her arms. "Shush now father, medical doctors from the assemblage are here, and medics from the center will be with you momentarily. They will look after you."

He looked up into her eyes. "Why are you so irreverent Dr. Masters? You are making a mockery of mans…" Father Donnely lost consciousness.

Several nuns made their way onto the stage. Many were weeping. One non-weeper, her eyes ablaze, came up to Lana and slapped her face.

"There you strumpet," she bellowed. "Release our beloved father." Lana simply turned her other cheek.

Security had the stage cleared in minutes. Father Donnely was hastened away by ambulance.

Lana returned to the lectern and asked if the attendees wished her to carry on. As one they shouted, "Yes."

"Thank you Ladies and gentlemen. I am sorry for this frightening interruption. Too, I am heartbroken over Father Donnely. I can understand his rejection of me because I know I have interfered with his life long theological beliefs. No doubt I have caused his thinking to be skewed to reckless anger, however he did seem to come to this meeting well prepared for violence.

"Let me assure you, my friends, father Donnely will be up and about, unscathed in a matter of hours. You see my gun was loaded with rubber bullets, they hurt, but they don't injure.

"Now back to business," Lana stated, her right cheek smarting.

"How long will our earth be bountiful?" she mused. "How many millions of people are starving unnecessarily?

"How many humans can our planet sustain?

"How many years will pass before our planet becomes sterile as a result of our mismanagement?

"How many years will pass before our planet becomes sterile under sound management? How many years will pass before we use up non-replenishing resources such as oil? Perhaps if earthlings put their minds to this fact oil and other fossil fuels could be substituted by other power sources. This could result in major changes in the world's present status. Such innovations could create worldwide, never before seen, increases in employment.

"How many years will it take to make space travel economical?

"Will space travel become a viable solution for extending human existence on earth?

"When will we decide to provide sufficient funds to science in order for scientists to unmask the secrets of bringing unproductive waste lands and the like to productivity.

"What do our Controllers consider to be good or bad?

"And, keep in mind that fucking 99-1/4 percent being held over our heads by our Controllers.

"Now, now," whispered Adam One in Lana's ear, "your incessant swearing, for shame."

Lana paced. She looked up at the ceiling, then over to the head table. She returned to her dais. She blurted out smiling, finger tips to her right cheek. "Sister whomever hits mighty hard."

No response came from the attendees.

* * *

"*Exodus, Chapter XX,*" Dr. Lana said.

"*Exodus XX* and surrounding chapters...let's look at some of the verses in Exodus and quote from them. For instance, *Exodus XIX, verse 10: '...and the Lord said unto Moses', "Go unto the people and sanctify them today and tomorrow and let them wash their clothes."*

"*Verse 11: 'And be ready against the third day: for the third day the Lord will come down in the sight of all people upon Mount Sinai*.

"*Verse 12: 'And thou shalt set bounds unto the people round about, saying take heed to yourselves that ye go not up into the mount or touch the border of it: whosoever toucheth the mount shall be surely put to death.'*

"Tough talk by our God. And to quote Chapter XX: "*Verse 4: 'Thou shalt not make unto thee any graven image or any likeness of any thing that is in heaven above, or that is in the Earth beneath, or that is in the water under the earth.'*

"Verse 5: '*Thou shalt not bow down thyself to them, nor serve them: For I the Lord thy God am a jealous God, visiting the iniquity...*("iniquity ladies and gentlemen, wickedness, unrighteousness")...*of thy fathers upon the children unto the third and fourth generation of them that hate me.'*

"*Verse 6: '...And showing mercy unto thousands of them that love me, and keep my commandments.'*

"And of course, *Chapter XX of Exodus* includes God's Ten Commandments, which, in brief are:

—'No Gods before me

—No grave images

—Not take the Lords name in vain

—Remember the Sabbath

—Honor Father and Mother

—Shall not kill

—Shall not commit adultery

—Shall not steal

—Shall not bear false witness

—Shall not covet they neighbor's house, neighbor's wife, his man-servant, his maid-servant, his ox, his ass, nor anything that is thy neighbors.'

"And note, the last commandment appears to pertain only to thy neighbor, but what about somebody across town, is that justified? And Lordy me, what about his man-servant, his ox, his ass. I'm just kidding.

"In any event, Exodus is quite fulfilling, satisfying, and judicial, yet I must say that I am inalterability opposed to some of the bible's pronouncements of God," Lana continued.

"My few quotations from Exodus provide a little of God's methods and his personality. His commandments to honor Father and Mother, not to kill, not to steal, nor lie, are righteous.

"The laws set down by God in Chapters XXI, XXII and XXIII as written by the scribes in Exodus are alarmingly close to some of today's laws. I shant take time to analyze them today. They are clear and succinct, and are quite self-explanatory.

"In Genesis too, the Bible's scribes appear to make God into a God who favors some, regardless of their idiosyncrasies, and chastising others regardless of their idiosyncrasies, for instance Cain and Abel. The scribes insisted God did not respect Cain's offering to him of the fruit of the ground but he did respect Abel's offerings of the firstlings of his flock, and, great Scott, of all things, of the fat thereof.

"Fat…cholesterol…my, my!

"As well, ladies and gentlemen, while God, as the scribes propose, in the beginning created the heaven and the earth, day, night, waters, land, grass, fruit, fish, fowl, cattle, creeping things and man. Yet, with all his omnipotence, he couldn't find big old Adam and the luscious enticing Eve who were hidden in the Garden of Eden. No…he had to call out to find them. As well God had to ask Cain where Abel was after Cain had slain Abel.

"God could create the Heavens and the Earth in just six days but, with all his or her powers could not find the hidden Adam and Eve, nor Cain.

"Am I missing something?" Lana asked.

"Please understand my friends," Lana smiled as she looked out over her attendees, "as I said this afternoon I am not attempting an exegesis of the scriptures at this time. I am simply trying to make manifest some of the obvious inconsistencies brought forth by the writings in the Bible. In addition, I am pointing out the obvious that God was not the original cosmos creator. That God was an understandable invention by those idealists years ago who needed to have an explanation of the advent of the Universe and more important…to comfort themselves death was not the end, and there was life after death. Now, ladies and gentlemen as to this latter point, life after death, Eve One has assured me after people's bodies expire their energies, psyche and soul are relocated in other parts of the Universe by the Controllers.

"I had not intended to speak on this subject this week, thus my brevity in alluding to life after death. Of interest let it be known that the average good person joins other deceased members of his or her family who were themselves decent law-abiding citizens during their lifetimes. It is rather interesting to note Shirley MacLaine's belief in the process of reincarnation does occur from time to time. This happens when certain humans have been relocated back into an 'Earthly Body' because the Controllers have deemed them not ready to be taken from planet Earth. And, damn it all, the Controllers would not give me the lifetime we could expect after departing this world. Bummer eh?

"Now to get back on track, Mr. Chairman," as Lana nodded to Dr. Carruthers. "I will outline the Controllers list of Good and Bad."

"Not so quick Dr. Masters," a woman called out from the audience, "With brevity you have teased us with your life after death postulation. This, you know is the most confounding question ever in the mind's of people. Heaven, Purgatory, Hell. For thousands of years people have been searching for an answer. Most humans are terrified at the thought of dying. Death is so final. Religions are prophetic on this topic but, by and large, have no proof of their divinations. Prayers do console some. You…you seem so matter-of-fact about it Dr. Masters."

"Well, m'lady, Eve One left no doubt in my mind as to its authenticity," Lana answered. At that moment Lana once again was enshrined in an aura, an aura so breathtaking, so beautiful that the attendees were spellbound. "Believe me my friends," Lana said with an angelic smile. "Eve One has assured me of life after death, but she gave me no further details."

Slowly the aura around Lana vanished like the dissipation of a soft morning mist.

The convention hall was without motion or sound for several moments.

Lana continued her exposé. "First, let me present **the good things** ordained by our Controllers and directed to us Earthlings. They are so simplistic they need no explanation.

"One: The family tops the list. The ingredients to make families achieve ascendancy include love, care, happiness, respect and attentiveness.

"Two: Love of people and the environment
"Three: Humane, compassionate, benevolence
"Four: Scruples, morals
"Five: Trust, truth, reliability, honesty
"Six: Kind, thoughtful
"Seven: Decent, propitious, respect
"Eight: Productive
"Nine: Wholesomeness, fun, laughter
"Ten: Cleanliness, physical and mental
"Eleven: Competitiveness, spirited but not detrimental to others
"Twelve: Good sportsmanship
"Thirteen: The weak, the mentally and physically handicapped to share equitably in the world's goods and services
"Fourteen: Sex to be enjoyed by heterosexuals, homosexuals and bisexuals
"Fifteen: Cooperation, humans working and living in harmony
"Sixteen: Jesus' teachings in his Sermon on the Mount
"Seventeen: Responsibility

"These seventeen items are not onerous. They are far less complex and much easier to follow than the wiles needed to be devious and wicked," Lana said. She looked at her audience and stated "Now I should like to recite **the 'bad' things**, as told to me by the Controllers.

"One: Topping the list of wickedness is men and women's inhumanity to men and women…present and past. Man's inhumanity to man covers the entire list that I am about to enumerate. Bigotry and racism are two of the ugliest components of man's inhumanity to man.

"Two: Wars of any kind. Be aware of atomic bomb threats by the Far East's religion.

"Three: Killing under any circumstance including wars

"Four: Inequities between the rich and powerful and all the classes of people. In particular between the rich and powerful and the meek, weak and the poor.

"Five: Thou shalt not steal.

"Six: Thou shalt not lie.

"Seven: Child and other abuse. Child abuse is ranked as the most heinous of man's inhumanities. Rape, harassment

"Eight: Cruelty and mayhem

"Nine: Greed

"Ten: Substance abuse...drugs of all kinds, including tobacco and alcohol

"Eleven: Gossip

"Twelve: Cheating

"Thirteen: Charity in place of social responsibilities

"Fourteen: Religious hypocrisy. I will expand on this topic later

"Fifteen: Heinous gangs

"Sixteen: Crime

"Seventeen: Pollution of any kind

"Eighteen: Laziness

"Nineteen: Malicious savagery

"Twenty: Unnecessary waste

"Twenty One: Servitude, bondage of any sort

"Twenty two: Rudeness, insolence, disrespect

"All these faults should be recognized by the majority of peoples on earth. Yes, and these are only some of the negatives we face today.

Ladies and gentlemen, life should be fun for everyone. That is how it was intended.

For 40,000 years the Controllers have let us make our own way without interference by them. Simply, we are their experiment. So far the experiment has been a fucking dud. Can you imagine people fucking killing one another over who's God is *the* God? What bloody nonsense, that's not fun.

"Yet somebody pointed us that way. It wasn't the Controllers, so who was it?

"In my view it was the first person who understood the superstitons of others, and, who knew superstitions were sheer bullshit. The Controllers are letting the hand of this dude be played out. Hell it only takes a few seconds for the experiment to take place as measured by universal time. I can imagine the sport this *clever* dude had in convincing his unwitting brethern about the frightful spooks who abounded on mother earth. I can see the sanctimonious bastard waving his arms frantically as he promised them only he could be their savior, and, at a measly cost of about $100 U.S. each. Yes, I'd bet in no time the *clever* one had his followers kissing his bountiful ass. 'You', he would preach to the masses, 'will be beholden to me forever. You will do my bidding, and you will do it for a pittance, and you will do it loving me as your God. And, incidentally, you will pay me a tithe for your right to worship me, say a buck U.S. a week.

'In addition to worshipping me you will worship my chosen ones. The chosen ones will be called High Society. They will be rich. They never need worry about you poor lowlifes rebelling, because you poor lowlifes shall be as frightened of them as you are of me. The chosen ones shall, in fact, heap scorn on you. They will thumb their noses at the stinkholes you shall live in. But be assurred, forever they shall be grateful to you for your busiess. Now *ye* lowlifes, be forewarned, if ever you stray from my bidding I shall see you burn in perpetuity in a place I shall call hell.'

"Now that's not fun as seen by the Controllers. In fact it's kind of a drag for the lowlifes. Fun…maybe for a few, but what about the millions of starving wretches throughout the world?

"The Controllers would be delighted if we had chosen a life of productivity and fun. But, unfortunately, from the beginning of the Stone Age people have not had the mental ability to choose compatibility. Yet look at some areas where we humans have excelled; worldwide communications, education, sanitation, health habits, scientific achievements, some environmental successes, wondrous inventions for the pleasure of people and for saving unnecessary back breaking toil, productivity, leisure time activities, human care through medical practitioners, hospitals, clinics and the like, publicly run medical and hospital programs, government warnings, intervention and punishment as to tobacco use, unsafe sex, drunk driving, illicit drugs and so on." Lana paused.

"Some say the 1990's are *the* times, like no other times in history, for sheer excitement and enjoyment for people of our great planet. That moving into the 21st Century will bring even more excitement and pleasures for people. Yes, how true for those who live comfortably above the poverty line, but what about lowlifes? There are about 3 billion of these plus poor suffering souls. How inane and inhumane we fortunate ones are.

"We are inane from an economic standpoint. Some 3 billion earthlings are yet to become equivalent to those more fortunate people living in highly industrialized nations. Wealthy nations must come to their senses and begin to provide meaningful assistance to the needy. What a boon it would be to the world economy if 3 billion people became active beneficial consumers and producers. They would not only be in a position to enjoy some of earth's bounties, but they would become participants in producing the earth's bounties. Just look, ladies and gentlemen, at what the European Recovery Program, widely known as the Marshall Plan following W.W.2, did for Great Britain, France, Italy, the Netherlands, Belgium, Luxembourg, Greece, Austria, Denmark, Norway, Sweden, Republic of Ireland, Switzerland, Turkey, Portugal, Iceland. And look at the boon the U.S., Britain and France bestowed on Germany when these countries occupied Germany.

"What if the 3 billion souls finally get pissed off with us and say fuck ya, ya bunch of greed mongers. We ain't gonna' buy one fuckin' thing from ya from now on, and we ain't gonna work another day for ya. We're gonna' steal what we need. Go ahead and arrest us. We won't give a shit. Ya, and if you arrest all of us where-n-hell are ya gonna' put us? Wouldn't such a move frazzle the pants off the genteel?

"We are inhumane because most of us who are more fortunate than others simply give lip service to the woes of the wretched. To ease our consciences and, by the way, reduce our income taxes, we make donations to charitable organizations. There, by the saints, we have been benevolent. We have done our bit say we and away we go brushing our more basic moral responsibilities aside.

"Friends," Lana said, "I have been in the stinking trenches of the poor for six years now. I have found only a handful of people who have the spirit, heart, guts, determination to get into these fucking penury hell holes. Nuns, other religious peons, social workers, volunteers and organizations such as the Salvation Army and the Red Cross get right in these trenches and work like Trojans in an attempt to comfort downtrodden souls. But they have no chance whatsoever in correcting this ancient worldwide scandal.

"This scandal can be overcome only with the cooperation and resoluteness of everyone.

"Please forgive my sermonizing, dear associates, but be forewarned, you will find me in this mode from time to time during the next three days," Lana professed.

"Dr. Masters," someone called out, "what about cloning…?"

Dr. Masters interrupted, "Yes, what about cloning?"

"Is it something you favor?"

"In certain instances, yes, in others no."

"Do you care to elaborate doctor?"

"I would be delighted to give you my views on the subject, sir, but I think we have only ten minutes left for this evening's session. If time permits in the next few days I may try to bring you my views on cloning."

"Dr. Masters," someone quipped, "Be sure you consult your nice little leprechauns, you know your Twelve Controllers re cloning. I suppose you think we are a 'bunch' of school children who believe your drivel. I still think you are a flaming fraud."

"I thought we had agreed on the Controllers this morning?" Dr. Masters questioned.

"You may have thought so…Lord Jesus Christ…what's happening to me! My God, what have you done to me you witch?"

Most of the attendees sucked in their breaths with abject horror as they saw the loathsome sight of the man who had just spoken to Dr. Masters and who now was standing next to her on the stage nude and skinless. His hideous body was pulsating. His face hung together by fleshy gobs of meat. His hair spiked out form his skull. His forehead was bluish red from visible capillary blood vessels and convulsing veins. His ears were ugly gristly protrusions. His eyes, huge, round and bloodshot, stared through skull holes. Forlorn eyes, blobs of pulpy egg like substances inside the skinless skull peering at the attendees through sunken holes. Good Christ, even snot was visible inside the hole where the poor bastard's nose should have been. No lips, just teeth jutting out of red saliva covered gums. And a tongue, fucking white on top, should be pink not white. His breath must be like rotting garbage based on his huge unsightly white-topped tongue. His cheeks were raw flesh, blood-filled with long hair growing out of the quivering mass. The skull itself moved disgustingly on its skinless neck. His face resembled the skinned face of a buck or a doe shortly after the "mighty" hunter's slaughter.

His body, arms and legs were like a freshly skinned seal pup, pulsating with every heartbeat. His heart, lungs, guts, bones, intestines, testicles, anus all moved and jerked as his life's blood throbbed through his body.

When the miserable soul saw himself on the big screen he vomited. Everyone in the audience who hadn't covered their eyes saw the hellish routine of vomiting—gut convulsing, spasmodic, pushing undigested food and bile in a violent stream, through a gullet then gushing out of a lip-less blood-red gaping tooth filled mouth. Revolting. Some of the puke spewed through those holes that once were his nostrils. The spew missed Lana. Many attendees watching this obnoxious display joined in and spewed their own streams of vomit. Some of the women used their purses as receptacles.

The hall became one big stinking mess.

"Believe," Lana preached, "believe in the Twelve Controllers lest this man remains skinless for the rest of his days."

Television viewers across the world had been dumbfounded several times during this day with Dr. Lana Masters. They had accepted the uncanny sights of the morning and afternoon. Now this revolting scene. This was too much for even the most callused of people. Millions rushed to their bathrooms.

"Dear me, won't they ever learn?" Eve One questioned.

"As we linger in the minds of all of our people in this auditorium and all those watching on television, and, without us influencing their thoughts in any way, many still remain cavalier about us Eve." Adam Four responded. "Would you like me to step in and convince them of our reality?" Adam Four winked.

"No Adam Four, don't be nasty." Eve One laughed. "We will let Lana, our erudite beauty, carry on and see how she makes out with just a 'wee' push from us from time to time."

Again in a trice, Eve One cleared up the Hall's awful mess, then as the attendees and viewers watched in awe, the skinless gentleman began to become whole again. His scalp began to crawl over his forehead and down the back of his head. Skin worked its way down the sides and the front of his head covering his ears, outlining his eyes, creeping over his rather bulbous nose, giving him back his lips, wrapping his chin and his pulsating neck and his bobbing Adam's apple. Christ this was insanity. Like a monstrous grafting his skin unfolded moving down his arms, chest, belly and over his skeletal digits. The poor soul bowed his head down and watched in terror as his skin crept silently over his body. "No, oh God no," he cried. His penis remained raw. He felt behind himself

"God no," his anus was raw. The air was stinging these exposed areas. "Please Dr. Masters I believe you." he croaked.

"Please, Eve One, restore him completely," Lana begged.

"Child," Eve Two answered, "look, now he is whole, and clothed."

Lana walked over to the terror-stricken man. She took his hand in hers, she touched his cheek with her fingertips. The man cowered. He went down on his knees. Beseeching he looked up into Lana's eyes. Lana took both his hands in hers and with a celestial smile beckoned him to stand. The gentleman stood. The terror left him. He felt warm, comforted, whole. While he knew Lana was not a goddess, he knew she was somehow connected to the cosmos.

She led him to the stairway down from the ample stage. She released his hand and whispered, "Now go back to your seat. I assure you, no one will feel any different toward you than they did before you had your breathtaking experience."

Beauty, once again, enveloped the majestic convention hall. The atmosphere turned serene. A fragrant aroma filled the air. The attendees were at ease.

* * *

Lana returned to her lectern. She thanked the attendees for their kind attention to her day's address and said she looked forward to seeing them at the evening's social and dance. She wished them all a pleasant good night.

Dr. Carruthers had the meeting adjourned. He reminded the attendees to watch the upcoming eleven o'clock news as requested by Dr. Masters, and reminded them that the 'morrow's meeting would be convened at 9:45 a.m. He wished everyone a pleasant evening.

Clark St. James vaulted up the stairs to the stage to claim his precious Lana. Tenderly he kissed her lips. He put his arm around her waist, held her close to him and awaited security.

She looked up at him and teased, "I have instructed security to stay close to our attendees as they leave the hall and as they go to their rooms or as they go to tonight's social. I want them to leave us alone.

"You what," Clark scolded, "you are too dammed vulnerable to be without body guards. What were you thinking Lana?"

"I know this ticks you off Clark, but with you, my Herculean superman, I feel as safe as a church mouse."

"You're a real little shit, aren't you?" Clark responded.

"Of course I am. C'mon Clark, first I want to visit 'Henry.' Then, my love, I want to go to the ballroom. I want a coupl'a drinks, a coupl'a dances then mosey off to our room, go potty, shower, brush teeth, fuck gloriously, kiss goodnight and sleep 'til seven. And, hey Clark, nice profit your brainchild had. Seventy-three mil'. I can't wait to see our beautiful 'scum bag' shareholders." Lana chortled, "I miss them."

"Thanks baby, let's go."

The crowd was merciless. They too wanted Lana. They pushed and shoved to get near her. Many begged Lana to sit at their table during the social. Many men near Lana were delighted to be pushed by others behind them so that their bodies rubbed against hers. Questions came at her from all directions.

The media personnel were becoming more and more frustrated as each moment passed. They tried to worm their way closer to her. Damn. It was impossible. They had questions, many questions. "You are a better magician or illusionist than Ziegfred and Roy. How did you master those uncanny sights? And the Twelve Controllers, when did you dream them up? Which do you rely most to captivate your audience, your physical endowments, your oratorical wizardry or your befuddling illusions? Dr. Masters, when did you dream up this bubble theory? Do you suffer from hallucinations, delusions, schizophrenia? Have you written a treatise on your theory pertaining to the origin of the Universe and the advent of your so-called Controllers? What do you think God feels about you? Do you enjoy rebuffing religion? Do you hate the rich? Do you hate the right? What's this eleven o'clock stuff, another of your illusions? Did Steven Spielberg dream up that sickening skinless repugnant prop? Do you expect brilliant physicists and able theologians, to accept your suppositions? How big are your tits, Lana?

Abruptly their questions stopped. Media personnel spoke no more. An eerie hush fell over them. Adam Three had taken over. Adam Three, was a loving, kind, thoughtful Controller but unlike the eleven others he was wont to be ruthless. In each of the media members ears he boomed out "BELIEVE HER YOU SCAVENGING HYENAS or I will change you women into ready-to-use toilet rolls and you men into ready-to-use menstrual pads. Look at yourselves you leper ridden gargoyles."

"No," Adam Three," Eve One interjected. "Please let them be. Leave them as they were. I do not want any of us to tamper with their minds in any way. Let them speak and write what they wish without one wit of interference from us. Lana will have to handle the media on her own. We will, of course, be at her side when she faces the media. Let's all relax now and mix in with those who are attending tonight's social. We will go in as good looking 'gals' and handsome 'guys.' Thanks gang. Let's all have fun as earthlings tonight. Stop by and say hi to Lana at the social…she will get a 'kick' out of seeing us."

Lana was polite and most ladylike to everyone who crowded around her as she made her way to her various destinies. In due course she was at her table along with the members of the council. The council invited Clark to join them." He did.

Lana had her two drinks of vodka over ice, danced with several men from the council; one with Adam Six; a chat with Eve Three and her dance partner; a wink from Eve One; smiles from all the other Controllers but not a single dance with Clark.

At two minutes to eleven, the orchestra stopped playing. Dr. Lana Masters was at the orchestra leader's microphone. The lights in the grand social room dimmed, three large 20 feet by 20 feet television screens on three different walls came on.

Dr. Masters asked everyone to view the program that was about to show up on the big screens. The incidences forthcoming she said, would be as she had described them earlier in the day. They were. In a space of 21 minutes the 'show' was over. The invitees were speechless for several minutes.

Lana broke the silence. "Thank you for your kind attention my dearest friends. What you have just witnessed was Controllers' driven. I should like to inform you that the Twelve Controllers are here with you now in the form of humans. Have fun trying to identify them." Lana smiled. "Ta Ta I must away to bed. I shall be with you tomorrow morning, good night and sweet dreams."

The applause was thunderous. The media was perplexed. "How the fuck?" They shook their heads, they hurried to telephone their respective editors and producers to report the phenomenon. They become even more perplexed when their editors and producers told them they had just viewed the same 21-minute news flash. Christ! What next!

Lana's last statement finally 'sunk in' to the partygoers and the media, "the Twelve Controllers are here with you." Everyone looked at everyone else, searching for a clue as to the Controllers' identities. They touched one another. Some became frightened. A few guests somewhat intemperate from the good wine asked brazenly of anyone, "Are you a Controller?"

Eve Three sidled up to one very handsome man, and said, "You must be one of the Adams, sir, you are so attractive, are you?" The man was speechless. "Show me some of your wizardry, take me to your love nest in the cosmos, and I will be your lover forever," Eve Three said as she smiled an impish smile.

"No, No," the man responded in a timid voice. "But, oh dear, would that I were a Controller. You are so beautiful. Please forgive me for being so forward Miss…"

"Miss Koslosky," Eve Three teased. She stood on her toes and kissed his cheek, then moved off into the crowd.

Dr. James Bell-Irving stood dumbfounded, touched his cheek where Eve Three had kissed him and reached out for her. She had disappeared into the crowd. 'Damn,' he thought.

A large group of people seated at two tables pushed together shouted, "Controllers, please, show yourselves." Leading the group was Adam Six who called out again, "come on Controllers, show yourselves."

Suddenly a warm fragrant breeze feathered its way over the partygoers. As it drifted across the room it whispered softly in everyone's ears, "Yes, we are among you, chatting with you, dancing with you and sipping wine with you, but you will not be able to identify us. I am Eve One. Please, continue your party and forget we are here." People sighed.

As Lana glided past guests on her way to her table peoples hands came out to touch her. She reciprocated. Everyone's eyes were glued on her. She bubbled with life.

After excusing herself to the council Lana put her fingers to her lips, threw everyone a kiss, then with Clark at her side made off to her room.

*　　*　　*

Lana undressed to her bra and panty. Clark sat transfixed. She came to him and pulled his head into her lower body and stroked his thick black hair. "How I love you Clark," she said looking down at him as he lifted his head and looked into her eyes.

"Lana, how in heaven's name can I ever express how much I love you?" He paused, stood, took her in his arms, "No love will ever be as deep as mine is for you."

"Don't be so serious Romeo," she replied tickling him, "you are so dramatic, so charming, yet so boyish." She nipped his ear then wrestled him down onto her bed.

And big boy, to prove to you that I am just an ordinary farm girl I am going to go to the washroom, take off my panty and bra, go potty, shower, brush my teeth, climb into bed, fuck you every which way, kiss you goodnight then go to sleep."

Clark blushed. He took off his clothes, except his shorts, went into the bathroom after Lana was in bed, did his thing, stripped off his shorts, and like a shy kid covered his rigid penis with his hands. He shuffled over to the bed, sat at the bed's side ready to climb in with Lana.

Laughing Lana pushed his hands aside, grabbed his penis, kissed its tip, mouthed it, then like a naughty girl, pulled his head down to her delectable "y." "French kiss it kinda, my shy superman," Lana giggled. "Ahh good boy, that's soooo nice, don't stop. Ooooh yes, yes," she moaned.

Clark reached under her buttocks, lifted her hips up, pushed his tongue inside her, carressed her clitoris with it, moved his mouth tenderly in every direction. Lana moaned, "Oh Clark, don't ever stop…no…yes…no Clark. No Clark, stop now, put your you know what…yes, yes…ooooh Clark…please do not stop…please…ooooh…" Her intoxicating orgasm was indescribable. Clark put her rounded buttocks back down on the bed. Lana reached for his erection and steered it into her vagina. Clark entered her. She came again in exotic rapture. Groaning, Clark exploded. God, how could anything in the whole Universe match this, he thought.

Like a cute little pixie Lana smiled, at him. As she kissed him goodnight she could smell and taste her female juices on his lips. This intrigued her. It was twelve o'clock midnight. Lana slept soundly until 7:00 a.m.

CHAPTER 34

LANA'S FRUSTRATION

At 9:45 a.m., Tuesday May 6th, 1997, Dr. Philip Carruthers welcomed the 2,100 guests and called the meeting to order.

"Dr. Carruthers," a woman from the audience called out, "how in the name of our good lord did that...that episode at eleven o'clock...occur as predicted by Dr. Masters? How did she fabricate such a fantasy? I understand it was headline news across the world on radio, television, on the Internet, and indeed in this morning's Turkish press and radio. Who, pray tell, is this Dr. Lana Masters? Look at her Dr. Carruthers. Have you ever seen anyone like her? Look at her clothing, white slacks, simple pink cotton top, three quarter length sleeves, nothing special, but, my god, she looks beautiful, like, like a goddess in her attire. And her face and figure, is she of this planet? She orates without so much as one note, no cue cards, who is she, I beg of you who is she?

"Thank you Fraulein Stoltz," Dr. Carruthers acknowledged. "First, my dear Ms. Stoltz, our Dr. Lana Masters is of this planet. She was born on a farm just outside a small city called Swift Current which is located in Canada's wheat province, Saskatchewan. I know her parents very well. She is a genius. Her intelligent quotient is a startling 205-plus. Her beauty, what can I say? She stuns everyone who lays eyes on her.

"She is not a fraud, and I know, Fraulein, you were not intimating such. Last night's 21-minute episode did occur, it was not a fantasy. Dr. Masters did not predict these events. No, all my friends out there, she knew nothing about them until Adam One informed her so. The Twelve Controllers, by their majesty, had the six events take place at the exact time Dr. Masters announced them. At that precise moment Adam One informed Dr. Masters of these happenings. What more can I say Fraulein Stoltz?"

"Thank you Dr. Carruthers. I am still hopelessly confused." Fraulein Stoltz shook her head in amazement. How will we ever know the mystique of Lana Masters, she thought.

Dr. Carruthers called upon Dr. Lana Masters to proceed.

Lana did her welcomes and thank-you's. "Before I get to the topics listed on your agendas for today, I want to say I hope you enjoyed the social last evening. As well I hope some of you were fortunate enough to meet the Controllers. This morning Eve One told me the Controllers enjoyed themselves. They had fun. Did you know each of them danced with various guests during the evening? They chatted and joked with many of you. Some of the Eves were asked for dates. And Eve Three told me she stood on her tiptoes and kissed the cheek of a very handsome but shy gentleman."

* * *

"Over the next few days, ladies and gentlemen, I should like to bring you my views on the mysterious world of finances, religion and politics."

I recognize many of you will find my discourse on finances to be passe. Please bear with me. Finances, financial statements, monetary subjects, financial planning, financial instruments and the like are shunned by most people because they are too boring, too incomprehensible, too obscure and downright perplexing. Yet friends, we live among these mysteries every day. Money. All 'of the above' perplexing 'things' are drafted in terms of money. Money, something every person wants and needs. That people work hard to earn. That people require for the purchase of day-to-day necessities, housing, clothing, recreation, family raising, health, education, and for retirement. That people steal, cheat, gamble, counterfeit, beg, kidnap, and kill for. Wars are fought over money. Yet money, the so called root of all evil, is nothing more than a medium of exchange, a price setter, a store of value and a measure of value. In simple terms that is what money is and those are its functions.

The development of our modern day civilization and our modern day knowledge came about as a result of fiated money. Our modern world and its progress or regress remains contingent on various forms of money, paper, plastic and book entries. How simple. As one economist so aptly put it, 'money is a unique and functional device for measuring economic values and for performing the awesome tasks of exchange in a world of heterogeneous goods and services. A monetary system performs these functions much more expediently than any other arrangement and with no necessity for detailed controls except the regulation of the number of nominal money units to be minted.'

Lana continued. She said it took over 2000 years to get to where we are now with fiated money. In our so called barbaric beginning pure barter was the trading process practiced. The basic problem with barter is the double coincidence of wants. In addition, specialization is required in today's complex economy. Consider the professions, doctors, lawyers, accountant, dentists, architects, engineers, computer specialists, athletes, painters, writers, hair dressers, finance specialists for example in a barter society. And what about Bill Gates and Warren Buffet in a barter society, how would they go about trading their services for food, shelter, clothing and luxuries. In a pure barter society specialists would make up the ranks of the destitute. Our world would still be pristine if it wasn't for efficient mediums of exchange. We would still be living in a tribal society.

Modern day economies require men and women to spend their whole working lives in one career. The current economic efficiency of nations' industrial giants is based on the staggering increase in scientific and technological knowledge over the past 50 years. But knowledge can be improved only if men and women 'specialize' by spending their professional lives working in one limited area. The modern world could not survive as it is without economic specialization. Yet specialists cannot live on what they produce. In a barter society, how many cows would equate to a loathsome root canal. Specializing professionals depend on a complex monetary system to reward them in money for their services. With money in the hands of his patient the dentist can trade his root canal service for a few hundred bucks. Now the dentist has a few hundred bucks to buy whatever he needs. Otherwise the hapless dentist woud end with a herd of cattle.

Industrial giants cannot exist without an enormous network of monetary exchanges. They must purchase raw materials, pay for the manufacturing of their product, then sell and distribute their product to final users. Can you imagine the monetary compexities facing industrial giants such General Motors, General Electric or the like. Monetary systems must be extremely sensitive in order to meet the colossal demands of trillion dollar economic segments. Yes the modern world depends on economic efficiency, specialization, and money exchanges.

Next Lana referred her audience to the beginning of the middle ages where very little progress was made in science both in inquiry or experiment. Communication systems were almost non-existent. That's just a mere 20 grandfathers ago. Intellectual activity began to accelerate during the high middle ages from about the 10th century through to the 14th century. This period formed the basis of modern history. Geographic exploration and discovery, the printing press, gunpowder for more efficient killing and the progress of the natural sciences occurred. A new class of bourgeoisie arose, professionals, scholars, administrators, independent merchants and with this new class of thinkers arose the need for more efficient techniques of production and voila, the need for an efficient money exchange system. Fiated money, mediums of exchanges agreed upon by governments and its citizens, became necessary to accommodate the burgeoning economics of the time. Hence, back about 10 or 12 grandfathers ago, the growth of our modern monetary systems began. But in today's society the appropriation of wealth measured by money is somewhat askew. "Fuck," Lana said in her her inimitable way, "the distribution of money holdings is bloody awful. $100 billion in net worth between a couple of gents compared to zip for a few billion hand to mouthers. Doesn't that grab you. Do you think the good Lord Jesus' breasts would swell with pride knowing that millions of his people live like shit while others are awash in money.

*   *   *

Lana was remonstrative in her diatribe against the obvious inequities between the rich and the poor. She said the basis of these inequities was beyond human reasoning. From the beginning of time, with few exceptions, the poor have touted the rich. The poor bitch and moan about the rich but by and large savor them as unavoidable and worship them subliminally as a singular seraphic deity. She reminded her attendees of her supposition pertaining to the *clever one.* Wasn't the advent of the *clever one* a reasonable hypothesis? Over the centuries the rich have found that, by and large, they need do nothing to enhance the worship of their penurious suck-ups but sit back and enjoy. Yet without question, the rich need the poor just as the poor need the rich. Can you imagine how the rich would endure if there were no poor to look down on. It would be hell on earth. And who could the poor look up to, to worship and adore if there were no rich, rich people like Gates, Buffet, Queen Elizabeth, Oprah, the Sultan of Brunei. Even folks like Air Jordon, Ken Griffy Jr., Oscar De La Hoya, Wayne Gretsky, movie stars and movie moguls, C.E.O's of banks and other industries. It's mind boggling how this all came about.

Lana hesitated for a moment as she looked out over her audience. She feigned a look of consternation for her forgetfulness in commenting on Ms. Stoltz's questions of Dr. Carruthers. "Is Dr. Lana

Masters of this planet? Who is she?" Lana had not forgotten to support Dr. Carruthers' reply to Fraulein Stoltz. No she had not said a word at the time because she wanted her mystique to be solidified among her attendees, viewers and listeners. She felt had she backed Dr. Carruthers' reply earlier it would look like overkill.

Lana felt now she could respond to Fraulein Stoltz. "Please forgive me Ms. Stoltz, and colleagues, I intended to follow up on Dr. Carruthers' answers to you regarding where I'm from and who I am. I must say the good Doctor's responses were correct in every respect, every respect, dear lady, except one. One that is unknown even to me. One I know is real but is abstract and elusive. It's possible I may never know its make-up or its consequences as an earthling. But, believe me my friends, this obfuscation in no way denigrates from the fact that I am as you are…a human being. Again please accept my apologies Fraulein Stoltz."

People in the audience stirred and whispered to one another about Dr. Masters' secret. Damn her, why doesn't she tell us what this exception is? We know she knows. She's just covering up. Is she of this world?

"Dr. Masters, was it necessary for you to chide us with your 'exception?' Sir Reginald Chalmers of the Council scolded. "Why did you leave us in this dilemma? Surely you could have kept this to yourself and saved all of us from conjecture."

"Sir Reginald, I did this on purpose. I have these consuming, burdensome, unanswered questions about myself. I was selfish, I wanted people to share in my frustrations. I can add nothing more."

Dr. Carruthers interrupted. "With your leave, ladies and gentlemen, I should like us to break for coffee. Please be back in your seats in 20 minutes.

Some attendees moved out to the convention center's large anti-room for their coffee and other refreshments while others remained seated. Lana Masters walked over to the council's head table. She was mulling over her provocative words. Some unknown mystery has been inside her since childhood telling her that, dash it all, she did have some vital unanswered questions about herself. Lana supposed this dichotomy was the reason the controller's hadn't 'come down' hard on her.

"Yes Lana, you were right in your supposition" Eve One stated. "We Controllers will answer this riddle for you in due course."

Lana did not question Eve One's words. But now, her anxiety level spurted upward passing even her frustrated audiences. Shit, Shit, Shit! I need to know what the hell I'm all about, she thought. Fuck everyone else—this not knowing is fucking awful.

"Now, now, Lana," Eve One scolded.

On reaching the head table Lana saw the looks of consternation in the eyes of several of the council members. Her Honor Marie Du Charme' of Montreal, Quebec and Sir Reginald Chalmers of Manchester, England seemed to be seething, not just with consternation but with anger. They sat side by side at the head table. Both of them were in their mid-forties, she was stunning and he was handsome in a 'stuffy' sort of way.

'They are really pissed off with me,' Lana mused. 'I know damn well they're fucking each other even though they're both married, I can tell by their phony prudishness.

"Lana behave yourself. Goodness, while we all cherish you, we feel you are a reprehensible brat sometimes. You know full well we can rule your mind anytime we wish and relieve your mind of your tiresome cursing and sex." Eve one scolded.

"But," Adam Six interrupted, "you are such fun, Lana, our sweetheart, what would we do without your awful tongue and your priceless thoughts? We have no intention of taking over your mind…at least not in the 'foreseeable' future," he teased.

"I love each of you," Lana said. "I will try to unbrat myself."

"We know you do and we hope you will." Eve One responded

Lana addressed the council. "Please excuse my impulsive, selfish statement about the one 'exception' I passed on to our audience a few minutes ago. I admit I erred. I understand your anger with me Sir Reginald. I beg your forgiveness for these misguided words of mine. I deem all of us to be friends. I would do nothing to jeopardize this friendship…"

"Lana, good gracious, to me sometimes you are an uncontrollable 'loose cannon.' Often I shudder wondering what 'next' will come from your pretty lips. But you are daring, rebellious, spirited, you are brilliant, exciting, ebullient, you could charm the pants off the Pope himself. Keep it up Dr. Masters," replied Thomas Cooper, a self-made billionaire from Rancho Mirage, California. "Before your upcoming tirade against the necessity of charity, I want you to know I am going to remit a cheque in the amount of 500 million dollars to my federal government. I will propose these monies be used solely for the purpose of feeding hungry children in my beloved country, the USA. And Doctor, I want you to know that you, and you alone, are the reason behind this donation. Truly, you are a humanitarian. You inspire me. I love you for that. I wish I could help you find the evasive answer to your exception.'"

"My goodness, Mr. Cooper you are so gracious and thoughtful, I thank you." Lana walked over to Thomas Cooper. She took his hand, bent down and kissed his cheek. "Thank you sir," she repeated.

"Lana, what a prize you are," Thomas Cooper replied smiling.

"I should like to point out, ladies and gentlemen of the council, I am living a wonderful life. But this unknown exception gnaws at me without let up. Tantalized, I await, *quod erat demonstrandum.* My sincerest apologies to each of you."

"Lana dear, I can say that your apology is accepted by all of us on council," replied Marie Du Charmé.

"Thank you Madame, your honor."

After Dr. Carruthers reconvened the assemblage Dr. Masters took time to explain her own frustrations to her listeners regarding the unknown exception that has plagued her mind since childhood. She said she felt her subliminal threshold slowly was giving way to her extrasensory processes, and that within the next few years her extrasensory processes will give way to reality. At this point in time she said she should know the answer to this elusive secret. And yes, ladies and gentlemen, then I shall let the world know my secret, providing of course it isn't just some frivolity."

CHAPTER 35

LANA LECTURES ON MONEY AND FINANCES

Lana had had a huge screen installed next the screen that portrayed her every move. The screen was 36 feet tall and 50 feet wide. It was large enough to provide for easy viewing by the center's attendees and media. Lana intended to use the screen to place special emphasis on certain exigencies of her upcoming words. As well, she had seen to it that brochures, which outlined the topics Lana would cover that day, were given to everyone as they entered the assembly room.

Now Lana wove her way into the mysteries of money matters just as easy and effective as Adolph Hitler had woven his innocent scheme to Neville Chamberlain one grandfather ago.

*　　　*　　　*

She loved what she had done in Istanbul.

'Fuck the bloody rats,' she mumbled to herself as her mind kept her entrenched in the memories of her meetings in that great city.

*　　　*　　　*

Lana looked at her audience to see if sleep had overtaken any of them. Damn, she thought, I have to speed things up so that I can stimulate my attendees with my political and religious sentiments. The shit I am peddling now is important but boring.

"Friends," Lana shouted, "did you know that the human brain is still the most competent, complex wondrous computer of all computers. But unlike today's man-made computers, which require highly skilled technicians to produce, the brain is still capable of being mass produced by unskilled labor."

A couple of giggles could be heard. But the audience came alive with Lana's 'shout.'

She continued her topic on money.

The real value of money, Lana said is determined by its purchasing power. Money sets the price consumers are willing to pay for goods and services. Money prices for all goods and services in a country is referred to as a price level, and the purchasing power, that is the value of money, is expressed by the level of prices. Thus, as the price level rises the value of money falls and the value of money rises when the price level falls. Doesn't that just grab your ass.

Adam Six knew Lana would finish her morning discourse in a matter of ten minutes, and that he would utilize the last five minutes to stir up the attendees before their lunch break. He would inject some excitement in the audience. 'Cool,' he colloquialized.

Lana pursued the topic of money by defining money by its six constituents, a medium of exchange; a standard of value; a store of value; a unit of account; a price setter and a bearer of options. She was in the process of explaining in detail each of these constituents when she hesitated as she saw the lights in the beautiful hall dim and the screen depicting her and the huge 36 by 50-foot screen light up. Adam Six entered Lana's mind. He told her the screens would hold some of life's divergent images. These images he said would last for 5 minutes.

The big screen divided itself into four equal parts while Lana's remained whole. Lana's screen was vibrant and raucous—it displayed a colorful swinging casino on the opulent Las Vegas strip. Slot machines were ringing, singing, swallowing and clanging. They were the epitome of mass money circulation. Velocity! The machines were sucking in thousands and spitting out hundreds. Screams erupted from jackpot winners. The craps tables were bouncing along with occasional yells. One tousled gent, who looked like wet shit, eyes glazed from lack of sleep, found he could still holler.

"YEA! COME TO PAPA! HIT ME WITH TWO LITTLE ROWS OF RABBIT SHIT.

"YEA BABY THANKS FOR THE SIX, YOU GAVE ME THE KICKS; IT'S FORTY TO ONE ON MY FIVE HUNDRED BUNS.

"THAT'S TWO HUNDRED, HUNDREDS OF LOOT I SO CLEVERLY WON…

"SO FUCK THE GREEN VELVET I GO HOME HOW I COME…NO BUS FOR ME NOW, NO, CROUPIER JOE…

"I JUST UNHOCK MY OLD CADDIE THAT'S BEAT UP AND CRAPPY AND PUT PEDAL TO METAL THEN OFF TO MY PAPPY…

"BUT WHO GIVES A SHIT THAT I'M UP TWENTY BIG ONES BUT SHIT A GOD DAMN I SEE THE FAT I.R.S. MAN'S A'COMMIN…

"HE'S HERE FOR SIX THOUSAND SO GIMME A BEER WHILE HE FUCKS UP THE COUNTING AND I SHED A TEAR."

"Get outta here," several gamblers laughed.

"Your poetry stinks."

Black jack tables, pai gow tables, poker tables, all the tables were full. Money and chips were everywhere. Lusty!

On the upper left hand corner of the big screen was a picture of a huge home awash in riches. Beautiful gardens, a breathtaking swimming pool, tennis courts, and three guest houses. It's worth, $20 million. A Rolls Royce and a Ferrari languished under the mansion's spacious PORTE-COCHÉRE. Wealth!

On the upper right hand corner of the big screen was a picture of the Vatican treasures. Palatial *cum riches cum inequity!*

On the lower left hand corner of the big screen was a live scene. Ugly, vicious. Rwanda's, stumbling puking refugees. Children trampled. Death by starvation. Human blood. Stinking fetid mess. Outrageous!

On the lower right hand corner of the big screen was another live scene. A skeletal, starving, bloated bellied baby girl crying from hunger and pain. Flies swarmed around her watery eyes, her runny nose and her cracked swollen lips. Her mother's breasts were vacant of milk. This baby along with millions like her is devoid of lifes simplest of pleasures. She will die in three days. Shocking!

The attendees sat without a whisper. In five minutes the pictures vanished.

CHAPTER 36

MORE MONEY AND FINANCES

A delicious lunch of fresh vegetables, fruit, carrot cilantro soup, refreshments and tasty *petits fours* awaited the guests for the noon break.

The session re-convened at 1:30 p.m.

Dr. Carruthers confirmed that the pictures seen on the two screens just before lunch were not part of the agenda. "Dr. Masters," Dr. Carruthers said, "together with…ahem…Adam Six, brought about these factual scenes. Clearly, they emphasize money inequities, and clearly they show the value of money. Dear me! Please continue Dr. Masters."

"Thank you Dr. Carruthers.

"It is important to recognize the fact that the value of money and the acceptance of money are two different things. The value of money is its purchasing power. Its acceptance depends on its utility value as a commodity such as gold, silver or any other metal, or, whether the citizens of a nation permit its government to decree a non-commodity as money, to wit, an inconvertible paper standard. The paper standard is used in most industrialized nations. The prime example is the U.S. dollar.

Lana paused.

CHAPTER 37

H&B FINANCIAL AND POORS, INC.

Vito Apostli and Washington Jefferson's murder

Just as Dr. Masters paused, two of her fellow board members of H&B Financial and Poors in lower Manhattan were chatting. "Hey man, just over $1.8 billion in assets in five years," The yellow toothed, wop marveled. "Christ, I wish Clark was here," Vito Apostli nagged.

"We jes wait, ya rubby dub, 'til he does gits here," Washington Leroy Jefferson warned. "We uns jus wait."

"I know," Vito said as he sucked on the top of the bottle of 'Bright's Concord'. Some of the cheap shit dribbled down his stubble. "Ya, man, I knows." Dreamily Vito muttered, "With my share of the pot, I could buy a couple swimmin' pools full of the sweet 'Motha' nectar an stay fucked up drunk all day and night."

"That's true wopola, you ugly bastard, that's 'bout where yo brain stops—pissed up on bingo," Leroy scolded.

"What a guy Clark is, huh Leroy?"

"The best Vito."

"With what we got now, do you figger nigger we'll be goin' uptown to live, ya know, on Snot Hill?"

"I don' know, wop. Maybe." Leroy wondered. He turned from the hand warming burning barrel, unzipped his fly, yanked out his black dorque squeezed its head, aimed it upward toward Vito and leaked a hot stream of steamy piss 15 feet in the air, right over Vito's head.

"Asshole." Vito yelled jumping aside.

"Ha, ha ya two-bit eyety," Leroy laughed, "I can piss higher'n at."

"Fuck away and die ya fuckin' shine, ya black ass'ed piece o'hyena shit."

Leroy shook the wet tailings off his cock, stuck it back in his pants, zippered up all the while laughing at the angered 'wop.'

"Ya know Leroy, when yor cock is outta your pants like that, you be half naked…you big pricked whoremaster."

"You got that right man," Leroy responded.

Vito Apostli and Washington Leroy Jefferson were members of the Board of Directors of "H and B Financial." They were each other's best friends. They would die for one another. Vito was once an esteemed doctor, a neurosurgeon, while Leroy was once a successful stockbroker. Each one of them hit the skids because of their drinking and drug problems. Their use of the English language and its niceties were used only on rare occasions. They couldn't wait until Clark got back from wherever he was. Clark knew he had meetings coming up at the end of May with H&B's auditors, brokers and bankers. "By damn," Vito said, "maybe all our board members, including Clark, should get some new store bot duds for the meetings. After all, our company is rich, $1.1 billion is in liquid assets, $600 million more is in top grade small Manhattan properties, while $100 million is invested in one big hockey franchise. We better ask Clark about this. Shit though, the annual general meeting of our scum bag shareholders is coming up on June 10th, 1997, and we uns wont need no new clothes for that meeting. Christ we'd be booted out on our asses if we showed up in suits and ties."

The May night was cooling down. Vito and Leroy tossed more sticks and papers into the barrel. The flames danced on getting a refill of 'stuff' that burned. Three more scum bags joined Vito and Leroy. They all had their hands extended over the flames.

"That's better," they all agreed.

Two shots rang out. Vito and Leroy were dead before they fell to the pavement. The three frightened scum-bags ducked behind the barrel, no more noisy shots, just the hum of traffic on fourth avenue.

CHAPTER 38

GEORGE WASHINGTON TO BILL CLINTON...U.S. DEBT

Holly Hoxdale, stunning hooker

Lana, over the past few months had mapped out her whole strategy pertaining to the Istanbul seminar. Her intent was to bring the topics of her five-day lectures to a bottom line much like financial statements do, a single bottom line figure anyone can read, like any entity that measures its success by its bottom line.

Lana was determined to bring her audience through a maze of heady topics, money, economics, religion and politics and lead them to the bottom line of her demographics with but one word anyone could understand...humanism. Humanism, the bottom line of life!

* * *

She maneuvered her way into the huge build-up of many nations' public debt. She had used the United States as an example. The U.S. federal debt amounted to 4.3 trillion dollars in 1996, while non-federal debt amounted to a staggering 10.4 trillion dollars. Amalgamated, the outstanding debt of the public and private sectors was just under 15 trillion dollars.

Lana remembered scolding the debt harbingers for their incessant one-sided story telling. These harbingers she had said refrain from explaining two vital realities. One, that the U.S. debt began with President George Washington in the year 1792, so it's not just a recent phenomenon the negative pundits would have you believe. Two, that much of the debt occurred as a result of government spending over the past 200 years on infrastructures vital to the needs of its citizenry, infrastructures which only the government could fund.

Lana brought out some startling facts pertaining to the United States of America. She noted that for a 206 year period, beginning in 1791 and ending in 1996, government surpluses occurred in 107 of those years, a balanced budget occurred only once and 98 of those years resulted in deficits.

She knew many in the audience would see her views as political rather than economic. She smiled as she placed her hands on her hips, parted her legs causing therefore her white slacks to stretch. These moves she knew all too well would clear the minds of all her attendees. Anyone out there who believed she took 'overloaded government debt' too lightly would have such thoughts expunged in a trice in favor of the wonderment of the riches which were hidden by her simple attire.

"President George Washington," Lana said, rang up the first deficit in the year 1792, a piddling amount of $1.4 million. And guess what my dear associates, early in Thomas Jefferson's presidency, 1800–1808, President Jefferson had his administration apply 70% of the nation's national revenue against its national debt. So you can see even back then the federal debt was a nasty issue. Mr. Jefferson was a democratic republican…ostensibly a republican in today's parlance. Under his leadership he had his envoys conclude the Louisiana Purchase, a whopping 800,000 square miles, for a mere $15 million in 1803, from France. What is the market value of this massive piece of land now? Trillions, I dare say. What ever happened to this huge property? Is there an accounting of disposals by way of sales, grants or gifts over the years? Can an American citizen find what happened to the 800,000 square miles? What dollar value is there for any residual ownership by the U.S. government, if so where is this residual value recorded?

"In any event four big years of deficits occurred in the years 1812 to 1815 totaling $68.3 million, while the total public debt rose from $56 million to $127.3 million, an increase of $71.3 million during the same period of time. All of these setbacks occurred under republican presidential rule. Mind you, the war of 1812 to 1814 occurred causing, I'm sure, some justifications for the annual deficits and the increased debt load for this new hearty, bouncing nation.

"A long reign of republican presidents began in 1860, starting with Abraham Lincoln in 1860 and ending with James Garfield in 1883. From 1860 to 1865, deficits for those six years totaled $2.6 billion and from 1866 to 1883…17 years…surpluses of $1.1 billion occurred, resulting in a net deficit of $1.5 billion for the whole 24-year period. It was during the Civil War years from 1861 to 1865 years that the annual deficit soared.

"The republican rule saw carpetbaggers infiltrating the southern states. These wily fellow's objectives were to gain money in whatever manner suited them. Unscrupulous devils a lot of them. The carpetbag state governments spent extravagantly individual states' incomes with millions of dollars going to carpetbaggers in the form of graft, while republicans in the north enjoyed kissing the fat asses of big business. For example, Northern Pacific Railroad was given 47 million acres from the government. Frauds took place. Unscrupulous politicians and corrupt businessmen raided without remorse the cookie jars known as the public treasury and the public domain. The total public debt of this great new nation grew from $65 million in 1860 to $1.7 billion in 1883."

"Woodrow Wilson, a democratic president for eight years, 1912 to 1919, ran up deficits of $23.26 billion during his tenure. Almost 100% of these deficits occurred in the last two years of his administration, the result of the war to end all wars, the First Great One. Total public debt grew by some $24.3 billion during Mr. Wilson's presidency and reached $24.5 billion by the year 1919.

"Franklin Delano Roosevelt, also a democrat, took over the reins of president for the longest tenure of all presidents in the U.S.A. past and present. Thirteen years in all, 1932 until his death in 1944, from the midst of the dirty 30's through most of World War II. At the beginning of President Roosevelt's term of office, the nation's public debt amounted to $19.5 billion. At the time of his death in 1944, the debt had risen by $184.6 billion to a staggering $204.1 billion. The annual deficits for those 13 years totaled $150.8 billion.

"During the stormy tenure of President Richard Nixon, from 1968 to 1973, the gross national debt grew from $369.8 billion to $541.9 billion…an increase of $172.1 billion. It was under President Nixon's term of office that the last of the federal government's annual surpluses occurred. The surplus amount was $3.1 billion and the year was 1969. Remember President Nixon had that dreadful Vietnam War to contend with during his tenure.

"President Carter's four-year regime saw the annual deficit decline from $70.5 billion in 1976 to $38.1 billion in 1979. However the federal debt increased by $200.0 billion under President Carter's administration and totaled $828.9 billion in 1979.

"Now came the Big Boys, the Conservative Genteel Elitists from the Grand Old Party led by Big Ronny. The man who stated that you can't make the poor richer by making the rich poorer. Not kosher math I'd say. But by golly, you sure knew how to spend the good old Yankee dollar on big business with just pocket change going to the poor. In any event you were classic as a leader, physically tough and your performances on TV were all award winners—and your supply side economics. Supply side, a new, breathtaking, economic masterpiece that will obliterate that devil, the federal debt. Let us non-wasteful Conservatives show you how it's done. With God on our side, we will demonstrate the fine art of fiscal fairness and sound financial management. Even though those irresponsible democrats spent money helter-skelter over the last four years on frivolous escapades, we, the champions of righteousness will stop such frivolity. During President Reagan's term in office, 1980 to 1987, the eight annual deficits ballooned as follows:

$72.7 billion in 1980
$73.7 billion in 1981
$120.0 billion in 1982
$207.9 billion in 1983
$185.6 billion in 1984
$221.6 billion in 1985
$237.9 billion in 1986
$169.2 billion in 1987

This adds up to a grand total of $1.2886 trillion. Tilt! The federal debt stood at a whopping $2.345 trillion. Good work, supply-siders!

"Then along came George Bush, another conservative. President Bush had a four-year stint from 1988 to 1991. He did have the desert war to contend with in 1990. During President Bush's administration the combined total of the annual deficits amounted to $889.2 billion and the federal debt had swollen to $3.6 trillion.

"Handsome Bill Clinton powered into the presidency in 1992. The annual deficit hit an all-time high that year, reaching $293.3 billion as the federal gross debt ballooned to $4.19 trillion. Under President Clinton's administration, however, the annual deficits have fallen steadily. The Federal Gross Debt stood at $4.3 trillion at the end of 1996. However, it would not be surprising to see the annual federal deficit disappear as early as 1998 or 1999.

"Interesting is it not, my friends? The information contained in your brochures regarding the federal debt build-up shows the build-up runs parallel to the colossal advancement and modernization of this great nation. Mind you, many disruptions occurred along the way and still occur today and, without question, will occur in the future. But, by and large, they have been overcome rather well. I should like to make one final observation before we break for coffee and that is, only public funding through its elected government representatives can fulfill the continuous demand by a nation's citizenry for mighty infrastructures. Insufficient funding through revenues must result in debt. While the debt load of the U.S. will be the responsibility of future generations, future generations will have the ownership and the use of publically held infrastructures which, I must say, created the ponderence of the debt in the first place. Kind of a wash wouldn't you say?"

It was agreed by the council and the attendees that a 15-minute break would suffice.

* * *

Within minutes into the break, Clark St. James was delivered a cable from Trent Logan, his associate in Manhattan,

The cable read: *Vito and Leroy dead. Murdered at 10:33 p.m. May 6. Sorry Clark. Trent.*

Clark winced, he doubled over in shock after reading the cable. 'No, God no, it can't be.' Tears filled his eyes. 'Who would want to kill these two harmless men?' He left the assembly hall. 'Vito and Leroy, they are irreplaceable friends, why?' Clark exited the building, found a bench, sat and with elbows on his knees, his face in his hands and sobbed.

After several minutes Clark took control of himself. He sat up, lowered his hands and shook his head. Anger began to share a spot in his mind along with sorrow. 'I'll get whoever did this. They'll suffer.'

Still with disbelief in his mind he re-read the cable. "Why and who" he said to himself? Clark knew many people were jealous of the 7,000 scummers who made up the shareholders of H&B Financial, but to kill? He doubted it. But Clark knew there were people out there who would kill for the opportunity to take over H&B. H&B was a very wealthy organization. If someone could garner a controlling interest in H&B

and change its corporate structure, he or she would become instant multi-millionaires. But why kill Vito and Leroy? Sure they were on H&B's directorate and they were damn competent men, but by killing them did not assure the killer or killers of anything. The takeover of H&B would require a very complex plan, not the killing of two shareholders. Perhaps it was a scare tactic. Frighten the whole board of directors. Have them resign. Elect a whole new board, a board who would follow the instructions of the killer or killers. Damn.....

He got up from the bench and hurried to an unused telephone booth. There he dialed direct to Trent's home in Manhattan. Trent answered in his usual abrupt manner,

"Ya."

"It's me, Trent."

"Hi, Clark."

"Vito and Leroy dead?"

"Yes, Clark. Sorry."

"Any idea who did it?"

"Maybe."

"Trent, while I'm broken up because of Vito and Leroy, I'm scared to death for Lana. Someone will be out to get her too, I'm sure."

"Ya, Clark, but we'll take care of her. By God no one will dare touch her."

"I'm going to call Holly and have her make all of the arrangements for"—Clark's voice stopped, "take care Trent and please help Holly."

"I will Clark."

They hung up.

'I can't believe it. Dirty rotten bastards.' Eyes red and body shaking, Clark started to make his way back to the convention center. He stopped. 'No, I better call Holly first.' Holly Hoxdale, former gorgeous street down-and-out hooker, tall, just over six feet, long straight light-brown hair, sleepy blue eyes, unbelievable ass and long legs that went all the way from here to there. Holly was now Clark's private secretary as well as H&B's assistant general manager and information officer. Clark had rescued her from near death. She was being gang-raped by some snot-nosed ivy-leaguers after they had spiced up her drink. Just before agreeing to go with one of the leaguers for $300 bucks, she had as usual pumped herself up mainstreaming on some of her pimp's shit.

Two female scummers quite by accident saw the rape taking place. They had just left the 'big handsome dude' Clark St. James with whom they had had coffee. Doris, the younger of the two female scummers rushed back to the run-down coffee shop just in time to intercept Clark from boarding a bus. "Clark, you're needed NOW!" Doris screamed. She grabbed his hand and led Clark to the scene of the drunken orgy.

Clark broke the arms of a 'coupla' of the ivy leaguers, blackened a number of eyes and crushed some fingers under his size 14's. He had left them a sorry mess. He carried Holly back to Vito Apostli, not yet drunk at this juncture and told him to take care her. Clark returned to the rape scene and found Holly's pimp, one Lenny Chimos. Clark beat the crap out of the foul excuse for a human being. He toyed with him like a cat toys with a mouse. After 20 minutes of torturing the low life, Clark hit him with a tremendous punch full in Lenny's mouth, dislodging eight of the pimp's gold capped teeth. Clark rushed back to Vito and the girl. Holly proved to be an invaluable addition to H&B Financial and Poors Inc. She, Vito and Leroy became inseparable friends.

* * *

From the time Holly first saw Clark St. James she fell madly in love with him. She kept this her secret. But my, how she ached over wanting his love in return.

After she got to know Clark well enough, Holly flirted and teased him. He was so shy and boyish. It was fun to watch him blush and hear him stammer when she snuggled her curvaceous body up against his big frame. She would smile, look up into his eyes, and murmur, "Is there anything more I can do for you master? I am, you know, your loving servant. I will do anything, positively anything your greatness wishes, tee hee." She would wiggle into his arms, pout, touch his lips with a slender finger. Only once did Clark succumb. This was just before he had met Lana. Holly had succeeded in getting him into her bed. She ravished his whole body. She kissed him everywhere all the while knowing she would finalize her assault on him in her favorite hold, the scrumptious 69.

She brought him to the edge of ejaculation in many ways, sucked his cock, sucked his toes, put the end of his mighty organ against her nipples, opened the crack at the end of his penis with her fingers and put her nipple inside. She had him perform cunnilingus. It was dizzying for Clark. He in turn ravished Holly. He was rough on her. He bit parts of her body. She would yelp and cry out. He would rub the transparent liquid drops that formed on the end of his penis on her lips and on her nipples. Clark was ready to explode. Before he knew it, Holly had maneuvered their bodies into the erotic 69 position, they came and they came, they exploded in each others mouth, the climax went on and on. Exhausted they slept for several hours in each other's arms.

That was the first and only love making session for Clark and Holly. Holly continued to love and cherish Clark. She knew Clark loved her, but only as a friend. To help cover her sorrow she found mental solace in befriending, caring for and nursing hundreds of H & B's seedy shareholders. She adored Vito and Leroy. She loved her new job with H&B as assistant general manager and information's officer. While she missed the streets and her profession as a prostitute from time to time, she never returned to her former life willingly.

*　　　*　　　*

Clark dialed the office of H&B Financial and Poors Inc., which was located on the main floor of an old warehouse building. The office had been walled off in the northwest corner of the building. Its interior was clean and spacious. It was up to date in the latest electronics. The office was plain, but Holly and other lady staff members had made the interior bright, cheery and colorful with lots of flowers, pictures and trinkets.

Holly answered in a quivering voice. "Oh Clark, it's you thank God. What are we going to do without those two…"

"Please Holly," Clark said.

"Sir, why would anyone want to harm Vito and Leroy? They were so gentle and kind."

"Holly please."

"I get sad, then angry. I can't control myself. We've got to catch those f—ing bastards."

"We will Holly."

"When are you coming back, Clark?"

"As soon as possible Holly. I want you to arrange the first flight out of here for me tomorrow morning Istanbul time, and get me into J.F.K. or La-Guardia as quick as possible. Please let me know the times and, oh, Holly would you pick me up at whichever airport I am to arrive at?"

"I'd love to."

"Holly, I know this will be asking a lot of you, but I want you to arrange for the funeral and all other necessary details, and stall off the media if you can.

"I will."

"Call me at any time if you need me."

"I will. I'll get on about your flights now. I am so distressed. I can't imagine life without those two."

"I feel the same Holly, bye."

"Bye."

Holly never did meet Clark at J.F.K.

Clark made his way back to the assemblage. He took his seat and looked up at Lana. He was sure he saw her wink in his direction. She looked stunning in her simple attire. How, he thought, will Lana take the news about the murders of Vito and Leroy? Damnation.

CHAPTER 39

ATROCITIES

Lana's mind strayed from her memories of her days in Istanbul. "Damn," she thought, "that was just a scant two weeks ago." Now her eyes were fixed on her shackled guest and his two remaining tormentors. The two male rats' bellies were beginning to look bloated. Should she pursue the execution of this man in the manner she had chosen? Fucking rats, and the two new visitors, the snakes, how gross. Gross! What an understatement! Her death sentence of her prisoner was just as diabolic as those Nazi Gestapo bastards who stuck garden hoses up the ass of certain of their prisoners and turned on the water.

Lana could not find it in her heart to absolve her prisoner of his sentence just as those fucking Nazis could not, nor would not absolve their sentence of the ones who were garden hosed. 'Am I as satanic as Adolph Hitler?' she asked herself. 'No way! If I had that cocksucking Hitler here right now I would have him lying alongside lover boy hosting more starved rats.'

Lover boy was a brute just as Hitler was. He deserved no better. At one time her guest was the typical All American, strong, gentle, truthful, sensitive, caring. But something inside him snapped a few years back. He became a killer. He found pleasure in mayhem of all kinds, rape, scoring pre-teen girls, causing hellish chaos in a few small Asian countries, torturing men, women and beasts alike without remorse. It titillated him to see animals suffer. Once he bragged to Lana about drugging a huge Brahma bull at an all-star rodeo being held in Dallas, Texas. The drug caused the bull to become blind just as he was about to be ridden. When the gate opened to release the bull and his rider, the bull panicked in fright and blundered into the arena. He ran amok, blind and terrified. He threw his tormenting cowboy aloft as if he was a fly. The riders and clowns who were there to assist the cowboy didn't realize the bull was blind. One clown, who had years of experience in sidetracking enraged bulls, stepped in front of the huge Brahma expecting the bull to swerve but the big bovine just kept on charging headlong, catching the clown on his horns. The bull pounded straight ahead, until he crashed headlong into a wire-bound board fence crushing the clown, breaking the boards, goring three spectators who were behind the fence and tangling itself in a maze of barbed wire. The huge beast fought a hopeless battle against the merciless barbs, its head and horns twisted and tossed, it's hooves flailed, it's massive body bucked. It screamed. The frightful scene was new and horrifying even to the most callused cowboy. Finally the wretched beast was shot. Lana's guest had caught the whole episode on tape. Bastard. Others of his tortures of animals were far too gross to even think on.

Lana switched her mind back to Istanbul.

She remembered spotting Clark in the audience. She felt he looked different somehow. Something was troubling him.

Hmmmmm, back to the topics she wanted to brief the world on. Yeah, some topics would deserve 'blasting' while others would deserve praise; Topics that should be common knowledge but are not.

She remembered Dr. Carruthers adjourning the assemblage until 8:00 p.m. She remembered the crowd pushing and jostling to get near her. She remembered the anguished look on Clark's face as he reached her side. She remembered the detailed lecture she had given to her attendees pertaining to various money matters as well as the history of the Dow Jones Industrial Average.

The attendees surrounded Lana. "How do you keep such detail in your head, Doctor? Why do you put down we God-fearing conservatives so?

Why do you carp at the rich? The poor deserve their lot. When will the Dow exceed 10,000? What about Euro-dollars and Petro-dollars? How big are your tits oh gorgeous one?" And on and on the questions came.

Lana smiled, unperturbed, even at the same reporter who was so insistent about her bust size. She high-fived some, shook hands with others as she and Clark made their way out of the prestigious hall.

Dr. Masters looked regal. She was breathtaking.

CHAPTER 40
LANA AND CLARK ST. JAMES

As Lana and Clark neared a huge exit corridor, Clark took her hand and picked up the pace to get her to himself as quick as possible. At last they were alone.

On hearing about Vito and Leroy, Lana stood for a moment dumbfounded. Tears began to roll down her cheeks. "Vito and Leroy? Who would kill such…?" she trailed off. Lana broke down and sobbed. Clark waited until she had cleared some of her emotions. He escorted her to a telephone booth. There he telephoned Holly Hoxdale on a special line. Holly answered.

After some sobbing by Holly, Holly told Clark that she had made all his travel arrangements. His flight was on Delta Airlines, departing Istanbul at 1210 p.m. Istanbul time, arriving at J.F.K. at 1600 New York time. She would be at J.F.K. to meet him. Clark thanked her. "Please stop crying Holly. I will see you at…"

Holly snuffled, "I can't wait for you to be here Clark. Bye," she said.

Bye Holly," Clark responded.

Holly would not be at J.F.K. to meet Clark.

"Will you be all right for tonight's session Lana?" Clark asked.

"Yes, of course Clark, you know me. I will keep Vito and Leroy out of my mind until we are together after tonight's session." Lana replied. Damn bastards, Lana thought, I'll catch the killer or killers. They'll pay for this!

The dinner served by the assembly's Turkish host was superb. Turkish bean salad, turkey apricot-glazed drumsticks, vegetables, a dessert to end all desserts, and wine from Turkey's finest vineyards, truly a Turkish Delight.

The assembly was called to order at 8:00 p.m., Tuesday,

May 6, by Dr. Carruthers. He invited Dr. Lana Masters to continue her discussions.

Lana thanked Dr. Carruthers. She welcomed the attendees to the evening session. She startled everyone with her changed attire. She wore a soft cream fine wool mini skirt, very breathtaking, topped by a light green formal cotton shirt, open at the neck, and a lovely one-button, soft cream form-fitting jacket that flowed over her hips. Her tanned legs were bare. Her shoes were made from a spun cream cloth with heels three inches high. She wore plain opal earrings, and a medium length, small pearl necklace. She was the queen of all beautiful women. She was born a high spirited prairie farm girl. A horse back riding, animal loving child who played in her father's granaries, ran with her dogs, toyed with her cats, fed the chickens, drove the tractor, climbed trees, generally in bare feet accompanied by a runny nose who grew into this exquisite woman. As a child she was a youthful Madonna, graceful, peppy, energetic, always smiling, always happy, always bubbly, always polite and charming. She grew up maintaining all these wonderful attributes.

While her opening volley was a potpourri of financial topics, Lana expressed them with amazing clarity. She put them all in perspective. She joked, she lambasted certain of the entities that control people's finances, she used theatrics, she was flattering in some instances and insulting in others. She carped on that mysterious thing called money supply. She tied the subject of moneys to interest rates.

She made an interesting observation about interest rates. In years past, the offering of interest on moneys to be borrowed had been looked on by some economists as a necessary bribe by borrowers to induce lenders, the recipients of income, to consume less than they might otherwise consume, thus leaving residual funds for lending. As well, she pointed out, some of the parlance handed out by some bygone economists was that interest as a reward compensated for the pains of abstinence suffered by a lender 'for fuck sake!' Good old boys from the socialist hoards heaped scorn on the notion if interest was a reward for the pains of abstinence, then the Rothschilds and other rich lads and lasses must have suffered monumentally.

Some laughter followed. A few people in the assembly carped "commie."

Lana's eyes flashed angrily. Dumb pricks, she thought. She carried on ignoring the 'commie' carping.

"As an aside, you may be dumfounded to know Homer found in ancient times interest rates declined when a society prospered and reached maturity, and rose when the society became chaotic and slumped. European rates fell from around 10% in the 12th century to 4% to 5% in the 15th century, then rose in the 16th century followed by a sharp fall in the 17th. Does that not sound familiar?" Lana exhorted. "Even in Ancient Greece, interest rates were as low as 6% and as low as 4% in Rome."

"Who told you this Lana, Eve One, Two, etc, etc? Did they take you back to ancient Greece so you could find out for yourself Lana?" Off came the jeerer's head. It flew once around the hall. Eyes popped open in disbelief. Then a sickening splat as it nestled back on the unbeliever's neck. He sat silent. Adam Five had fixed that dink.

Lana delved into interest rates, over heated economies, punishing recessions, inflation and deflation, the macro deflator, credit pools, hoarding and dishoarding. She held nothing back as she spanked the world community for allowing starvation to take place as meat spoils, as produce rots in fields, and as subsidies are paid to keep supplies low. We are not Samaritans, we are not our brothers' keepers, hell no, we must preserve our monetary principals above all else. Starvation so be it. What would the Lord Jesus do if he was faced with this delimma? The good old religious right don't seem to care.

Lana stopped and looked down at her wristwatch.

"Good Gracious, ladies and gentlemen, I see it is ten o'clock. I am sure Dr. Carruthers is ready for tonight's adjournment. I look forward to seeing you at tonight's social." She threw everyone a kiss.

Dr. Carruthers called for an adjournment of the assemblage. He welcomed everyone to the evening's social, and he announced it would be held in salon three. He said all of the Eves and Adams would attend as well. "Look for them," he said.

* * *

Dr. James Bell-Irving found he had difficulty containing himself. "I must find Miss Koslosky," he thought, "I won't let her out of my sight tonight. Damn, why am I so enamored with her?"

* * *

As usual, Dr. Lana Masters was surrounded by hundreds of attendees the moment she left the stage. She was gracious, courteous, polite and grateful for their kindness, but she had to explain to them the necessity of returning to her hotel room for an hour or so for business reasons. She promised everyone she would be back to 'Salon Three' not later than 10:30.

She and Clark St. James left for the Grand Hotel just one block from the Convention Center.

* * *

Clark dialed Holly.

Holly was expecting his call. "Yes, Clark, everything has been arranged, the funeral, everything. I will meet you at J.F.K. 7:45 p.m. Thursday, May 8th. Clark, I need you."

"I know you do Holly," Clark responded. "I will be with you tomorrow. Please try to relax, take care of yourself. Lana and I love you. I must be away now, so good-bye my dear."

"Damn you Clark," Holly blurted out, "I just want your love."

"Please Holly, say good-bye now."

"Good-bye Clark," she snapped and hung up the phone.

"Fuck him," she said angrily.

Her doorbell rang.

* * *

Clark held Lana's hand. He told Lana of Holly's love for him. He confessed his one and only escapade with Holly happened three years ago. "This was before I met you as Lana. I know we have known one another for nearly six years, but remember, for over the first three-and-one-half years I knew you only as Polly the Bag Lady. For those three-and-one-half years I had no idea under all those ragged, God awful wraps was the world's most brilliant, wonderful, beautiful girl. Anyway Lana, damn it all, Holly still thinks she loves me. You know I love only you. It is perplexing though, loving you that is. Everyone wants you…every one. How can I keep you loving me, how in heaven's name can I. How, Lana, how, when every man and half of the females in the world dream and fantasize about you. No girl, woman, female, lady worldwide can match you. You stand alone on this planet! In every sense of the word you are desirable. Good gracious, Lana, I can't imagine how my life would be without you."

Clark looked miserable. "Dammit, it would have been better for me had I never met you. It would be better for me if I could be one of those poor souls who could only dream about having you."

"Please Clark, no more. Be fair. You have no right to say things like that. Have I no say about our relationship? I could say the same about you. Women look at you and fucking flip. Be fair. I only want you. As you feel about me, that's how I feel about you. I know too, how you feel about Holly. So don't be silly. You're not exactly hyena bait. C'mon, kiss me. I looove yoooou. Understand. Now we must get back to the social!"

* * *

Lana was overcome with guilt. "Damn me and my life. Why me, Eve One, why me? Can't you let me go and find someone else to take my place as your choice? I want to be just like other women. I didn't ask to be like I am. I want love, marriage, kids. I want to be married to Clark. I don't want to be who I am. Please, Eve One, free me."

"Lana dear, I have no hold on you. You are free. You are at liberty to do as you wish. At the present time I play no role in your life."

"But you know exactly what I will do when I am on Stone King's talk show on Thursday evening. Clark will be devastated. Istanbul will be devastated. The whole TV viewing audience will be devastated. Please, Eve One!"

Silence surrounded Lana like water surrounds a drowning victim.

Eve One had left her.

"Clark, my darling, I love you so!"

CHAPTER 41

DR. JAMES BELL-IRVING AND EVE THREE: COSMIC LOVE

Dr. James Bell-Irving spotted her. She was chatting with some ladies. They were all smiling. They seemed to be trying to out-talk one another. Hah! The female of the species! Thank the Lord! He stared at Ms. Koslosky. Eve Three knew he was trying to get her attention. She giggled to herself. She knew everything that was taking place in his mind. She liked him…a lot. But let him work a bit.

James tried to look nonchalant, cool. He leaned his long body against a corner, put his right leg out in front of his left leg. This would show off the sharp crease in his Verducci slacks and would portray him as a man of the world. It didn't work. Ms. Koslosky glanced over in his direction only once. She didn't appear impressed. 'Damn it, I don't want to waste precious time cat and mousing, I want to be with her. Dang it. I'll just stroll over to her and say good evening.' And that's what James did. Pretending not to tip his hand (that she had him smitten) he strolled over in her direction (just as Eve Three had planned it).

The ladies were discussing Dr. Lana Masters.

"Well, good evening Ms. Koslosky, how very nice to see you," said the smitten one.

"Dr. Bell-Irving, a good evening to you." Eve Three smiled.

The good doctor's heart thumped.

Eve Three turned and came a step toward him. She glowed with femininity. She prevented James Bell-Irving from fainting. He looked quite unsteady from his longing for her.

"I don't want to interrupt, but I see your glass is empty Miss…"

"My first name doctor is that what you wish?"

"If I am not being too bold?" he said, his cheeks reddening.

"It's a Ukrainian name. It's funny, you may laugh at it."

"One so stunning as you can get by with any name," Dr. James replied.

Eve Three put on a pouting, little girl smile. She engulfed his whole being. She was vibrant, alive, mischievous, fun, enchanting, impish.

He wanted to take her in his arms and never let go of her.

"Go easy," Eve One warned, "unless you intend to take control of him."

"Darling mother, I want just ordinary everyday earth like fun with him."

"Knowing you, you will have fun you wretched girl," Adam six laughed.

"You're a wretch Adam six, who are you going to subterfuge tonight you handsome devil you?"

"Ha, ha, sweet sister, guess?"

"Be nice to Dr. James Bell-Irving Eve Three," Eve One said.

"Romantically, I will be unparalleled," Eve Three sighed.

"My first name doctor comes from a long line of Edmonton Albertans. It is Itanya, pronounced, Eye—Tan—Ya." Eve Three said.

"How entrancing, just as you are Ms. Koslosky, it's such an exciting name. You are—oh! I'm so sorry, shall I call you Itanya?" he blubbered. "May I bring you a…"

"Sherry please. Yes, do call me Itanya. May I call you…"

"James," said the doctor.

"James," Eve Three repeated. She had known his name from his birth.

Dash it all, Eve Three thought, he is so handsome, so charming and so shy.

"That's enough Eve Three," Eve One admonished.

"Too bad sister whoever. How do you pronounce your fancy new name, Eye –Tan—Ya? Adam Six teased.

"Up your galactic orifice," Eve Three laughed.

"That is quite enough Eve Three," Eve One cautioned.

"Yes Mommy," Eve Three giggled. For 51 billion years Eve One has cautioned and scolded Eve Three, you'd think she'd learn.

"Your sherry, Itanya,"

"Thank you James," Eve Three replied, smiling like a naughty girl. "Where do you practice James? I see the AMA insignia engraved on your fraternity pin so, I presume you are a medical doctor?"

"How observant of you Itanya," he said looking down at his pin. "I practice in the charming city of Santa Fe, New Mexico. I've been there eight years now, and I must say I love it. It's so laid back, clean and liveable."

"Do you have a family, doctor?"

"No, I've never married and I'm almost 35. Slow aren't I?" he replied. 'Good, God,' he thought, 'I would marry you on the spot if I could, Itanya.'

"See," Eve One said.

"Yes, Eve One, I see, and I'm loving every moment of it."

"Just be nice now dear"

"I will. I'll be real nice…ohhhh soooo nice," Eve Three said provocatively.

"You Vixen," Adam Three piped in, "you tart."

Other than Eve One, each of the other ten Controllers were having a 'ball.' Because Eve One was all 12 Controllers combined, she was enjoying the evening in 'multiplicity.'

"And you are from Edmonton Alberta?" James asked, frowning trying to think of where Edmonton Alberta was.

"Yes, Edmonton, Alberta, Canada, Doctor."

"Edmonton, Alberta…ummm," the doctor said. "I know, yes indeed, at least I think I know, That's where the Great One played hockey isn't it? Wayne Gretsky?"

"You're right James, he played his greatest hockey ever with the Edmonton Oilers."

The good doctor hesitated for a moment then said, "let's dance, Itanya, before I embarrass myself."

"I'd love to." she replied.

They brushed past Lana and Adam One as they whirled to the music. Lana smiled as Adam One winked at Eve Three.

They danced twice. The second dance being a beautiful waltz by Chopin. He could feel every move of her lithe, graceful body. On the frequent eloquent twirls they made, Eve's inner thighs would snug up against his legs. Eve Three would hold these positions a few moments longer than was necessary. James would hold his breath and gasp. She would stretch up to whisper something in his ear and in so doing would pull down the silver satin night-like dress she was wearing away from her bra-less bosom, exposing the tops of her amazing breasts. James could only gulp to keep from choking. He dare not let his penis rise…but it did damn it…he knew at each twirl it would be felt by Itanya. He was flustered. Once when Eve Three turned her head to nod at Clark St. James, she brushed her moist delicious lips against James's. This made him even harder. His jockey shorts were useless in this scene. His hardness found its way out of his shorts and now pushed against his Verducci slacks. The disobedient uncontrollable damn thing now made a tent out of the front of his expensive trousers. Eve Three was amused at James' predicament. Because she wanted to spare him further embarrassment, she clung tighter to his big frame in order to get the center pole of the tent flattened out against her body. This only made it worse. James thought of diseased bladders, appendix, innards of all kinds, anything to get his mind off this gorgeous creature. Nothing worked. It got stiffer.

He devised a plan. Eve Three laughed, she knew of course what his plan would be and she allowed it to come to fruition.

James maneuvered them through the dance floor to a large opening in the salon, which led to a beautiful garden. A garden arranged with flower edged walks, beautiful shrubs, elegant palm trees resplendently lit, and tiny lighted ponds alive with colorful fish. Streams flowing as gently as Sweet Afton. Emblazoned waterfalls and fountains. A veritable Garden of Eden.

His damn trousers still jutted out.

He grasped Eve's arm and hurried her out into the garden. He found an uninhabited dark walk into which he steered Eve. His anxiety was so overwhelming to hide his bulge that he found himself pulling and pushing Eve Three rather roughly.

He stopped and looked down into her incredible face. Her eyes were soft, her smile gentle. She looked up at James her eyes begging the question what's next in store for me sir?

Eve Three's eyes were translucent. They sparkled with life and intelligence. They were beautiful. Her body was voluptuous under that exquisite dress. Her nipples pushed against their silk covering, saucy, pert and delectable. The satin dress hugged her flat tummy. It revealed the exact contours of her hips. The dress rounded her full curvaceous buttocks—it left nothing to the imagination. It pulled itself in, into the top front of her thighs, into her mysterious womanhood. Most of her dazzling legs showed. Her dress, a mini dress, did its thing. It showed off the impossible dream.

He found a bench. They sat. Phew, they sat. The doctor was lost for words. He fussed. He wished he smoked so he would be able to move or do something.

"I'm so glad you don't smoke Doctor, its such a filthy habit."

"I agree Ms. Koslosky. I never will."

Eve Three took his hands in hers. "My, we are formal aren't we doctor?"

"Yes, Ms. Koslosky, please call me Jim."

"Jim?"

"Yes Jim."

"Okay, I will, if you call me Itanya."

"Sealed with a kiss, okay?" With her full lips parted, the tip of her tongue out between them, she kissed the doctor. She moved her lips on his and pushed her tongue gently into his mouth.

The good doctor was ruined. He was relegated to nothing more than a sack of goose bumps. He was jelly. Eve Three took her mouth off his.

"There," she said, "sealed with a kiss."

Sealed, My God, The good doctor was obliterated.

"Itanya," he gasped, "are you an angel?"

"I suppose so Jim," she said, winking at him. Her breath was clean, refreshing, sweet as an angel's would be. Has she no flaws? Dr. James Bell-Irving stood. He took her hands and had her rise. She stood close to him. She blew her warm breath over his face. He felt giddy. Eve Three began to unbutton his shirt. Jim put his arms around her. She removed his shirt. Her silk-covered nipples touched his chest. His knees shook and all but buckled. Within his arms, she wiggled out of her dress. Now her bare breasts touched his skin. They sent shock waves through his whole body. His penis was bursting with life's blood. Eve Three reached down and felt his penis through his slacks. She unbuckled his belt, unzipped his zipper, and with warm deft hands, pulled down his trousers. She knelt down and removed loafers, then his socks. He stood nude now all but his shorts. His organ pushed so hard against his shorts that it popped out one side, bare in all its glory. Eve Three lifted her head and looked up past his manhood into Dr. Bell-Irving's eyes. He was shattered. She reached up with fingers in each side of his shorts, eased them down, watching as his cock sprang back to attention after she had slid the shorts over it. She raised herself up on her knees, her face a scant inch away from the doctor's penis. She took it in her small warm hands, played with it for a few moments, kissed it, then stood.

James-Bell Irving stepped back a pace and watched. He stood affixed as Itanya wiggled out of her scant mini silk panty.

There they stood naked, she smiling, he gasping for air.

They melded.

James' strength returned. He lifted her in his strong arms, his hands cupped her remarkable buttocks, and entered her. She moaned.

With him inside her, he carried her to a marble outside table. There he placed her on the still warm (from the day's sun) surface of the table allowing her legs to fall freely from it. Eve Three closed her eyes bit her lower lip and sighed with pleasure.

Now he was lost in an unknown sexual ecstasy. Yet he was able to hold back ejaculation. He drifted into a fantasy so erotic that he felt certain it was not of this world. His rigid penis explored every part of Itanya's womb. It moved in and out against the tightness of her uterus. He had never dreamt anything could be so beautiful, so fulfilling.

Eve Three was enjoying this magnificent feeling too. Yes the beautiful cock that was inside her. The cock she and Eve Two had dreamed up for men beasts millions of years ago. She congratulated herself on her wise choice. Now just enjoy. "Oh that was a nice one…so was that…oh take it out harder it hurts nice…oh…oh," she moaned. "Let's fly off into erotica near galaxy two trillion." she mused. "Oh, that was the best one yet." Another goody, and yet another.

James's feelings were ecstatic. Frank Sinatra's sensuous strains of "Fly me to the moon and let me play among the stars" enveloped his thoughts. James was in heaven. He was flying to the moon, flying to the moon with his angel in his arms. Their intimacy was celestial. Eve Three was taking James through her mysterious Cosmos. She stroked his hair, she sent tingles up and down his spine as she kissed his eyes, his cheeks and his mouth. Rhythmically she revolved her hips. In a matter of seconds James and Eve Three were on the outskirts of the Universe. Now Sinatra's rich baritone voice filled the whole of the firmament with its romantic request, just as Eve Three had planned it. Eve Three and

James held one another in a frantic embrace. Every beat of James' heart was dedicated to this wonderful woman. He looked out over the firmament. The Universe below him was indescribable. It was diffused in a maze of colors, its awesome depth unknown. Now he knew Itanya was one of the Eves. How else could his satisfaction be so complete? His mind, soul and loins were lost in cataclysmic ecstasy. At Eve Three's bidding they were back on earth with James' mind oblivious of the strata venture he had just shared with Itanya.

"Push hard, Jimmy Boy, yes my darling man. That's it, kiss me, play with me. Oh that's it Jim, darling, that's it. Just a couple more of those wonderful moves and we'll be back on…whooie, where did you find that one my good doctor, and that one?….the table.

"Eve Three," Adam One piped in, "is he as good as Moses?"

All six Adams laughed. Eve Three answered her 'brothers' by sticking her tongue out at them.

"I had better bring James back to reality then we will finish together. Now, yes now," Eve Three moaned, "Now, James, now, now yes now, oh, oh yes—b-e-a-u-t-I-f-u-l," Itanya purred.

Doctor Jim blew like a howitzer. He came like an avalanche. He gritted his teeth. His sperm cascaded and filled her vagina. He dropped his head on Eve Three's soft white shoulder, exhausted, delirious. "Wherefore," he gasped, "wherefore."

A 51 billion year old immortal had now been loved by a 35-year-old mortal.

Lana and Clark were in bed and asleep by 11:00 p.m.

CHAPTER 42

MESOZOIC ERA AND UPPER PALEOLITHIC PERIOD

Clark kissed Lana good-bye as she was about to leave for her third day of lectures. He would meet her at J.F.K. airport on Monday morning, May 12th next. Both were sad.

Dr. Carruthers had the assemblage come to order at 9:30 a.m., May 7th, 1997. No seat was vacant. All 2,100 attendees were present including the errant priest who had shot at Lana on the first day of her sessions. Lana had insisted that he be pardoned by the Turkish officials. They agreed, provided the priest be searched before entering the assembly hall and he answer any charges laid against him by anyone who had attended the meeting the day of the fiasco. The priest assented.

Dr.Carruthers explained to the attendees that Dr. Masters would not be able to finish her lectures by this evening. He stated she would need all day Thursday, May 8th to complete the topics scheduled on the agenda. There were no repercussions from the assemblage.

Dr. Lana Masters thanked Dr. Carruthers and her audience for their patience and understanding. Dr. Masters knew there would be no 'to-do's' from her audience for taking an extra day. She knew she had everyone's attention. How could she not? Was she not an orator of Churchillian excellence? And her presence, well for today, she had selected her attire from a boutique which specialized in fashionable Turkish wear.

She thrilled the media when she agreed to be interviewed for two minutes prior to the assemblage. Cameras, both TV and still, clicked and hummed in a frenzy. They filmed Lana from head to toe. Modern Turkish women's clothing shops should be the ultimate beneficiaries of this unrehearsed fashion show. Crowds gathered around pushing and shoving to get near her. Women were awed and men were impassioned. Her outfit showed just enough 'skin' to cause a touch of mayhem in the crowd. Security men and women surrounded Lana. When her interview ended the security guards formed a wedge with Lana in the middle, by which they forced their way through the throngs of people to the convention center.

* * *

From her lectern, Lana stated that today she would cover various subjects with respect to banks, both public and privately held, as well as some outrageous inequities pertaining to the distribution of wealth.

* * *

Lana smiled as she watched the snakes eyeing her guest. The rats she noted were enjoying some sort of a respite. She watched her guest squirm wondering if he was coming around. She dropped herself off the bales, went to her guest, took a capped bottle of orange juice off the floor, removed the top, inserted a flexible straw in the bottle then placed the straw in her guest's mouth. Half comatose he sipped the juice. He stopped. Lana removed the straw. He groaned then began to snore. Lana climbed back up to her 'nest' on the bales. She noted that her guest's penis was almost chewed off by the rats.

* * *

Lana's mind again was back in Istanbul.

"As I said earlier ladies and gentlemen, Governments in the past have not kept records of their capital expenditures. Has the big U.S. of A. a record of all its capital acquisitions and disposals from George Washington's time to date? No. What is the value of various levels of governments (Federal, State and Municipal) ownership in capital items? The Federal Government of the U.S.A.'s financial statements show Property, Plant and Equipment at its year-end in 1996 to be $969 billion. Hell, Bill Gates' and Warren Buffet's combined net worth at various times in 1997 exceeded $60 billion and by the new millennia Mr. Gates' net worth will exceed $100 Billion. Come now, wouldn't you think the capital assets of the government of the mighty U.S.A. would be more than 16 times greater than Messrs. Gates' and Buffet's combined net worth. Hell yes! The asset value of government-owned assets in the U.S.A. must be in the high trillions of dollars and, if so recorded, would cause the government's balance sheet to show a whopping surplus rather than the deficit it showed at its year-end.

"So what, you ask? Well, it seems to me if the U.S.A.'s Balance Sheet reflected its assets at market, or cost for that matter, its total liabilities of $6 trillion in 1996 would be most tenable and, in fact, the government's balance sheet would be a most enviable one. The government's Income and Expenditure Statement should begin, in my view, to show a 'profit' in the next year or two. So, the mighty nation should be in a strong financial position by the year 2,001. Then, my friends, the U.S. government should be able to enhance the lives of those 38 million people who now live below the poverty level. Jobs, education, health and the sciences should flourish. Debt reduction should be possible."

She pointed to the big screen, which showed the United States Government's Financial Statements at its fiscal year ended September 30, 1996.

"Friends", Lana said, "is full employment in the United States a result of low minimum wages, or is it the result of economic prosperity? Or, is economic prosperity a result of low minimum wages. Think on it, if minimum wages throughout the U.S.A. were a mere two dollars an hour higher would the U.S. still be enjoying this prosperity. Is its prosperity founded on the backs of low income earners? Are wages in America sufficient to provide all workers with a decent standard of living? Should we ask the Fed. this question or should we ask Amos and Andy? Lets ask Amos and Andy."

Amos—"Holly Mackerel der Andy, wha'd yo make in yo sallary last yer."

Andy—"Amos, why you ax?"

Amos—"Cause."

Andy—"Okay, I made over $3,000 dolla's Amos."

Amos—"My, my, I only made $2,600 dolla's last year. Yo rich Andy."

Andy—"But why you ax Amos?"

Amos—"Well, when I wuz sittin' on de post office steps a white man throw'd a magazine in de trash and I go's and picks it up. I reads good, Andy."

Andy—"I knows Amos."

Amos—"Well, I picks up a good stubby still smokin' the same guy throw'd away, parks meself on de step and reads whar some big shot sellin' clothes out of de 'Gap'...whatever de "Gap' is...and he picks up $104.8 million greenies las yer."

Andy—"Dats all de money in de worl' ain't it Amos?"

Amos—"Guess so Andy. Mabbee dat's why we'uns didn't git much."

* * *

The time was now 11:00 a.m. Dr. Carruthers called for a

15 minute recess. Lana stood looking a bit somber as she waited for the recess to end. Her mind was on those two wonderful scummers, Vito and Leroy.

Lana looked at the head table. She walked over to Dr. Carruthers. She leaned down and kissed his cheek. She then proceeded to kiss the cheeks of everyone at the head table. She turned, walked to the stairway leading to the main floor and descended.

"I love all of you here," she said. "I wish I could kiss each one of you to show you the respect and adoration I have for you."

Bowing she made her way back to the stage.

"I want to deviate for the moment from my main topics and point out something I think is most poignant. I want to warn you ladies and gentlemen my language and flippancy will be uncensored. I realize I am known as an unrepenting curser and my warning to you as a result is unnecessary. But I want all of you to know I do have the utmost respect for you and my incessant scourging of the King's English is in no way intended to be rude or disrespectful.

"Let's assume, my dear colleagues, we knew nothing about the possibility the universe's Controllers may displace us in the next few years with some other life form because of our disgraceful behavior from the time Genesis was written by the scribes in the Bible to modern times.

"Then let's look at our predecessors who lived during the second period of the Mesozoic Era…the Jurassic Age…and the Mesozoic Era itself which lasted some 155 million years, and compare that age's life span to our scant Upper Paleolithic period, of 40,000 to 50,000 years. You see the 40,000 years is a mere.000029 percent of the time good old Tyrannosaurus Rex and his kin ruled the world. Shucks folks, we have only 154,960,000 years to go to match the dominance of our reptilian forbears.

"What do you think? Will the 'Age of Humans' still be abounding

154,960,000 years from now?" Can we outlast 'Good Old Dinny'? If not, what did those mothers know we humans don't know?"

Lana paused, a look of consternation on her face. She looked angry and puzzled. "Are we not our brothers' keepers?" she asked.

"Again I apologize to each of you for my deviation from the subject of economics. But I must interject with some of the thoughts which enter my mind when I think about money and people. I feel obliged to pass these thoughts along to you.

"Are we without fault? Are we pure, good Christians, Jews, Muslims, Hindus, Buddhists, Shintos, etc etc?

"Are we thoughtful of others?

"Are we gentle?

"Are we adverse to cheating, lying, warring, fighting, moral destruction, crime, violence, abuse of others and so on?

"Do we have sisterly and brotherly love for one another?

"Do we respect life and property of others?

"Do we abhor racism?

"Are we not the most intelligent life form on earth?

"Are we the greatest?

"Is money the sole instigator of ambition, pride and productivity?

"We all must answer these questions without equivocation.

"Damn it friends, with our present day technology we humans can cause our own extinction, as well as most other species without needing the Twelve Controllers to expunge us.

"Can't the world's peoples live in harmony, and co-exist in peace just as the cosmos does?

"Why must we rob, kill, abuse, fight wars, hate, cheat, lie and worship money?

"We've got the bomb.

"We've got AIDS and ebola as well as other hot zone virus's.

"We've got all manner of death dealing devices.

"And, damn it again friends, these terrifying killing devices are held in trust by people, people of all things. Isn't that frightening?

"If we humans do plan on destroying ourselves say by nuclear devices, just before we do so let's have a booming worldwide party where everyone gets drunk, so drunk we all get 'palsy walsy' with one another. We all get so inebriated we put on a show of overwhelming love and friendship.,A show so fucking overwhelming we find Catholics hugging Protestants; Hindus hugging Muslims; Agnostics hugging Televangelists; Croats hugging Serbs; Serbs hugging Albanians; Nazis hugging Jews; Poles hugging Russians; Anti-Semites hugging Semites; Semites hugging Semites; Netanyahu hugging Arafat; Holyfield hugging Tyson; Whites hugging Blacks; Japanese hugging Chinese; heterosexuals hugging homosexuals; Bill hugging Newt; (Starr hugging Lewinsky) (Lewinsky hugging Trapp); rightists hugging leftists; Lady Aster kissing the ass of a scum-bag; foresooth, everyone hugging everyone! Wouldn't that be a sight?

"And just before we blow ourselves to bits, we find we do love and care for one another, but drat, we are too late, someone pushed the button, BANG!!!!! It's all over.

CHAPTER 43

ISTANBUL, LANA AND STONE KING, THE BIG U.S. NETWORK

The big U.S. network was ready for the 90-minute interview to be given by Dr. Lana Masters to its top talk show host, the charming, handsome intellectual Stone King.

The studio, which was in one wing of the Convention Center, was like the Convention Center itself, tastefully decorated. The Host City of Istanbul again could be proud. The studio's maximum seating capacity was 250. It had been agreed beforehand by the network, and at Lana's insistence, admittance into the studio for the 90-minute program would be $2,000 U.S. dollars per person, and the gross proceeds therefrom would go to the Minister of Social Programs in Turkey's senior government. It was agreed as well the 90-minute program would have only three 5-minute commercial breaks, and the last one would be timed for 8:10 p.m. The program was to start at 7:00 p.m. Thursday, May 8th, Istanbul time and continue through to 8:30 p.m.

All of the seats had been pre-sold six months earlier, just moments after it was announced Stone King would be interviewing Dr. Masters in Istanbul during her five-day conference there.

The glamour world was 'a twitter' at the thought of the dashing Stone meeting the goddess. Something fiery was sure to happen. Mr. king had been asked a thousand times how he would react on meeting the sylphic beauty. "I will be no different with Dr. Masters than I am with any other of my guests," he said. Once however, he made a much publicized Freudian slip, "I will meet her hard on," he had said.

Lana was grieving. She was not at all nervous about the interview itself, it was what she knew she was going to do following the last five-minute commercial. Hell, no one can 'stump me' on any fucking topic she reasoned. But Clark, what was he going to think on viewing the last several minutes of the program. She loved Clark. She admired him and was proud of him. Their love and devotion for one another made them like one. While she knew marriage to him was never to be, still she would die for his love. Their lives together over the past three years were 'made in heaven,' Eve One's sylphic heaven. Lana knew she could live with Clark to the end of time. "Clark," she whispered to herself, "forgive me. I love only you! Why does Eve One want Stone and me to—to…? What is its significance?"

Stone King had faxed Lana a series of questions he was proposing to ask her during his interview of her, and he asked if she would be so kind as to review them and advise him if any were objectionable to her.

"None," Lana had answered.

They met for the first time at his office May 1st, just past. Like everyone else who had first met her, Stone was fixated. She 'smoldered' him with her eyes. His mind could think of only two apt words to describe her, *fucking apoplectic.* She was beyond beauty. He was so stricken by Lana he had to excuse himself from her for a moment, feigning he had left an important envelope on his secretary's desk. He fumbled his way out of his office. Once away from Lana he pumped air into his lungs by puffing and huffing. "Get a hold of yourself Stone," he said to himself, "she's only human."

"What's that Stone?" his secretary asked.

"Hard on," came his stricken reply.

"What?" said his secretary, her eyes aglow at her hunky boss.

"The day so far has been hard on me, Mick, that's all I meant."

"Oh, I'm sorry Stone. Can I get you something?"

"No, no, everything is fine, thank you." 'Like hell everything is fine,' he thought in misery. 'This Dr. Lana Masters oozes. Damn how she oozes. She sucks your brain dry of reasoning and leaves it a gooey, mushy blob.'

He made his way back into his office without an envelope.

"You didn't find your envelope?" Lana asked.

"What envelope?" Stone replied. "Oh, the envelope, yes, yes." Dammit, he thought, what's gotten into me? "Well, Doctor, my secretary informed me she had put it on my breast, no I mean desk. Ah! Here it is. Goodness, Doctor, you seem to have me titillated." 'Son of a gun, why did I use the word titillated?'

Lana almost burst out laughing at this hapless hunk. Lana noticed the envelope Stone had picked up from his desk was from Sears Roebuck, Automotive Division. She giggled, but kept a straight face. She crossed her long legs, smoothed out her mini-skirt, then flashed Stone a beguiling smile. She acted so innocent, so very innocent, knowing full well she had the Mr. King wishing he could be anywhere else but here now, even if it meant disappearing up his own fundamental orifice. A Sears Roebuck mailing piece of all things.

After he fumbled his way around his office knocking two golf balls on brass stands off his desk and stubbing his toe on one of his rich leather office chair's leg, finally, thank Christ, his butt was able to find its way into the office chair's seat. Quite an accomplishment under the circumstances!

'Ah shit,' he muttered to himself. 'I haven't even introduced myself to Doctor Masters yet. I've made a total ass of myself up to this point. Now I gotta go through the whole damn issue again.'

He stood.

Lana stood.

He shook.

Lana knew his problem. Stone King, like most other men who met her for the first time, was blatherskited. She must unblatherskite him so he can return to normalcy. But not before one more little 'jolt,' she thought. She walked around the handsome one's desk then snuggled herself up to his nattily attired body. She took him by the shoulders and turned him so his butt was up against his desk. He was trapped. She placed her body against his. In fright, or whatever, he pulled his head back.

"Stone King, I presume."

"Yes."

"I am Lana Masters."

"I know."

She put her hand on the nape of his neck then pulled his head toward her. With her mouth partly open she kissed his lips. Somehow Stone King survived.

Other than a few more hapless blunders by the polished sophisticate, Mr. Stone King, and the odd tease by Lana Jean Masters, their meeting went well.

* * *

The night had come. Thursday, May 8th, 1997, 7:00 p.m. Istanbul time.

The studio was quite lavish. A colorful display of flowers had been placed around the two principals' seating area. Two fountains languished near the back wall of the stage. The stage itself was on ground level and was set back about 20 feet from the front-row seats. The semi-circular seating for the audience was amphitheater-style, enabling therefore everyone in the audience to have a splendid view of Stone King and his guest Dr. Lana Masters. Lana was seated on an embroidered love seat across from Stone who was seated in a medium back sofa-like chair. Between them was an elongated coffee table, which held a beautiful sculptured cut-glass pitcher, filled with ice water and two matching glasses.

The stage was set for the meeting of the two famous celebrities. TV cameramen were ready to catch on video everything that was to transpire during the 90-minute interchange. Lana had insisted the cameras roll on taking in she and Mr. King regardless of the scene before them, no blackouts, no fuzzies, just straight camera work on the two principals for the whole 90 minutes. The network agreed.

* * *

"Ladies and gentlemen," a deep, resonant voice sounded throughout the theater, "NBC is pleased to bring you *Newsline* this Thursday evening from the beautiful Convention Center here in Istanbul, Turkey. Please welcome your host, Mr. Stone King."

Stone King made his entrance onto the stage amid an exuberant round of applause. "Good evening," he said cordially. "Welcome to tonight's NBC special broadcast." More applause. "I should like to welcome you in our studio audience and our inter-stellar viewers to this city, the enchanting, historic, cultural masterpiece, Istanbul." More applause!

"Tonight I shall be bringing you a 90-minute program one-half hour earlier than our network's normal broadcast time and one-half an hour longer. My guest, as you all know, is Doctor Lana Masters." This he said amid a thunderous applause.

"There will be three 5-minute breaks in our video content to allow for messages from our several sponsors. I wish to assure viewers during the three 5-minute breaks no questions will be asked of our guest. Now, ladies and gentlemen, please join me in welcoming to our broadcast Doctor Lana Jean Masters."

A hush fell over the studio as Lana entered. Stone King's whole body tingled as the goddess made her way onto the stage. Lana was dressed in a light wool, all-white suit. The skirt, as was Lana's trademark, was very mini, yet everything about her attire was pure sophistication. This woman could wear a gunnysack and make it look like a Geovana original. Her hair was incredible, her face inimitable, her figure exceptional.

The audience began to stir, it stood, it erupted into an ear shattering applause. Finally, it quietened.

Lana shook Stone's hand, then kissed his cheek. She turned to the audience, bowed, threw them a kiss, then sat as everyone gasped. Another hush! Lana Jean Masters had won over the whole fucking crowd by her presence and she damn well knew it.

Stone King sat. He braced himself as he readied himself to enter into the fray.

As usual Lana was composed.

* * *

Lana's guest jerked, snored and blabbered. He blabbered about an Asian monetary crisis. He shouted at the Jews and the Arabs. He warned Bill Clinton. "Jessica Flowers," he said in a muffled voice, "Paula Jones, Tripp, Starr, Monica something or other…"

"Yeah," Lana said, "lover-boy may be letting me in on some top secrets he'd learned about on some of the missions he'd been commissioned to do for the Feds. Carry on McDuff," she whispered. Damn, lover-boy fell silent.

"Okay, back to Istanbul and Stone King," Lana said aloud.

* * *

After getting by with some light-hearted niceties, Stone began to feel more at ease, and indeed, quite comfortable with the *nonpariel* Lana Masters.

His first serious question had to do with the goals Dr. Masters had set for herself.

She answered that family cohesion, worldwide human rights, worldwide humanitarianism, elimination of worldwide poverty were foremost in her mind. Population control was one of her goals. Others included full global employment, freedom for all peoples of the world, expansion on scientific research for the planet's productivity, its people's health, worldwide education for everyone, and a cared for universal environment. And, for Eve One's sake, worldwide religious and political reform. Lana stated an objective needed in order to effect her goals was to have all borders worldwide expunged. Hell, she had stated, after three generations had gone by no one would care about silly borders. Today's technology has made all of us neighbors even though we may be thousands of miles apart. One world country, and one worldwide medium of exchange. Then what could we fight about on a global basis? We could still squabble, mutter, argue and fart around like ninneys, but we would have no basis to take up arms against one-another.

"Essentially, my goals are endless,"

"Yes indeed they are endless. Good luck in accomplishing them, Doctor."

"I thought we had agreed you would call me by my name, Stone."

"Sorry, Lana."

"You are forgiven," Lana said, winking at him.

"Thank you, Lana. I have watched the telecasts of you from my office and from my home in New York City on numerous occasions and, of course, your discussions here in Istanbul, and I must say your divulgence last Monday pertaining to the Controllers was most intriguing. I realize from what you have said, Lana, about your so-called Controllers that, in your view, they are real, not divinities, while the various God's people on earth worship are, in fact, fictitious. Fictitious and conjured up years ago by scribes and priests for the purpose of easing people's fright of death, to teach righteousness as these scribes saw righteousness, to worship these scribes and priests, and to pay homage to them both spiritually and monetarily."

"You are correct, Stone. The messages I brought this past Monday to the assembly are true. If your network wishes, it is welcome to all the transcripts for the details of my discussions pertaining to the Controllers."

"Thank you Lana. Can your Eves and Adams show us some proof of their existence?"

"Just look at your surroundings, that should be proof enough."

"You can say 'look at your surroundings' without concern because you know I have no way of rebuking you other than by way of Genesis as described in the Old Testament. Personally, I am quite at east with the teachings in the Bible, as well as the scientific theory of the big bang."

"The big bang, sheeeit, Stone, childish. My dear sir, did I detect a gleam in your eyes when you said the big bang?

Stone's face reddened.

"I suppose you want some magic from the Controllers for proof, right, Stone?"

"Yes."

"Well why don't you stand up and call out to Eve One and ask her to perform her magic? Who knows, she may respond to you."

"I would feel foolish calling out to some, what should I say, some figment of your imagination?"

"Cool, Stone. Now I am unable to rebuke you because I cannot command the Controllers to show you a miracle. In fact, the Controllers have made it clear to me they do not give one whit about people's belief in them. Whoops!"

Suddenly Lana's love seat bounced. "Whoops," she said again, knowing it was Adam Six playing games.

Adam Six was there unseen. "Stone King, I am Adam Six of the universe. I am a part of Eve One who is the Universe. I enlarge the cosmos on a continuous basis by displacing its greatest enemy, *nothing*. For your purposes I have brought a bit of nothing to display to you. Please look down at your legs. Stone looked down, paled, gasped, then tried to stand. He had no legs. He remained seated no matter how he tried to stand. From his waist down he was nothing. Suddenly his chin was gone. Now he was back in his studio in New York, legless and chinless, blubbering at Tom Brokaw. "What in God's name has happened to you Stone?" Tom asked. Before Stone could reply he was back in the studio in Istanbul. He was whole once again.

"Please Stone," Lana whispered, "carry on with some other topic."

The audience was agog at the happenings, but the whole scene had happened so fast the audience had no time to question its authenticity.

Tom Brokow shook his head. "Damn," he said, "forsooth and all that shit."

Stone King was in a state of shock. He was frightened. He looked at Lana. Through her eyes she soothed his battered psyche. After a moment of silence, he cleared his throat, reached over and took Lana's hand and stated to her and to his audience for the time being he would not pursue further this particular topic. His audience understood. Stone hid his panic and his perspiration well.

He took a deep breath before asking Lana any further questions. Lana, eased his mind again with a reassuring smile. Stone, eased by Lana's inner strength queried her about her views on the world's banking systems. In particular commercial banks strengths, weaknesses and their influence on economies ranging from village aggrandizement to world wide international money markets. Lana delved into this topic with vigor.

Today's economies could not exist without well run financial intermediaries. Their evolution as a monetary service made possible the present advanced state of the industrial nations. She flattered the banking system from time to time even as she nagged at their financial weakness. Her nagging included huge national banks from Europe, Asia, the United States and Canada. Their weak foundations, known as shareholders equity, are woefully inadequate to support the obesity of their blubbery torsos. The combined net worth of the world's two riches individuals is greater than the combined net worth of the three largest banks in the United States.

Lana referred her attendees to the large screen on her left on which the most recent financial statements of the major banks of the United

States, Canada and one huge German bank were shown. Core capital ratios were emphasized in bold red figures.

She reviewed the importance of various countries central banking systems and the enormity of their monetary policies. She stressed the paranoia central banks governors often suffer over the elusive monetary devil known as "inflation". On your mark set go, run up interest rates and pull back transaction money as soon as an economy seems to be overheating. Central banks objectives are few, but vital Lana said...regulate a country's credit and currency operations...protect the external value of a country's currency...mitigate fluctuations in the level of employment, production, trade and prices, and protect the economic and financial welfare of a nation.

* * *

Lana and Stone chatted for a few moments during the first of the three five minute commercial breaks, then Lana walked off the stage to mingle with the audience. There she greeted people, shook many hands, sat on the lush carpeted steps and talked with others, then returned to the stage.

Stone, in the meantime, was feeling a mild turbulence in his mind. He had a wild feeling that following the last five minuet commercial break something bizarre was going to happen. His psyche was sure of this. He knew he was going to play a major role in whatever? This women! Good God! This women LANA.

Stone flashed his winning smile as the cameras began to roll once again.

"And what about this bank called The Bank for International Settlements? Is it not a central bank, too, or at least a central bank of some sort?" Stone asked.

You mean the B.I.S., the old boys' banker club. No, it is an international bankers club whose shareholders are primarily central banks. This bank was created for the purpose of facilitating World War I reparations payable by Germany to the Allies, not for the purpose of formulating global policy for central banks.

The purposes and functions of the B.I.S. 'are somewhat clouded and mysterious.' Did the B.I.S. collaborate with the Germans in the 1930's? And was it not the B.I.S. who mandated central banks to do away with their compulsory reserve systems required of commercial banks?

"Just prior to the elimination of the reserve system in the latter 1980's commercial banks were obligated to place funds in their respective central banks as reserve requirements, and as I am sure you know, Stone, no interest was paid on these reserve funds held by the central banks.

"Isn't it a chilling fact the B.I.S. in 1988 announced the complete dismantling of the reserve system? My goodness, the reserve system was not only a safety valve for commercial banking proprieties, but the system was a splendid mechanism for controlling debt, thus most helpful in stemming inflation. Now the Reserve System of Central Banks is extinct. It has been replaced with minimal equity based ratios and multiples called core ratios.

"Commercial banks everywhere complained during the 1980's high interest rates had smashed many of their borrowers into economic oblivion...defaults on loans...bankruptcies...desertion of assets held as security by banks...leaving financial institutions in financial distress. Commercial banks whimpered the reserves they were compelled to keep in Central Banks earned them no interest. This, they cried, was unfair. Their howls of "foul" were successful. No more reserve requirement as announced by B.I.S. in 1988.

"When did the actual abolishment of reserve requirements occur, Lana?" Stone asked.

"The abolishment was complete in 1992," Lana answered.

"That long ago? It certainly is a well-kept secret.".

CHAPTER 44
LANA AND DR. JAMES BELL IRVING

"The world wide distribution of purchasing power is a disgrace." Lana said to Stone. "Despicable conditions exist in varying degrees in every nation in the world. Conditions brought about by religions, class distinctions, political tyranny, extreme right-wing fascism, unworkable depressing communism, and the general contempt most people have for the working class...including the working 'stiffs' themselves. Look at religious hierarchies; take for instance the Catholic Church. "Wouldn't it be something to see a revenue and expenditure statement and a balance sheet of the mighty non-bordered nation called the Catholic Church. How many Catholic worshippers are there around the globe, one billion? All paying some manner of tithe to this huge organization.

"What is the value of the Vatican itself, the palace and official residence of the Pope in Rome? How would Jesus react if he was on the earth today. Would he rejoice at the finery of the Vatican and the ostentatiousness of some of the incomparable worldwide Catholic Churches? Jesus seemed to be a simple soul...brilliant...kind... sympathetic...without question, the finest person the world has ever seen. Would he swath himself in silk and other rich adornments? Would he live in hiding in pompous splendor, rarely showing himself to his faithful following? Would he have allowed the paying of millions or billions of dollars in hush money in order to cover up heterosexual and homosexual wrongs and abuses certain of his clerics perpetrated against children?

"Sorry, Stone, the topic of religion is for my lecture tomorrow not for tonight. I have strayed, but my oh my, what a best seller the consolidated worldwide financial statements of the Catholic Church would be.

* * *

Lana's mind went back to the dinner break two hours before her interview with Stone King.

A stranger, a tall fine rather shy-looking man had come to her and took her arm. Without a word he whisked her away from the crowd. In the large, flower-adorned hall, Dr. James Bell-Irving excused himself to Lana for his audacity in taking her away form her adoring audience.

"I must talk to you, Dr. Masters," Bell-Irving said. "Please give me just a few moments. I, I am so confused, troubled, I…"

"Do I know you sir?" Lana asked, smiling.

"No, Doctor, you don't. My name is James Bell-Irving. I am a pediatrician from Santa Fe, New Mexico. I have seen you several times on television, read all of your books and works, and I must say you are on a plateau by yourself. You are above all others. You are refreshing, unique."

"I don't think you are here to award me with praises, Dr. Bell-Irving. I can see in your eyes you are here on a personal matter concerning someone you have met during the last few days. A girl of your dreams perhaps…right, Doctor?"

"Yes, Doctor Masters, I have. This young woman means everything to me yet I have just met her. And Doctor…"

"Please call me Lana."

"Are you sure it's all right to call you Lana?"

"Of course it is."

"Well, Lana," Jim said, "I believe she is not of this world. I believe she is an angel, one of your…ahh…Controllers. She is so perfect, so utterly out of this world!"

"What is her name, and where is she from, James?" Lana asked.

"Itanya Koslosky from Edmonton, Alberta, Canada."

"I'm afraid I don't know her, Doctor."

"Do you think she is not one of us?"

"Oh no, I am certain she is one of us, James," Lana replied.

"I hope you are right, Dr. Masters."

"I suggest we go to our guest register and check out this Ms. Koslosky, Dr. Bell-Irving, and see if she is registered as an invited guest. Come, let's go and see if we can solve this exciting mystery."

She took Dr. James Bell-Irving's hand and led him to the registration desk. Once there Lana asked the registrar to look up Itanya Koslosky's name, address and occupation. It took the registrar just a moment to bring up Ms. Koslosky's name and address on the computer. She had registered on Sunday, May 4th, 1997 at 9:00 a.m. as Itanya Margo Koslosky, M.D., Edmonton, Alberta, Psychiatrist. She had not missed one of Lana Masters' sessions.

"Poor Doctor Bell-Irving," Adam Six whispered in Lana's ear. "Eve Three has done this before a number of times. She has seduced Moses, Samson, two Pharaohs unbeknownst to you, Mark Antony, and most recently Thomas Jefferson and J.F.K. She has had similar pleasures and acquaintances in other galaxies. She seems quite taken with James Bell-Irving. As you know, Dr. Masters, whilst there are 12 of us Controllers in your earthling's conception of division, we are in fact one, known to you as Eve One. But we do have individual independence in our cosmic functions. Each of us has singular duties to perform, second by second, in order to assure the whole universe's delicate balance, its harmony, its uniformity, its precise performance, its overall management. But Eve One is forever, as your forefathers spake in Latin, primus inter pares. She is one being, just as is your body, and just as your body has independent moving parts—your arms, legs, fingers, mouth, eyelids and so on—so does Eve One have we eleven controllers as her body parts who act independent from one another in each ones exigent activities. Yet we are one. It's somewhat more complicated than I have just explained, but what I am coming to is the fact that Eve Three is, you might say in your limited parlance, transcending her independence in this instance with her flirtations with Dr. Bell-Irving. Eve One and we ten others are permitting Eve Three to have this indiscretion. We are not, as you, our earthlings put it, killjoys. We love, love fun, enjoyment, independence, a little teasing, games, accomplishments, respect, humor, repartee, pleasantness, playing, wit, scintillating living. We deplore wars, gossip, fighting, inequities, anything that isn't nice. In any event, Lana, we can permit Dr. Bell-Irving to spend his mortal years with Eve Three if he is worthy of this permittance. Of course, we know the answer to this question now, but Dr. Bell-Irving does not. You must just wait the outcome.

"Incidentally," Adam Six said, "Eve Three signed in the registry as Itanya Margo Koslosky on Sunday past and, my sweet Lana, Eve Three took a moment of her time to be born to Viktor and Itanya Koslosky some 26 years ago in Edmonton, Alberta. There she attended school and university. She was always an 'A' student, and the most popular in her class. Eve Three had fun. Never has she acted as one of the Controllers whilst playing out the part of Itanya Koslosky. Always she acted as an earthy human, poor sister, I felt so sorry for her on hundreds of occasions as she took on the role of an inelegant frightful human."

"So," Lana said, "It is clear Itanya is of this world, Jim."

"Yes, but…"

"Ah ha, but what, Jim?"

"Well, Doctor Lana, sorry Lana, she seems far beyond this globe of ours."

"Jim, for Christ's sake, have you fucked her yet?"

Dr. Bell-Irving was shocked at Lana's switch from a serene beauty to a foul-mouthed minx. He had heard her unusual swearing from the stage, but he seemed able to take her stage talk. But this question of him, a person who rarely said damn, made him step back from this goddess.

"Pardon," he said blanching.

"Have you banged her, Jim?" she went on, "you know, stuck your thingamabob into her doojigger." She laughed, seeing Jim the physician flush. "Did she give you a blow job?"

"Dr. Masters, shame on you. You, you shouldn't…"

"Cut the crap, Jim, did you or didn't you have sex with Itanya?"

"Dr. Masters, you are terrible, you…"

Lana giggled, grabbed his ears, pulled his head down to her level, kissed the tip of his nose, winked and said, "So you have, haven't you, you naughty boy."

"Yes…yes…yes I have, last night. It was heaven. It was heaven oh dear God, it was heaven. Lana, she made me feel my maleness. She was exciting, extraordinary. She is so alive, so vibrant, yet gentle, loving, caring. I cannot be without her." Tears filled his eyes. He put his hand over his eyes. "Lana, I can't be without her."

"Truly, Lana, is she of this world?"

"Yes, Jim, she is."

Lana took his shaking hand in hers and began to make her way to her dinner table.

"Jim," she said, "Itanya will be with you this evening."

Someone from behind tapped his shoulder. Jim turned. It was Itanya. She was smiling, adoration in her eyes. Big Jim nearly fainted again. He fought to stay on his legs. Eve Three was breathtaking.

Lana (knowing Eve Three and knowing Eve Three knew that Lana knew the story) introduced herself to Itanya, then said, "See you, Jim," and left.

CHAPTER 45
LANA AND STONE KING INTERVIEW CONTINUED

By the time the second break occurred Lana had reviewed the enormity of remuneration, stock options, conversions, bonuses and the like paid to executives of major corporations in the United States as compared to those employees who earned government sanctioned basic wages. She remarked on the startling fact that Bill Gates, the world's wealthiest man, the man who owns over one billion shares of Microsoft, earns some $4.5 million per hour. She noted that if a person earned an average of $100,000.00 per year it would take that person 45 years to earn what Mr. Gates earns in an hour.

She stated the earnings of the ten highest paid American executives of opulent American corporations is $100 million annually while its top forty athletes earn well over $20 million dollars annually. These figures she said compare to 14.5% of United States residents, 38 million people, who must get by on just over $4000.00 annually. Employers, she noted, fought against minimum wage laws of $5.40 an hour, $5.40 an hour, just $4,4999,994.60 less than Bill Gates hourly earnings. I must say Stone, while I feel Mr. Gates' stipend may be a bit generous, I have no argument with him and his booty."

"I agree with your last statement, Lana, but as to your feelings about the rich needing the poor in order to exemplify their station in life, I'm from Missouri on that one. And, Doctor, how do you see the world accomplishing zero destitution?"

While the temperature was a comfortable 70 degrees, Stone felt perspiration on his face, forehead, neck, and under his arms. He squirmed a bit, trying to get comfortable. It was Lana, damn her. Her legs! That's it, her legs. She crosses them then she uncrosses them. Her sexy actions remind him of that old drolly, 'she crossed her legs and broke his glasses.' God, Lana, his mind swirled how I would love to love you.

"I have an answer, Stone, and I believe if there is the will by the politicians, the religious, business, union and labor, it is possible to eliminate poverty worldwide.

Dr. Masters went into details in her answer…$72 trillion worth.

* * *

When Lana finished her answers to Stone's questions (with all her in depth explanations, her various hypothesis, and thoroughness) Stone responded somewhat breathless,

"Pheeeuuu, Lana, your thematic will need to be studied, analyzed, critiqued…"

"Hell no, Stone. Everything I have said can be accomplished by the methodology I have just outlined. What is needed is will. The will of people! The will of politicians, the religious, business and labor! And this 'will' better come soon lest the Controllers dispense with all of us in favor of some other life form. You know my good man; the process of people's elimination is already taking place by way of the computer age. Just think on it. Once man injects independent thinking into machines along with super intelligence, humans will be at the mercy of machines. Then what? However Stone, the Controllers have given me no such hint. They may just fry all of us when they decide they have had it up to here with our shenanigans."

"So, back to the Controllers are we? Ladies and gentlemen, I see it is time for our second 5-minute break. Beverages will be brought around to everyone."

Again Lana left the stage to stroll among the studio audience and chat. This time Stone joined her. Everyone enjoyed his presence as well as Lana's. He was so charming and so sophisticated. However Stone's eyes could not stray away from Lana. Suddenly his mind became a theater. A theater where he and Lana were the performers! Christ, now what's happening? They were alone in Stone's world enjoying life to its fullest. Napili Bay, Maui. Hand in hand they laughed as Lana squealed with delight as he chased her down a beautiful sandy beach. They splashed bits of water on each other; they stopped long enough to hug and kiss as she tousled his hair. He lifted her in his strong arms and nuzzled her tummy with his nose and lips. They tried to entice shore birds to come join them. The sun was radiant as it shone on the azure ocean. The world was theirs. They kissed again. They hugged. The contour of their bodies melded. Stone looked into Lana's eyes. He saw unending depth in them. He felt swallowed up by their dazzling beauty. He entered her very sole through them. "I am a part of her now. Our lives are one. Our bodies are separate but our lives are one." Their bodies met. They clung together. Stone ran the tips of his fingers down her back and onto her buttocks. He kissed the side of her mouth. He ran his fingers back up to her shoulders and over onto her breasts. He ran his tongue between her breasts, down her firm belly until he reached the secret entrance to her body. He stayed there for a few moments. He stood, picked Lana up in his arms and carried her to a nest of fronds hidden beneath some palm trees. Gently he laid her on the inviting nest of soft flower petals. He knelt down beside her. Lana pulled him to her. They kissed and fondled one another. Soon they were making love. Their beautiful bodies moved with excitement as they sought out each ones pleasure. Lana nipped at his chin and lips. She pushed his shoulders up away from her breasts so she could look down and see his erection enter her. She moaned as she moved her hips up to him. They changed positions. Like a tigress Lana purred out her pleasure as she romped and played with his body and genitals. She was tireless. She made love with such energy and verve that all he could do was to lay back and capitulate. What a way to capitulate. Ecstasy. What an incompetent word ecstasy is. Ecstasy alone doesn't make it. What word will make it when a man is in the clutches of this supreme love machine?

'What is happening to me?' Stone said to himself. 'Why couldn't Oprah or Larry or Rosie have had this 'chore' of interviewing Lana Jean Masters, and what about Barbara, she would have been terrific? This damnable woman will never be out of my mind.' He trudged back to his seat, smiling mechanically as he offered his arm to the temptress.

"Do you wish to carry on, Lana?"

"Thank you, Stone, I would."

* * *

Lana spoke of the strange paranoia everyone sinks into when it comes to wages for workers. Incredible as it seems workers themselves sometimes argue against workers rights. She noted that society in general gets a "bad taste" in its mouth when it comes time to attend to workers' wages.

"Costs, as they pertain to people, seem to gather more controversy than any other cost globally.

"People are the producers of goods and services," Lana said to Stone, "not machinery, land, buildings, and equipment, not even the mighty computer. Capital goods, machinery, et al., are dormant, without life, and cannot on their own produce consumer goods. They can be productive once they start up, but who starts them up in the first place…people do. Who designs and makes the machinery, equipment, buildings, waterways, bridges, ships, airplanes, computers, TV's, it is people. Land becomes fertile and productive year after year only because of people's ingenuity, diligence and hard work. Machinery, equipment and buildings are lifeless, inert and dormant without peoples' input.

"It is not until men's and women's labor, energies and expertise are injected into the system of production that capital goods become operative and produce consumer goods for the benefit of society.

"It is obvious labor is the single most important ingredient in bringing prosperity to a nation and, of course, labor is exchanged for money which in turn enables labor to exchange its money for goods and services.

"When the preponderance of the labor force (in all positions from the unskilled to the top executive) is employed the preponderance of business big and small, under able management will enjoy health, prosperity and fulfillment.

Lana predicted that 50% of the world's work force would be unemployed by 2050. Shoppers will be a scarcity. Who will grace our grocery stores, our clothing shops, pharmacies, travel agencies, theaters, etc? Endless hours of spare time will be weighty and intolerable. Spare time will become the enemy of those not working; all manner of indecencies will become commonplace.

"Perhaps space travel, searching for substitute energy sources, attitude changes, mandatory birth control, selective controlled death dealing diseases instituted in over-populated areas, carefully planned atomic wars, death penalties for the most minor of legal infractions, mandatory euthanasia at age 65 will help solve the spare time problem.

Vexed Eve One said, "Lana, you are horrid for saying some of those things even though I know you don't mean them."

"Sorry, Eve One."

"Space travel, searching for other cleaner energy sources, a return to personalized services in those enterprises where clerks are 'conspicuous by their absence' and those unbearable telephone answering voices which say 'if you are using a touch-tone telephone…' go back to the good old telephone system which used people services. Reduce income taxes on people's incomes who are middle class or below; institute taxes on machinery and equipment (that'll slow down substituting people with machinery) sufficient in amount to replace taxes on income of those just spoken of. Spend dollars. Get the scientific community in high gear. Provide scientists with the funds necessary for them to make productive those properties that hitherto were unproductive. Increase teaching facilities and teachers in order to 'beef up' education, get the unskilled skilled. Slow down population growth (get the lady who whacked off her husband's dick to manage this one) through education and understanding. Get rid of some of the machinery, equipment, tools and the like and replace them with people.

"It troubles me not one whit Stone to echo over and over again people are the ones who permit businesses to succeed. They are the only forces who can 'make' or 'break' a business entity by their veneration thereto or their lack thereof. People stand first in line in all matters of the world. Consider in wartime, if the fighting forces of the armies, navies and air forces, allies and axis, put down their arms simultaneously and said 'fuck it, no more,' all the armaments and war machinery and equipment would become 'hunks' of useless killing machines. They would be inert without people's input.

"Stone let's get to the question of who and what is business. This will just take a minute or two. It is rather interesting to note, in general, executives have been able to shield themselves behind their businesses names and logos for years. It gives the individuals within a corporation a vast amount of freedom from criticism. This has been done so convincingly that the public makes reference to the entities themselves as if they (the corporate entities) were the purveyors of all business activities. Ford Motor Company has a new product, Chase Manhattan has lowered its interest rates, Seagram's makes the best whiskey, Wal-Mart has the lowest prices. Phillip Morse ups its nicotine content in cigarettes in order to hook better present and prospective users. Yeah,

Phillip Morse et al. It is the people working for cigarette companies who deliver the death penalty to children, not the companies themselves.

"It is fascinating to note 'all of us' make reference to business entities as if these entities are something other than people driven, that corporate giants are operated by some mysterious force unknown to us 'the unwashed.' That their decision making processes pertaining to operational activities, price setting, staffing levels, wages, dividend payments, senior management remuneration etc. etc., come about by some unseen ontology totally foreign in nature to all of us. When we read of giants such as General Motors, Exxon Corporation, Mobile Oil, Citicorp, Alcan and the like we lose sight of the fact that they are run by human beings. Their incorporation documents are just that, documents, gathering dust somewhere in a government file. They are as lifeless as is their machinery, buildings and equipment. All artificial entities become active and productive only when men and women are employed to start up the activities of production, a labor force which encompasses the entire gamut of personnel, right from board of directors, senior management down to the most servile staff member.

"All undertakings good or bad, horrendous or pleasing in business are the actions of people. So keep in mind corporate leaders are people. It is these very people who make corporate decisions that have over the years caused mayhem in so many ways. Dramatic examples are the wanton destruction of much of our world's precious environment and the destruction of countless numbers of species in the animal world. Yet, these corporate leaders have provided some societies with the most wonderful pleasing, life sustaining, comfortable, and enjoyable living standards imaginable.

Lana turned her head toward Stone. She saw a look of consternation in his eyes. She knew what was troubling him. It's me damn it. He's off on a tangent about me. She reached across the coffee table and took his hand in hers and said, "Thank you, Stone, for your patience for hearing me out. You are remarkable, as are you my friends," Lana said, as she nodded at the studio audience and at the TV cameras.

Stone acknowledged Lana's kindness with a smile. He hesitated for a moment then stated, "We have come to the last of the messages from our sponsors, ladies and gentlemen. We will be back to you in five minutes."

He smiled at his audience even though his mind was swirling over his thoughts of Lana.

Lana left her love seat but this time she strolled over to the cameramen and other stagehands rather than to the audience. She chatted, joked and rapped with them. The crew loved every moment of it. She reached up to one of the cameramen who was on a lift and whispered something in his ear. Stone eyed her jealously. As she stretched up to the cameraman her beautiful rounded bottom was just covered by her mini-skirt. Stone gulped. Her movements caused his mind to pick up some crude 'ditties' he swore he had never heard before. Damn her.

"With her arse against the barn door riggy giggy gig," for Christ sake. Yeah, and a fine old Scottish melody that went "They were stuffin' in the parlor, stuffin' in the micks, you couldna' hear the pipers for the swishing of the pricks, coom 'a hi diddly hi de hi diddly hey…"

Stone knew he was a sophisticate, then where in heaven's name did those little squalid tunes come from?

Lana returned to her seat.

The last commercial ended.

Stone was about to speak. He opened his mouth but no sound came. The audience gasped at the scene that began to unfold in front of them. Its beauty took their breath away.

Lana and Stone were removing their clothes as the stage changed to a wondrous live theatre setting. While shedding his attire, Stone's voice came back. He asked Lana if she was the only person ever to be visited by the Controllers?

"No," Lana had replied, as she understood from Adam Six, "Moses, Maria Sanchez, Will Rogers, Ghandi, Albert Einstein, Joan d'Arc, Madame Currie, Louis Riel had all been visited by them as well as a selected few from other origins and religions. Jesus was at one time a part of the Controllers. Allah and Mohammed may well have been too," she explained.

"What is happening to us Lana?" Stone asked, bewildered.

"I don't know," Lana replied.

"Just be yourselves," a melodious voice said.

"Eve Three, is that you?" Lana asked.

"Yes," Eve Three replied.

The scene viewed by Lana and Stone was not artificial, it was real. There were no props, no make-believe sound effects. The stage was no longer a stage; it was in fact a real land and seascape. It was Napili Bay on the Hawaiian Island of Maui. Breathtaking and beautiful! The pounding surf was breaking a few hundred yards out to sea. The leftover waves were making their way into shore as far as the sand of the beach would permit. The sea, mist and shore met 'tenderly.' There was a deep feeling of peace and tranquility pervading the air. Lana and Stone stood nude, silent and alone. The loveliness of nature held them breathless.

They took one another's hands as they marveled at the sight of the Island of Molokai just a few miles away. They began to run through the leftover waves. Then splashed each other with the ocean's warm water. They laughed, frolicked and played with one another stopping only to hug and kiss. Lana would tousle Stone's hair. He would lift her in his strong arms and nuzzle her tummy with his nose and lips.

Suddenly they stopped. At the northern end of the Bay, amid a grove of palm trees was a nest made of flower petals and fronds. They were entranced by it. It beckoned them. It looked so romantic, so enticing. It captivated them. Their eyes met. They knew what was about to happen. Stone lifted Lana in his arms and carried her to the "bed" of petals.

Stone was unable to imagine the delight he was about to feel. Gently he lowered Lana onto the petals. She reached up and pulled him to her. They kissed as they ran their hands over each other's body. Their mouths and tongues met. They made love. They made all fashions of love until their cup runneth over.

* * *

Lana was back with 'lover boy,' her battened down guest. And what a bloody mess he was. Horrible! How she had enjoyed Stone King, and now this monster.

Lana squirmed and wiggled in her nest in the hay bales. She squirmed not from physical discomfort, but from puzzlement. What was the need for the romantic scene with Stone King?

"Eve One, please," Lana asked hoping Eve One would answer. "Why the theatrics with Stone King, making love in front of the studio audience and those watching TV, what was its significance?"

"For the time being, none my dear," Eve One answered.

"But…?"

"Just think of the theatrics as something deep and loving. Our planet earth needs much more of this. Not hatred, wars and greed," Eve One whispered into Lana's ear.

Then silence.

Lana's mind returned to Istanbul and her 2,100 attendees.

* * *

This night she allowed her bodyguard and security personnel to take her to her private room in the beautiful amphitheater. The crowds waiting to see her and be near her seemed more numerous than usual. While being polite and thoughtful as usual, the crowd appeared to be more congested, more mob-like. Lana guessed she felt this way because Clark was now back in New York. She always had a feeling of great comfort when she was with him. Big Francois, her huge bodyguard, seemed to sense Lana's feelings. He took her hand in his big paw and squeezed it gently. This gesture told Lana he understood her jitters, and for her to feel safe and secure with him. He would see to her safety 'by gar.' Feeling better with Francois at her side, Lana joked, laughed, and lifted the spirits of the crowd with her wit, her inspirational charisma and charm.

Francois took her to the room, checked its interior to see that all was well. "Bon," he said as he stepped outside her door into the hall. There he stood; arms folded and awaited her exit from her room.

Lana telephoned Clark at the offices of H. & R. Financial in New York.

"Hello, Clark."

"Hello, Lana."

"How are things Clark, you sound so somber?"

"Holly was not at JFK to meet me."

"How come, did she leave you a note?"

"No. Nothing! None of the staff has seen her today. They're frightened for her Lana. Since Vito and Leroy's murder, everyone is sad, depressed and frightened."

"Damn it all, Clark. What are you going to do?"

"Well, I've already called the police and Trent. I'm going to go to her place in a few minutes and I'll take Jenks with me. He can open any door anywhere without leaving a trace of any kind."

"I'll let you go. I'll call you tonight at your home after the social. My usual parting."

"Mine, too, Lana. I hope I will have located Holly by then." They hung up.

Slowly Lana and Francois made their way to the social room. Lana had freshened up for the evening. She wore a fine rich wool deep blue mini dress that featured light semi diagonal stripes. The dress accentuated her full breasts and her long tanned legs. Over the dress she had on a magnificent full-length jacket made out of the same material as her dress, the same dramatic color but with the stripes running vertically. The jacket was wide open at the front, and its length was two inches longer than her skirt. She wore no necklace. Her shoes were soft colored deep blue, topped by a tiny broach on each one. Her long tawny golden hair flowed down the front of her jacket and halfway down her back. Her high cheekbones, her sculptured nose and her glistening full lips slightly parted (which accentuated her moist inviting mouth) could not be equaled, she ranked several levels above the next most beautiful girl in the world.

Lana sat with a group of people from Istanbul. She was able to carry on a conversation with them in both Turkish and English. They were delightful. She danced with three of the gentlemen from the table. They were excellent dancers. She danced too with Adam Six who whispered in Lana's ear that Itanya Margo Koslosky would soon wed Dr. James Bell-Irving.

"What?" Lana sputtered.

"Yes, she will marry him September 10, next."

"Fuck me," Lana blubbered.

"Lana, you are so charmingly gross."

"I'm sorry Adam Six. But who will fulfill her cosmic duties?" Lana asked, searching Adam Six's beautiful teasing blue eyes.

"Lana, the time it will take from Itanya's birth until her death in 2072 is just a matter of a split second to we controllers. In addition Eve Three will not miss any of her cosmic duties during her 'side life' as Ms. Itanya."

"What does Eve One think Adam Six?" Lana questioned. "I get a little angry at her," Eve One responded, "but Eve Three is such a cute charmer, just like you Lana, I can't stay angry with her. I will, as you our Earth people say, bless her marriage. The children she will bear, two girls and a boy, will be earthlings just as Dr. James Bell-Irving is. Eve

Three knows all this, but Dr. Bell-Irving will never know anything pertaining to Eve Three's cosmoses."

"Thank you Eve One and Adam Six. It sounds so romantic and exciting. I am so happy for James Bell-Irving," Lana said.

Eve Three and James Bell-Irving danced through the entire social. At the close of the evening they departed to the good doctor's hotel suite, made love then Eve Three left. She promised she would see him at the close of Dr. Lana Masters' session on the 'morrow.' She knew he would propose marriage to her tomorrow evening. She giggled with delight.

"You are such a Rag-a-muffin Eve Three, or should I say Itanya," Adam Six laughed.

"I love you too, Adam Six," Eve Three beamed.

Lana telephoned Clark at midnight Istanbul time at Clark's hideaway in the big warehouse that housed H & B's offices. Clark responded with "Hi darling."

"Hi, sweetheart," Lana said. "Any Luck?"

"None, babe. Nothing! not a clue, even in her flat. I'm getting frightened for her. She's never missed a day at the office in three years. The police are baffled, too, although they said it wouldn't surprise them if she has gone back to the streets."

"No way," Lana said.

"I know, Lana. What should I do?"

"Just keep looking, darling, and send Trent out to look and, you know, have him use his convincing ways. He'll scare the truth out of somebody. There're lots of our scum-bag friends who will check every nook and cranny in the big apple for you too, Clark."

"I know. Not only have I got Trent on the go, I've got Jason, Freddy, The Count, The Ripper and Ann out searching now. Tomorrow Ann and Samantha are going to go to each Ivy League School and are going to try to set themselves up as bait for those same jerks who gang-raped Holly. Personally, I will try to get through to some people I feel may be involved. God how I miss you, Lana—Monday seems like years away."

"I know Clark. It doesn't seem fair that we are apart, ever."

"No, Lana and Clark, we know what you are thinking, but we are not going to help you solve your mysteries," Eve One said.

"We know," Lana replied.

"I will phone tomorrow Clark. In the meantime, take special care of yourself. I love you, here's a kiss good night." Lana made a kissing sound.

"Oh! How I love you, Lana." Clark sent her a long distance kiss, too.

CHAPTER 46

LANA'S SISTER MARGARET'S PLEA

Lana's mind erased several hours of her time in Istanbul. At the close of the day she remembered she did not leave the stage immediately. She remembered the crowd awaiting her. Francois and security personnel, too, awaited her. She looked troubled as she placed her elbows on the dais then cupped her chin in her up-stretched arms. Someone in the crowd called softly, "Are you okay, Dr. Masters?"

"Yes! Yes! I'm fine thank you," Lana answered. "I'm kinda in dreamland cogitating. I shan't be many minutes. Francois, please wait for me. Ladies and gentlemen, I will be at our fun time in a half an hour at most." Something was troubling Lana, she was very ill at ease. Was Clark safe back in Manhattan? Clark was after all, *her man*." Enemies of H & B, the scum-bag company, would search out Clark for elimination. Was he safe? Think now, our closest friends at H & B Financial, Vito and Leroy murdered. The botched up robbery some months back. Holly missing. The need for such a wicked bastard as Trent, one ugly mean son of a bitch! Her bygone lecherous lover she thought was her friend. The Ivy Leaguers, they've snooped around H & B's premises many times, they are slick and without question they are seeking revenge against Clark. They conned the 1995 Annual Report of H & B out of a shareholder named Billy Wheaton, age 19, one truly fucked up junky. Are the Ivy Leaguers after something big, like taking control over H & B? The priest who took a shot at Lana! How does he fit in? Where is he from? Lana swears she recognized him from somewhere. Does he have a connection somewhere back in Manhattan? Or is it any of the above? Is it someone unknown to the executive of H & B? Is it someone who is trying to pirate the shares from H & B's weakest shareholders and take control of this wealthy organization by having a block of votes sufficient in size to elect a new board of directors? Christ, so many of H & B's shareholders are drunks and/or junkies, who will sell their shares at next to nothing to supply their habits.

There was no doubt in Lana's mind someone, whomever it shall be, intends to be at H & B's annual general meeting, holding share certificates and registered as shareholders with the intent of taking control of this rich entity. Fucking reverse scalpers.

"Francois, please escort me to my room."

"Oui, mademoiselle." He was up the steps to the stage in two big bounds. Francois took Lana through a back entrance to her room.

Lana called Clark. He answered, thankful to hear her voice. Lana recited her concerns. Clark knew what she was talking about, except for the priest. "Trent must get on this now, Clark," Lana ordered, "and get him some reliable scummers to help him."

"No, no trace of Holly yet."

"Shit," Lana said, "I so wish I was with you now. I love you Clark St. James."

"I love you too, Lana Jean Masters."

"Clark, I am going to leave Istanbul on Sunday the 11th, the same flight you took, please, if you can, meet me at JFK. And my darlin', bring Trent along with you for safety's sake." Lana begged.

"We'll see," Clark said. He gave Lana a kiss over the telephone then hung up.

*   *   *

Lana changed into something comfy for the social. White designer jeans by Lindon Ex, a white western-style silk blouse, buttoned down the front with white exquisite horseshoe shaped buttons. The top button reached just above her bust line revealing the tops of her tanned breasts. The wrist-length sleeves ended in a trendy imitation white fur. Her black belt was a wide classic piece scrolled in a western motif. She wore tasteful Hillary designed white western feminine boots. Her hair was pulled back from her face then caught up in a clip behind her head allowing her tawny hair to free-fall three quarters the way down her back. She wore a western black string around her neck tied at the end in the shape of a saddle. Her earrings were black one-inch circles emulating coiled riatas. This dress mode was new for many at the social. The fit of Lana's jeans was most indecent. In total she was the essence of sublimity, an exquisite lovely piece of human splendor. When she walked her hips and posterior rocked both men and women into a state of hyperbolic hypnosis. Many women craved Lana. They would give up their religion to be able to make love to her and to be loved by her. Sleep with her at night, debate worldly issues by day and fuck any *old* time. Jesus, what a life it would be with this woman. This woman who should have been born Queen on the Aegean Island of Lesbos. Her poetic beauty unquestionably would subvert the castings of Sappho.

Lana could feel the penetrating looks of many women. She knew their desires, she knew too many of these women were straight, but on viewing her anatomy they lost their sexual equilibrium. These 'straights' wanted to fuck or be fucked by the 'Queen' of the sultry Isle of Lesbos. Christ, Lana thought!

And what about the 'switch hitters' the AC-DC's? They would switch to me as quick as the blink of a tiki-tiki turtle's eyes. You know, the tiki-tiki turtles on display at most zoos? The turtles, as vociferated by the turtle's attendants, "Yes ladies and gentlemen, the unique tiki-tiki turtle, when it gets sand in its eyes its foreskin rolls back with a click. Come now ladies, stop throwing sand in the tiki-tiki turtle's eyes…" Yes these gals would switch in a second if I gave them the come-on eye, and as for the down to earth lesbians, they would be all over me in a flash if I gave the green light.

Lana's mind went back to her stunning honey blonde-haired sister Margaret. The day 10 years ago when Margaret, who was studying medicine at the University of Saskatchewan, Saskatoon, telephoned Lana pleading with her to come to Saskatoon! "I need you Lana. I have to speak to you face to face, now. Please Lana, get the earliest flight possible to Saskatoon."

"What is it Margaret? Mom, dad, our brothers?"

"No, God Lana no, they're fine. It's just me."

"Are you sick Margaret or pregnant?"

"No, no, nothing like that. I need you, that's all."

"OK baby, I'll be there by noon tomorrow."

"Thank you, please hurry. Lana I'm as happy as I can be, I promise you, but I'm in a dreadful quandary. I need your advice. Margaret had hung up crying.

Jesus, Lana thought, what's with my sister?"

CHAPTER 47

MARGARET MASTERS and CHRISTEEN BARLOW'S LOVE AFFAIR

The score was 81 to 79 in favor of Washington State over the University of Saskatchewan. The date was December 29th, 1986. This game was game number three. Four games out of seven would give the university women students the North American Basketball Championship. The play was physical. There were no holds barred. Each side's determination to win was so overwhelming that everything, including a few fisticuffs, took place. Washington State's players had the height advantage averaging six feet one inch, while the U of S girls were just over five feet eleven.

There were three minutes left on the clock. The U of S team had just laid-up a two pointer, leaving them two points behind the much favored Washington State.

Margaret Masters at six feet, the U of S's number one center, was the best standing jumper on her team, very athletic, very strong. She was held captive in a graceful radiant body. She was 136 pounds of sheer beauty. She had three more years to go at the U of S to receive her degree in medicine.

Her opposing center from Eureka, California, Christeen Barlow (in her third year of medicine) stood six feet one and one-quarter inches. She too was very athletic, very strong and she was gorgeous. Christeen's body pushed the needle on the scale to a solid 137 pounds. Her raven black hair and piercing brown eyes her three-quarter-inch (natural) eyelashes together with her perpetual scowl made her look wicked.

"Okay Blondie, I'm going to fuck you good," Christeen sneered at Margaret as the referee approached them. All through the game Christeen had manhandled Margaret. She had her right elbow stuck in Margaret's ribs most of the night. She slapped Margaret's hands every time Margaret went for the ball or had possession of the ball. Christeen bodied Margaret when they jumped for the ball, or if Margaret dribbled the ball anywhere near Christeen. She even smacked Margaret's cheek with an open hand, claiming innocence of course, quite accidental in the excitement of the game. She hip-checked her; she trod on Margaret's feet. On more than one occasion she had one of Margaret's tits in her hand. Christeen had been charged with only three fouls during the game, three, she should have had 33. In the meantime she was Washington State's leading scorer putting 28 points on the board. She was a one-person wrecking machine. She made Xena look like Ann of Green Gables. Her references to Margaret were obstreperous.

"Blondie, you wimp."

"You blonde-haired air head."

"What you got up your ass girl?"

"Nice tits for a retard Canuck."

"How would you like a face full of my twat you tantalizing tart?"

"I'll be fucking you good by ten o'clock tonight pussy, pussy Maggie."

"These tits are made for sucking and they'll flop all over you." To the tune…These shoes are made for walking and they'll walk all over you.

"Hey cunt, I'll call the Ref if you keep on trying to hurt my little bod…ha ha."

"Just think, Maggie, by tonight I'll have my arms around your ass and you'll have your arms around mine."

"Fucky, fucky baby…whooeee…a suckin and a fuckin…a lick'n and a kickin, drool baby, drool cool baby."

Being a farm girl, Margaret could take the pounding from Christeen without too much ado. Even Lana's Sir Galahad quite by accident had once stepped on Margaret's foot with no consequences except for a swollen big toe. And what about the time she fell off the combine while it was running. It could have been game over if Tim Thompson, the quick thinking driver of that $150,000 machine hadn't turned the whole machine off within a second of her fall. She bumped a coupla' times against something before she hit ground. She hurt but she didn't cry. Tim gathered her up in his arms scolding and asking at the same time if she was hurt. No she said, gulping. Tim sent her home and told her to tell her mother everything. But Christeen's cursing and innuendoes, now that was something else! Margaret was leading her team in scoring too, 27 points in all.

The whistle had gone for play to begin. Christeen glowered at Margaret as they stood ready for the Ref to toss the ball above their heads. She put her glistening thigh between Margaret's legs and moved it back and forth and murmured see you at the bar in the Besborough at nine-thirty tonight. Wiggle your cunt on my leg if you agree."

Margaret, frightened, lost, sexually excited wiggled. God what have I done, she thought?

The whistle blew as the referee put the ball into play. Margaret made first contact with the ball and tipped it back to her point guard. The point guard made her way slowly up the court, which gave her teammates time to set up their formation. Margaret ran up the center of the court, turned as she got near Washington State's basket, arms outstretched she called for the ball. Susan Strong, U of S's most physical player, fired the ball at Margaret. Margaret grabbed it, made a move ready to arch the ball to the basket ala Lou Alcindor (Kareem Abdul Jabbar) when crunch, Margaret flew one way landing tummy first on the court with a 'whoooooof' while the ball flew into the arms of a Washington State guard. Christeen rushed down the basketball court stopping under the U of S's basket and on receiving a pass from her guard she stuffed a two-pointer.

Score 83 to 79.

The whole U of S team was on its feet as their coach roared down the court calling, "Foul, no basket ref, No. 69 (who just happened to be Christeen) charged my center, she's been fouling my No. 37 all night, where are your eyes?" Margaret got up. She strode over to big No. 69, who had a happy sneer on her face. "I'll see you tonight at the bar," Margaret said, then she hit Christeen with a short left hook to Christeen's gut, followed by a vicious overhand right to Christeen's jaw. Down went Christeen in a sprawl, long legs in the air, a surprised look on her face. Damn, Christeen was one tough broad Margaret thought, no tears, just a hand rub on her jaw. Christeen struggled to her feet looking as innocent as a new born child. She did not retaliate, she was too smart for that, she wanted the two points to count, and more to the point she wanted the sweaty Margaret to be her subservient sex slave. She smiled sweetly.

"The two points count!" The referee yelled. "Charging!…#37 the University of Saskatchewan. One free shot…#69 of Washington State. Because there are only two minutes left in this game I will not give #37 a game misconduct. She can stay on and play but one more infraction by #37 and I will toss her out of the game."

Coach Palmer could not believe his ears. The Saskatchewanites booed and jeered. Like an angel the big center smiled at the crowd, blowing kisses at them, with a look on her face that said, me do anything wrong? I am far too nice to play dirty! she chortled to herself. These antics enraged the crowd even more. A riot was close to erupting. Coach Palmer stood nose to nose with the Ref, his words harsh and uncomplimentary, his finger waving, his face beet red, with spittle flying everywhere but mostly in the Ref's face, howling "Bloody outrageous call, it was my player who was fouled. She should have three free shots. Are you blind you…"

"I've heard enough," the referee roared. "One more word from you Coach Palmer and I stop the game now, disqualify the U of S squad and proclaim Washington State the winner." Mouth agape Coach Palmer stared in disbelief at Referee Freud for a few more seconds, then turned and strode back to his team. "Okay gang, we will make a formal request for a review of this infraction with Board of Governors of the league. Are you okay Margaret?"

"I couldn't be better coach."

The referee whistled for the game to continue. Margaret again won the toss as Christeen whispered, "You're going to be a delicious yum-yum tonight Maggie Baby." This time Margaret's right forward took the ball and swept down the right side of the court. She was covered by a Washington State guard who lunged at her to take the ball, but the classy forward feinted to her right, then passed the ball back to one of her guards who was just back of the three point circle. The guard made a spurt up the center, turned her back just under the basket and handed it off to Margaret. As Margaret leapt to jam in a two-pointer her feet were cut out from under her. As she was falling she threw the ball back to center court to her point guard. Again no foul was called. The crowd screamed. Even the coach of Washington State shook his head in disbelief.

The play went on!

Thirty-five seconds had elapsed. A scant one minute and twenty-five seconds remained. Coach Palmer was about to call a time out as he saw Margaret leap out past the three-point line. The point guard faked a shot then shoveled a pass to Margaret, who in one electrifying moment put the ball in the air which dropped through the basket for a three-pointer.

83 to 82

The crowd cheered, stood and echoed hey, hey, Masters, Masters, Masters.

One minute and six seconds remained on the clock.

It was Washington State's ball. The ball was put into play. Christeen rushed to the U of S's end trailed by Margaret. The ball carrier looped a long high pass to Christeen who caught it in mid air and jammed the ball through the hoop for two points.

The crowd booed. Then complete silence.

The score was 85 to 82, Washington State.

Washington State's Coach called a time out. "Girls great score, but damn it all, you used up only three seconds. Quit showing off, use your heads, eat up the clock. Do what I say now, get the ball back in your possession." He clapped his hands. His team made its way back on to the court.

In the meantime Coach Palmer set up a new formation, a formation that would have Masters hang back as her team worked its way up the court. Masters was to follow the right forward as if the forward was a blocker, she would then burst past the forward, take a hand-off from her and just before reaching the three-point circle she would take a jump shot and hope for the best. The play was executed perfectly. Masters shot, a little lower this time, hit the back rim. The ball bounced to the forward rim, hovered for a second, bounced back to the back rim then fell through the hoop. Margaret dropped to one knee, "yes," she yelled. The crowd couldn't contain itself. It whistled, clapped, pounded its feet for a full two minutes. They loved their team.

85 to 85

It was Washington State's ball.

Thirty-nine seconds left.

Washington State had one girl who was a joy to watch as a "dribbler". She was a magician with the ball. The pass out was to her. She wove her way down center court, pivoting, on her knees, squatting. She watched her teammates for an opening. She spied Matilda Osterly somewhat unguarded in the left corner of U. of S. territory. She caught the U. of S. team off guard by looking in the opposite corner from Matilda. Twenty seconds left. She fired the ball to Matilda. Matilda picked off the pass.

She had an opening. She dribbled three paces then jumped high releasing the ball in a feather-like fashion. The ball soared toward the basket. Margaret, with Christeen all over her, gave her mightiest, full-powered jump ever. Straight up in the air she went, Christeen went sprawling, Margaret's right hand swatted the ball out of bounds. The crowd cheered.

"Foul," yelled Referee Freud pointing at Margaret Masters. "No. 69 Washington State, one free throw."

One second left.

Now the crowd went ballistic. "Referee Fraud."

"Bullshit. Stone the pompous prick." They stood and stomped their feet. It was bedlam for 10 minutes.

Coach Palmer beseeched Referee Freud to reverse his decision. God, Coach Palmer found the Ref to be an obnoxious snot. Freud looked at Palmer as if he, Palmer, was some unimportant worthless twit. An ignomatic annoyance. Referee Freud turned his back on Coach Palmer and walked toward the timekeeper. There he sat. When things began to quiet down Referee Freud got off his chair and began to walk out on the court.

The crowd jeered and booed again.

Finally the crowd was spent.

Play in was called.

Christeen took her time. She sank her shot.

Time had run out.

The score was 86 to 85 Washington State.

The crowd was silent.

* * *

A frightened, hesitant yet curious Margaret met Christeen at the bar in the Besborough that night at 9:30.

Christeen was alone in a semi-circle booth toying with her gin and tonic. She looked too good to be true. Her thick black hair was piled on top of her head, her bangs came down to her long lashes. Her makeup was exquisite! Her high cheekbones made her look exotic. Her eyes, my God, how do you explain such eyes. Her miniature Roman nose could not have been more suitable for the remarkable face, and her lips and mouth, deliciously moist, were made for romance. Her flawless chin completed an inimitable face. Margaret knew Christeen's body. Sculptured. Faultless! Sexy! Mean. Christeen did not look like that damnable Amazon who had molested Margaret just three hours ago. No, she looked like a movie star. A sophisticate! Someone who would not dream of working up a sweat on a basketball floor! No, a ballroom dancer perhaps, not a rough and tumble guttersnipe talking two-bit whore.

Margaret approached unseen by Christeen. "Hi champ," Margaret managed to squeeze out.

"Margaret, how nice to see you. Please sit down. My you look lovely!"

"So do you Christeen."

Margaret slid into the booth. She was doe-like. Insecure! Near nausea knowing that she was going to bed down with this amazing she animal sometime, probably tonight. How she ached with frustration. Her stomach as well as her hands trembled. God how she wanted to be touched, played with, fondled by Christeen, foul-mouthed, dirty Christeen. 'I want to experience wickedness with her, get soiled, spoiled and sweaty with her. Damn, my panties are soaked already.'

"Would you like something from the bar Margaret?" Christeen asked.

"Yes Christeen, that would be nice, but only if we go halves on the tab. Okay?"

"No way, mon cheri. My father spoils me. So darlin' its on me tonight, no arguments please."

"Cool. But only if it's on me tomorrow night, oops! if there is a tomorrow night?" 'Damn me anyway for taking for granted tomorrow night. I'm just over anxious. Christeen may have another chick lined up for tomorrow night. Damn me anyway,' Margaret thought.

"Oh there'll be a tomorrow night for us all right, and it will be at a friend's house. A friend who just happens to be leaving for Dallas tomorrow and who will be away for 10 days and who has asked me to house sit for her. And you, my sweety-cake, will be my guest for those full 10 days. So if you wish you can bring your favorite drink along with you when you move in with me, but, it's not necessary, my friend has a cupboard full of booze."

"Christeen how dare you assume that I will move in with you just with the snap of your finger. Who do you think you are? I just met you today, not fucking formally…excuse my use of that word…but rather nastily as you roughed me up on the court." Margaret was mad. Damn Christeen's self-assured egotism, Margaret thought.

"A dry white wine waiter," Margaret snapped.

"Yes, madam, a glass or a carafe."

"A whole damn bottle of Cote Rotie."

"Yes madam, thank you madam."

"That's better Margaret. Mad looks good on you."

"Fuck you Christeen."

"That's what I intend to do you tonight my dear."

"Let us change the subject Christeen?"

"Okay, what would you like to talk about?"

"You."

"Me?"

"Yes you."

"Cool."

"Well lets see, do you want my whole life story Maggie darlin' or just some exciting excerpts?"

"Whatever you like, you gorgeous stud," Margaret responded.

"Stud! That's a new one! What's wrong with Butch, Queen or Dike?"

"Never mind Christeen, let's hear your story."

Christeen laughed. Her laugh was loaded with arrogance.

"Jesus you're annoying, Christeen."

"I hope so pussy cat. Let's see now. I was born Christeen Charlene Alexandria Barlow January 13th, 1966 to Marshall and Charlene Barlow, M.D.s in the pretty little town of Yreka, California. I went through primary school in Yreka, and, I loved every minute of my life there. The school was the best in the whole world, and the kids, all of my friends there, were the best in the world. It was a world of nature, a world of good clean fun and adventure, no bad stuff just good stuff.

"Then my parents sent me to a private all girls school in Sacramento for my secondary grades when I was just 13. I was frightened, homesick and so lonesome for my parents, my brother and sister and my friends. I did everything imaginable to convince my mom and dad to let me stay home. But no, I had to stick it out for four years, dressed in my little uniform, living in the school's little dorm, learning my lessons from my prim little teachers and crying night after night in my little bed.

"I did, however, do well in all my grades. Well above the entry requirements for medicine, which, incidentally Margaret, is what I wanted, because on my own volition, not by my parents directives, I wanted to become a doctor. So there!" Christeen smiled.

Christeen finished her drink, then ordered another. The waiter refilled Margaret's.

"Well," Christeen went on," after the first Christmas break in nineteen whatever, I became a little less jaundiced about being away from Yreka. I found some new friends, all girls tho', 'cause no boys were allowed in the school obviously. Nice girls, too. We played all kinds of sports, softball, soccer, tennis, ice-skating and, la de da, basketball. And, honest Margaret, without being braggy, I was the best in all of them. I was tall, lean and mean.

"There was a private school for boys just a few blocks away. We girls got to meet a lot of them. We had fun parties with them, weekend hikes, and some inter-squad basketball games. We had a ball. Just one problem, boys fought over me. I was flattered by their attention and their adoration of me, but my oh my I was baffled. I used to wonder, when are my horny hormones for boys going to kick in? The boys' school good lookers were targets for our girls who without shame chased them, but these 'hunks' wanted me. Me! Me, not the other girls! At school dances the guys would line up for me. On slow music, guys who danced with me used to hold me tight, and some would even put their hands on my butt and pull me into their hard-ons. The reaction on the part of my psyche was "nil". But I was a good actress. I made them think that I enjoyed their pre-adult passions.

"But damn it Maggie my eyes were on Miss Adams. She was my mathematics teacher about 27-years old who was my room teacher in grade 11. She was pretty and among all the teachers and students her T's and A's were, supreme. The feelings I had for this teacher were not anything but sexual. She was shorter than me and rather plump. Jesus, Margaret, I used to sit on the can and masturbate thinking about her. Lots of times I placated myself in my classroom, in bed, in theaters and a couple of times in church.

"I hated myself for this feeling. I tried so hard to get it on with boys. I couldn't. As time went on I would see many women, all strangers, nameless, who would turn me on. When shopping for clothes I would insist on a woman clerk being with me, including helping me dress and undress in the cubicles. It was all I could do to control myself from feeling them up.

"God, it was horrid. Was it just a passing phase? No. It couldn't be. Its been going on too long. God, am I gay? Am I a lesbian?"

Christeen's eyes flooded with tears. But the lady's grit was unwavering. She was one pragmatic gal! She accepted her lot and woe betide anyone who tried to second-guess her. She was a proud woman. "Don't anyone stand in my way or I'll break your fucking neck. Right wing conservative bigots, burn at the stake religious inquisition loving farts, bible thumping obdurates—go suck cocks.

"I decided to go to my doctor and pour out my whole story to him. Find out, if at 16 a person's sexual preference could be permanently molded. If so, how do I tell my mom and dad, my sister and brother, my dear friends, how for pity's sake?"

Christeen hung in there. This gal has guts.

"My appointment date was seven whole days away. It might as well have been seven millenniums. I was so frightened, so, so much at a loss. I needed to blurt out my story now, not seven days from now. Margaret, those were the longest seven days I have ever endured.

"Lets have another drink. Oh waiter, here please.

"In any event I tried two experiments during that time. I still thought I might be exaggerating my sexual nuances. Maybe I just hadn't given boys a chance. Heavens, unless I've broken something, I'm still a virgin at 16. For the last three years I've been with girls, not sexually Margaret, and, at that point I had never had sex with a girl either, but you know what I mean.

"My first experiment was with a guy from the boys' school. His name was Robert something or other, I can't remember. That's how impressed I was with him. Anyway, he was 'the' All American Hero to all the girls at my school. He was cute, I must admit. He looked a little like Kevin Costner. Well Margaret he had dated me a few times, the movies, school dances, things like that, and I think he thought I was his steady because of those dates." Christeen giggled. "I even let him do a little petting at times. Okay, the Saturday before my appointment with Dr. Chaney, who, by the way, was a good friend of my parents, Robert escorted me to a dance being held at the boys' school. All the girls as usual were envious of me, but me I would have preferred being with Miss Adams.

"Are you getting bored with my life so far Margaret? Cause if you are we can talk about something else?"

"No Christeen no, I'm fascinated. Don't stop, please."

Christine sipped her drink, toyed with her glass again, looked around the bar then continued. "Robert was from a well-to-do family and, while I don't remember his last name, Finney…that's it…Finney…ha, good for me, I remembered. Anyhow Margaret, he was a good guy, not a snob or anything like that and, frankly, he was a lot of fun, and I decided, man tonight's the night."

* * *

"You girls looking for some fun tonight?" A young brash, half-corked man interrupted. Christeen and Margaret looked up to see who the interloper was.

"I'm a fun guy and you look like fun girls. May I join you, you know a menage a trois?" Christeen smiled at him. "I got a buddy over there, see," he said, pointing a wavering finger toward the bar, "manage a quarter or whatever?" he said laughing like a perfect ass.

'Jesus, what a rube,' Christeen thought.

"That's very kind of you to be so gracious with us," Christeen mocked. She wiggled herself out of the booth, stood right up to 'Mr. Rube' and towered over him by a good five inches.

He looked up and said, "you're a big beauty aren't you?"

"Yes, I'm big, and I'm mean. Now run along little boy before I get angry."

Mr. Rube persisted.

Next thing you know Mr. Rube was dumped sans ceremony on his pratt.

Christeen leaned over him, her breasts half exposed to his bugged out eyes, and whispered, "I said run along little boy before I get angry."

"You'll be sorry you did this to me bitch," he said, as he struggled to get up.

Christeen ignored Rubes remark and seated herself again.

Several staff members appeared after spotting the mild ruckus. They assisted Mr. Rube to his feet and were quite apologetic to him.

"What's happened here?" a somewhat authoritative one among the staff questioned.

"She," pointing to Christeen, "unprovoked, jumped out at me, for no reason. She caught me by surprise and dumped me on my ass. Throw the bitch outta here she's a fucking menace. Get her, and her," pointing to Margaret, "outta here or I'll call my father, and he'll close down your whore filled bar."

"Wait one minute, Mr. Perlhomme," the authoritative one said, "leave your father out of this. I'm sure you don't want him to see you like this."

"Like what Matt, are you threatening me? My father's the mayor of this city. Don't fuck with me."

Christeen got up again and once more dumped the mayor's son on his ass.

"Jesus," Mr. Rube Perlhomme screamed, "she done it again."

Before anyone could stop her, Christeen pushed Mr. Rube Perlhomme on his back, placed a foot on his chest, banged her clenched fists against her chest and screamed the blood-curdling howl of Tarzan of the apes.

The whole bar erupted in "yea's, good stuff, give that two-bit bully the what-fors." Then everyone in the bar gave Christeen a standing ovation.

Christeen gave the 'thumbs up' sign, then bowed.

"What happened Miss?" Matt, the authoritative one asked.

"Nothing much," Christeen replied, "he just pestered us a bit, then he started to come on to us, he was drunk, so I floored him."

"Sorry ladies, I'll get him out of here. But be warned the guy has a powerful father and he'll look for revenge."

"Thank you Mr.?"

"Matt Stennard."

"Mr. Stennard."

"We will be here 'til about 11 if that's okay with you Matt?"

"No problem ladies."

God how I hate people saying 'no problem,' Christeen thought.

The people in the bar settled back and began their low buzzing conversations.

"My, that was quite awesome Christeen," Margaret said.

"Twarn't nothin' Chile," Christeen twanged.

"Okay, Margaret, where was I?"

"Robert Finney," Margaret responded, "man tonight's the night."

"Well to shorten the whole messy story, about a half an hour before the dance was to end I suggested to Robert we go out in the school's garden and find a cozy spot for some heavy petting. Robert, poor chap, flipped.

"He asked me if I was serious.

"Oh yes Robert, I said to him, I winked, moistened my lips with a suggestive tongue, I am more than ready. He took my hand and almost dragged me to a secret lair in the gardens. He kissed me with a drooling mouth and stuck his tongue inside my mouth, he wasn't going to waste one second, no, he was going to get right at it. First, Margaret his kiss made me nauseous, I thought I might throw-up. He reached under my mini skirt and grabbed both cheeks of my ass. He kinda' shoved me onto the ground. He was panting, and whimpering like a dog. I thought he was going nuts. His mind was all over the place. I watched him in bloody wonderment. Is this how men act as they prepare themselves for sex? As far as Robert was concerned I was just a cock recipient like any other twat. Throw a gunnysack over our heads and we girls are all the same—cunt. He grabbed at my panties with both hands, then squatted down on his knees, took one fumbling shaky hand away from my panties reached for his zipper, started to yank the silly thing down and, guess what, the zipper caught on his tucked-in shirt. Christ, you would think the end of the world had come. He cried out like a disappointed child, he whimpered ever harder, spittle was running down his chin, his hips were revolving. Now he had both hands working feverishly at his zipper. The thing wouldn't budge. I watched bewildered but amused too, because I couldn't believe what I was seeing. He stood up and yanked his pants down with a mighty jerk. Christ, at this point he could have pulled a two-ton-truck with his teeth. Then he flopped down on the ground tugging at his pants, his shirt ripped where the zipper had caught, and down came his pants. By this time he had rolled onto his back.

"He got up, tripped on his pants which were hugging his ankles. He whimpered for God's sake. What a dink I thought. He struggled to his feet, shuffled toward me, his cock waving like a fistless arm, tried to straddle me, which, I must say was impossible with his downed pants binding his feet together. He fell again, dork first into the grass. He yelped, whimpered and drooled. What a fucking sight! He yanked his pants off over his shoes jumped up, straddled me, tore my panties off, pushed my legs apart, got between them then tried to jam his cock inside me. The twip found me dry as a bone and tighter than a bull's ass in fly season. Christ, what next! He got on his knees, took both hands and with his pointy fingers he tried to pry my vagina lips apart. That didn't work. He put drooly spittle on my clit, then tried to part 'it' again and this time it worked. Now it was my time to suffer. He drove his cock inside me, broke my maidenhood and then he came his lump. He flopped like a wet fish on top of me. His come together with my blood flooded out of me. While I hurt like hell, I made no sound. So this is sex with a man! Great mother of Mary! It's about as much fun as picking dung balls out of a hairy ape's ass. It's awful. Wherefore art thou Miss Adams.

"Experiment one was zero, nil, obnoxious. So I tried my second experiment, Margaret, this time with a full-grown adult male but knowing in the back of my mind that it, too, would be a failure." Christeen lamented. "At the boys' school there was a good looking phys. ed teacher. My guess he was about 30-years old, unmarried I believe, in any case I was pretty sure he had the 'hots' for me. When we played basketball against the boys team, I noticed how he…Troy was his name…glued his eyes on my tits and my ass, and finally my face. Just like a man huh Margaret, tit's, ass then face?"

"I guess so, Christeen."

"Well we had an inter-school game against the boys' team on a Monday night before my doctor's appointment. I don't think I mentioned my doctor's appointment was for the coming Thursday. Anyway I was determined to get 'Troy Boy' in bed with me that Monday night. I had it well planned, sneaky broad that I was, and still am, right Margaret?"

"I guess so Christeen."

" I made sure my number 69 jersey was loose at the top so when it was appropriate for me to lean in Troy's direction my tits would be impossible for him to ignore, my bra was tiny. Jesus how that worked! His eyes went buggy. And as for my basketball shorts, I shrunk them as much as I could, so my ass would be, well, almost like I was wearing a thong. God, Troy was fucking agog, just like his whole team was. The whole fucking boys' team guarded me, hands, arms and legs all over me, Christ, they lost 78 to 42 to us because they didn't guard the other girls on our team. Coach 'Troy Boy' didn't seem to care. He spent the whole game eyeballing me. Crazy huh, Margaret?"

"I guess so Christeen."

"Let's lighten up for a moment pussy cat, and partake of our booze juices," Christeen said.

"Okay Christeen," Margaret replied.

"You know Margaret, I had a great, great grandmother who played basketball on a girls' team way back in 1907, 1908. She was a very good player I understand. She had the neatest first name, Silken, Silken Hendricks. Apparently she was a beauty. Old rumors have it she had a secret lover for a whole year. A married guy called Phillip. Yeh, and this Phillip dude was a phys. ed. teacher at a school, a snob school called Santa Monica High in LA, Yeh! Silken, believe it or not, was a student at the school and she, using her sexy wiles got it off with Phillip, and, believe it or not, honey chile, Silken became a doctor. Same for me hey, pussy cat? Except'n Silken wasn't gay. Ain't that the berries?

"Anyway, my Troy was ripe for the pickin' after that sex show I put on for him. Jesus, was he ever. Before all of us left the court I ran over to the boys' bench where Troy was sitting. I asked him if I could come and see him at his suite before the girls' curfew, and bring my math lesson with me so he could help me with it. I told him I understood he was a marvel at math and I could sure use the help. 'Well Miss Barlow, your request is somewhat unusual,' he said. 'Are you not able to be helped by your own instructors?' he asked. 'To my knowledge,' he said, 'your math instructors are excellent.' Mr. Wentworth, Troy's last name, I said, it is this particular part of the math program no one seems able to help me with. Please, I beg of you, please help me."

"All right my dear," he agreed, "please be at my suite at 8 o'clock sharp. I believe you know where I live?"

"Yes I do sir, and thank you so very much sir, I will be at your home at 8:00 p.m. Thank you.

"The fornification that night, Margaret, was different from the Saturday night fiasco, but in some respects more sickening. Again to shorten the story, I arrived at his suite at 8 o'clock in tight short shorts, skimpy top, no makeup, hair flowing over part of my face, over my shoulders, down my back, and I had bathed in an exotic perfume. Shit kid, when I looked at myself in the mirror I made myself horny.

"He was in shorts and a tee shirt. Good lookin' dude! We worked at math for awhile, I sat right next to him, we rubbed knees, played footsies, totally innocent hey Margaret, yeh, in a pig's eye. Poor Troy, he gasped his way through the lesson I had brought. I would lean over his shoulder so he could smell me good and see my breasts. With my face just inches away from his I would ask him questions about the lesson. I would do this with the most innocent pleading eyes. Eyes that said to him, my hero, my king, I must have you. The poor guy. He fell into my spell. Yes Maggie baby, much like you are now, he fell into my spell. I stood and pulled his handsome head into my bare midsection. I stroked his hair, moved my body back and forth then pushed his head down toward my…well you know what, Margaret. He was breathing as if he was climbing Mount Everest. I had him stand and embrace me. I swayed my hips every which way and thrust my, you know what, against his rock hard dick. I licked his quivering lips, stuck my tongue in his mouth and continued to writhe my body against his as if in sexual ecstasy. He could stand it no longer. At that time, Margaret, I was six feet tall and weighed 130 pounds. Troy was about six one and weighed, I'd say, 190. He picked me up as if I was a child, carried me into his bedroom, laid me on his bed, stripped me bit by bit, then took his own clothes off. My God, his thing looked vicious. He caressed me, and he kissed me all over my body. But shit, I didn't respond sexually as I had hoped for, but physically I 'done' good'. I moaned and I groaned. I whispered to him, what a he-man you are, fuck me please, please fuck me hard. He was smart, Troy was, damn it all he was smart, he put some vaseline on me. Knowing I was just 16, he knew, or he had a hunch I would be dry. Dammit Margaret, I was dry because I wasn't turned on, not because I was only 16-years old. He entered me. Christ it hurt. But I was and still am one tough broad. I faked and I faked. I made all the right noises. I bucked like a bronco hoping he would finish. Again, he was some cool dude. Just as he was about to blast-off he withdrew his big cock and spurted the shit all over me. What a mess! But at least it was over.

"Now his come was everywhere, under my chin, in my hair, on my boobs, all over my stomach, dribbling down my sides, one hell of a mess of it in my pubic hair, some even reached my mouth. I had a terrible time keeping from throwing-up but by damn Maggie, I toughed it out.

"Troy, after he had finished, was drained of all strength. He lay on top of me. Then came my next ploy. I began to cry. I sobbed out 'what have I done? What will my mommy and daddy say? How will I tell them? Will I be expelled from school? Mr. Wentworth, it was wonderful, but what am I going to do? I should kill myself.' I sobbed, cried, and carried on like a wailing child. 'What am I going to do Mr. Wentworth, what?' Please God help me.

"Troy, realizing his folly, jumped off of me. Gadzooks Margaret, some of his come was now stuck to his body…ugh. He looked down at me and said in a quasi controlled voice, 'Christeen, don't be silly, I will think of something I promise you. First, let me clean you up, I'll get a towel and a face cloth.' He turned to go, then he looked down at his crotch, spied his dick flopping back and forth and, shit, he realized he was nude. He covered his cock with his hands then rushed over to where his clothes had been dumped, dressed, then returned to me."

"No Christeen, I want you to shower, yes shower, that will be much better than a sponge bath by me, yes Christeen a shower, a shower. Take my hand Christeen dear, come to my shower."

"He reached his hand down for me and helped me to my feet. God he was in agony. He spied my tits, he gasped, Margaret my sweety-cake, the poor fucker was getting horny all over again. Oh my God, I thought, I couldn't stomach another man screw, I better wail even harder to discombobulate this unfortunate male. My wailing worked. He became discombobulated—phweew. He led me to his shower as I moaned 'oh mommy and daddy, mommy and daddy.' He turned it on, tested the water then without thinking put his right hand on the left cheek of my butt to guide me into the shower stall. I wailed even harder. He jerked his hand away from my posterior and panted, 'sorry Christeen.' Just as I was about to enter the shower, I turned to him and blurted out, 'sir, am I now pregnant?' Troy's faced paled. 'No, no Christeen I didn't let any of my, my, liquid get inside you.' But sir, my friends all say if you let a man get inside you it will start a baby to grow, I don't want that sir, I'm still just a baby myself, I don't want a baby growing inside me.' Waaaaaa I cried. "Maggie dear, was I being cruel to Troy?"

"No…yes…I don't know Christeen" Margaret replied.

"Well, Margaret, we got everything sorted out to his satisfaction. The poor guy, he never did nor never would know the reason I seduced him.

He was terrified I would go to my parents, my teachers and my friends and accuse him of rape. After Troy outlined the reasons I should never, ever, tell anyone of this ever so pleasing but private occurrence he seemed satisfied I would be as discreet as he. And I was until now.

"Damn it, Margaret, those two experiments proved I was gay. I was miserable. Yes, Miss Masters, in both sexual encounters I had, I had but one person in my mind during those encounters, my masturbation icon, Miss Adams. I was so devastated I thought there was only one direction for me to go and that was to the 'streets.' To become a street person, that's all I deserved to be, a rag-tag street dweller, maybe even a prostitute. I was sure my life as I had in mind, a damn good doctor, would never materialize because I was different. I was a fucking queer.

At that point the time was nine forty-five, the right time for another drink. The waiter obliged.

After a few moments of silence, Christeen took up her story where she had left off.

"I had heard that if a girl can't get it on with smoked meat, an Afro-American guy, then she is gay without a doubt. I never went that route thinking one more male of any race floppin' his dick around me would be one too many.

"When I visited my doctor on that Thursday I unloaded everything on him, Miss Adams, my horniness around women and my sexual repugnance of men vis-à-vis Robert and Troy. And I told him how I loathed myself for my feelings. How I thought my sexual preference would screw up my career. How my family and friends would hate me. I wouldn't go to heaven when I died. No kids! You know Margaret all those awful feelings and disgust you have about yourself."

"My story is similar to yours Christeen, but please go on."

"Margaret first, are we going to sleep together tonight?"

"Yes," Margaret said her eyes downcast.

Christeen put her hand on Margaret's hand and whispered, "We're not going to the gallows you know Maggie. We are going to enjoy each other. We can make love, talk, have a snack, whatever, for as long as we want tonight. Remember there's no game tomorrow night, just an afternoon practice. Don't be gloomy."

"I'm not gloomy, Christeen, I'm just nervous. You are so attractive it scares me. I don't know whether I'm just concerned about what happens to us when the basketball series is over, or what?"

"C'mon Margaret, we won't know what are feelings toward each other will be until we have a few days together. My guess is we will be very happy together. Do you want me carry on with my story?"

"Yes, I really do, Christeen."

Their glasses were empty, but they had that corrected. Both girls were beginning to feel their drinks.

"Okay Maggie, I better hurry with my off-beat life, 'cause I'm getting tipsey from these drinks. Are you feeling your drinks, too?"

"Yes."

"Maggie, you're sure a talker aren't you," Christeen said laughing.

"Yes."

"Okay, sweet stuff, I shall get on with it," Christeen said winking at Margaret. "The doctor was very sweet about it all. He gave me a thorough examination including blood analysis, x-rays, everything, and Margaret as it turned out I was in top physical condition. Mentally, Dr. Chaney said since my childhood he had never known anyone with a better attitude about life than me. He said my psyche was the essence of stability. He said my brain was just fine. He said I would make a fine doctor. Dr. Chaney reminded me that he had been my doctor, including my birth, for these past 16 years, that my father and mother were very close friends of his. Salt of the earth people, all of us he had said.

"He was however somewhat 'surprised' at my sexual inclination. Surprised but not disgusted or angry with me, just surprised. He then went into some detail about homosexuality with me. He kept religion out of the picture. He stayed with his belief people are born with their sexual tendencies already in place. He said most scientists adhere to this belief.

"God love him, he did get a little paternalistic with me, almost to a point of pity, but Maggie, "pussy cat", I wheeled him away from his paternalism. In some ways even at sixteen I could manipulate people."

"You joke, Christeen?" Margaret said sarcastically.

"Touché Margaret," Christeen said laughing.

"My doctors advice was sound. He urged me to discuss my homosexuality with my mother and father soon, on my next visit with them in fact. 'Your mother and father may blame themselves for sending you to an all girls' school,' Dr. Charney had said, 'where lesbianism presumably exists. Where some lecherous young women and many of their teachers are homosexuals who prey on innocent wholesome neophytes turning these idyllic babes in the woods into sex-crazed sylphic monsters. To my knowledge Christeen,' he said, 'people who are born heterosexual remain heterosexuals all their lives. They will not switch to homosexuality through persuasion. They may experiment once or twice in same sex but they will find the experiment to be abhorrent. Your mother and father know this to be true but they may grasp at straws hoping you are an exception. Homosexuals are not nurtured from heterosexuals, no my dear Christeen, homosexuals are born homosexuals and they remain homosexuals all their lives. Please, my dear, don't think any less of yourself over this characteristic. You are a wonderful person, a young lady I would be so proud of if I was your parent. You have a marvelous brain, your health is superb, your physique is most enviable, your personality is exciting, you are charming, caring, polite, and to top it off, you are beautiful. Christeen dear, do not waste your time trying to change your sexual psyche. It will bring only heartache to you if you try to fight such a hopeless battle. Just be you. I know you will become a scientific wonder in the world of medicine. I love you child'

"I love you too Dr. Chaney" I replied. 'So speaketh my doctor, Margaret. He was terrific. I love him dearly."

"And did you tell your parents on your next visit, Christeen?"

"Yes I did. And was I scared? Jesus I was scared and you know me even tho' we just met, I am bumptious, Jesus am I bumptious. As soon as I got home to Yreka, inside our house, mom and dad beaming at me I blurted out 'I am a lesbian' mom and dad'. Not one minute had passed after I stepped through the threshold and closed the door behind me when I hit my parents with that homecoming cheerful 'nice to see you mom and dad greetings, here I am your meritorious fucking 16-year-old lesbian daughter'.

"With their arms outstretched to greet me, huge smiles on their faces, tears of happiness glistening in my mother's eyes, dads eyes glowing with pride…bang! You would think I had hit them with a stocking full of diarrhea. They stood stiff, unmoving. Then their smiles began to ebb, ebbing into toothy grins, you know, Maggie, like the grinning cat of Tweety's, 'I tot I taw a puddy tat.' Their arms stayed outstretched for several more seconds. I moved toward my mother. I entered her outstretched arms. I hugged her and kissed her. I stepped back and looked into her eyes. My eyes told her 'Mom, I love you.' I turned to Dad. I hugged and kissed him and professed my deep love for him.

"Whoooeee lover girl, I'm sure feeling my gin and tonic. Let's lay off the booze now Maggie Baby. I've got another half an hour of tales to wend your way and I sure don't want either of us pissed when we hit the sack."

"Oops, Margarita, look who's coming, the Mayor's son and two other bully boys.

"Hi Rube," Christeen laughed, waving at Stanley Perlhomme. "Come sit by my side little darling."

Stanley Perlhomme, glowering, walked to Christeen's and Margaret's table followed by his two bully boys.

"Please sit, your honor's son," Christeen offered.

Stanley sat.

"You foreign-born bitch," Stanley snarled, "I know you're a 'Yank' I saw your name and your picture in tonight's paper. Six foot one and a quarter she-male basketball player, right? And you," turning to Margaret, "I thought I recognized you too, you're Margaret Masters, our team's prima donna elitist, right? Well you fuckin' broads, you better take care. I'm going to make sure I get each of your ass's before your series is done. I'm sober now girlies, and I bloody well mean what I say. Meet Chester and Willy, my two best buddies, they're gonna get your asses too."

"Please sit Chester and Willy," Christeen said.

Chester and Willy sat.

"Now fellas, cool down. I meant no harm to you…"

"Stanley," Stanley said.

"Stanley. I was just protecting myself. I was frightened of you. I knew you had one too many, so I took advantage of you. I know you could have hurt me if you had wanted to, but I could see in your eyes then you were a true gentleman and you would spare me."

Christeen put her hands to her face and feigning fright and sorrow, she begged Stanley's forgiveness for her earlier theatrics.

"I would be so honored if you would let me buy you a drink Stanley, Chester and Willy. I deplore my impulsiveness and ungraciousness, which in most instances I can control. But when I saw your rippling muscles and your square jaw I thought you were going to abuse Margaret and me. I was scared Stanley. Please forgive me. Shake?" Christeen said, offering her hand to Stanley, "Friends forever."

"Before I shake your hand and forgive you, you fucking siren, you must agree to two things I wish."

"And what are these two things Stanley?"

"One is that I get to fuck each of you in the same bed tonight. And two is you get the best tickets in the house for us three for the rest of your series."

"Goodness Stanley, the first request is quite impossible. You see sir, each of us have our monthly visitor and we are flowing like hell tonight as a result of the hectic pace of our game this afternoon. Do you want to see?" Christeen began to pull her dress up to her crotch while spreading her legs apart for Stanley and other nearby patrons to see.

"No, no, Christ no, forget it. I don't want to ride a wet deck with blood. Forget it."

"I'm sorry Stanley, if what I did was revolting to you," Christeen apologized, "But in any event, please do come to our next game. It will start at 7:30 p.m. December 29th, at the U. of S. Sports Arena. I will see to it you have passes to the best seats in the house. Stanley, you will sit behind me in the first row. Shoot, we will be able to banter back and forth while I am benched. You will have a 'ball,' and why shouldn't you, being the Mayor's son and all. Chester and Willy will be seated at the opposite side of the court sitting behind Margaret. They can chat at Margaret. They, too, should have a ball. Would you like to shake on it Stanley?"

"Yeah, I guess so."

They shook hands.

"Christeen and Margaret, I will want to fuck you two in tandem after your visitor goes."

"We will see what we can do Stanley. Who knows, it might be a thrilling possibility after a few days have passed and when we can dismount from our cotton ponies."

"You're some broad Christy," Stanley said.

"Yeah, and I'll bet you're some kind of a stallion when you get your harem of mares in place," Christeen said, with a sly wink.

"I make an exceptional stallion my dear girls. You will be in awe of my pecker when you see it. In my shy modest way I deem it to be the eighth wonder of the world. Would you care for a peek at it now in its soft unagitated state? I can unzip my fly, pull down my shorts and let you admire it while it's unconscious, but, I must warn you girls, if either of you touch it, it could rise up in a raging furor ready for a devastating penetration into any female orifice."

The two girls looked at one another feigning fright, tense trepidation, and alarm. Oh how they wanted to burst into laughter.

"Please do," they echoed holding one another's hand in wonder, eyes popping, pretending.

Stanley within 30 seconds had himself exposed to Christeen and Margaret. The nerd had not been bragging. His soft cock was immense. Ten inches of soft bulky meat! Both girls touched it. They couldn't help it. Just like warnings 'wet paint'. It exploded into 12 inches of sheer beauty.

"My God," each girl gasped, this time not pretending. While neither Christeen nor Margaret had ever been purveyors of men's phalluses in the past, they knew the sight before them was unique. Unique, my God, what an understatement, this ramrod could, by rights, earn the title 'the eighth wonder of the world'. It was remarkable. Huge! Meaty! It had a healthy red tinge. It pulsated. Dark ominous veins ran through it. Its amazing head was perfectly forged for the purpose of leading the charge into any mysterious cavern, no foreskin, just a shiny pate. A marvelously shaped instrument, with an ever so slight dog-leg to the right. A phenomenal prodigious prick! The girls' eyes were glued to this monster.

Is it the drinks? Margaret thought, no man's thing could be that big. How could any woman accept this into her womanhood? Goodness, it would render her asunder. This phallus should be considered a lethal weapon, not a tool for impregnation. Perhaps it should be disconnected, taxidermied, then displayed in a museum. Whilst I marvel at its size, agog in fact at its size, I am not turned on by it in any way, just dumbfounded.

"Startling, Stanley. It is startling. I have never seen or heard of a man thing that fucking big. Has it been on steroids Stan? Or have you played with it so often it grew to that breathtaking size? Christ, a girl could chin herself on it," Christeen clucked.

"You can play with it if you like girls. It loves to be played with!"

Christeen chuckled, grabbed it in her right hand and pulled it in rapid jerks. In about 30 seconds that gigantic bazooka spurted a geyser of come clear over the booth's table landing in a huge glob on the bar's colorful carpet. The monster shuddered, dribbled out some excess semen then began its collapse. Christeen jerked it less frequently now. She felt its rib-like hardness begin to ebb. Finally the thing dropped its mighty head, then settled itself back into a nest of pubic hair.

"There Stanley," Christeen said smiling.

Poor Stanley was rocked. He tucked in, zipped up and murmured, "I think I've died and gone to heaven."

"Well, big boy, Margaret and I must leave you now. I hope I didn't injure your noble eminence in my excitement. Stan Baby, I implore you, do preserve your monolithic masterpiece for posterity."

"Bye-bye fellas, see you in a coupla days at our next game."

Margaret and Christeen got up from the booth, stepped over the glob and walked to the cashier. Christeen signed the tab and added thereto a $10 tip. They took the elevator to the sixth floor, strolled the hallway without saying a word to one another, and at room 609 Christeen inserted her card key, opened the door and stepped inside.

Margaret stood in the doorway looking bewildered. She shook. Christeen held out her hand to her. Margaret balked. Christeen reached down and took Margaret's hand in hers. Margaret didn't budge. Christeen smiled at Margaret and took a step toward her. Margaret seemed immobilized. Christeen touched Margaret's body with hers. Margaret tensed. Tenderly, she kissed Margaret's lips. With that, Margaret's eyes began to dampen. Christeen kissed her again, this time moving her moist lips on Margaret's lips. Margaret's eyes, while filled with tears, began to brighten. Christeen ran the tip of her tongue over Margaret's lips. Margaret's body began to tremble. Christeen's tongue parted Margaret's lips and entered Margaret's mouth. Margaret moaned. Christeen's tongue moved inside Margaret's mouth. Christeen placed her hands on Margaret's rounded hips and pulled Margaret to her. Margaret's stupor began to subside. Their ample breasts were pressed against one another. Now Margaret opened her mouth wide and accepted Christeen's roving tongue. Margaret reciprocated. She entered Christeen's mouth. They were now lost in their eroticism, forgetful their Lesbian embrace was taking place partly in the hotel's hallway.

Smack! Margaret's saucy ass was the recipient of a man's swat.

The man laughed, put his arms around both of them and snuggled up against Margaret's writhing delectable derriere.

"Jesus, what a pair of Amazons," he said. "Lesbos eh? How would you like eight inches of a real prairie prick stuck up your juicy asses?"

"Piss off Buster," Christeen growled.

"Fuck you lady."

At that moment a middle-aged couple got off the elevator and began walking toward the threesome.

"Please sir," Christeen yelled, "call security, this man is trying to rape us."

"Cunts," the man whispered to Christeen and Margaret, then turned to the middle-aged couple and countered, "I just got off the elevator myself folks, and I saw these two women wiggling so much I thought they were fighting. I was simply trying to break them up. Now I find they are a couple gays, ya, gays, making time in their doorway. Brazen hussies, disgusting. There is no need to call security. I'm on my way to my room where my wife is waiting. Hussies!"

He turned on his heel and left.

Margaret stepped into Christeen's room and closed the door.

Christeen put her hand to her mouth and snickered. Margaret looked frightened again, only this time it was over the swat she received and the verbiage that followed.

"Harrumph," scolded the middle-aged man as he and his wife strode by. Christeen broke into gales of laughter.

"What a night pussy cat," Christeen howled. "What a crazy mixed up night." Christeen held her sides as she laughed and stomped her feet.

"Whoooeee—I tell you part of my life, we drink, we get propositioned by a nerd, I flatten the fucker twice, he threatens us. I tell you about my men experiences, the nerd returns, we see his monumental pecker, I whack it off, we get to my room, you balk, a prairie cowboy horns in, tries to get his rocks off up your ass, the odd-couple come along and our secret is known. Whoooeee!

And at last, here we are, ready for a night of 'love-making.' 'I vant yor' bloood Margarita.' and a taste of your…"

"Yes Christeen, a night to remember. Please don't make me bleed—please?" Margaret purred.

"How about a nightcap my darling, a tot of sherry perhaps?"

"Delightful my queen. I beg of you, your greatness, finish your life story before we bed down."

"As you wish my child."

Christeen poured them each a wine glass three quarters full of Beaujolais sherry.

"Now Maggie, where did I leave off before I was interrupted by Stanley? Let's see now, ah yes, I remember, my nefarious confession to my mother and father, your child is gay, their stunned shock. Well Margaret, following their shock came dismay and a ton of other feelings. After I got settled in my room, I came downstairs into our family room where my mother was seated crying while my father was pacing. I felt horrible. How could I do such a thing, this abomination, to the sweetest, kindest persons in the world, my mom and dad. God how I wanted to die to spare the two people whom I loved, cherished and respected most in the whole world, from this horrid being called Christeen.

"Where did the evil gene come from that made me into an aberration. Did Beelzebub plant it in my mother's womb while she slept, had God taken his eyes off Lucifer for a moment allowing therefore the Prince of Darkness to lay this tainted seed into my mother's child growing garden." Christeen began to cry. Soon she was sobbing.

Margaret sat, not knowing what to think or what to do to comfort Christeen. She was non-plussed on seeing Christeen upset and showing emotions.

'Good heavens, Christeen is human after all. She suffers from her feelings like everyone does. She is living a life of make believe. She truly thinks she is evil,' Margaret thought.

"Christeen, please don't think such awful thoughts. You are not evil. You are wonderful." Margaret stroked Christeen's hair. She held Christeen's head close to her bosom.

Christeen sat upright. "Sorry Margaret. Enough of my blubbering." She tried to dry her eyes with her hands. Margaret offered her a Kleenex.

"I want you to know, Margaret, that I love my parents so very much. I know it hurts them to know I am gay, gay, what a horrible word, but I know they love me as much as I love them.

"We discussed my oddity the first weekend I visited my folks following my Doctor's appointment. They called and talked to Dr. Chaney in my presence, they searched my upbringing, they gave thought to the all girls' school I was attending. They looked back over their family trees. Maybe 40 to 50 grandfathers ago, ancient times, some ancestor was a good old homo, certainly not in recent times. We even laughed a bit talking about some ancient guy dressed in metal wearing under it, a Cleopatra bra and panty. The guy holding his saber, pinkies extended, saying to his commander, "Thir, I just hate the thight of blood, can't I just kith the nithe Phillistines to death, they are tho pretty. Pleathe spank me if you dithagree thir, I just love to be thpanked."

"Anyway Margaret, mom, dad, my brother and sister and all my friends in Yreka now know that I am a Lesbian. All of them love me regardless, just as I love them. And what is so very important Margaret, is they all respect me, love me and they all admire me for my guts, determination, abilities and the goals I have set for myself. So there Maggie, me darlin."

"Christeen you are a gem. A veritable diamond," Margaret said.

"Thank you sweety, but please bear with me for another few minutes as I relate to you one sexual session I had a few months ago I wish you to hear about. I know the girl I cavorted with loves me, but I promise you, Margarita, I couldn't care less about her. She is very jealous of me. I feel certain she will do anything to try to get me as her lover. And Maggie, while I have known her for two or three years, she's taking law at Washington State, I have never pursued her even as a friend. I used to see her on the campus from time to time, and I always acknowledged her when I saw her with a 'Hi' or something. On occasion groups of us including Betty, Betty Goldstein is her name, would stop and chat about this and that, but nothing more. Then in October of this year at a big Halloween campus party, Betty got me aside and came on strong about her adoration for me. She wasted no time in propositioning me. Christ, she's a cute chick, about five one, 105 pounds and while she came on strong she looked to be very, very vulnerable. I knew I could eat this little cheesecake whole.

"Shit Maggie, a few drinks, a cute sacrificial bod, a long, long lack of nooky, I was ready for 'Freddie,' I was ready to steam roll this fragile defenseless lamb. I fucking licked my chops.

"We went to her place. A small, cute one-bedroom suite in an apartment building just off the university grounds. She had it delightfully appointed, comfy, cozy, pretty. Her selection of paintings, in my view, was exquisite. Pricey, I'm sure. I gather her parents are loaded. Her dad is the senior partner of a huge law firm in Los Angeles, called

Goldstein, Levinson, Abram and Lipsieg. Jewish I'd say. Anyway Maggie, she wasted no time when we got to her 'flat.'

"To begin she had me stand in front of her brick fireplace with my legs spread apart and my fists on my hips. She placed a mannish kind of crown on my head. She stepped back to look me over. She smiled, came close to me, flipped off her shoes, stood on her tiptoes, jumped up and kissed my lips. I swear the little broad was purring. Next she stripped down to her panty and bra, they looked pricey too, and real "femmie". Damn it, Maggie my sweet, how I wanted to rip those scanties off her and get down to business. But I was patient, I stood there like a fucking Amazon, stony faced, angry eyed. Betty removed my tight hugging sweater. She had me lift my arms, and before the sweater was removed, she slid her pink tongue over my underarms. She purred, licked and moaned. My armpits were ecstatic. She got a footstool to stand on so she could remove my sweater without my help. She giggled when she finally got it off. You know why she giggled Maggie? Cause I stuck my tongue under her bra when she was reaching up to pull the 'wool over my eyes.' She stood back again, stared at my brassiere filled with boobs then came to me, undid the zipper at the back of my mini skirt letting it fall to the floor. She had me lift my feet so she could dispense with my skirt. I was now in my thong panty and bra. She removed my shoes then skipped off to her bedroom.

"I stood motionless.

"Betty 'Boop' now returned with spike-heeled black leggings and a pair of scissors.

"What the hell I thought?

"She removed my bra. She sent shock waves through me when she sucked my nipples. While she was sucking she reached inside my panty and found my clit. Maggie that almost did it, but I stood my ground.

"Now she put those black leggings over my shins, you know Maggie, somewhat pointy at the top and running down to those daring spike heels. I lifted each foot so she could get them on me.

"Again she stepped back and ogled me with glowing passion. There I was towering over six feet seven, crowned, bare bosomed, on six inches of black sexy boot leggings. My eyes were heavily mascaraed, my face tanned (from a weeks holiday in Mazatlan) my tits browned from the sun, a diamond stud in my navel, skimpy, and I mean skimpy panty, thong black panty and lush red lipstick.

"Betty snipped off my panty with her scissors. Now I stood nude. 'A female titan!' The clever little lesbo ran to her bedroom again and wheeled out a huge full-length mirror. A mirror encased in beautiful French 'provincial' carvings. Quite apropos for the occasion I dare say. She placed the mirror about six feet from me so I could see how I looked.

"What Playboy wouldn't give for this," I thought. I, in all modesty Maggie darlin, looked like a goddess. I was astounding, breathtaking, awesome. Christ, I was a sexy skyscraper.

"Betty Boop now removed her bra and panty. She looked good, nice full pointy tits, good shoulders, trim flat belly and a cute navel decorated too with a diamond stud, good hips, perfect pussy and nice legs.

"Again she disappeared into her bedroom, nice derriere, I licked my chops again. In a moment she was back with me holding, a soft white cushion. 'Hookay,' I said to myself, 'what's next? Well, sweet stuff, she put that cushion on the fireplace's hearth right under me. Then she lay down on her back, head on the cushion looking straight up at my orifices.

"I watched her antics in the mirror. Well Margarita, this little fluff now began to play with herself, yeah Maggie, play with herself as she looked up at my bare legs into the promise land. That kitten, meowed, groaned, moaned, purred, even growled tiny growls as she activated her sex organs. I perspired like a long distance runner as I watched her. My whole body glistened from my sweat. I must say, sweety cake, I looked positively indecent.

"Do you know, Margarita, we had never said a single word to one another from the time we came to her suite, over an hour I'm sure, to this moment of Betty Boop's sightseeing of my hidden secrets.

"I didn't want her to come. Shit no, I wanted some fresh juice for myself.

"I took off the crown and threw it in a corner.

"I reached down and grabbed the little broad under her arms. I lifted her to her feet. I snarled at her. She looked frightened, helpless and horny.

"I picked her up in my arms and marched into her bedroom. I threw her on her back onto her bed. I turned her over on her belly, I stuck my tongue and fingers between her buttocks. She gasped. I bit one cheek hard. She squealed. It bled. I roughed her up pretty good. I assaulted her whole body. It was fun molesting her. The more I hurt her the harder she climaxed. I forced her to blow me, cunni fucking lingus, I damn near drowned her. Like 'Lil Abner's' shmoos she came back for more, she couldn't get enough, the more shocking the things I did to her, the more she cried and the more she crawled back for encores. The sex we performed was the essence of depravity. Miss Betty Boop loved me to be her cruel master. She was a wily little thing too. She knew how to satisfy me that night, eight times to be exact. Maggie, my sweet, she had a mirrored ceiling above her bed.

"Thus, we saw, we loved, we conquered. The orgy went on until five in the morning. Five full hours of sex! Betty was small, but she was mighty. Despite all her bruises, teeth marks and the brutal treatment I had laid on her, she was the one who wanted to keep going. I, the titan, had to cry 'uncle.' I capitulated at five a.m. spent, exhausted. I slept like a baby until ten. And you know, Maggie, that little fuck had one more go at me before I departed her company at 11:00 a.m.

"I got home at eleven-thirty. I showered and slept 'til nine that night.

"Okay doll, I see the consternation on your face. I suspect you think I'm an easy pick-up by any gay babe after you hearing me tell you about

Betty. Right? I didn't have to tell you about her, but Maggie, I wanted to. I have no amorous or any other feelings for Betty. She was just an incident. From the time I was 16, six years ago, when I confirmed to myself that I was a gay I have had only two relationships with other girls and, including Betty, only two one night stands. I've had dozens and dozens of opportunities over the last six years for affairs. But no, Margaret, I have kept my nose to the grindstone. I don't want meaningless affairs. I want a lasting love, I am the absolute antithesis of promiscuity, I want us to be together. I want to find out how suited we are for one another. And not just sex darlin' but the whole ball of wax. Are we compatible? That's the question. I promise you, Margaret, there will be no skullduggery on my part. I know we will hit it off baby doll, I just know it. We would make one splendid team in both our personal lives and in our profession as Doctors."

"You are something Christeen. I have never met anyone like you. You are refreshing, candid, soft, hard, loving, a physical marvel. Goodness I would be a fool not to give us a good try at being a devoted twosome. Even tho' I have known you such a short time, what is it now, including basketball, twenty hours? I felt pangs of jealousy when you told me about Betty. Christeen I do trust you, so please, I beg of you, respect that trust. And for goodness sake quit trying to kill me on the court. Three friggin' fouls the ref called on you today—three. Chris baby you should have had at least 33. I am bruised all over my body from your antics. And what an actor you are on the court, me, tender me, Christeen Barlow playing dirty, not me."

"Right Maggie," Christeen replied. "I am a tender soul. Now, my dear, tell me about your life as a gay."

"Christeen, other than a Betty, my life story is a composite of yours. I had intercourse with three men trying as you did to get my sexual footing. Each of these experiences where dreadful. The actual act itself with each of the men was without gratification. Each act was messy, sweaty, hairy, smelly, undignified and painful. I vomited from revulsion on each occasion.

"And believe me Christeen, the men were all charmers. Handsome guys. They were the popular ones sought after by all the girls in our sororities. And wouldn't you know it, one of the three was my teacher. They were polite, caring and decent men. I did as you did Christeen, I flaunted my beauty at them and literally, I cajoled them into bed. And Christeen, like you, I was always the most sought after girl in my school years. In many respects I had often wished my younger sister Lana was a student at the schools I attended because she would have captured every man's attention ahead of me. Without question Lana is the most beautiful woman in the world. Instead of the boys chasing me they would have chased Lana."

"You mean Dr. Lana Masters, Maggie?" Christeen asked in amazement. "**The** Dr. Lana Masters?"

"Yes Christeen, she is my younger sister."

"My good God, Margaret. She is phenomenal. She's a genius. She's a...a...goddess."

"I know Chris, I know."

"Is she straight, Maggie?"

"Yes."

"Damn."

"That's enough Christeen."

"Just joking, Maggie," Christeen laughed. "Carry on my dear."

"Honestly Christeen, my story is so emulative of yours there's not much more to tell. I've had a few sexual experiences with girls and frankly I found each one most fulfilling. However I have not talked to our family physician in Swift Current..."

"What the hell is a Swift Current, doll?"

"It's where I was born crazy. It's a jewel of a little city Chris, about 130 kilometers southwest of Moose Jaw."

"Moose Fucking Jaw," Christeen laughed.

"No Christeen, Moose Jaw."

"Sorry sweety," Christeen said putting a hand over her mouth to stifle guffaws. "Moose Fucking Jaw," Christeen whispered. "Do you Saskatchewanites have a town called 'Horse's Dork' too, by any chance?"

"Christeen, behave, of course not."

"'I shall behave, my illustrious beauty from Speedy Creek."

"That's Swift Current, darn you Chris."

"Yes, of course, Swift Current, a hunnert and some kliks southwest of Moose Fucking Jaw, right Maggie?"

"Your impossible Christeen."

"God, you're gullible Margarita. Okay doll, no discussions with your doctor. Right?"

"Right, but if we hit it off tonight and tomorrow night, I intend to call my sister Lana, who now lives in New York City, and ask her to come see me and to meet you, and to advise us. My family doctor is not as knowledgeable as Lana."

"I guess not kiddo. Sounds cool."

"Do you want to tell me some details of your sex life, Margarita?"

"No Chrissy baby. Let's go to bed now. Then I can demonstrate my sexual prowess to you. Two titans! Two big beautiful she-male specimens going tit to tit, belly to belly, mouth to mouth, and ending up with an arm around each others billion dollar asses. Are you ready for a tear-ass-knock down—drag 'em out—excuse the expression 'fuck' Christeen, you gargantuan sex-pot?" Margaret challenged.

"Oh, I'm more than ready, you big broad. Yeah! Leeeeettts get ready to rumble."

They rumbled and tumbled all night long. There was no winner or loser. They tied. The night was a roaring success. They bonded.

Then the two girls slept.

CHAPTER 48
MARGARET AND CHRISTEEN

They awakened just in time to get to their afternoon practices.

Washington State practiced in the main auditorium of the University of Saskatchewan while the U. of S. team practiced in the engineers' school arena. They were just three buildings apart. Christeen and Margaret, happy as larks dominated each of their team practices. They were awesome. Their coaches were overjoyed.

Following their practices, Christeen and Margaret met in the lobby of the Besborough. Christeen had already checked out of the hotel and was sitting in the hotel's lobby when Margaret arrived. Margaret had packed her bag at her room in one of the university's residences. She drove over the beautiful Fourth Avenue Bridge, which spanned the mighty, frozen North Saskatchewan River. She parked her car under the hotel's porte-cochere. It was a chilly 20 below zero Fahrenheit outside with a wind-chill factor of 40 below. Snow blew jaggedly across the pavement. Margaret hustled into the lobby. She spotted Christeen and walked over to her. Christeen rose when she saw it was Margaret. As they met they hugged briefly exchanging pleasantries and loving looks. People in the lobby, which was quite full from an arriving charter flight out of Brussels, were taken aback on seeing these tall stunning beauties. Had Marilyn Monroe and Jane Russell been re-united?

'Maggie' and 'Chrissy' made all other people look so ordinary. With their clog-heeled shoes they both stood well over six-feet-six. What a pair! They loaded their suitcases and their other paraphernalia into Margaret's classy little BMW. Then, off they went, back over the bridge spanning the North Saskatchewan River to Christeen's friend's beautiful four-bedroom home on University Drive in Saskatoon, Saskatchewan.

The girls made their own dinner. A pleasant pasta dish, a green salad, tea and a non-fattening dessert. They watched TV for awhile, and by 10:00 p.m. they were in bed. They made love, kissed one another good night, then slept until 7:30 the next morning. Their time together was delightful.

Margaret decided to call Lana 'this' very day. She knew she was in love with Christeen, she 'just knew' they were compatible. But what about Lana, her father and mother, her two brothers, her grandparents, her aunts, uncles and cousins, her friends ad infinitum. Would they hate her for her sex preference? Doesn't the Bible condemn homosexuality? Would Lana understand? Lana, the genius, the all time good Samaritan! Good God, Margaret thought, if Lana abandons me because of my sexual quirk, hates me for it, forsakes me, then I know all to well no one will forgive me. Everyone will find me disgusting. Dear God, why me?"

But surely not Lana, Lana is far too big to be hung up on such a trivial thing as sex predilection. She's just too intelligent to be influenced by bigotry. She hates hate. Still I'm so frightened, why me? Why couldn't I have been born straight? God, how I despise myself. C'mon, get a hold of yourself Margaret Tricia Masters. Quit your sniveling. Phone your sister now. Remember, you've got a big game tonight and you don't want anything on your mind except winning. Your team's down two to zip already. Call your little sister, then if you know she will be with you by tomorrow then you can put your mind solely on tonight's game.

Margaret dialed Manhattan and in a trice she heard the eloquent deep-throated voice of young Dr. Lana Masters.

Lana will be with me tomorrow, so watch out my big lover Christeen. Led by me, the U. of S. team will stomp your horde of Yankee Doodle Dandies into our good old Saskatchewan clay.

And that they did. U. of S. 92, Washington State 84. Christeen had bounced Margaret from pillar to post all night long. She flattened Maggie six times. She swore at Margaret. She intimidated, spooked, elbowed and badgered Maggie. But after the dust had all settled Margaret had scored 37 points, assisted on another 16 and collected 12 rebounds. Star number one, #37, Margaret Masters, star number two, #69 Christeen Barlow, star number three, #12 Susan Strong.

The teams shook hands. When Christeen got to Margaret she smiled, winked and said, "Fantastic game Maggie. You were awesome."

Maggie gave Chrissy's hand an extra squeeze and responded, "Thanks champ."

Stanley, Chester and Willy ran out on the floor with hundreds of others.

"Hey Stanley," Christeen yelled, grabbing Stanley, picking him up and giving him a big sweaty kiss, "How's by you?"

"Christeen, I've never seen anything like it. What a thriller! Shit babe, you and Margaret could make the Bulls."

"Chester…Willy com'ere, Christeen's handing out kisses." Chrissy gave them each a big smacker.

"Guys, let's go get Margarita…where is she?"

"She's talkin' on TV, radio, everything, she's being mobbed," Stan hollered.

The crowd was still celebrating with raucous victory calls, "We're number one, ya, we're number one"…the U. of S. team was supposed to be simply 'grist for Washington State's mill,' a pathetic piece of dog meat compared to a huge red juicy New York steak. Not tonight baby, not tonight.

Christeen led Stanley, Chester and Willy's charge toward Margaret. They barged right in on the sportscaster. Chrissy screaming, "If that Masters Babe hadn't been so dirty, fouling me at every turn, we'd a won, yeah, we'd of whipped the U. of S. girls' butts easy if she wasn't so unsportsman-like. Can't you biased broadcasters see that? If #37 had played a clean game like me, the outcome would have been different."

Christeen put her nose an inch from the interviewer's nose snarling like a tiger. The crowd booed, hissed, "the broads a phony" they screeched. Chrissy knew she had riled everyone, everyone except Maggie that is. Maggie knew Chrissy was now acting, without doubt an Academy Award performance. Maggie knew she was to be a part of it. Just like the W.W.F.

The broadcaster tried to speak, but before he could say a word, Chrissy grabbed his microphone and turned to Margaret screaming (The TV cameras zoomed in), "You 'bleeping' farmer's daughter. Where did you learn your filthy tricks, in a pig pen? Did your hay seed dumb nut cowhands teach you on their Saturday night drunks, how to fight dirty? You scum bag. You backward Canucks, you should visit the great USA sometime and get some class. God, your poor sportsmanship is disgusting Ms. Masters. You snowbound snot dripper. Yeah, when ya' walk down the street in this Sooskatoon or whatever, all you see are snot-nosed dripping Johnny Canucks freezing their butts off in this ice-bound country. You, Miss Dirt Bag of 1988 are a disgrace to the fine sport of basketball, you chippy creep."

The crowd howled. They were all for lynching Christeen.

Christeen raised her hands above her head proclaiming in her shrillest voice, "I am the greatest. I am the essence of clean play. She," pointing a finger at Margaret, "is the rotten apple who interrupted me so blatantly by her foul tricks. She destroyed my usual graceful, angelic athletic talent by her despicable antics. I could have scored 40 points or more tonight if Miss Goody Two Shoes hadn't been so dirty."

"Shame on you #69," bleated several fans, mainly women who tried to get at Christeen. They were incensed. Some even screamed obscenities at her. Security and others held them at bay. Margaret gave Christeen a good shove right into Stanley and Chester's surprised arms. She grabbed the 'mike' from Christeen and stood toe-to-toe with her.

Shit! She could hardly contain her laughter. This Christeen, what a gal she is.

"Ms. Barlow, it is difficult for me to even respond to your silly accusations. Look, look at my bruises from your rough play." Maggie lifted her jersey to show the tattooing her ribs had taken from Chrissy's elbows. She showed the crowd the bruises on her thighs, calves and arms. Not the finger nail scratches on her back, nor the bites on her inner thighs…no…those were from the games she and Chrissy played two nights ago.

"You are without question, Mzzz. Barlow, a dirty scrapper. You will stop at nothing to win a game. Absolutely nothing! You would trample your own grandmother for the sake of two points."

"You're a whiner, a spoiled brat, a poor loser. On the court you shove, elbow, trod on your opponents feet, charge, slap, pinch, punch, hold, grapple, you even feign injuries to have your opponents get fouls. You intimidate everyone on the floor. You are worse than a brat, you are a menace."

"And Mzzz. Christeen Barlow, your profanity during the game is shameful, blasphemous, crude, un-Christian."

"Profanity, me?" Chrissy howled, "I, farm girl, am not a person who would dream of swearing. You lie girl, you lie. My oh my, my very soul has been hurt by your dreadful accusations." Good old Chrissy squeezed out a couple of tears.

"Look everybody, look at the whiner's forced tears. She's a ruddy flake," Maggie taunted.

With that, Chrissy punched Maggie in the gut. It looked harder than it was. No way was Chrissy going to damage her precious Maggie. Maggie retaliated by grabbing Chrissy around her waist and pulling her to the floor. The girls put on one hell of a show. No hair pulling, just a damn good fake fight like the W.W.F. They rolled, twisted, punched and growled like two tawny female lions. Even some blood appeared on Maggie's nose.

Stanley, Chester and Willy egged them on knowing the fight was faked. They hooted and shouted encouragement at their idols, Stanley for Chrissy, Chester and Willy for Maggie. "Hit her. Kick her. Bite her. Bash her a good one. Fight gals, fight."

The TV cameras caught it all.

The sportscaster retrieved his microphone and gave a blow-by-blow description of the fight. The crowd booed Chrissy and gave thunderous "oles" to Maggie.

Finally the police stepped in just as every guy in the auditorium wanted the tussle to go on. Chrissy had torn off Maggie's jersey and Maggie was some sight.

"Tear it off, tear it all off," the crowd shouted. Maggie looked delectable, her ample breasts almost bared by the struggle with her lover. Maggie retaliated, she grabbed Chrissy's shorts, and off they came. Chrissy's scanties barely hid her delicious front and back. The crowd howled, "Yeh, yeh, this is 'the' game, no other sport like it, damn put one on every night."

The two six-footers stood glaring at one another. Each one held by one of Saskatoon's finest. God they were gorgeous. Hair askew, glistening from perspiration and so scantily clad.

The crowd, which had now turned neutral, gave them a huge ovation.

The two Titans bowed to the crowd.

Then, once again they glared at each other.

For the next half an hour Christeen and Margaret signed autographs. Occasionally they would look up at each other and scowl.

Washington State went on to win the series, four games to two. The teams played to standing room only crowds for the next three games. Each game was loaded with excitement. The athletes received standing ovations for their outstanding performances. Christeen and Margaret kept everyone agog with their remarkable skills and theatrics.

CHAPTER 49

LANA MEETS WITH MARGARET AND CHRISTEEN

Lana Masters arrived at Saskatoon's municipal airport at 2:30 p.m. December 30th as promised. Margaret, on spying Lana's entrance into the baggage claim area, rushed to her sister, kissed her, and hugged Lana with all her might.

"Lana, Lana, I'm so glad you're here. I love you and miss you so very much."

"I love you and miss you too Margaret," Lana said, standing back and looking at her sister. "My Goodness, you've grown. You're a knockout. How tall are you?"

"Just a touch over six feet."

"Wow, I'm only five-eleven."

They stood admiring one another for several moments. People gawked at these two beauties.

Lana found her suitcases, picked them up and with Margaret's help they made their way to Margaret's car. They chatted about their family, the weather, how the flight was, everything except the reason for Lana's visit. Lana was anxious to know why Margaret had asked her to come to Saskatoon, but Lana was patient. She knew Margaret would tell her soon enough.

"And how's my Big Buster, Marg?" Lana asked.

"He's feeling his age Lana. He hasn't the energy to kick up a fuss any longer. He just lies in his stall eating, chewing his cud, bellowing now and then and quite frankly, enjoying the attention he gets from everyone. He misses you Lana. I know he would be more active if you were at home. I think too, the injuries he suffered in his battle with Sir Galahad way back when has started to catch up to him. He's so damn lovable."

"I'm going to go to Swift Current for a day or two before I go back to New York Marg. I'll see mom, dad, Ray, Steve and Carl, visit some friends, and I'll see if I can perk up Big Buster when I'm there.

"I know Lana."

"Lana, before we get to where we are going, I have to tell you something I love and despise all at the same time. I am so much at a loss. I don't know if I'm being fair with you asking you for your help or not? But Lana, you are so clever, I can't think of another person in the world I'd rather discuss my problem with than you. I hope you won't hate me for it," Margaret said.

"Margaret, I could never hate you, you know that."

"I hope so Lana."

"Damn it all, how do I say it?" Margaret frowned as her car caught some bare ice on the road and skidded sideways. "Damn winter driving," she said.

"Margaret, if you are going to tell me in any event, you may as well tell me now," Lana answered.

"I'm in love sister, I'm crazy in love."

"Wonderful?"

"Shit Lana—bloody roads," as the car skidded again.

"I'm in love, passionately in love."

"Wonderful"

"With another woman," Margaret blurted out.

"Oops," Lana said, shocked.

"Yes, another woman," Margaret repeated.

Lana remained silent.

"I knew you'd hate me Lana, I just knew it."

"Hold it Marg, hold it. I don't hate you. I could never hate you. I love you. Before I arrived here today, I was certain you were going to tell me you were pregnant. You kinda caught me off guard that's all."

"God, how I wish."

"C'mon Marg, clue me in."

"It's simple Lana, I've known of my lesbianism since I was 15. I never did have to confirm it. I tried sex with boys a few times to test the water and each time I found it God-awful. I tried sex with girls a coupla' times and found it to be heaven. I like boys as people. I find they are much more fun, more open and not so f…ing picky as girls, not so devious or scheming either, but sexually they are nauseous to me. Only women arouse me sexually."

"Well, well, sister, without question you have kept your privacy private."

"Secret you mean, Lana."

"Okay, secret sweetie."

"Well?"

"C'mon, Margaret, give me some time to collect my thoughts."

"Sorry Lana."

"Don't be sorry Marg. Let's be pragmatic. All people's sexual traits are biological. You know that. People, as to their sex drive, are born with that drive as an inherent part of their biological make-up. Heterosexuals cannot deviate from their heterosexual status because the preponderance of their sexual genes are fixed, not variable. Bisexuals have genes with some 50 percent of them being attracted to the opposite sex while the other 50 percent are attracted to the same sex. Homosexuals can not, by any method alter the physical status of their sex cells and become heterosexual or bisexual. Science to date has not been able to accomplish such niceties. Therefore my beautiful sister, if you are homosexual, that is how you will remain."

"Gee, thanks a lot Lana. Just what I wanted to hear," Margaret said sarcastically.

"Honey," Lana said, "you know these facts as well as I do. I'm just confirming what you already know. Marg with your brains, vitality, personality, beauty and your imposing gorgeous six-foot body, no one will ever stand in your way regardless of your sexual preference. You are one breath-taking brilliant biological genotype."

"You're something else too little sister," Margaret said.

"Margaret, I am proud of you. I always have been and always will be."

"One more thing, Lana. We are not going to my room at the residence, we are going to..." pointing to a picturesque, two story house, "that house right there."

Margaret stopped the car, faced Lana and said, "in that house is my lover. Her name is Christeen Barlow. She goes to Washington State University. We are the same age. She is one inch taller than I and she is gorgeous. She is in her third year of medicine. She is a terrific athlete. She is one exciting gal. I think you will like her. She is very anxious to meet you, she knows you are coming to 'that house right there.' You will stay with us, and you will have your own room and bath. And I have made Christeen promise me she will not rape you—aren't I a good girl?"

Both girls laughed.

"C'mon Lana, let's get this part over with, let's go meet Christeen."

They took Lana's luggage from the car and started up the walk to the front door. The snow, salt and ice crystals crunched under their feet. It was a little slippery too. But being prairie girls a little ice and snow was old hat to them.

Christeen had been nervous all day. Christ, meeting 'the' Dr. Lana Masters. The world renowned Dr. Masters. Yeah, the famous one. The Michael Jordan of brains, and only 19 friggin' years old. Yeah and too, Dr. Masters is thought to be the world's most beautiful woman. I know some people despise her but most people worldwide adore her. She's a medical doctor, a lawyer, a professional accountant and a scientist all wrapped up in one. She's a fucking genius. God, I hope she's nice.

Why am I so nervous? Christeen thought, Lana Masters is just one 'itty-bitty' person on this planet like the rest of us. Why fret? Goddam Maggie anyway for getting the idea of having her sister come see us. Lana Masters cannot change our feelings for one another. The most she can do is threaten Maggie with exposure of her lesbianism to her parents and her brothers if she doesn't 'straighten' out. Maybe even have Maggie disowned by her parents. Goddam her. She can holler and scream at Maggie all she wants the miserable witch. I'll fight for Margaret, Miss Lana Masters, tooth and nail. So don't try to coerce, frighten, blackmail or intimidate my Maggie. Damn you Lana Masters, who do you think you are threatening my Margaret? You're despicable. I hate you already and I haven't even met you yet. Shit, there's the doorbell.

Christeen sauntered to the door. No cow-towing to Miss Prissy by me, no fucking way, Chrissy promised herself as she opened the door. "Hoooly Sheeit," Chrissy quipped to herself. "This can't be. This is an illusion. No one can look that good. Jesus H. Christ, is she real? Those eyes, they own you." Christeen blinked. She looked again. "My my, my my, my my," Chrissy hummed under her breath. "She's right there in front of me. She's fucking radiant. She's real. She's…"

"Aren't you going to let us in, Chrissy?" Margaret teased.

"Yes, oh yes, pardon a moi, excuse eh, do come in, Miss Masters, Dr. Mixmaster." Abruptly Chrissy closed the door. "Asshole," she said to herself. "You twerp, remember, she's human, just like the rest of us. But you 'ditz,' you haven't even seen her body yet, you've only seen that face. Jesus, I called her Dr. Mixmaster…what a dweeb I am. Get a hold of yourself, ya dumb broad."

A gentle knock came on the door.

Sheepishly, Chrissy opened the door once again. "God, she's there all right. She's astonishing. Stupefying. Bloody hell," she muttered to herself. "Please forgive me, Doctor Masters. You obliterated me. I…I have heard about how your loveliness…you know," Christeen stammered, "How your beauty mesmerizes people...well you blitzkrieged me. I do apologize Doctor, please, please do come in," Christeen said, extending her right arm with a flourish followed by a slight bow. Lana entered with a polite smile on her face. Even though ignored, Margaret crossed the threshold too.

"Thank you," Lana said.

"Nice going Chrissy," Margaret said. "Cool."

Christeen gave Margaret a peculiar look. Margaret couldn't quite make it out.

"Lana, I would like you to meet Christeen Barlow, Christeen, please meet Lana Masters."

Lana and Christeen shook hands and using the old cliché, said, "How nice to meet you, I have heard so much about you."

"Dr. Mixmaster," Margaret reiterated, smiling.

"I know, I know," Chrissy said.

"S'okay," said Lana, "I thought it was cute."

"Come Lana, I will show you to your room while Chrissy makes some tea," Margaret said laughing.

"Thanks sis. I could do with some refreshing. See you in a few minutes Christeen."

"Take your time Lana, I'll make up a dish of goodies too."

Margaret led Lana upstairs to a lovely-furnished guest bedroom. A charming bedroom with an ensuite bath.

"Beautiful," Lana said, giving Margaret a hug. "It's a delightful room." And looking out a large bedroom window Lana spied a huge spruce tree decorated by Mother Nature with snow and icicles. The tree was inhabited by several tiny, white breasted, super active chickadees all enlivening the cold crisp wintery day with their delightful chick-a-dee-dee-dees. "They are so cute," Lana gushed. "Chickadees are one of my favorite tiny birds Marg. They are so busy, they burst with life. They're adorable. 'Oooh, I'd love to hold one, wouldn't you sister?"

"Yes darlin' I would."

"Do you want me to stay with you as you freshen up Lana?"

"Sure, stay with me."

"Okay baby sister."

Lana went into the bathroom with her toiletry bag. As she emerged she said, "You two must turn a lot of heads when you're out together. People must gasp when they see you?"

"Yes Lana, it always happens when we are together in public even tho we've been out so few times. But wait until people get to see you, they'll flip!"

"No, you two will outdo everybody. Goodness, with your awesome size, people will go crazy over you. Men are going to go ga-ga when they see you."

"Okay Lana. I know. But you turn heads worldwide."

"Have you seen mom and dad recently?" Lana asked, changing the subject.

"Yeah just 10 days ago. They're great. So are our bro's and their families. I saw Aunty Pat and Aunty Maybell too and guess who else sis? Mom and Dad's friends Bruce and Glady. I even went to a Bronco's hockey game with Bruce and Glady, played against Lethbridge. Great game. Just like the N.H.L. Good fights too. And big. Those juniors 16, 17, 18 are huge, all 200 pounders."

"Good for you, sis!"

"All set?"

"Yup."

"Let's go then."

Christeen had everything ready on a huge glass topped mahogany coffee table. The goodies looked scrumptious. So did Lana. No matter what Lana was dressed in, she always looked scrumptious.

"Those are the neatest little sandwiches Christeen, may I?"

"But of course you may, Lana."

"Tea Lana?" Margaret asked.

"Please Marg."

"Jesus we're formal," Christeen said.

"Fuckin' right we are," Lana answered. "Just like we've got broom sticks stuck up our asses. No need for formality around me."

Christeen laughed. Margaret looked embarrassed, seldom did Margaret swear, in particular the 'F' word.

"Ya, okay, Maggie?" Chrissy said, laughing.

"Ya, ya, Christelena. Be vulgar if you want. My little sister has cursed since she was two years old. Mom and dad couldn't believe it. They did everything but cut Lana's tongue off, but no 'ceegaar.' Lana just went on cussing. She even embarrassed our farm hands, eh Lana?"

"True Marg."

The girls were quiet for a few moments while they sipped their tea and ate some of the nice tidbits Chrissy had whipped up.

"So, you're lovers gals, right?"

"Right," Maggie and Chrissy responded in unison.

"Good," Lana said.

"Is it just a passing fancy between the two of you now or do you feel, at least at the moment, it will be lasting? I'm assuming both of you are certain you are homosexuals."

I know I am homosexual," Chrissy said.

"I know I am too," Margaret agreed.

Christeen averred as far as she was concerned, in spite of the fact they just met as friends in the last three days, they were compatible; it was as if they had been lovers for years.

"We have known each other for three years Lana, but only as athletes on basketball floors. I have had a crush on your sister since the first time I saw her. It's not just a passing fancy, I assure you."

"I feel the same as Chrissy, Lana."

"Good, but Chrissy, what if Margaret wasn't here, and you and I were alone and I said I wanted to fuck you?" Pause. "What would you say?" Lana questioned.

"Lana, that's dreadful. You don't have to answer Christeen. Lana, please don't be crude."

"Ignore Margaret," Lana ordered, her piercing eyes overpowering, her voice authoritative.

No one could ignore Lana Masters' orders. She dominated whomever she wished by sheer mental supremacy. She ruled when it was her wont to do so. "Answer me Christeen," Lana demanded.

Margaret stiffened. Christeen's blood ran cold for a moment. Lana then eased her hypnotic ascendancy. Margaret sat passively. Christeen's fright left her. She was ready to proffer an answer.

CHAPTER 50

TEN YEARS AGO

"Son of a gun," Lana reminisced, "It was 10 years ago I asked Christeen that question. Ten long years ago! Her answer still haunts me.

CHAPTER 51

THE IVY LEAGUERS

Trent had followed different students from Columbia University for two days now. He felt certain the Ivy Leaguers were responsible for Holly's disappearance. He was convinced if he could find the 'guys' who had raped Holly, he would have the bastards who kidnapped her. No luck to this point. But today, Friday May 9th, 1997 lady luck smiled for a change. Trent knew for a few bucks, some of the H&B's 'loose' shareholders would give a coupla' slick dudes like the Leaguers confidential information pertaining to H&B.

He had talked to a number of H&B Financial and Poors Inc. shareholders whom he deemed to be 'loose.' In due course he met Billy Wheaton. Billy a 19-year-old junkie, who had given 'two young university guys' his copy of H&B's 1996 annual report. Billy was shaken up by Trent's threats as he tried to describe the two students. For a junky, he did a pretty good job. But first Trent had to ask Billy how he knew the two of them were university students? Billy had no difficulty with the question. Billy himself had been a student at Columbia University for two years before dropping out in December 1996 as a hopeless addict. His well-to-do parents, reciprocated, they dropped him. Billy was an above average student, a good athlete, personable, but helpless when it came to his habit. His friends and his instructors all had tried to get him 'to get' off the stuff and 'get on with his life.' Billy consoled himself by reasoning his 'highs' were one hell of a lot better than studying his brains out to become a frustrated, stressed-out runner in life's fucking moronic marathonic rat race. Screw the establishment. Get back to the good old 60's. Christ, Billy was minus 13-years-old in the mid 60's. He wasn't born until 1978.

"The two guys were pretty ordinary sir," Billy said. "Both about five-eleven, medium build, both had blond hair shaved up the sides of their skulls. Conceited looking. Both are from Columbia. I know. I recognized them. I had seen them on campus. They were seniors in their early 20's. I can tell you they didn't know me from shit when I gave them H&B's 1996 annual report."

"If you wish sir, I can ride along with you and I can take you to where I had seen them when I was a student and maybe pick them out for you."

"I wish, kid."

"But first sir, I'll need a little scratch for a batch."

"Here's a 'C' note kid," Trent said. "Before two months are gone I'll have you off the habit. Leastwise, I'll pull your lips off and shove them up your ass!"

"Thank you, sir. I look forward to that."

"I hate feeding a youngster like you with cash to buy junk. Anyway kid, I'll meet you at H&B's office in two hours. Be cool kid or I'll beat the crap outta' you."

"I'll be cool, sir."

They met at 2:00 p.m. in Clark's office. Clark had met Billy before and knew Billy was hooked on drugs. Clark thanked the 'kid' for offering his help to find Holly. He told Billy it was possible there could be some danger in the search and if Billy wanted to retract his offer to assist Trent, he would understand.

"Yeah, with the return of my hundred," Trent growled.

"No, no, sirs. I want to help. Here's your hundred back Mr. Trent. I want to do this. I like Holly a lot. I want us to find her. I'm sorry I even asked for money sirs.

The two men looked at one another unbelieving. "Holy shit," Trent said, "I can't believe my ears. You're a good kid Billy. Keep the fuckin' money. Just don't buy any hi-test with it."

They left Clark, went to the parking lot and got into Trent's '85 Mustang. An '85 Mustang Trent had gorged with power. This mother could scat. Five seconds to 60. It picked up a lot of broads too. Yeah, some heap.

Columbia University is located just to the northeast of the most northern part of Central Park. It's assessable from lower Manhattan by catching Broadway at 14th Street and staying on Broadway north to 116th Street. This is the route followed by Trent, and within 35 minutes, Trent was parked in a section for visitors parking on the campus. Billy and Trent walked toward an area where Billy had seen the two leaguers on a few occasions.

"For Christ's sake, I'll be a monkey's uncle, there they are sir," Billy said surprised to see the leaguers first off.

"Careful don't be conspicuous," Trent cautioned. Billy pointed to the two young men who were dressed campus style and who were both looking very attentive as they chatted with one another. Trent took a small camera from his pocket whose lens pointed downward from the normal position. If, in fact, he did look straight ahead through his camera he would photograph the ground rather than the subjects ahead of him. Trent had this little camera made just for him. In order for him to take pictures of the two leaguers, Trent raised his camera as if he was taking a picture of the top of the building they stood beneath. His lens now was on his subjects, and he snapped several pictures of his subjects in various positions by moving around as he looked upward at the different campus buildings. He grinned nerd like as if he was a tourist shooting pictures of anything he thought he could brag about back at his home on the range.

"Excellent," he said to Billy.

He made his way toward the two students. He looked this way and that. He smiled like a 'rube' as if he was taking in every sight possible so he could bullshit his rural friends about the sophistication he had gained while exploring the wondrous higher education facility known the world over as New York City's Columbia University.

Just as he got to the twosome, like a dolt, he tripped and sprawled in there midst. His tourist sunglasses went flying, his hands scraped on the sidewalk, they bled. The right knee of his trousers was ripped open as he skidded on the sidewalk. He managed a 2-inch scratch on his knee.

"Ooomph," he blew.

"Ya' okay," one the two leaguers said. What a geek, they thought.

"Don't know fellas. My hands, knee and dignity are hurt, dang my clumsiness. Did you happen to see where my bi-focal sunglasses went?"

"Charlie help the guy up while I get his glasses."

"Sure Stu. Here take my hand, mister."

"Thanks boys, darn decent of you. You must be taking theology to be this helpful. Whar I come from people say New Yorkers are downright unfriendly to strangers. Not true, you boys're shore great."

Stu handed Trent his glasses.

Trent tried to clean the grass and moisture off the lenses with his blooding hands.

"Here man, let me do that," Stu said.

"Mighty kind of you son," Trent replied. "I've been enuf of a nuisance to you boys. Please let me have your college's name and I'll send a few thousand dollars as a grant to it. Just give me your last names and I'll be certain you fellas are inscribed as the Samaritans who earned it for the college. And boys," Trent said as he fumbled in the pockets of his trousers trying to find his wallet. "Here," he pulled $400 from his found wallet, handing $200 to each leaguer. "I'm sure a couple of students could use money anytime. Right boys?"

"Hey, thanks man, you got that right, here's our cards. The name of our college and its address is on the cards as well as our names."

"Thank you boys," Trent said as he brushed off his clothes with his torn hands. "Thank you boys, good luck with your studies. Yore good boys." The bumbling tourist was still mumbling as Charles and Stu disappeared into a crowd of students.

Trent waited until he saw the two dudes enter the faculty building. He then made his way back to the car where Billy was waiting. "Sure fucked up my hands and my knee for that show, kid. But it was worth it. I've got those suckers names on their personal cards. Dumb fucks."

As they drove back to H&B's offices, Billy read off the names of the two students to Trent. The cards were headed Columbia University, College of Commerce, New York City, New York, 3022 Broadway, Uris Hall, New York, N.Y. 10027.

Charles Putnam Watkins (Student) allocated to Men's Dorm Room # 763. The other student's name was Stuart Cleatus Williams. He resided also in the men's dorm, room #768.

"I'll get those clowns to talk, by damn," Trent scowled at Billy, I may get you to tag along with me for the first couple of times I tail them. But, kid, when I'm ready to deal with them under my rules, I want to be alone, understand?"

"Yes sir."

"Can you drive?"

"Yes sir."

"Do you know the city, I mean the city and its five boroughs very well?"

"Not bad sir. But to tell you the truth, I do get lost."

"Hmmm," Trent thought for a moment.

"The reason I want you along is so I can have you drive when I need you to and, park the car where I tell you to, and be ready to pull away in a hurry in case I need you to. Can you manage that stuff punk?"

"Yes sir, aarrgh sir, your servant sir."

"Fuck up on me kid and I'll drive a corkscrew up your nose. You got that motherfucker?"

"Yes sir!"

Trent gave Billy a playful punch.

"I'll teach you to grow up without using drugs, alcohol or tobacco. You got that too motherfucker?"

"Yes Sir!!!" Billy hollered.

"Good. Here's what we're gonna' do kid. We're gonna' be outside the men's dorm at six-thirty tonight. We're gonna' phone up each guys' room on my cell when we get there. If they answer, I'll have my cell phone squawk by pressing this button right here as if we have a bad connection. If they don't answer, we know they are out of their rooms. So, it's no sweat either way. We just set up our surveillance and watch for them coming or going. If they are going, we follow. If they are coming back to the dorm, depending on the time one or both of them arrive, we will decide whether to maintain our surveillance or not. Say they came back to their dorm at eight, nine or even ten o'clock, we will hang around for at least an hour to see if they are going out again. We might even hang around 'til midnight, I'm not sure yet. You see, Billy, I have a hunch about these guys. You don't know this but Clark beat the shit out of four or five university dudes who were gang-raping Holly some time back. Clark didn't know Holly at the time, he just knew she was in deep trouble. That same night he went back to where Holly had been gang-splashed, he found her pimp and he re-arranged the fuckers' countenance."

"My hunch is the pimp and the leaguers are connected. Why I think that, I'm not sure. No doubt Holly was a good producer for the pimp, and that may be all there is to it. Christ what 'john' wouldn't want to bang her for a coupla' hundred bucks. But my hunch goes deeper Billy. Pimps are cowards, and Holly's pimp would think twice about angering Clark again by grabbing Holly back. Is she worth that much to him? I doubt it."

"Then why do I still think there is a connection between the pimp and the leaguers? Well let's think on it. The leaguers are smart dudes. They're taking commerce at Columbia. They were down in the skids when they took turns fucking hopped-up Holly while all the while they could have afforded to be with a call girl. The pimp returned to the Holly scene, I'm damned sure on orders from the leaguers, otherwise he wouldn't have gone. I think the commerce boys are now putting their studies to practical use. Let's make some easy bucks on prostitution and drugs while we're here at school. They hang around different skid roads, maybe Grand Central Station, until they find a likely prospect. They want someone who's in the trade. They like the looks of Holly's 'old man.' They strike up a conversation with this dude and cross his palms with some meaningful bucks. The dude likes the deal. The leaguers see some of the pimp's hookers and figure they're okay, good producers. They take special note of the six-foot Holly. Holly they reckon can charge up to $300 for a short time, $500 to play around a bit and a couple of grand for an all night stand.

"The leaguers, I would guess, calculate gross revenues on prostitution to be 10 girls each grossing $1,200 daily for 268 days each year. One day a week off, plus annual sick leave of 30 days and 14 days holiday, no statutory holidays off, just Christmas day, if you're Jewish, Hindi or whatever else, to fuckin' bad, to be $3.2 mil per year. They figure the pimp's payroll to $2,555,500 per year less $292,000 protection money, split, depending on each girl's gross production of course, but on an average of $226,000 per year per hooker. Follow me?"

"No," Billy said.

"As for tips, the leaguers will be ambivalent on this matter. Too much trouble to police. The annual net cost of girls would be therefore $2,263,000. The pimp would pay all annual miscellaneous expenses of $292,000 for protection, insurance, auto costs and the like. Leaving him with a net profit of over $650,000 give or take a few bucks. The prick could report whatever he wanted for tax purposes."

"The leaguers figure the pimp brings in around $300,000 a year in drug trades too.

"Jesus Christ Sir, it sounds like you know what these dudes are up to. How come?"

"Just hold it a minute Billy. These leaguers now hear good things about H&B Financial and Poors while slumming around in the world of scumbag pimps and druggies. The bastards also think about the pimps annual tax free income of $950,000."

"They figure, let's eliminate the pimp and black knight H&B. They figure they could make millions. And, of course, they know too they could choose between enlarging the basic prostitution herd to get their gross revenues up to 10 mil annually, or, simply selling the illegal pimping business. Now Billy, these dudes, if they decided to sell would evaluate the worth of the 'going concern' hooker business to be about $725,000. The $725,000 would be then the selling price. They would arrive at this figure by capitalizing the net revenue of $650,000 at 90%. Ninety percent into $650,000 is about $725,000. Are you with me kid?"

"No sir, I'm not sir, it's just ordinary everyday fuckin' gibbly guck to me sir."

"Hoookay. Then Charley and Stu would try to sell the drug end of the business too. In this deal, because the drug business would be deemed to be a more stable enterprise with fewer risks than pimping, the capitalization rate can be lower than the cap rate for prostitution, thus fetching more for each dollar of net revenue for the leaguers. I would suggest a cap rate of 50% would be used for the drug department of the enterprise. You see Billy the drug end of the business does not have the continuous moving parts the sex end of the business has. You must realize kid, dreadful asset depletion occurs daily in sex enterprizes. The careless, insensitive and callous wear and tear brought on by the pimp's clientele have a most profound effect on these earning assets' productivity. Also, these damaged assets cannot be repaired or refurbished at an ordinary every day repair shop. No. In most instances these assets become irreparable and cannot even be sold as scrap. In many cases when an individual asset is terminated as a result of an unhappy customer, the chain of efficiency is broken until a new link can be found. There are no storage facilities for these links. The pimp must not, by 'thieves honor,' pirate from another establishment. Thus he must go search for others of these assets to replace the worn out and terminated ones through public exploration. Schools seem to be a strong source of recruitment for prospective candidates, as well as malls, night clubs, bored housewives and the streets."

"In any event Billy, the selling value of the drug business would be $600,000. The $600,000 is arrived at by capitalizing $300,000 at 50%. So now kid, if these two smart asses are successful in effecting these sales they will have $1,325 mil available for investing.

"Now comes H&B Financial & Poors. Where is there a connection between the leaguers, the pimp and H&B, Billy boy?"

"Well, I've just explained the possible "pimp—leaguer" connection. But as I said earlier, I may be 'all wet' about the pimp and the leaguers. If so, I've started my investigation on the wrong premise. I know I've got to keep my mind focused on what I'm doing for Clark. Find Holly Hoxdale. Maybe I'm just dreaming up an exciting intrigue, you know kid, a fancy mystery to solve. But dammit, I think the crunch of the matter goes one hell of a lot deeper than just the leaguers and his honor the pimp. I think the two college boys stumbled onto something big regarding H&B quite by accident while playing their college game of money smut in searching out whores' nests and illicit drugs. My bet is these leaguers either shot or had hired a hit man to 'whack' Vito and Leroy. I'm positive the leaguers thought Vito and Leroy had cottoned onto their scheme. And maybe they were right, maybe Vito and Leroy had gotten wind of something and were waiting for Clark to get back to New York and were gonna run the shit by him. Damnit Billy, that may have been what got them shot."

"But, if that's the scoop, why hadn't the leaguers got to Holly a lot sooner?" Trent blanched. He sat straight up. He banged his hands on the steering wheel. "Shit no, Jesus fucking Christ no, was Holly just a plant…a whore mongering plant?"

"Good God almighty, a plant. Here kid, quick, change seats with me. Don't get out of the car, just switch seats." It was a struggle to drive in the sea of yellow cabs and switch seats at the same time.

But they made it. Billy got goosed a couple of times by the pumped up Mustang's gearshift while he struggled under Trent's bulk. He sputtered, "Ooooops-a-daisy."

"What's that kid?"

"Never mind, Trent sir."

"We're goin' back to the campus now, so make a friggin' 'u' turn. Don't waste any time, but don't get a ticket either. Git now."

"Yesss sir!" Billy snapped, as if he was a marine. He then did as he was told. Horns honked. Other drivers screamed obscenities at him. The yellow cab drivers suggested various indecent places Billy should go. Billy laughed. He made that Mustang dance. The kid could drive. They were back at the university in 15 minutes. Billy knew where to park so that he and Trent could see the movement of people coming from and going into the student's building. The time was 5:30 p.m.

In the meantime Trent had tried to get Clark on his cell. Pam, H&B's night receptionist answered. "H&B, F and P., here to serve you yes-sirree," she chirped. "Open 24 hours a day, seven days a week. How may I help?" she warbled.

"Pam, it's Trent. I need to talk to Clark now. It's urgent."

"He's not here Trent. Let me try to get him for you. On your cell Trent?"

"Yeah sweetie, it's damn urgent."

"I'll do all I can."

"Thanks Pam." Trent closed off his cell.

Billy leaned over to Trent. Billy's face had turned a sickly gray.

"Trent, I need a fix."

"What?"

"I need a fix or I'll puke."

"Where the hell would I find you a fix?"

"Don't know. Shit, I feel it coming." Whurrp.

"Don't heave up in the car."

"S'okay, it went down again."

"Would an aspirin do?"

"Maybe. But sir, I've got some shit on me. Enough to do me 'til midnight."

"You've what?" Trent yelled. "In my car?"

"Yeah."

"You little bastard."

Billy had a long sleeve tattered shirt on with the sleeves partly rolled up. He rolled down one sleeve and out popped a small cellophane sealed bag with white 'stuff' in it. He placed it on his lap. He rolled the sleeve back up. He then rolled the other sleeve down and out popped a slim tapered straw. He placed the straw on his lap. Suddenly he began to shake. He muttered to Trent, "please man open the glove compartment door, open the bag and whurrrp." Billy closed his eyes and with every ounce of gullet control he swallowed his gorge. Tears squeezed out from under his eyelids and streamed down his cheeks. Another whurrp! Another swallow! Billy held his breath. He pointed from the bag to the open flat glove compartment door.

Trent understood. "If this kid's going to be of any use to me tonight, I better help him with his goddam fix." Trent opened the bag of 'coke' and placed the contents on the flat surface of the glove compartment door. Billy took the tapered straw in his spastic fingers and tried to find his nose with it. He whimpered. He couldn't do it. He shook too much. Trent took the straw in his fingers and put the narrow end in the 'stuff.' Billy leaned his head down, as still as possible, and stuck the straw held by Trent in his right nostril. His pointing finger found the left nostril. He pushed his finger against his left nostril thus closing off any air that might gush through that nostril as he sniffed air in his right nostril. In a few moments he had Trent switch the straw to his left nostril. Billy was ready to complete the procedure on his left nostril when Trent called out, "Billy, Billy, there they are. Shit man, They're getting in a car."

Trent dropped the straw.

Billy hollered, "Holy fuck…fuck them, I need the straw." A crazed Billy searched the floor of the car for the straw.

"Drive Billy, get on the tail of that damned Honda." Billy ignored Trent's order and continued to grope for the straw. Trent smacked Billy's face with an open palm. Billy struck back. Trent was ready to throw Billy out of the car just as Billy opened his car door and puked a hot stream of steamy leftovers splashing onto the car next to him. Billy gagged. What a stinkin' mess, Trent thought.

"Billy, you get the hell out of the car, I've got to follow those pricks." Billy swirled back into the car, leaned his head down, steady now, placed his nose over the remaining 'coke,' snuffed in like an imploding television picture tube.

Sumbitch, if the kid didn't snuff up most of it.

He started the Mustang, winked at Trent, backed the car out of the stall, geared it up and the chase was on.

# # #

Charles drove the speed limit. He took 116 Street east to Madison Avenue, then turned south on Madison. Billy followed. Trent guessed Charles and Stu were headed for the Grand Central Station area or possibly to Washington Square. They had no difficulty following the carefree driving Charles.

Charles and Stu were chatting about their future riches. They congratulated themselves on the shrewd investment they had made just seven days ago in Lenny Chimo's hooker and drug business.

They would get their first of many weekly payments in cash, non-taxable, ha, tonight at 9:00 p.m. in Pippin Pizzas' Pizza House on East 41st and Park Avenue.

"How much do you figger man?" Stu said.

"The deal is $310 per day, so Stu it'll be $2,180. $1,090 each."

"That's cool," Stu said, "Let's park at the Pam Am Building and just stroll down to Pippins. Shit man, we may even see some of our meat stock, yeah, our ass-ettes-maybe even our pricey, prima donna Holly. God that Holly, what a broad. If I was her pimp I'd keep her all to myself."

"Yeah, and you'd be givin' up $2,000 plus a day."

"Hey man, it would be worth it."

"Don't get any ideas Stu, leave Holly alone. Lenny just got her back a few days ago. Don't you remember, Lenny gave her up for nearly a year, well, seven months anyway. I'll bet our nemesis, Clark St. James got a lot of freebees off a' Holly.

"Lucky Bastard!"

"That dude," Charles said, "He may have to go." Charles thought for a moment. "Fact is, he must go. Yeah, he must go before H&B's, A.G.M. The guy is just too powerful. His shareholders think he's God. And that rag with him, Polly I think her name is, apparently she's a brain. We'll get the priest to stiff Clark, maybe Polly too. We'll have to go to Lenny's church tomorrow to see his priest."

"I can't get over the priest. He's weird. Lenny tells me the priest gets one of our pre-teens every Saturday afternoon for free." Charles pondered. "I guess it's worth it, you know he whacked those two scumbag directors of H&B as neat as you please." Lenny found out from two previous H&B directors who were jailed for a screwed up heist of H&B's cash some time back, and whose knees were shot out by somebody, and who the most loyal board members were of H&B. Turned out to be Vito Apostili and Washington Leroy Jefferson. The priest gunned them down while the two weasels were warming their hands over a fired up oil barrel."

"Why am I telling you all this stuff, you know the story as well as I do? It amazes me why Lenny would tell us all this crap?" Charles said.

"I think I know why, Chuck. He wants to impress us. He needs our brains. By stiffing those two reprobates, Vito and Leroy, he figures he proved two things to us. One, he's got an efficient killer on his payroll, so don't mess with me type of thing, and two, he evens up a score for those two buddies of his; his payola buddies, those two previous loser directors who fucked-up the heist. So don't screw with my buddies type of thing."

"O'course by telling us all about his hitman the priest we've got old Lenny by the balls. That's why he went back to where we were 'gang-bangin' Holly. When we said go he went, then Clark busted him up good."

"Anyway, Chuck, we know Lenny the pimp wants part of H&B's action, but he's too stupid to know how to go about doing it. That's why he needs us. He knows we know how business takeovers are done. So, good buddy, he's our partner for the nonce. And, Chuck, as far as the priest is…"

"Yeah, he is one weird dude," Stu replied. "I'm glad I'm Protestant."

"Same here Stu."

"Good old W.A.S.P.'s"

"Yeah, good old W.A.S.P.'s"

Charles found a parking spot not far from the Pan Am building. It was now 7:00 p.m. The sun was disappearing behind some soft white clouds. It was a pleasant sight. Vibrant sun rays were streaming through openings in the clouds creating colorful beams throughout Manhattan's skyline. Smiles began to overtake the scowling faces of the mass of humanity walking the busy streets. What magic nature's beauty possesses. Its slight of hand transforms dark forebodence into cheery brightness. Even Charles' and Stu's gaiety and gloating stepped up a notch or two.

"It should be a hot time in the old town tonight," Charles chortled.

"Yeah, beam the johns down Scotty," Stu said rubbing the palm of his hands together. "Girl sales should be brisk tonight, Chuck baby."

"Yes indeedy do," Charles replied. "Stu, seriously, we have to think on a date of when we blow Lenny away. We've got to take over his businesses so we can sell them, cash out, and have the funds to buy proxies from the stupid shareholders of H&B. We need the proxies for H&B's upcoming A.G.M."

Billy found parking within a block of Charles' car. Under Trent's skillful guidance, they were able to follow the leaguers without being spotted. Charles and Stu doddled! They looked in windows, eyeballed every pretty lady that they passed. Stopped for a Latte in a charming little outdoor cafe. Cheered on a couple of drunks who were engaged in a fist fight. Spat in the hands of some of the numerous panhandlers, then laughed.

The minutes seemed to take hours to pass by for Billy. "What the hell are we hoping to find out by following these guys?" he wondered. At least the 'coke' had now removed his nausea and shaking. Billy felt quite fit from his fix and proud to be part of Trent's investigation and detecting. This is the first day in many years that he felt he had some utility value. By damn a responsible citizen. But poor Billy still didn't really know what he and Trent were doing. Oh well, it's fun, he thought.

Now Charles and Stu picked up their pace a bit. The time was now 8:20 p.m. Lenny had told the leaguers where five of his hookers were to be stationed this night. Not far from "Pippins Pizza. "Yeah, Holly'll be there. She starts at seven," Lenny said. "But I doubt you'll get to see her. She's always busy. I told her 300 bucks minimum per john, and I told her 10 hours of business time. I told her I want her to produce $3,000 on her shift tonight. I got my enforcer Henry to keep tabs on her. "Henry's not gentle, she'll behave, she'll produce." Charles and Stu stood on the corner of East 43rd and Park. They recognized some of the basic herd. Two of the girls in tight shirts and slacks, one in a V-neck sweater and short shorts wearing six-inch spikes. The two not there, busy to be sure, were Holly and a pre-teenager.

Trent and Billy stopped when they saw Charles and Stu on the corner. "We must be getting hot Billy boy, yes indeed," Trent said. "We'll just sit and talk and make like nothing's going on."

Several minutes passed without any action.

"Hi boys," Holly whispered as she leaned her head down between Trent's and Billy's. They jumped. "Stay cool," she murmured, "I'm surprised it took you so long to find me. I've seen and talked to lots of our shareholders since I went missing last Wednesday. I've only got a second Trent, so hear me and hear me good. I was hauled out of my suite last Wednesday night by Lenny's enforcer. A guy called Henry. He took me to Lenny Chimos' pad. I worked for Lenny before Clark saved me. Lenny threatened me with everything, unspeakable things, if I didn't come back to his stable. He said, too, he would whack Clark if I didn't stay. I kissed ass man, did I kiss ass. I said, 'Lenny, I will never disobey you again.' I told him I loved him, that I couldn't live without him. My act was so good I even cried. And I even did a couple of 500 buck tricks for him that night. But Trent, I have learned a lot of what's coming down. I've got to tell everything I know to Clark soon. There's more I've got to find out from Lenny and his new partners…a couple of those leaguer clowns who gang banged me…their names are Charles and Stu…before I desert Lenny and come back to H&B. Please believe me Trent, there's a lot at stake here. Come by tomorrow night as a john, you know, dressed like a john and pick me up right here at seven. Be sure to come by cab, don't use your car. It's too easy to recognize. Bring 500 bucks Trent, you'll be my first trick tomorrow night. I gotta fill you in. Gotta go now. Don't let me down Trent, please sweetie, be here."

"I'll be here Holly. You can count on it. Holly?"

"Yes Trent," she replied.

"Be careful."

Holly winked.

She disappeared into the crowded streets.

Trent and Billy sat for several more minutes chatting. They didn't want to arouse any suspicions by hustling away. Trent was ready to break some necks when he saw a child get out of a car, skimpily dressed, cute as a button, and join the other hookers. Billy swore. He wanted to run and grab the little girl and take her back to H&B's offices and see to it she was properly looked after. For the first time Billy saw the streets out of caring eyes. Christ, Lord Jesus Christ, he thought, there are child prostitutes all over the place, I've seen them before, but I paid no attention to them. I thought only about my habit and myself.

At nine o'clock they saw Charlie Boy and Stu disappear into 'Pippins Pizza House.'

"Billy do you think they would recognize you if you went in and looked around?"

"No, they wouldn't sir."

"Good, they'd know me from this afternoon if I went in and they happened to spot me, my scruffed up clothes and all."

"I'm on my way boss."

"Good man."

Billy sauntered over to the Pizza Parlor, gawked at the outside menu, whistled a non-tune, looked inside, stepped through the doorway and almost bumped into the backs of the two leaguers. There they were, talking to a tall slim rather handsome swarthy man. Billy stopped and peered through the glass encasement pretending to be searching for a special tidbit. He was a smart kid. He would look up at the parlor's patrons as if he was trying to make up his mind what to buy. But, in fact, he was seeing only Mr. Swarthy one.

After storing the image of this swarthy man back in the theater of his mind, Billy walked over to the other side of the narrow Pizza house. He looked up and down at the mouth-watering array of goodies displayed in the display cases. I'm starved hungry, he thought to himself, everything looks so friggin' good. I've got five bucks, I'll get a coupla muffins before I leave. But he wasn't ready to leave yet. No. Not until he was certain that Mr. Swarthy was Lenny Chimos.

Lenny led the leaguers to a small booth. It was reserved for him. The students and the Swarthy One sat. Billy followed them as close as he dared to, and, as the leaguers sat, he overheard one of them say, "Thanks Lenny."

'Yeah,' Billy said to himself.

Billy made his way to the cashier. He paid her for two raisin muffins, and got back his buck-fifty change. He left the parlor happy as a fox in a hen house.

'What a dick I am,' he thought proudly. Then he laughed at himself. 'A dick's a dork asshole, I mean dick as in Dick Tracy, a detective. Yes. Trent'll be happy.'

Trent stood as he saw Billy emerge from Pippins Pizza. The kid had been gone 15 minutes. Trent had begun to worry about him. What if the kid is recognized? What if the whore mongers got suspicious and nabbed Billy the kid. Damn me, why didn't I go closer to the joint so I could keep an eye on him.

"What a relief to see you Billy. You look like the Cheshire Cat. What didjado in there, whip up a pizza, make friends with the leaguers, what?"

"No boss man sir. I saw the great meat vendor himself, Lenny Chimos. I'd know the sucker anywhere now. Ain't I a first rate dick sir?" Billy laughed.

"Yeah, you got that right kid."

"Now you gotta keep me as your partner, because I know what this dude looks like."

"Maybe so Billy, maybe so." Trent was beginning to like Billy Wheaton.

They got back to H&B's office at around ten. There were quite a few winos inside the warehouse all getting looked after by H&B's staff who themselves were once drunks and misfits.

CHAPTER 52

H&B FINANCIAL AND POORS

Most of H&B's 7,100 shareholders were no longer charity cases as they once were. The board of directors, headed by Lana and Clark St. James, had met with the mayor and council of the City of New York together with business leaders, Better Business Bureaus, Chambers of Commerce and the A.F.L.C.I.O. three years ago when H&B's financial affairs were skyrocketing. H&B had introduced a plan to the mayor and councilors regarding its shareholders and other unfortunates who were not yet H&B shareholders. The plan, as defined by the directors, was a mini financial structure that, on proof of its success, could be adopted statewide and in due course nationwide.

The plan was not complex, nor were its intent and goals. The plan called for government and industry to pay for individual services rendered by H&B shareholders and other unfortunates, and H&B would, until probation periods ended, reimburse government and industry 50% of labor and related costs. Individual services rendered by scummers would blanket every nook and cranny of unattended to jobs, uncompleted jobs and overlooked jobs in the great city of New York. Science would play a major role in the plan. Its function would be to make those resources considered to be waste into productive resources anywhere in the city, state or nation. Science would use many of H&B's unskilled shareholders and other unfortunates as its plow horses. Not slaves, but well paid working people. Skilled and professional down-and-outers would, with effort, be pushed back into a state of productivity.

Helpless scummers would remain at the expense of society while lazy, uncaring ones would be the financial responsibility of H&B.

Lana, the instigator of the plan, felt the effects of the plan would be noticeable within a few months of its introduction. Manhattan Island's roadways, bridges, sidewalks and other basic amenities would be made whole again. Its parks, seaways and the like would become cleansed. Repairing infrastructures would become a regular process in the day to day activities of H&B's scummers. Lana was certain H&B's shareholders would be integrated into Manhattan's society within 20 years.

* * *

Lana knew H&B was just a Band-Aid solution benefiting only a handful of Greater New York's homeless population. She was delighted with H&B's successes, but she wanted more people to become its beneficiaries. Lana wanted H&B to branch out to New York City's boroughs, to the state, to the nation and to the world. In Lana's view, she saw two viable solutions to the problem of arriving at a degree of equity for the world's citizenry. One, a worldwide H&B Financial and Poors Inc. or two, a $100 trillion investment in the global economy.

Lana knew a worldwide H&B Financial would in due course become the biggest monopoly ever dreamt of. Its shareholders, limited to those people around the world whose net worth was less than $1,000 U.S., would number some 3-billion. Its financial size could become mind-boggling—its power overwhelming. Literally H&B with 3-billion shareholders could become, in time, the rich and the famous, while the current rich and famous could falter and become the poor and downtrodden. Thus Lana knew, unless otherwise controlled, H&B would not be a moral solution. She knew as well the whole scenario could change within a few years, hell, those who are destined to be rich under any scenario would, in due course, take over H&B. The cycle would then have been completed, and, for fuck sake, we are back to 'square one.' Ain't that a banger.

However, to bridge the current inequitable gap between the super rich and the poor, Lana felt H&B should shoulder as much of the burden as possible for now and expand H&B to the boroughs, the state and as far into the country and world as possible.

CHAPTER 53

TRENT LOGAN, THE EQUALIZER AND BILLY WHEATON

Trent and Billy were met by Clark as they entered H&B's office. Pam hooted out, "Hi Trent and Billy, I told you I'd find Clark. He tried to call you on your cell Trent, but the reception was awful. Trent, you look terrible, what happened to your clothes, your hands and your knee? And Billy, you look so pale. Whatta' you guys been doing?…oops sorry boys…H&B, F and P here to serve you, yes-sireee…"

"That Pam, ain't she sumpin?" Billy said smiling.

"She's our sweetheart all right," Clark answered.

Pam Gottelig was a recovering alcoholic, she had been abused by her father and uncle for eight years until she hit the streets at 14. From 14 to 19 she drank, used drugs and prostituted herself. One night two years ago, Pam was brought to H&B's office by two policewomen. Hyperventiliating from lying in the snow on a wind swept street, boozed and drugged she was near death. These same two officers had brought quite a few scumbags to H&B. They liked what they saw at H&B. Their chief was supportive of their actions. Over time Pam was cleaned up and given the job as receptionist. She has never looked back.

Trent and Billy followed Clark to his office. They all sat. Shivering, Billy asked if he could be excused so that he could go get some coffee and food from H&B's Foodateria.

Trent gave a full account of his and Billy's day's activities. Clark was astounded at their accomplishments and overjoyed they had found

Holly. "Damn it all, I should go to that Pizza house, grab Holly, beat the shit out of Lenny again, kick-ass those leaguers and haul the pre-teener back here with Holly. Bastards."

"No Clark, forget it. Let me get back to Holly tomorrow night. I think we have to use Holly as a go-between for awhile yet. I know she's in danger being with that fucking pimp. But I think she's got the moxy to hang in there 'til we bring her back here. If I feel she's in over her head tomorrow night, I'll make sure she's safe. You know Clark I was convinced at one point today Holly was a goddam plant. Son of a bitch, hey.

"My best guess Clark, is that you and Lana are on the leaguers hit list. They're cute fuckers. Slyer than Lenny Chimos. Now that their semester's finished, these lions have nothing but time on their hands to plan and connive. They're rich kids from rich families. They don't have to work between university years. Not like that shit-heel Lenny who has to mind his herd of prosties and play it safe in his drug dealings. Lenny's gotta work, he can't take the time to plot out a business plan like those students can. Those students, I'd say, are going to have Lenny whacked, by whom I don't know, take over Lenny's affairs, sell the businesses, then I would guess they would use the cash to try to buy up H&B proxies and shares for voting at H&B's upcoming A.G.M. You and Lana could get murdered Clark. (Billy was back now) I'm serious."

"OK Trent," Clark responded, "I hear what you say. Lana must be protected at all costs, no question about that. As for tomorrow night, you've got my okay. I'll get 600 bucks from petty cash for you. Now let's look at the whole scenario and see what we're facing. Oh, gents, before going over our problems step by step, I want to tell you Lana phoned today from somewhere and said she would be here at the office Sunday.

"Oh yeah, and she wants me to pick her up, I don't know where or when yet, but she'll call and let me know." Clark gave Trent a knowing nod. Trent now knew Lana would be back from Istanbul on Sunday.

"Billy, Trent tells me you are a good man even with your habit and your propensity to toss-up. He says he will need your help for the next few days and hence he would like you to stay with us now while we discuss the current situation. Is that all right with you?" Clark asked.

"Yes sirs," Billy bellowed like a raw recruit being berated by a tough Sergeant. "But I need a fucking fix sirs, now sirs."

"Jesus Billy, I thought you said you were good 'til midnight," Trent replied.

"No sir," Billy roared, "Between the two of us we lost some of my shit, sir."

"Billy, for Christ's sake, you're not in the U.S. marines," Clark said.

"I know sir, but I want to make an impression on both of you sirs, sir." Whuurrp.

"Yeah, the kid needs a fix all right Clark. He's Whurrping."

"Pam darling," Clark called, "Get a mainline out of emergency and bring it here quick please. I'll sign for it. Hurry Pam, or Billy's gonna barf."

"I'll be just a moment Clark, tell Billy to hang in there."

Billy started to shake. He shook like a dunking duck's ass. "My God, he's going to come apart," Clark said.

"Whuurrp," said the Duck's ass.

"Oh fuck," Trent said.

Billy held back so much he farted.

"Nice impression you're making on the boss," Trent said.

"Whuurrrp," Billy shook so hard his pecker pissed.

Pam rushed in.

"God Billy, you peed yourself," she said.

She rolled up his sleeve, found a good vein, Clark and Trent held down his arm. She squirted the syringe and pushed in the needle. All eyes were glued on Billy. Some shit bags came to Clark's office door to watch, their mouths agape in toothless grins. "Shoot 'em up good

Pammy," they gummed. "Hee Hee," they twittered like some alien mucked up mutants.

"Hey guys, we need some privacy for a while, okay," Clark said.

"We're gone," they cackled, "Have a good ride Billy."

They shuffled off tee-heeing.

Within seconds, Billy's body responded to the hit. Pam stood over him.

"Hi Pam, I didn't 'fro-up' did I?" Billy asked baby-like.

"No sweetie-pie, but you did jobby number one in your pants," she said laughing. Billy looked down at his crotch. He not only saw what he had done but now he felt the cold wet urine oozing in his pants. Even his bottom was awash in pee.

"Awe heck," the kid said, revolted, "What a dork I am. What a bleeping dork." He looked up at Pam.

"Pam I'm sorry I'm so crude."

"Inelegant you mean," Trent corrected.

"That too Pam," poor Billy whispered. Billy had had his eyes on Pam since he came to H&B. He was sure now he had messed up any chance he might have had with her.

"Billy its okay, believe me," Pam said, "Come with me and I'll help you clean up."

"You're kidding Pam," Trent said.

"No I'm not Trent. Clark, Lizzy is out there tonight, I'll get her to relieve me on the switchboard 'till I get Billy back to you. Okay?"

"Okay Pam. Just leave the requisition for the drug on your desk and I'll sign it before I turn in. And thanks Pam. Your terrific."

"Thanks Clark. Come sweet William, mama will take care of you," she said.

Billy rose flushed, picked up his chair, held it in front of himself and followed Pam.

The shit bags pointed bony wart-covered fingers at Billy as he passed them and laughed like dingos. Pam addressed the shit bags. "Now

George, Lena and Jack, leave Billy alone. His accident was simply an accident." Pam could no longer hold back her laughter. She grabbed her sides and laughed. She laughed and laughed. The shit bags laughed with her. Even Billy snickered. Pam pulled the chair away from Billy stood on her tiptoes and kissed him on the mouth. The shit bags hollered their approval. 'What a fuckin' day,' Billy mumbled to himself.

In just 20 minutes Pam returned Billy to Clark's office all spit and polished. Billy still looked sheepish and subdued. But he even looked a little frisky. Was his friskiness the result of his hi-test fix or the red lipstick mark on his neck Pam, in her excitement, overlooked? Probably Pam's kiss.

"Siddown ya bloody nuisance, and quit wasting my time whuurrping, shaking, puking, farting and pissing. You're a fuckin' one-man disaster. Clark has agreed with me that you need special help. You're only 20-years old kid and by God, by the time you're 21 you are going to be clean. H&B has some tremendous counselors, and you're going to be their baby. You hear me?" Trent hollered.

"Yes Trent sir, I hear you sir" Billy barked.

"Sorry Clark, let's get at it."

"Right. Billy I assume you will work with Trent then?"

"Yes Mr. Potter, Clark, whoever, I will."

After an hour of looking ahead and synthesizing what might occur over the next few days, Clark summarized the items the three of them had just discussed and must attend to, "Control over H&B's Annual General Meeting. What Charles and Stu may be plotting? Lenny's role and life span? Will Charles and Stu take over the prostitute ring and the drug conduit business? Will the leaguers keep these enterprises or sell them? Charles and Stu's interest in H&B...is it control through equity holdings...proxy voting or is it positions on H&B's directorate? Holly's role in obtaining answers to the above? Who is Lenny's, Charles' and Stu's hit man? When are Lenny, Clark and Lana due to be whacked?"

"Jesus, that's heavy stuff gentlemen," Billy said. "How come you trust me with this information? I'll bet I could flog it off for thousands. What makes you so sure about me?"

"Billy, H&B has been built on trust. Our 7,000 shareholders have earned respect through trust. When you became a shareholder, one of the prerequisites before H&B issued shares to you was that you sign a covenant of trust. You signed such a covenant," Clark said.

"Yeah, and Billy Boy, you break that trust, and I'll have your nuts," Trent warned.

"Well I'm flattered sirs. You have my word of honor I will never betray you Clark, you Trent, H&B, its shareholders, no one. I swear I will never let you down. You have my complete trust."

"Thanks Billy," Clark said.

Saturday evening at six fifty five, Trent had his taxi driver pull up and park at the spot he and Holly were to meet. There she was, strolling toward Trent's cab. "All six-feet of her." Swinging those incredible hips. Her body was covered richly in a Kurdish maroon mini dress which met her shoulders only half way. The dress proceeded downward hugging every inch of her curvaceous figure stopping just below her womanhood.

"God," Trent thought, "She has to rank second to Lana."

"Hi Girly, want an all day sucker?" Trent asked.

"How kind of you sir, that's exactly what I want," Holly replied.

"Then jump right in my sweet."

"Thank you. I will."

Holly squeezed in beside Trent.

CHAPTER 54

CHRISTEEN'S ANSWER

To Lana's Seductive Question

"Damn you Margaret, why did you ask your sister to come here and why did I encourage you to do so? We could have worked things out even including telling your mom and dad about us. We're not kids. Now see the impossible spot I'm in? Look at your sister Margaret, look at her. She's a fucking doll. Now she's asking me if she and I would make love if we were alone. It's like asking me if I would like to live in paradise at age 22 for eternity. Would I take a billion dollars if it were offered to me? Would I like to walk over a square mile of tits in my bare feet? Would I like my monthly visitor to be a thing of the past—no strings attached? Would I like the Taj Mahal to be the parking garage for my mansion?"

"Jesus Christ Lana, who wouldn't want to be bedded down with you?" Christeen answered. "You are heaven on earth. It's hard to believe you were born a mortal. You exude life. You are delicious, delectable, de-lovely. I met you about two hours ago, two flippin' hours ago, and my impression of you is incomprehensible. You are fucking luscious. Yeah Lana, I'd make love to you if we were alone," Christeen snapped. "You are the ultimate of sex and you are just out of your teens. Satisfied Lana?" Chrissy barked. "But let me say this Lana, I am in love with Margaret. I want Margaret as my life's love and companion, no one else. When we are in our 60's we will look back on this day and Margaret and I will say, Lana, we told you so." Christeen turned to Margaret and said, "I love you Maggie."

"Excellent Christeen," Lana said.

Margaret squirmed. "So Christeen, you would sleep with Lana, would you? Damn both of you."

Margaret rushed out of the room crying, feeling small and insignificant. Christeen got up to follow.

"Stop Christeen. Let her cry and think things out herself." Lana commanded.

Ten minutes went by and still no Margaret. The loud sobs began to ebb. Margaret had heard all the words spoken by Christeen, and in particular the horrid, 'Yeah, Lana, I'd make love to you if we were alone. Yeah Lana. I'd let you make love to me if we were alone. Yeah Lana. I'd let you…goddamn her."

Margaret lay silent for a few minutes then began to think, "What would I have said if the shoe was on the other foot. Say, Chrissy's sister was of Lana's caliber, and was blessed with the same mental ascendancy, and loaded with wild animal attraction, wouldn't I agree to fornicate this imaginary creature, just for the sake of fornication? No love, no companionship just unadulterated lust. I think I would."

"And didn't Chrissy quantify her reasons for agreeing that she would make love to Lana? Yes she did. And didn't Chrissy say she wanted me as her life's love and companion? Yes she did."

"So why am I lying here jealous and angry?" she asked herself.

"Damn Lana, why did she ask the question anyway."

"I suppose the queston would be on my mind even if Lana hadn't asked it. I know damn well every man, woman and probably child would make love to Lana if they had the chance. So I guess Lana in her f…king wisdom stopped my wondering in its tracks as to whether Christeen would prefer Lana over me with that question and answer. She is so goddamn smart, so far sighted. So far ahead of we mere mortals. Sheeit"

With her frustration somewhat eased Margaret got off the bed, straightened herself out, corralled her composure, opened the bedroom door and strode out to the living room.

Christeen watched Margaret's entry with hope. Lana watched her sister's entry, wondering if Margaret had come around? Had Margaret seen Christeen's answer as a response by an insincere sleep-around-trollop, or a sincere friend and lover?

"Chrissy, while I still don't like your answer to Lana's question, I do appreciate your candor and I do understand the reasons you gave to arrive at the answer and Chrissy, what the hell is this 'walk over a square mile of tits in your bare feet,' you're weird Christeen. I love you too, Chrissy, you gorgeous skyscraper."

"And you little sister, you may be numero uno worldwide, but I can still take you over my knee and give you a good spanking." Margaret said.

"Oh, please do Maggie," Chrissy said. "Wow."

"Fuck you Chrissy."

"Maggie I was just kidding." Christeen said as she came over to Margaret. "I love you baby." She put her arms around Margaret and held on tight. Margaret reciprocated.

Lana sat pristine as 'things' unfolded. The girls broke up their embrace. But they continued to face one another, their pretty eyes relaying messages of affection between them. To this point, Lana was satisfied with their mutual devotion. "Now I hope it lasts." Lana thought.

"Did we pass your test oh great one?" Margaret questioned.

"Yes darlin' you did." Lana answered laughing.

Christeen and Margaret each told Lana of their sexual experiences and experiments. They did this much in the same manner as Christeen had told Margaret a few days earlier.

Lana knew now that Margaret was gay. It made her sad. She was certain her father and brothers would be devastated by the news. She felt her mother would be heartbroken, but pragmatic about it. "Damn the luck," Lana mused. Why did this have to happen in our family? I just wish Maggie could be heterosexual for mom's and dad's sake. We kids can accept it. Margaret will have to live her life as it is yet she has nothing to be ashamed of. She is a wonderful person. Sexual preferences as far as I am concerned have no bearing on a person's propriety and moral standards. Morals have to do only with humanitarianism, goodness, honesty, integrity, caring about others. Morals are the essence of homogeneity, spiritual as opposed to matter, spiritual as opposed to physical. Was Jesus, the most moral person who ever lived on our planet, a homosexual? We don't know do we? Then what about J. Edgar Hoover a double standard moralist. Was he not a homosexual? Homosexuals morally come in as big a variety of packages as do heterosexuals, good, bad and indifferent. Margaret is one of the good ones as is Christeen.

'Lana' she said to herself. 'You know gene domination and hormone regulation in a person's body and brain are the factors which determine a person's sexual preference. Physical characteristics only, not spiritual. A person's moral standards, good or bad, sometimes are inherent within, but more often than not, proper teaching and training are the essential factors needed to mold a person's morality.

'Goodness, far to many people are ingenious and verbose at paying lip service to morality. This lip service is close to the bottom of the hypocritical deceit barrel as far as I am concerned. Animals, while they have their share of homosexuals, are magnificent when it comes to morals. They don't gossip, fight wars, trap humans in leg hold traps, murder, terrorize intentionally, kill-off other species, loot, rape, lie, cheat, etc.

'And money! Human greed for money is monstrous. Are these not the important factors to consider, not sexual preferences?' Lana thought, not sex. Then without thought Lana said aloud "yes" startling Margaret and Christeen. "Sorry gals I was just thinking out loud."

"Margaret, are you going to approach mom and dad and your brothers about being gay? Are you going to tell them of your love for Christeen? Are you going to introduce Christeen to our family?" Lana asked.

"Yes Lana, I am going to do all those things," Margaret replied. "I intend to do my best to make my family understand me, and maybe even accept the fact I am a lesbian. I know Mom will be quasi receptive. Dad, he may want to take me out in the field and plow me under. I don't know if Dad will ever accept the fact I'm gay. I know he'll always love me. The boys, they'll just give me shit, they will try to make me change, they will have a hard time understanding my sex choice. They may even string me up, who knows?" But in time they will accept me. Let me tell you this Lana, they will flip over Christeen when they see her. Christeen will ride with them, cold, snow and all, explore the whole farm with them, help them repair the machinery, drink beer with them, wrestle with them. She'll have our brothers wrapped around her little finger in no time. She will win Mom and Dad over too, with her charm eh! Christeen? All our family will be proud of both of us because of our professional goal, medicine. Yes Lana, I intend to tell everyone next week. Christeen and I will be driving down to Swift Current on Tuesday and we intend to stay at the farm, if Mom and Dad let us, and while there we will 'bust' out of the proverbial closet."

"I think that's wonderful girls," Lana said.

"Now kids let's get on with something else, enuf about sex."

It was late afternoon. Chrissy and Margaret earlier had made up some cabbage rolls, fresh buns and apple pie. They were going to complete the menu with whipped potatoes and steam-cooked carrots. Their beverage was to be a choice of tea, coffee or Chateauneuf-Du-Pape. No salad tonight! Forget our figures. Pig-out! Yeah!

The doorbell rang. Chrissy jumped up and answered it. "Well Maggie look who's here, Stanley, Chester and Willy. Come on in you sweethearts." The boys took off their shoes, came indoors, gave Chrissy and Maggie a beautiful bouquet of long-stem red roses, a 40-ounce bottle of Tanquery Gin and a huge box of Purdy's chocolates. Maggie and Chrissy smothered the boys with hugs and kisses. Chrissy wrestled Stanley to the floor and pinned him. Stanley, in a draconian voice growled, "careful girl or I may call on the eighth wonder of the world to eviscerate you."

"Some shit Stanley boy," Chrissy giggled.

"Holy, Mother of Christ, who is that?" Stanley gasped pointing to Lana. Please, please, pretty please tell me she is not gay. If she is I will commit hari kari in front of all of you. I bow before you Oh Goddess of Beauty, who, pray tell are you?" Laughing, Lana said, "No, I am not gay so you can put away your hari kari blade. My name is Lana Masters."

Chester and Willy stood speechless gawking at this unbelievable beauty. Not gay eh! Fantastic! What a ravenous beast!

Margaret introduced the boys to Lana.

"Your sister mayhap?" Stanley said.

"Yes, Lana's my sister."

"You're not?" Stanley fumbled, "Dr. Lana Masters, the mega one, are you?" he asked.

"Yes Stanley, she is," Margaret answered.

"Oh my God, my folks won't believe me when I tell them I have met you. You're, you are, lord almighty, you are the one people either love..."

"Or hate," Lana filled in.

"You are world famous for everything. You are so very young for all your accomplishments. Just out of your teens, are you not Doctor?" he asked.

"Yes, just two months ago," Lana said smiling.

"You are younger than all of us then?"

"That depends on how old you gentlemen are?"

"We are, oh God, I'm speaking to the girl, woman...oh god...the goddess of beauty, how do I address you, anyway....all 22."

Chrissy laughed. "Lana, he is mowed down by you, just like the rest of the world. But Lana you are talking to the Prince of, Maggie is it okay to tell Lana about Stanley's, you know what?"

"Chrissy you are so bad. Isn't she boys?"

They nodded.

"Chrissy, Lana wouldn't even blink an eye if you told her" Margaret answered.

Stanley reddened.

"Come on Christeen tell me, you've aroused my curiosity."

"Well Lana, let's see, how do I put this without sounding inviolate? Hmmm, his thingumagig, you know, his dong at full erection is slightly over 12-inches long and its girth is awesome." Christeen said. It's a f—ing lethal weapon as your sister describes it."

"Girls, you had me convinced you are gay. Then voila, along comes these three fella's with gifts and poof, you kiss them, Chrissy wrestles one of them to the floor and now you brag about the size of Stanley's penis. What's up? Sorry Stanley, no pun intended. Have you played with it girls?"

"Yes, I have" Chrissy said smiling, "I whacked it off in a bar, in public."

"You what?" Lana said taken back. "Okay, go on."

"Well we tricked the guys at first Lana. They wanted to lay us and we said we'd love to 'cepten' we both had our visitor. They didn't want to ride a gooey deck. We gambled and won. So, meany me jerked Stanley off. Actually, there was more to it than that Lana. You see I dumped Stanley on his ass earlier in the night, I didn't know him then, he was being a jerk. Stanley's dad is the mayor of Saskatoon. Stanley made the bar's staff and Maggie and me aware of this fact. He threatened all of us, didn't you big Stan?"

Stanley nodded.

"Stanley then left the bar. Later on in the evening he returned with Chester and Willy. We invited the boys to join us for a drink. They agreed. Then Stanley began to brag about his yahoo, he showed it to us, and we damn near fainted. He warned us about touching it. We both did and just like he said it would, it stiffened into this, this behemoth. The rest, Lana, is history."

"They know we're gay sister," Margaret said, "we are now the best of friends. They love us and we love them, and we'll be their friends for life. Right guys."

"Right," the boys chorused.

"Now Lana," Christeen interrupted, "would you care to observe Stanley's monstrosity close at hand my dear."

"It's up to Stanley."

With pride, but red in the face, Stanley unzipped his fly, unraveled his dick, looked up at Lana and saw her run her pink tongue over her moist luscious lips. This was too much for 'Stan the man,' his great dick went rigid. Slight dog-leg to the right, huge and pulsating!

"My-oh my," Lana said in a whisper. "My-oh my, my, my."

* * *

The boys stayed for dinner. The six of them played George, a card game played in Saskatchewan. Lana won every game. The boys left at midnight. The girls turned in at one, Lana in her bedroom, Margaret and Christeen in another.

Lana left for Swift Current the next day. Margaret cried when Lana left. Lana had a wonderful visit with her family. She stayed three days. She spoke not a word about Margaret's private life. Lana perked up her favorite pet, the aged Big Buster with her care and affection. She departed for J.F.K. airport from Regina, Saskatchewan's capital city.

CHAPTER 55

THE IVY LEAGUERS CONTRACT FATHER DONNELY

To assasinate Lenny (the pimp) Chimos

Chuck and Stu decided they had to move fast if they were serious about their takeover of H&B Financial & Poors Inc. Its annual general meeting was only three months away. In that period of time these lions would have to have Lenny Chimos, Clark St. James and Polly whoever eliminated. Lenny Chimos 'would go first' they agreed.

So, a meeting with the good father must be arranged post-haste to work out the details of the hit. Stu was given the chore of finding out from Lenny, in some circuitous way, the name of the priest and his telephone number. If Stu was asked by Lenny 'why he needed the priest' Stu had to be able to "stick-handle" around the question so as not to arouse Lenny's suspicion. Stu was good at "stick-handling."

After Lenny's unfortunate demise, the students then would have to determine if they should maintain Lenny's businesses, manage them and expand their activities to increase revenues or sell one or both of them. Shit man, if they kept both of them and took over H&B Financial, too, they would have a 'kind-of-a' built-in clientele for their hooker and drug enterprises. Hooker and drug revenues would increase from such a venture because, social assistance moneys received from governments by the shit-bag shareholders and their dividends on shares from H&B

would funnel right back to Hooker and Drug Services Inc. if, of course, Hookers and Drugs' public relations were handled properly.

"Stu, you and I could hire a coupla' tough dudes to handle the hookers and to take care of crooked creeps who might try to horn in on our businesses. We could have the funds received by these enterprises laundered through H&B. We could pay ourselves a few thousand dollars a day as CEO and CFO of H&B and, man, live the good life."

"Problem is Chuck, we would need two or three million dollars to buy our way into H&B," Stu said.

"Yeah, I know, that's the problem Stu," Charles replied.

"I know we could raise the financing if we could get our fathers' to act as covenantors for a big line of credit. But," Charles said, "they would want every detail about our proposed business. Business plans, budgets, cash flow, the whole shebang."

"Imagine chuck," Stu said laughing, "the list of assets we would have to provide our sires, Holly, Suzanne, Blow-Job Katy, Lard-Ass Amber, Titty, Dawn, Spook, Anal Anny, etc.,etc., and our subsidiary, two kilos of dark shit, a half kilo of white shit, a coupla bales of hash, man we'd be fucking keel-hauled by our paters. However Charles, if our fathers sign as covenantors without their knowledge, and we operate the line in accordance with its terms and conditions, our fathers may never know they were backing it."

"So Charley boy, if they do happen to find out it would be too late for them to do anything about it unless, of course, they took us to court and, because of forgery, have their covenants made inoperative. Do you think our dads would do that to us, especially if we had the line transferred over to H&B and if the line was current and up to date?" Stu questioned.

"That's a tough one to answer Stu, but I know my dad would be so pissed off he'd do something. My dad's a straight shooter. He can't stand cheating. I'd be disowned, ergo, out of my family's will. And think on it

Stu, why would our fathers even go to court? I know my dad would tell the bank his covenant is inoperative, and that would be that."

"So," Stu answered, "then what would the bank do Chuck? It would demand repayment of the amount of the line being used by us. Right! Then it would cancel the whole line of credit. Right! And Chuck, my boy, we would simply pay the used portion of the line off by way of a loan to us from H&B Financial. Yes. Then we would be good boys and repay the loan to H&B over the next few hundred years. Or if you would feel more comfortable going another direction, Chuck Baby, we could do as I said a moment ago and have the line transferred from us over to H&B once we become H&B's principal shareholders. Now in doing that we could have our fathers false covenants discharged without fuss, and in place of personal covenants we would hypothecate some of H&B's assets in favor of the bank, and the bank, God bless it, then would have hard assets as security for the line."

"Christ, you're devious Stu."

"I know. But Charles, you haven't asked me 'the' critical question, how do we do the forgery in the first place, without our papas being present at the signing?" Now getting around this, Chuck old chap, is what I would consider being devious and clever.

"Okay man, how do we do the forgery?" Charles questioned.

"Good Chuck, I thought you'd never ask," Stu said smiling.

"Well, the actual forging of our father's signatures is a real snap. First we each get a current specimen signature of our respective paters. Okay? We can go to our homes and dig one up, or whatever way we want to get the signatures. Now with the specimen signatures we can do one of two things. One, we can practice forging the signatures until we are satisfied we can do it right. And by the by Chuck, the proper way to emulate a signature almost to a tee is to practice the signature while it is upside-down. Or two, we could use any number of up-to-date technologies to transcribe our father's signatures onto the bank's lending documents. As I say, the actual forgery is not a troublesome issue. It becomes an issue if the bank's lending officer requires our fathers' to be present at the signing. Yeah Chuck old chap, our fathers' presence so 'the insipid lending officer' can act superior as he lectures our fathers as to their moral responsibilities and their legal liabilities in the event we the borrowers default on any of the terms and conditions of the loan. Dumb turd! Our fathers would ring the little bastard's neck if he got paternalistic with them."

"So, Charles me lad, how do we overcome this obstreperous problem?"

"Yeah, how do we Stu?" Charles replied.

"Again Charles, I thought you'd never ask," Stu laughed.

"Okay. This may frighten you a bit Charles and, frankly, it may not work. I feel certain it will with my dad, because I know his psycho inside out. But while I know your dad quite well, I don't know the depth of his ego like I know my dad's. You are going to have to make that necessary assessment pertaining to your pater's egotism. In any event here's the 'poop' partner. We find a copy of our fathers' latest net worth statements, yes, and we make a photocopy of them and have them at our disposal. Incidentally, Charles, if your father's C.P.A. is as fussy as my father's is, your father's signature will be on his net worth statement authenticating thereon its propriety. Hookay? Now I know my dad's net worth is over one-half billion dollars, and I know your dad's is about the same, right Chuck?"

"Right Stu."

"Now, are these two wealthy barons of industry going to go sit in some two-bit office of a half-baked lending dink, and let this dink give our know-it-all fathers a lecture on their moral and legal responsibilities as covenantors? No way! Right Chuck."

"Right Stu."

"Now, we go get one more thing from our great sires. Some copies of their personal stationery, you know, their letterheads!"

"Yeah."

"So, Chuck, what have we gathered up to this point in time for the line of credit, of say, three mil from our fathers' banks? Well, we have our fathers' forged signatures, their egos, their net worth statements, and their personal stationery. Now, my boy, can you think of anything else we might need?"

"No Stu, I can't but why the personal stationery?"

"Because Charles, our fathers must send a letter to their respective bankers explaining certain things pertaining to our loan application and, as well, our fathers' inability to be present at the signing of the agreements. We, good buddy, shall draft these letters in a most explicit, no nonsense and demanding way and forge our fathers' signatures thereon. The letters will be explicit in explaining to the banker the line of credit loan is so insignificant, that they, the covenantors do not want to be bothered time-wise or other-wise with the details of the $3 million loan. The letters will go on to say, 'please accept this letter as my unequivocal approval to provide a line of credit, not to exceed three million dollars in United States funds ($3,000,000) to my son Stuart Cleatus Williams, student at Columbia University, C.O. Graduate School of Business, 3022 Broadway, Uris Hall, New York City, New York, 10027, etc. etc. and please be advised that in the event of default by the borrower(s), any unpaid balance of the line of credit, not exceeding three million dollars, plus accrued interest thereon may be contra'd against my savings account held by me in the bank, etc. etc. Please accept this letter as my unconditional guarantee to act as my son's covenantor for this loan, dated this day of, etc. Yours truly, etc.' And as I said a moment ago, Charles, we will sign the letters with our fathers' forged signatures. And, of course, the wording contained in the letters may be written with more sophistication than what I have just described albeit, my dear Charles, the message and content will remain the same."

"Gee whiz Stu, did you think all this stuff up in just the last few minutes, or did you have it all pre-planned?"

"No Charles, it just came to me as I went along."

"Well Stu, why wouldn't we just go to our fathers and ask for their guarantee on a loan to buy up H&B outright?"

"C'mon Chuck, surely you know better than that? C'mon, if we couldn't buy H&B for some reason or other, then we are fucked as to working capital. I realize that when we whack Lenny we won't have to lay out much cash when we take over his businesses. But if we wanted to do everything on our own we would have to sell the money printing, hooker and drug businesses to take a stab at buying out H&B. Personally Chuck, I'd like the whole cotton pickin' conglomerate as ours."

"OK man, I see your point. I agree."

"You know Chuck, we could drop the whole scheme and be just ordinary guys. We both graduate in 1998 with our MBA's. We can hire ourselves out for $60,000 a year or more. Shit, our dads would hire us in their companies for probably $80,000 a year. But, damn it all, look at the lucrative businesses of Lenny's, Charles. Christ, all cash, about one million dollars a year. With our expertise, God, we could build that income to one million each. Report a coupla hundred thousand each for tax purposes if we choose to, or, Chucky baby, report nothing 'cause we haven't had to file a return yet with the IRS 'cause we've never earned any reportable income before. And, laddy buck, if we were able to buy up control of H&B, we could sell off 'hookers and drugs' for big money and set it aside, you know, for that proverbial rainy day. And with our control over H&B we could pay ourselves five or six mil a year. Now, I'm positive H&B's shares cannot be traded in any market presently, so their selling values are non-existent, although I would imagine using a price earnings of 18, their market value could be in excess of $300 each. So, if we took control of H&B, one of the first things we'd do would be to amend the company's by-laws allowing therefore the company to be listed on the New York stock exchange. We then would increase the authorized capital to say 200-million common voting shares and introduce out of treasury, say 10 million shares at a $100 each and 'hock-em' off through a well connected broker. This would give good old H&B close to one billion dollars after brokerage fees to buy…hmmmmm…let's say, a reasonable size casino in Vegas. What say you to that old bean?"

"I'd say you are one big dreamer and schemer Stu, but I like your style. So far, in the last half hour you have had Lenny stiffed; taken over his enterprises; established a $3 million line of credit for us through our fathers' bank, everything forged; taken control of H&B, sold off 'hookers and drugs;' got paid as H&B's top executives $5 five mil per year each;' amended H&B's by-laws; got its shares listed on the NYSE; got a well-connected underwriter; increased H&B's authorized capital to 200 million common shares; sold and issued 10 million shares at 100 bucks each through the underwriter, and bought a casino in Vegas. What took you so long Stu baby?"

"Aaahh, I'm just a little sluggish today Charles. So Charles, are you satisfied with the path our business activities should follow as you so eloquently outlined?"

"Yes Stu, I am."

"Okay, should we now go the first step and meet with Lenny's executioner, today if possible?"

"Why not man?"

"Good, I will away post-haste my trusty pard, and see if I can find Lenny. And of course if I find him I will get the priest's address and telephone number from him, one way or another. "

Stuart Cleatus Williams left Charles's room, departed the student's building, climbed into his '97 Cobra G.T. red convertible Mustang and drove to Pippins Pizza.

Lady luck was with him. Seated in the same small booth as last evening sat the bejeweled Mr. Swarthy himself, Lenny Chimos, with one of his bigger assets, Lard-Ass Amber.

"Hi Lenny, Amber."

"Hi Stu," they chorused. "How's it hangin' man."

"Loose baby, loose," Stu replied as he high-fived them.

"Can I join you and Amber?" Stu asked Lenny.

"Why, are we cummin' apart Stu?" Amber answered laughing.

Shit, Stu thought, a Henny Youngman reply. Ya know the neat old comic who was famous for, 'I take my wife everywhere, but she always finds her way back.' 'Ya know, the half-baked terrorist who was told to 'blow up the consulates car and burned his lips on the tailpipe.'

"Lenny, I've gotta see you for a moment in private."

"Sure pal. Beat it Lard-Ass."

"Yes your highness," Lard-Ass replied. She gave Stu a wink, smiled at Lenny and left.

"She's a good producer Stu. Hits her target or more on every one of her shifts. Some customers like blimps, so I give 'em blimps. She doesn't do drugs so she stays cool. I like her. I haven't had to smack her around for weeks. Her bein' good gives Henry more time to ride herd on the rest of my cattle."

"Good," Stu acknowledged.

"Okay, Stu man, wha-da-ya need?"

"I've got a job for the priest. Bloody important job. I gotta have a 'horse's ass' whacked. Private deal! Nothing to do with you or Chuck. I'd prefer it if you and Chuck be scarce on this hit. As I say a private but 'must be done' matter. So, Lenny I need the priest's phone number and address."

"Just like that?"

"Yeah, just like that."

"Okay baby, you got it."

Lenny obliged. He gave Stu all the information he needed. He even described the priest's face and build. But he said the priest was not in town. "In Istanbul, whereever that is Stu. He'll be back on Sunday. You won't get to see him 'til Sunday."

"His name Lenny?" Stu asked.

"Father Donnely," Lenny replied.

* * *

Trent told the driver to take Holly and him to Citicorp Center and drop them off in front of the Citicorp building. Trent had a suite of offices on the seventh floor. Trent called security. The main door buzzed. Holly and he entered and took an elevator to the seventh floor. Trent held Holly's arm and escorted her to suite number 7007. He retrieved his passport key, opened his office door and switched on a light.

Holly gasped, "Trent, this is beautiful. What in the world are you Trent, a spy, a lawyer, a loan shark, a rich playboy, what? Your offices are so gorgeous. Even flowers. Imagine Trent and flowers,? they just don't mix. Yet when I look at you now Trent you don't have that 'mean old Daddy' look and, by gosh, you and the flowers do look good together. The offices suit you to a tee. You must be rich Trent to have such, such lavishness, what do you do?"

"It's a deep dark secret Holly," Trent said.

"C'mon, Trent, tell me?"

"Sorry kid, no."

"I'll give you head if you do."

"Holly, be a good girl now."

"I don't want to be a good girl," Holly said pouting. Trent picked her up in his arms as if she was a feather.

"You're strong, aren't you big guy?"

"Yeah, I'm strong. C'mon baby, we have only 40 minutes left to get you back to 'Pippins.' Let's get at it."

"Let's get at what big boy?" Holly continued.

"Okay darlin." Without ceremony, Trent sat Holly down on his office's richly finished couch and said, "Now Miss Tease, we get to the reason for this rendezvous, understand?"

"Yes Sir."

"Good, so what do you hear Holly?"

"Well Trent, all kidding aside, this is what I gather from snooping on Lenny, hearing from my cohorts and news from my stoolie. Lenny and the ivy leaguers intend to take over H&B. That's one thing. But in the meantime the ivy leaguers plan on having Lenny whacked, whacked by 'the priest' whoever he is, and then they, Charles and Stu, will take over Lenny's prostitute ring and his drug trade. Then the leaguers are going to try to establish a sizable line of credit with a bank, and guess how I found that out Trent?"

"I have no idea Holly," Trent answered. "How?"

"Well, I sexed a guy two nights ago who I found out was a Columbia business major. The trick was supposed to be only a half-hour one but when he told me he was a student at Columbia Business School I gave him extra time so I could quiz him. I told the guy he was a sensational fuck. I told him I had never enjoyed it before but that he had changed all that. I told him I had come three times when he had his big thing inside me. He was so proud. Actually Trent, he was not bad. But man, was he an egotist. When I told him he could have a free-bee because I enjoyed him so much, his chest went out to here. I said he was so good he played me out. 'Could we just sit for awhile 'til I got my breath back.' That's when he started to brag. He bragged about every thing he had ever done. Then he told me about a couple dumb guys at Columbia he chummed with who he said were planning on buying out some seedy worthless business for two or three million dollars. Can you imagine he said to me some worthless piece of shit for three million? He understood, he said, these guys were going to set-up a line of credit at their fathers' bank for financing the deal.

"Am I a good girl now, Trent?"

"Yes you are, Holly."

"Anyway Trent, I let the leaguer screw me for another half-hour. And Trent, I stole his personal business card from him. Here 'tis, all yours. His name is Robert James Coleman. His phone number is on the card, too. I thought you better have it in case you needed to, hmmm, shall we say, convince him if you had need to. Right Trent?"

"Right Holly."

"Now to go on to the scary parts. You won't believe this Trent, but the one known as 'the priest' is the person who murdered our Vito and Leroy." Holly hesitated. She was still teary about Vito and Leroy.

"Just a moment, Holly, is this priest a real Roman Catholic priest?"

"Yes, I believe so."

"Jesus H. Christ."

A few moments lapsed.

"And this priest is the dude who whacked our two buddies?"

"Yes Trent, that's right."

"Jesus H. Christ. Go on Holly."

"Well, as I said earlier, Lenny is scheduled to be the priest's next victim. Sometime next week! I don't know the day, Trent, but I know it's next week."

"Okay Sweetie, then?"

"Then Trent, it is Clark's and Polly's turn. God how I hate this, it's so frightening. Clark and Polly are the next targets of those ivy leaguers, those snot-nosed bastards. If they so much as touch one hair of Clark's head I'll kill them both with my bare hands," Holly whimpered.

Trent put his arm around her to comfort her.

"God-dam bastards," Holly sniffled.

"Anyway Trent, Stu and Chuck are their names. Oh yes, you already know that. They intend to take over H&B, change its by-laws, go public, get H&B's stock on the NYSE, sell a swack of new shares and make themselves a bundle. They even plan on buying a casino in Vegas if they can get control of H&B. Bastards."

"Anything else, Holly."

"Yeah, Just one minor detail. These leaguers intend to forge their fathers' signatures on the $3 million line they're going for."

"Fine young men," Trent muttered.

Silence.

"Trent?"

"Yes Holly."

"Will you, hold me and hug me. I am so scared. I want so bad to be back at H&B. I'm so sad. I miss everyone so very much. When do you think I can come back Trent. I hate being away." Holly cried, she was hurting.

Trent held her tight. Damn. He wished he could take her back tonight.

*　　　*　　　*

After taking a cab back to Pippins, Holly got out, threw a kiss to Trent as if he was an ordinary every day john and tucked the $600 Trent had given her into her bra. She strolled like a sex doll into the pizza joint, walked over to Lenny's booth, handed Henry, Lenny's bodyguard, the $600 bucks, bought herself some 'Clearly Canadian' and sat her butt down next to surly 'Hank's.' After she finished her refreshing non-alcoholic drink she thanked Henry for his scintillating conversation. Big Hank had not said a word to Holly, he only grunted a couple of times. She rose, then drifted out of 'Pippins' back onto the horny streets. God, how she hated this. I love H&B, she thought to herself. Will I ever get back there. Tears wanted to flow, but Holly held them back. A limo drove up. A rich looking john in the back seat beckoned her in. With disgust, but with a sexy smile on her face, Holly climbed in.

*　　　*　　　*

Trent had the cabbie let him off two blocks away from H&B's office. He watched the cab disappear before walking to the office. Trent reported everything Holly had told him to Clark. They discussed the report in detail. Their first decision was to send Billy back to Pippins Pizza so he could keep an eye on Holly and see to her safety.

"Yeah sirs, and what do I do when she's with a john?"

"Just do whatever you have to do Billy," Trent replied.

"Okay, sir, sorry I asked."

"Billy here's $500," Clark said, "for cab fare, food, whatever you need to watch over Holly."

"What about a fix if I need one, sirs?"

"Well Billy, I can't give you any of the stock we keep here under permit for two reasons. One, if you're picked up by the police and they find the drug on you, you'll be jailed for possession of a narcotic. Second, if we happened to be questioned by the police as to your 'possession' we would have to admit to supplying it to you, then H&B could lose its permit to keep drugs on its premises which it uses 'for emergency purposes.' Maybe you can't handle this assignment Billy. If you feel you can't, please say so."

"I can handle it, sirs. If I need a fix I'll buy a small dab with my own money. Is that okay?"

"I didn't hear that Billy," Clark whispered.

"Okay, I'll get Pam to get me a cab, sirs. I'm gone great masters," Billy said saluting. And off he went.

"He's such a great kid," Trent sighed, "But what a fucking flake. Here we are Clark, sending out a boy to do a man's job. He shakes, he pukes, he farts, he pisses himself and yet I have faith in him. I think he'd give his life to protect Holly. I don't lack any confidence in the young buck."

"I feel the same Trent but, man, we have to get him off that rotten stuff."

"We will Clark, we will."

"Clark, with your permission, I'm going to try to locate this hit man. The priest."

"You've got it Trent, "Clark replied, "And Trent, I pick Lana up at JFK at four o'clock tomorrow afternoon. God I miss her. And Trent she wants you to come with me so you can protect me."

"D'ya want me to go with you Clark?"

"Trent, I'm a big boy, surely you jest?"

"I'm coming with you man, no arguments."

CHAPTER 56

FATHER DONNELY DOESN'T MISS

"Let's find out when the good priest's flight arrives Chuck. We can phone La Guardia and JFK and find out arrival times. It may mean we will have to split up, one of us to La Guardia, the other to JFK if arrival times are close at both airports."

Charles phoned JFK first. He called information and found that Delta Airlines, flight number 73 from Istanbul would arrive Sunday, May 11 at 1600 hours. "Great," Charles said, "4:00 p.m., perfect."

When he called La Guardia, he found the only arrivals from Istanbul were via Heathrow in London, and the times were mid-morning and late evenings. The boys decided they would go together to JFK. They felt certain the four o'clock Delta flight would be the flight the priest would be on.

* * *

At 4:00 a.m., Sunday morning Billy Wheaton took a taxi back to H&B's office. He left 'hooker haven' only after seeing that Holly was back safely from her eighth and last trick of the night. Holly had seen Billy meandering around on the streets. She knew why he was there. Good old Trent, she thought, he's being sure I'm okay, at least between tricks. And Billy, what a sweetie! Poor kid. I know he'd die for me. When her shift ended, she strolled by Billy and whispered, "Thanks darlin' my shift's over. See you tomorrow."

"Ta ta," Billy murmured looking straight ahead.

That night, not including Trent's $600, Holly had grossed a whopping $4,000 for Lenny's enterprize. In addition, she was tipped $500. Christ, at H&B she got paid only $900 a week. But she loved H&B. She loved its directors, staff, clientele. Above all, she loved Clark. $900 bucks a week was a fortune to her as far as she was concerned compared to the filth of hooker money.

Holly went into Pippins, walked over to Lenny's booth where the rest of the girls were and plopped down beside bull-necked Henry. Henry the Grunt. "Hi, O'talkative one. How'd we do tonight?" she asked.

"You five grossed $13,450. The other five grossed $10,200. Now all of you get in the fuckin' van, we're goin' home. And 'shad-up' about the green."

"Jesus your a bundle of fun Henry," Blow-Job Katy remarked.

"Ya! I am," Henry replied.

"Hospitality Hank at your services proud maidens," Spook spoke.

"Watch you're fuckin' black-ass mouth, you black bitch," Henry warned.

"Yaaaazzzza' massser' sir," Spook said laughing.

"You fuckin' coons, you're all the same. Horny and stupid," Hank barked.

"Fuck you, you goddam kraut," Lard-Ass Amber shouted. "Leave Spook alone. Blacks are a hell of a lot nicer than whites."

"Shad-up and get in the van or I'll kick the shit out of all of you," Hank warned.

To the girls' shock, he grabbed the pre-teenager's long ponytail, slapped her face hard and dragged her into the van screaming. Once all of them were inside, he tore the child's teeny dress and panties off, took out his thick cock and tried to drive it up her slim ass. Led by Holly, they jumped on Henry's powerful back and began flailing their fists on him.

Suzanne grabbed his cock and pulled it away from the child. She gave it a hard twist with both hands. Henry yelled.

"Stop now you bunch of cunts and I'll stop," Henry hollered.

"Promise us you fucking pig," Lard-Ass screamed.

"I promise," he yelled again as Suzanne now squeezed his balls, "I promise."

"Okay, let's all be nice now," Lard-Ass continued.

The girls sat. Henry brushed himself off, sat in the van's driver seat, mumbling to himself. He turned on the ignition, slapped the van into gear and sped off to the girls' residence. The child cried. She was just 12-years old. Holly and Suzanne tried to comfort her.

* * *

It was three-thirty Sunday afternoon, May 11th, 1997 when Clark and Trent arrived at Delta's terminal at JFK airport. Clark had a valet take his car. He and Trent walked into the terminal and headed straight to the luggage area where Lana would arrive. Clark was so nervous and filled with anxiety that the back of his tongue nearly filled his throat. He almost gagged two or three times. His beautiful Lana would soon be in his arms. Mixed in with all of his other emotions for Lana, was his gloating. Gloating over the final remarks she had made to her attendees in Istanbul. Three billion people begging, borrowing or stealing one hundred equivalent US dollars each and investing the funds in H&B…300 billion US dollars…all equity funds…great living Jesus. No private industry in the world would have such a formidable equity base.

"Hey Clark, where-ya at?" Trent asked smiling.

"Aahhh, Trent, miles away on a desert island alone with Lana," Clark answered.

"Hold it Clark, don't move. Stay right where you are. For shit sake if I don't see those two ivy leaguers. I see them over your shoulder. Yeah it's them all right. Charles and Stu, stay still Clark. I don't want them to spot me. Christ, they're cummin' our way. Just move a little to your left Clark 'til I tell you to stop. You'll be hiding me from them—glad you're six-five and I'm only six-one. That's it Clark, they're only about 30 feet from us now. Keep talking and be cool.

"Okay, they've stopped, pheeu! Let's you and I mosey along now over to the other side of the carousel. I'll tell you when to stop Clark. I want to have a clear view of them. I might have to shoot them. They're in shirtsleeves, so I don't think they're packin heavy. That's good Clark, stop right there."

"Maybe I should just go over there and break their bloody arms, Trent."

"No no," Trent said.

"What if they are going to try to kidnap Lana, or kill her here on the spot, or…?"

"Clark, they won't try to gun her down, not here in front of all these people. No, they would be risking everything by doing that. But they might be here going for the kidnap. Turn around Clark and keep talking to me and I'll point them out to you." Clark turned until he was facing Charles and Stu. "Yeah, I see them Trent, short sleeve green shirt on one, white short sleeve shirt on the other, both wearing white golf shorts. I've got 'em."

"Good," Trent said, "Now lay five on me and then stroll over toward them. Try to get in listening distance of them. When you spot Lana, go to her fast. I'll take care of the lions. I've gotta' find out what they're doing here. Clark, the monitor shows Lana's flight has landed. She'll be here in about 20 minutes."

Clark ambled over towards Charles and Stu. He picked at his fingernails. He stopped about five feet from them. He listened to what they were saying.

"Yeah, we'll know whether our guy is on the flight in a few minutes. Are you sure he'll be in his priest garb, Stu?" Charles asked.

"Yeah, I'm sure!"

"He's about six-two, medium build, handsome, a bit of a scar over his right eye, pale complexion, gentlemanly looking? Right dude?"

"You got it."

"A fucking priest hitman. What next?"

"Quiet Chuck, for Christ's sake."

"Sorrreeey."

"I'll be damned," Clark thought, "it's the ruddy priest they're meeting, Father Donnely. Coming in from Istanbul. 'The hit man.' My God, that's the priest who took a couple of shots at Lana last Monday. The one she floored with her 'rubber shot' gun. Lana hurry, hurry baby, get here. There's no extra police buzzing around, so there can't have been any problem on the plane. But what if that sacrilegious bastard's got to her, with a gun in her back?"

* * *

"Yeah Chuck, Lenny first, Clark second, Polly third. Yeah, all of them sometime next week, now quiet."

Clark heard that comment. "So, all three of us next week. Brazen pricks those two."

Disembarkees from Delta flight #73 began to stream through the doors coming from customs. Clark left the ivy leaguers and rushed towards custom's doors. To Clark, the passing of seconds took hours. "Where are you Lana, where in heaven's name are you? Hurry Baby hurry."

Clark saw the huge shoulders of a big man backing out of the custom's door. He was making the way out for someone. He stood still, forcing passengers to walk around his huge body. He glanced to his side.

"Francois," Clark called out recognizing Lana's bodyguard. Francois didn't hear Clark's call through the hub-bub. Clark bulled his way through the oncoming wave of passengers. He got to Francois' side. Francois smiled at Clark. Clark saw Lana surrounded by admirers. In behind the admirers was the unmistakable face of the priest.

A shot like explosion erupted in customs.

People dropped in their tracks. Screams came from everywhere. The only ones left standing were Lana, Clark, Francois, who grabbed Lana, and the priest.

The priest turned around facing where the din came from.

"Sorry everyone. Sorry. My goof. Nothing to worry about," shouted a workman atop a hydraulic lift some 30 feet up near the ceiling. "I just dropped a big gas filled light globe. They make one hellova' racket when they're dropped. All's okay, I promise you."

Slowly everyone got to their feet, some remained skeptical. In a few minutes everything was back to normal. The snarling crowd went back to its snarling.

Francois let Lana go to Clark. Clark held her but his eyes never left the priest. Lana kissed Clark's chin. She knew the priest was there. Why is Clark being so strange about him? Lana had seen him on the aircraft. As a matter of fact, Lana and the priest had a brief visit during the flight. They had exchanged cards. Lana had promised to visit him. Lana was not one bit afraid of the priest. Lana in fact was not afraid of anyone or anything. Lana was the very essence of cool. Lana knew it was Father Donnely, the same man who had shot at her twice while she was behind the podium last Monday.

Clark held Lana around her waist. He kept his eyes on everybody, Lana's admirers, the press, radio, TV as well as plain ordinary everyday nosy gawkers. All were oblivious of her comfort. They all pushed to get nearer to her. Francois was a great bodyguard. Without heed, he manhandled those who came 'too close' to his charge. Clark and Lana had little room to move in the huge crowd but still they were able to make some progress toward their carousel.

In the meantime, Trent was trying to conjure up the most powerful ESP message he could in an attempt to get Clark's attention. By God he did it. Clark's eyes met Trent's. Trent motioned he would try to get near Charles and Stu. Clark understood. Clark could no longer restrain himself, he kissed Lana on her lips. Lana reciprocated. The crowd howled its appreciation. Now Francois, followed by Lana and Clark, bulled his way through the crowd to the carousel. Clark and Francois shielded Lana from the mobs of people both front and back. Polite, ladylike and smiling Lana tried to answer at least some of the tirade of questions fired at her.

The airport's security personnel had now broken through the myriad of people and had gotten to Lana. With Lana's permission, security escorted her and Clark to Delta's first class lounge. Here she awaited Francois and her luggage. Clark excused himself without giving Lana a reason. He rushed back to where Charles and Stu should be. He spotted them. They were talking to the priest. Just to the right of the threesome, his back to them stood Trent. Clark felt certain Charles and Stuart had not seen him with Lana. He walked toward them.

* * *

Stu was the first to recognize the priest. Both he and Charles had spotted Father Donnely when the big mother who was guarding someone had backed through custom's door. They wondered who the prima donna was getting all the attention.

"Christ, wasn't that a shot Stu?" Charles yelled.

"Yeah, hit the deck man."

Down they went. They looked through the open custom's door where the sound had come from. There they saw four people still standing, two big dudes, a breathtaking, beautiful broad and the nonchalant priest. Then they heard the workman's voice. "Fuckin' false alarm," Chuck whispered.

"Yeah, and you know who that broad is, Stu?" Chuck asked.

"Course I do. It's that day dreaming commie, Dr. Lana Masters. Gorgeous broad! Imagine a night in the Ukraine with her. She's been on

TV the last few days. Good speaker, sacrilegious broad, great tits and glorious ass! C'mon let's get over to the priest and introduce ourselves."

"Hello Father," Charles said, "We are very sorry to interrupt you after your long flight from Istanbul. But we have heard so much about you from your clergy it was imperative for us to come meet you and greet you, and to offer you a ride back to your parish. We are in dire need of your help Father. We would be so obliged to you if you would agree to help us. Hallelujah, great sire, we have seen the light.

"Yes Father," Stu said, "One of your most ardent followers has made us see the light. Praise the Lord Father, yes Father, the gifted healer himself, Lenny Chimos. We have large sums of money to donate to your most worthy "causes" sir. We would be so indebted to you if you permitted us to drive you to your home. I have an envelope here containing several pieces of testimonial paper which shows our propitious intent. Please take it Father."

The priest accepted the envelope graciously. He peered inside it and saw many U.S. $20's, $50's and $100's. With a pious smile on his face, he tucked the envelope into his robe. He raised his hands and placed one on each of the student's heads intoning, "Gentlemen, I am pleased you have found the errors of your ways. God welcomes you into his domain of righteousness. Bless you my sons, and may the good Lord keep you safe and on the path of morality." He took his hands off each of the students heads and said, "I would be honored to have you drive me to my home. You seem to be such nice lads. Perhaps you would be kind enough to assist me with my luggage?"

"Of course we will help you with your luggage Father, please, lead the way," Charles offered.

"Thank you my sons," the priest countered.

*　　*　　*

Clark and Trent overheard much of the conversation between the priest and the ivy leaguers. Someone was going to be fingered as the first one on the hit list. It seemed obvious to them that 'the first hittee' would be the herdsman, Lenny, The Meat Vendor, Chimos. They saw Charles and Stu join the priest as he made his way to the carousel.

Too, they saw Francois gathering up Lana's luggage. They knew Francois would take the luggage to Delta's lounge.

"We've overheard enough now Trent, don't you think? We better get out of here before those lions recognize us."

"Yeah Clark, we better get back to Lana. She's going to be wondering what's going on out here."

Lana had been waiting patiently. She was certain whatever Clark was doing, it would have to do with Father Donnely. She brightened the moment she saw Clark enter the lounge.

My, he's so damn handsome, and he's such a good man too. I'm one lucky woman to have this great guy, Lana thought.

She jumped up to greet him. She was made even happier when she saw Trent was with him. After fussing over Clark, Lana hugged and kissed Trent.

* * *

Stu gave the valet his card for his car plus a $5 tip.

Soon the three-some where on their way to West 52nd Street and Tenth Avenue in Manhattan.

"Okay, now that we have introduced ourselves gentlemen, what is it I can do for you?" the priest asked.

"Well, first we would like you to peruse the contents of the envelope we gave you," Charles replied.

"Thank you, I shall," Father Donnely retrieved the envelope, took out its contents and counted out $15 thousand dollars.

"Mmmmmm, quite a tidy sum lads. Are these moneys being offered me as a penance for your past indiscretions? If they are laddie-bucks, just carry on with your indiscretions and, from time to time, have them forgiven by me with offerings much the same as these," the priest said waving the bills in front of Charles and Stu's noses.

"Yeah, I bet," Stu said with a notable twinge of sarcasm in his voice.

"Father, we have heard about your fame as a whacker," Charles explained, "We have three requests of you. Three hits as a matter of fact."

"Do you now, boys?" the priest questioned.

"Yes," Chuck replied.

"And where, pray tell, did you hear of these thrilling exploits I have supposed to have done?"

"From Lenny Chimos. We understand you whacked a couple of directors of H&B Financial & Poors just last week, when you were supposedly in Istanbul. You did this killing as a kind of revenge or something for a coupla' former directors."

"My, you boys do get around."

"Perhaps you would be kind enough to do these three jobs for us Father?"

"You see, there's $21,000 more in it for you, and in any denomination you prefer I might add, when you have completed all three tasks. The total funds you would receive for your work would be $36,000. That's $12,000 per whack. Does this interest you Father?"

"Well boys, let me put it this way. You are beginning to tickle my fancy. But Charles and Stuart, you both must realize I do not take on any such tasks until I am made privy to certain things."

"We understand, Sir."

"All right Stuart, you can stop the car in front of that white stucco house. I own it." Stuart stopped the car moments later. All three got out of the car. Charles and Stu carried in the priest's luggage for which they were thanked. Once inside the house, Father Donnely had the two boys sit in his tidy front room. The house was quite delightful. It was decorated as one might expect of a man of the cloth with numerous reminders of Christendom, yet not overwhelming. The furniture was exquisite French Provincial, chesterfield, love seat, two comfy chairs, coffee table, end tables, lamp tables. The wide picture window had as its cover white pleated sheers, while its drapery was light muted gold velvet which stretched from wall to wall. The room was two steps down from the tiled vestibule. The living room's hardwood floor was covered in part with a Persian rug. In all, the room was quite splendid.

Father Donnely took his luggage to his bedroom. He freshened up, donned a pair of Dockers as well as a black shirt with a priest's collar. He wore slippers. He was quite a handsome gentleman. Before seating himself he asked his two guests if they cared for a drink. They declined.

"All right boys, these are the things I must know," laughing at the absurdity of the first question, "The names of the three eliminees?"

"Yes, Father, now please don't be too shocked when I name the first one on the list," Charles said.

"Good grief, not the Pope dear lads?" Reverend Donnely remarked laughing.

"No sir, not the Pope," Charles chuckled, "Lenny Chimos."

"Lenny Chimos?" the priest gasped.

"Yes, Lenny Chimos," Charles repeated.

"Well bless my soul boys. Why my good client Lenny? I doubt you are aware of the fact he's an excellent provider for both me and my flock" the priest said.

"Yes, we know he is good to you father," Stu remarked.

"Well then?"

"Well, on poor Lenny's demise we, good fellows that we are, will take over Lenny's businesses."

"I see," said the good Father, "And…"

"And, we will expand Lenny's enterprises for the good of all of us," Stu said.

"And gentlemen, what about my regular Saturday afternoon tidbit. Are you aware of Lenny's thoughtful gratuitous 12-year-olds he lavishes on me weekly?"

"Indeed we are sir. It is our intent to expand on this 'perk' if it so pleases you sir."

"Thank you lads. You are most thoughtful. Now when would you wish this service rendered?" Father Donnely asked.

"Let's cut the bullshit speechifying, Father Donnely and Charles. We know what we are planning to do is not fucking kosher. No later than Wednesday, May 14th."

"Dear me Stuart, I do not, and I repeat do not abide by swearing. Most particularly that dreadful 'F' word. Nor do I abide by taking the Lord's name in vain. However, sir, Wednesday next will be just fine."

"I do apologize to you on Stuart's behalf Father Donnely," Charles said. "He can be crude and obnoxious sometimes."

"Fuck you," Stu mumbled.

The priest pretended not to hear Stu's mumbling.

"Then lads, who is the next after poor Lenny, pray tell?"

"It is a gentleman who's name is Clark St. James," Charles replied. "He is one of 'the' powers behind H&B Financial & Poors Inc. H&B is a very wealthy organization owned and controlled by a bunch of seedy vagabonds, a bunch of useless, godless wretches."

"Yes I know of the organization. I have heard of its wealth. I do believe I have seen this Mr. St. James, Yes indeed I have. Now gentlemen, why him?"

"Well Father, Stuart and I wish to take over H&B and then run it in a more capitalistic manner. We want to have H&B pay its dividends on a regular basis to its shareholders just as it does now. But we want to obtain the controlling interest in the company by acquiring most of its outstanding shares at a dollar or two each. Once we have controlling interest in the firm we will list it on the New York stock exchange. Then, sir, we will offer H&B's shares to the public at a steal of $100 each.

We believe our plan is a sound one Father, but two people stand in our way before we can bring the scheme to fruition. One is of course Clark St. James. The other is that outrageous glamorous commie, the pussy of all pussies, Dr. Lana Masters."

"Verrrry interesting. Dr. Lana Masters you say? My! My! My! Dr. Lana Masters, very, very interesting! Dear lads, her extermination is exotic to think on to say the least. I will be more than delighted, let's say ecstatic to send the good doctor to hell," the priest verbalized wringing his hands in delectation.

"Just one catch to the execution of sweet Lana Masters Father," Charles said, "Both Stu and I want to play all manner of naughties with her while she is held captive by you before you kill her."

"Splendid idea chaps, I believe I would enjoy partaking in a little hanky-panky with her myself. She is a dazzler. She is a woman who is equally engrossing whether she is walking t'ord you, or walking away from you. Yes lads, she must be ravished as she quite deserves. Yes, this hybrid female species must be scourged by us in the name of everything that is Holy. I am so pleased Charles and Stuart you have given heed to removal from our wonderful world this debauched harlot. Now gentlemen, have you determined an execution date for Clark St. James and our dearest Lana?"

"Yes Father, as to Clark St. James, we should like his life to end on Monday, May 19th next. And as for Lana Masters, we would like us to spend this coming weekend with her, fucking her brainless, you know sir, coming as often as we can with her. Doing any damn thing we choose with her. We don't even have to feed her, we can supply her with all the nutrients she needs. When she gets hungry, she simply has to feed on our big juicy cocks." Stu said.

The good priest covered his ears and closed his eyes mortified.

"I realize how necessary it is to defile this godless witch, to, to exorcise this pitiful conjurer's evilness, to ream out her devilish soul with the seduction tools given us by our maker, but good gracious Stuart, must you be so crude?"

"Your fuckin' right I must you Quisling," Stuart barked.

"Shut up, Stu. What are you trying to prove man? We're all shooting for the same goal. Why traumatize Father Donnely with your filthy mouth? "Cool it."

"Okay, okay, sorry Father."

Casting hate filled eyes into Stuart's sneering eyes, the priest said solemnly, "Your tasks shall be carried out with dispatch. You will hear about Lenny's and Clark's demise through the regular media, not through me. I will insist on $7,000 be paid to me following the media coverage. The payments made by you will be in 70 one hundred US dollar bills. No thousands! One of you will deliver the first $7,000 to me in person in the men's wear washroom in Bloomingdales precisely at two o'clock next Thursday afternoon. Do you understand me gentlemen? Do not try to swindle me or lie to me, cheat me, rat on me or in any way provoke me. If you try any skullduggery whatsoever, I shall see to it that each of you will suffer. And gentlemen, I mean suffer. I warn you now gentlemen, from this moment on your very hides are mine. I am exhausted now, so I bid you both farewell. Please leave."

Shocked, Charles and Stuart stood, looked at the priest who, without doubt, had them spellbound and under his control. The priest had the hellish look of Satan in his eyes. Beside the priest's countenance, Lucifer would look like little Lord Fauntleroy. This motherfucker looked mean.

Charles and Stuart drove back to their university subdued. Charles' only comment was, "Well Stu, you cranky son of a bitch, we've now got the old ball rolling." Stu only nodded his head in agreement.

* * *

Lenny never felt a thing. His driver had dropped him off in front of Pippins. Lenny had a sweet thing holding onto his arm, his name was

Ocelet. Ocelet screamed when Lenny dropped. The only sound heard on the street was the street's normal hub-bub, taxis, people's foot steps, the constant hum of people chattering, the endless throngs of people and their noises. No gun shot or shots. It was 8:30 p.m. May 14th, 1997. Lenny had gotten out on the street side of his limo and had walked around the back of the car to the sidewalk. His driver had come around the front of the car and opened the rear door to let the gorgeous, mini-skirted transvestite out on the sidewalk. The driver said his 'good nights' to Lenny and Ocelet, returned to the car and had driven off. Lenny stood with his back to Pippins facing the street, his man-girl clutching his arm when, splat, a clean hole appeared in the middle of Lenny's forehead while the back of his head blew away in pieces. Lenny dropped to the sidewalk while the back of his skull, his parietal lobes, occipital lobe, temporal lobes, cortex, skin, hair and shit flew wildly in the air. Most of the stuff landed on many hungry pizza eaters pizzas' who were standing or sitting behind Lenny munching on their favorite Italian guck. Christ, Lenny's splattered disassembled brain blended in well with all the other pizza toppings. This topping, however, did not titillate many of the fast fooders. In fact it had quite the opposite effect. Many, discourteously disgorged the contents of their repast without penitence

* * *

Lenny was buried at Saint Angelica Catholic Church Friday, May 16th, 1997. Father Donnely presided. His service was reverent. Amen.

Father Donnely received unnoticed his 70 one-hundred-dollar bills (US) from Charles on May 15th, 2:00 p.m. in the men's wear washroom in Bloomingdales.

CHAPTER 57

LANA'S TWENTY-THIRD BIRTHDAY

It was seven-thirty on the evening of October 29th, 1990. Lana's 23rd birthday. She was putting the finishing touches on her already stunning face. Her attire was not lavish nor was it ostentatious. Yet her appearance was overwhelming. She wore a close fitting golden dress sprinkled with patterns of non-obtrusive scintilla. The dress delivered a hint of sex by baring just the top of her tanned breasts. The dress's slender straps left open an unobstructed view of her lovely shoulders and back.

She was awaiting the presence of Franklin Foster. This night was going to be the night that would send Dr. Lana Masters into the depths of hell.

CHAPTER 58

LANA'S TWENTY-THIRD BIRTHDAY PARTY

Franklin Foster et al.

Her doorbell rang.

When Lana opened the door there Franklin stood, smiling and looking very handsome dressed in a light tan woolen suit. He looked so mature, so sophisticated since she last saw him three years ago. They embraced. He smelled of Ralph Lauren's Polo. He was bigger but not fatter. He looked to be physically fit. Lana had read about his meteoric rise in diplomacy. His demeanor underscored the perfect job fit. Franklin was not a person where an employer fits a job to suit the person, no Franklin's personality, abilities and training instead were suited for the requirements of the job. Nor was his ego 'stressed-out' by the lengthy hours of work he gave to his job. Quite the opposite, his ego appeared to feed well on his tough intricate time-consuming workloads.

Franklin entered Lana's lavish condominium. They exchanged light kisses. Lana, because of her anxiety to see how Franklin's presence would affect her after three years without seeing him, had not taken notice of the gentleman who accompanied him. After a few polite words and another hug and kiss, Franklin introduced his companion to Lana, "Lana I should like you to meet my cousin from Los Angeles, Jay Foster." Lana and Jay recognized one another immediately. Both looked shocked. Lana had Franklin and Jay make themselves comfortable while she poured drinks.

Lana returned, sat, toyed with her drink for a moment then said, "We've met before, haven't we Jay?"

"Yes, we have. Small world," he sneered turning to Franklin. The pompous ass remarked, "Franky baby, this here broad kneed me in the crotch a couple months ago after I had offered her a weekend of sport in my home in Malibu. We were at Club 24 in LA when she did it to me. Right Ms. Masters?"

"Whatever you say Mr. Foster. But why don't you tell Franklin the whole story sir?" Lana said.

"It's not worth my time baby. So you're the infamous commie, Dr. full of shit Lana Masters. Ain't that something?"

"You've got it big shot."

"Hold it Jay, what's this all about?" Franklin asked.

"She kneed me. Caught me by surprise. That's it."

Lana laughed hypocritically.

"Fuck you Dr. Commie."

Lana punctured his supercilious face with her compelling eyes. Good ole Jay's brain was not garbled by drugs this time. Lana's piercing stare rocketed through him. Jay faltered for a moment then turned to face Franklin.

"Franky baby, this broad's a hoodoo. Look at her fuckin' eyes. Let's get the hell outta here. She gives me the creeps."

"Don't worry about Lana, Jay, I've known her for years and she's a great person."

"Like hell, Franky, she's a stinkin' commie."

"No she isn't Jay."

"I thought we were cumin' here for some fun tonight Franky? A few drinks then 'whammo' but with this broad?"

Lana looked surprised. She had understood when Franklin had called her about this date just she and Franklin were going out to dine, then they were to return to her condo to spend the night together.

"What's he talking about, Franklin, a few drinks and then whammo? What about our date?"

"Nothing really, Lana. Jays just a loud mouth," Franklin said winking at Jay.

"Yeah I'm just a loudmouth Dr. Commie."

"Level with me, Franklin, or Jay goes."

"Lana, I said he's just a loudmouth, nothing serious."

"Why is he here anyway Franklin? I thought tonight was to be our night together alone?"

"I lied Lana."

"You lied, why for chrissake?"

"Because I can't get you off my mind and it's beginning to get to me. I can't think straight when you're on my mind. It's even beginning to affect my job. I know I can't have you so I reason with myself, am I going to let my job suffer because of Lana Jean Masters? A job I love, where the sky's the limit for me. Am I going to be smart, you know, intelligent about this whole thing and remove you from my mind? What better way than by making you someone whom I loathe. Someone whom I find disgusting! Disgust, Lana Jean, so any memory I have of you will be just that, disgusting. Or do I mope along year after year thinking of you as a forbidden treasure. So Lana Jean I have chosen disgust. And who better to assist me in this matter than my disgusting cousin Jay?"

Lana sat for a moment eyeing both Franklin and Jay. Both men rose and strolled over to Lana's well stocked bar. They poured themselves doubles. They chatted about Lana's lovely condo and how it would suit their evening's intent. They ignored Lana.

Lana was a fearless woman, but she wasn't foolish about it. She knew when she was into something over her head. She knew she wasn't the bionic woman who graced television several years ago. Lana was a scrapper, but no bionic woman. Franklin's a big strong man. No way can I handle him. And Jay, I imagine he's a wild man. And of course, my damn handgun is in my purse in the hall closet, damn it. I've got to think of something. But what in hell has happened to my long time sweetheart Franklin? He didn't smell of liquor when we kissed, so he's not drunk. I don't know if he's doped up on coke or something? He's never used drugs when we were together before. I'm sure he means what he says about doing disgusting things with me. He didn't imply killing me, so, what is his intent, is it to disfigure me?

"Franklin, are you serious? Good Lord, we've been friends and lovers for years, what in hell are you talking about?" Lana asked as she eyed him.

"Just what I said Lana."

"With no remorse?"

"No remorse Lana, because I have taken some junk which will keep my mind free of remorse, and darling, keep me from falling under the spell of your eyes.

"And what about later when your mind clears?"

"Well babe, my last memory of you tonight will be so repulsive it will last forever. Yeah Lana baby, fixed in my subliminal 'til I die."

"Will it not trouble you to think about my Mom and Dad and my brothers and sister after whatever you are intending to do to me?"

"I'll force my memory of them to fade."

The doorbell rang.

"Sit Lana, I'll get it." Jay said.

"Like fuck you will you gutless asshole," Lana snapped. She rose to go to the door. Franklin rose too, and intercepted her. He put his strong arms around her and squeezed her to him. She fought like a tiger and managed to loosen herself just as Jay opened the door.

"Welcome my friends," Jay said, "c'mon in. You're in for one big blast tonight. Yeah good buddies, and ladies come right in." Franklin covered Lana's mouth so she couldn't scream.

Lana was dumbfounded. Entering her condominium were her sister Margaret, Margaret's lover Christeen, three husky young men and a tethered male German Shepherd dog.

Jay closed, locked and bolted the door. Margaret and Christeen rushed to Lana, Margaret crying and Christeen cursing at the three husky young men. The three girls hugged. "Bastards," Christeen bellowed.

"This," Jay said rubbing his hands, "is going to be the summer and winter Olympics of sex all in one. I'll bet any mother here the dog wins the gold going away."

CHAPTER 59

THE TWENTY-THIRD BIRTHDAY RAPE

Warning! Orgies. Rupulsed, Lana becomes a Manhattan Bag Lady.

Lana sat up on the bales and looked down at her guest. It was now 6:15 a.m. She thought back on that dreadful night. No question, it was sheer madness. She was just 23 at the time.

"One thing is certain," she said to her sleeping, chewed up guest, "Franklin sure as hell disgusted me. And good old Jay, he was right on when he said the German Shepherd would run away with the gold medals. The men sucked."

Lana permitted her mind to think back on the bloody, unbelievable sexual atrocities which 'graced' her 23rd birthday. How proud she was of Margaret for the grit she displayed throughout the unspeakable sex inflicted on her during the night by the five men. Lana had whispered to Margaret to, "Stay loose, be docile. Let the men perform their rape uninhibited. As a physician you know if you tighten up your muscles when these fuckers enter you, you will end up a bloody mess, so stay loose. Remember sis, I'll get these dudes, they'll pay for this." Lana, at this time did not know a week from now she would meet a man who would become her devoted mercenary. Trent Logan. A man no one with a brain in his head would cross. When riled Trent was a brute. Too, Trent was a man of loyalty. He was one hellova find for Lana.

When Jay hollered out, "Let the sex begin," things got into motion. Margaret screamed when two of the young husky men entered her. Her whimpering excited the two men. They became frenzied. Neither had experienced sex with a gorgeous six-footer before. When they found out Margaret and Christeen were gay lovers, big beautiful gay lovers, Jay and his three young huskies found this fact to be of unparalleled ecstasy.

Christeen, who came close to crying and begging for mercy on a few occasions, hung in there. She was tough. At one point she hammered Jay with a walloping punch to his nose spraying blood every which way. Jay sat, mewled like a spoiled brat as he held his bruised and bloodied nose. Two of his buddies pinned Christeen's arms. Jay's eye for an eye and tooth for a tooth became a thing of revulsion. Just what Franklin wanted, disgusting revulsion of women. Jay violated Christeen's body every way possible. Christeen whimpered but held back tears.

Lana was the main target of assault by Franklin, his 'merry men' and the German Shepherd. Lana could still see the anguished faces of Margaret and Christeen as they were forced to watch the disgusting things being done to her. Margaret had the horrible feeling she would shoot her sister if she had a gun. Such a killing would be a merciful one. No one, Margaret thought, could stand up to the gross iniquities being brought upon her sister by these monsters. Better dead than this wicked disparagement. Margaret was certain Lana's mind would be scarred for life by the unthinkable things being done to her. But Lana's mind was impervious to any repulsiveness when her inner being took command. Lana never quavered. She never cried out. Her brain had such inscrutable control over her ego that she could keep both pain and shame at minimal thresholds.

Lana knew the object of Franklin's exercise was to exorcise Lana from his brain through disgust. Lana, unbeknownst to her tormentors, put on an 'Oscar' performance in making certain parts of her anatomy reeked with disgust.

She knew the men were weakening. The dog had become a non-entity several hours ago. He just lay in a corner watching his superior brained males rollicking and sexing the females whom, in his dog mind, were in heat. Quite a display, the dog thought, as he watched the males gang-up on one female. Odd too, the German Shepherd thought, to see the males pump their 'doggy dicks' with their front paws then squirt whitish milk like stuff out of the ends of their 'doggy dicks' all over the females, the carpets, chairs, everything. Once too, he noted the three females licked each other's hidden secrets. Doggies do this, too. But when doggies finish they spray on things to 'mark the spot.' The females didn't.

All night long the fearsome sex storm raged. At about 5:00 a.m. the men's penis' would no longer react.

Each of the men during the long session took turns at taking both stills and action video camera shots at the 'swishing of the pricks' as Jay named the night's activities. But by 5:00 a.m., the men were spent.

Lana knew the men were spent. Other than for a fair amount of scrapes, bruises, bleeding orifices as well as the feeling of degradation by Maggie and Christeen (who had put on a stunning performance of gay love), the girls were in a more active state than the fucked out men. Maggie and Christeen emulated everything Lana did. Lana lay on her back, legs spread apart unladylike displaying the mess the men had made of her vulva and anus. Margaret and Christeen followed suit. To a new set of suitors this sight would have been heaven on earth, but to the sex spent macho men and in particular Franklin the sight was nauseating. Disgusting. The men started to clothe themselves, tidy up a bit, and gather up their paraphernalia, including the now sleeping German Shepherd dog.

"That has done it for me Lana Jean Masters. You are no different than any other female. You look revolting. Come all over you. Female musk.

Your cunt smells like crank case oil. You look pathetic. Like a fucking cow. I'm glad I did this. Shit lady, after seeing you like this and smelling the three of you as you are I may just become chaste, or maybe gay. Anyway bitch, I'm glad I won't want to be a part of you anymore. You are out of my mind, gone, kaput, toast. Goodbye you smelly, oily, cocksucker. C'mon guys, let's go."

Just as Franklin was about to step out the door, Lana called out to him. "Be advised, Franky baby, the dog was better than all of you he-men. Yeah, he was the gold medalist. And you "jerks", you haven't seen the last of me yet. And, Franky baby, be advised the whole stinking escapade has been videotaped by my hidden cameras from the time you and Jay first stepped through my door. The film through automation has been sent already to my private offices. Have a nice night."

Tears welled up in Franklin's eyes. Despite his so-called disgust, he knew he could never forget Lana.

Lana was devastated by the night's obscenities, not just for herself but for Margaret and Christeen. She was shocked at Franklin's behavior. What happened to their love? Was his mind warped from being convinced I would never be a permanent part of his life? Goodness, before this happened I still had strong feelings for the guy. While she was now, as always, in complete control of her faculties, her faculties were now informed by her ego that she had had it with this thing called love.

As she lay there alongside her sister and Christeen she decided she would exit her present way of life. She would exit her life of preaching and teaching. The thought of men's and women's maneuverings, skulking, fraternizing, peeping, cheating, patronizing, sucking up, gossiping, oblique hinting and disparaging double meaning scuttlebutting of others sickened her. She'd hit the skids. Yes, she would find out how those people she fought for lived. Yeah, but only on her terms. Franklin's antics that night sewed up Lana's decision. Yes, his sick antics was all it took to push Lana off the edge of conventionality into the maelstrom of deprivation.

Lana's remorse and sorrow over the night's sadism was for Margaret and Christeen. Why did Franklin have to include them? They had nothing to do with Franklin's hang-up about Lana. "The s.o.b." She wondered why he hadn't gotten her alone, he and his merry men? Busted her up maybe. "Franky baby, don't ever show up in front of me again. If you do you'll die.

She got up. Christeen got up. Margaret wiggled into a fetal position. She sobbed and shook—she was traumatized. Lana and Christeen lifted her and carried her to a bed and covered her. Lana, who had completed her medical degree, and Christeen, who like Margaret had another year of study to complete before beginning their internship, knew how to treat Margaret's trauma. Margaret was a strong person, a tough prairie girl, a bright girl, all of which were reasons why she should make a quick recovery from her trauma. But Lana could not in the wildest of her imaginations, dream-up such cowardice and inhumanity by such a sweet guy as Franklin. And his pals, what fucking planet were they from? The dog, she thought, was nowhere near as 'filthy' as these bastards.

By eight o'clock that evening Lana's front room had been scoured clean. Christeen and she had showered at least a half a dozen times. Margaret, who finally shrugged off her shock, had hardly left the shower.

Now they were seated in Lana's library drinking tea. The conversation between them was sparse until Lana decided to liven things up. She didn't feel like livening things up, but she knew in order to get Maggie and Chrissy at least part way back to normality she would have to do something.

"Now girls, that was an orgy. A full-fledged sock-it-to 'em drag em out orgy.' We'll never need lectures on that bleeding topic. Between the five men I'll bet they spewed out a pound of semen in and on us chicks. Great men each of them wouldn't you say?"

"Yeah. They remind me of a bouquet of torn assholes," Christeen said. Christeen had taken nearly as much abuse as Lana had because of the haymaker she had landed on Jay's nose. One of her eyes was swollen shut where Jay had hit her when her arms were pinned by two of the 'huskies.'

Sneering, Christeen said, "Lana you and I must have broken some kind of record when we diddled five of the guys at one time. When I saw you do it I thought, now that is pure sagacious salaciousness. Under any other circumstances, say for Ripley's Believe It or Not, or as a "show-stopper" in Vegas, that manipulation would be hard to beat. It would deserve and get a standing ovation in Vegas I'm sure. While I wasn't jealous of your feat, it did cross my mind whether or not I could perform it so ably as you? Well, as you know, I was put to the test by Franklin and his buddies and, by damn, if I didn't pull it off—no pun intended. So Lana, as the law society members would put it, we shared our wizardry *pari passu*, right?"

"Right Christeen."

Margaret gagged.

"Sorry," Christeen apologized

"Please girls, forget about the whole ordeal. Let's not talk about it ever again." Margaret begged.

"Margaret you should know better than that. You can't just leave it without discussion. Damn it sister, if you don't get it out in the open, air it out, it will fester in your mind for years."

"Yes Lana, I suppose you're right"

"Then Maggie, get on with it. Blurt the whole sordid affair out. Cleanse your mind of the ordeal."

Margaret cleansed her mind all right. First, she tore into men in general, then ripped Franklin and his fornicators into shreds. She cried, cursed, shrieked and stomped around and in and out of Lana's library.

Lana and Christeen egged her on. Margaret's language became so foul even Lana was shocked from time-to-time.

Euphemistically Margaret's most profound description of the five fornicators was:

Five
Useless
Cocksucking
Knaves
Perverted
Orgasm
Tit
Squeesers

Christeen and Lana laughed. Margaret was unstoppable. Lana's recommended therapy had begun to work its wonders.

The next morning Margaret, still shaken, was more like her old self. Christeen was taking the abasement in stride. Lana was pissed off with the world.

The three of them decided they would dress up in the most suggestive manner possible. They would stroll up and down Fifth Avenue, Madison Avenue, Park Avenue and the Avenue of the Americas teasing and showing off their towering exquisite bodies to all the rotten males who were marching the busy Manhattan streets. They did. The girls stunned everyone, their stylish hats, tight knit red sweaters which displayed their plentiful bosoms, tight white mini skirts which left little to anyone's imagination, bare tanned legs that never ended and six-inch spikes which elongated their normal height to six-foot-seven. Like Moses and the Red Sea, the heavy-laden streets parted to let these Amazon beauties through. These girls were well above Bo's ten. They skyrocketed well into the hundreds. Their feet killed, but it was worth it. The torrid trio reduced subjunctive males from prince charmings to stupefied bozos.

"Let the bastards drool," Margaret said.

Manhattan was dazzled as never before. These femmes smoldered.

* * *

Lana would dress normally on very few occasions over the next three years. On her walk with Margaret and Christeen that morning she spied a bag lady. A bag lady who was swathed in all manner of clothes! She wore rubber boots. She pushed a grocery cart, which carried all her worldly goods. The bag lady's pock marked face showed little emotion. Here was Lana's answer to this fucking jungle of a world. Become a bag lady. Damn right, enter the murky depths of degradation occupied by scumbags. Learn first hand their day to day proclivities. Eat their food, sleep in their rat infested quarters and share their lice. Shit it would be one hellov'n experience.

* * *

The next day Margaret and Christeen boarded a plane for Rochester New York. It was there where they were to complete their final year of medicine at the Rochester School of Medicine. Both were taking obstetrics and depending on the degree of success they had in their final year at the university, they would commence their internship in New York's General Hospital.

* * *

Lana became a bag lady. A rich bag lady!

CHAPTER 60
LANA'S QUESTIONS

The abrupt end to Franklin and Lana's long on and off courtship festered in Lana's mind. What caused him to change from a real nice guy to a brutal s.o.b. At one time she had loved Franklin. They were so compatible. Now she deplored him. But should she deplore him? Was he sick? She had met his parents on a number of occasions. She found them to be gracious and loving. She knew Franklin's grandfather Charles at age five together with his mother and sister had moved to New York from Los Angeles in 1918. Grandad Charles was an academic. He had taught in a small college in Queens from 1939 to 1976. Franklin's father Lawrence was born in 1939. He had attended N.Y.U. and had graduated with his L.L.B in 1962. Franklin was born in June 1963. Everything appeared normal. No family break-ups. No apparent family dysfunctions. The guy seems to have come from good stock, so why would I think he's sick. Lana's mind continued to be troubled by Franklin's behavior. She would not be satisfied with Franklin's propriety until she checked further into his family history.

CHAPTER 61

LANA'S TRANSITION INTO POLLY THE BAG LADY

Lana's transition into a bag lady took some planning. She had to find enough old rags to swathe herself in. She had to make certain the rags she wore would cover her head and most of her face. What about her eyes! Her beauty could be hidden, but what about her eyes? They were devastating. Old sunglasses! No. After a few hours of wearing "sunglasses" images go wobbly and even headaches occur. She resolved this problem by buying a gray ugly wig she could tousle around her face and forehead to obscure those power laden eyes. Her feet were not a problem, emulate the bag lady she saw on the Avenue of Americas wearing rubber boots. A cart for her 'worldly belongings' was easy, she bought a big old grocery cart from a second hand store. She stored it in her locker until she needed it. She bought all her other bag lady needs from the second hand store, too. As well, she bought an old comforter. A comforter she had dry-cleaned. Subsequent to the drycleaning Lana grubbed it up with her own sanitary grub. Yeah, an authentic looking old comforter but clean.

Next, Lana decided to chart out the territory she was going to cover. Was it to be just lower and mid-Manhattan, or would she make jaunts into Harlem and upper Manhattan? For the nonce she decided on exploring only mid-Manhattan until she mastered the ropes. Once she felt proficient, *pro hac vice* you might say in her new lifestyle, she would stray further afield.

Lana was finding the planning she was going through for her upcoming life as a bag lady to a blast. Yeah, this was going to be the life, yeah, 'specially' when I know I can go to my beautiful condo whenever I want. I'm a spoiled brat I guess. But who gives a shit? Fuckin' world anyway. Genteelism, and its propitious cohort riches, is pretty damn comfy. It's fun having lotsa bucks. But, damn it all, I get feeling so damned guilty when I know about those poor peons out there with no riches. Franky baby, you slob, my money's on the poor. How long will it take for the tables to turn? I guess a person's gotta ask the Lord Jesus himself about that one 'cause He's the one who said "Blessed are the meek: (I suppose he meant the poor) for they shall inherit the earth." I guess too, a person's gotta ask Jesus what he meant when he told his disciples, "Blessed are the poor in spirit: for theirs is the Kingdom of heaven." And by damn, I've got my interpretation of the 'poor in spirit' and I'm going to stick with it until I can be convinced otherwise.

Anyway, for now, I've got to get onto the streets; obliterate my thoughts of the world in general; learn about the 'rejects' and just wallow along beside them. Who knows, maybe I'll meet somebody on the other side of the tracks who I can love and respect? Yeah, but first thing on my agenda is to search out Franklin's family background. His attitude bugs me. It'll be an interesting project to do as a bag lady. I imagine I'll run into some strange situations when I, as a bag lady, ask those all too often haughty snots the whereabouts of various archives, old newspapers, library info, microfiche, etceteras, and especially when I pay hard cold cash for services from a wad I'll carry. I'll have a ball. I'll flabbergast them. Maybe I'll find some poor s.o.b. on the streets who I can take along with me as a gopher. What a blast! Two down-and-outers, one with a big wad of cash! Fuckin' supercilious broads and dudes will shit themselves when I bribe them with C-notes, pay big tips, fly first class to LA or Frisco, or wherever.

Lana's first chore was to get her housing council's security personnel to know and to swear to secrecy about her charade as a bag lady. She told security her stint as a bag lady was for the purpose of studying, understanding and finding the underlying reasons why street people were street people and why the poor were poor. She told them she would visit her condominium unit at least once each week. Too, she told them she would telephone them two or three times each week to assure them of her safety and well being. She stressed the point her mission was one of great importance and one of great secrecy.

The only other persons she informed of her intention to be a bag lady were her parents, her brothers, her sister Margaret, her banker, and Trent. Ah yes, Trent.

She had a dreadful time with her parents. They demanded she 'come to her senses' and 'forget this frightening idea.'

"Lana Jean, you will be killed or raped. Any horrible thing can happen to you on the streets."

"Sorry mom and dad my mind's made up." Lana told them she would phone them every two or three days. *Not* to worry, she could take care of herself anytime, anyplace. Her dad wished her well. Her mom scolded her then cried.

CHAPTER 62

POLLY'S FIRST SORTIE ONTO MANHATTAN'S STREETS

Lana's first 'sortie' onto Manhattan's streets had her nerves tingling with a combination of trepidation, verve and daring. She taught herself how to cackle, to talk with a pitch above her normal voice and with an annoying rasp. Too she monotoned her words.

How the hell do bag ladies walk, do they slouch, do they slump over? How and where do they go to the 'can?' Where do they sleep? How do they feed, and where do they get their feed? Lana had everything 'taped' as far as she was concerned. After watching their movements for a few days she knew how they walked, shat, fed and slept. She had her bag lady paraphernalia stored in a small space she had rented in the sub-structure of the building where her multi-million dollar condo was domiciled. The space was large enough for her to have room to change, wash-up, whatever, for comings and goings. Her first day, changing from a glamour doll to a hag, then out onto the streets, went without any untoward incidents. It was a snap. As she shuffled south on Fifth Avenue she noted that no one noticed her. She was simply a part of the scenery. On purpose she jostled a couple of young 'Turks' who were rushing, jawing, briefcases swinging, off on some multi-million dollar venture. They took no notice of her. They just barreled along going about their business as if she was nothing more than a fart in a windstorm. She crossed over to Madison Avenue between 47th and 46th Street, mid-block, harassing the cabbies and all other vehicular traffic between Fifth and Madison. Here Lana got some attention. Horns blared, fists came out of windows, she was cursed at, threatened, all manner of dire suggestions were directed at her by the busy, angry drivers. Lana looked straight ahead. She offered no apologies to the plaintiffs. She just doddled her way over to Madison as if she was strolling in the park. But upon reaching mid-way twixt the two avenues she stopped and bowed at her tormentees. That rankled the traffic-jammees 'real good.' The whole undertaking seemed to stem the nuisance of her tingling nerves.

Lana was not in her disguise to rankle people (although she found it fun). She was out to sample a new way of life. If she found it to be good, she may stay with it for life. In the meantime she must concentrate on finding a gopher. A gopher she could trust. She wanted a gopher to help her in her research of Franklin Foster. The gopher wasn't a necessity instead the gopher was a luxury. A luxury to be part of her 'show-off' of the poor. Lana knew she would have her gopher within a week of her becoming a bag lady and she was right. Even wrapped in her bag lady swaddlings, monotone squawky voice, shuffling along in her over-sized rubber boots, ugly wig akimbo she had an unexplainable aura about her. Within three days she had a following of "scum-bags." Ten at this point! She hadn't invited them to accompany her on her march to nowhere. They just tagged along, eight men and two women.

It wasn't until the second day out that she spoke to them. Just a simple "hello."

"Yore sumpin' else ain't cha," one of the male scummers said.

"What do you mean?" Lana replied. Lana had decided she would not change her grammatics. Whilst her voice would be different, her use of the English language would remain the same as it was in the past.

"I dunoo." We just like you. We don't know you. But we figger yor sumpin' else. So this here US of A., bein' a free country and all, we're gonna tag along with you if its okay with you."

"Yes of course, you can tag along with me providing you don't bug me."

"We won't bug you," one of the women said.

"Good."

After rummaging around for something to eat for supper that evening and being rewarded with some leftovers from a pizza place called 'Pippens' the ten followers invited Lana to their 'maggot hole' near the docks on West 49th. Lana accepted. They talked, all ten of them. They told Lana their life stories. The reason they were down in the skids was because of bad luck and maltreatment by all and sundry. Except for one man their stories sounded like unadultered b.s. to Lana. They were just lazy no-goods as far as she could make out.

Oddly enough, it wasn't the man who didn't sound like a teller of tales who Lana selected as her gopher, it was a skinny no-account grub whose name was Peter Klutz. Klutz for Chrissake! A perfect name fit, Peter was a klutz. He tripped, stumbled and bumbled along like Dorothy's scarecrow. His story telling was so superb it was absurd. But Peter Klutz didn't intend for anyone to believe him, he told stories because he figured it was good for the imagination. Peter was 25 years old. He came from Detroit. He graduated from high school when he was 17. He came to New York when he was 18. He had chosen acting to be his profession, but opted for the streets after finding acting was 'too tough a chore' and the work to be too laborious. But the guy was trustworthy. Lana read this in him, and she was right. He was just lazy.

Lana was able to talk to Peter alone on several occasions. On November 8th, 1990, Lana discussed the matter of trust with him. She found Peter to be spontaneous. He spoke to her with candor and sincerity. Lana decided he could be trusted. Therefore she told him he would help her with her project re Franklin Foster. She told him she had sufficient funds to finance the project and that she would pay him a stipend by way of direct deposit into a checking account in Citibank, an amount of $1,000 per week for a minimum period of eight weeks. As well she told Peter she would pay all his expenses whilst he assisted her with the project. Expenses would include air, bus or train travel, taxis, hotel and meals. She said their travel would be to the city of Los Angeles or to any other destination required to complete her project. When she finished her outline, Lana pulled her straggly hair aside revealing therefore her eyes, her compelling beautiful eyes. Peter gulped. He had expected her eyes to be watery, mushy, cataract-filmed with ugly tidbits of catarrh glued to the corner of each eye. Not these pools of beauty! Holy mackeral, he thought, these orbs own whoever they look at.

"Now Peter, please look at my eyes and whilst doing so swear to me you will keep secret all of the information I give you pertaining to the Franklin Foster project. As well the confidentiality thereto be solely between you and me. Any breach thereof by you will entitle me to retrieve all of the funds advanced to you as stipends, expenses or any other outlay made by me on your behalf. Punishment for any impropriety you are guilty of, which affects negatively the outcome of the project, I, Polly Smith will have the sole right of retribution against you. The retribution will be in any form of punishment I choose, including one hundred cat and nine tail lashes on your skinny ass and back or tweaking your nose."

"Jesus Polly, I don't mind the tweaking the nose bit but don't you think the other is a mite harsh?"

"Never mind, swear you louse-infected skinny shit?"

"I swear...cross my heart and hope to die."

"Good man," Polly cackled. "Peter I am dead serious about the secrecy and confidentiality of my project. I need your trust Peter."

"You've got it Ms. Polly Smith. "Polly...your eyes...good God they don't belong on an old hag. I wonder what the hell is under your funny clothes?"

"Never mind Peter. I want to get on with my project starting now. I want us to get over to Queens and find out if a small college called McMasters College of Arts and Sciences has kept old records of its teaching staff. I want to know the background of Franklin Fosters' grandfather, Charles Foster Jr., and I'm hoping McMasters will be a good starting point. And, by the way Peter, I'm just an ordinary everyday old broad under my charming clothes. And to answer the question swirling around in your mind, Pete, I am just under six feet tall when I'm not slouching like I am now and I'm tough. Damn tough. And I carry with me at all times a.38 caliber pistol that holds twelve deadly shells in its cartridge. And, as I've warned many others who are not aware of my marksmanship, I can shoot the testies off a squirrel running lickedly-split up a tree at 30 paces. So don't worry my lad, vis-a-vis Allstate, *you are in good hands with Polly*."

"Thanks ma'am, but I know damn well you are not just an ordinary everyday old broad under your duds. I'll bet you're a beauty. And thanks for tellin' me you're tough and you're a top-notch gunslinger. It makes me feel guooood."

"Now come with me," Lana said.

She took Peter to the rear of the exquisite high-rise building, which housed her multi-million dollar condo. She unlocked a back entrance doorway with her special code ID. The back entrance led to a small cubbyhole sized room whose walls were made of thick concrete and whose doorway was just a plain sheet of steel…no doorknobs…no hinges…just a plain sheet of steel. Nothing happened until the back door closed. Now Lana, her cart and Peter were alone in the cubbyhole as bright lights came on. Lana stood still, Peter froze. Then Lana mumbled something. The steel door creaked open. Lana pushed Peter and her cart through the doorway. "Stay here Peter, I'll just be a moment." Peter stood as Lana pushed her cart into her rented storage room.

Peter was dumbfounded. 'Damn, like a scary fairy she gets into the back entrance of a luxury high rise. Who is this dame anyway?' he thought.

"Who in hell are you Polly?"

"Peter, remember trust and confidentiality."

"Yes."

"Well. Aw, forget it."

"You mean you gotta be able to trust me, but I ain't expected to trust you? Right Polly?"

"No Peter, you're right. The trust has to work both ways. But Peter you tell one soul about what I'm going to tell you and I'll have your ass."

"I promise. Scout's Honor, I won't tell no one."

"It's, I won't tell anyone…not no one Pete."

"Huh?"

"Forget it. In any event, I own a big suite of rooms on the 29th floor in this building, Peter."

"You what?" Peter said awe-struck.

"Yes, Peter my sweet, I own a big unit in this high rise."

"C'mon Polly what are you all about for shit sake?"

"I haven't time to tell you now, Peter, but I promise I'll tell you all about me as we struggle through this project. Deal man?"

"Deal," Peter said disappointed.

Lana gave him a hug. Peter looked happier.

When they got out to Fifth Avenue Lana tried to hail down a cab. None stopped for her. She laughed. "No cabbie's going to stop for us'ns reprobates?" She tried over and over again knowing full well that the cabbies would ignore her and her skinny "scum-bag" tag along.

She stepped out into the traffic raising her left arm like a policeman would, bringing the outside lane of traffic to a screeching halt. As Lana had planned, she stopped a line of traffic headed by a taxi.

"Fuck off lady," the cabby hollered as horns began to blare.

"We need you to get us over to Queens, asshole," Lana hollered back.

"D'ya think I've got shit for brains lady?"

"I know you have dickhead."

"Find some other sucka' ya loser," the driver said as he put his cab into gear and began to drive toward Lana. As his cab got to within inches of her she put her hands on its hood. The cab continued to move until it touched her body. Lana stood her ground. The next thing she knew a big guy with a face of a pugilist was standing beside her.

"Hey man outta the way," the cabbie yelled, his voice a little less bold than before.

"The lady and her friend need your services so let them in or I'll break your face."

"They won't have the fare for chrissake, with a tip it'll be over $40 bucks."

"I have the money sir." With that Lana reached into her layers of clothing and produced a wad of bills that would choke the proverbial horse.

"Holly Jesus lady, you shouldn't be carrying money like that around. You could get rolled," the big guy said.

"Thank you sir, but I can take care of myself," Lana responded.

"Let her in driver."

"Okay, get in the two of ya."

"Lady, here's my card. You're gutsy. I like that. If you ever need me give me a call." He patted her head then stepped back on the sidewalk. Lana and Peter got into the cab. At last they were away on the first leg of the project, McMasters College of Arts and Sciences near Forest Park in Queens.

Lana perused the pugilist-looking gentleman's card.

TRENT LOGAN
The Man
#721 City Corp. Building Manhattan
Tel (212) 854-1959
Fax (212) 854-1960
24 hour service

"Succinct," Lana murmured. "I've got to get to know this man. He appears to be very interesting."

Lana paid the $40 fare, gave the driver a $20 tip, then asked him for his card.

"Why lady?"

"Because, I need to have you at my beck and call, and sir, because you are such a gentleman." They both laughed. He shook Lana's hand. Lana parted her hair and looked at him. Steven Crossiti, like everyone else who saw Lana's eyes, gulped. He was caught in her web.

CHAPTER 63

McMASTER COLLEGE OF ARTS AND SCIENCES

The bursar at McMasters was quite pleasant. He was most helpful after the initial shock of seeing the two scummers. As he listened to the bag lady, he found himself to be quite enchanted with her because she spoke so eloquently about her project. Lana turned her charismatic charm up a few notches as she had done so often in the past. As well she exposed her eyes. That fixed the Bursar. He became so caught up in her aura he would have mooned the school's chancellor had Lana asked him to do so.

"Please follow me Ms. Smith and Master Peter to our rather tiny but well conceived archives room. The information contained in our archives covers the history of the school right from its inception to date. You have inquired about one Professor Charles Foster Jr., I believe. Well let me go to our index wherein I will locate his name, address, tenure and his file number from which I will be able to advise you whether his file is an open one or whether his file is by way of microfiche. Please give me a moment or two as I scan the record." Lady like Lana waited as the nattily dressed picture perfect pompous Bursar ran his finger down the record of names. He mumbled to Lana. "As soon as the school's budget permits all of the school's archives will be put on computers. My, won't that be a blessing, Ms. Smith?" he said busily scanning the names.

"Aha, dear lady, here we are, Charles H. Foster Jr.'s complete history. And lucky you it is in an open file, not on microfiche. Please, come with me and I shall retrieve the file or files for you. I do believe there are five open files on Professor Foster." They walked down a narrow walkway between ledges of files until they reached the 'F' section. There the Bursar found the five files, and with a look of pride on his face, he handed them over to Peter.

"Now my dear lady and Peter, please make yourselves comfortable at this table. I see you have no note pads or pens. I will be pleased to supply you with some if you wish."

"Thank you sir, you are so thoughtful and such a gentleman. However I do have a pad and some pencils tucked in my attire." Lana thrust her hand into her skirt like wrappings and unceremoniously pulled out two pads and several pens and pencils.

"Please do call me if I can be of help," the Bursar said fanning his fingers daintily at Lana.

"You are too kind sir."

Blushing, the Bursar turned, left the archives room and returned to his own office. Those eyes! my good God those limpid but flashing compelling gorgeous eyes. They rule a person. "Tch, tch," he muttered, "an extortive bag lady and a good for nothing bum, tch, tch. Should I have been so willing to help them? tch, tch. Those marvelous eyes, tch, tch."

Lana was pulled into the files as if they were magnetic. She went through all five in less than 20 minutes. She stored all pertinent information therefrom in her mind. "In-fucking-triguing! No shit! Well I'll be damned! Charles Jr.'s mom was sweet but his dad must have been a stompin' ground for horse dung. Charles Jr. was like his mom. He was highly thought of. A good man." But, Lana wanted a written record as well. Turning to her associate, she said, "Okay, Master Peter, write." Lana dictated as pathetic Peter wrote. Before Lana had said a single word, Peter said, "Don't go so fast." Lana thumped his arm.

"All set you skinny shit?"

"Yeah, I guess so."

"Okay, write."

"Franklin's granddad did not go to New York City in 1918...he went with his mom's parents and his brother to Santa Barbara. Charles Jr, went to UCLA...Grad...Dr. Poly ScEc...then McMaster 1939 to 1976. Charles Jr's father Phillip Rupert Foster was killed by someone called Mousey in 1914...why? Maria St. James (sounds like a bloody carnage...my comment)...Robbery of Maria. (Bull)...Rape, I'll bet." (My comment.)

"Also involved at Phillips death...Dr. Schnider, Sheriff O'Flarity, Hymie Lipschit, Mousey...later on, Bat Masterson, Harley Earp...Phillip Rupert Foster, teacher...Santa Monica High. Handsome big dude...Phys-Ed + Math...7 or 8 yr. tenure. Who was Silken Hendricks? Bat Masterson...New York's Morning Telegraph.

"That's it Peter. We've got one hellova good start. Let's go say our thank you's and bid farewell to Bursar Higgins. Our next stop, you bag of bones you, Los Angeles, the City of Angels."

Peter rubbed his brow. Lana's vivacity and dash dazzled him. Christ almighty LA. "When?"

"First thing in the a.m."

"How?"

"Classic air, First Class. You can come home with me tonight. We'll catch our cabbie, head to 'maggot hole,' pick up your shit then off to my condo."

"Jesus Polly. Slow down. My shit consists of toothpaste, toothbrush, shaving stuff, deodorant, one old pair of pants, a copula shirts, shit like that."

"Good. It should wow LA."

Before leaving the school Lana made her way into the outer office of the school's administration department. The staff ogled the pair of scummers as if they were extras dressed like lepers in some old movie. No one wanted to serve Lana or Peter. Surely the two of them were hosts for lice, probably infected with some dreadful disease too.

"Bravehearts, will one of you come to me? I have something in this envelope for the school." Lana croaked. Now, somewhat embarrassed, the staff members looked around at one another to see who would make the first move. None did.

"Okay, you bunch of bravehearts, I will send the contents contained in this envelope par avion." Lana opened the envelope, removed a piece of paper, made it into an airplane like kids do, threw it into the outer office, then called out, "Mr. Bursar sir, please come to the outer office."

In an instant an office door opened and Mr. Higgins appeared. Everything was quiet. The airplane landed on a red haired prissy's desk. She pulled away from it as if it was contaminated. The Bursar called out, "What is it everyone?"

"We're non-plused about these two Mr. Higgins," one man answered.

With that the frightened prissy redhead picked up the paper airplane between her thumb and pointing finger and eyeing the airplane with misgivings she marched it over to the Bursar.

"Thank you Ms. Gillis," he said as he took the airplane from her. He unfolded it back to its original state. He stared at the paper. First his knees wobbled then his face paled. He reached out to the closest desk for support. His eyes stayed transfixed on the paper.

"My God sir, what is it?" one of the male staffers asked with a trace of fear in his voice.

"It's, it's, good gracious, it's, I cannot believe it, it's a certified check in the amount of $250,000 made out to McMasters College of Arts and Sciences, signed by Polly Smith and counter signed by a name I am unable to decipher, Dr. L….someone or other. The bag lady, that's' who its from." Under the signatory's names was the word, 'Thanks.' Everyone looked over to Lana and Peter, shocked.

"Use it wisely. Toodles everyone." Lana the bag lady said waving. She took Peter's arm and whisked him off to Steven Crossiti's waiting cab.

CHAPTER 64

POLLY'S FLIGHT TO LOS ANGELS, FIRST CLASS, SHOCKING!

The next morning was a 'hoot.' Lana knew it would be. She had learned that only three of the 12 first-class seats in Classic Air's Boeing 767 were to be occupied for the flight from JFK to LAX. She and Peter sidled up (dressed in their disreputable rags) to the first class ticket sales counter. The salesclerk looked up at them rather contemptibly and in an unfriendly voice said, "The washrooms are down the hall to your left." She pointed in their direction then continued her work on the morning's Times crossword puzzle. 'Tough fucker this one, all about operas and authors.'

"Excuse me Irene (Lana saw Irene's name on the nameplate pinned over Irene's left breast), we should like to fly first-class on Flight 201—departing at 10:12 to Los Angeles this morning. We have no need for the washrooms."

"Yeah, and my Aunt Mary has no need for Richard Gere's dick."

"I beg your pardon Irene?" Lana said shocked at the clerk's remarks.

"C'mon, the cans are down the hall I said."

"Irene, my good friend and I have no need for your comfort station. We simply want first-class tickets to Los Angeles on Flight 201."

"All right your highness, how do you and your prince charming intend to pay for these tickets, with food stamps?"

"No my sweet one, with cash."

"With cash?"

"Yes, with cash you piece of sloth snot."

"What did you say, you horrid woman?"

"I said yes, with cash you piece of sloth snot."

"Well we'll just see about that now won't we, you, you despicable hag?"

"I suppose so you contemptible cunt." Lana said hoping to inflame Irene further.

"You, you…thing, you have forced me to call my supervisor. How horrid of you to call me a…"

"Good, do so my sweet. In the meantime, here are the funds necessary to pay for a round-trip to LA, with an open ticket, back to JFK, first-class." Lana produced the prodigious wad of bills she always carried with her and peeled off $2,900 and placed the money in front of Irene.

"Yes, Mr. Kelso, I have a bag lady and a bum at my station. They are a despicable pair, and I'm afraid I need your help"…pause…"yes, the bag lady has a huge roll of cash, yes, thank you sir." She hung up.

"My supervisor will be here in a moment."

"Thank you, Irene."

Lana and Peter waited at the counter for several minutes. Other unreserved first-class customers came to the counter in the meantime and received their tickets. In time Mr. Kelso and a big security guard appeared.

"What seems to be the problem here?" Mr. Kelso asked.

"This lady and her friend insist on flying to Los Angeles in first-class, sir. As you can see, they are not of our first-class quality you might say. I feel they are not fit even for our economy section."

"And whose moneys are those in front of you Miss Stemple?"

"The bag lady's sir."

"Hmmm. What is your name ma'am?"

"Polly Smith."

"And Ms. Smith, I understand you have quite a large sum of money on your person. Is that correct?"

"Well Mr. Kelso, while it's none of your business, yes I do have a fairly large sum of money on my person."

"How much?" The big security guard asked.

"Seven thousand dollars."

"Christ. That's a big swack of dough Ms. Smith. Where did you get it from?"

"From the fucking tooth fairy your lordship. Where do you think I got it from?"

"Don't get smart ma'am or I'll have to call the police."

"Good, call the police, Batman."

"Just answer the question ma'am."

"I do not think I am obliged to answer your question, sir. You see I am an attorney and under Section 82-1001-ii of the Civil Code I am under no obligation to answer such a question except in a court of law. By the way, under the Criminal Code, Section 7, part ciii, I do not need to answer this question, except in the presence of my attorney. Right Mr. Kelso?"

"I'm sure I don't know Ms. Smith," he gulped. "An attorney?"

"Ms. Smith do you expect us to believe you're an attorney?" the security guard asked.

"I don't give a shit what you believe, sir. I simply want my friend and I to get to Los Angeles, first-class on Classic Air at 10:12 this a.m."

"Look me in the eye when you answer my next question lady."

Perfect, Lana thought, just what I wanted.

"I shall be delighted to," she said. With that Lana drew back the hair which covered her eyes. She put her whole ego into her stunning, authoritative eyes.

"Did you steal? Oh, I'm sorry my dear. Of course you didn't steal. Please forgive me. Mr. Kelso, I implore you, let the good folks fly Classic. Please issue them first-class tickets."

Lana turned to Mr. Kelso, her eyes penetrating his. The poor bastard would have flapped his arms and flown the two on his back to LA.

"Oh my yes. Irene, be a dear and provide Ms. Smith and her associate with first-class round-trip tickets to Los Angeles. I am so sorry for any inconvenience we have caused you Ms. Smith. Please my dear, do take my card and call me at any time for service. Thank you and God bless."

Lana turned to Irene, smothered Irene with incredible eyes. Irene all but kissed Lana's ass.

CHAPTER 65

POLLY VISITS SANTA MONICA HIGH

And St. James, Rogers, Struthers and Co. C.P.A.'s

During the four-hour and 20-minute flight to LA, the first-class passengers and flight attendants on Flight 201 were very suspicious, solicitous and even a bit horrified by the two 'blighted rag bags' sitting in the spaces that should be occupied only by the elite. Bizarre! How dare the airline allow riff-raff to sit among those who occupy the seats of the mighty?

Lana couldn't help herself. She enjoyed playing the part of a low class crone. She sat in an aisle seat allowing Peter to sit by the jet's window. Peter was in awe of the far-off sights below. Lana opted for the aisle seat, first to allow Peter to experience the pleasantries of a window seat and second to allow her to torment the 'stuck-ups.'

She cackled at the slightest nuance. She hacked sneezed, coughed and sniffled. She burped in a most unladylike manner after guzzling down her champagne. She broke her fast in an appalling, irksome fashion. Several times during the movie she stood and stretched making certain she did so in front of viewers. She visited the lavatory ten times in that four-hour and 20-minute flight and each time she went she left the toilet doors wide open. Agitated flight attendants rushed to close them. As drinks were being served, following the movie, Lana completed the well-planned finale of her irritating production. While seated, she lifted her left leg up as far as she could allowing therefore her layers of clothing to fall away (just short of being obtrusive) from her limb, then after catching the other passengers attention she farted. My God, how she farted. She laughed, Peter gawked, the attendants froze, the passengers groped for oblivion.

On arrival at LAX Lana and Peter were the first to de-plane. She stood to leave the first-class cabin. More than once she thanked the attendants for their attentiveness, then turned to the passengers and told them how she hoped to have the pleasure of flying with them again soon. As she left the aircraft she farted again. "Damn," she thought, "this was one hellova flight."

Lana hired a limo. The task was testy, but after tipping the limo's hook $100 the hook made certain that Lana and Peter had 'comfortable transportation' to the Regent Beverly Wilshire hotel in Beverly Hills.

When she and Peter arrived at the swank hotel, she attended the check-in for Celeb's, showed the clerk an elaborate piece of plastic and immediately was swished off to a beautiful suite of rooms. All the while she and her gopher were the recipients of jaundiced eyes by guests, staffers and security.

It took her and Peter about one minute to unpack their pathetic belongings. Peter had his own bedroom, bath and Jacuzzi. The poor slob, from the time Lana had hired him his mind was agog in wonderment. Everything happened so fast. So fucking fast! Just a few days ago he had been inhabiting the dirt and filth of the streets, waiting for time to go by, sleeping at the 'maggot hole' and eating wasted food being thrown out in the garbage. Now for chrissake he was living like a king. Buzzing around in taxis, limos and jets, going to all the right places, mind agog trying to keep up with this whirling, astounding benefactor who had brought him to this scampering world. "Son of a bitch" who is this Polly woman? Her intelligence! Her vivaciousness! Her speed and morality! Holy shit who am I tangled up with? I mean, this lass moves. Nothing stands in her way. Her money, she must be a drillionaire. But she's an effing bag lady. She's been on the phone the last half-hour, now what is she up to?

"Peter."

"Yesssumm?"

"C'mon, we're on our way to the school district where Santa Monica High has its archives. Hustle baby."

Within five minutes they were away from the hotel in a long white Lincoln limousine. This limo was to be for their exclusive use all the while they were in Los Angeles. Six-grand a day. Their first stop was the Bank of America, Santa Monica Blvd. Here Lana stopped to pick-up a certified check made out in the amount of $500,000 payable to the Superintendent of Schools, Santa Monica School District. Next stop the Santa Monica School District building. She had her driver park the limo and wait for her and Peter.

The superintendent's staff was unaware of Polly Smith and her consort's attire. The receptionist expected Ms. Smith and Mr. Klutz to be regular people. When she and Peter arrived at the receptionist's desk in their 'rags' they were welcomed much in the same way Joe McCarthy would have welcomed a mob of Bolshevists.

"My dear lady," Lana said, "I have an appointment with Mr. Klemke at this exact moment. He is expecting me. Please let him know I am here."

"Who shall I say is…?"

"Polly Smith."

"Polly Smith?"

"Yes, Polly Smith."

"Oh my yes, Ms. Smith, you are the lady who wishes to explore our school district's archives and who is bringing a cashier's check in the amount of $500,000 to Mr. Klemke?"

"That is correct."

Acting the pompous one she said, "May I see the check before I call Mr. Klemke?"

"Yes my dear, after I wipe my ass with it."

"Oh my, Ms. Smith, that kind of vulgarity is uncalled for."

"You know Miss Stanford, I presume you are Miss Stanford as the name plate indicates, just because Peter and I are not attired to your fancy, we do not expect to be treated irreverently. You treat us with respect and we shall reciprocate one thousand times over. Here my dear is the $500,000 cashier's check, now please tell Mr. Klemke we are here."

Miss Stanford informed Mr. Klemke that Ms. Smith and Mr. Klutz had arrived for their appointment.

Mr. Klemke showed up in his golf clothes. He had just completed 18 holes at 'the club.' He was in a most jovial mood. He had shot a 76 from the blues. He apologized for not having changed yet.

"It is so nice to meet you Ms. Smith and Peter," he said fibbing and wondering about their dreadful appearance. 'Where in heavens name did they come from? But who cares. A $500,000 gift to the district, damn, the trustees will be as ecstatic as I am. Five hundred thousand dollars from a bag lady, out of nowhere, out of sight, pheeeouu, nice bag lady,' he murmured to himself.

Mr. Klemke ushered Lana and Peter into a large room full of archives. Within minutes he had located all the files pertaining to Santa Monica High back in the early 1900's. He assigned Miss Hutton from his staff to assist Ms. Smith for so long as Ms. Smith needed her.

As usual, Lana went through the files in a trice. Her keen mind sorted out all the pertinent material contained in the files. "I'll be damned," Lana whispered to Peter, "this is more than I had bargained for. Christ, talk about a "soap opera." Shakespeare, you are a whimp when it comes to violence, mayhem and sex compared to Phillip Rupert Foster."

"Okay Peter, I should like you to photocopy all the pages I have tabbed with yellow stickers, then give them to me. Miss Hutton, if you please, I should like you to take some dictation. And, please Miss Hutton, do not take offense at my expletive etymology. Thank you."

Lana dictated…"Phillip Latham Foster, born San. Fran. 1884…MA in Phys Ed + Math…. Married early 1907…Headmaster P.E.& Math. S Monica High Aug/07…Womanizer. Fucked many unknowns (my thoughts)…Silken Hendricks, 18-year-old student. Gorgeous silken blonde! Other comments…torrid affair twix Phil & Silkin…spied by some schoolmates copulating orally and other ways with Mr. Foster. Lovers from Oct/07 to June/08! Silken 1908 onto School of Med NY, Grad 1915. Wed Bernard Barrow same year. Practiced Med LA…two kids…boys, Marshall & Samuel. Marshall born 1916, Sam 1918. Last info…Marsh grad Med UCLA 1945 married 1950. Divorsed 1960! Remarried 1963 to 29-year-old Dr. R. Tulsa, practiced Eureka, CA. Child Christeen Charlene Alexandria Barlow. Born Jan/66…. Christeen…beautiful Christeen, she must be the girl who is Maggie's lover. She is!…See notes re: Maria and Simon St. James and Maria's bros. Jose AKA Mousey…Oct 26, 1914…P.R. Foster admitted to Miss Gloria Stevens (B B girls coach) that he was crazy about Maria St. James…. Oct 26, 1914, P.L. foster attacked Maria St. James in her office, tried to steal…demented. Such mayhem! Phil tried to kill Maria, Mousey killed Phil, Phil killed Mousey. Mousey was Maria's brother Josè. Guck kept from newspapers…Phil had switchblade, leather strap, chloroform and artificial penis in possession sounds like molestation not robbery…could be a cover-up for Phil's wife and family. N.B. time of attack Sat. aft when office closed. Maria and her husband Simon owned CPA firm. Phil's sons, Chas Jr., and Lawrence…. Chas Jr., father of Lawrence F…. Lawrence F Begat Franklin June 3, 1966.—Reported LA Trib Nov. 1914 Bat Masterson and Harley Earp (related to Wyatt) came to LA to comfort Maria and threatened anyone who touched her…. Masterson and Earp guardians of Maria from age 13…Maria born Maria Nancy Sanchez, July 8, 1886.

Lana at this point was finished at the school district. Lana thanked Miss Hutton, gave her $200 for her time, then she and Peter made their way to Mr. Klemke's office. She thanked Mr. Klemke for the help she had received from him and from Ms. Hutton. She parted her false ugly hair from her eyes and looked into Mr. Klemke's. The poor 'lamby-pie' melted, he stood stupefied. At last he was able to say how pleased he was he could help her with her project and how kind and thoughtful she was toward the school district with such a generous grant.

It was not yet 3:00 p.m. when Lana and Peter returned to their rented limo. She instructed her driver to drive them to the offices of St. James, Rogers, Struthers and Company, CPA's in downtown LA. The driver dropped them off at 3:20 p.m. in front of an attractive high-rise, which housed the firm. Lana instructed her driver to meet Peter and her in front of the building at 5:00 p.m. If they were not there at that time, she asked the driver to drive around the area and to be in front of the building every ten minutes following 5:00 p.m.

During the 20-minute ride from the school district, Lana had convinced herself that Phillip R. Foster was a sex-crazed 'chap'. She felt certain Phillip had selected Saturday afternoon for his attack against Maria because he knew Maria was to be alone in her office that day. She was certain, too, Phillip intended to rape Maria that afternoon. And Lana surmised he had set up some sort of an alibi—an alibi which would fault Maria, not good old Phil for the afternoon's delight—that would exonerate him from any blame in the event Maria accused him of rape. At this point it looked as if Franky baby had inherited his great grandfather's genes. Lana was sure a gory story would unfold itself by the time she completed her investigations.

They took the elevator to the 37th floor of the office building, the floor where St. James' et al Administration Department was located. Here she was to meet (by previous arrangement) the firm's Managing Director, Christain Farley St. James.

Lana shuffled her way over to the receptionist. Lana was in no mood for further fiddle-faddle regarding arguments with underlings. Lana noted the receptionist's name, by her pretty brooch-like tag, was Karen. Lana swept her hair back from over her eyes, looked directly into

Karen's eyes and informed Karen that she, Polly Smith, and her associate Peter K were here for their appointment with Mr. Christian St. James. Karen put up no defense. She rang Mr. St. James' line, and on hearing Mr. St. James voice, she informed him his three-thirty appointment was now at the reception desk.

"Please have a seat Ms. Smith and Mr. K. Mr. St. James will be just a minute or two, he's on the telephone at the moment. May I get you something, tea, coffee or some other beverage?"

"No thank you my dear, we had coffee just awhile ago."

"Please make yourselves comfortable."

"Thank you Ms. Karen we shall."

Holy fuck, Lana thought to herself, who is that hunk?

Strolling in front of Lana was a tall handsome dark-haired tanned Californian, eyes glued on some papers he held in his hands. So engrossed was he he was unaware of the world around him. He stopped for a moment to study the papers. He turned to Karen, smiled, and told her he was going to the firm's library and he would be there for an hour or so.

"Okay Clark," Karen replied. Clark moved on.

"Who is that handsome young man Karen?" Lana asked.

"That is Clark St. James. He is the son of Mr. Christian St. James, the gentleman whom you will be meeting with. Clark St. James' great grandfather Simon St. James began the firm as a sole proprietor in 1909. The firm and the St. James have had an enviable and a distinguished background since its beginning way back then. St. James, Rogers, Struthers and Company is the finest CPA firm in the country, thanks to Simon St. James and his wife Maria who together set down the etiquette, ethics and service goals so many years ago. Clark St. James is like all of the past St. James'. He's a brilliant, caring, responsible man."

"Well thank you for your comments Karen. Its very thoughtful of you."

"Ms. Polly Smith?" A tall, distinguished handsome gray-haired man said, as he walked toward Lana.

"Yes, Mr. St. James?"

"Yes," Christian St. James took Lana's hand in his and said how pleased he was to meet her.

"How kind of you sir. You are most gracious."

Lana and Peter were escorted by Christian St. James to his office. Once seated he said he understood from her telephone call she would like to peruse the personnel files of his grandmother Maria and his grandfather Simon. Too, he understood the information therefrom was solely for Ms. Smith's edification, not for publication of any sort?

Lana looked into his eyes with remarkable directness. Her eyes relayed a straightforward message to him. "You have my word sir." Mr. St. James was frightened by this transmission and yet satisfied with its propriety.

"Perhaps Ms. Smith you would be kind enough to tell me why and what sort of information you need from the files? There is some very personal information contained in one particular file that is unspeakable. It has to do with my grandmother, Maria Nancy St. James."

Lana said she had an unpleasant entanglement with a certain family, the Fosters, which she needed to unwind for her own peace of mind." She asked Mr. St. James to be kind enough to keep the story she was about to tell him confidential. She said she was certain her story would answer all his questions about why she was doing this research. He agreed to hear her out.

Lana then removed the swathing around her face and her awful wig. Her face now was exposed. Christian St. James sat transfixed. He was mesmerized by her stunning beauty. 'Good God, she is the most gorgeous woman I have ever seen,' he said to himself.

"Ms. Smith, your face, your eyes, your hair, your, your mouth, you are, well, what can I say? You are lovely. No, you are radiant. No, you are beyond lovely and radiant."

"Thank you kind sir," Lana said, "my face looks good to you simply because I am a bag lady"

"No, no, not at all."

Lana began to restore her disguise. Then she started on the complex story of her life.

She told him of her nine years off and on relationship with Franklin Foster and its dreadful ending on her 23rd birthday. She said it was that dreadful day which caused her to 'jump the traces' from the world of the rich and the famous to the world of the poor. She explained to Mr. St. James it was necessary for her ego to find the reason or reasons for Franklin's progressive uncalled for nasty behavior over the years which culminated on her 23rd birthday. She said she knew Franklin's family history back to and including Charles Foster Jr. and she saw only strong loving family ties flourishing over the years. She said she felt it necessary to go back at least one more generation in search of a possible culprit who may have been rife in bad genes. After all she had loved Franklin Foster over those nine years and her heart strings had been tugged rather abruptly on that terrible night. Christian St. James listened to Lana's dissertation of the Fosters. Had this Lana stumbled onto the Foster family by luck, or was she a competent sleuth. When Lana had recounted her findings about the Foster family from her research at McMaster College and at Santa Monica High School's school district, and had come up with all the 'right' names Christian St.James knew nothing could stop her from 'digging up' the whole damn story.

Christian St. James stood up from his chair, walked over to a wall safe, opened it, reached inside it and retrieved a large golden colored accordion file held together by a slender golden soft silk rope. He took it to his desk and set it down. He then handed Lana a 12-inch framed picture that sat on his desk facing him. Lana took the picture. She studied the picture in minute detail. Her eyes flushed.

She wept.

Christian St. James came from around his desk to her. He knelt down on one knee in front of her. Quietly he said, "My dear Dr. Masters, as lovely as she looks in her picture, the beauty inside her was even greater. She was precious, kind, thoughtful, caring, loving, energetic, lively, so personable, so human, so humane, loving, loving, oh my God, so entirely a decent…" Christian St. James voice quivered. They remained silent. Peter put his arms around Lana.

"Maria Nancy Sanchez St. James, now I have met you," Lana said. "You are the person who brightened everyone's life who knew you. I must know your life story, forgive me, but I must."

"Well," Christian St. James said as he dried his eyes. I haven't had tears like that for many years, but the way you looked at my grandmother's picture, well, I think even the stoniest of persons would have broken down and wept."

"Mr. St. James, all photographs I have ever seen of your Grandmother replicate the image of a very special person. This picture of Maria not only replicates her personage but more than that, it captivates her soul, her being, her very presence. My God, it's like meeting her in person."

"Yes, I know, Doctor."

Christian St. James returned to his desk. He handed the golden colored accordion file to Lana and said, "I'm sure the contents of this folder will answer most of your questions, Doctor. Please feel free to make notes of any matter contained therein and in Great Granny's diary. And Doctor Masters, make copies of any relevant material you find in the file, but with respect, I beg of you not to make copies of anything in Great Granmother's diary. I'm sure you will understand about the privacy of her diary."

"Of course I do. Thank you sir."

Lana dictated the information she wanted to Peter. "Born Maria Nancy Sanchez, Tij. Mex, July 4, 1886…Jose only living sibling…born 1885 lived horrible life till met Maria 1903 or 04?…Maria's mother died

1899…Maria to S.M. High…met H. Earp and Bat M. 1899. Great story…met Simon 1899…married him 1907…great life (Jose AKA Mousey) excpt 1914…1914 rape of Maria by P. R. Foster: ghastly…. 1914 death of P. R. F. & Jose…. Maria…died peacefully 1983. As she died she was heard to speak in hushed tones to an Eve One. Interesting. Incredible life! Incredible woman! How I'd love to have known her, and…the abysmal note left behind by Phil R. Foster…found later by Sheriff O'Flarity among Foster's hidden stuff. His alibi…Maria wanted his body…he complied to save her from suicide. Real bad ass!

* * *

Lana removed her wig. She kissed Christian St. James' cheek. She hugged him. Then, smiling, she replaced her wig.

"I do hope to see you again, Mr. St. James."

"I'm sure we'll meet again, Doctor."

CHAPTER 66

LANA VISITS THE MORNING TELEGRAPH, MANHATTAN

Lana and Peter flew back to New York. She had all but completed her project. Just one more source to investigate…the Morning Telegraph re: the great American icon, Bat (William Barclary) Masterson.

For this part of the investigation Lana decided to go it alone, and to present herself as Lana Masters, Ph.D. She was anxious to wrap the whole affair up. She knew now Phillip Foster's genes had leapt past a couple of Foster generations and landed in the womb of Lawrence Foster's wife Hedda. The little fuckers, they aborted remission as they surged out of Lawrence's testicles into Hedda's baby manufacturing plant. Franklin was assembled therein in nine months out of good old Phillips's rejuvenated genes. 'Sumbich eh?'

When Lana walked into the newspaper's reception area she was met by the receptionist. Quite a change from her experience as a bag lady. I guess when you walk like a grub, talk like a grub and look like a grub, you are taken by folks as a grub. However when you dress in a smart, well-tailored, maroon mini-skirted business suit, you are accepted as a member of the human race. The huge windows in the reception area were next to the newsroom. The activities in the newsroom came to an abrupt halt when the staffers saw Lana. Now Lana had to be certain she would not be recognized. She turned her back on the 'newsies.' The outline of her ass drove the poor fools into "a frenzy". A smart looking, middle-aged lady came to her rescue. This smart looking lady took Lana to a room filled with scads of newsworthy memorabilia. She knew where to find the files of the late great 'Bat' Masterson. A whole shelf was devoted to his life and times. Lana was permitted to peruse the entire inventory of papers, letters and pictures contained in his files. However Anna Hershold, the smart looking middle aged lady, was required by company policy to remain with Lana or for that matter any other person seeking information from this room of 'treasures.' Anna, as well, would do any photocopying required by an inquirer.

These files were extraordinary. Two complete sets had to do with Maria Nancy Sanchez St. James. Lana could not believe the detail Mr. Masterson went into regarding his beloved angel. Lana learned the entire life of Maria from Masterson's copious notes. As far as Masterson and this other man, Harley Earp, were concerned Maria was their Godchild. He wrote about her childhood as told to him by Maria. He told about the wonderful times Maria, Harley and he had together. Their tears, their adventures, their heartbreaks, Harley and his scolding of Maria, their joy at her marriage, their love and respect for her husband Simon. How they persuaded Santa Monica High's headmaster Dr. Bartholemew Westwiggins to accept "our little Mexican spitfire" into his snobbish school. Maria's pathetic, gut wrenching cries when Harley and he would have to leave her—the child thought she would never see them again.

"This broke Harley's and my heart. Nothing on earth means as much to us as does our precious Maria."

"The rape of Maria by Phillip R. Foster took a huge part of our lives from us. Both Harley and I blame ourselves for the savage attack on our angel. Had we kept her with us as she had wanted, this atrocity would never have occurred. Damn us. Anyone, anyone who lays a finger on our Maria will die."

Mr. Masterson said Phillip Foster was fortunate he died at the hands of Maria's disabled brother Jose. Had Harley and I got to him first the 'bastard' would have been strung up on the nearest tree.

Again, Lana wept.

The files contained many pictures of Maria, Simon, Harley and Bat. A stunning woman surrounded by three handsome men. There was a large stack of letters to and from Maria and her heros.

Pages and pages were devoted to the pride Bat Masterson had for his beloved protegé. Bat Masterson's final entry into his journal read simply, "God bless Maria."

Lana, accompanied by Peter made three more trips back to Los Angeles. She was drawn there because of the inordinate impact the life of Maria St. James had made on her. She visited the site of the brutal rape. The building in which the incarnate Phillip Foster had brutalized Maria was left standing by the City of Los Angeles as a heritage site. She visited the sheriff's office and with guidance had found Phillip's alibi note as well as the history of the event as recorded by Sheriff O'Flarity. She found that Dr. Schnider's children's children were scattered throughout the USA. His office building was a thing of the past, a housing complex now was situated on the site. As well, Hymie Lipschit's deli was gone. Mr. Lipschit's only child David, who was born in 1918 and who had become a fighter pilot in the Royal Air Force in 1940, was killed in a wild aerial battle against overpowering German numbers in 1942. David was awarded posthumously the Distinguished Flying Cross for his bravery. Lana spent many hours at the gravesides of Maria, Simon and Jose. Lana's psyche knew Maria's spirit would live on forever.

Lana took time on her last visit to LA in 1990 to locate the whereabouts of Jay Foster and his merry men. She had no difficulty sniffing them out. She knew what Trent Logan's first assignment by her was going to be.

CHAPTER 67

LANA MEETS WITH TRENT LOGAN

Lana sat at her desk in her condo's den. The calendar told her it was Wednesday, November 16, 1990. She wanted Jay Foster and his three 'bully boys' brought to justice. She had no intention of going back to Los Angeles to even up Margaret's, Christeen's and her score, but in no way was she going to leave the score lopsided in Jay's et al favor. She reached for her wallet, opened it at the slit that carried others' calling cards and pulled-out 'the man's,' Trent Logan.

I wonder, she thought, if this guy's for real? He looked cool, he looked tough, too. Face of a pug. He looked a little like pictures of the old Manassa Mauler, Jack Dempsey. If he does what I ask, not kill the pricks, just maul them, bust them up a bit, kick their butts, make them bleed, that'll even up the score as far as I'm concerned. My gut feeling is he can be trusted. She dialed his number.

"Yes," a rather rough voice answered.

"Mr. Trent Logan?"

"Yes."

"I need some information about the services you offer, I have your card but…"

"Yeah, yeah, I know, my card is vague.

"You're not terribly polite are you Mr. Logan?"

"Ma'am I'm a second Sir Geoffrey Snodgrass."

"Like fuck you are."

He laughed

"What can I do for you?"

"Do you want it straight?"

"Absolutely."

"I want four dudes brutalized, not killed, just brutalized."

"That's easy ma'am, I'm an expert at brutalizing."

"Mr. Logan?"

"Yes?"

"Do you mind coming to my place? I'm not far from your office, in say half an hour, about ten?"

"That's fine."

"Okay my unit code is 1435. My name is Lana and I live at the St. Pierre across from Central Park. Twenty Ninth Floor."

"Thanks, ma'am. See you."

Trent Logan wondered why this broad wanted some guys busted up. He'd know soon enough. He donned some jeans, put on his thousand-dollar brown leather jacket over a white Perry Ellis shirt tucked his magnum in its shoulder holster, put on his Italian Camprii brown loafers and began his15-minute walk to the St. Pierre.

Lana was at her door waiting for him. Damned if he wasn't the spitting image of the great heavyweight. Pug ugly handsome. Six-one, one-ninety. Kind of scary. They shook hands. His were steel.

He commented about her condo. Then…

"You are without doubt the most beautiful woman I have ever seen," he said in a matter-of-fact tone.

"Thank you, sir, you look like Jack Dempsey when he was in his prime."

"Yeah, I get that a lot."

They discussed the Malibu project.

"It's a deal. Fifteen hundred a day plus expenses and a five grand bonus if the pictures of the four show the quality of my work to be satisfactory to you."

They shook hands. "Jesus Mr. Logan, I thought Roberto Duran had hands of stone."

"Lady I'm hard all over."

"I'll bet you are."

They laughed.

"Incidentally, Ms. Masters, I know who you are. You are the well-known intellect, Dr. Lana Masters."

"You're right, sir."

"And for chrissake call me Trent."

"Okay, and in private please call me Lana. But in public—just sit tight for a moment." Lana rushed off to her dressing room, shut the door behind her then in two minutes she re-appeared in her bag lady swathings and her ugly gray wig. "And in public call me Polly Smith. Do you recognize me?"

"For fuck sake, you and the cabbie. If I'm not......"

"Cute eh, Trent?" Lana said, as she modeled her outfit.

"Yeah, the scrappy bag lady."

"Right on baby."

Confidentiality was discussed and sworn to.

CHAPTER 68

TRENT LOGAN EVENS THE SCORE

Lana saw the article on page one of the Los Angeles Times. "Jay Foster, well known fast-laner, found along with three of his stooges, beaten and mauled in his Malibu mansion...robbery not a motive...police think a gang of hoods broke into his home around midnight..." She smiled.

That evening Trent reported. Lana saw the pictures Trent took with his Polaroid. They were sickening. "Good work Trent. You've earned your bonus. I've decided to add $2,000 more and, with your leave, I want you to have it as a retainer. I want us to be good buddies both personal and in business, okay?"

"I'd like that," Trent said. They dined. A new friendship was born. Like Maria, Bat and Harley.

CHAPTER 69

POLLY'S ENTOURAGE

Polly meets Clark St. James

Lana's following grew as she wandered the streets of New York. Wherever she went at least 50 or 60 scummers trailed along behind her. However the numbers grew to 100, then 200 and then 500. The city of New York tried to keep the numbers down to 300. Much to the city's chagrin the numbers often exceeded 1000. Seldom did she talk to them for any length of time. She led and they followed. When she stopped they stopped. She roamed from one end of Manhattan to the other. She spent most of her time around Park Row, Rockerfeller Center, Central Park, Greenwich Village, the old Sub-Treasury building at Wall and Nassau, St. Patrick's Cathedral, and Grand Central Station. From these austere places she would lecture her pathetic, tattered, homeless group. She fed them no bullshit. None of this "bless you for your kingdom awaits you." She'd tell them outright, "this right here is your kingdom. If you want to be Kings and Queens get off your sorry asses and do something about it. Don't just traipse around after me grinning like a bunch of morons. Gather up your fucked-up buddies and tramp your way to Washington DC. Get thousands and thousands of you to mill your asses all around the White House, Capital Hill, the Washington Monument, the Lincoln Memorial and demand work. Block the doorways of big businesses. Tell business big-wigs you will get millions of down-and-outers to obstruct, clog and boycott their products until they open their employment doors.

"If you don't like this approach try to do something on your own. Earn independence. Be fruitful. Get together, thousands of you. You've got the most precious thing in the world on your side…time. Shit, you've got nothing but time on your hands. Get industrious, hustle and bustle. Be vigilant. Wake up, pool your few resources, set up your own businesses, and work your butts off. Compete, it's fun, it's healthy, it's challenging. Don't sit around and bitch, unless of course, that's what you want to do. If you want to be lazy and accept your present station in life, so be it." Abruptly Lana would stop her lectures and once again trample on into time using up worthless seconds.

Several months passed without anything too dramatic happening in Lana's life. However, her lectures on self-help were beginning to take a hold on many of the scummers. Some felt massive marches on Washington DC to be the answer. Peaceful marches. But demanding. Demanding a decent degree of equity and employment. But the preponderance of the scummers liked the idea of independence through free enterprise and a consolidation of their measly resources to fund some fucking thing or another.

Fate! By damn if fate didn't 'drop in' on Lana in October 1991. October 21st to be exact. Lana had heard some gossip via the scumbag grapevine about a big dude who was trying to get scummers to pool their resources for the purpose of creating a scumbag bank or something. Coincidence to be sure, just as she was putting the final touches on her plea to get her scummers to scramble for their own financial independence.

Lana decided she wanted to meet this big dude. She had heard he hung around Grand Central Station. She decided she would make the trek to Grand Central on October 23rd. She was told the big dude was easy to spot because he was so tall, so handsome and quite tanned and he always had two ordinary scummers with him. They were well known scummers, Vito and Leroy something or other. One was a little dago, the other a ponderous black. She heard the big dude's first name was Barney.

Lana's faithful followed her from West 49th past Ninth, Eighth, and Seventh Avenues to the Avenue of Americas then South on the Avenue of Americas to East 43rd. This brought her and her entourage into the vicinity of the Grand Central Terminal. All the while she made the trek her following grew. Lana was patient, she trundled back and forth between East 41st and East 45th Streets, around the Pan Am Building searching for this tall man. One poor wino seated on the sidewalk playing the pavement with bonafide drum sticks told Lana a bum called Barney Potter a.k.a. Clark something or other showed up at noon daily in front of Grand Central. "Lately," the wino said, "Vito and Leroy were with him." Lana slipped the wino ten bucks and thanked him. The wino said to Lana's surprise, "Thank you Polly."

Lana along with her faithful were in front of Grand Central at noon and right on time, as the wino had said, the three vagabonds showed up. Lana, ever the aggressor, marched up to the tall one and all but flipped her lid. Holy sheeat, she thought, this Barney Potter is either Clark St. James or his identical twin. Christ, even the small scar just above his right eye is the same on both men. Lana's agile mind worked wonders as she walked up to the big man, extended her hand and said, "Clark St. James I presume?" Now the big one damned near 'flipped his lid.'

"No, no," he stammered, "you have mistaken me for someone else. My name is…"

"Jose Jaminiz," Vito said laughing.

"No. Barney Potter is my name."

"Excuse me," Lana said. "So you are not the man to whom I am speaking."

"No. Yes. Yes, I am the man to whom you are speaking, Barney Potter. My name is Barney Potter, not Clark whoever."

"Come on Clarke St. James. I know who you are. Your alias 'Barney Potter', has been a dismal flop. Everybody knows you are Clark St. James. Why the bulldurham? My name is Polly Smith."

"It's nice to meet you, Ms. Smith." Clark said, still flushed. (How in hell does she know my real name? She's just a flea bitten old bag lady. Maybe she's seen my picture in one of the rags when I was dating Michele, Melanie or Kim or Sharon or…damn it, I'm not ready to give away my identity yet.) "And I should like you to meet Messrs. Vito Apostli and Washington Leroy Jefferson."

"How do you do gentlemen, it is my pleasure."

"You have quite a following, Ms. Smith." Clark said, still flustered.

"Yes, I do. Most of the time my group adds up to 500. But today it looks like 1000 or more. They just puddle along behind me. Once in a while I lecture them on economics. But by and large we just walk the streets. In any event, Clark or Barney, whichever is your pleasure, we have come all the way from West 49th and 12th Avenue to find you. I have heard some rather favorable comments about you."

"Oh, have you now? Perhaps you would be kind enough to tell me about such comments."

* * *

Lana knew this man was Clark St. James. She decided she would call his office in Los Angeles later in the day to find out if Clark St. James was still with St. James, Struthers et al. There was no question in her mind about who he was, but being a thorough investigator she felt one phone call should be made just to make sure.

Lana made the call. Just as she expected, Clark St. James was no longer with the firm, and no, the office was unaware of his whereabouts. Mr. Michael Scott, Miss Marlee Aitkens and Miss Allyson Morrow had taken over his files. Yes, they are most competent.

CHAPTER 70

H&B'S MANHATTAN OFFICE

Clark St. James and Polly were dynamos in money matters. Both had extensive financial training, both had front line experience in security trading, both were accounting professionals thus able to dissect financial statements, notes thereto and annual reports, and both had uncanny senses of accurate timing. And Lana, as always, was Lana. Leroy Jefferson added to their strengths. He knew the brokerage game inside out.

Polly was a master sales person. Over the years her super-natural persuasiveness garnered in thousands of shareholders into H&B Financial and Poors Inc.

Polly had explained to Clark when they first met outside the Grand Central Terminal back in October 1991 she had heard about his idea of a financial organization owned and controlled by the poor. She told him fate had to have intervened and put the two of them together, because whilst he was pursuing his thoughts she had been promoting on a similar basis her thoughts to her followers. So when the good old fickle finger of fate saw two alike thoughts running parallel to one another it said, "sumbitch, these two must follow one power path," and "voila" their thoughts became one. Polly congratulated Clark for his foresight in incorporating H&B Financial & Poors Inc. in the manner he did.

They became close friends and associates. Lana introduced Clark to Trent Logan. She convinced Clark that H&B needed a handyman, a non-sniveling good all around tough SOB who would stand up for any "rag-tag scummer" against any and all odds. Lana told Trent the big secret that, in fact, Barney Potter was really a rich dude whose name was Clark St. James. Clark and Trent became close friends and associates.

Shit, Lana thought, good stuff.

Lana found herself becoming more and more attracted to Clark every time she was in his presence. She had contemplated on many occasions to reveal her real self to him. But the thought of Franklin kept her back. Franklin had been a nice, sweet man for most of the years she had known him, just as Clark appeared to be to her now. But, damn it all, Clark could turn out to be as possessive as Franklin, as jealous as Franklin and as perverted and as cruel as Franklin. Fuck it. My safest lover is my right hand. Yes baby! my right hand. Yeah, and for a real tumultuous orgy my sneaky old left hand gets in on the fun—but Clark, you are such a dreamboat!

In the Spring of 1994 Clark and Polly were in a rare verbal battle over two important items. One H&B's investment policies and two whether H&B should provide pharmaceutical products, including some heavy-duty drugs free of charge to its shareholders. As to the pharmaceutical products, including soft and hard drugs, H&B had received in February of 1994 permission from all government authorities to dispense all manner of drugs 'under the strictest of conditions' only to its shareholders. Everything was in place for the installation of a 'drug center' in the big warehouse owned by H&B. Clark was apprehensive about such a move in spite of the fact the shareholders at a special meeting had gleefully approved of the 'drug center.'

He was certain the center would become nothing more than a junkie haven for H&B's shareholders. It could even be an open invitation for robberies and lootings. "Many of our shareholders lives could be in danger because of the drug center." he cautioned. While Clark had given lip service to the project in the beginning, he now was against the move. He knew if he blocked the center's introduction he would risk the chance of being thrown out of H&B because, after all, the shareholders had voted unanimously for the creation of the center. But Clark was a strong, influential and moral man. Unless his mind could be changed he would do the proper thing and divorce himself from H&B if it became a necessity.

Lana tore into him. "No, it would not become a junky haven. For goodness sake! Too many safeguards will be instituted and put into place to allow the dispensary to become abused. You know that's correct Clark. Robberies, hijacking, kidnapping, all sorts of things are possible, and no doubt, some will occur. But, be reasonable Clarke, our shareholders are in far more danger of being hurt or killed by doing street trades than by coming here to do their thing under controlled conditions. The bullet proof caging around the dispensary will save harmless the druggist on duty. And Clark, who knows, stressing the foolishness and danger of drug abuse H&B may be able to reform many present-day addicts. And, Clark, as you know one of the conditions pertaining to 'hard drugs' is the user must take the drugs here on the premises and not carry them out onto the streets. And heck, 'handsome' if the experiment doesn't work H&B can shut the center down. Remember Clark the dispensary, too, will carry soft drugs for headaches, toothaches, upset stomachs, injuries, vitamins, coughs, colds, the flu and the like. Let's go all out and give it a try."

"Yeah your right Polly, we must give it a try. But one too many slip-ups and its bye-bye hard drugs, agreed?"

"Agreed."

"You like the stock market Polly, but I have a real concern stock prices now are too high. Goodness Polly, look at company price earning ratios. Getting out of whack I'd say. Companies' profits can't just keep going up. I mean, expense cutbacks can only go so far. Companies, and in particular retailers, must start giving service back to its customers. Hence up go expenses and down goes profits. Growth in sales now must be given priority over cutbacks and, damn it Polly, there is no evidence this is happening. Business must begin to think globally. But damn it here again, Polly, the big Asian markets who for the nonce are enjoying substantial growth in their GNPs could begin to dry up if their heated economies falter. This could spill over and be a detrimental factor to us here in the United States. And, Polly, look where the Dow Jones is…3,800 plus. Can markets continue to go on unrestrained? I don't think so. And, Polly, I'm not just talking about a market correction, I'm talking about a 10 to 15-year stabilization of stock prices with little potential for capital appreciation except of course in rare cases. Dividends alone cannot induce people to buy. Pension funds, big players and the average American want to play the stock market. It's the magic of the capital appreciation that keeps the ball rolling. And what about ruthless speculators?"

"Jesus, you are a happy one aren't you, Barney?"

"Just the facts ma'am."

"Yeah, yeah. Look Clark, surprises are not necessarily surprises. While historic and present day facts cannot be held as realities in the future…other than the cosmos itself which, I dare say, will itself burn out and die about one trillion years from now, give or take a day or two…they can provide humans with the tools necessary to make judgmental estimates with a good deal of accuracy in many of life's turn of events. You don't know what lies beneath my swaddlings other than a body do you? But, is the body male or female? Is it scarred? Is it hairy? Is it flabby, skinny, big bosomed, yellow, healthy, whatever? You don't know until you see it. And when you do see it you may find it to be somewhere between gross and gorgeous. So now we try to make an educated guess at what lies under my swaddlings (the stock market). Are my underlying principals healthy or sick? We uns gotta strip that 'mother' the bestest way we can for us'ns to see if she's dosed up or 'fundamentally well.' Right? First we look at the atmosphere around her. We want to see what kind of an environment she lives in. Is it clean or smoggy? Is she publicially acceptable? ain't I a breath of fresh air?" Lana said as she curtsied, "wouldn't the public love to have one like me in their home? Great Scott Clark, you know what I mean. Are interest rates stable and low enough to allow for economic growth to be on a steady incline? Is inflation under control allowing therefore the consuming public to buy goods at reasonable prices? Will capital spending be reasonably consistant? Is another world war eminent? Christ Clark, you know the schematics. And what about the lady herself, has she got a good share of the market, has she got a good product, is she liquid? Has she got a prodigious net worth, how about her current and fixed assets, are they in good shape, how about her cash flow? Are her significent ratios propitious? What is her history of dividend payments. Does she operate under strict regulations or does she go about her business unregulated. And is the general public optimistic or pessimistic about her wares? Well Clark, my phony Barney Google, I think she is in damn good shape and should stay that way for quite a number of years. Her Dow Jones body will go from its present 3.8 on the scale of one to ten, to nine or more before the next millennium. Yeah baby, the Dow will reach the 9000 plateau in the latter 1990's. I say have at least 60% of H&B's investments in the stock market."

Clark agreed, yet with some degree of scepticism. After a few minutes of wonderment he said, "You know, Polly, I have known you for about three years now and I have no idea what you look like. You keep yourself so covered up. I know you are a brain, I know you are charming, I know you are caring, and my dear secretive one, I know you go to the St. Pierre at least once each week and then 'ppwhist' your gone. I am so mystified by you. Who in hell are you?"

"Good question. So you know about me and the St. Pierre? Hmmm, I suppose it's only fair for me to level with you about moi because, handsome, I know exactly who you are. That's why I have kept calling you Clark over the years. You sir, are the rich, good looking Californian, Clark St. James. Right?"

"Right. God you're annoying. You're always right. Now who the hell are you?"

Lana stood, took Clark's hand and said, "Come oh great one, fly away with me to the Casbah. She smiled, "lets be off to the St. Pierre and I shall bare my secret to you."

CHAPTER 71

POLLY DISROBES

And discloses her secret to Clark

Off they went, Clark wondering what the heck to expect from this cackling floozy. He didn't have to wait long. He was shocked at every turn of the journey to her 'flat.' The cabbie's presence and joy on seeing her, the doorman's friendliness, and then her flat—what a flat, my good God. Polly had Clark sit down. She brought him a juice, turned on some sexy music, wiggled her way to the middle of the room, her back to Clark, and began to disrobe.

First, off came her wig. She shook her head, her tawny golden hair flew around her magnificant face then settled gently over her shoulders and down her back. She turned until she faced Clark. His mouth dropped. He was dumbfounded. He could not believe his eyes. Polly's face was stunning, beautiful. Her remarkable eyes mesmerized him. Who is this beauty? Clark was breathless. Second, off came her ugly rubber boots, then her socks. Even her feet were beautiful. Third, off came her swaddlings. Now she stood smiling ensconced only in her panty and brassiere. All five-feet eleven of her. Her breasts rising and falling with every breath, her hips placed in such a position so as to reveal her long smooth glistening legs. And, oh Lord, where the inside of her thighs met, a slight mound, a mound of mystery and intrigue. A triangular mound hidden beneath soft tawny hair beckoning the male of the species to dare to discover and explore it. This woman was without equal. Not one square inch of her whole anatomy had a flaw. Now Lana turned revealing her back. Her loosened hair had fallen to the top of her panties. Her back had an inward arch that emphasized her full, rounded derriere. No posterior anywhere could match this 'beckoning' rump. No words yet had been coined to describe Dr. Lana Jean Masters' loveliness.

"You like, senor?"

"Don't. Please don't ask such a silly question."

"You no like senor?"

"Polly, or whoever you are don't, don't please don't. You are breathtaking."

Clark was hypnotized. He just sat and stared at this magnificent female.

Lana closed the distance between Clark and her. She moved toward him like a prowling lioness. Clark imagined he could detect a smoldering guttural snarl coming from her throat, a snarl of a wild beast, a beautiful tawny wild beast. Now her astonishing legs touched his. He quivered. She took his hand and tugged gently to have him stand. Shaking from uncontrollable excitement, Clark stood. Lana looked up into his eyes. Like an impish vamp, she said, "are you all right, big guy?"

"No, heavens no I am not all right. I have never been so un-all-right. My lord Polly."

Now Lana's right leg moved between his legs. Then she did her wicked, sensual thing. The thing that had tied so many people up in knots, yes, when Lana parted her full moist lips and ran her pink tongue over them. Her mouth was pure sex. This move filled people with unbridled passion. This she did to tease Clark. Then she kissed him. She nipped his quivering lips. Her tongue moved into his mouth searching. She rolled her hips. She disengaged their mouths. She undressed the big man just as if he was a baby. He stood still eyes only partly open. Zombie-like, he would lift an arm or a leg as she required. His body was shaped like a Greek Adonis, tall lean with flowing muscles. He was bare except for his thick tousled head of hair, his underarm growth and the fortress of hair that stood guard over his loaded cannon.

Lana allowed Clark to remove her pretty underthings. They made love. Finally, Lana said, "Oh by the way, Clark, my real name is Lana Jean Masters."

"The doctor Lana Masters?" he said, jumping from the bed. "The real, Dr. Masters?"

"Yes."

"My Good God."

They made love off and on until the following morning. Clark proposed marriage over and over again to her. His proposals were made at every hiatus and during their sexual explorations. Lana just giggled. Lana found Clark to be a most patient caring lover. No brutality, just adventurous, rollicking and fun.

'How easy it would be to just say, yes,' Lana thought.

Clark was stunned for weeks after finding out his three year acquaintance with Polly the bag lady was in fact with *the* Dr. Lana Masters.

She was to be his…his alone. God, she was earth's most radiant product. She was to be his until death do us part.

Their life together in all respects was as if they were one. Their repartee was all inclusive. Two great minds. Two great lovers, devoted, caring, generous. They enjoyed exploring the great State of New York together, and from time to time visiting 'the spread' in Saskatchewan. They continued to live in squalor yet always they cherished one another's love. They were happy.

CHAPTER 72

THREE YEARS LATER POLLY DISROBES TO WALL STREET YUPPIES

Polly discloses her secret. Hold on to your hats!

Strange feelings had begun to come over Lana's psyche after leaving Istanbul…feelings cluttered with serious and impish thoughts. Her ego demanded she forego her life as Polly the bag lady, and it said, "have a ball doing it. Unswaddle your swaddlings, give Wall Street a show to remember, be dangerously piquant."

*　　　*　　　*

May 16th1997, 11:58 a.m. Friday, the best day of the week. It was sunny in Manhattan, a delightful 76 degrees with a pleasant breeze wafting its way in from the northwest. The weekend weather forecast was for more of the same.

People poured out of the financial districts mighty skyscrapers jostling, pushing, smiling, and clamoring to buy the street vendors' luncheon offerings. The 'guys' were in shirtsleeves the 'girls' in dresses or light slacks. Most of them were rushing to Wall and Nassau. They knew 'Polly the bag lady' would be at the top of the steps of the Sub-Treasury Building by noon and they knew the old broad would be her usual turgid self. She never let them down. It was more fun listening to this old tank-o-shit than going to the best show on Broadway.

A cheer went up as Polly was spotted. Everyone stepped aside as the old witch made her way up the steps. Everyone near her gave her the 'high five.' She reciprocated.

The young 'Turks' laughed. "Hey Polly," they yelled, "what's up your ass today, you old crone?"

"Two billion dollars worth of junk bonds and a glycerin suppository," she cackled.

"That'll clean 'em up, Polly baby."

Everyone cheered and laughed. Polly stumbled on until she reached the top of the steps. She turned to the throng. The hooting and hollering was deafening. "C'mon Polly, give us shit. It's a great Yankee Doodle day, yeah Polly fuck it up for us." To quieten down the crowd, Polly raised her hands above her head. This caused strands of her ugly wig to flip into her mouth. "Quiet you futherfluckers," she snorted as she tried to blow the hairy ugliness out of her mouth. Everyone laughed. They guffawed so hard wieners slipped out of their buns, cokes and beer splashed everywhere and food spluttered out of their mouths. This was going to be one "hellovan" hour of laughs.

"Futherfluckers?" They yelled.

"Thut you mealy moufs you intellectual deserts," Polly yelled back. She brought her hands down and yanked the loose strands from her mouth.

"There, that's better. Hair in your mouth when you're busy is a pain in the butt, eh fellas?"

"Right on Polly baby!" the boys hooted.

The girls booed.

Polly saw several of New York's finest scrutinizing the goings on. Polly waved to them. Some waved back.

"Hey you money mongering shit for brains out there, I gotta tell ya somethin' that happened to me years ago when you were still young ass wrapped, diaper wearing primates. The bulls out there bring back memories."

"Yeah Polly, lets hear it," the lunch crowd crowed.

"I used to drive a Studebaker. I was parked downtown."

"Yeah."

"And the time ran out on my parking meter."

"Yeah."

"And I got a two dollar ticket stuck behind the Study's windshield wiper."

"Yeah"

"And I was so busy hooking, I didn't have time to go to the police station to pay the two bucks."

"Tough noogies Polly."

"No Problem. God how I hate that saying, 'no problem'" she spat.

"Yeah, no problem Polly"

"Fuck you you ape apples. Anyway, so I put the two dollars in a stamped envelope with a note and mailed it."

"That's not funny you old bag," the mob hooted.

"Shut the fuck up a-holes, I'm not finished yet. In my note, I waxed poetic."

"Yeah, how did you wax poetic?"

"I waxed as follows you bunch of toads…"

"Hickory Dickery Doc,

"The cop is up the block,

"The time has struck,

"And I am stuck.

"Enclosed you'll find two buck.

"Now you rich young farts out there, what do you think of that for sheer majesty?"

Laughter rollicked up and down Wall Street.

"You are the greatest you old goat," they screeched.

"Merci you bunch of bozos. Now my children, I must get serious, I must get on with my topic for today, yes children my topic for today."

"And what is your topic for today, oh great one?"

"Aha! it is a topic near and dear to your hearts you soul-less bunch of horse turds. Forsooth my children, harassment in the work place," Polly boomed.

"Yeah brethren, harassment in the work place."

"Wild, you old hag Polly, wild. Give it to us m'lady," the crowd bellowed.

"And you juicy coke sniffers, I've got a secret thing to show you at the end of my sermon today."

"Wild, Polly, Wild."

The police looked skeptical.

"But, before I start my sermon my wealthy 'nose bags' we must pay homage to our God of riches. This you know is only right according to our great moguls, you noble bunch of money grubbers. Now do you remember how to do the rites, oh miserly ones?"

"Yes, we know the rites, oh great crone."

"Then begin now your opulent chicanery—look down with disdain at any scum bag near you—good—now push them down on their knees and have them thank you for allowing them to breath the same air as you. Have them kiss your bountiful butts. Piss on them if you must. Hallelujah my wealthy sisters and brothers. Hallelujah."

Polly let 30 seconds roll by.

"Now you infelicitous morons, on with harassment," she croaked. "To begin do you know dudes, women dress for women in the main and not for men. Yes, jealously they look at other women's attire and jewelry and stuff, not at the appeal their rags have for men," Polly clacked.

A mixture of "bullshit" and boos erupted.

"Yes, dudes, they do. Clothes designed by "tootie-frooties."

"Boo, hiss. You're nothing but a tootie fruitie yourself Polly!" the gals shouted.

"No sisters, I am not. Look at me I'm normal."

"Yeah, you're about as normal as hemorrhoids on a fly's ass," some woman screeched.

"Stone the crone," someone yelled. "Women dress for themselves, then for men. Not for other women."

"Oh no men, our girlies carp. Hear them? Hey dudes didja know girls became domesticated just 9000 years ago, yeah, only twice as long ago as kitty cats? Maybe that's why they are so different from men. When they do dress for men they dress in such a way as to excite mens weak minds. They become cock teasers."

"You're a fuckin' turncoat dingbat," the girls screamed.

"Keep it up Polly," the guys hooted.

Now the police had to move. The women were mad, they were ready to assail Polly. "Fuck you—you old goat, you miserable old traitor."

Polly herself halted the charge.

"Stop you heathen sluts, lest I lay a curse on you. I am about to advise men on how to expunge harassment in the work place. So don't screw this up. Oh, and by the way how many of you are wearing tight mini skirts now?"

"Damn near all of them, Polly" The good lads called out.

"No shit?" Polly feigned surprise.

"No shit Polly."

"Well ain't that a titty."

"You're horrid," a few ladies screamed.

"Now boys you are about as smooth at your harassment of girls in your work place as my ass is at skeet shooting. Yeah you empty headed morons, and, quite properly so, you end up paying monetary judgements to these pretties because your arrogant, ceaseless stupidity."

"Hold it Polly. Careful," some guys uttered laughing.

"You are one cool 'matha' Polly but stay cool or we'll have your ass!"

"Okay, boys, here's my advise to you at the workplace. (1) Do not pay any attention to any woman who is working for the same company as you. (2) Say good morning and good evening only. (3) Only speak when spoken to by a female, unless you must ask a question pertaining to the business of the company. Then be terse, no eyeballing, stand erect, eyes front then when answered repair back to your own work station. Never, under any circumstance, lean over a woman's desk. (4) Address all females formally vis-a-vis, Ms. (5) If a 'teaser' comes to your desk and leans down facing you, breasts glowing under a skimpy bra, look her in the eyes only. Do not massage her tits with your eyeballs. (6) Do not pick up after them. (7) Do not help them on with overcoats or the like. (8) Never, ever touch a female fellow employee. (9) Never offer them drives to their homes. (10) Do not buy any female fellow employee coffee, lunch and never ever suggest drinks or dining out. (11) Ignore sexy attire, glistening gams, pumped up breasts, and gorgeous faces. (12) If you men ever discuss between yourselves sophicated remarks such as 'what a lay Mary would make' or 'how would you like a handful of her ass,' do it quietly so no female can hear you. No snide, suggestive remarks should be made aloud.

"Now boys, on the streets it's a different story. You can howl like a horny Cro-Magnon man at any broad, whistle, even pinch the odd skirt so long as she is not a fellow employee. Take me for instance, any of you dudes here today want to come up NOW and pinch my ass?"

"No, good God Polly, no, you're too uugly."

"Okay cowards, you may be sorry!"

"Polly, you're a miserable example of a female, you old pussy. You piss us ladies off. We take harassment from the Neanderthals every day of the week," said one beauty standing near Polly in the tightest mini dress possible.

Polly eyed Ms.Mini Dress then said, "I'll bet you do."

"Ladies, subliminally all women think along the same lines. While in general you dislike one another, nevertheless, you form a profound, secret alliance between yourselves so deep-seeded, so powerful, so patriotic that without overt signals you know what all other females are thinking. You have it fixed in your minds so that…not as you do now in subterfuge, in secret nor with formal planning…by the year 2033 you will rule the world. Men will be nothing more than listless perfunctory wanderers."

"Boo you vagrant old hag," some screamed laughing.

"You're our heroine oh great crone," others hooted.

"In any event you bunch of heathen primates. You women, if the men comply with my 12 directives, can dress in accordance to your fancies then, hallelujah, you can breathe easier in the workplace because men will distance themselves from you and will ignore you."

"You've got shit for brains, Polly Wolly," the crowd roared. The bag lady just stood until the crowd silenced.

"Hey everybody, I am now ready to show you my surprise."

"Wild," everyone chorused. Two of New York's finest moved to the top of the stairs, came within two or three feet of Polly and stationed themselves there. They were suspicious of this side show wonder. Polly threw them a kiss.

"Now, my children, I need two willing male volunteers to assist me." Hundreds yelled, "Me Polly me, I'm the one, take me."

Polly selected two hunky exec's named Jerry and Bobby-Ray.

"Okay everybody this is what I want Jerry and Bobby-Ray to do. I want them to undress me, slow and easy, as I direct them." Jerry and Bobby-Ray looked stunned. Christ, undress this old hag. They eyed each other. What in hell did we get ourselves into?

The crowd went into hysterics. "You old piece of shit you, we can hardly wait, will we need barf bags Polly?" the massive bunch shouted.

"You might," Polly replied cackling.

"Okay Jerry and Bobby-Ray let's get to it—off with my wig."

With misgivings and whilst holding their noses the two young turks removed her wig. Polly looked face down then flipped her tawny mane over her back and down past her shoulders.

She looked up smiling. The crowd stilled, Jerry and Bobby-Ray blinked, looked, blinked again, looked at one another, at the stunned crowd, at the two policemen. They stared at Polly's astonishing face, then mumbled "It's Venus, it's...The Madonna...it's" The crowd became silent, spellbound.

"Okay boys off with my rubber boots and socks."

They obeyed. Again they were stunned. Even Polly's feet were beautiful.

"Now boys, my swaddlings."

"Good God dare we?" they whispered. "What if she's nude?"

"Now boys" she ordered, "NOW."

Again they obeyed. They started at the top unraveling Polly's layers of clothing. They stopped, agog as they unfurled the swaddlings down past her breasts. They could see, as did the crowd, that Polly was not nude. She was wearing a slip-like red 'thing' beneath her bag lady clothes which left her shoulders bare and which allowed everyone to ponder the size of her incredible 'boobs.' Jerry and Bobby-Ray stood as if their feet were stuck in concrete, stone like, bewitched by Polly. The crowd was silent.

"Common cowards," Lana demanded, "get these fucking clothes off me."

Again they obeyed. Their hands fumbled. As they unfurled her swaddlings they touched her body. That rendered them useless. The clothes now lay in a heap at Polly's feet. Like a stealthy lioness, Polly stepped away from the heap of clothes and as she did, she brushed one of the policemen. He paled, gulped, but never moved. There she stood; taller than Jerry and Bobby-Ray, the most beautiful woman in the world. Her red slip-like 'thing' clinging to her body. It showed every curve and fissure of her magnificent body. The crowd, Jerry, Bobby-Ray and the two policemen stared enchanted, transfixed, debilitated.

After a few moments Lana broke the silence, "Now would anyone care to come up here and pinch my ass?" Using sex as her tantalizer

Polly turned her back to the crowd. Gulps and gasps gushed out of the mouths of every soul on Wall Street. Her posterior was the final straw. A strange silence fell over the crowd. Who is this being? Now it began to stir. A few hands clapped. A few 'Polly's' were heard. The huge throng began to rumble like a volcano readying itself to erupt. Polly strutted. The enclave roared its approval. Polly threw in a few impish wiggles as she strutted. That did it, in a heightened frenzy the big crowd shrieked out an impassioned "Paully, Pawllleey, Pawllleey…"

Questions were rained on her. Why have you covered yourself up these past years? Who are you? Are you a Goddess an angel or what? Are you for real, touch her Jerry and Bobby-Ray, find out if she's real, and on and on until Polly silenced them.

"Yes, you grandiloquent grubs, I am real, go ahead Jerry and Bobby-Ray touch me, see if I'm real."

They did. "She's real. She's really, really real. She's……." Both men shook."

"Doyawanna pinch my ass you handsome cops?" she purred.

Polly walked over to them and kissed each one's lips. They were numbed, lost, tongue-tied. Their blood pressure soared. They had been kissed by a Goddess.

"Okay guys and dolls my real name is Lana Jean Masters."

"Not…" Some in the crowd started to yell.

"Yes, Dr. Lana Masters."

"We saw you on TV from Instanbul earlier this month," several in the crowd called out.

"That was me, big shots."

"Holy Sheeet."

"No more questions please, 'evabody' I have a brief interlocution to discuss with you."

"Dr. Lana you are the one."

First, I want to apologize to all you wonderful people who accompany me on my walks for not telling you of my true identity. I love all of you. Be assured my great friends, I will be with you, when possible, just as I have in the past. I may dress a bit different, but I will be there for you.

"I see you Wall Streeters have only five minutes left before you must return to your offices, so I shall 'hustle.' I'm sure most of you have heard of H&B Financial & Poors Inc?"

"We have"

"You know its beginnings?"

"We do"

"I am a shareholder of H&B, I am on its board of directors and, too, I am one of its finance advisors."

"Great, Polly-Lana."

"As of today's date H&B has 7,112 shareholders. All of my 'scummer friends' here with me today are shareholders. Neat eh?"

"Great Polly-Lana."

"2300 of H&B's shareholders now are employed in private business."

"Yeah Polly-Lana."

"Another 1,900 are now employed in various levels of government."

"S'okay, Polly-Lana."

"H&B employs 300 "streeters," while 2,612 are yet to be rehabilitated."

"Excellent, Polly-Lana."

"And, 30 of our young men and women will become politicals some day.

Those are some of H&B's accomplishments to date.

"Hey all you guys and dolls out there, its been a ball bandying words back and forth with you over the past three years. You're great. Maybe I'll come back every few Fridays just to get Wall jived up with our bandying. S'ok with you guys?

"Yeah baby. We want you. You are *the* one, so don't leave us danglin'."

"Keep the faith you'ns."

"As long as you're with us we will."

She threw the big crowd kisses. She kissed and hugged Jerry and Bobby-Ray, then thanked them for undressing her. They reddened. Both in the matter of minutes had fallen in love with Lana.

The huge throng roared its approval for Lana. Even the two big cops joined in. She picked-up her wig and swaddlings, then began her descent down the steps. She milled in with everyone, high-fived, chatted, answered questions and hugged many. She charmed everyone. She was like Muhammad to the Muslims, Jesus to the Christians, Marilyn to the Kennedys' and like Tinkers was to Evers was to Chance. She owned Wall Street. TV cameras captured the whole event. Clark had informed NBC, CBS, ABC and the CBC of Polly's 'coming out debut' that morning. He promised each network the 'show' would be a winner. It was. Millions tuned in for the six o'clock news. They heard and saw unedited, the full hour of The Bag Lady's Exit.

CHAPTER 73

LANA'S RAPE BY FATHER DONNELY AND THE IVY LEAGUERS

Lana was anxious to meet with Father Donnely. She had his card. She knew Father Donnely was the one who shot at her during her first day of lectures in Istanbul. She had to get to know this man. He seemed vaguely familiar to her and this vagueness bothered her. Too, she had a bad feeling about this man. Devil-like. Hawkish, shiny bald pate, thin, good-looking, but evil. She felt as if he was carrying a personal vendetta against her. Just like Franklin. I wonder whatever became of Franklin? she mused. He was such a Jekyll and Hyde. Franky baby, I categorize you along with Uncle Fred, evil. Forget Franklin, on with Father Donnely. I know on occasion clergymen can become devil incarnates. They want to worship God, but the devil's influence becomes too persuasive. Yes, it will be interesting to meet this man. Chat with him. See if I can psychoanalyze him. Maybe its nothing but a 'hang-up' I have with the good reverend. Anyhow here goes. She dialed Father Donnely.

"Good morning, this is Father Donnely."

Surprised at getting him, Lana hesitated a moment then said, "Good morning Father, this is Lana Masters. You may recall me, I met you once or twice in the past."

"Yes of course I do child. Dear, dear, I must apologize to you again, Dr. Masters, for my dreadful behavior while in Istanbul. You wouldn't know the number of times I have chastised myself for that awful incident and the number of times I have asked God to enter your soul and scour my misdeed from your mind. I have asked for absolution through numerous prayers. I beg of you to forgive me my child," Father Donnely said, as he crossed himself.

"Please Father I do forgive you. You have my sympathy. I must say, many of the words I speak cause infuriation with some people. I know I can be a big pain in the, excuse me Father, butt. Please try to forget the incident, I have."

"You are most gracious Dr. Masters."

"Thank you Father."

"Now what is it I can do for you Doctor?"

"Well sir, remember when we chatted on the aircraft coming back from Istanbul and we thought it would be nice if we got together sometime."

"Yes, of course I do."

"Well, I would be so delighted if I could meet with you, perhaps even tonight at 7:00, if you are free?"

"That sounds splendid doctor, but give me a moment to peruse my daytimer to see if, tonight, umm May 16th, 7:00 p.m. is open… mmm…7:00 p.m., yes it is, yes child it is. Please doctor I should like you to come to my house rather than the church, you see the church has bingo on this evening. You will see my address on the card I gave you. I look forward to seeing you tonight my dear."

"Thank you father, you are so kind. I look forward to seeing you as well. Goodbye."

'This could be a 'rip-snorter' tonight,' Lana thought.

The priest dialed Charles'and Stu's number. Charles answered.

"Charles, it's Father Donnely."

"Well hi Father, we wondered when you were going to call. Remember, Friday, Saturday and Sunday are to be the days for our rendezvous with Lana Masters?"

"Come now gentlemen, have faith in your Father. Our rendezvous is on. Doctor Masters telephoned me just as I was about to call her. She will be at my home at 7 o'clock this evening. I should like you chaps to be at my home no later than 6:45 p.m. You shall stay out of sight until 7:30 p.m. At that time you shall make your presence known, and voila, the party will begin. Of course in order to be proper and polite, I shall introduce both you and Stuart to Dr. Masters. Following my introductions one of you must grab the good doctor's purse and be away with it, well out of her reach. She carries a Derringer in her purse, so chaps don't fail. The lady is a sharpshooter. She can split an Eskimo cunt hair in two at 20 paces. Then she must be grabbed and searched by the two of you. Knowing her, she could conceal a weapon someplace on her body, so do not be shy boys, search her everywhere. My recommendation to you before you begin the search is to render her naked. One final word of warning for you each of you Charles, do not, and I repeat do not look into her eyes. She can spellbind you with her eyes. Be vigilant my boy, heed this warning."

"Right on padre, we will be at your house at 6:45."

* * *

Lana arrived at Father Donnely's home at 7:00 p.m. Charles and Stuart had arrived 20 minutes earlier. They had made themselves at home in the priest's bedroom.

Like a gentleman Father Donnely welcomed Lana. Lana told him it was so nice of him to see her on such a short notice. She commented on the gentility of his home. The priest said he was quite comfortable and he was more than satisfied with its trappings, therefore found his home to be a fine place to live.

He had Lana sit in a large easy chair then he offered her a drink. Lana chose a sherry—the priest selected a port.

Lana showed great interest in his life. Where he was born, what his parents did, where he lived most of his life, did he go to a public school or to a separate school? How were his years in the seminary? Winking she asked if he had ever dated and did he ever miss having a girlfriend? Did he get good grades in school? Was his decision to become a priest a difficult one? The priest seemed quite flattered by her attention. They chatted about Lana's dissertations in Istanbul, but neither made mention of the Twelve Controllers, the shooting incident nor the mysterious events that took place in the large assembly room.

A short hallway led from Father Donnely's living room to his bedroom. At 7:30 p.m. the bedroom door opened. Father Donnely, from where he was seated, was able to look down the hallway. On seeing Charles and Stuart emerge, he beckoned them to come to the living room. As they entered the living room Lana turned in her chair to face them. She smiled. Father Donnely stood and said, "Please come in lads, there's someone here I would like you to meet."

Charles and Stuart smiled. They looked every bit the ivy leaguers. They were introduced as two young men visiting Father Donnely from a seminary just outside Boston. They both looked so clean cut, so All American.

Without wasting any time, Charles snatched Lana's purse just as Stuart grabbed her.

"What's going on Father?" she called out to the priest.

"It's not what's going on my dear lady, it's what's going to be coming off. Hurry boys, I'm getting quite stiff." In the next instant, Stu found himself under the pressure of a wrist-lock and, as they say in wrestling, he was taken to the floor by a hair pull. Lana sat on Stuart, but she was unable to fend off Charles who grabbed her from behind and pulled her to the floor.

"Don't damage the merchandise boys, she's precious," the priest cautioned, smiling. Stuart cursed as Lana twisted his wrist one last time as Charles got on top of her. Lana wasn't beaten yet. She raised her long legs and gave a mighty heave with her body as she straightened her legs. Charles was dislodged onto the carpet, but before Lana could reach for Charles' throat, Stuart was on top of her. Bastards, she thought. She threw one hell of a right cross at Stuart from the floor, but good old Father Donnely stuck his foot out just in time to thwart off the blow and to save Stuart from getting a 'thick lip.'

"C'mon chaps, don't let a woman beat you up. Get her arms behind her back, tie them, then you will be able to disrobe her." Stuart grabbed Lana's right arm and her right leg. Charles did the same with her left arm and leg. Lana bucked like a bronco. The two 'lions' were flipped around by Lana's powerful legs. Her dress was now pulled up past her hips. Her pink bikini panties showed. The 'ivy leaguers' held on despite the shaking they were taking. Finally Lana ran out of steam. Fuck it, she thought as she saw the priest standing above her ready to enter into the fray. While Lana knew she was unable to overpower three men, she knew she could outwit them. By the grace of Eve One this ladies great brain had begun a plan of redemption at Charles and Stuart's first move. She let them stand her up. "No bonds are necessary," she said, "I'll be a good girl."

"What do you think Father should we tie her?"

"No, I think not, I believe her. So undress her and search her."

They did.

"Jesus Chuck, we could hire her out at $10,000 a pop."

"No doubt we could Stu, but we are going to stick to our plans. Let's just lay the broad 'til we're sick of her."

The priest and the ivy leaguers ravaged Lana for 15 hours, until Lana decided to put her plan into action. She did this at 10:00 a.m., Saturday morning, May 17th. The two ivy leaguers were asleep. The priest was milling around in his kitchen.

Quietly, so as not to rouse Charles and Stuart, she slid from the bed, wrapped herself in a housecoat left lying on the floor by the priest, then tiptoed to her purse and fetched her Beretta the foolish men had left unhidden. Too goddamn stupid horny to hide the gun, assholes, she thought. She slipped the tiny gun into a pocket of the priest's housecoat then made her way into the kitchen.

"Shh—shh Father Donnely. Don't waken those two leaguers. They are terrible lovers. Very sadistic, very selfish." Lana shivered as if she was being attacked by nausea just thinking of them. "But you Father, you were delightful, I could be loved by you forever. You are like a dream come true. May I kiss you?"

"Yes you may my angel. I find you exude eroticism. You are so beautiful. Making love to you is heaven my child."

They kissed. "What are we going to do about those two leaguers?" Lana asked. "They are so foul. I want only you Father."

"Well my dear, I don't mind letting you in on a little secret. You see, sometime tomorrow I am going to kill you. The leaguers, as you call them, will pay me well to dispose of you—dispose of you in a most discreet manner."

Lana began to cry. Tears flowed down her cheeks. "This is so horrid," she said, "the man whom I could love is to kill me. Is it for money?"

"I'm afraid so dear."

"Just because of my love for you Father, I will offer you $100,000 not to kill me. You will not regret it. I will stand by your side always. I need your love. Oh God how I need your love. Do not kill me, I beg of you. We would be so compatible not just as lovers but as intellectual logicians. I will give you $100,000 today if you spare my life. Too, Father, I would give anything, anything to have you come to a beautiful love nest I have on the prairies in Western Canada. You would find it enchanting, pristine and oh so romantic. I am to leave tomorrow, providing you don't kill me Father. We could arrange a flight out for you on Monday or Tuesday…"

"No, no my dear, if I decided to go to your little love nest, I would not be able to leave until May 23rd. I have meetings that day in Chicago at 8:00 a.m."

"That's fine Father, please, let me look after your travel arrangements."

"And the $100,000?" he asked.

"I will have a cashier's check for $100,000 in your hands by noon today, and I will have your travel arrangements, tickets and itinerary to you after your morning mass tomorrow."

"Splendid, I think I should like to see your vast prairies, yes, indeed, I would. Now please excuse me Lana. I wish to go in and discuss various options with Charles and Stuart. Don't run off now when my back is turned, my angel."

"No, of course I won't, I love you to much to run off Father."

Satisfied the priest departed to his bedroom. The 'ivy leaguers' were still asleep, snoring.

"Sorry boys," the priest said under his breath, as he asphyxiated them with pillows. Their bodies jumped hideously whilst suffocating.

He returned to Lana. "The boys are most understanding my dear. They have agreed to let me out of their contract. I am free to meet you at your love nest."

"Oh thank God," Lana said.

By noon Lana had handed the priest a cashier's check in the amount of $100,000. The next day after mass, Lana delivered the priest his travel documents.

He was amused at Lana's care in covering his trail from Chicago's O'Hare. 'It will take the constabulary months to find the skeletons of Charles and Stuart.' He mused, smiling.

Lana assented to Father Donnely's wish following Mass. She fucked him.

CHAPTER 74
INSTANBUL

MAY 8, 1997

Lana relates to Clark St. Jame's journey into privation.

"I should like to discuss an incredible topic with you before I plead my thoughts to you regarding religion and politics," Lana said.

"Earlier in the day I spoke of the 3 billion people worldwide who were living in deplorable conditions, and about an investment in these people of 72 trillion dollars.

"Well, now I feel compelled to tell you a story about some homeless vagabonds on Manhattan Island who have created and built one of the most successful business enterprises I have ever seen. They are drunks, junkies, petty thieves, whores, misfits and schizophrenics, down-and-out professionals, and of all races, creeds, and religions. There are over 7,000 of them now. They all have a minimum of 100 common voting shares with a par value of one dollar each in their company. The largest single shareholder is a 42-year-old lady of the night who holds 630 shares. The total outstanding shares issued and fully paid amount to $910,500. One of the originators of the company at the time of the company's incorporation donated $990,000 as contributed surplus.

"The name of the company is H&B Financial and Poors Inc. The 'H' stands for hobos and the 'B' for bums. Its fiscal year-end is March 31st. H&B, as I will refer to it during my talk, was five years old on March 31st, 1997. From its first fiscal year-end to date H&B has been most successful. At March 31st, 1997 the company's total assets exceeded $1.8 billion. Its liquid assets exceeded $1.18 billion, its investments in high grade small Manhattan rental properties was approximately $500 million, its fixed assets amounted to one million dollars, and its ownership of a National Hockey League franchise at cost amounted to $100 million.

"Its gross revenues for the 12-month period ended March 31st, 1997 totaled $446 million, which included gains on sales of stocks of just under $200 million. Its expenses were minimal. It's after tax profit was $73 million.

"Shareholders were paid $293 million as wages. Income taxes amounted to $48 million and $73 million was transferred to retained earnings. Government and private business wage subsidies together amounted to $32 million.

"Liabilities consisted of amounts payable to shareholders of

$283 million, $48 million re various income taxes, $32 million in wage subsidies, and $20,000 of ordinary monthly payables leaving something in excess of $1.436 billion in shareholders equity.

"Succinctly, ladies and gentlemen, that is the current financial condition of Hobos and Bums. Now, I should like to tell you of its roots and its dynamism."

Dr. Masters told her attendees how a man from California put H&B's wheels into motion. This gentleman had been a part of the 'good life' from the time he was born. But something from his childhood gnawed at his inner feelings. In his own right after becoming a professional accountant he became wealthy. His family's fortune was in excess of one billion dollars of which his entitlement was one third thereof, amounting to some $350 million.

Two things continued to engulf his mind as he grew into manhood. One, was his loving relationship with his great Grandmother Maria and his great Grandfather Simon. They had taught him selflessness, honesty, integrity, forbearance, respect for others, forgiveness and love. Whilst he loved his great grandparents equally his adoration for Maria was indescribable. Without ego or braggadocio his gentle Maria had told him, in fascinating detail, the life stories of her and Simon. An indelible scar resulting from the knowledge he had of Maria's troubled childhood and the poverty she had lived in were engraved deeply on the man's soul. His goal in life, it seemed, was to erase the scar he bore on behalf of his great Grandmother by going to war on the side of the world's destitute. Two, his memories of the deplorable conditions thousands of people lived under. Ghettos, urban slums, drunken reprobates sprawling, begging, wearing filthy pissed and shat in clothing adorning the streets like maggots. Young children living in hell, prostituting themselves. Little ones with snotty noses, playing without underthings, skinny, poorly clothed.

The gentleman, after much soul searching, made the decision to drop out of his feathered bed and get on with his life battling the war against poverty. He was smart, he made certain he had at his disposal funds in excess of $5 million. These moneys, he promised himself, would be used only for the benefit of the poor. He left home September 1st, 1991. His path to glory in the name of the poor was not without hazards. He had made a covenant with himself that from the time he left home he would live like the wretched. His destiny was New York City. The chap was hale and hearty, he stood six-feet-five, and his hard muscled body weighed in at 235 pounds.

Lana informed her listeners the gentleman's first night out was a disaster. The month was September, so the weather on his departure was warm. He had made the decision his mode of transportation to the city of New York would be by way of walking, hitch hiking, sneaking his way on eastbound freight trains, any dashed method available to him as if he was a hobo. No personal vehicles. No paid for transportation, unless of course he earned some money as a hobo allowing him therefore to buy a Greyhound ticket from about here to there.

The gentleman had made the decision to take interstate 15 north through to the southern half of Utah then west on Utah State Highway 50, then catch interstate 70 through to St. Louis, Missouri. Once he reached St. Louis, he would make the decision there as to the final leg of his journey.

He left home at 9:00 a.m. September 1st, 1991. The morning was beautiful. A west wind was blowing across Los Angeles at a pleasant ten knots. The air seemed clean. Traffic in front of his 12,000 square foot home was negligible. Except for a household manager (a maid) and a maintenance manager (gardener and handyman) the gentleman lived alone. He had left them a detailed letter of instructions as well he assurred them of their continuing employment and monthly pay. He told them they could continue to live on his property rent free, and he promised he would be in touch with them twice each month to find out how 'things were going.' He said it would be impossible for them to contact him but if they really 'got stuck' they were to contact his father. He informed them too, they could use his Land Rover and his Lincoln Mark VIII. He had wished them both well.

* * *

'What the hell am I doing leaving home?' he had anguished.

'Why don't I just change my will and have all my assets directed to the Salvation Army at the time of my death? In the meantime I could send regular contributions to them. Why leave all this comfort for a ruddy seedy one? It's not my fault people are poor. Damn me, why wouldn't my donated money suffice? The dent I will make as a vagabond in the wall between the rich and the poor will be minuscule. My money would be much more beneficial to the needy than my meager presence in their midst. Why am I doing this, why?'

Off he went, backpack over his shoulders, a few bucks in his pocket, old runners on his feet, a gut full of butterflies and his karma awash in turmoil.

He arrived in Barstow at ten in the evening. What a cruddy time he had getting there. It took him five hours just to get out of Los Angeles.

He had been harangued, sworn at, damned near clipped by a dozen cars, propositioned by some women even some gents, saved by a few 'born agains,' scoffed at by Promise Keepers and at last given a ride by a sympathetic soul who was on his way to Etwanda. It was now after two in the afternoon. Damn, at this rate of speed the gentleman guessed he wouldn't get to New York City 'til the year 2005. Etwanda was off Route I15 by a few miles, so our man was left standing on the interstate in 98-degree heat. Our man was hungry, discouraged, and angry. He was so far out of his element.

Why not just turn around and go home? I've had enough of this already. He mumbled expletives as he trudged onward. What would 'Gram Maria' do in this situation, he wondered? No wondering necessary, she would carry on, she wouldn't throw in the 'sponge.'

Some goons pulled up beside him at around 5:00 p.m. Nice guys. They drove on the road's shoulder beside him mocking him in every way possible.

"How about a blow-job faggot?"

"How would you like eight inches of red juicy cock stuck up your keester?"

"You're a big fucker aintcha? Did mommy kick you out because you're a faggot?"

"Gimme ten bucks and I'll let you play with my balls."

"Okay buster, we're through fuckin' around, give us whatever bucks ya got on ya and we'll leave ya alone."

Our man just kept walking, looking straight ahead trying to ignore the thugs.

"I said give us your fuckin' money faggot or we'll get outta the car and take your fuckin' money the hard way."

Our man noted there were two guys in the front seat of the car, and one guy in the back along with a slutty looking girl. Our man seldom swore, and if he did it was never smutty swearing. Shit was about as blasphemous a word as he ever used and he used it only when he was at the end of his patience. But now the gentleman was damn good and mad, yet somewhat apprehensive of these hoods and downright ticked off with his grandiose pie-in the-sky dream.

He reached into his pocket, looked up at the miserable bastards in the car with phony frightened eyes, eyes that said, 'sure fellas, I'll give you all the money I've got.' He walked around to the driver's side of the car while he fumbled in his pocket. He leaned close to the driver of the car and remarked, as he reached in the open window grabbing the punk by his hair, "Fuck you buster." He yarded the driver half way out of the car's window, still hanging onto the dude's hair, and with care not to kill the guy he drove his hammer-like fist full in the snot-rag's face. Blood spurted from the guy's nose and mouth. Then without the nicety of opening the car's door, he pulled the piece of shit out of the window, broke his right arm, then threw the screaming driver over the car's hood into the ditch.

The punk in the front passenger seat was scrambling for his switchblade when a vice-like hand took hold of his right wrist. Our man pulled the switchblader over to the driver's side of the car and using both hands, broke the guy's wrist with a sickening snap. He opened the door of the driver's side and pulled the mewling puke toward him then slammed the car's door on the puke's other hand crushing most of the bones therein. He pushed the howling dude back into the car and closed the door.

He looked at the man and woman in the back seat and asked in an affable manner, "May I be of service to either of you folks? I'm sure, sir, it was you who wanted me to give you ten dollars so that I could fondle your testicles. If the offer is still good, I will give you the ten dollars my man, then I will rip out your testes, shove them through your anus and drive them up into your rectum. Deal?"

"God no, please, I'm sorry. Jesus, man, I am sorry."

Our man reached in the back seat, grabbed the punk's left hand and snapped a couple of fingers. He looked at the terrified girl and said,

"You're a lucky woman 'cause' I don't hurt women." He told broken fingers to get out of the back seat which broken fingers did.

He retrieved the moaning driver and put him in the back seat with Ms. Slut. He told her to buckle Mr. Driver up as well as buckling up herself. Our man buckled-up the punk whose wrist he had just broken. He then told broken fingers to get in the driver's seat, buckle-up and drive off. Broken fingers did just that, he slammed the machine into drive and sped away.

Damn me, the gentleman thought, why would I do that to those punks? I had no right to do what I did. If I had just kept ignoring them, they might not have tried to rob me. If only there had been more traffic or if a highway patrol person had came along. For goodness sake don't ever let your temper get the best of you again. Your mission is to help people not harm them.

Our man kept walking toward Barstow. He didn't get another ride until 8:45 in the evening. The man who gave him the ride had to turn off about three miles out of Barstow. The walk into the little city was hot, dusty and painful. His feet were blistered, his shin splints ached. He needed a shower and food—food and wine—food, wine, coffee and desert. Jesus, he was hungry. And tired. He needed sleep. "What a bozo I am, I've got everything I want at home, what am I doing here? Where do I eat and sleep tonight, shit, shit, shit?"

He found the bus station. He used its washroom. He scrubbed his hands and face clean. He went into its coffee room and ordered scrambled eggs, toast, and coffee. After eating, our man felt a little better. He went into the bus station's waiting room, found a bench away from the station's ticket wicket, put his knapsack at one end for a pillow, lay down and fell asleep. About two o'clock in the morning he was awakened by the ticket master's rough shaking. He was told to leave. Struggling, our man got to his feet, put on his knapsack, sipped some water from his small cooler, shook the ticket master's hand and left. He was still exhausted. He needed more sleep, he had to urinate. "What in the hell am I doing here?" He trudged back to Interstate 15, clamored through the ditch, put down his knapsack, took a leak, then laid down. He slept.

He heard a strange droning sound and even the odd swishing noise. He reached for his eider-down comforter to pull it up over his ears in order to drown out the sounds. It wasn't there. He opened one eye to look for his comforter. Damn, all he saw was sand. Am I dreaming he wondered? He pawed at his bedside. More sand. He opened both eyes. Yeah it was sand all right, and the droning and swishing noises were the noises being made by the vehicular traffic on a big freeway.

"Where the hell am I?" He went to sit-up, but every bone and muscle in his big anatomy were on strike, or on sick leave, or some wretched thing. He struggled to sit up. He made it. Bloody hell, he was surrounded by desert, a ditch, a freeway and here he was laying in the center of it. God no, no beautiful home, just sand and tumble weeds. And the dreams he thought he had had were not dreams at all, they happened. Yes, he remembered. He beat the hell out of some guys the day before but damn he was supposed to be on a mission. A mission to wage war against poverty.

Finally he stood, stretched, looked around and within seconds of his rising, his frustrated psyche crashed down to about his knees. "Now what do I do?" he said to himself, depressed and lost. Lost like a tragic soul in purgatory. "I've got to go to the can, jog, shower, shave, dab my face with Ralph Lauren's Polo, underarm myself with Right Guard, eat a healthy breakfast then drive to the office and gross another five or six thousand. In a pig's eye. I don't know what to do the poor man said as he shouldered his knapsack again. This time he took a big 'swig' from his water cooler. Next stop Las Vegas, or maybe with a little luck, St. George, Utah.

He saw a MacDonald's in a nice setting just outside Barstow. He went in, used its washroom, washed…no shave…then came out and ordered the biggest breakfast 'Big Macs' had. While he ate he took out his map of the US studied it and agreed with himself. Yes, Vegas or even better St. George by tonight. Before hitting the road again, he had his water cooler filled to the brim.

It was 8:30 a.m. The morning was a touch on the cool side, about 60 degrees. There wasn't a cloud in the sky and the winds were beginning to pick-up. He walked along the freeway and thumbed every vehicle that passed him. At about 11:30 a big 28-wheeler stopped. The driver leaned over to the cab's passenger seat opened the window and asked our man where he was off to. "New York City, via Vegas,"our man answered.

"Are you packin' heavy, or are you on the lam, what?" the driver asked in a rather high-pitched voice.

"I don't know what you mean by packin' heavy, and no, I'm not on the lam or anything else, I'm just trying to get to New York in the next two or three weeks."

"You don't know from packin' heavy, big dude?"

"No sir, I don't."

"Are you a rapist, serial killer or any other fuckin' excuse for a man?" the driver asked laughing.

"No sir, I'm not."

"Do you like women?"

"Yes sir."

"And you don't know what 'packin' heavy means?"

"No, but I guess it means guns or something."

"Right big boy." The driver removed her baseball cap, shook her head and let her long reddish hair fall over her shoulders.

"You're a girl?" the gentleman gasped, "a pretty girl, a girl girl."

"That's right handsome, I'm a girl. Is it safe for me to let you in the cab with me?" the driver asked.

"It certainly is."

"How do I know you're okay?"

"Please," our man said, "if you have even the slightest hesitation about me, just carry on."

"That's a great line cutie."

"No, I'm serious, if you have any hes..."

"I haven't cutie, climb in."

The gentleman climbed in the big rig. He sat. He looked at the very attractive driver and said, "My you are a beautiful girl."

"Aren't you suppose to refer to us gals as women, not girl, dame or broad?" she said.

"I'm sorry if I've slighted you Ms., I just think you look like a girl, a cute girl."

"Well then, can I call you boy. Because even though you are a big dude, you look like a boy."

"That's fine with me woman," he responded smiling.

"Fuck you boy." She said with a throaty laugh. "Don't call me woman, it sounds awful. My name is Gerry, short for Geraldine, what's yours?"

"Just call me, er, Rodney," Clark said wondering why he lied about his name.

"Didja' forget your name for a moment big dude?" she said laughing. "Did I twitterpate you Rodney old chap?, Rodney, what a whoose of a name. You should be a Michael, Steven, Barney, some manly name, not Rodney."

"Sorry Geraldine, but that's my name. However Gerry, you can call me Rod."

"How sweet of you Rod," she teased. "You don't look like a hitchhiker Rodney. You're tanned, sophisticated looking, bright as hell and rich too I bet. Are you slummin' just for the fun of it?" Gerry questioned. "I kinda hope you're a horny slummer, baby boy. I'll bet I could give you a lesson or two. Are you just doing it for kicks?"

"Well..."

"Never mind, Rodney old chap. By the time we get to Vegas I'll know what you're about. And Rodney, don't worry about AIDS or any of that shit from me, I do not sleep around, I don't slum fuck, I don't do drugs, I don't drink and I don't smoke. So if I decide we are going to make love today, tonight, whenever, it will be bareback not saddle. What about you Rod, are you clean?"

"Yes Geraldine, I'm clean. But…"

"Good, I've fooled around long enough. Now Rod it's time to get this big Fatha rollin'."

Our man had never been in a rig like this before. It was awesome. The cab like the trailer was spotless. The dashboard looked like it belonged on a Boeing 747. The view from the windshield was unbelievable, nothing to hamper the driver's view. It was like a wide-angled camera, perfect for safety.

Geraldine drove the monster out into the right lane. She looked serious as she guided the huge carrier out into the traffic. The mileage to Las Vegas was 150 miles, about three hours away including lunch. She planned to stop at Baker for lunch.

Geraldine and our gentleman rode without a word being spoken for several minutes. She was busy getting the carrier in the mode she wanted. She checked her odometer, fidgeted with sun visors, the tractor's running lights, its sound system, air conditioning, brake tests until she was satisfied the big rig was 'A-okay.' Then she began to chat.

"So, Rodney, are you just slummin'?"

"In a way, yes."

"Just for kicks?"

"No, Gerry, I'm deadly serious about what I'm doing."

"Are you big guy?"

"Yes."

"And, what are you so 'deadly serious about' Rodney?"

"Well, remember you mentioned earlier that I was probably rich. Well I am. But I'm a little sick about rich. I want to live with the poor, you know, down-and-outers, addicts, drunks, deadbeats, whatever, and see if I can resurrect some of them into being productive people."

"Good luck, Rod baby. Millions of people have tried to do what you are hoping to do but have failed. What makes you think you can do it?"

"I don't know, Gerry. I'll probably fail too. But I'm going to give it my best shot over the next number of years."

"I believe you, handsome. You look like you are a fighter."

"Thanks Gerry!"

"Do you want to tell me about your plan of 'resurrection' Rod, or would you like to talk about something else?"

"Whatever Gerry. If we talk about something else I do want to mention something to you before we change the subject. I would like you to watch for a name that should hit the financial pages within the next five years. It's called H&B Financial and Poors Inc. It'll be good, sweetheart, believe me, good!"

"Yeah, why?" Geraldine asked.

"Because H&B Financial is going to be the vehicle which will carry the poor out of bondage." Clark said with a dramatic flair, raising his arms much like Moses did when Moses spoke to the children of Israel.

"Praise the lord, Rodney, Hallelujah." Gerry sermonized. They both laughed. "Anyway Rod, I hope you have success in helping people." Gerry said.

They rode in silence for awhile. Clark kept looking at the stunning Geraldine. She noticed and said to him "Do you like the way I look?"

Clark blushed, kinda squirmed embarrassed as Gerry took her eyes off the road and looked into his eyes. "Yes," he mumbled, "I do."

"Good," she said, "I like the way you look too."

"Thank you," he said.

"So'kay," she said.

"Rodney we are going to stop for lunch at Baker, about ten minutes from now. That'll mean Vegas between two thirty and three. How's that with you?"

"Geraldine, it sounds great. You're a very kind person, do you know that?"

Geraldine did not answer. Then she said, "Half of the cargo I'm carrying is for the Flamingo Hilton on the strip. It'll take about an hour to unload. Then I go to a big warehouse on Las Vegas Boulevard North and fill the trailer up with some mining material, that'll take another hour and a half, so by the time I'm finished in Vegas, traffic and all, it will be about six o'clock. Time for dins. I left San Diego at five this morning so I'm going to bed down in Las Vegas for the night. Then Rod, I'm off to Salt Lake City. Now handsome, you are invited to stay with me the whole time. Unloading, loading, getting the tractor gassed up, dining with me and sleeping with me tonight and hitching a ride with me tomorrow to wherever."

"Goodness Geraldine, I'm supposed to be roughing it. Getting used to the world of destitution. Christ, you're willing to serve me up a platter of goodies so enchanting I might say 'to heck with my plans' and stay with you. By the way, you're not married are you?"

"No I'm not. C'mon Rod, let's have some fun tonight. You can start roughing it up again tomorrow night. We won't stay up late. We can gamble for an hour, hit the sack around nine-thirty and then you can play with my body 'til eleven. How's that sound?"

"Fantastic," Clark said.

CHAPTER 75

CLARK'S JOURNEY

He hated himself for it, but he had had a most memorable night. He didn't want to leave her. But he was determined to give his plans a try.

Our man left Geraldine at the intersection of I15 and state Highway 50 at 10:00 the next morning in Utah. They had left Las Vegas at 6:00 a.m. Geraldine had begged him to stay with her but she knew Rodney was on a mission, a 'mission impossible' perhaps but nonetheless a mission. For a 'tough' truck driver she had tears when Rodney kissed her good-bye. Clark didn't feel so good about it either. Geraldine stayed on his mind for months after their parting. Goodness, he thought, if this is how the homeless live, I'm all for it. What a wonderful person Geraldine is, kind, thoughtful, lively, mischievous, bright and a buzz saw of a worker.

He spent the next night, September 3,rd in a small town called Rifle. It was a storm filled night, heavy rain, lightning, booming thunder, bloody awful. Our gentleman slept under a raised loading platform attached to an old warehouse of some sort. He knew the night was going to be a nightmare. Cold, wet just damn well shitty. No Geraldine to cuddle up to in a nice soft bed, hell no, just lightning, thunder and hail. And what about food, he didn't have any, not a scrap. Lesson one, our man discovered, was to keep a few reserves in the old 'nappy.' Too, he learned quick, was to wash wherever you can, take a crap 'any old place,' shave if you can, brush your teeth and get used to being lonely, cold, hot, uncomfortable, sweaty, dirty, hungry, thirsty, useless and frightened. And what do you do if you get sick?

When he awoke the next morning nothing seemed right. He felt he hadn't slept a wink. He was stiff and sore from sleeping on his earthy, bumpy, stone-filled mattress. He had to urinate. He was still wet from the night's rain. He was hungry. He had refused to take any money from Geraldine. His funds were down to a measly two bucks. Yeah, that's what our man intended, no extra cash. If he was going to be a bum he had to live like one. Run outta cash and you either work for some money or you 'beg, borrow or steal.' He was tired and hurting. He bumped his head on the overhang when he got up. That was the last straw. He threw a stupid punch at it in anger, bruising therefor his knuckles, and his placid psyche.

'Dumb bastard,' he thought as he shook his injured hand. He looked around, saw no one, yanked out his dick and leaked. He sat down and thought about his woeful financial position. No money, no food, sweet diddly squat. So what should be his next move, work, beg, borrow, or steal? He couldn't borrow any money around here, so that was out. He would not steal, and his ego would not stoop to begging, so only one thing left, work. He remembered seeing a Chevron station sign last night on his way to this 'shitty' overhang. He stood up looked and spotted the huge Chevron sign just a few hundred yards away. He shouldered his knapsack and made his way to it.

He went inside noting the food and all the other goodies in the station's store. 'I'm sooo damn hungry. Maybe I should steal some of the goodies then make a run for it. Naw, don't get stupid.' He walked over to an attendant who looked like he might be the boss and asked if he was the manager. The man nodded his assent.

"Sir," our man said, "is there any chores I can do for you?"

"Yeah son there is as a matter of fact. The washrooms need cleaning, the grounds could use some raking, the trash receptacles at the pumps need emptying. Yeah, go ahead, tidy everything up and you get fifteen bucks."

Like most Chevron stations, this one was clean to begin with, but our man made it spotless. The manager was so pleased with the way everything was done he 'shelled out' two ten dollar bills. Our man's pride bounced up a couple of notches. Followed by his thank-you's he traded back $5.90 of his earnings in exchange for that amount of packaged food. 'Yeah. $14.50 left over, I'm rich.' Off he went to a small diner next to the station.

His pride somewhat appeased our man now was ready to carry on. First he devoured a huge breakfast.

Next stop Denver, about 190 miles from Rifle. That was his goal for today. Find Denver's worst slum area, spend a couple of days there, get some down in the gutter experience and hopefully come out alive. Thrilling and chilling, he thought. He had been to Denver many times before, not only on business, but for pleasure, skiing, hiking, partying, the whole gamit. He loved Denver and its fine hotels and restaurants. Beautiful. "Yeah man, but not tonight. Tonight, shit for brains, what?"

It was 10:45 a.m. when he made his way to Interstate 70. There was plenty of traffic going his way. But this time the gentleman saw a freight train just starting to move out of Rifle toward the east. That's the ticket, he thought. He raced toward the lumbering behemoth and just as if he'd been doing it all his life, he caught one of the moving train cars as nice as you please. He had been in so much haste he hadn't looked to see what kind of freight car he had caught. But our man could smell it. It was a ruddy cattle car full of hamburgers on the hoof. "Man oh man," he said to himself, half laughing and damned near crying, "a bedroom fit for a king."

The trip took four and a half hours. There were three 15-minute stops along the way to Denver. Cripes, our man had been so far out of his element since he had left home he'd even forgotten to set his wristwatch one hour ahead. By the time the train arrived in Denver it was 5:30 p.m. Our gentleman artfully had dodged the train's working personnel during the trip, but he didn't dodge the cattle odor. After nearly five hours of hiding among the bovine beauties, he smelled like cow dung. 'Maybe even the slum dwellers will rebuke me because I smell so bad.' he though. After he had made some inquiries of reluctant, stand back inquiriees, he found his way to Denver's most indelicate slum.

* * *

The two days' experience our man had in the slums of Denver were dreadful. Drinking, drugs, needles, sickness, insanity, human filth, disease, and open running sores on men and women. Has-been prostitutes doing it for a buck. Whites, blacks, Hispanics. Old codgers, middle-aged, thirties, twenties, teenagers and some as young as ten. All intermingling sharing needles, squabbling, fighting, cackling, fucking, laughing, most of them toothless. Many passed out from overdoses of alcohol and drugs lay in drunken heaps. Some men had their balls hanging exposed as they lay in their comatose state and some comatose women whose hairy vermin ridden twats were revealed through spread legs and panty-less rumps. Most of the slummers were half-starved.

Much of their food stock came from garbage disposal containers. Many charities did their best to keep at least some of these pitiful pieces of shit clothed and fed. Of course at Christmas most good old Christians came out of hiding and 'gave.' "Yes," say our generous givers at Christmas, "it makes us feel so wonderful to be able to help these lonely, poor, poor souls. My how they must appreciate our hand-outs." Fuckin' paternal poppycock.

Our gentleman found the major portion of the Denver slummers were from broken homes, whose parents were drunks, addicts and/or abusers. The next largest group was mentally handicapped people—people who needed special or professional care and attention. 'Cleanliness is godliness' crossed our gentleman's mind.

Cleanliness is godliness. If that's a fact then all these wretches, and all others like them in the world must be the children of the devil. These people are the epitome of filth and degradation. They couldn't even qualify as agnostics. They must be atheists, or at best, heathens. How in heaven's name could these pathetic people keep their bodies and souls clean in their station of life? How would the Pope or the Archbishop of Canterbury, the Dalai Lama or whatever 'big wig' servant of their God 'make out' living in the stinking conditions of these slummers? Our man was certain only Jesus could endure these poor people's plight, stay among them, and remain whole.

"Should these human dung heaps receive proper attention from the world's populace, or should they just be left to die like godless mongrels in their squalor? Who gives a shit anyway? Yeah my Buddhist brethren, long live Nirvana at least for these poor fuckers."

Our gentleman found that some of the people of the streets and slums were at one time productive workers. People employed all the way from the top of the heap (scientists, professionals, business people and the like) to the unskilled. These people 'hit the skids' because they allowed certain happenings or substances to rule them. Many had lost their families, jobs, friends, and their dignities because of unswerving drug and alcohol habits, some because of family break-ups and others because of laziness.

These two days were eye-openers. Could these people ever, even with a hefty push, help themselves to improve their lot? Would they just say 'fuck it, no one can help us,' or would they say they are perfectly happy with their lot? 'Even if you think we should be something different, we want to remain as we are, so piss-off. Leave us alone.'

That's a tough one to get around. If these slummers don't want help then, by God, leave them alone. But there are millions of others world wide living in poverty who want to be productive. They want their pride along with a more equitable share of the world's riches. 'So keep on truckin,' our man said to himself.

The gentleman had tried begging on a busy street corner in Denver to see if he could do it. Damn tough way to make a living. Everyone he tried to put the touch on, even those who gave him money, looked at him as though he was sub-human. Some cursed at him while others cursed and spat on him. "Why don't you get out and try to make an honest living?" was a common comment. Our man was even propositioned by two well-dressed young women who were taken with his good looks. He had gathered in $21.60 in one hour of begging. 'Shit, that's one heck of a lot better than minimum wages of $4 an hour,' he said laughing. 'Imagine me begging? Pheeeuu I feel different somehow.'

The last night in the slums a fight broke out between some blacks, hispanics, and whites. Yes man, even in the slums racism can rear its ugly head. The ruckus started when one white guy pushed a black woman who was yelling "Ya white mother-fucker, ya owes me two bucks for that blow job."

"Bullshit I do, what blow-job ya ta'kin' 'bout, ya black whore?"

"The head I jus' gib yo, yo whitey pissin' jerk-off!" She took a wild swing at her client after he pushed her. She missed and stumbled to the ground. There were quite a few other slummers around the makeshift camp. She had knocked a white drunk flying when she missed her client with her roundhouse swing as she went sprawling. The white dude who owed her the two bucks gave the black whore a couple of feeble kicks as she lay akimbo on the tarred surface. A black brother shoved whitey from the back and whitey fell on top of the black whore who was still screaming for her two bucks.

A toothless hispanic, who began to cackle a wheezing laugh-like noise, pointed a filthy forefinger at the downed couple. "El fucko, ya dirty black pussy an white cock-sucker, el fucko," he squeaked encouraging a free-for-all-orgy. Then he pushed the black brother on top of the squirming duo. In a few minutes everybody was shoving, pushing, tripping and punching everyone else. Drunken cries of spook, coon, wetback, spic and whitey filled the smelly air.

One white dude was heard to splutter out, "kiss my ass ya' ape-faced coon juice." The ape-faced coon juice was heard to holler back, "Youse all ass yo allbeeno prick, warre'll I begin."

Our gentleman felt he should stop the fracas, but being a greenhorn at this lifestyle, he decided to stay out of it. Besides this little set-to was damned funny to watch. Too bad all wars couldn't be fought like this. Lots of arms flailing around but no one getting hurt.

Our man just stood his distance and watched, fascinated. After about a half an hour everything had subsided and gotten back to normal. No one was hurt, not even a scratch could be seen, not a trickle of blood. One old fart who had stayed out of the melee went to the blow jobber and gave her a dollar and asked her to quit hollering. She gave the old fart a toothless smile and whitey the finger. That put the seal on the 'cease fire.'

The gentleman had learned a lot in the two days he spent on skid row. There was a good degree of honor among the scummers, an unhealthy sharing of bottles and needles, but nevertheless sharing. The anti-racism was not done perfunctorily, it was done from the heart in spite of the meaningless ethnic shoving match that occurred as a result of a two dollar economic dispute. Our man felt these kind of people could be gotten together as a group and could work for the benefit of the whole. A fun-style democratic entity. A true laissez-faire economy with a touch of hard-nosed capitalism if any outsider tried to horn-in.

"Yeah."

CHAPTER 76
CLARK'S JOURNEY

Our man left Denver Colorado on September 7th. He had begun to get a little hardened regarding the lifestyle of the down-and-outers and clued in on the obstreperous tenacity of hitchhikers. "C'mon man, I need a f—ing ride!"

He arrived in Kansas City at midnight, September 8th. He was proud of himself. He had been picked up only twice from Denver to Kansas City, both being long hauls as far as he was concerned. He had made another 30 bucks or so panhandling along the way. Nothing new transpired as he traveled via the thumb. He was getting used to the ugliness of slums and skid rows. He still hadn't become used to being dirty, sweaty and no clothing changes, and bathroom regularity, forget it. But he plowed on. Our man was tough. During his life as a 'richo' he had played every rough sport possible and he had trained and body built assiduously. He had spent much of his spare time in the 'gym' boxing, skipping rope and learning karate and other exotic Asian fighting styles. He jogged, walked, rode his bicycle, skied, skated and mountain climbed. The girls, including some Hollywood sex symbols he had made love to, found him to be the find of all finds. They cherished his sexual prowess, the man could 'come' as often as they did. And his anatomy, it was a thing of beauty and power.

Our man arrived in St. Louis at 3:00 p.m., September 9th. He was sleepy and hungry. He still had 22 bucks on him. He opted for sleep first. He knew St. Louis well. His firm had several clients in the city, and whilst it had no office there the firm had allocated auditors to its clients' offices several days each month. Our man had visited St. Louis at least six times each year to serve his firm's clientele. He loved St. Louis. Too, he knew where its public parks were. He hastened to the nearest one, found an unoccupied bench off the park's core, laid down and slept for six hours. When he wakened he found the night to be warm and serene. While our gentleman was well rested he was rather 'kinked-up.' He got up, stretched, did a few push-ups then made his way to the public washrooms. There he removed all of his clothes and gave himself a thorough scrubbing. Now he was ready for a good meal.

He ate heartily, even a little dessert. So now he needed more money. He found a lounge nearby. He stationed himself near the lounge's entrance. He was begging again, panhandling. He spied six young women coming out of the bar, all of them well dressed and cute. He moved closer to the exit/entrance glass doors. He saw the 'cuties' were all a bit tipsy. Good, he thought to himself, when people are a little drunk they get a little more generous. I'll take these chicks for some 'bobs!' He pushed the sleeves of his shirt right up to his shoulders baring his smooth muscular arms. He unbuttoned his shirt down to his pants' top displaying his magnificent chest, his flat rippled gut and a touch of hair just above his pants' top buttons. His deep tan glistened from the beads of perspiration on his face and body. He put on the 'cool dude' look.

The women came out of the lounge's door chattering as if there was no tomorrow. They looked so delectable. They spotted our man. Their chatting stopped. "Well lookie here gals, it must be Tarzan himself?" one of them remarked. They sidled their way over to our Tarzan. One of the pretties chucked his chin, another cupped one of his peck's, while another felt his ass. "What a fuck machine, girls," one of the lovelies said, "let's rape the s.o.b." They all laughed. Our Tarzan put on a 'cool dude' smile.

"Can you talk, Tarzan?" one gal said. "Me, Jane."

"Yes me talk Jane," Tarzan replied.

"Can you fuck?" Jane asked.

"Yes Jane, Lord Greystoke can fuck like Numa the lion." Tarzan boasted. "Tarzan mighty Lord of the Jungle, can fuck Tantor the elephant or Hista the snake so, no trouble fucking six Janes."

The girls broke up laughing.

"But Tarzan need money to fuck. Tarzan need 60 bucks. For that Tarzan fuck one Jane in park over there. Tarzan not prostitute, Tarzan out of 'coconuts.' The girls broke up again. All six women opened their purses, reached inside, pulled out their wallets and gave Tarzan money, $90 in all. The gals then stepped away from our man and went into a huddle. They whispered mischievously, peered over their shoulders at him all the while giggling. Then five of the ladies hi-fived the sixth. They giggled as the sixth girl turned from the others and slunk over to Tarzan.

She reached up to his shoulders and pulled his head down close to hers. She stood on her tiptoes touched his mouth with hers and said, "Me Jane."

Our man knew what that meant. Jane took hold of one of his hands and began to lead him toward the park as the other girls re-entered the lounge. Our man didn't have to be told what the 'score' was. He was to take Jane to the park, make love to her, then take her back to the lounge where she would join up with her friends again. Tarzan didn't let Jane down. She 'came' and 'came' as our man romanced her. He was gentle with her yet he let her know he was all man. He performed such exquisite cunnilingus on her secret parts she cried from sanguine erotic ecstasy.

"Don't ever stop," she moaned. By the time Tarzan thought she had had enough she was in a frenzy, biting him, scratching him, her mouth all over his, fighting him for more, tears streaming down her face, begging him to stay as part of her. "Please don't stop doing these things to me."

By damn, the girl has taken leave of her senses, he thought. He picked her up in his arms. She was crying hard. "Sweetheart," he said, "you've had enough now. Please. I'm going to take you back to your friends now."

"No," she begged, "No!"

Our man dressed her as she whimpered. He led her back to the lounge zombie-like, took her inside, spotted her friends, led her to their table, sat her down, and said, "Here Jane ladies."

"My god, what have you done to her?"

"Just what Jane want"

"Did you drug her?"

"No Tarzan not drug Jane"

"Then what?"

"Tarzan just make love to her!"

"Cindy are you all right, dear?" one of them asked the zombie-like girl.

"No Bonny-Lee, I'll never be the same. I—I have never experienced anything like it—he's an angel—he's a prince—he is the Lord of the Jungle. You poor things, you'll never have what I just had" she said, "the man is a demigod. He took me to another world, I mean, girls, sex is overrated, but not with this god. He takes you to heaven and back" she purred.

"C'mon Cindy, stay with us," Bonny-Lee said laughing.

"No girls, I'm gone again," Cindy said, putting the back of her hand to her brow and feigning a swoon. "Come to me my Romeo."

They looked up. Tarzan was gone.

"No!" Cindy cried, "where is he?" This time she was not feigning. She got up and ran to the lounge door, the girls following. "Where is he?" she shrieked, yanking open the door, stumbling on her way out and yelling "Tarzan! Tarzan!"

The people in the lounge wondered about this sensational looking girl.

"Who spiked her drinks? She is so gorgeous. She looks familiar."

Her friends caught her. She struggled to get away but they held onto her. One of the girls rushed back to the lounge. In a few minutes she was back on the street with her friends. Cindy had regained some of her composure. Still her friends held her tight. Soon a limousine pulled up beside them. The limo's chauffeur got out, hurried to the side of the six ladies, helped them get Cindy inside then held the door open for the other models, yes models, then returned to his driver's seat and sped off.

Pheew! our man thought, what a fantastic group of beauties.

* * *

"Ladies and gentlemen," Lana said, "I have taken you through this afternoon's break with my story of 'our man.' I'm sorry," she apologized as she turned to Dr. Carruthers for direction. Dr. Carruthers took the cue from Lana.

"Friends and associates," he said, "would you like a coffee break now, or just a leg stretch? Please give me your wishes."

"A leg stretch only. We want to hear about our 'hero' now," was the unanimous reply.

"Fine my friends, let's take a five-minute stretch." Dr. Carruthers offered. It was 4:15 p.m. The crowd stood, did their few little exercises, chatted and, almost as if they were tuned in with one another, they all sat awaiting Lana's story.

"Thank you ladies and gentlemen," Lana said. "You may wonder why I have given you such detail pertaining to our man's travels from Los Angeles to St. Louis. It is because I want to acquaint you with the tenacity of the man. As well I want to point out things which we already know but choose to turn a blind eye to, to wit, the dreadful degeneracy of the slums that tarnish the nations of the world. A slum is a slum whether it be in the United States of America, Canada, Britain, Australia, India, whatever nation. Our man is a proud American. He is using his country as a test case in his mission. He is not intending to insinuate that slums exist only in the USA. In fact he knows America is one of the leading countries trying to exorcise inhumanity and indignities. One significant problem the USA and Canada have in their fight against poverty and degeneracy is the ever widening gap between the rich and the poor. We all know the answer to the problem, but we don't have the will to activate the answer.

"In any event my dear listeners, I shall go on with the true life adventures of our man.

"He remained in St. Louis for 2 days. He wanted to 'check out' its most formidable slum. He found it. While the slum area was ramshackle like all others, it proved to be different from Denver's in that it had a definitive 'people' hierarchy. Our gentleman found this out soon after arriving at the slum. He had gone around the back of a long-deserted seven-story dilapidated sinful looking tenement building to urinate. He heard some footsteps and voices coming his way. At first he paid no attention to the noises, just some scummers cooking up some hijinks, he thought. He waggled his dick to get rid of the dew drops still lingering on its head, tucked it in his bikini shorts, zipped up his fly and marched out from behind the foul-smelling old building. Christ, a few minutes ago, the open space beside the building was vacant. Now there was a crowd of 50 or 60 unsmiling people looking his way. The footsteps and voices he had heard belonged to two Afro-American men and a surly brutish looking white man. The three of them looked as if they had just washed themselves in a slop pail.

"Wadd'ya doin heah white boy?" the bigger of the two blacks asked with a sneer on his face

"Just stoppin' on m' way to New York City. Why you ax, brotha?"

"Yu ain't no brotha man, 'sides I as de questions here motha-fucka!"

"Sorry."

"Yu cop white boy?"

"No fuckin' way black boy!" our man responded thinking he was doing the right thing acting tough.

"What yu calls me ya white cunt?"

"Black boy, brotha!"

The big black was mad. He wasn't used to anyone standing up to him. "Black boy huh whitey. Dat's wat yu sez? I'z goin' to de-nut yu, yu fucka!"

"Wa' fo' lil' black sambo?" our foolish gentleman said.

"Wat 'chu calls me fucka?"

"Lil' black sambo!"

With that the big black stuck out his arm, finger pointed at our man and said, "Yu one daid man sucka!"

The white brute stepped behind our man, but before he got there the big black was on his knees looking shocked at his finger our man had just destroyed. Our man drove his right elbow into the brute's ample midsection, then stomped his size-14, hob-nail onto the brute's right foot. The brute roared like a wounded bear and lashed out at our man with his huge right fist. Our man blocked the errant 'overhand' right, stuck out his hip and as nice as you please flipped the cursing brute over onto the big black. The other black grabbed for his knife, but before he could use it a couple of bystanders were on his back. In another instant the whole crowd of scummers were at the threesome. They looked ready to kill the three men.

'What's going on?' he thought, 'these scummers are like a pack of wild dogs.'

"Stop, hold it!" our man yelled as he began to pull the mob off the three frightened bullies. "Let them go, you're going to kill them!" he bellowed. As fast as he pulled a couple of people off their quarry two more would pile on in their place.

A police siren was heard.

The crowd broke-up and as if by magic it dissipated into the surroundings just as fog dissipates from the heat of the sun. One middle-aged ratty-faced scummer took our man's arm and rushed him into the old seven-story apartment building. He led our man into the building's broken down furnace room, thence through a secret panel into a smelly hide-away. A few other people were there. The place was dank, strewn with old wine bottles, food wrappings, shoe polish cans, cigarette butts, used needles, dirty clothes, every-bloody-thing. The ratty-faced man told our gentleman of the dictatorial treatment the scummers lived under, under the dictation of those three bullies.

"We have to pay them three dollars every month for protection," he said. "They steal from us, beat us up, make us do their dirty work, you name it we do it. We were non-pulsed when we saw you stand up to them. They are real bastards. Maybe we can come to our senses now and gang-up on them if you aren't around, hell, maybe they'll even hi-tail it out here? Anyway man, we thank you for what you did."

"It was my pleasure sir," our man responded, "Now what?"

"Well, we just wait for another half-hour or so then look out and see if the cops are gone and if the coast is clear."

"Cool," our man said. He had quite a chat with the people in the hide-away. No, they didn't like their life on skid row.

"But whadda' we gonna' do? Nobody wants us, nobody cares for us. We get our few bucks from welfare every month and because no one gives a shit about us we spend it on wine and drugs. There's lots' talent among us, 'cept for the loonies, but nobody wants to gamble on us…we're not too reliable I'm told."

They all laughed at the 'not too reliable' statement. The speaker was a skinny woman of about 40. Her hair was a mess. Black and gray tousled strands going every which way, uncombed and dirty. She had a few teeth, no breasts to speak of, toothpick arms and legs. Her dress was far too big for her; it was dirty and wrinkled. She wore crumpled 'bobbysox' socks, which oozed out from around the unpolished straps of her white sandals. While her grammar was 'wanting' she made good sense. Our man thought the rat-faced man and this skin and bone woman would make excellent shareholders in H&B Financial and Poors Inc.

The people in the hideaway all seemed like decent folks even though they stole, begged, rummaged through garbage cans, inter-mingled their diseases, pissed their drawers, drank anything that would give them a boost, lied, cheated—just like the rest of the world. Our man got a lot of valuable information from them pertaining to his mission.

He gave all of them his card and told them to watch for news about H&B, his dream company, in a few years from now. Some of them laughed at his latter statement 'in a few years from now' and looking at one another crowed, "we'll all be dead a few years from now!"

Tim, the rat-faced man, led our gentleman out of the 'stink hole' back outside to the spot where the melee had taken place. All was clear. Tim told our man where he could sleep tonight. "Yeah, on the second floor of this old tenement building—you can't miss it. I'll be there drunk to my teeth by five this afternoon. Come see me. Even though I'll be hammered I'll know you. I'll see to it you get a nice spot all to yourself. Now, you sure you won't share a drink with me from my bottle of fine vintage wine?" Tim said winking.

"No thank you, Tim. Truly, I don't drink."

"Good man," Tim said turning and waving his hand as he re-entered the run down old building.

Our man made his way to the center of town. He was certain he knew an excellent corner uptown St. Louis which had endless possibilities for panhandling.

CHAPTER 77

CLARK'S JOURNEY

Warning…one loathsome scene

He decided he would make himself as sexy looking as possible, short of exposing himself, of course, so that females would be enticed to put up some meangingful bucks. He was right. His handsome face, his torrid torso and his engaging smile caused many a lady into putting quite significant sums of money in his outstretched hands. In three hours he had weaseled out over $600 from the passing crowds, at least $550 of it from women. He had numerous propositions of good times too, again mostly from women but from a few gents as well. Several ladies had crossed his palms with their cards during the afternoon, had winked at him trying therefore to entice him to their lairs. He wasn't going to succumb to sex this night.

Our man retreated back to the beaten-up old seven-story structure after supping, and made his way to the second floor. Propped up against the wall, head flopped down on his adams apple was a totally inebriated Tim. Pinned to his shirt was a note which read, 'Clark, Room 202 is yours. Thanks pal, Tim.'

The next morning at 6:30 our man was on his way to Indianapolis. This part of the trip turned out to be slow. It took him two days to make it there. While our man was far less homesick now and his skin was beginning to *thicken* he still heard and saw confounding conditions that turned his stomach. Perhaps the most horrid of all the rot he had come across to date happened in a hell hole in Indianapolis. A hell hole probably unbeknownst to the citizens of Indianapolis. The dreadful place was located in an old unused sewage tunnel. Our man had been taken there by an old derelict, who promised to show our man the most revolting of all Indianapolis slum habitats. The putrid place must have had a special designer design its foulness. No scummer, however filthy and foul, could make a place so rotten. Dangling from the ceiling were slimy, yellowish white chunks of frayed moss alive with slow moving, blind, albino rat-like creatures that squeaked as they fumbled their way around.

The walls were plastered with damp packs of human feces. The floor had watery potholes full of fresh human waste…urine, feces, spittle, mucus, snot and vomit. The four feet wide ledges above the floor were adorned with more human waste and half-dead humans. Strewn about in huge piles were empty brown paper-wrapped bottles of every size. Some of the humans who were sitting on the ledges were dressed like ancient lepers. They mumbled, giggled and wept as they drank their rotgut.

Our man vomited when he saw the most vile, putrid sight of sights. An obese nude woman sitting with her blubbery back against a wall. Her fat grotesque legs were stretched out sideways from her body. She held a bottle of rot-gut in her shaky liver-spotted hand. Spittle drooled in slimy strings from the corners of her fat lips. Her vein smeared eyes bugged out of their sockets. She made pitiful squawk like sounds out of her maniacal grinning repulsive mouth. Her nose was a bulbous mass of flesh covered with clumps of hair. Black bits of hair formed an ugly mustache on her upper lip. Crud dripped off her chin landing on tits that dangled almost down to her inner thighs. Our man could handle this part of the sight. It was the remainder of the woman's ghastly appearance that made him retch.

The flesh on her back had begun to grow onto the walls. The wall was now part of her back. When she moved her torso, the skin of her back would peel away from the wall and bleed. The sight defied all reason. How could this creature's flesh enjoin and grow on the wall. Our man got on his knees lowered his head and covered his eyes. Christ, even medical people would be sickened by this foul sight. Her lumpy varicose veined legs and her wrinkled fat ass, like her back, had attached themselves to the ledges and grew as part of them. When she tried to move her legs they remained stationary. The walls and the ledge were now just as much a part of her stinking carcass as were her teeth or her ears. The back of her right arm had begun its fusion with the wall as well. Only a sucker size part of her arm was attached to the wall at this point in time. The consequences of these demonic mutations were that the feces and urine discharged from her bowels and bladder oozed out of her orifices in a constant stream causing a lava like flow to drip off the ledge into the excreta filled water hole below her. From time to time large chunks of feces she released from her anus would block the smooth flow of urine emanating from her bladder. These chunks of shit would either sail along undisturbed in her stream of piss or would break down from the force of the urine being released by her and would thence cascade down the abominable waterfall.

Our man had seen enough. He ran from this horror show as quick as he could. In his haste he stumbled over a pile of old tiles and almost ended up in one of the loathsome water holes. Inane giggles broke out around him from the ruptured throats of the uglies when they saw him scramble to keep on his feet. One of the monstrosities cackled out to our man, "Have a nice trip?" The whole room erupted in fucked up laughter at this hackneyed line. Many of the 'laughs' turned into phlegm-filled coughs and sputterings as the uglies' mucous membranes became disturbed. This along with their despicable countenances made the whole sewer room look like a scene from hell.

Our man kept running from this tormented place until he spied an unused telephone booth. Here he stopped, his face drained of blood. He opened the booth's door went in and sat. He bowed his head between his knees in an attempt to fight off the faintness he felt. Slowly he came around as he fought off his nausea and lightheadedness. He grabbed a tattered telephone book attached to a chain and therein he found the telephone number of the City Health Department. He dialed the department's number and after the usual run around of pressing this, that, and the other thing, he was put in touch with a live human being. Our man described the hell hole he had just left, gave the live person he was talking to the location of the Stygian Gehenna and hung-up.

Our poor man had a dreadful time trying to erase from his mind the awful image of that fat woman who sat perpetually in her own waste. Will he ever be able to enjoy sex again after seeing this sub-human putrid sight? My God, he thought, I could be in the midst of a sexual encounter with a stunning beauty and on the verge of ejaculation when 'bam' my poor subliminal could light up with the sight of that horrid woman's large, fat, shit smeared orifice.

Why dear God did I ever go to that stinking place. Will I ever be able to forget it?

CHAPTER 78

CLARK INCORPORATES H&B FINANCIAL AND POORS

"Our gentleman departed Indianapolis September 13th at 6:00 a.m., his mind still inflamed and sickened by the 'hell house.' He arrived in Pittsburgh the same day. While he felt downright morbid from those ghoulish sights in Indianapolis he did feel rather proud of his successful panhandling in St. Louis. He treated himself by spending the night in an old run down motel…cost $15 per night. The room included a shower and a toilet. Our man got into the shower and soaped and soaked himself for a half an hour. He would have stayed in longer if the hot water had not run out. He did all he could to scour out the images of the putrid hell hole. He had bought a Pittsburgh newspaper at the motel's front desk, which he read from front to back. By damn, the world's greatest hockey player would be practising the next day with his mighty Pittsburgh Penguins. Big Mario Lemieux. 'Gotta see him,' our man said. By pulling a few strings he was able to take in a Penguin's practise. The fat lady was forgotten when he saw how the athletes plied their skills. They were fast, intent, reckless, fearless and tough. They'd fire the puck back and forth before shooting cannonading shots at the poor goalie. As for big Mario, our man could not believe his eyes. Lemieux, he reckoned, was in a league by himself.

"He departed Pittsburgh on September 14th."

* * *

"Our gentleman arrived in New York City on September 18th, 1991. His first stop was to be the Grand Central Station area in Manhattan. It was from this location where he intended to begin his plan of action. He knew New York City well and in particular Manhattan Island. He had made many visits to the 'Great City' primarily for business reasons but often for pleasure. He stayed at the Plaza Hotel during most of his visits but from time to time he would lodge in one of the other of the city's grand hotels or in the penthouse of a beautiful co-op condominium owned by friends.

"He had been fortunate enough to have visited many of the great cities of the world. Often he had accompanied his parents on holiday or business trips to London, Paris, Rome, Singapore and Hong Kong. But he, like so many travelers who had the opportunity of seeing New York City, had experienced a charisma, or charm, or excitement no other city anywhere could offer.

"Many other cities of the world were more scenic, had finer weather, less crime, less poverty, less racism, more fascinating history, more cultural centers, more culture and were cleaner. But they lacked New York's esoteric aura. New York's big town personality, it's ego, vibrancy, Wall Street power, titillating excitement, awesome skyline and the city's incomparable people were unique.

"Yes, by damn, this 'Big Town' is unique, our man thought. His first night was spent in Grand Central Station. Nothing of any consequence took place during the night. Yet he was restless because of his anxiety to get started on his 'mission' and because of the odd night-stick being poked in his ribs. When he awakened he repaired to one of the huge station's men's rooms and freshened up. He went back into the station, found a cafeteria, ordered a hearty breakfast and whilst sipping his coffee he perused the plan he had plotted out.

"Our man was a 'doer.' He wasted no time on frivolities. He found the public telephones ensconced in Grand Central, sat, took the phone off the hook and dialed a number he knew well from his business practice.

The party he was phoning was a Wallace K. Brown of Hilliard, Brown and Associates, Barristers and Solicitors. This law firm was big by any standards, having some 700 practicing lawyers and over 100 partners. The firm was fully integrated as to the services it provided its clientele. Right from corporate law to litigation from cases of petty thievery to horrific criminal offenses, from incorporation of companies to the most intricate of business mergers, from municipal law to giant government cases, from marriages to divorces, insurance disputes, suing your dentist and for fucking your dog."

"Lana, you just can't quit shocking people can you?" Adam Five said, laughing. Lana smiled. Her audience tittered too. The attendees were getting used to their tawny-haired bombshell's naughtiness.

"Our man knew the firm well. It acted as St. James, Rogers, Struthers and Company CPAs law firm since the early 1940's. Wallace Brown was the lawyer our man had sought legal advice from for the past seven years.

"He telephoned Mr. Brown. The two of them spent a few moments chatting about the big Californians adventure as a 'bum.' Wallace Brown had been informed of our man's mission several weeks ago. Mr. Brown at the time had given his covenant as to the priviness of our man's intent and whereabouts. He had been instructed to look into the legality of a company as envisioned by our man, and in particular the type of common voting shares the company wanted to sell. The share certificates were to be available only to buyers whose net income was less than $5,000 per year and whose assets were not in excess of $10,000 and whose net worth was under $5,000. Further our man wanted the maximum share holdings of any one person to be limited to 1,000 and proxy voting to be limited to 1,000 votes per shareholder. Except for a few minor amendments to the proposed incorporating documents, everything on our gentleman's 'docket' pad was a-okay and ready to launch. Mr. Wallace was instructed to proceed with the state incorporation papers and the registration thereof of H & B Financial and Poors Inc. and the printing of the share certificates. The head office address of the new company temporarily was to be the lawyer's offices on East 32nd Street and Madison Avenue. Mr. Wallace expected the registrations and all filings to be completed by September 30th, 1991.

"Now our man could get the ball rolling.

"He was ready.

"He was pumped."

CHAPTER 79
CLARK'S SKID ROW COMMITTEES FOR H&B

"To begin, our gentleman roamed the streets of Manhattan day and night. He did some 'odd jobs' for anyone who would employ him. From this he often earned enough money to do him for the day. He still had $457 left from his successful panhandling in St. Louis. Even with the $457 tucked in his jeans, in order to fit the exclusiveness of the *slum society* he panhandled alongside scummers. At night he slept where hobos, bums, drunks and addicts slept. He would stay three or four days at one spot to get the scummers accustomed to him and he to them. He would listen to their chatter in order to acquaint himself with the style and character of the big city's skid row denizens. Sometimes he would hang out with bag ladies, cart-pushing men, prostitutes, 'fruit cakes' and retards. After three weeks of wandering, watching, listening and attending to the habits of Manhattan's scummers, our man felt it was time for him to befriend a few select people among them and apprise them of his mission. He had telephoned Mr. Brown on October 1st, 1991 in order to find the stage of completion of H & B incorporation. Mr. Brown informed our man that all the documentation, registrations and filings had been completed as of September 29th, 1991. And yes the share certificates had been printed and numbered sequentially and were now ready for issuance. The authorized common voting shares of the new entity had been set at 100 million.

"Our gentleman had been most circumspect in selecting the scummers he thought would make the grade as emissaries on behalf of H & B. What a chore it had been. He needed two representatives from the lesser-populated slums of Manhattan, three from each medium-size slum and six from the big ones. Yes, indeed, representation by population. No fuckin' aristocratic, fascist, totalitarian émigré allowed in this group. No Tammany Hall high jinks either. Just straight up democracy.

"The selection process had been brutal in some instances," Lana remarked. "For example, our man whilst going about his selection business in a lower Manhattan mid-size slum thought he had found just the person to be a selectee. He had met the fellow a few times and was impressed with his demeanor and intelligence. He knew the man was a junkie, but our gentleman expected each of his emissaries to be 'untoward' one way or another.

"Our man had taken Horace Oakely, the junkies name, aside and had outlined to him his entire plan re financial independence for scummers. Horace had asked all the right questions pertaining to the plan and he appeared to comprehend its complexities and benevolence." Dr. Masters said.

"The idea is splendid, Horace had commented, a magnificent conception. 'What a shock we would be to the community. God, how I'd love to shove a successful financial entity of us scummers down the throat of the bourgeoisie. Yes sir, I would be proud to serve as a representative on H&B's start-up committee.' Horace and our man had sat on the lower steps of the post office as they chatted. Then Horace lost it. He slipped back into his true ego, a leprechaunic nut. He flipped his lid. He took off one shoe then scurried up the wide steps of the post office building dodging the multitudes who were lunching there. He reached the top and in a flourish turned to face the throngs of people below him and on the streets. Two soap-box orators were at the top of the stairs bellowing their brains out at each other, one denouncing the capitalistic imperialism of the United States of America, the other calling the denouncer a lazy communist suck-up, a hypocritical Stalinist and a disbelieveer of human rights. Horace snuck in behind them then gave each one a mighty shove sending the pair sprawling down the stairs onto some of the lunchers. The squeals, hollers and curses could be heard a block away as the orators tumbled through the diners. Hot dogs, sauerkraut, sausages, spaghetti, burgers, veggies, coffee, beer, fruit juices, milk were dislodged hither and thither among the dislodgers as arms, legs, feet and torsos flew everywhere.

"Good old Horace laughed like a hyena. Some poor dink held his arm above his head, in the confusion, trying to save his plastic glass of beer from being wasted when Horace, measuring with his shod foot, booted the thing. Beer and froth flew indiscriminately. The plastic glass drifted through the air, landing feather-like on another poor dink's empty plate. The crowd, covered in grub began to turn into an angry mob. They slipped on the food and drink-laden steps as they went for Horace. Horace stepped back a pace or two, whipped out his dick and pissed into the mob. The mob stopped its clamoring as it ran headlong into Horace's discharge.

"The people on the street, in particular the yuppies, cheered and egged Horace on. What a lunch break, I mean, this is fun, better than Letterman and Leno. It should be done daily, it takes away stress.

"Laughter cascaded up and down the block. Horace was last seen leaping down the post office steps fumbling at his fly, laughing like an imbecile, hooting and hollering, 'I'm not a fig plucker nor a fig plucker's son, I'm just plucking figs 'til a fig plucker comes. Say that fast ye squalid feasters,' he roared.

"Horace, without his other shoe, ran zig-zag down the street, arms flailing, yelling 'fig plucker' as he disappeared into the noon-day crowd.

"Our man wrote Horace Oakley off as a contributing member of H & B's start-up committee.

"His search's first success for the selection of committee members occurred in lower Manhattan where our man had, had his encounter with Horace. He had seen a pasty-faced drunk and a sober, disreputable-looking black slouching on a park bench. He had noticed them a few days back and while the impression they made on the world was woeful, our man saw something in them that appealed to him. They appeared to be arguing. The pasty-faced one, who took frequent sips from his 'brown papered' bottle, was waggling a finger and mouthing off at the black. The black looked quite undisturbed and patient with the grungy white. Our man moved behind the bench a few feet away from the scummers, put his knapsack down on the grass, laid down, closed his eyes and feigned sleep. The white scummer didn't miss a beat.

"Why should we Americans care one iota about our domestic poor and the world's poor? God chooses the rich. He gives them the ability to reach the top in any situation. He gives them unbridled intelligence. Ergo the rich know what to do. They work hard, stomp on the weak, cheat when prudent to do so, market their wares intelligently, take well-studied risks and they make good use of lady luck. They deserve their station in life; they've earned it. While on the opposite end of the spectrum we have the witless, lazy good-for-nothing poors. You know who I mean, Leroy? We see the stupid, dull, incompetent idiots every day.

"Yes Vito, the black replied.

"C'mon, Leroy, show some spunk, don't just say yes Vito, get with it man.

"Yes Vito, Leroy repeated.

"Yes Vito, yes Vito, yes Vito. Is that all you can say ya' black turd? Have you no argument against my hypothesis re the genteel rich and the mongrels?

"No Vito.

"You must have an opinion, Leroy. Do you think as I do that the rich are the world's movers and shakers, the very people who have made our lives so plentiful in material and spiritual things? The deserving ones. God's children so to speak?

"I think you are full of dingo dung, Vito, Leroy said, smiling.

"What? Vito screamed. Me full of dingo dung?

"Well, sort of Vito.

"Sort of? Vito screamed again.

"No, I go back to my first answer, Vito. You are full of dingo dung.

"Explain yourself, you black assed nigger, why am I full of dingo dung?

"Because only a handful of the mega-rich earned it through their intelligence and ingenuity. Most of them inherited their wealth or had it handed to them on a silver platter or were just plain lucky. Some of the rich, vis-a-vis chief executive officers of large corporations, some businessmen, certain professionals, brokers, some speculators, professional athletes, movie and television stars, you know who I mean Vito, are deserving. But are all of them or at least some of them not over-compensated when one considers their true value or worth to society? Yet Vito, fair game if society has no complaint as to the enormity of salaries or earnings of the rich. Who am I to judge? And Vito, you screwed up 'Wop', you and I are the poor. Shit man we are the poor, we gave up our other station in life years ago.

"Yes I know Leroy, Vito said.

"Remember Vito, we agreed many years ago if we stayed in the lifestyle we are now ensconced in for over ten years we would never re-enter our professions again. Essentially Vito, your practice as a neurosurgeon 16 years ago is now a thing of the past just as my career as a stock broker is a thing of the past. Christ, for 16 years now Vito we have been bums. You drink and I shoot-up. Like a pair of nit wits we gave up our old lifestyle—assholes that we were, Washington Leroy Jefferson remarked to his long time friend Vito Apostli.

"For 16 years now, other than the few good things we have done during those years for our pathetic brethren, we have been a drag on society. Mind you, the burdensome federal and state taxes we paid on our million dollar earnings back then should more than look after our use of park benches and alleyways and our miserable fuckin' daily up-keep. Goodness, Senor Apostli, if we didn't drink and shoot-up, we might be the kings of shit hill.

Vito grinned his toothless grin.

"Are you a misled pinko weak-knee'd socialist, Leroy? Vito asked. You sound like one.

"How many times yu gwine ax me dat massah? Yu no's I's jes a pure god fearin' pragmatist, Leroy replied.

"That's how I like to hear you talk to me you heathen savage, Vito said.

"Ya you Sicialian catholic 'mafa' mafioso. You pope brown-noser. You're the ruddy savage, you and your white-robed cowardly K.K.K.'s. Leroy said.

"God, if I could, I'd start-up a K.K.K. here in Manhattan right now just to keep you coons in your place. Yeah man, I'd be one happy dude.

"Duke you mean you prissy sissy white puke. It takes ten of you pale-faced dicks to match one of our proud males. You gotta' hide your peach fuzz faces behind your K.K.K. doilies' so your yellow-belly eyes don't show you as gutless wonders.

Both sat quiet for a few minutes.

"You gettin' hungry Leroy? Vito asked.

"No, not yet Vito, are you? Leroy replied.

"It's too nice a day to go grubin' for food yet.

"It is a beautiful day, Vito. Do you want to discuss anything else now, or should we just sit here and relax? Leroy asked.

"Let's just relax, Vito said, taking a gulp of his cheap 'bingo'. Yeah, just sit here in the sun and enjoy.

"Our man could not believe his ears. One minute enemies the next busom buddies.

"Our man got up from the grass, made his way to the front of Vito's and Leroy's bench and said, 'Sirs, I must talk to you.'

"Who're you? Vito asked surprised by the interruption.

"Just a friend, our man answered.

"Sirs he called us. Sirs. Leroy nudged Vito. Now, Leroy said to Vito, that's the respect we should get from all scum bags around here, right Vito?

"Right Leroy, Vito agreed.

"They laughed.

"What must you talk to us about pray tell my son? Vito said. And son, by the by, this gentleman beside me is known as Washington L. Jefferson the third, whilst my name is Vito Alberto Alfonse Apostli.

"Well gentlemen, with your leave, I should like to propose to you a fascinating idea pertaining to a financial institution for the poor, our man stated.

"My how intuitive, Mr. Jefferson said, a financial institution for the poor. How quaint. I"m sure with all the spare funds the poor have hanging around just itching to invest, the entity, without question, would be an overnight success. Would you agree Senor Apostli?

"Smashing idea Mr. Jefferson. Vito responded, I'm so sorry we never thought of that ourselves.

"Please young fella, fuck-off, we're trying to rest, Vito said. There's a guy on the corner over there selling shit. Maybe he'll sell you some cheap.

"Just a moment gentlemen, I've got 20 bucks for each of you if you agree to hear me out. Our man reached in his pocket and showed the two scummers his wad of bills. I'll give each of you $5 now, and another $15 when I'm finished talking if that's agreeable to you.

"Hey man you're on," Vito said, thinking vino.

"Yeah, Leroy said, thinking a fix.

"Please listen to what I have to say. I am dead serious. To begin with, I have overheard you two gentlemen talk twice, once three days ago and once again today. Frankly, I have been very impressed by both of you. You discuss those matters which pertain to the reasons for the formation of such an entity. For years now I have put my mind to a method the poor could use to create an independent society of wealth for themselves. The poor have been given lip-service by governments, religious groups, politicians, do-gooders for centuries. Follow us your beloved leaders. If you do so your souls shall forever prosper in the eyes of the Lord thy God. Hallelujah! But it's never been more than lip-service. The poor still remain poor. The religious connivers, in my view have been the most hypocritical of all those I have mentioned. They lie to the poor, they manipulate the minds of the poor all in the name of God. The religious connivers promise comfort to the poor through God. They have the unmitigated gall to tell the poor not to despair about physical hunger, pain, mental anguish, squalid living conditions because he god loves them, he comforts them, and he keeps the devil away from their door. Pray to him my son and my daughter for his love and for your misgivings and by the by contribute some moneys to his goodness.

"It really angers me about how the poor have been hornswoggled by so few from man's beginnings. The few appear to have no conscience about gouging out the last penny from the lowly masses and stripping them of their last vestige of pride. Ah, what the hell!

"My plan simply is this. One, get a group of 30 intelligent scummers from various slums and skid row areas of Manhattan. With your leave gentlemen, people like yourselves. You two gentlemen would make perfect representatives of the group. I know Dr. Apostli you were once a practicing physician. Good lord sir, you would fit so well and you Mr. Jefferson as a broker you are made for the committee. Two, the committee's function would be to discuss the proposed financial entity's plans, goals, aims and objectives. In so doing the committee would determine if the plan had potential and truly had utility value for down-and-outers. If the committee feels the plan is a viable one and should be pursued then three, the committee would commandeer as many scummers it feels is necessary for the purpose of going out among all scummers in Manhattan and selling the scheme.

"Please now, gentlemen, let me give you the corporate set up of the company. First, its name is H & B Financial and Poors Inc. The 'H' in the name stands for Hobos and the 'B' stands for bums, okay?" Vito and Leroy nodded okay?

"Sounds descriptive to me," Leroy commented.

"Our man then explained, H & B's corporate structure. He told them the company was incorporated on September 29th, 1991. It's fiscal year-end was to be July 31st. He stated he had purchased 100 common voting shares at $1 each on September 29th, 1991 and had loaned the company $500,000.00 that same date as a shareholder's loan. He said if the committee and its chosen members were able to sell 2,000 shares at $100 each by November 30th, 1991 to scummers, our man would transfer the $500,000.00 out of his shareholder's loan account into an equity account called contributed surplus at November 30th, 1991. This, of course, would mean our man would never have a claim against H & B Financial for the $500,000.00 he had gifted to it.

"Yeah, meathead. $500,000.00 huh? What a fuckin' dreamer, Leroy said, looking at Vito and laughing.

"Why didn't you make it a million bucks, big shot, rather than a measly 500 'thou'. Christ, big Leroy and me could make it two million bucks each only we forgot our checkbooks at home. Right O Zulu King?

"Right Ginney, Don of the Wops, Leroy agreed.

"Let's get outta here Vito, this dude is beginning to annoy me. Look at him. He's a piece of scum shit just like us. $500,000.00 bucks, what a crock.

"They got up to leave.

"Hold it fellas," our man said. "I can prove I made the $500,000.00 contribution to H & B in a matter of minutes if you wish me to do so. We just march to those telephones over there, call the State of New

York's Public Affairs, or the Securities and Exchange Commission, or my lawyer Wallace Brown of Hilliard, Brown and Associates, or Burroughs Hanlon and Bentley my CPA's and ask any or all of them about my $500,000.00 contribution.

"As well, our man produced a duplicate receipt from Hilliard and Brown authenticating our man's $500,000.00 loan to H & B Financial. The sincerity of our man's voice and the receipt he produced ameliorated to a large extent Leroy's and Vito's concern about him.

"Okay man, carry-on, Leroy said. We will act as though we believe you, right Vito?

"Riiighht Leroy, Vito responded. By the way, big shot, where'd you get the half million bucks?

"Some day I'll tell both of you about myself and my bucks but for now let's just let it ride, our man said.

"Okay, but how come you don't enjoy your wealth yourself? Why for Christ sake give up the good life, why are you giving the money away? How come?

"Well gentlemen, I could ask you the same thing, couldn't I? Why did you give up your practices and your wealth to become skid row junkies? Do you want me to continue? he said.

"Ya go on, Vito and Leroy responded.

"Our gentlemen went on to explain that H & B's authorized capital at the time of its corporation was 100 million common voting shares with a par value of $1 each. He informed Vito and Leroy he had made a few investments in the bond and stock markets in the last few days. He said he was certain interest rates would be falling during the 1990's because of favorable economic factors. Thus bond prices would increase as interest rates fell, so, holding a position in the bond market seemed sensible. As well, our man had taken a strong position in the stock market. He felt as interest rates fell investments in the bond market would become unpopular, and, alternatively the stock market would strengthen. In any event our man said if H & B Financial did get rolling its investment activities would be handled through a three-person investment committee.

"He told Vito and Leroy he had made another direct contribution to H & B's 'Contributed Surplus Account' of $490,000. $290,000, of the $490,000 had already been spent on the purchase of an old warehouse building located in Soho in lower Manhattan. The building, our man said, "has 80,000 square feet of useable space." The buildings basic structure was fine, but its interior was a shambles. Our man told Vito and Leroy that the warehouse was to be the head office of H & B Financial. The $200,000 held back by H & B was to be used to upgrade the warehouse into H & B's offices, a pharmaceutical dispensary, a games room and a coffee bar for scummers. As well, showers, bathrooms and some sleeping rooms would be built into the structure.

"Our gentleman went on to say if H & B was successful in selling 2,000 shares to Manhattan's riff-raff by November 30th, 1991 that H & B would have to call a special meeting of its shareholders soon after that date.

"The purpose of the special meeting of shareholders would be several fold. It would include the approval of any special bylaws, the election of directors, the naming of H & B's external auditors and a report to the shareholders as to H & B's financial status. And, of course, a thorough report would be given to the shareholders as to H & B's goals, aims and objectives, its services and its benefits to shareholders.

"Our man then began his recitation of H & B's goals, aims and objectives. It's goals he said are simple: Self-help, financial independence and humanitarianism. Its aims are to amass as many of the world's poor and homeless into its corporate being as possible and to gain power for them through massive numbers. Worldwide, the ultimate aim would be to amass three billion of the worlds poor with each person holding an investment in H & B's share capital of two-hundred equivalent American dollars providing H & B therefore with an equity base of six-hundred-billion dollars.

"Holy shit, Leroy said, wild, bizarre. An organization with that kind of an equity base could buy controlling interest in one hell of a lot of the major corporations in the world. H & B at that size would be able to impose its wishes almost unfettered on worldwide business. Its influences would be unmatched. What a thought.

"Yeah, our man said, but Leroy, that would not be the purpose of H & B. Its purpose would be to open up new avenues of industry in farming, manufacturing, mining, fishing and the restoration of declining capital assets. To clean and restore the globe's environment, including therefore the deletion of the greenhouse effect, and to restore and protect its wild life. To build hospitals, education centers, homes for the aged. The promotion of scientific research and space programs. On the humanitarian side, H & B would fight for worldwide democracy, human rights and freedom, environmental livability, and full employment.

"Who do you think you are my friend, Jesus Christ himself? Vito said, laughingly. What a dreamer you are. For your information, whoever you are, half the fuckin' scum bags who adorn our slums think like you do. They all have hallucinatory dreams of grandeur.

"Okay sir, I understand what you're saying. But as you know unbelievable things have happened in our world since the beginning of the 20th Century. In 1899 the United States Government was so positive nothing more could take place in technology it felt it could repeal and do away with it's patent laws. The world had reached its apex in new inventions by 1899. It was not possible anything more could be invented. If those parliamentary gentlemen could see the world now out of those 1899 eyes, my oh my, how they would burble. Anything, Mr. Apostoli, is possible.

"Our man went on and explained his views on H & B Financial's current objectives. H & B's first objective, he offered, was the legal creation of the entity itself. That, he re-informed Leroy and Vito, had been done on September 29th, 1991. The second objective was to be the gathering of Manhattan's scummers into H & B's fold as shareholders.

Get the scummers excited, stimulated, energized and boiling over with enthusiasm about a financial organization of their own. Their company would hunt for jobs for them; help educate them in various skills; help them in re-orientation; care for them to the extent possible with the resources available at H & B; provide them with a source of income, limited of course to the extent of H & B's ability to earn revenues, and to accept without denunciation the maintenance of the lifestyles of those scummers who wish to live as they are.

"Our man went on to explain that all the positions to be filled as employees of H & B Financial would be chosen from among the shareholders of H & B.... hiring of H & B's staff would be done by a committee of shareholders.

"Future objectives would include the branching out of H & B's activities to New York City's other boroughs.

"Finally our man explained that if the company did become operative, it would require the appointment of a firm of external auditors, a selection of a firm of solicitors and a stock brokerage house. He stated that if H & B was able to sell 2,000 scummers each $100 worth of its shares, the company would have a start up base of $200,000 in share capital and an equivalent amount in cash. H & B would have a total of $700,000.00 at its disposal for investment, $200,000 in share capital and $500,000.00 in contributed surplus.

"You're getting closer to reality now my friend, but how do you think us poor turds can raise one hundred bucks? Shit man if I had a hundred bucks now I'd buy as much cheap wine as I could with it. I wouldn't give the fuckin' money to your little dream company for a bunch of worthless shares.

"Well, our man said, if you haven't the money now you have four ways of raising it. You can work for a few days, or you can beg, borrow or steal." Then our man said, "Have some faith in the proposed enterprise, get some pride back in your bones, show others in society that scummers can succeed. If you have to buy one hundred bucks worth of booze, then, work, beg, borrow, or steal $200. Raising a coupla' hundred bucks on the streets now days should be easy. It could work out to be a fun kind of a challenge for a bunch of scum bags to compete with the rest of society in money making.

"He's right, Vito, Leroy said, it might be fun to give it a shot. I'm all for it mister, count me in. C'mon Wop.

"Okay nigger, Vito said to Leroy. He then turned to our man and in a whinny voice said, yeah, count me in.

"Thank you gentlemen, our man said with a smile.

"Here's the fifteen dollars I promised you.

"We are now a threesome.

"We'll make H & B rumble. He shook their hands.

CHAPTER 80

H&B'S FIRST SHAREHOLDERS MEETING

3000 skid row derelicts attend

In just seven days the trio had garnered 21 men and seven women to form the start-up committee. The committee was a scruffy group of low lives. Lost businessmen and women, former policemen, professional athletes, prostitutes, a bag lady whom a few days ago introduced herself as Polly and had called him Clark St. James, petty thieves, bible preacher fall-outs, long-term scums, even a former Miss America. They were all colors and races. Six of them came from Harlem, one was a Jew, five Hispanics, four Asians, two Native Indians, the rest were mongrel whites. All of them were enthusiastic. Fifteen of them had even put-up $100 to buy shares in H & B.

The committee was charged with the responsibility of finding 2,000 investors. The committee members could use whatever methods they deemed necessary to sell the shares. Our man had prepared a prospectus many months ago. The prospectus had been approved for distribution to prospective shareholders at the time H & B was incorporated. Each person who was approached to buy shares was given a prospectus. The committee and its nominees had sold 2,800 shares…fully paid for…in just 21 days. They had a ball doing it.

Our man had selected the bag lady for the start-up committee. She was a case. Our man had seen her the day after he had arrived in New

York. He was 'taken' with her. She always had several scummers straggling along behind her like sea gulls following a boat. She didn't pay them much heed, but when she spoke they listened. In spite of the warm days, the bag lady was clothed from her ankles up past her nose. She wore an ugly old wig to cover her eyes. Other than her distinctive female voice, it would be impossible to know if she was in fact a she.

Our man had followed her in secret for a few days and he found she had no daily pattern. He had listened to her orations to her pitiful followers on occasion and each time he was impressed by her words. Most often she and her group slept close together at nights in various skid row locations. He wondered how she knew his real name when she introduced herself as Polly. Damn mysterious, how the hell does she know who I am. One late afternoon our man overheard the bag lady dismiss her group for the balance of the day and for the night. She instructed them to meet her the following day at noon at the main entrance of Madison Square Garden. She then trundled off alone up Fifth Avenue toward Central Park. She had left her herd on East 47th Street and Fifth. Our man followed her. She stopped at an ATM midway between 51st and 52nd. She looked around to see if anyone was near. She inserted a card into the machine. She punched in her pin numbers and in a moment or two she retrieved her card, $200 and a slip produced by the machine. Unbeknownst to our man, when the bag lady glanced at the bank slip, the balance of her account showed $63,683,700. The bag lady then retrieved a box of matches from her belongings, lit one, then used it to burn up the bank slip. After she satisfied herself the slip was now just pieces of ashes blowing in the wind, she continued her trudging toward Central Park. What in hell he thought?

The wretch stopped in front of a plush high rise apartment located just a short distance from the Plaza Hotel. She glanced around to see if anyone had paid heed to her, seeing none she moved closer to the high rise's elegant doors. The doors opened and a uniformed doorman beckoned her in. Whilst our man could not hear the conversation between the bag lady and the doorman, he saw the doorman bow to her as she entered the building's palatial lobby, took care of her cart and saw to it that she got into an elevator. Our man, who now was getting to be quite proficient as a sneak, saw the elevator was being directed to the 29th floor.

"Jesus Christ," our man muttered, "who is this person? A suite in this part of New York City had to be worth seven to ten million dollars." He wondered if she was a maid. No she couldn't be. Only owners of a suite would be permitted through the front entrance of the building. Are she and the doorman thieves? Are they co-conspirators in some grand larceny scheme, whilst the true owners of the condo are away from the city? Or is the bag lady some rich, senile old woman?

I've got to find out, our gentleman thought. This is a puzzler. Son of a gun!

Our man followed the bag lady many times after this first sojourn, and each time she left her flock she came to the same classic apartment building where she was greeted like a queen by whomever was at the door.

In the meantime our gentleman found a reason for talking to her. She and her piteous entourage were grubbing their way around Times Square, panhandling, checking out garbage receptacles, chattering when suddenly they were accosted by three men. One of the men began pushing some of the bag lady's followers around, demanding them to get "the hell" off the streets. Two of them went for the bag lady. In spite of the crowds of people about, the three bullies became physical with the group. The two who went after the bag lady were getting ready to dump her over-stuffed cart when, as cool as you please, she kicked out with her right foot connecting with one of the man's shins. He let out a yelp. He looked down at his leg and saw blood. "You bitch," he yelled, "ya got a fucking' blade in your shoe."

"You got it Toyota," she mumbled.

The other dude reached for her throat. She grabbed a three-pronged garden tool from her cart and was about to rake it across his face when the bleeding one hit her flush on the chin knocking her to one knee. She didn't utter a sound. Her heavy facial clothing absorbed much of the punch. Her followers screamed for help but the crowds of people on the street ignored them. This was nothing unusual for Times Square. The bag lady was on her feet in a trice. Both men went for her as she lashed out at them with her garden tool. One of the tines caught the corner of one of the punk's mouth. She yanked the tool hard ripping his mouth into a gaping wound. Blood spewed from the five-inch gash. The wound went from the right corner of the punk's mouth almost to his ear. A slab of his lip hung down past his chin. He screamed. The man who was pushing the bag lady's entourage around took a run at her. Next thing you know he was flat on his face. A size-14 hob-nail boot had tripped him up. Our man stood towering over the fallen punk. Slowly our man walked over to the bag lady took her hand and looking back at her followers beckoned them to follow as he marched them down the street. They left the three bloodied bewildered bullies behind.

Our man asked the bag lady if she was okay?

"Yes," she said, "I'm just fine. I enjoy a little fracas from time to time. It keeps me sharp. Thanks for the trip you put on the one dude."

"Your welcome."

"You can let go of my hand now Sir Galahad."

"Oops, sorry your ladyship."

They both laughed.

"You really messed up the one guy."

"Yes I did. It teaches punks to respect me. My theory is if I mess some of the assholes up good they'll either respect me and leave me and my contingents alone or they'll blow me away."

"Doesn't that scare you?"

"Naw, I'm too stubborn and mean to be scared. By the way Clark St. James how come you follow me so often? You know what I'm saying, up to the big sexy apartment I go to once in a while?"

Our man felt like he'd been hit by a two-ton truck. Again she called me by my right name.

"Pardon?" he bumbled.

"C'mon, Sir Galahad, fess up."

"I don't know what you're talking about," our man said with a straight face.

The bag lady turned, looked up into his face and smiling said, "sir I can tell you the dates, days, hours and minutes you shadow me. Do you want me to recite them to you, or are you going to come clean Mr. St. James?"

"Yeah, ma'am, I've followed you," he confessed. Christ, how does this old witch know my name?

"Why?" she asked.

"Because you intrigue me."

"How do I intrigue you?"

"Because of your get-up. If it wasn't for your voice no one could tell whether you are male or female."

"That's no answer handsome. But it'll do for the time being. Now Sir Galahad, what do you think when you see me enter that swanky place?"

"I think you're a rich…ummm…martyr perhaps. Someone who wants to join the ranks of skid row people to see how they live. But you keep that luxuriant back-up place just in case, I mean when you need to get cleaned up or you get a little sick and tired of the street filth, or whatever, you traipse back to your luxurious haunt for a few hours. Right?"

"Wrong Clark," she called our man. "I saved the lives of three of the owners of that complex a couple of years ago, and as a reward the housing company's council has given me free access to the building.

They let me stay in a cubbyhole of a place which is located on the top floor of the building."

Our man had guessed the bag lady would have an appropriate answer to his dilemma. But secretly he had hoped for a more exotic one.

After a brief conversation about the streets, they re-introduced one another to themselves.

Then our man got right to the topic of H & B Financial and his proposal for the selling of H & B's capital stock to the street people. They had made their way to Washington Square, found a bench and sat. Some of the bag lady's followers sat around the bench on the grass looking up to her while others milled around the square waiting for their matriarch.

Our man discussed the topic of H & B with the bag lady. She tuned in easily. She required no repetitiveness. She grasped its underlying principals and practicalities without the necessity of foraging for answers. Our man, on completion of his presentation to her, had an eerie feeling she was more aware of H & B's intricacies than he was. It wasn't her words alone that gave him the feeling, it was her whole demeanor. This person, he thought, could sway people to her thinking as if they were under her spell. She lives in secrecy, yeah, in a luxurious high rise apartment, she fights like a tigress, is fearless, is compos mentis and brilliant. Our man tested her ego on matters so complex that only those with university training could answer. Shit, this bag of rags was a genius. Something very serious must have gone wrong with her sometime during her life to cause her to live on skid row. Did our man have the courage to ask her about her past life and her apparent lofty qualifications? No, he thought it would be more intelligent to hold back his intimate questioning of her now. Later perhaps as he gets to know her, but not now.

* * *

Polly the bag lady was in fact *the* start-up committee. Her incredible brain power together with her charisma, spellbinding parlance and compelling ego made it simple for her to convince scummers to invest in H & B's shares. She together with her herd sold 2697 of the 2,800 shares sold. Our man's deadline of November 30th was beaten by 12 days. God, he thought, things are looking good. He never would have guessed in his wildest dreams he would find the brainy people he had recruited for the start-up committee, Polly, Vito, Leroy, Mary, Peter, Klaus, David, Joseph just to name a few. They were incredible.

It had been agreed all 2,800 subscribers would meet at H & B's warehouse building at 200 W. 4th on November 30th, 1991 at which time a special shareholder's meeting would take place. A notice of the meeting had been given to each of the share subscribers at the time the subscribers had paid for the shares. The time was set for 2:00 p.m.

The meeting was a 'hoot.'

This wasn't your ordinary meeting of shareholders you see at formal get-togethers. Just calling the meeting to order was a chore. Our man's 'start-up' committee had arranged for 2,500 folding chairs to be rented and delivered to the warehouse. Money up front, of course. The committee members thought maybe, just maybe 1,500 shareholders would attend the meeting however, they ordered the extra 1,000 just in case. They were wrong. Over 3,000 fuck-ups showed up. Friends of shareholders, drinking buddies, shit-using buddies, junk-heaps, whores, all looking for something free. Nearly all of the 3,000 skid rowers were either pissed or pumped. Jesus-H-Christ, our man thought, what kind of a show is this going to be? The place stank of cheap wine, and body odor. Just like a rancid armpit frolic. Noisy, staggering fuck-ups vying for seats, stumbling, shoving, pushing and cussing at each other all clamoring for a chair. At last Washington Leroy Jefferson, who was part of the head table (he as well as Vito, Polly, Mary, Peter, Klaus, David, Joseph and our man) had had enough. He grabbed the microphone the committee had bought on sale and bellowed out, "shut your dumb fuck up faces you vile smelling shit bags. We just sent out for more chairs, so cool it."

The clamoring stopped.

"Did you all sign the official registry when you came in?"

"Yeah," came a gigantic response, "we did tar baby." They laughed.

"Fuck you, you bunch of maggot brained arse wipes." Leroy hollered back.

The crowd burst into a spontaneous maniacal laugh. "Whoeee" they shouted, "Good old Leroy. Are you still buggering your Wop buddy Vito up his ass?" one scummer seated in the front row yelled up at Leroy.

Vito jumped up, ran off the makeshift stage and hurled himself at the accuser. There was one hellova scramble. Arms, legs and more maniacal laughter. Our man now left the stage and got in the middle of the melee. The bag lady took the microphone away from Leroy. Like magic, her voice filled the warehouse. It was spellbinding. The din in the building stopped. The bag lady handed the 'mike' back to Leroy and whispered to him, "call the meeting to order—now!" Leroy didn't, he was too tongue tied.

Somehow the media had heard about the fact some people had convinced nearly 3,000 skid row juice-ups to buy 'a hundred bucks' worth of shares each from a rubby-dub company called H & B Financial and Poors. Another scam to hose the poor the media thought. Several newspaper reporters, television crews and radio personnel decided to cover the meeting. The start-up committee had been ambivalent about the media's presence at the meeting and to settle the question the committee left the decision in the hands of the media itself. NBC, CBS and ABC all came. Cameras were set and ready to go. What a 'ball' the media had. Wars, riots, earthquakes, tornadoes and hurricanes are far more intense than this bizarre affair, but by the Lord Jesus not as outlandish as this one. The media licked it's chops with glee after getting involved with the show. TV cameras zeroed in on the mongrels as they staggered into the warehouse. It was a blast just watching the drunks trying to sign their names at the registration desk. "Why do I have to sign this friggin book anyway?"

"Because slime ball, I said so," replied one of the three hookers assigned by the committee to act as registrars.

The three prostitutes doing this job were required to get the name of each person who was attending the meeting, check the persons name against a computer printout in order to verify his or her status as a shareholder. The 'prosties' after satisfying themselves as to each the signers bona fides gave each shareholder a white and black piece of cardboard paper for voting purposes. White for yea and black for nay, and a copy of the meetings agenda as well as H & B's opening balance sheet. What a hope. Most of the attendees understood only one thing...free sandwiches and coffee..."Yeah, but what, no vino?" The three hookers were intelligent meeting-wise. Before taking to the streets the three of them had worked for companies which held shareholders' meetings. Each one had been involved acting as registrars for their respective companies hence had previous experience in this function. All of them were in their mid 20's. All three were hard looking glamour girls. They weren't above asking some of the media 'guys' about a 'good time' right at the meeting. The media 'guys' found this hilarious.

The show went on at the registration desk. Some shareholders whose bladders were full of beer and wine didn't trouble themselves in finding a men's 'can' to relieve themselves. Hell no, they just took out their wrinkled dorks and pissed in the doorway passage. Cameramen zoomed in on this rarity. Our man realized from the mayhem taking place at the entranceway and in the bowels of warehouse that he should have had ushers for the meeting. The place was a drunken bedlam. The din was like a zoo at feeding time. Scummers hollered back and forth to each other greetings, threats and propositions. The swearing was obscene.

After about an hour the place was beginning to settle down. More chairs had arrived...just in time too...the melee had gotten so out of hand people and chairs were being knocked akimbo in the wild pursuit of a seat onto which a butt could be placed. Politeness, thoughtfulness…forget it. TV cameramen got right into the middle of the muddle. They got pushed, shoved, cussed at, peed on, but no way were they going to miss this for the six o'clock news. The bedlam was "spirited" but it wasn't ferocious. Other than a few scratches and bruises no one was hurt. As far as the media was concerned it was fun to watch because of its kinship to the Keystone Kops' bumbling. But our man was mortified. Once again the bag lady took the microphone from the stupefied Leroy.

"Ladies and gentlemen," she called out. "Slow down…now," she demanded. The din and clamoring began to subside once again following her order. The bag lady continued, "It upsets me to see all of you behaving like wild beasts. I don't like being upset. I do nasty things when I get upset—so don't annoy with me." With that she took an ugly looking handgun out of her wrappings and fired a shot just above everyone's head. (A blank cartridge mind you, but no one but her knew that.)

Even the 'drunkest' among the people 'came to' following the echoing blast of her handgun. Jesus, the media types thought, dropping to the floor scared of what might happen next. From their position on the floor they heard the bag lady say "Now sit you heathen mothers and pay heed to your chairman, or I will lay a curse on all of you."

The cameras were manned once again. They focused in on the bag lady. While she looked like a wretch, her voice was overwhelming. It's tone and possessiveness held complete domination over all its listeners, including the media. "Who the hell is this broad?" one media type asked another. "I have no idea," his cohort replied, "but I feel like a grade three'r listening to her."

"Yeah, right."

The woman investigative reporter in front of camera 2 was trying to determine whether she should be laughing or hi-tailing it out of the wretched place. She 'hung-in' there, commenting on everything her cameraman shot. The cameraman zoomed in on the head table. In his mind, other than the bag lady and a big tanned dude, they looked like a bouquet of torn arsholes.

Vito was back in his place after his set-to with the clown who inferred he, Vito, was Leroy's buggeree. This still pissed off Vito who was now guzzling on his bottle of wine just as the camera caught him, and just as Peter stood up from his head table chair and scratched his ass. A fine group they made. Perhaps the Directors of City Corp, Exxon or Ford Motors would like Vito or Peter on their respective Boards.

The bag lady made one more comment to the subdued mob before handing the microphone back to Leroy.

"My friends," she said, "please try to listen and to understand what today's meeting is all about. You may be in the process of making an historical turn-around for mankind today. If your company is successful in its deliberations over the next few years, it could become the base for a statewide organization of the homeless, thence mayhap nationwide and perhaps even worldwide. Some three billion people on our earth today are needy. Just think of the immense power of three billion humans. Financially they could become enormous. If three billion people invested $100 each, over a given period of time in H&B Financial and Poors Inc. they would create an unheard of equity position of $300 billion. Using a 20 times multiple of the $300 billion under today's bank laws, H&B would be allowed to take deposits of $6 trillion. Now, if one converted the $6 trillion into bottles of wine at two bucks apiece, one would have three trillion twenty six's of lush." The attendees cheered and stomped their feet at the thought of oceans of wine at their disposal.

"Quiet," the bag lady bellowed.

"You must take heed of today's undertakings as sensible, mature adults, not as a bunch of useless boneheads. We want H&B to participate in a free marketplace. Government intervention must be kept to a minimum. Freedom of the individual is paramount. So my friends, let's show the world we can compete. Let's admit we may be a little shy of decorum. Pointing toward a far corner of the warehouse, the bag lady said, "see the two men and the lady over there urinating. That's not what the genteel would do. No the genteel would either repair to a bathroom, or they would hold it. Not just get up and piss.

"So we not only have economics to learn, we must learn also to have some savoir-faire.

"Now, by damn, be attentive you ill-bred heathens." For some unknown reason the bag lady got a standing ovation from the scummers.

Leroy was now out of his trance. He was ready to chair the meeting. Good ole Polly, like an angel she had set the stage for him.

Banging his gavel on its wooden base, Leroy called the meeting to order at 3:29 p.m. The meeting's secretary Betty was a matronly looking overweight drunk. She had raised three kids by herself, put them through college, now two were teachers and one was an electrical engineer. As soon as her offspring's were financially independent, Betty went off the 'straight and narrow.' She was now doing what she always wanted to do—be a skid row drunken, irresponsible bum. She was enjoying every minute of her life in spite of the fact her children had now forsaken her. "Yes, Mr. Chairman," Betty confirmed, "the time of day is hereby, burp, excuse me, noted in the minnn, minnn, minit book."

"Thank you," Leroy said. "Since this is the first meeting of shareholders there are no minutes to be read so ladies and gentlemen, I would like to introduce you to the man who came up with the idea of creating a financial organization for us. He is one hellova guy. He's a straight shooter. He put his money where his mouth is. Yeah. He donated one half a million dollars cash to H&B Financial in what shows in H&B books as contributed surplus. Then he bought this warehouse for $290,000 and put up another $200,000 aside to fix it up, a total of

$490,000 and, by damn if he did'nt give this to H&B as more contributed surplus."

"Do any of you here know what I'm saying?" he said, looking out at the sea of deadpan faces. "Those of you who do understand what I am saying, please raise your hand." What a surprise, about half of the shareholders raised their hands.

"Are you sure you know what I just said?" Washington asked astonished.

"Yes," came a voluminous reply.

One seedy looking woman stood up and called out, "Yeah brother, we know what you just said. The philanthropist, whatever, gave our company $990,000."

"Yeah," another yelled. "How come not an even million?"

"Jesus you're stupid," the seedy woman hollered back. She continued on saying, "Of the $990,000, I assume $500,000 is for investing, while $290,000 of it has been used to buy this property and the remaining $200,000 will be used for upgrading this building. Correct?"

"Correct" Leroy replied.

"Where did he get this money?" another scummer asked.

"Ya, where'd he get the money, and why'd he give it to H&B Financial?" another asked. "There has to be a catch."

"He's a fucking crook I wager," an English accented hobo stated. "I says he's gonna sell our live bodies to some government or scientist, the bleedin leech is, I says."

"Why didn't this dude just give us the $990,000 big ones? We'd know what to do with it, wouldn't we my fellow Americans?" one grubby slob said, emulating Richard Nixon.

"Yea, yea," the crowd erupted.

"Stone the son-of-a-bitch," another grub screamed.

"He's a slick bastard. How much money did he get out of us for christsake? Let's see? Hey yer lordship chairperson, how many of us dumb fucks donated $100 bucks each for our so-called shares?"

Leroy looked stunned.

"C'mon asshole, how many?"

"Two thousand eight hundred and twenty one," Leroy answered.

"That's, lets see now, that's over $280,000 bucks," the grub shouted. "Fuckin' crooked bastard is what he is. He'll now wind up the company and run off with our money. I'll wager he didn't buy this old warehouse at all. He probably just rented it for the day and claimed he bought it. Have any of you dumb-asses up there on the stage seen the title or deed for this property? None of you I'll bet? Shit he's spent maybe $5,000 bucks tops organizing this scam, and he's going to rip us off of $282,100 bucks."

"Let's get him," another yelled, jumping from his seat springing open a stiletto.

Several drunks and hopheads struggled out of their seats and began to fumble their way toward our man.

"Hold it, hold it, everybody," our man called out, "Keep your cool. I thought this might happen, so I came prepared. I have all the documentation to prove the facts about your company H&B Financial and Poors Inc. The documentation includes an audited opening balance sheet of H&B and a verification statement from Citicorp confirming that all of the funds donated by me and the paid-up capital you folks have paid in for shares are in a Citicorp trust account that cannot be redeemed by anyone without the approval of the Securities and Exchange Commission. This approval will be waived only after you shareholders have elected a 12-person board of directors and after you have approved of various signing authorities. As well, ladies and gentlemen, I have the deed to this warehouse property here in my hands. The deed is made out solely in the name of H&B Financial and Poors Inc. You can view this deed anytime you wish. On viewing the deed you will note it is free of any encumbrances. Now if you look at the reverse side of your agenda you will see a copy of your company's opening balance sheet. Please note the auditors opinion statement pertaining thereto and my confirmation of its propriety.

"I am not a thief folks. I am on your side. I want the best for you regardless of your choice of living. I will not be paternalistic. I do not want any special favors from you; I just want to work for you. I purchased $100 worth of the stock of H&B just as you did.

"I want H&B to be a model company, free of political infighting. I want your company to go out in the marketplace and succeed. I want it to be the base and forerunner of much bigger things. Damn, I want all of you to be winners.

"This building is yours, open to you 24 hours each day. All of you are welcome to go through the files of H&B that I have here with me. I don't care how long it takes you to peruse these files, I will remain with you until every last one of you have satisfied yourselves as to the propriety of my words."

The belligerent ones stopped their advance as our man spoke. When he finished, the big crowd threatened the belligerent ones with all manner of punishments if they didn't return to their seats. They all did except for a stiletto carrier, he continued his charge toward our man. Our man walked off the stage, down the steps toward the knife yielding scummer.

The TV crew were having the time of their lives covering the whole event. Now this drama was unfolding. A vicious looking knife wielder walking menacingly toward a big 'easy going' man who was advancing (like a John Wayne) towards the ugly would-be killer.

The attacker sprang at our man. He was agile and quick. Our man didn't expect the speed the scummer showed. Before our man knew it, he was bleeding from a superficial chest wound. The scummer slashed at our man's face but missed by a fraction of an inch. The scummer threw a thunderous left hook to our man's jaw. Our man reeled. The scummer leapt forward ready to plunge his stiletto into our man's gut, but just before the stiletto reached our man's skin, the stiletto wielder's wrist was caught by our man. Our man slipped his hand down from the scummers wrist to the scummers hand and squeezed. The scummer screamed. Our man compressed the scummers hand so tight that blood vessels broke through the scummer's skin and blood juices flowed between the fingers of our man. Hand bones were heard being crushed. The scummer fainted. The bag lady telephoned for an ambulance. The TV cameras caught the whole sickening episode.

The crowd applauded. Almost all of them had a big gulp from their bottles in honor of our man's triumph.

Leroy rapped his gavel several times as he called the meeting back to order.

The remaining business of the meeting carried on with only minor infractions occurring. Twelve directors were elected, signing authorities were approved and the date for H&B's first annual general meeting was set for June 15th, 1992.

CHAPTER 81

POLLY'S FINANCIAL EXPERTISE

Lana went on to explain that H&B Financial made millions upon millions of dollars in the bond and stock markets over the next few years. Bond prices soared between 1991 and 1993. H&B stacked up several millions of dollars on bond trades in both Canada and the United States during that time. Stock prices as measured by the Dow Jones industrial average rose from 3000 in April of 1991 to nearly 8000 by May, 1997. Our man's selection along with H&B's three-person investment committee, Polly, Leroy and Peter, of individual stocks from '91 to '97 was uncanny.

It was, in fact, Polly who was the 'seer,' the brains and the mastermind behind all of H&B'sinvestments. The committee took but two fliers during the six-year period. In one case the committee bought two million shares of a particular mining stock for a few pennies per share and sold the shares over a six-week period at an average price after brokerage of $23.05 producing therefore a gain of over $45 million. In another case H&B had purchased two million shares of a multinational computer company in mid-June of 1992 at $18.00 per share, sold them in November 1992 at a net after brokerage of $22.10, repurchased them again in August 1993 for $18.10 sold them in May of 1994 at a net of $32.15, bought them again in December of 1995 at $42.00 then sold them in October 1996 at a net of $81.50. These transactions alone netted H&B $115 million. H&B did not realize in the beginning of its stock and bond market transactions our man had used his substantial net worth as the back up for buying equities on margin by H&B. This our man did until H&B's cash position was sufficient on its own to either purchase marketable securities outright, or buy on a 50% margin or deal with brokers wherein the broker guaranteed any unpaid portion of purchases made by H&B. H&B from time to time sold short on stocks if it felt the stocks were overpriced. In one case the committee studied a blue chip stock whose earnings per share was $1.90 and its current price was $65 5/8. The committee knew even if the entire earnings per share were paid out in cash dividends the return would be only 2.89%. The price earning ratio was a rather high ($65.5/8 / 1.90) 34.54. Could this stock see some profit taking by current shareholders? With the bag lady's OK the committee felt "yes". Yes the stock price would likely fall—to as low as $52.00—if this did occur, H&B would profit by $13.00 per share. H&B did sell 65.5/8 million shares at an average price per share of $65.5/8 dollars in June of 1996 and did buy the stock three weeks later at an average price of $51.50 and gained $13 million dollars on the transaction.

"Selling short, ladies and gentlemen, is not a complicated mechanism," Lana stated. "When H&B sold this stock, H&B did not own or have any of it in its portfolio. On orders from H&B's investment committee, the broker sold H&B's non-existing stock at $65.5/8 to one or more purchasers and in order to fulfill the sale and deliver the stock to the purchasers, the broker 'borrowed' the stock from another or others of its client's portfolio. Then when H&B bought the stock for $51.50 three weeks later, H&B's broker replaced the stock back into the portfolios it 'borrowed' the stock from in the first place. At no time did H&B have any direct contact with the stock it bought and sold. H&B received checks totaling $13 million dollars from the two transactions.

H&B's single most profitable gains took place in a mega bank stock. Its final net return from the time of its first purchase of the stock in November 1991 for $10.00, until it finally sold out it's position in August 1996 for $107.00 was a whopping $123 million dollars.

H&B dealt in stocks of a major soft drink company, in several oil stocks and it had a rather classic ride in a high priced $9 thousand dollar per share it bought into in January 1992. It sold the stock for $33,900.00 per share in May of 1996. In all, H&B had had gains of over $1.8 billions dollars in bond and stock transactions for its six-year period ended March 31st, 1997. H&B's stock at March 31st, 1997 was made up of those companies who have paid, or have had the financial ability to pay dividends for the past five years.

The scummer shareholders were proud of themselves. Yes, we are a smart bunch. Just look at our company's financial statements for proof.

CHAPTER 82

ISTANBUL, LANA DISCUSSES RELIGION

It was Friday morning 9:30 a.m., May 9th, 1997 when Dr. Carruthers called the meeting to order. Dr. Carruthers thanked Dr. Masters for the fascinating story of the successes of H&B Financial and Poors Ltd.

"I'm sure," he stated, "the dramatic growth of H&B over the past six years, its financial well being and its attainments are beyond the belief of most people. Our man, whoever he is, and the bag lady, whoever she is, must be proud of their accomplishments."

"Yes, they are sir," Lana replied.

Lana told the gathering it was her intent today to discuss her feelings toward religion and politics. In particular she said she would comment on leaders in those fields.

Religion. What a sham it started out to be, and how it has remained a shocking sham. It all started about 150,000 years ago in the latter part of the Old Stone Age. Neanderthal humans began to develop a degree of intelligence, particularly in the making of tools and utensils that were useful to them. They even began to sketch out markings in caves and on stone walls which have provided our modern-day historians with valuable data. Some of them began to wonder and question the mysterious things around them. Things such as how they stuck to the ground and didn't fly off into space. How some things could flap their long feathered arms and stay off the ground, then come down again, how some things could stay in water without having to come up for air and how some other things liked to eat them up. How did all the things around them get there like the big, tall, woody things that moved only when air around them moved. And what about those pretty little things that came out of the ground so often and smelled so nice. How the big blue stuff way up there with a small yellow little thing hanging in the blue stuff sent down warmth and light and would always, always fall off the ground at the end of the day? Then it would be dark and scary. Then instead of a little yellow thing up in that blue stuff everything got black and another hanging thing that was once a warm yellow thing would be there but would now be white and would change from only being partly there to all there. And way up in the black stuff there would be a whole bunch of little wee white dots that would sparkle. And how some awful thick gray stuff would come along and cover up the blue stuff and that nice little yellow thing, and then big noisy scary flashes of white wiggly stuff would come out of that stuff that covered the blue, then a whole bunch of wet things or icy things would fall down on the ground? And how come the yellow little thing in the blue stuff would always come up on the other side of the ground unless that other stuff that leaked water covered the blue stuff. And how come it is so fun when one of us sticks our sticky-out thing in a shorter one of us who doesn't have a sticky-out thing but who has a nice little warm inny thing? And how come many times after the little yellow thing falls off the ground, the one of us who has the warm little inny thing gets a big round thing in front? Then how come after many more times the little yellow thing falls off the ground the smaller thing of us with the round thing in front would make loud scary noises until a little wee one of us would come out of the inny thing's inny thing. And how come the little wee one of us would yell loud once it found its way out of the inny thing's inny thing?

How come all these things? "I know," said one old gnarled sage, "a big thing made all of this. The ground, the blue thing, yellow thing, dark thing, white thing that changes when its dark, white little dots, gray things that cover the blue thing and makes noisy scary flashes then leaks water all over the place, big wet things that taste salty other wet things that taste good. I know where all these things come from. They come from a great big thing who has an inny thing, no, who has a sticky-out thing. Yes a sticky out-thing. The big one brought all the things to us on this ground. The big one with the sticky-out thing sends all things to us on a metal thing that does not flap its long arms with feathers. No, instead the thing comes fast from out of the blue stuff then comes down and lands on the ground. Lots of funny-eyed things come out of metal thing and run around on the ground and make strange things. The funny-eyed things take some of us things into the metal thing. They look at all our things and play with our sticky-out things and inny things then go back fast into blue stuff."

"And," the sage went on, "long before us things came to be on the ground, the big thing sent on that thing that comes fast from the blue stuff, one who has a sticky-out thing and one who has an inny thing. And these two things made many little things who got big like us things. So that is why us things are here."

All of the sage's tribe were happy and relieved to hear his answers. Now they could go about their day-to-day business without troubling themselves with these weighty matters. The sage had all the answers to the universe's mysteries. The sage said it was someone by the name of God who owns the metal thing and that God is an almighty thing. The old sage, proud of his intellectual accomplishments and of his education of his brainless brethren, now felt he must determine the finality of each of us things. Ah, he conceptualized, if he could reason out finality for us things, something grandiose for us things he said be good and something hellish for those us things he said be evil he could become the ground ruler of all. He could have slaves, wives, concubines, mistresses...all these things and 'hard assets' too. For my intellect and my dictation all us things will be required to pay me the sage thing valuable things forever. "Those of us things," he preached to his tribe, "who do my bidding and be good will leave their body things on the ground when they become dead and they will go up into the blue thing and they will be happy things forever. But, the sage preached with fire and hate in his eyes, "those of us things who do not 'be good' and who do not do my bidding and who become dead will leave their body things on the ground and they will go into the ground where hard things get so hot they melt and gurgle and rumble and burble and these hard hot things will have us bad things grow horns on each side of our head things and us things will cry and sputter and howl and screech forever in agony," he warned. "Us bad things that have sticky-out things will have our sticky-out things fall off and melt in the hot hard things and those of us who have inny things will have our inny things melt shut by the hot hard things forever. So the 'it is so fun' thing that the taller thing and the shorter thing do with their sticky-out thing and their inny thing with each other will be gone forever.

"Now all of you us things must give me, your divine sage, some of your valuable things when the yellow thing falls off the ground this many times," the sage held up his fingers ten times. "And each of you us things who have a young inny thing who has never had a sticky-out thing stuck in her inny thing must bring this inny thing to me for me to be able to stick my sticky-out thing in her inny thing whenever I wish.

"Now all of you us things hear me well. I, your sage thing have been given a message by the thing that does not flap its arms and comes out of the blue stuff fast, that the big God thing gives me the all mighty power to rule everything on the ground. Those of us things who do not obey my every word will fry in that hot place thing forever. Yes fry in brimstone stuff and fire thing. I am God's divine thing on ground. I have supremacy and divinity over all you us things."

"Hallelujah...praise thee 'O' God thing. Us things will do your bidding lest us things fall into fire thing and be in agony forever. Here God thing, take our money, our brains, our souls, our hard assets, our soft assets. Us things will saturate the world with your words of goodness. Us things will fight wars and kill other us things for you. Us things will terrorize people on trains, airplanes, ships, and in buildings for you. Us things will steal lands, bomb, sacrifice, torture, brainwash unbelievers, savages, pagans, heathens until they do your bidding. Us things will build palatial palaces from which us things can worship you thing. Us things will fight other us things for riches so that us things can have moneys to erect these palaces. And God thing us things will keep the lowly us things in poverty forever so that those us things will be like dumb animals and never know how to improve our us things lot nor will us dumb things ever want to improve our us things lot. The lowly us things will eat only what rich us things give us lowly things to eat and us things who are in poverty will worship you and sacrifice lambs for you rich us things. The poor dumb us things will never ask for any nice things so as you 'O' God thing will have all the fine riches you want from the ground thing. All of these things us poor dumb us things promise you forever and ever if you promise for ever and ever to let us things worship you "O" God thing."

"Does not that little bit of folklore sound familiar to you my dear friends?" Lana said.

"The words I speak about religion most often are not intended to reflect on the world's masses. When religion comforts people and gives them a feeling of well being and brings them joy and guides them along the path of virtue, decency and understanding, then religion is a blessing. Religion must be pure. It must not be adulterated. But my how we humans have adulterated it.

"Statistically, the world's composition of religions is made up of 1.928 billion Christians and 3.788 billion non-Christians. Roman Catholics number 968 million and they account for 50% of the world's Christians, while 1,099 billion Muslims make up 29% of world-wide non-Christians. Atheists number 220 million people, while the non-religious number 842 million. Ladies and gentlemen, it is interesting to note that South America has 448 million Christians of which 403 million are Roman Catholic. Latin American Catholics account for nearly 42% of all Roman Catholics worldwide.

"Does this latter statement not say something about the close tie between the poor and the Roman Catholic church?"

CHAPTER 83

ISTANBUL, LANA ON CELIBACY

God's Banker, Catholics and Muslims, grand theft.

Celibacy in the Catholic Church among priests and others in loftier hierarchies may be deemed to be moderately well adhered to. The cases of homosexuality among priests or nuns is not known, but has been estimated to be about 40%. Is homosexuality among these religions an evil thing? Are not priests and nuns born with inherent sexual desires just like any other male or female? Are priests not taught from childhood that sexual abstinence has to do only with the opposite sex? Are not most young males taught that having sex out of wedlock with a female is wrong, even evil? Do parents lecture their kids about not fucking a female if their kid is a boy or not to fuck a boy if the kid is a female? Yet in most cases nothing is said about fucking someone of his or her own sex. So, the heterosexual priest says to himself, I must be celibate when it comes to a she. I must not even think of sex with 'that voluptuous comfy piece of womanhood' over there, but maybe, just maybe it's okay to stuff a boy. No one has told me screwing a boy is wrong. Screwing a girl is evil for a priest. I am married to the church, so I will be overcome with guilt if I sex a woman. But to sex a boy, all it takes to obliterate guilt is confession. Screwing a boy is not really sex, the guilty priest may self rationalize, it is just a matter of ridding myself of an anxiety.

"Shouldn't priests or nuns be allowed to have sex with a consenting adult? Of course they should," Lana said. "The act is so innocent. If all of you in the audience are so convinced God made man in his image and made sex so much fun and pleasure for humans then you should be convinced all male and females should have the right to partake in sexual activity.

"The Twelve Controllers have no objection to consensual sex be thee priest, nun or otherwise. But woe betide all those perpetrators who molest children, engage in incest, rape, enslave or treat sex as a punishment for on their demise they shall be dealt with by the Controllers.

"Now friends, what if the sex act was repugnant for all men and women? What if it was a boring, unexciting, foul, offensive, disgusting, loathsome act. An act so foul it would make chewing on a hairy baboon's dungballs yummy. Yet an act which need be carried out if we humans believe in procreation. So for the sake of procreation somebody would have to do it.

"I wager we humans would be a scarce commodity in that kind of a scenario.

"We would be backward, listless wanderers. Cities would not spring up, there would be little if any transportation facilities, no cars, no jets, no television, radio, computers, movies. No class distinction, very limited wealth disparities, few wars, limited hatreds, no gossip, no sex abuses of any kind, few novels, few magazines, certainly no Playboy et al, no skimpy clothing, no shyness of exposing male or female genitals.

"And what about the religious? What could the religious carp about? Murders would all but disappear. Coveting someone else's wife wouldn't be, because no one would get married. So 'nes ce pas' coveting." No gays to desecrate, abuse, harass and kill. Who would want to marry and raise a family? The list goes on and on.

"Think on this my friends. The world would not be an exciting place for humans to enjoy for their limited life span if it wasn't for sex. Sex makes the world go 'round. Yet sex has been and always will be a most perplexing problem. It's each individual's problem. Until men and women show respect for one anothers sex drive the problem of sexual abominations will never subside.

"Yes sex is a most perplexing problem. But when treated with respect it is incredibly gratifying, and morally responsible. Do you ever wonder if popes masturbate, do Imams masturbate, did Jesus, did Adam (sorry about 'did Adam' Adams One to Six) did Abraham in his seventh heaven, masturbate. What about Mohammed, God's messenger and Ali, Mohammed's friend? In my view I hope they all have, or at least have had a wet dream.

"You are impossible Dr. Masters. Have you no religious morals? You defile God and his millions of earthlings.

"Shame on you. God is the glory of life, its goodness, its righteousness, not sex you obloquious contemptible witch," cried a totally angered religious one.

Lana smiled. She stepped out from behind her lectern. She glowed with beauty. She placed her hands on her hips. She was wearing a black netted dress that rode just past her knees over a white silk sheen slip. The dress's bodice was just below her bosom. Its string straps held the dress so that her ample breasts were held high. A black string centerpiece ran from the middle of the bodice down to the three-inch black hemline of her snug dress. She wore no wristwatch, nor rings. A simple gold chain adorned her lovely neck. Her tawny blond hair flowed in abundance down the front of her shoulders.

"Friends, I have no hatred of anyone. I have animosity for very few. However, I do have disrespect for many religious leaders. The Twelve Controllers are without fault. They are the essence of goodness. They are not divine, they are real. If you wish them to be referred to as God so be it. They are the cosmos. They see the monstrous physical and mental burdens religions place on those employees whom the religious say must be chaste. The Controllers accept those people who choose, without outside influence, to be chaste. But to be subjected to such an order is base in the Contollers view, and, in fact, fraudlent. Fraudlent because it deceives the natural function of a person's physical and mental activities.

"Yes friends, the matter of being forced to be chaste is wrong, and the dreadful consequences that occur from time to time because of it are heinous. Child molestation and abuse by the religious. Is there anything more vile than child abuse?

Ladies and gentlemen, not very long ago, only 40 to 50 of our grandfathers ago, *Jesus Christ Superman* was abused by the religious. Then he was killed in a most vicious, cruel, debased way. The greatest human being ever to grace our world was tortured, humiliated, taunted by both Semites and gentiles then put to death by the religious. Why? Because the scribes and priests were terrified their 'flocks' would turn to Jesus as their savior. And what about the rich, even then the rich were *sucked up to* by the priests and the scribes as icons? Consider James, Chapter V, the New Testament, 'the wicked rich 'ye rich men, weep and howl for your miseries, etc. your riches are corrupted, etc., your gold and silver is cancered, etc., the hire of the laborers which have reaped down your fields, which is of you kept back by fraud, etc., ye have condemned and killed the just.' Jesus was and remains to this day, the essence of purity, humility and kindness. But the very fact he drew together all manner of people through his teachings, he became a threat to the Jewish chief priests and scribes who feared for the loss of their power and riches. Whilst Rome's Pilate was cavalier about Jesus, Herod, Caiaphas and their bunch of religious thugs claimed Jesus to be a perverter of Herod's people. Jesus, the thugs said, claimed to be the King of the Jews. He must be crucified. And, of course, Jesus was crucified by the religious of the time."

Lana went on to discuss the Catholic Church, the church's hierarchy, not its followers. Lana stated over the past seven or eight hundred years the Catholic masses had been threatened, cajoled, tortured, executed and brainwashed into submitting to the rules and orders of its oblate. Spiritual purity (Cathari), puritans (Waldenes) and heretics (Albigenes) were considered dangerous to the religious and the state.

"Initially, under Pope Paul III's tribunal, a heretic or a rebellious or obstinate one was yielded to the civil courts for punishment. That was the beginning of the Inquisitions. The year was 1230. The Inquisition escalated in Spain under Ferdinand V and Isabella, the king and queen of Spain in the year 1480. The proceedings, and the severity of the methods to extract confessions from those deemed guilty of a multitude of religious sins were brutal. Burning at the stake, executions, all manner of punishments were frequent under the Spanish Inquisition. The Spanish Inquisition was abolished a mere 163 years ago.

"Then along came Benito, Adolph, Francisco and Joseph, better known perhaps as Il Duce, Der Führer, Generalissimo Franco and Stalin. Other than Joseph Stalin's communists, Benito Mussolini's fascists, Hitler's nazis and Franco's rebels (Pope Pius XI supported Spanish Dictator Francisco Franco) were accepted as credible by Pope Pius XI and Pope Pius XII. However, when the Vatican City was bombed in 1943 by Germany, and when the Vatican was certain that the allies would defeat the Axis powers, Pope Pius XII became an ally of the Allies. One wonders whose side Pope Pius XII would have taken had the Axis powers won World War Two? Pope Pius XII did continue and intensify the anti-Communist policy of Pius XI. In 1949 Pius XII issued a proclamation which declared that any Catholic rendering support of any kind to communism would automatically incur the penalty of excommunication.

"Now, this immense religious power with no geographic boundaries to deal with, and with a following of almost one billion faithful, recently had the world's multitudes guessing at three conspicuous Catholic questions:

"One, the church's administrative annual financial losses and the need for contributions through Peter's Pence to cover the losses and the omission of full disclosures through the church's financial statements.

"Two, the Vatican's scandal-plagued bank…The Istituto per Le Opere De Religione.

"Three, wherefore Archbishop Paul C. Marcinkus and Roberto Calvi (God's banker).

"The Catholic Churches published losses of $56.7 million in 1986, $59.3 million in 1987 and $61.8 million in 1988 were retired through Peter's Pence contributions. As you know, ladies and gentlemen, Peter's Pence is a voluntary contribution made by Catholics to the papal treasury. The published losses have to do only with the Vatican's administration, it's diplomatic services, its administrative and diplomatic social expenses and the Pope's expenses. The Holy See budget, the papacy, represents only a fraction of wealth and activities of the mega Catholic Church. The financial omission of the Vatican bank, the Vatican's missionary system, religious orders, Catholic parishes and its investments, stocks, its huge real estate holdings, its diocesan districts and its art and architectural treasurers is unknown publicly. Are the consolidated assets of the church in excess of $100 billion, $500 billion, $1 trillion. Do you remember Jesus' entry into Jerusalem? 'He rideth upon an ass.' He had no material wealth. He didn't own acres and acres of land. He was poor. Did Jesus instruct Christians to build gigantic entities vis-à-vis the Catholic churches for him? Did he believe in a world of devilish discrepancies between the pampered rich and the stinking poor?"

* * *

Lana spoke of the Vatican Bank, God's banker one Roberto Calvi of the Banco Ambrosiano and the untouchable Archbishop Paul C. Marcinkus. Roberto Calvi was found hanging under a bridge in

London, England in June of 1982, his pockets stuffed with various countries currencies. Italian judges concluded that his death was murder, not suicide. Others claim suicide. If it was suicide, Senor Calvi would have had to be a stupendous athlete or a Harry Houdini to manage a boat in the Thames' swift currents, toss a rope over the Blackfriars Bridge underpinnings, and do all the things necessary to hang oneself. Sometime later, Michele Sindona, a 'crooked' Italian financier, who had introduced Mr. Calvi to Archbishop Marcinkus, was killed in jail by someone who allegedly laced his coffee with cyanide. Whoops a daisy," Lana said.

"The scenario was most intriguing. Banco Ambrosiano, Italy's largest private bank crashed in 1982. The Vatican was a 1.5% shareholder in Banco Ambrosinano. Archbishop Marcinkus was the head of the Vatican Bank (The Instituto Per Le Opere Di Religione—founded about 100 years ago for 'works of religion and Christian piety'). Marcinkus and Calvi were intertwined with one another. It happened that Banco Ambrosiano controlled a maze of 'offshore operations.' Marcinkus gave Calvi 'comfort letters' as backup for (security) for £800 million in loans made by Banco Ambrosiano to offshore companies. The 'comfort letters' appeared as though they took responsibility for the propriety of the loans by the Vatican. At the same time Marcinkus made Calvi give Marcinkus written promises that the Vatican would not have to repay any losses should losses occur. The £800 million disappeared. Now, those offshore companies, were they ghost companies of the Vatican? Was the Vatican involved in the £800 million fraud? Did the £800 million find its way back to the Vatican? A good question. If so, how was it accounted for in the books and records of the Vatican? Too, is it true the Vatican bank was used by well connected clients to escape income taxes by sending millions of unchecked funds to the bank—a-la the Cayman Islands? And why in 1984 did the Holy See pay nearly £164 million to unsecured creditors of the failed Ambrosiano Bank. The

Vatican claims the £164 million was not to be construed as an admission of guilt, rather, it was simply a good-will gesture.

"Would Jesus be proud of his pious representatives for the past 40 grandfathers?" Lana continued, "Would he say, 'blessed are my followers for their bloody religious wars; their burning of people at the stake; their persecutions; their racism; their torture of people; their fraudulent practices; their taking of tithes from the poor; their amassing of riches; their splendid robes; their priceless art treasures; their inexcusable cover-ups of child fornication and child abuse by their holy employees; His Holiness Pope John Paul II unswerving support of Archbiship Marcinkus? You name the evil and immoral acts against people over the centuries and you will find the religious front and center leading the pack.

"Churches of all denominations and faiths, and in particular the mighty Catholic and Muslim domains, have done little except pay lip service to world wide decency." Lana exhorted. "These two faiths have over two billion followers. Their influence over the abolishment of wars, deprivation,bloodshed and hunger could be so very positive if the hierarchy of these two faiths had the will and guts to demand peace, harmony and equity among all humans. They never have made a booming, demanding stance on world equity as did Jesus. Whilst Jesus was a peaceful man, he was not one to defraud. Can you imagine friends, if two billion religious demanded equity in one massive voice how the world would take notice. And what if the two billion Catholics and Muslims were joined by the remaining religious of two billion six hundred and fifty million people? What a voice would be heard. The majority of child abusers, murderers, rapists, war mongers, greed mongers, racists, bigots et al would cease their iniquitous behavior if the religious were serious about human equity. Wouldn't Jesus smile and bless them if the churches demanded equity? And folks, why must so many of the religious be so deceptive, so two-faced? Many attend their churches professing purity then throw every ounce of their purity to the wind the very next day, thence to absolution, thence to church, thence to…and over and over again. We people at this convention center must send a forceful message to all religious leaders…White Anglo Saxon Protestants, Muslims, Catholics, Buddhists, Ethnic religionists, Hindus, Jews, Sikhs, every last religion…demanding politicians to ensure world wide equity eliminating therefore poverty. Universal equity among several billion people may seem farfetched, ladies and gentlemen, but the alternative, the demolition of we humans by the Twelve Controllers if we do not enshrine humanitarianism, is so final, and I might add without the right of appeal.

"What thinkist thou, my fellow humans, to my recommendation? Do you think four billion people could get the attention of the world's political leaders if they, the four billion, demanded equity 'or else?' Or else to mean ignore our demands politicians lest we rise up in fury and squash you like bugs.

"Now business tycoons, wealthy professionals, et al do not despair. As I see it, there must be exciting challenges available at all times for those people who have entrepreneurial skills and ambitions. No communism. No bloody communism. No fucking communism. The rich and super wealthy should not be constrained. Excessive riches must be available to everyone. The only change from today's economic society would be that no one in the scenario I perceive would be living in poverty.

I do hope it isn't the case where the rich can feel rich only if there is poverty, slums, ghettos and so on. My oh my, what if the rich only feel rich if they are able to look down on the lowly masses? Essentially, a class distinction measured by wealth. Would the rich feel cheated if poverty was eliminated? I hope not. But in my view today's wealthy need the suck up middle class and the poverty stricken for comparison purposes. So the rich need the poor psychologically. And I dare say, the middle class and the poor need the rich to look up to, worship and adore. What the hell would the world be like if everyone was equal? It would be a big fucking bore. So in my view there must be a class distinction measured by wealth. But not so shockingly bizarre as it is now. The rich and the super rich don't need changing, the change must come for the poor. The earth can sustain comfortably up to 8 billion people. My goal in life is to push for a decent living standard for all 8 billion. Hell, the super rich can become super super rich as long as everyone else lives comfortably. I just hope the rich would accept the elimination of poverty.

"Pope John Paul II chairs a position of enormous influence. His subjects outnumber the total population of the USA by 720 million people. Interesting 'what.' But his blessings to the multitudes are meaningless in the scheme of things. Blessings do not fill empty bellies. Blessings do not provide proper shelters, education, hospitals, health care facilities and playgrounds. His Holiness' undertaking is to carry on the work of Christ. His pilgrimage should be devoted to the elimination of privation among people. So why is it that so many millions of his followers live in poverty? Millions upon millions in Africa and Latin America have nothing. Over 500 million Catholics live in these two countries alone. While millions live in poverty adults are still encouraged to breed more little Catholics to be raised in unspeakable conditions. But what about his Holiness' housing, the Vatican, and places of worship, the fine richly appointed decadent churches. What horrible discrepancies twixt the splendors of the Vatican and many of the Catholic churches compared to the slop so many millions of the Catholic faithful must live in. Does the Vatican not recognize these unholy discrepancies? If it doesn't, the Vatican must be terribly blind. If it does, it should be ashamed of its pathetic attempts, if indeed it ever has attempted, to rid the world of inequities. What would Jesus think of all this? Would he falsify himself by enjoying the glitter and comfort of the Catholic riches while so many of his worshipers wallow in the stench of poverty? No, not he, the greatest of all earthlings ever. Jesus would not permit inequities. He would stand tall, ferocious alongside the needy. His voice would rumble throughout the world demanding equity, dignity, along with physical and mental comfort for all the earth's people."

Dr. Masters went on with her discussions of religion, but now she heralded the splendid efforts and heroics of so many of the world's clergy, priests, reverends, and nuns. She marveled at the unselfishness of these people. How they devoted themselves in comforting those who needed love and attention. How they took up altruistically their assignments in every corner of the globe. How they have accepted the most brutal of living conditions in stagnant, merciless hell-holes. How they cleansed so many hell-holes with physical and mental labor under hostile conditions. Only a minute number of these devoted people have strayed off the path of humanitarianism. Unfortunately their leaders often have used them as pawns. Their leaders have let them and billions of their worshipers down. The global reverends who have devoted their lives to decency and their legions of followers by and large are free of the Controllers' criticisms. The wretched must be brought to a state of dignity and well being. They must become world participants in global enjoyment by sharing in productivity, through efficacy, inventiveness and work ethics. They must be brought to a state of mutual trust and camaraderie. No charity, no, no charity, instead of charity, have fulfilling rewards for productivity.

"Just one more thing on the subject of religion," Lana stated. "World population. But how does world population fit into the subject of religion? Is it not a subject for science? No friends, it is a problem all of us must face. I spoke earlier this week about science being given full rein on the enhancement of global fecundity. I stand by that. What a boon it would be to see infertile lands brought into fertility and despoiled waters brought back to prolific life-giving sources of food and other resources. I'm sure scientists, given time and adequate resources, can make the globe more fertile. But unfortunately as resources are consumed…and even if the resources can be fully reclaimed…the distasteful problem of waste and refuse continues to rear its ugly head.

Again science must be given full rein on the effective resolve of this dilemma.

"As populations grow, so do the problems of the scarcity of food, shelter, health, education and the like grow. The problem is not one of the diddling arguments between pro-abortionist and anti-abortionists," Lana went on, "but of sensible population control. Worldwide population must not exceed eight billion people. No doubt the age curve could become skewed as a result of population control. This would cause the unproductive elderly to be at the heavy end of the age curve with fewer and fewer younger people supporting the oldsters. What a conundrum. One answer to the problem of age disparity would be to have oldsters continue to work in some productive capacity for part of the year after they reach the age of 65. Another answer to the problem is for federal and state (or provincial) governments to give greater incentive for people to reduce their income taxes through tax deferral savings plans to enable people to build extra funds for retirement purposes. In this whole scenerio it is mandatory to have a minimum base income for all working people well above poverty thresholds with stipulated portions of their incomes to be set aside in properly funded pension plans. Dr Masters found herself moving away from the subject of world population and religion. So she did her usual thing. She paced up and down the stage before she hypothesized that religious leaders would have a more positive effect on the subject of birth control than would governments. Even if governments suggested smaller family sizes, its citizenry would construe such a suggestion to be just another government entry into their private lives. If the request was by way of government edicts, then of course, anyone acting outside the edict would be breaking the law. In any event, Dr. Masters challenged religious leaders to introduce and command their subjects to abide by maximum family sizes. Scientists should complement the religious' request by explaining how the earth's resources can support only seven to eight billion people at any given time. Science would postulate that populations in excess of eight billion people could cause a precarious strain on food supplies and other resources needed to provide the world's citizenry with adequate living standards. Thus, Lana emphasized, "Common sense must prevail as it pertains to global population."

Enough on religion for now friends," Lana said. "As much as I would like to go on and on my thoughts thereon, time does not permit. I am convinced however that the religious are in a position to make things right for humans. They, the religious, have more influence on world opinion than any other global entity including big governments. Hitler for goodness sake, one little unknown rat went from his beer hall Putsch to the Führer of Germany in just over one decade. One mustachioed little loud mouth prick convinced millions of people they were a superior race; that his Third Reich would reign for 1,000 years, and he damned near pulled it off. Millions upon millions of people died as a result of Hitler's influence. And we sanctimonious sacrosancts don't even try to push the power packed religions into forcing equity for our world's people nor do we demand our religious to lend their formidable weight to population control. What a bunch of cowardly, uncaring milktoasts we are. What about the religious themselves, are they cowards too? Are they satisfied with the status quo pertaining to human inequities and the helter-skelter population growth?"

CHAPTER 84

ISTANBUL, LANA DISCUSSES POLITICS

"Politics. My what varied forms politics come in. Democracies, fascism, communism, sovereignties, nazism, aristocracies, dictatorships, socialistic, social classes and so on. Democracies are the fairest form of government conceived to date. Whilst we are all aware of the fact that democracies are anything but perfect, they are the world's most tolerant and most representative of their citizens wishes.

The day to day business of most governments is run by it's bureaucrats. Elected officials are transients. Some linger in office longer than others. Lana explained it was pointless for her to discuss the intricacies of government entities and their duties, because all her attendees were well versed on these matters. But as to the transient aspect of elected officials, their flitting in and out of office gives them little time to attend to important global matters. Most of their time is spent on debating and enacting legislation. Proposed legislation which comes from self-interest lobbyists, bureaucrats, public opinion if strong enough and on rare occasions from private member's bills. The elected persons have to devote ample time to their home constituents, make public appearances, travel to and from their homes and legislatures, attend social gatherings and keep up their good will for future elections.

In a democracy does the average citizen feel the effects of federal legislation whether a left wing, center or right wing party is in power? Personal income taxes generally rise no matter what party forms the government. Whilst conservatives claim to be more responsible on fiscal matters compared to their opposition parties, their record over the years has proven otherwise. In general they have more financial scandals than other parties. And they boast more about their religious righteousness than others do. Certainly the religious right kiss conservative butts more often than they do the other parties. Liberals like to profess everything under the sun while the left likes to profess honesty and integrity. Liberals and conservatives favor big business while left-wingers favor big labor. But at the end of the day average citizens go about their business no matter which party is in power feeling therefore little or no change in their lifestyles.

It may be a pity that senior bureaucrats run the government's day-to-day business without daily consultation or reference to their elected politicals. However, if bureaucrats were required to report daily to their elected bosses peoples in most countries would still be riding horseback. Red tape does not come about purely as a result of government forms, legal interpretations, fitting within government acts and regulations, falling through unintended cracks and the like. No, red tape can come from attitudes of those civil servants who take pleasure in stalling citizens, businesses and others thereby showing their power.

Still bureaucracies are vital entities for any form of government. It's the bureaucracy's size and at times the attitudes of the bureaucrats which causes concern for the electorate. In a democracy the civil service is charged with the responsibility of carrying out the dictates of its elected officials. Some of the civil servants have enormous powers while in the employ of their elected officials. In the United States these positions of power include the president's respective secretaries, the governor of the federal reserve banks, the heads of the FBI and the CIA, the heads of the military, the Pentagon and so on. Government (the public sector) activities account for 30 to 60 percent of the various industrialized countries' economies. That's big government. How can a few transient politicians control the activities of tens of thousands of civil servants who by and large operate a country's business on a tenure basis?

Lana made reference to the great United States of America as to its politicians' attention span over its massive bureaucracy. She noted that elected representatives federally amount to a mere 537 people, the president and vice-president, 100 senators and 435 congressmen. The task of controlling the civil service through political representatives, truly, is a vast impossibility.

Despite the fact the civil service of most democracies run the big government ship, the elected politicians ultimately have the hammer. Without question, the president of the United States of America is the most influential political person in the world. He represents the world's mightiest nation, a nation of some 270 million people, yet a mere 4.6% of the world's total population. But the US is such a powerful entity, not only by way of its armed forces, but by way of its self-sufficiency, its financial dominance, its productivity dominance, its monetary unit dominance, its freedoms, its respect for human freedom, its exciting psyche, its world leadership and its domestic wealth. It is the United States firm belief in democracy that makes it the political leader of the globe. Again, whilst the civil service of the USA is powerful, the politicians are mightier. United States' show of power can be evinced through its president, its congress and its senate. Just the way it should be.

But now this mighty nation must power its way through the unjust way it appears to condone its own human inequities. Lana pointed out some glaring examples to her attendees. There are four to five million homeless Americans, 38 million below the poverty threshold, while the country boasts of numerous billionaires. For instance, Disney's chief executive in the latter part of 1997 enjoyed an estimated profit of $500 million on the sale of stock options granted him in 1989, whereas Disney's earnings in 1995 were only $24.6 million. Occidental Petroleum's CEO was paid a cash remuneration of $95 million in the latter part of 1997 while it agreed to pay a measly $375,000 for damage to birds and fish after dumping toxic waste in Love Canal. Further, in the year 1996, the average pay increase for US workers was 3% whilst 54% pay increases were granted the average US top executive. The source of this information, Lana explained, was the Canadian edition of Time dated December 15, 1997. Lana reiterated the fact that it takes a retail clerk 16 months of labor to earn what Gap's CEO earns in one hour. As Lana had evoked earlier in her discussions with the attendees, her argument had not so much to do with the wages paid top executives, it had to do instead with the skin flint wages paid to minimum-wage earners. She pointed out wage disparities are a worldwide problem and not unique to the United States. Sure the highly paid person does not eat an appreciable amount more than does his or her forlorn brother or sister, better quality and more exotic yes, but quantity, comme ci, comme ça. The rich will buy at the best of outlets while the poor shop around at thrift stores and while scummers most often dine on garbage. So, a rich individual may pay 25 or 30 thousand dollars every year on staples while a poor individual can afford no more than 4 or 5 thousand dollars. The rich, other than for housing, furnishings, clothing, autos, insurance, travel and entertainment do not consume a great deal more for groceries that do the poor. So the rich do not make an economic impact on the purchases of foodstuffs. This, of course, allows the rich to argue they are not responsible for any over consumption nor the cause of any shortage of any particular food product. Thus the rich have little or no effect on inflation. It's those nasty plebes out there who create food shortages. But the rich by and large own the production and distribution facilities for foodstuffs. So they can't be too nasty with the plebes...they don't want to alienate their products with the gluttonous plebes...no...they want to sell, sell, sell for more and more profit.

The rich do contribute to society in other ways. They invest some of their massive fortunes in debt and equity instruments. Investing in debt instruments of course provides additional credit sources for lenders to lend and thus for borrowers to borrow. The rich as well are players in the stock market. Their investments in stocks provide important long-term sources of funds for corporations.

But in no way are the mega rich the foundation of society. It's the middle and the low-class society members that make up foundation of all business activities worldwide. Without their productivity and consumption there would be no rich. Assume that a few billion of the world's masses said, 'Fuck it, we aren't going to spend one red cent on anything for a couple of months. We'll simply beg, borrow or steal for food. We won't pay our rent, our mortgages. We won't work, we won't run our cars, we won't buy clothes, pharmaceutical products, sweet fuck all—so stick that in your pipe and smoke it.' "The world's economies would shudder and collapse under the weight of such a calamity. The rich would be the only buyers of goods and services. Just think of the huge shopping malls, no clerks, no janitors, no security personnel, no buyers. Maybe one rich dude or gal in every tenth mall searching for goods and services but,alas, without success. It's enough to make one cry. No airplanes, taxis, ships, subways, buses moving. Nothing. Just because those thankless peonic pricks out there have said, 'Fuck it. Ungrateful pricks all of them,' our sad-faced scrouges would lament. Now money is not circulating, mines, farms, orchards, dairies, factories, warehouses, banks, brokerage businesses, construction, wholesale and retail businesses are all at a standstill. Pricks."

Dr. Masters carried on this plane by insisting that if reasonable equities were granted to all people of the world by government, business, labor and the religious great benefits would inure. Crime would drop dramatically; health and education standards would rise; government size could be reduced; individual freedoms would be enhanced; individual injustices would be reduced; racism could become a thing of the past; taxes would be reduced. These rewards would be most bountiful. Those members of society who wish to strive for great riches would not be hindered in any way. People's aspirations, drive and competitive spirits would not in any way be jeopardized. Businesses would flourish because people would have more disposable income to spend on goods and services. "Such a boon," Dr. Lana Masters asserted, "would cleanse the world of most of its corruption and decay. Good citizenship would flourish among the globes populace if inequities were expunged. My," Lana said, with a feigned look of surprise on her face. "Respect, love, trust, and kinship could be spawned throughout the world. An Utopian world. A return to family values, families where children are exposed only to love and respect. Where children grow and mature with their lives full of excitement, fun and happiness. Where children are burdened with nothing more than growing up, becoming educated, and preparing themselves for their future.

"The religious and the politicals must lead the way in the fight against inequities," Lana asserted.

"You know, ladies and gentlemen, we humans are a strange lot. We laugh and make light of politician's promises. Promises after promises. We should take their promises seriously. We shouldn't let them sidewind. Sidewinding is a snake's lot. When political wizardry through Churchillian oratory sounds good (not necessarily believable, but convincing) and keeps the party faithful, we the faithful not believing our politicals are as guilty as he or she who lets the bull shit fly. Promises, promises. We laugh and make light of our general feelings toward politicians that they can't be trusted. Isn't that dreadful? However I believe most politicals in a democracy are hard working dedicated men and women. But they get mired in the party line, and when the party line strays into tempting territories that are muddied, the good men and women become muddied as well, unless of course, they divorce themselves from the party and become independents. By becoming independents they may lose some of their constituent power. Their brief encounter with fame may vanish. Mayhap their pensions become smaller. By and large they become unwanted fungi wallowing in a sea of politics. Most politicals don't want to jump party lines nor do they wish to abandon their party by becoming independents. They are serious in their belief in their party's propriety. They are serious in their belief their party is the best for the common good. The United States democratic formation permits bipartisanship. In general this permits the scrupulous political to step outside the party line without the necessity of resignation or opting to becoming an independent. Other democracies become quasi dictatorships from the time the elected party takes office until the next election four or five years later. There is no one to stand in the way of this democratic dictatorship because unlike the United States there are no 'built in' checks or balances available to disencumber the elected majority. We the public allow this dictatorship to govern. And what about those gallant politicals who jump from party to party and back again as they guess which party will form the next government. Like rats abandoning ship. Dreadful. No political loyalty for their own feelings let alone their parties.

"Just a few more thoughts pertaining to politics," Lana said. "Politicians are the neon signs of governments. They flash. The electrical currents running back and forth along high power lines are the entrenched bureaucrats, unnoticeable, yet surging and pulsating. The media often is blasé about these electrical currents. It wants the neon signs, the stars, the performers. Ergo, that's what the public gets, a spectacular view of the transients. Damn it all, it is up to the transients to use the media to their advantage for good, and, like superman, fight evil. Lead the way to equity for the world's forgotten.

"Pay politicians properly. Their incomes are far too low. There aren't that many of them to cause a noticeable nick in the revenue and expenditure statements of a nation such as the USA or Canada. Triple or quadruple their salaries, provide for substantial pensions. The transients must be of various backgrounds, not just lawyers. Lawyers are professional at drafting bills and legislation, but as businessmen often they are inadequate. The transients must be capable people. They must realize the Controllers of the universe are close to pulling the 'plug' on humans. Politicals, together with the religious, can effect a world of justice and freedom.

"Make politicians more accountable for their actions, but for goodness sake pay them decent stipends for their responsibilities. Otherwise payola will settle in the minds of some politicals and their first responsibility will be for their own monetary aggrandizement. Political patronage must be eliminated. No political jobs should be created artificially for political hacks. Government jobs should arise only out of necessity and should be filled by the most qualified people. And it must be clear that civil servants, while on the job, must attend to that job. They must refrain from influence peddling.

"Political parties must not be self-interest groups. They must be representative of everyone.

"In the US and Canada, the senior governments permit monetary policy to be under the jurisdiction of their central banks while the politicians maintain jurisdiction over fiscal policy. There must be more interplay between the two. Central banks must be more aligned with fiscal activities of politicians so as to correlate spendings activities made from the public treasury, matching therefore—as close as possible—current costs with current revenues. While inflation control is necessary it cannot be the abject paranoia as displayed by central bank governors. Unemployment must be given a higher priority on central bank's agendas which in fact is one of its mandated powers. Politicians must be ready to take action if they see their central banks are focusing in on inflation and price control at the expense of other sound economic factors such as unemployment.

Lana voiced her displeasure with individual politicians' obvious self-interest in being re-elected. Throughout their elected tenure their minds appear to be focused on the next election. During the first half of their tenure, they are as busy as little mice covering up and excusing themselves for not fulfilling the bulk of their pre-election promises.

Then by the third quarter of their tenure they begin to trumpet the wonderful things they intend to do for the masses and the unwashed when next elected. More promises. Perhaps even lies. God forbid.

"Politicals, get some corporeality, some sensitivity, some emotion, tenderness, kindness. You along with the religious can make this beautiful world of ours a garden for everyone. Doubtless you will refer to the lazys and hangers-on as being unchangeable. Perhaps so. But for the sake of humanity do the noble thing, bring in a propitious equity base for all the world's citizenry."

CHAPTER 85

ISTANBUL, LANA SUMMARIZES HER FIVE DAYS OF LECTURES

"Dr. Carruthers, I see I have gone past our morning coffee break, our luncheon, and now I see it is three o'clock in the afternoon. My, how time flies." Turning to her attendees, she apologized to them for her intemperate gluttony of their time. She smiled an enchanting, bewitching smile at her audience. Most were captivated. Most stood cheering and applauding her. Others sat, their eyes flaming with hatred, ready to tear her and her plea for worldwide equity and her religious blasphemy into shreds.

"Dr. Carruthers," Lana whispered, "I have a brief summary of my week's talk. It will take a matter of 30 or 40 minutes. I should like to leave it in your hands when you wish me to give this summary."

"Thank you, my dear Dr. Masters. I shall confer with our audience."

"Ladies and gentlemen," Dr. Carruthers called out to the assembly, "please be seated." The applause still thundered through the assembly hall. "Please my friends, be seated," Dr. Carruthers begged. Lana walked out from behind her lectern, lifted her arms above her shoulders, then slowly brought them down. This move indicated that she wished the attendees to be seated. It worked. They did.

"Dr. Masters has just informed me that she needs but 30 to 40 more minutes of your time to sum up her week's dialog with you. I suggest we take a 20-minute break for coffee and be back in our seats at 3:20. What say you?"

The attendees approved. In 20 minutes all were seated once again. Lana was back at her lectern. Damn, her 'enemies' thought, she is so 'right' looking. She dazzles, she sparkles, she makes 'you' feel alive. She's so intelligent. God, if we could get her on our side, we could control the world. None of this equity bull shit. We could keep the status quo, even widen the gap between the genteel and the dogs. How the hell can we lure her to our side? A big good-looking, bright stud perhaps.

"Ladies and gentlemen I have made a list of items that have been said about me in the various media. By a succinct comment or answer to each of these items, I believe I will have then summarized my five-day dialog with you. I will recite the item to you first, then I shall comment thereon. So friends, voila.

—"One. Is this Masters woman just a boor who swears ?

—"I don't believe I am a boor, but I do know that I'm a cusser!

—"Two. Is this Masters woman a communist?

—"No, no bloody way!

—"Three. Is this Masters woman a nut?

—"I have an IQ of 205, so there's a good chance I am. But, I feel anything but a 'nut'. I want people to live happy and fulfilling lives on a garden-like planet. No, I am not a nut!

—"Four. Is this Masters woman just an unparalleled beauty who earned her reputation by being unparalleled between the sheets?

—"Yes and no! I am a beauty and I fuck for pleasure, not for favors!

—"Five. Did this Masters woman get to her elite position by being a slick, compelling actor?

—"Partly. I like to 'speechify good.' I like to be emphatic, lovable, shocking, play act and to be 'incorrigibly' truthful!

—"Six. Is this Masters woman an atheist or just someone who claims to know the origin of the universe through a word or a thought not yet discovered nor defined in any global language?

"I am an atheist only as to the bible's rendition of God and Genesis. I know the origin of the universe. I know the universe is the Twelve

Controllers. I know the universe is encircled by a super force, a nonchalant, frightening 'nothing.' I know the Controllers continue to expand themselves out into the vast 360-degree abyss of nothing. In the event the Controllers collapse, the universe will shrink back to nothing. The Controllers are not divine; they are real. They are indestructible." At that moment a celestial hush fell over the attendees. Lana, her lectern, the head table, all vanished as Eve and her eleven Controllers appeared in their place. The beauty of this mystique was breathtaking. The scene was calm. A fragrance never before breathed in by earthlings filled the air. Gently the Twelve Controllers took the hands of everyone in the assembly. At that very moment every child, woman and man on earth felt one of their hands clasped in an unimaginable comfort. Tender, warm, humble. A message of love and peace traveled through their bodies into their souls. A message understood by everyone, a message so profound, so warm and affectionate, it needed no interpretation.

Lana, her lectern and the head table returned as eleven of the Controllers faded away. Eve One remained. She spoke, "Jesus was real. Judicious equity for all my people on earth is mandatory before the year 2250. Lana Masters speaks the truth. If human inequities are not expunged by the year 2250, all of you shall be displaced by another form of life. I have given you 8,327,000 years to reach your present degree of maturity and intelligence. But you have been a bitter disappointment to me. From the time I gave you life those 8,327,000 years ago, I have permitted you to evolve without my interference. I have no intention of intervening in your future actions. You must do what you must do. Survive equitably or disappear." Eve One vanished.

The attendees were spent. Lana gave them time to revive from their paradoxical bliss. They looked at the hand that moments ago gave them complete fulfillment.

"Perhaps," Lana said, "the answer to this question has been done to your satisfaction?"

The assemblage was quiet. Tears moistened most eyes throughout the world. No act of God...earthquake, tsunami, hurricane...nothing could have had the impact on humans as did the brief presence of the Controllers. Eve One's awesome ubiquitousness was exhilarating. No words in earth's language yet have been formulated to describe the omnipresence of Eve One and her Controllers. As Eve One had said, "I have no intention of intervening in your future actions." In just 10 minutes after Eve One's departure, the globe's inhabitants returned to their pre-controller's visitation. No, Eve One would not intervene.

'Damn,' Lana thought. 'What dumb fuckers we earthlings are.'

"Lana" Adam Three said, "what a girl you are. Your language, my, my."

"Sorry Adam Three," Lana whispered. Adam Three laughed.

—"Seven. Is this Masters woman just a kind soul who is blessed with the brain of a productive genius, but whose brain is garbled leaving her a misguided misfit?

"I leave that for you to judge my friends." Most of the two thousand and ninety nine attendees rose and called out, "Dr. Masters, you are a saint." Their applause was thunderous.

—"Eight. Isn't her hope for kindliness among all the earth's populace just wishful Utopian thinking?

"I hope not. What is wrong with such a goal to strive for?" Again most attendees rose to their feet and applauded.

—"Nine. How dare this Dr. Masters attack today's religions?

"I believe I have covered this with you today. I do not attack the various religions' parishioners, although religious terrorists, religious people who make a mockery of righteousness I deplore. I am astonished at the religious for their lack of guts to fight for the improvished, and, at their hypocritical love of Jesus. I implore the religious to use their immense power and influence to demand equity for all humans and to still population growth.

—"Ten. Dr. Masters, you are ripe for a religious terrorist's bullet.

—"Yes. One just missed me earlier this week, remember. The thought doesn't frighten me. Jesus, Joan of Arc, Luis Riel all were 'taken out' by terrorists. Their memory lives on," Lana said smiling.

"Dr. Masters, you are blasphemous...linking your Godless self with Jesus," one 'injured soul' called out from the audience.

Most of the audience rebelled against the 'injured soul' shouting, "Sit down...quiet." The 'injured soul' sat. Lana carried on.

"-Eleven. Dr. Masters, how dare you attack big business?

"I do not attack big business unequivocally. One of my thrusts pertaining to big business is that big business is not some mystic ontology. Big businesses are nothing but entities related through letters patent or the like. They come to life only when people put them into motion. The corporation itself doesn't dump waste into the world's soil, air and waters, its people do. Corporations don't convince youngsters to smoke cigarettes, its people do. Corporations don't lie about their products, it is its people who do. Corporations don't allow for poor working conditions, cheap labor, belt tightening for the sake of profits, its people do. Corporate entities are artificial beings created by law. They are creations that can mobilize vast sums of money from the public's investments in both debt and equity. These funds are put into productive use through investments in labor, buildings, factories, and equipment. But ladies and gentlemen the corporation doesn't gather in these funds then expend them, its people do. Corporate entities are wonderful creations by and large. They provide economies with vehicles wherein massive amounts of money can be pooled by thousands of investors which in turn allows corporations to invest in capital assets of immense magnitude, something that otherwise would be prohibitive for individuals. But it's the people within the corporation's confines who invest the funds of the corporation. Productivity, research, the whole gamut of an economy's activities are done by people. The world would not have all the amenities it now enjoys without big business. The person who sired corporations in the first instance was a brilliant one. But damn it all, people in big business worship their corporations as if the corporations were divinities."

"-Twelve. Dr. Masters how can you be so naive as to think global problems...people...territorial disputes...religion...human respect... dignity...politics...economics...the wealthy and the poor...etc., can be overcome through simplistic solutions?...good gracious Dr. Masters get real."

"I suspect, friends, the answer to that question is rather simplistic. As Eve One said a few minutes ago...'you must do what you must do. Survive equitably or disappear.' I am not about to summarize the information I have dispensed to you over the past few days. All things contained in this twelfth question are surmountable if the people of the world have the will to overcome them. One hundred trillion dollars seems to be an interminable objective. Think ladies and gentlemen, just 30 or 40 years ago it was thought that an Irish Sweepstakes win of $100,000 would keep the winner in the lap of luxury for a lifetime. Now $100,000 wouldn't last a person three years. Millionaires were scarce at that time. Executive salaries of $100,000 annually were unheard of. Now billionaires world wide are not a scarcity. Sales of many giant corporations top 100 billion dollars with ease. Some government budgets now top one trillion dollars. Many bank's assets will reach the trillion dollar mark in the next few years. Some peoples net worths will reach 100 billion dollars soon. So a 100 trillion dollar spectacle is just around the corner. Less than one grandfather away.

"Yes, my friends, the world can become Utopia. Thrills and excitement can be enhanced. New discoveries, space travel, regenerating our mighty globe, fulfilling leisure time, computer challenges, reclaiming waste land for productivity. A myriad of exciting challenges face us.

—"Thirteen. Dr. Masters, you are an angel. You may be God's daughter just as Jesus was his son."

"No, I am not an angel nor a daughter of God. I am however, a disciple of Jesus. I believe only in the Twelve Controllers as being supreme.

"Ladies and gentlemen, that concludes my address to you. I must say we have had an exciting five days together. My closing statement is a simple one, academic you might say. I bring it to you with every ounce of my personage. I chill thinking of the sordid debasements we earthlings have perpetrated throughout our history. Think on the scribes recounting through the bible of God, the merciful one, and his family Adam and Eve. Do you remember that the merciful one's grandson Cain slew his other grandson Abel? So God's family, if one believes in the bible, was not only the first family on mother earth, but also it was the first family that suffered murder and abuse. Was God's family dysfunctional? Cain slew his brother Abel because Cain's grandfather, God, liked Abel's offerings better that he did Cain's. My intent is not to be derisive as it pertains to God and his family. No, my intent is to drive home in everyones mind that the family is and always will be pre-eminent over all other global matters. No other entity of any kind can compare to a family's pre-eminence. No sin is as evil as family abuse. The inimitable family unit and its values are without equal.

* * *

Lana moved to the center of the stage. She threw everyone a kiss. Her eyes were radiant. They charmed her attendees. She called out in her most alluring way, a way which was her's alone, deep and throaty, "I love all of you. I am so appreciative of you attendance to my words and for your patience with me for these last few days. I am grateful to all of you for attending each of my sessions. You are wonderful, for which I thank you with my heart and soul. Adieu until this evening." Lana bowed.

Dr. Carruthers closed the five-day assemblage first by thanking Dr. Masters for her emphatic, remarkable parlance, the attendees for their attentiveness, the host city for its graciousness, generosity, hospitality and its friendliness. He thanked the personnel of the grand convention center for their courtesies, thoughtfulness and heed. A thunderous applause occurred as Lana bowed showing her gratitude to the City of Istanbul and the convention center's personnel. As she stood at center stage bowing and throwing kisses, balloons covered in hearts began to fall from the ceiling. Now the entry doors to the assembly hall began to roll quietly into their secret hiding place. An eight-piece Turkish band appeared and began to play delightful Turkish melodies. Glistening streamers fell among the balloons from the ceiling as beautiful strobe lights intermingled their graceful rays through the falling streamers. The Turkish band struck up some rhythmic melody that soon had everyone in the hall clapping to the music. A lovely Turkish lady made her way to the front of the musicians and taking a microphone in hand began to sing, just like Barbra, "Happy days are here again." All applause stopped. The massive hall was silent. The songstress captured everyone's heart with her charming, cheerful rendition of the song. Now waiters and waitresses made their way to the convention center's huge public area carrying food, and all manner of beverages. The strobe lights ceased as a distinguished looking gentleman made his way up the stairs to the stage and to the lectern. He motioned for Lana to join him. Lana did. He put his arm around her and kissed her cheek. He spoke with a very broad but pleasant accent. He thanked everyone for selecting and honoring Istanbul with their presence. "Please take a little of your time to visit our lovely city. I am sure you will find it interesting, educational, mysterious, beautiful and historic. I am Istanbul's mayor; I am its chief supporter. I love Istanbul. It is a vibrant, exciting, charming and friendly city. Its past is unique, today it is spellbinding and its future is destined to be as you say in American, awesome. My name is Jon Tramir Ammand. Dr. Lana Masters, while I have a few differences of opinion with you, I find you to be the most straightforward person I have ever met. I am amazed at your brilliance and verve, your untarnished ethics, your care for the other half of the world's people and, of course, your allure. My sincerest good wishes to you. As one small person in your immense planetary stratagem, without equivocation I join you in your quest for global equity." With that, the mayor of Istanbul clasped Lana's hand in a firm handshake. The audience roared its approval as the band struck up the corny, overused, For He's A Jolly Good Fellow.

The band played on with music from the world over.

The attendees left their seats and began to intermingle in the grand spacious open hallway. They were served beverages by uniformed waiters and waitresses. Long tables of food were decorated exquisitely with large bouquets of stunning flowers and greens, everything about the show being put on by the city of Istanbul was done with taste.

As Lana made her way among the attendees she was met with cheers of approval. Everyone wanted to be near her. Media types forgot about the most basic of etiquette as they shouldered their way to Lana. Francois, as ever, was at her side. Lana found time for everyone. In fun she mocked the untamed, impolite, disheveled, super-gossips, the paparazzi for their abrasive behavior. She answered all the questions they threw at her save for the question of one unsavory prick who for five days now had asked Lana how big her tits were. Shit, she thought. "Hey asshole," she called out to the unsavory one, "I've changed my mind. I'll answer your question. My tits measure the same as your IQ…38."

Cameras popped, TVs zoomed in, microphones were shoved all around Lana, people laughed…"38," the unsavory one yelled back, "Would I like to play 'come in Tokyo' with your 'ten fours' Lana…whoooeee!" Francois lunged for the prick. Lana held him back. "Down boy," the prick hollered, "roll over, play dead you big fucking mastiff!" That did it. Francois steam-rolled over the hapless paparazzi. He grabbed the unsavory prick by his shirt collar and with one hand lifted the slime-ball above his head just as Lana got to his side. "No

Francois, put the man down." Lucky for the man, Lana had just saved his face from being pancaked by Francois' huge right fist.

Lana and Francois made their way to many groups who were beckoning her following the paparazzi incident. Except for a few of the religious and some politicians, everyone in the convention center cherished, admired, and agreed with Lana and her oral treatise.

The cocktail hour ended at 6:15 in the evening.

By 9:30 that night the social was in full swing. Everyone was happy and enjoying themselves. As usual Lana was the center of attention.

Lana found she could not take her eyes off the priest, the one who had tried to assassinate her this past Monday. Something was so familiar about him. She was certain she knew him from somewhere. He was quite tall, probably six-feet-two-inches. He looked very athletic. He was quite handsome, yes, even attractive. His eyes…yes, his eyes…they were not familiar in any way. They were dark and foreboding. Perhaps even evil looking. He was young…probably in his late 30's. His pate was shaved bald. He had a ragged scar on his forehead…damn, she thought, that scar should tell me if I had met him sometime in the past. She thought about all the men she knew and had met in the past. None came to mind re the priest. Lana danced with each of the Adams'. Adam Five teased her. "No," he said, "I will not give you even the minutest clue or hint about 'the priest' my gorgeous sweetheart. You are on your own on this one."

Lana pinched his butt. "My, what have I done Adam Five? I have pinched you, the universe."

"That you have child," came a voice from the cavernous depths of the twelfth dimension, some hundred trillion, trillion, trillion light years away. "Behold, the universes' end and the beginning of nothing," he thundered.

Lana gasped. She reached out into nothing. Her hand and that part of her arm that ventured into nothing disappeared. She pulled her arm back. It was fully in tact.

"Adam Five, what?"

"Just having sport with you for pinching me," his voice rumbled.

"Are you going to take me back to earth?"

"Of course I am, see!"

She pinched him again as he swirled her around the dance floor. He laughed.

Adam Five returned her to her table where Dr. Carruthers was seated. She sat. She thought about the wonderful Controllers. She thanked them. She told them of her undying love for them. She cried. Dr. Carruthers understood. He too was deep in thought about the Controllers. Eve One responded. She told Dr. Carruthers they would not visit him again whilst he was an inhabitant of their planet earth. Tears filled his eyes. "Lana," Eve One said, "we shall visit you from time to time. But for now my dear, I should like you to meet someone very special to us. "A beautiful woman appeared in Lana's mind. It was Maria Sanches. Maria St. James, nee Sanches. Maria smiled. In a voice that enveloped Lana, a voice that was warm and enchanting. Maria said, "Do not give up your struggle against human indecencies." With those words, Maria was gone.

"Dr. Masters, what is it, you cry, why?" Francois asked.

"It's all right Francois. I'm just a little sad about the thought of leaving Istanbul, and happy too about seeing Clark on Sunday."

"I sit with you mon cheri, then you won't cry."

"You're so sweet Francois."

"Merci. Francois big et ugly. You kind to call me sweet. I look after you forever."

Lana kissed his cheek. "Francois, I want you to be with me all day tomorrow. I want to sight-see and shop."

"Tres bein, Dr. Masters."

Before going to her room, Lana sought out Dr. James Bell-Irving. She was not surprised to find him seated on a sculptured, wrought-iron bench out in the center's exquisite garden with Eve Three. They were holding hands. "Hi you two," Lana said on interrupting their snug little tête-à-tête, "I've come to say goodbye to you romanticists."

Dr. Bell-Irving rose to shake Lana's hand and bid her farewell when 'boompph' he found himself holding her in his arms. The next thing you know his lips were on Lana's. Eve Three had orchestrated the move. Play-acting Eve Three said, "Enúf James" a handshake will do. Dr. Bell-Irving fumbled, I…I," Eve Three winked at Lana. They laughed.

Their goodbyes were teary. They promised each other they would get together some way or another after they returned to America.

All day Saturday, Lana lugged big Francois everywhere she could in the short space of time she had to explore Istanbul's wondrous sights and its fabulous shopping.

Sunday morning saw Lana and Francois depart this fascinating city.

CHAPTER 86

FATHER DONNELY'S DEMISE

Warning! Abject horror.

Lana's mind came back to her guest. Her mind had raced through her life while she baby-sat him in the huge barn. Yes, Franklin Foster (aka) Father Donnely, the priest) was not long for this world. Soon his body would go to its final resting place. Not, mind you, in a 'pleasant' cemetery, no, quite the contrary. Lana had selected the perfect place for burial of her one-time lover. A place that would be discovered only after eons of time had elapsed. Perhaps the discoverers will not be of the human race. Perhaps humans may have become extinct by the year 2260 or so (say five grandfathers hence) as ordained by the Controllers. Perhaps the discoverers will be from another planet, who knows?

* * *

The second snake wriggled up to the lead actor's head. It raised itself above the barn's floor, using its three-foot long body as support, and waved its scaly head over the face of the tortured actor. On seeing his mouth wide open, with spittle and stale vomit drooling out of the corners of his bluish lips, tongue lolling, snake number two, drove itself into the gaping mouth of Lana's guest wiggling its way down his throat searching for food. Her guest gurgled, regurgitated and sputtered. Lana screamed, scrambled down off her perch on the hay bales, ran to her guest's rescue and yanked the slimy party crasher out of Lover Boy's gorge. "You sonofabitch," she screeched, "you try to fuck up my play will you?" She slammed the snake's head on the cement floor of the barn, ran to a door, and with all her might flung the dead reptile out into a lush stance of wheat. No way was that blessed snake going to end her guest's life by choking him to death. While being so involved with snake number two she was unaware of the fact snake number one had worked its way up Lover Boy's ass, into Lover Boy's bowels, and had ensconced itself there. Out of sight, out of mind.

* * *

Perry Como's, *I need no shackles to remind me* ground its way on. Lana nestled herself back onto her baled hay perch.

She noticed the two male rats were now staring out of the inside of the cage in bewilderment. They were looking at the female rat who now was outside the cage. The female rat at the same time was looking up into the eyes of the two male rats. Lana was certain the female rat, at least by the look in her eyes, was, by telepathy, telling the two-dullwitted males to escape their trap as she had done simply by burrowing through their host's body.

Now Lana almost threw up. Daylight was now passing. Thunder groaned in the distance. Perry Como kept singing.

Lana, as foul as it may seem, saw snake number one's head pop-up through the tattered skin on her guest's lower belly. It's head rose six or seven inches above the cage, peered at Lana, then flicked out its forked tongue and, once again picked off flies in a most expeditious manner. As well she saw its tail had not yet disappeared up Lover Boy's anus, instead it protruded out several inches and quivered back and forth in a most loathsome manner. 'Good Christ' Lana thought, 'I'm wittnessing this fucking sight…a snake with it's head sticking out of Lover Boy's gut while it's tail is sticking out of his butt.' Holding back her gorge, she leapt off her hay made 'settee,' rushed to her guest's side, grasped snake number one's head and yanked at it in an attempt to pull its body free of her guest's torso. Shit! She had yanked so hard the snake's head snapped off leaving its wretched body to squirm back into Lover Boy's anatomy.

Lana threw up. She staggered back, almost fainted, then knelt down in an attempt to get herself together. After a few moments she rose, still dizzy from her nausea, she made her way out of the barn to the outside. There she stayed for several minutes. She gulped down fresh air; marched around the farm yard in quick strides; jogged around the farmhouse, noted the distant lightning; then still a bit shaky made her way back to that hellish barn where just 18 years ago Uncle Fred had died.

Once inside Lana uncurled a water hose turned it on, and with great care cleansed the fetid mess that surrounded her guest's body.

Now fevered and delirious, her guest giggled!

Perry Como sang.

The two male rats began their escape through his body.

* * *

"Lana," her guest babbled, "thanks for getting rid of those goddamn rats. Awhile ago they hurt me 'pretty good,' now it's okay, no hurts."

In the meantime the two male rats, not as bright as the female, strayed as they gnawed their way through Lana's guest's body to freedom.

"Oh, bury me not on the lone prairie," he sang, "where the coyotes howl and the wind blows free. What's with Perry Como, Lana, I need no shackles to remind me? Don't I know? Ha, ha. Lana, a coupla things I want to discuss with you, one, I want to recite King of the Royal Mounted to you to see if I's got it right. 'Member you told me that joke years ago and it's still one of my fav-rits. And Miss Cunt Face I want to be able to tell it to some foreign gidnatories, no, dingatories… whatever…next week when I meet them at the UN Building in New

York. 'Not 'han'ona buusoom', Lana, so letzzz go eh Lana. King of the Royal Mounted just graduated as a Canadian Monted Poo-lic-man from his training in Regenia, Sasabush, ha ha, saskabush…to fucking canucks…notice Lana I's saying eh! like all crazzy can-a-dians eh Lana, and he wuz being sent to Washington, AC, DC on a special mission, on a choo choo twain," hee-hee, he twittered after calling a train a choo choo twain. "Only one seat waz lef on choo-choo car nex to a beautiful girl. Oh Lana 'fore I foget, I wanna tell yu'sumpin. Lotsa guys including moi think an that's that, even tho you are a geeniuss and you have beean a greate wourldy citizzan, a grate re-for-mer, you weer put on this planit, no, plaanet, you know, earth for one reeson and one reeson only, n'that's for you to be (hee hee) merely a ree-sip-ient of mens' cocks. Unnerstan' me Lana? ree-sip-ient of men's cocky-lockies. Thas 'cause of your peerdy face, you titt-lating tits and you're dee-liss-ours, darry-aire. And, Lana, how I've always luv'd to shove my all-amer-ican prick up your royal can-a-deen ass. Whoweee.

"Now back to King Mountee," her guest giggled, "King waks to the empy seat and says to the goorgish girl, mam, I'm King of the Royal Canadian Mounted Poo-lice, on an importtent speshal mission to Wash-ing-ton Dee Cee. I'm a bigg man, as he blows on his fingernails then proudly rubs them on his ches, no toonic. May I sit b'side youu? 'Of corse you may,' the ravissing one says. With dignatty, King sits. The twain pullls away. After some time King looks to the girl and repeets, "Mam, I'm King of the Royal Canadian Mountees, I'm bigg man going on speshal…secreet…mission to Wash-ing-ton Dee-Cee—blows on his figger nales then rubs them on his toonic…may I put me arm on the bak of your seat? 'Please do, sexxy lady says invite-ing-ly.' Choo Choo rumbles on. King's dorque begins to stand at attention. Several more minnits pass. King, getting braver, repeets, 'mam, I'm an important man, I'm King of the Royal Canuck Mounted po-liceey on…shhh…speshal seecreet mission to Wash-ing-ton Dee-Cee'.. proudly rubs his finger nales on his toonic again, may I put my hand on your 'nee.' 'Oh, I'd looove that hansom one,' she teased batting her baby blues at him. Choo Choo rumbles. King's hoorney dick stiffens. He put's his han on her 'nee. King's hoornied up good now.

"Shit, Lana, yore not lissening."

"Yes, I am darling boy."

"Okay, then I will enter-tain you further with King, not 'Han'on'a Booosoom.' Mamm, I'm King of the Rooyal Canadian Monted Police, gooing on veery speshal, secret hush hush mission to wash-ing-ton AC DC, blows on pinkees, rubs them on toonic, may I slip my hand rite up to your seecret dell-a-cusy. Yeah, King, ole pal, be my guest, and when you get there, scratch my balls, I'm Prescot of the FBI."

"How'd I do Lana, will the joke go over with the dip-la-mats I meet next week?"

"You'll knock them dead, providing you don't miss your flight good looking," Lana replied.

"Lana, oh my God," Lana's guest gurgled, "Lana, please wh'hs h'ppning...Lana...it feels like suzthing crawling up my throat...Lana, Lana, it's alive, Lana I can't talk. Lana," he choked. His bulging eyes pleaded with her to help, his eyes turned childish, they begged for mercy, for sympathy. His face took on the appearance of a helpless child, an innocent tortured child. Tears flowed down his cheeks. No longer was he non-compos mentis. He was fully aware of the fact he had, for whatever length of time, been in shock and out of control of his senses. But now he had a full grasp of his situation. He knew death was near.

"Why Lana, why?" he gasped.

Then there was silence as the adult male rat's head poked out of lover boy"s frothing mouth. The rat's head jutted out past Lana's guest's teeth while its body remained in his mouth. The rat squeaked and looked about with its beady bloodshot eyes in an attempt to find its female cohort.

Lana gasped and stared in horror at the scene now unfolding. This scene was not to be part of her play. She had no idea the play would become so hideous, so repulsive, so sickening, so vile, so…so ghastly. She covered her mouth with her hands and vomited geyser-like greenish yellow bile through her fingers.

As it happened, her guest, in one last brave effort to show that fucking rat what's what, and knowing his life span was down to seconds and in order to foil the cocksucking rat's escape, her guest with all his might clamped his teeth down hard on the rat's neck. The rat's skin held. Lover Boy ground his teeth back and forth through the bits of skin. Now the head was severed. Still squeaking, the rat's head parted from its body. Blood covered Lover Boy's mouth and lips and leaked down his throat. The severed head rolled down Lover Boy's chin, bumped its way down onto his torso then fell with a tiny thud on the barn's cement floor. Franklin Foster's (A.K.A. Father Ocravious Donnely) body convulsed then died.

It was now May 24thth, 1997, 10:30 p.m.

Lana sobbed. How could she have fabricated such a dreadful punishment to the man she had just executed? Even though he had become so cruel with her during their 'so called' courtship, he had been a productive, loyal and brave American. Just moments ago she had seen his pleading, childlike eyes. God, how they pleaded with her to stop this barbaric charade. He was once a babe in his mother's arms, a growing fun-loving child, a typical teenager, a responsible hard-working adult, a proud and dignified man. Now he was dead. He had died a horrid death, a death which had robbed him of his pride and his dignity; a shocking painful death.

How dare she be so almighty to think she had the right to carry out such a diabolic execution? Lana reached into her knapsack for her pistol. She placed the gun's barrel into her mouth. No, she thought, I am not suicidal but, she amended, if I choose to take my own life, I will shoot myself through my heart, not through my mouth.

Thinking back a few minutes, at least since her guest's recitation of King of the Royal Canadian Mounted Police, she had thought she heard sirens.

Her mind, however, now was focused on dispensing with her guest's disgusting remains, not on sirens, her squeamish stomach or the revulsion she felt toward herself. She knew she must continue on with her plan and rid the barn of her guest's disemboweled body and all the incriminating evidence therefrom.

But, she thought, before I make any such move I must reconsider what I shall do with myself because any clean-up may be redundant if I decide to sho…

At that moment the barn door crashed open, Lana twisted to see who dared intrude. Invading her privacy were two policemen from Swift Current along with the one man she has always loved, Clark St. James. Lana pressed the barrel of her pistol to her heart.

"NO, LANA, FOR GOD'S SAKE DON'T," boomed her lovers voice.

Finis

Author's Secret

....by dang...,was Lana just having a nightmare, and would she wake up in a cold sweat knowing the horror show just over (including Uncle Fred's demise) was only a bad dream?

Did Lana commit these dastardly deeds?

I can't tell you, because my computer just got a virus. Ain't that a tittie? And guess what, no ones got an antibiotic to fix up my ailing computer. The problem is, damn it, I don't know if Lana pulled the trigger or not.

Sombitch eh!

and

oh, yes, regardless of whether the foregoing is a dream or a reality, I'll bet all you readers are on the edge of your seats wondering what happened to the juvenile rat. Well, be jaabers, the little rat took a wrong turn in Lana's guest's body, couldn't find his way back and forsooth, ended up smothered in Lover Boy's 'twattle.'

and

remember back in Istanbul, Lana didn't know about herself? Remember how she frustrated Fraulein Stoltz and her attendees and the council? Remember she said "shit, shit, shit! I need to know what the hell I'm all about..."

Well forsooth, splendid readers, I called out to Eve One for an answer to this mind-boggling question, "Eve One," pleadeth I, "please, I beg of you, tell me who this Lana is and what she is all about?

I, Jack Bentley, author of this here book, need to know."

Postscript

MANDATORY READING!

Lana Masters is a twenty-nine-year-old genius.

Beautiful and brutal, she serves as a role model for all women.

Her story is made more relevant in today's world

as women continue to be victimized by terrorists.

I, Jack Bentley, am sitting here alone in my den. I am perplexed. I am sitting, preparing to eat a lettuce and tomato sandwich my pretty wife Jean is making for me. I like it with a touch of mayonnaise.

Jean brings me a glass of skim milk. I only drink skim mile when Jean and I go out to visit friends. But I always ask the hostess, 'I am wishing my skim milk in a dirty glass please.' This is proving I am a tough guy like the other dudes who are drinking scotch on the rocks.

Our den is small, but comfortable. Five years ago my pretty wife, who will not accept anything untoward even from guys like Harry The Horse, Spanish John or Little Isadore said to me, "Get off your lazy butt. I do not like this fading brown grasscloth wallpaper. Together we are going to paint over the wallpaper in cream paint. I paint, Jean paints. Seven coats. It is nice.

I am sitting in my den perplexed.

Beatuiful Jean is sitting on a chaise-lounge on our townhouse patio and looking happy.

I am not finding an ending to my book.

* * *

'Lana,' I say, 'I am perplexed. Are you shooting yoursef in the heart? Look Lana, Clark is perplexed. Clark, is booming out—"NO LANA! FOR GOD'S SAKE...DON'T!'

Now what Lana? Is this the end? Maybe millions of readers out there are saying...what the hell?'

* * *

"Jack!"

Huh? Is Jean calling me?

I do not answer.

If you do not answer men friends, your wife is thinking you be asleep or you be dead. Hence she is not going to call you a second time.

"Jack!" Again.

Huh? What is this? Nobody be in the house. Jean is sitting on the chaise lounge outside nibbling sexily on Chapatti. Where is this "Jack!" coming from? Maybe the skim milk I am drinking should'ov been drunk a few days ago. You know, best used before such and such a date.

"Jack!"

It be louder this time.

'Huh!' I say under my breath. I am putting my hands behind my ears and crying out, "Wherefore thou speaketh thou speaker?'

I am looking out at Jean. Pretty Jean is looking like a nap is coming on. SHE IS NOT CALLING OUT "JACK!"

"JACK!!"

Even louder it be this time.

I stand. Positively perplexed I am. 'Wherefore commeth this **"JACK!"**' I am asking indignant. I am asking concerned. I am asking, near filling my drawers. 'Show thyself or begone thou frightening sound, or whatever. Forsooth, do not fray me by calling my name.'

"JACK!" A hollow deafening call this time.

I sit. 'Who or what in the f...?'

"**YOU, JACK,** are making Lana a propagator of foul language, you foulest wretch, thou foulest of all beasts."

'Waaa,' I am muttering dunce like.

Now a delightful laugh is emanating from a very feminine throat.

Now Itanya Bell-Irving she be standing before me.

Like a frightened cur, I am flopping face down on the den couch. Quite a nice couch it is, twelve years old mind you. Each end of the couch is Laz-y boy to watch the TV. I like to watch the news; Jean she does too. Each night we are playing Scabble while we sittith watching the news. Then I watch E.T. Jean, she is thinking E.T. is too gossipy, too confabulatory. We watcheth Jeopardy. Oh, I forgeteth; Jean she be winning 82.7% of the Scrabble games. Jean, she be good, me I be diddle-squat. I do the dishes.

'EVE THREE!' I mumble into my end of the couch! 'Eve Three, I be only writing about you, you know, fictionese.'

"I know Jack."

'So do I dreameth at this present time Eve Three, or do I be awake?'

"You are awake, Jack."

'I am frightened.'

"I know Jack."

'Are you going to kill me Eve Three?"'

"No Jack," the Controller's voice rumbles.

Jean sleepeth. I am looking out the window at her.

"'Jean, she does not hear your big voice?'

"No Jack. Do you want me to awaken her? No, you do not do you? I know everything in your mind Jack. No, I am real Jack, not a dream, or an hallucination. See?"

Eve Three, she is strolling over to me. She taketh my hand. Her hand, it is warm. My hand it shaketh. She pulleth. I riseth. She kissith my cheek. She putteth my hand in her hair. Yah, she be real…OH SO REAL!

"Now Jack, I am going to tell you what has become of Lana and her guest."

'Waaa?' I remark like a dweeb.

"Lana and her guest live, but not uncle Fred. He is now living in Subcosmos One hundred and One T. Lech."

'Waaa?' I continue.

"Yes jack, I know I am ravishing."

'Indeed!' I think.

Eve Three mimics me, smiling. "Lana and her guest are dining at O'Toole's Restaurant on North Hill in Swift Current. They are feasting on sesame-topped perch and they sip Chateau Clinet Pomerol. Lana's puissant is in charge. Neither is dead."

'Waaa?' I say again.

"Yes, I have turned back time for Lana, her guest Clark, and the two policemen. Back three days in fact. I have not turned back the world, just Lana, her guest Clark and the two police officers. So now Lana and her guest dine and chat. Lana has not committed the crime of killing her guest. However, I must say, Lana is now contemplating her guest's future."

'Eve Three, Eve Three, don't go." I am pleading as Eve Three is beginning to fade away. 'I do not know the finish to my book. I am needing you to help. EEEEEVE THREE COME BACK! Please come back.'

Like in an echo chamber Eve Three answereth softly. "Here she is Jack."

'Who Eve Three?' I am asking worn and imbecilic.

Eve Three disappears.

Lana appears.

I am falling back onto the couch. I am coming apart. I am dizzying. I am now *non-compos.* Holy shit, I am shortchanging Lana in my book.

She is more than I am writing *vis-à-vis* pulchritudinous, she is a goddess. SHE BE ONLY FICTITIOUS.

"Hi Jack."

'Hi Lana.'

My stars, Lana, she be nude.

I faint.

* * *

Readers, sayeth I. Watcheth for LANA'S GOD CHILD, it revealeth everything.

Eve Three, she helpeth me write it…honest.

Jack Bentley

About the Author

Jack Bentley makes a stunning debut as an author with his novel **POSITIVELY INDECENT! The Story of Dr. Lana Jean Masters.**

* * *

A Canadian, he spends his winters in the California desert where he ves on the Executive Advisory Council of the Palm Springs Writers ild and its website: *www.palmspringswritersguild.com.*

He is completing his next book, a sequel to POSITIVELY INDECENT!

LANA'S GODCHILD.

ack Bentley joined the Canadian Merchant Marines as a teenager spent the better part of four years sailing on freighters around the be. He is the author of

THE OCEAN TURNED MILKY

scintillating record of his rollicking experiences as a young sailor.

entley graduated from the University of Saskatchewan with a nmerce Degree and subsequently became a Chartered Accountant. often traveled to New York City for business meetings with senior utives of The Federal Reserve Bank of New York, major brokerage ses, large New York commercial banks, the Wall Street Journal and ssociate Dow Jones. It was Bentley who recommended in 1974 to then Salomon Brothers economic department that a new fund be duced for sale to the public which would reflect precisely the ht and measurement of the Dow Jones Industrial Average. He eled to London to meet with professors at the School of Economics ondon University, major banks, money managers, brokers, and several groups of underwriters at Lloyds of London. He has writte extensively about his findings from these meetings.

Jack Bentley's other published writings include newsletter promotional programs, editorials, annual reports and the like.

Bentley is an accomplished orator and has spoken on vario subjects to large and small groups throughout Canada.

He lives in Richmond British Columbia with his wife Jean ar presently devotes his time, energy and vivid imagination to writi novels.

*   *   *

POSITIVELY INDECENT

The Story of Dr. Lana Jean Masters

Available from Barnes and Noble.com, Amazon.com, Amazon.U Borders, iUniverse.com, hyacintheart.com and **palmspringswritersguild.co** (Exerpts are available on major search engines and translated into ei languages.) and **other Book Sellers in the U.S.** and **Canada, and web sites the world wide web.**